In memory of my parents.
Sol and Rose Lubell, my sister, Bobbie Krasny and my nephew Barry.

To my nephew Michael
We were both named after Morris Lowenthal
(my grandfather, your great grandfather) but you got the better "M"
name

A special thanks to my cousin Sandy, for editing the manuscript and helping with commas, semi-colons, and dangling modifiers (whatever those are)—also to former classmates who enriched the book with stories and memories . . . Michael and Eugene Sharkey, Jack Bodne, Howard Levy, Arden Seigendorf, Richard Fenster, Bobby Ger, Milton Tupler, Ruth Gratz (Berger), Richard Swaebe, Danny Bakst . . . also to other classmates who read the manuscript and offered suggestions . . . Linda Kay Brown (Zilber) and Paul Ruthfield

I also dedicate this book to my wife, Yolanda, and my children, Steven, Stacy, and Luisa.

THE SIXTH BOROUGH

THE SIXTH BOROUGH

MYRON S. LUBELL

authorHOUSE®

AuthorHouse™ LLC
1663 Liberty Drive
Bloomington, IN 47403
www.authorhouse.com
Phone: 1-800-839-8640

Published by AuthorHouse   07/15/2013

ISBN: 978-1-4817-2973-4 (sc)
ISBN: 978-1-4817-3001-3 (e)

CONTENTS

Introduction...xi
About The Author xiii

EIGHTH GRADE

Chapter 1:   Goodbye Minnie Minoso 3
Chapter 2:   Porticos And Slaves 11
Chapter 3:   The Volume Of A Sphere 19
Chapter 4:   The Holy Ghost 28
Chapter 5:   The Giants Win The Pennant 36
Chapter 6:   Preparing For World War III 42
Chapter 7:   In Search Of Double Nymphs 49
Chapter 8:   Parting Of The Red Sea............................... 56
Chapter 9:   The Wonder Machine 62
Chapter 10: The Badge Of Courage................................ 68
Chapter 11: News From The Outside World: 1951-1952 77

NINTH GRADE

Chapter 12: The Move To Surfside 81
Chapter 13: ¿Qué Es El Burro? 91
Chapter 14: The Steinberg Twins 96
Chapter 15: Protective Custody Prisoners 100
Chapter 16: And God Maketh The Rules Of Syntax 107
Chapter 17: The Importance Of Being Normal.................. 117
Chapter 18: Stone Crabs And Kishkehs 125
Chapter 19: The Unidentified Pube 135
Chapter 20: Kibitzing At The Crossroads........................ 142
Chapter 21: News From The Outside World: 1952-1953 155

TENTH GRADE

Chapter 22: Think Pink 161
Chapter 23: Forward Typhoons 172
Chapter 24: The Final Voyage Of The Niña 177
Chapter 25: Biology: The Study Of Life 183
Chapter 26: Shop: Preparation For Adult Responsibilities 192
Chapter 27: B-56: The Bumpy Road Of Youth 200
Chapter 28: Kingdom By The Sea 210
Chapter 29: Myrons, Myrons, And Myrons 218
Chapter 30: Dreams, Canasta, And Overtown 227
Chapter 31: News From The Outside World: 1953-1954 237

ELEVENTH GRADE

Chapter 32: The Grand March 241
Chapter 33: A Tale Of Two Cities 251
Chapter 34: Xenocrates 263
Chapter 35: The Catch 269
Chapter 36: The Punch 275
Chapter 37: Black And Gold Forever 281
Chapter 38: Advanced Conjugation 287
Chapter 39: Rebels Rule Dolly's 295
Chapter 40: The Melting Pot 306
Chapter 41: Wheels To Freedom 316
Chapter 42: Sitting Shiva 327
Chapter 43: The Age Of Reason 332
Chapter 44: News From The Outside World: 1954-1955 347

TWELFTH GRADE

Chapter 45: Three Brains Are Better Than One 353
Chapter 46: A Night In The Slammer 362
Chapter 47: Rendezvous With Destiny 374
Chapter 48: The T-Shirt Rebellion 393
Chapter 49: Thanatopsis 407
Chapter 50: Banco De Portugal 421
Chapter 51: Music Of The Devil 438

Chapter 52: A Tigress To The Rescue 447
Chapter 53: Emphysema And Ventriloquism..................... 464
Chapter 54: The Senior Prom..................................... 467
Chapter 55: Polar Opposites 478
Chapter 56: Graduation 499
Chapter 57: News From The Outside World: 1955-1956....... 510

Epilogue 515
Glossary Of Usesful Yiddish Words................................ 519

INTRODUCTION

In 1951 Miami Beach, Florida was one of the most popular resort cities in America; the warm weather and tranquil beaches of this tropical paradise attracted thousands of winter visitors, mostly Jewish tourists who made the two day drive from New York. In addition, the resident population of this small island was primarily from New York. Thus, the city of Miami Beach was sometimes referred to as the SIXTH BOROUGH of New York. However, if you ventured off the island and crossed the beautiful expanse of Biscayne Bay you were in another world; you were in the deep south, where Jews were often envisioned as demons with horns, "colored" people were second class citizens, and racial laws were reminiscent of Nuremberg and Berlin.

Myron Lindell was twelve when he moved from Chicago, where he was a secular Jew, barely aware of his religious or ethnic heritage. But, In Miami Beach, on a Jewish Island, he had an odd feeling . . . he was "different." He "survived" the move by blending fantasy with reality, and if reality was more than he could handle, he escaped by writing adolescent observations in a journal, creating imaginative short stories and essays, which he rarely shared with anyone except his father, a few teachers, and a "street smart" female classmate. This compilation of memoirs is not a documentary; it is just a testimony to the value of simple memories. Too often, historians have forgotten the individual view, the poetic view, which might be closer to reality than the consensus.

Note: Since Yiddish was part of the popular street talk in Miami Beach during the 1950's a glossary of selected words is included at the end of the book.

ABOUT THE AUTHOR

Myron Lubell was born in Chicago (1939) and moved to Miami Beach, Florida in September 1951 where he attended Ida M. Fisher Jr. High School and Miami Beach Senior High School. He then graduated from the University of Miami and eventually received a Doctorate in Business Administration from the University of Maryland.

He worked for 32 years as an accounting and tax professor at Florida International University (Miami), published over 60 professional articles, and wrote a weekly tax column that appeared every Monday in the Miami Herald and over 40 newspapers, including the New York Daily News (1978-1997).

Doctor Lubell is now retired, reads incessentaly, is an ardent fan of the Miami Dolphins, Heat, and Marlins, and the Miami Hurricanes. His idols are Jefferson, Lincoln, Woody Allen, Jerry Seinfeld, and Stephen Spielberg.

He has three children and five grandchildren.

EIGHTH GRADE

CHAPTER 1

GOODBYE MINNIE MINOSO

It was supposed to be a dark, overcast day—gloomy, with thunder and lightning, and a werewolf howling in the distance—like the start of a Dracula movie; that's how I envisioned this day, that's how I fanaticized this ominous moment in my life. For the past six months I dreaded the morning of September 11, 1951, but as I looked out the window of my second story bedroom, I saw a radiant blue cloudless sky. This was supposed to be the worst day of my life; I did not want sunshine. It was not part of my script!

And my mother bounced around the kitchen with a contrived buoyancy; she did her best to keep the morning cheerful. She made my favorite breakfast and even served a peeled and quartered orange; she knew I loved oranges. We listened to "Don McNeal's Breakfast Club" on the radio, like we always did, and marched around the breakfast table . . . just my mother and me. My father never got into childish things like that; he was always on the serious side. I don't think he ever really acted silly.

I was twelve years old, and this was to be my last day in Chicago. We would be leaving after breakfast, moving to Miami Beach Florida. My father had a heart attack the previous year and the Chicago winters were too difficult for him to tolerate. So, he retired, sold his paint and wallpaper stores, and decided to move the family to Florida. I was heartsick about the move; I would be leaving my very close friend, Michael Bernstein, but I understood that we had to move, for my father's health.

3

He was sixty and seemed like a very old man to me; his posture was bad and he was somewhat unsteady when he walked, but he walked with dignity. Because of his heart condition he had trouble climbing the stairs to our second story apartment; he needed help, either from my mother or from me. And he was very concerned about the drive to Florida, a drive which a younger, healthier man could make in two days. He told my mother that we would take five days to make the 1,400 mile trip . . . stopping at 3:00 PM every afternoon. In 1951 my mother didn't drive, nor did she read maps, so my father would do all the driving and I was the designated map reader.

I banged a large wooden spoon against a pot as my mother and I marched around the breakfast table, a daily ritual with the "Breakfast Club." The radio program began with a "first call to breakfast," then a few boring guests, then a "second call to breakfast" . . . and finally . . . breakfast. My father just read the morning newspaper, the stock market pages.

The phone rang; it was Michael Bernstein. He didn't cry—but his voice cracked. "Damn! Myron . . . why do you have to move? I'm really gonna' miss you." Michael said he was coming over, by bike, to say a final goodbye. He lived only five blocks away. I made that walk many times, even in the snow and the biting wind of Chicago—which is the only thing about Chicago that I hated. The snow was OK, it was even fun, but the wind was horrible. I remember sometimes making the five block walk to Michael's house, walking backwards . . . to shield my face from that ice cold wind.

"Rose, turn down that damn radio," my father lifted his head from the Tribune, and growled at my mother. "I can't hear myself think."

"Sol, this is our last day in Chicago, who knows if they'll have this program in Florida, let us enjoy our final march."

My mother gave a look of defiance, which was unlike her . . . normally, she agreed with anything my father wanted. But, on this last morning in Chicago, she raised the volume a little louder and I continued banging the pot with my wooden spoon. I lifted my knees high in the air as I marched around the kitchen table, shouting: "second call to breakfast." I didn't want to think about the reality of the day. I loved Chicago and I would be leaving my sister Bobbie, who just got married a few years earlier, and my two-year old nephew, Barry. We had such fun in our apartment

4

when Bobbie and Barry came to visit. Barry was just beginning to walk, and we laughed as he struggled and kept falling, and Barry recognized that every time he fell, we all laughed, so he kept falling on purpose, just to get more laughs from his mother, grandmother, and me . . . . I was only 12, and it was fun being called "Uncle Myron." How many kids who are twelve years old are uncles?

The car was ready to go; my mother packed most of our personal stuff a month before the trip. So, after breakfast we just closed the door of our apartment, left the furniture for the new tenant, and went down to the car; no one was there to wave goodbye, not even my older sister; she said her goodbyes the day before. I urged my parents to wait a few minutes; Michael was coming over, and I wanted to see him, one final time. We sat in the car; my father lit a cigar as we waited for Michael.

"Sol, please," groaned my mother, "not so early in the morning, that stinkin' cigar makes me sick."

He got out, stood at the side of the car, and puffed away as we waited for Michael.

Several minutes later Michael came racing up the street on his bike. He hopped off; threw his bike to the ground and ran toward me. We hugged . . . and didn't know what to say, but neither of us cried. It was a sick feeling, an emptiness in my stomach. I tried to say something but a lump in my throat made it difficult to talk. Michael was older than me, taller than me, and knew a lot about many things, especially World War II; he knew all about Hitler and Tojo and Mussolini and the details of how each of them committed suicide or was killed.

Finally, I broke the silence: "I'll . . . I'll . . . I'll write as soon as I get to Florida."

Michael turned to my father: "Mr. Lindell, don't forget to bring the tape recorder, so Myron and I can send tapes back and forth to each other."

"Don't worry Michael, we packed it with the movers," said my father. "And say goodbye to your mother and father for us." My father had a great deal of respect for Michael because they both read a lot, and to my father, if you were a "reader" everything in life would fall in place. My mother thought Michael was a wild kid because he often wore a German helmet and raced in and out of traffic on his bike and because he was twice suspended from school for "unspecified violations." One of those

5

violations, I think, was for carving a huge picture of his dog on a desk.

We drove away and I looked back through the rear window of our 1947 Packard. I waved goodbye to Michael and to Chicago, and to the White Sox, my favorite baseball team. I was in the back seat . . . alone . . . and I buried my head in a pillow so that no one would hear me cry. We were on our way to Florida—to Miami Beach—a place which we had visited frequently, but only for short winter vacations. I was positive that I would not like living there. The beach was fun, but after a week of swimming what else was there to do?

As we drove to Florida my job was to read the detailed map and the information booklet prepared by the Chicago Motor Club. I was alone in the back seat, working as navigator, tail gunner, and bombardier . . . I imagined that we were flying in a B-17, on a bombing raid over the southern part of the United States . . . wiping out pockets of escaped Nazis. It was a secret mission; I was commissioned by President Truman. I couldn't even tell my parents. If I was captured I would have to swallow a poison capsule. I had a few hidden M&M's, just in case!

Michael and I frequently played war games. I was always the American; he liked to be the German . . . the commandant of an elite battalion of Storm Troopers. He said the Germans had a better disciplined army than the Americans, but we won the war because we could manufacture more airplanes and tanks; my father agreed with him.

We took the Outer Drive south; I loved that highway . . . the vista of the lake and the beautiful Chicago skyline . . . it was the prettiest view in the world . . . except maybe Paris when the American army, led by Ike, marched through the Arc D'Triumph and rescued the city from the Nazis. I saw pictures in Life magazine. I wish I was there, marching in that parade. I couldn't understand why Eisenhower had to run for president in 1952 . . . we should just appoint him as our next president.

Later that day we listened to the White Sox baseball game on the radio, but not until I finished dropping a few of my bombs . . . I "leveled" the giant crematories in Gary, Indiana. This ugly smoke filled city was a secret haven for escaped Nazis, a place for them to prepare for World War III. The word "GARY" was a clandestine acronym: "German Army Relocation Yard" . . . . not many people knew that, but I figured it out.

The White Sox were two games behind the Yankees in a heated pennant race, with only one week remaining in the season; Minnie Minoso, the new Cuban rookie stole two bases and the Sox were leading the Yankees by a run. It was a fast and exciting Sox team that year; many sports writers called them the "Go Go" Sox. We listened intently to the game until we were outside of Chicago radio range; the sounds of Chicago faded . . . replaced by Indiana grain reports . . . and the price of wheat and barley.

"What's barely?" I asked my father.

"Those are the little white things that float in mushroom barley soup."

"Dad," do you think Minnie Minoso will be as good as Babe Ruth?" Minoso was the most exciting baseball player in Chicago.

"Well, he is good, and he is fast, but I don't think you can compare him to Babe Ruth," said my father. "But that new rookie in New York, Mickey Mantle, looks like he might become a big home run hitter."

I hated the Yankees . . . . almost as much as I hated the Nazis. For a Jewish boy growing up in post World War II Chicago, the blue and white "NY" of the Yankees was the second most hated symbol, second only to the dreaded Swastika. I couldn't believe my own father was saying that Mickey Mantle, a New York Yankee, was better than Minnie Minoso. But, my father was very biased; he was born in New York and never lost his loyalty to New York teams. I loved my father, but wouldn't accept his opinion that Mickey Mantle would ever be better than Minnie Minoso. Impossible! I was a big collector of baseball cards in Chicago and had five full shoe boxes, the entire '49, '50, and '51 series, with doubles and triples of many cards. Of course, like most kids, I never chewed that sickening saccharine gum; it tasted like powdered cardboard. When my mother said that we wouldn't have enough room in our new apartment to save all my cards, it was like pouring salt into an open wound; she was destroying the last vestige of my Chicago identity. I could only keep one box; I had to make important decisions; which cards to save; which cards to cut. I saved five Orestes "Minnie" Minoso cards and dumped the two New York rookies: Mickey Mantle and Willie Mays.

"OK, here's a riddle," said my father, as he thought of a few geography questions to break the monotony of the boring drive. "What state is round on both sides and high in the middle."

7

"Alaska," I shouted.

"Wrong. Alaska is only a territory," replied my father.

"How bout' Colorado?" asked my mother.

"No, Colorado and Wyoming are square on the sides and high in the middle."

"OK . . . I give up," I responded.

"Ohio," said my father. "Round on both sides . . . O's . . . . and H-I in the middle."

"That's stupid," I groaned. "OK my turn. What's the longest word in the English language?"

"Antidisestablishmentarianism," said my father.

"No. Its SMILES . . . . an S on both ends and a mile inbetween." That even got my mother to laugh.

On the fifth morning, as we passed through Claxton, Georgia, I studied the travel booklet prepared by the Chicago Motor Club and informed my parents that Claxton is the "Fruitcake Capital of the World." We all laughed but refused to eat any fruitcake when we stopped for breakfast at a local truckstop. My mother, father, and I all agreed; we hated fruitcake, especially the green cherries, or whatever those little green things were. I had a few bombs left; I dropped one on Claxton. Lots of Nazis were walking the streets of this very clean little town pretending to be Americans, but I could see through their disguise, especially when they smoked. Real Americans hold their cigarette between the index finger and the middle finger, with the palm of the hand turned toward the face; Nazis hold the cigarette between the thumb and index finger, palm facing outward. I learned that spy trick in a Humphrey Bogart movie. One well placed bomb at the old courthouse would take care of the Claxton problem.

We were definitely in Nazi territory. Along the highway I observed a series of covert cryptograms from a Nazi organization known as Burma Shave. The signs were spaced exactly one tenth of a mile apart. I jotted them down to send to President Truman. He would have the secret code deciphered.

Hardy men *A Man, A Miss*
Were the Caesars *A Car, A Curve*
Instead of razors *He Kissed the Miss*
They used tweezers *And Missed the Curve*
Burma Shave *Burma Shave*

8

I don't remember how much longer it was after "Operation Claxton" but we finally reached the Florida border. We were greeted by a large billboard, **"Keep Florida Green,"** and a picture of a pretty woman in a bathing suit drinking orange juice. My parents cheered as we entered the state; I sat there quietly, consuming the pages of my Chicago Motor Club booklet, to see what important attractions we would be passing in Florida. Were there any good sites to drop additional bombs? I learned that Florida oranges outsold California oranges; I never knew that before. In Chicago we only ate California Sunkist oranges; I liked them better, much better; they tasted like oranges were supposed to taste. On the outside Florida oranges looked just like California oranges but that was deceptive. On the inside, they weren't even a real orange color.

Somewhere south of Jacksonville, as we scanned the radio, searching for baseball scores . . . I heard the devastating news. During the past five days . . . while we were driving south through rural America, completely out of touch with the world, while I was dropping bombs and eradicating enclaves of hidden Nazis, Mickey Mantle hit five home runs and the Yankees beat the White Sox four consecutive games. The Yankees had just clinched the pennant. I wanted to cry . . . but I didn't. Twelve year old boys don't cry. I just stared at the ugly billboards along the Florida highway . . . . more pictures of women in bathing suits drinking orange juice.

"Where are the coconut trees?" . . . . I broke the long uncomfortable silence.

"They're in south Florida," said my father, "they don't grow here in the northern part of the state."

"Goodbye Minnie Minoso," that was all I could think as I fell asleep. I slept for the entire state of Florida, until we reached Miami. The next voice I heard was my father, asking directions from a teenage boy, how to find the causeway to Miami Beach. The boy was barefoot, carrying a fishing pole, and he spoke with a deep southern accent.

"Y'all take this here road for two lights." He pointed his pole to show the way. "Then hang a right to the Beach, but be careful, that's where Satan lives."

And as we crossed Biscayne Bay to the tropical island that was about to become my new home, I would not allow myself to enjoy the spectacular view—the wide expanse of open water—the swaying palm trees that lined the causeway. I would not even read the Chicago Motor Club booklet. Nothing about Miami Beach could possibly interest me; how could I ever like a city where the oranges weren't even orange . . . and I was sure they never heard of Minnie Minoso; he was from Cuba, what did they know about Cuban baseball players in Miami Beach?

CHAPTER 2

PORTICOS AND SLAVES

"Wake me when we get to our apartment," I mumbled . . . secure in the protective bowels of my B-17, buffered by my pillow, a Chicago Motor Club map, two books about the lost continent of Atlantis, and three boxes of chocolate chip cookies. Armies always travel on their stomachs. Napoleon said that. I had no interest in marveling at the sights of Miami Beach. My mother and father were "oooohing and aaaahing" . . . . they gawked and raved about each beautiful ocean front hotel as we drove slowly down Collins Avenue—the main street of "Mecca"—the boulevard of their dreams.

"Sol . . . don't you just love the Casablanca. Look at the beautiful statues of Arabian slaves, holding up the portico."

"Whats a portico?" I thought . . . but to ask my mother that question would imply that I was interested in something about Miami Beach. (Mental note: When Michael comes to visit me . . . we will have an elite squadron of Storm Troopers obliterate the Casablanca.)

"Myron . . . look . . . there's the Atlantic Ocean," said my mother. "Isn't it beautiful?"

I buried my head in my pillow and refused to look, but I knew that the ocean was named after Atlantis. I just read it in one of my books. Finally, without raising my head from the pillow, I mumbled.

11

"I like Lake Michigan better, the water doesn't burn your eyes."

"You'll love the chocolate sodas at the Noshery," said my father. "Thats the coffee shop in the Saxony hotel."

My ears perked up a little . . . but I said nothing. (Mental note: when I drop my remaining bombs . . . make sure to avoid the Saxony.)

Herman and Aunt Pearlie were there to greet us when we arrived at the James Manor, our new home . . . . a disgusting little apartment where I would not even have my own bedroom. I would be forced to sleep on a sofa bed in the living room. Aunt Pearlie, my mother's sister, was very nice and had a giant Hershey bar for me, the one pound size. Aunt Pearlie never had children so she always acted like she was my mother. She greeted me with a huge smile and a warm, loving hug; she buried my head in her bosom. I could see gold fillings in the back of her mouth.

"Myron . . . this is Mitzie . . . our new puppy." The little black and white Boston Terrier was very cute . . . a stub of a tail wagged so fast it was a blur. Mitzie was so happy to meet me she left a puddle at the front steps of the James Manor. Aunt Pearlie was just as happy, but she didn't pee.

Herman was a deadbeat. That's what my mother called him. I didn't like him, and I refused to call him uncle . . . he was just my aunt's husband and he always had a cigarette in his mouth and he always coughed. My mother used to say, "families are like fudge . . . mostly sweet, with a few nuts." Herman was a former motorcycle cop from Chicago . . . back in the Al Capone era . . . and even at twelve years old, I knew not to trust him; he thought he was a good ventriloquist and liked to entertain, but his lips moved. Herman and Aunt Pearlie came to Florida a year before us; they were hiding from creditors and lived at the James Manor, two doors down from our new apartment. Herman did card tricks or whatever it took to get laughs, even if he got the laughs by making fun of friends or relatives . . . or me.

I asked Aunt Pearlie if I could take Mitzie for a walk; I wanted to scout the neighborhood . . . to look for hidden Nazis and I didn't want to watch Herman do card tricks and I hated listening to his constant coughing. Mitzie was very tiny; she had to take ten quick steps for every one of mine. She loved walking with me and she peed a lot. Dogs don't hold back . . . they show their true emotions. I also felt like peeing on every palm tree that I passed. Mitzie stared at me while I devoured the giant Hershey bar; she begged for a piece.

"Sorry Mitzie, but chocolate is bad for dogs."

Aunt Pearlie always had a refrigerator full of Hershey bars; she taught me that they taste better ice cold . . . but not frozen; they turn white when they're too cold and lose most of their flavor. She used to say . . . "when chocolate turns white it loses its gusto."

As I walked with Mitzie I stared at all the old people on James Avenue. I never saw so many old people in my life. They were Jewish; all of them . . . and most of them talked with thick New York accents. But, some had European accents—they were immigrants from the "old country." My mother called the immigrants "greenhorns." Where was I? Wasn't this the south? None of them said "Y'all" . . . not like the barefoot boy with the fishing pole . . . the boy who gave us directions to Miami Beach and warned us about Satan.

I think Mitzie read my mind; she started pulling her leash, dragging me behind a building, to an isolated palm tree, where I could pee and not be seen.

"Nah . . . C'mon Mitzie . . . lets go home . . . Aunt Pearlie and the deadbeat will worry about us . . . I can't pee here."

On the sidewalk in front of the James Manor Mitzie found a boyfriend, a little white poodle held on a leash by a young girl with a pony tail. We both stood silently and watched our dogs take turns sniffing each other. Then, the poodle put his front paws on Mitzie's back and the girl yanked on the leash and yelled: "No Pepe." Both dogs barked as the girl walked away; she turned toward me and smiled.

We went to dinner that night at Dubrows, a popular Jewish Cafeteria on Lincoln Road. It was Herman's suggestion. Dubrows smelled from pickle juice and it was packed with hundreds of old people. They kept talking about "The City" . . . an arrogant reference to New York city . . . as if New York was the only "city" in the world. Hey . . . Chicago is also a city . . . so is Peoria . . . . so is Berlin . . . and I'm here to rid this place of Nazis . . . so you better appreciate what I'm doing for you.

I wanted Southern Fried chicken . . . wasn't this the South? But they only had chicken in the pot at Dubrows . . . slimy chicken floating in soup surrounded by bubbles of fat.

"No Thanks . . . I don't like boiled chicken . . . tastes like rubber."

"What are blintzes?" I asked the Negro lady, who was serving at the cafeteria counter.

"Jewish crepes," she responded.

"OK . . . I'll have two; thanks . . . with lots of blueberry sauce . . . but no sour cream" Not bad; I really liked them. I never had blintzes in Chicago. Next time I'll try them with sour cream.

"Did you like the blintzes?" asked Herman

"Disgusting" I held my neck and feigned an imaginary vomit. I didn't like Herman and I wasn't about to give him the satisfaction of telling him that I liked his favorite restaurant.

"Next time you have to try the latkas," said Aunt Pearlie.

"What are those?"

"Those are Jewish style potato pancakes . . . eat 'em with apple sauce . . . deeeeelicious."

"Don't they have southern fried chicken anywhere in this town?"

"Yes," said Herman . . . "Pickin' Chicken, just down the block, has chicken in the basket . . . and I know the manager . . . he's a good friend of mine."

Herman was a "name dropper" . . . . always trying to impress people. He insisted that he knew everyone who was famous or near famous. He even had framed pictures of himself with Duke Ellington, the jazz composer, and Barney Ross, the Jewish boxer. Pickin' Chicken was probably run by gangsters. (Mental note: when I send my first tape to Michael, make sure that his storm troopers wipe out Pickin' Chicken.)

Dubrows was a Jewish cafeteria, but no one wore yarmulkehs, and the closest thing to a prayer was the popular pre-meal expression: "Ess gezunterhait!"—a Yiddish term meaning, eat in good health!"

"How come there are no colored people eating here?" I asked my aunt.

"Shhh . . . Myron . . . watch what you say; this is the south. 'Shvartzas' aren't allowed to eat in the same restaurants as white people."

"That's mean," I said . . . "but the women working behind the counter are all Negroes."

"They have work permits . . . otherwise they would have to leave Miami Beach by 6 PM," said Aunt Pearlie.

"What!! I don't believe this . . . this is America . . . this is a free country . . . . how is this possible?" I felt like I was in Berlin, just before the war, where anti-Jewish laws were accepted by the public. It was happening here, all over again, only this time the Jews were the bad guys.

"Myron . . . this is the South . . . this is not Chicago . . . shhhhh."

"How can you call this the South . . . everyone here is from New York . . . and everyone is Jewish?"

"You're right . . . we all know you're right," said my aunt. "but Miami Beach is just a small part of Dade county. We don't make the laws. If you cross over the causeway to Miami . . . you might as well be in Alabama. This is deep south."

"OK . . . I can understand that . . . the other side of the causeway is deep south. But, Miami Beach is all New York Jews . . . why do we have laws that force Negroes to have a work permit . . . or leave town after 6 PM? I can't believe this."

"Give it time," said my father . . . "its very upsetting to me also . . . but it will change. Most of those terrible racial laws were written years ago, before Miami Beach had a large Jewish population. Jews have only started coming here, a lot, since the war."

"Hey kid," said Herman, "I don't see eye to eye with your old man; I was a cop in Chicago back in the 20's, and anytime we had a murder, 'shvartzas' were involved. It ain't the same down here; we boot the god damn 'shvartzas' out of our town, 'cept for those who have jobs. You'll see, it ain't such a—

I interrupted; I couldn't listen to this anymore . . . "I hate this city . . . I hate it!" I started crying. For the past five days I held back tears, but finally . . . I couldn't control myself any longer. "This city looks bright and beautiful on the outside . . . all those pink hotels and phony Florida oranges. But . . . these people are just as bad as the Nazis."

"Rose, why don't you walk home with Pearl and Herman," said my father, "I want to show Myron the ocean."

We sat on a bench looking at the famous moon over Miami. The reflection of the moon on the ocean was beautiful; we listened to the waves and smelled the salt air. We just sat and ate ice cream cones. My father knew when to talk, when to listen, when to bring ice cream.

My father was the youngest of eight brothers and sisters. He went by the name of Sol Louis Lindell, but his birth certificate said his name really was Abe. Not Abraham! Just Abe! He was born in New York on December 1, 1890. However, he liked to glamorize his birth by saying that he was conceived in Russia and incubated in the steerage section of an ocean liner, crossing the Atlantic. His first marriage was to Sophie Stein; it lasted for twenty five years, until she died from strept throat at the age of forty seven. Sol and Sophie had no children. Three months after Sophie's death Sol married Rose Lowenthal, a feisty young woman who soon became my mother. Rose was previously married to Moe Stein, who was Sophie's brother. Thus, my father married his sister-in-law, who already had a child, Bobbie Stein. My half-sister Bobbie was eleven years old when I was born. These relationships were very complicated to me when I was a child. I always thought it strange that my sister called my father Uncle Sol, but she was related to him even before I was born. When I arrived in this world my father was forty eight; he had given up hope of ever having a child. My relatives often told me that he was so elated with my birth he felt like a "bright star" had risen in the East on March 20, 1939 to herald the arrival of the new messiah. My father sometimes called me his "sunshine." We had a very close and special relationship.

"Sunshine . . . I was miserable also when we moved from New York to Chicago. I was only fourteen at the time and begged my mother to let me stay behind, to live with my older brother Nathan. I know what you're going through."

"Dad . . . how can they be so mean to the Negroes in this city, it isn't right? I hate it when people call them 'shvartzahs'."

"When older Jewish immigrants use that word it's not so bad," said my father. "Shvartz means 'black' in Yiddish. But, when American born Jews use that word it's very insensitive."

"How can you be friends with Herman? He's so mean."

"You know the old saying," he chuckled. "You can pick your friends, but you can't pick your relatives."

I continued to complain. I was on a Jewish island comprised mainly of transplanted New Yorkers but racial bitterness was obvious. They wouldn't let go of slavery . . . and I remembered the four statues of Arabian slaves in front of the beautiful Casablanca hotel.

"It will change," my father assured me. "and I think changes are coming soon. President Truman just integrated the Army and baseball has also integrated. And Stevenson is proposing many social changes."

"Stevenson!!! Do you like Stevenson? . . . what about Eisenhower . . . how can you vote against Ike?"

"Ike is a war hero but I don't know what kind of president he'll be. Except for Washington, generals haven't been our best presidents. Did you know, Ike and I were both born in 1890? But, as a Jew I feel a little different about things. Minorities in this country must all stick together. The Negro, especially in the south, is treated like a second class citizen. As Jews . . . it's our moral obligation to support them." "Remember this Myron . . . no one supported the Jews in Europe and they were almost exterminated. All minorities must support each other . . . otherwise, what happened in Germany can happen here also."

Exterminated? What a strange word to use. I thought you exterminated bugs!

"So . . . what does that have to do with Stevenson?" I asked.

"Stevenson will probably lose," said my father, "he's too much of an idealist and too intellectual for America, but he is the voice of the future . . . he is in favor of civil rights legislation for the Negroes. And, any legislation that helps the Negro also helps the Jews. Never forget this Myron, even though you will look all around our little island and see mainly Jewish people we are a very small minority in this country. Don't ever think, not even for a minute, that the moral values that you will learn in Miami Beach represent the thinking of America."

"Dad . . . Are you saying that Americans are bad people?" I felt a terrible sense of hopelessness; my eyes swelled. I cried silently. Americans were supposed to be perfect—we saved the world from the Nazis.

"Unfortunately . . . many people are bad. But here in Miami Beach . . . things will be better." He put his arm around my shoulder.

"Sunshine—those people at Dubrows, those old Jewish people with white hair . . . . they've been through a lot; they've endured a lifetime of anti-Semitism, pogroms, and violence; many of them are survivors of concentration camps; they mean well and they know better, but they lost their will to fight. There is an old Yiddish expression: A yung baimeleh baight zich; an alter brecht zich." (*A young tree bends; an old tree breaks.*)

"But, its wrong . . . everyone knows its wrong."

"This is a fight for your generation." He paused and collected his thoughts. "It is the duty of your generation to end discrimination in America. My generation is too old to fight."

"Dad . . . I don't like being different. I didn't feel like I was different in Chicago. I was one of the only Jewish kids in my class and I wasn't different. But here, I live on an island of all Jewish people . . . and I feel different."

My father smiled and hugged me . . . "because in Chicago we were assimilated, even though we didn't eat mayonnaise and mom packed bagels or halvah in your lunch box. But here we are reminded, every day, of who we are . . . who we really are . . . and sometimes we don't like what we see."

"Dad . . . what's a portico?"

We walked back to the James Manor. We talked about porticos; we talked about baseball and Negroes and about being Jewish in America. My father told me about a book of essays by Ralph Waldo Emerson, "Self-reliance;" he thought I was old enough to understand them, he would help me with the difficult words. I told him that I really loved the blintzes. (Mental note: In my first tape to Michael . . . call off the Storm Troopers; we will not demolish the Casablanca.)

CHAPTER 3

THE VOLUME OF A SPHERE

The next morning I got up very early; it was still dark outside. I took forever deciding what to wear on my first day of school. Black chinos and a red plaid shirt . . . that seemed like it would be OK . . . and penny loafers, with a penny in each shoe . . . . new shiny pennies . . . . a new life!

My father drove slowly to Ida M. Fisher Jr. High, my new school. He told me to write down the names of all streets and signs so I could walk home on my own. Along our path we passed several kosher butchers with signs in Hebrew and Yiddish . . . . I couldn't read either, but I knew that Hebrew had little dots above and below the letters; Yiddish doesn't use any dots. And there were Orthodox Jewish men in beards and long black coats . . . even though it was a sweltering day. September in Miami Beach is always hot . . . even when it rains.

"The dots are vowels," said my father. "Yiddish doesn't use vowels."

"That's dumb," I responded, "like doing arithmetic with only the numbers and no signs. You'd be guessing whether to add, subtract, multiply, or divide."

I was supposed to be in 7A, the second half of seventh grade, but the Registrar informed my father that in Miami Beach, they only had "annual promotion." I had a choice; I could either be put back to the seventh grade or moved up to the eighth grade. The Registrar was a very pretty woman, probably in her early thirties, but she had sad eyes and didn't smile. Her job was to be guardian of the school, and I guess guards aren't supposed to smile. Wow . . . I could "skip" a grade; this was great. Before my father had a chance to ponder the options I jumped in . . . "Put me in the eighth grade."

"But Sunshine . . . maybe you won't be able to handle the work."

"Don't worry dad . . . if its too tough, I can always go back to the seventh grade."

"Well, we can look for a tutor if you have trouble," said my father. "And, don't get into any arguments with your teachers." He gave me a good luck hug and a kiss on the forehead. I was embarrassed; the attractive Registrar was watching. My father always found tutors for me if he thought I needed extra help. During the summer before our move to Miami Beach he hired my cousin Mandy to work with me, two hours a day, mostly on synonyms, antonyms, and homonyms. I learned the difference between "jerk" as a verb and "jerk" as noun, and read (pronounced reed) is the present tense, and read (pronounced red) is the past tense.

"So why don't we spell the two tenses differently?" I asked.

"So that I can make extra money tutoring you," replied my cousin.

I never could understand why 7A came after 7B . . . who designed that system? Shouldn't "A" come before "B?" Maybe B stands for "Before" . . . and A stands for "After."

"Are you sure you'll be OK walking home from school?" asked my father.

"Dad . . . didn't I do all the navigating from Chicago to Miami Beach?"

We lived on 19th street . . . the school was on 14th street . . . you didn't need a compass to find your way home. But, if necessary, I knew how to use one. Michael Bernstein, my old Chicago friend, had lots of World War II memorabilia, including a pair of binoculars from a dead German tank commander, and a compass; he taught me how to use the compass. Michael said he also knew how to use a sextant; Columbus navigated to the New World using only a compass, a quadrant, and the stars; sextants didn't exist then. I knew all about Polaris, the North Star, longitudes and latitudes, and about Greenwich Mean Time. Certainly, I could find my way from 14th street to 19th street, even if I couldn't read Hebrew or Yiddish.

The Registrar asked Harold Lorber, a student assistant, to escort me to my homeroom; I was assigned to section 8B-3. Harold was wearing a yarmulkeh; I never saw a boy wear a yarmulkeh in public before. In Chicago, only the religious Jews, the bearded old men, wore yarmulkehs in public. Except for his little beanie, Harold looked kind of normal. He wore pants and a polo shirt. He should be more careful . . . walking around like that. I'm sure he didn't know about all the Nazis that were lurking in Miami Beach; what better place to hide than on a Jewish Island. My work was cut out for me; President Truman would be proud. I wanted to tell Harold about my mission, but I didn't want to scare him.

"How old are you?" I asked. Harold looked like he was seventeen.

"I'm thirteen . . . I'm in your homeroom. Our homeroom teacher is in charge of student assistants; that's how I got this job."

The classroom for section 8B-3 looked the same as my class in Chicago, the same type of desks with attached chairs and ink wells. What was the purpose of the ink wells? No one ever used the old fashioned dip pens anymore. I guess they were relics from another era and the schools couldn't afford to buy new desks.

I stared at Linda Spiegel. She was much taller than me and she had breasts—big ones!. I handed her my file and asked where I should sit. I assumed that she was my teacher.

"I'm not the teacher," she laughed. "That's her . . . up there."

I looked all around the room; I think my father was right. I didn't belong in the eighth grade; these were adults. All of the girls had breasts; well, maybe not as big as Linda's and many of the boys were huge. I couldn't believe that eighth graders were so much more grown up than seventh graders.

"Boys and girls, I want you to meet Myron Lindell, our new student," said Miss Baker, our home room teacher. "He's from Chicago." Miss Baker smiled without showing teeth . . . and she had no breasts. I could tell . . . she was wearing a see-through white blouse; you could see her bra. Why was she even wearing a bra?

"Good morning Myron" the class responded.

I could detect a hint of sarcasm . . . especially from some of the big guys. Why did my parents name me Myron; I know I was

21

named after my maternal grandfather, Morris, but there were lots of better "M" names. Well . . . it could be worse . . . what if they named me Melvin or Maynard. How difficult would it be to transfer to the seventh grade?

Later, in math class, Miss Baker was explaining how to compute the area of a triangle. The students all looked lost and confused as she wrote the formula on the blackboard:

$A = \frac{1}{2} HW$.

"The Area of a Triangle is computed by multiplying the height by the width . . . and dividing the sum by 2." Lots of blank stares . . . bewilderment . . . none of the kids wanted to be called on by Miss Baker. I learned all about formulas for area and volume in Chicago . . . this would be easy; they were a year behind the Chicago schools.

"The volume of a sphere? That's simple," I responded . . . "V = four thirds Pi R Cube."

I then went to the blackboard and wrote: $V = 4/3 \, \pi \, r^3$

"Very good, said Miss Baker, "and what do you mean by cube?"

"That's when you raise the square of a number one more power."

"I see you are well prepared in math," said Miss Baker. "You can return to your seat."

I was faced with my first dilemma . . . should I stay in the eighth grade? I was definitely way ahead of these kids . . . but they all were bigger than me and certainly, more grown up. I guess thirteen is the age when girls grow breasts . . . none of the girls in my class in Chicago had breasts, not even the fat ones.

"Myron, can you stay a few minutes after school . . . I want to talk to you," said Miss Baker.

"Teacher's pet, teacher's pet," a few kids were chiding me at lunch.

"Only fags live in Chicago," said another kid—Norty Berkowitz. "And what happened to your Go Go White Sox?" Several kids started laughing. . . . most of these kids were Yankee fans. "I think they've Go Go Gone."

"Don't know why . . . I've got lipstick on my fly . . . . Sloppy Blowjob!"

Berkowitz sang to the tune of "Stormy Weather" . . . the boys all laughed as he sang and scratched his balls.

22

What's a Blow Job, I thought? But . . . I wasn't about to make a fool of myself and ask. Everyone else seemed to know what it was.

"Hey kid," Manny Lefkowitz tapped me on the shoulder. Manny was a big tough hoodlum looking guy, who wore a white T-shirt, with sleeves rolled up to the shoulders. "Around here we don't kiss ass to teachers. Learn that fast, or you got trouble wit' me." Manny had huge arms, with muscles; he had a thick New York accent. But, he was a Giants fan . . . not a Yankee fan.

Howard Lefkowitz, a little guy, around my size, walked out from behind Manny and started to say something, but Manny clenched his huge fist and held out his arm, to shelter Howard from me. "Howie, you stay outta' dis'; let me take care of dis' fag." Howie was dressed more like me; black chinos and a plaid shirt. Why was he hanging out with a creepy looking hood like Manny?

The girls ate together at lunch, at separate tables from the boys. The boys all stared at the girls to see which ones had the biggest "boobs" and which ones were wearing "falsies." "Boobs" was a new word . . . I never heard it before . . . it was the New York way of saying "tits." Linda Spiegel and a few of her friends were whispering about Joey Lefkowitz, how cute he was. They all hoped he would be at the school dance that Saturday night.

Manny Lefkowitz, Howard Lefkowitz, Joey Lefkowitz . . . this was confusing. How many Lefkowitzes at this school?

"Aren't there any colored kids here?" I asked Howard Lefkowitz.

"Shvartzahs? Are you nuts?" said Howard. "Manny's right; you are a fag."

"Are you two guys related?

"Nah! we just have the same last name . . . and we're both Giants fans . . . Manny can beat the crap out of anybody here and he protects me. He treats me like I'm his little brother."

"And don't act so smart around here . . . its just gonna' get you in trouble." Howard stood there and scratched his balls . . . and spit on the ground. "If you look weak they'll make life miserable for you.?"

"Who?" I asked.

"All of them . . . just make sure you scratch your balls when you talk to them . . . and forget about that volume of a sphere crap."

"Where you from Howie?" I asked.

"The name's Howard . . . only Manny calls me Howie, and I'm from 'Joisey' near Newark."

Newark? I thought he was saying New York . . . Howard had a way of slurring everything he said . . . in fact, most of these kids talked funny.

"No . . . I lived near NEWARK!" He repeated himself, and scratched his balls again "its in Joisey . . . not far from the City." Even Howard from "Joisey" called it "the City." Howard was my first friend and he wasn't even from a place, just from near a place.

"Have you ever heard of Minnie Minoso?" I asked Howard.

"Yeah . . . he's the Shvartzah that plays for Chicago."

"He's Cuban."

"So what . . . he's still a Shvartzah."

"And it isn't pronounced Chi CA go . . ." I told him . . ." its Chi Caww go."

"Who gives a shit . . . only fags live in Chi Caww go." (Mental note: Tell President Truman to look for Nazis in Newark . . . just outside of New York)

I also met Paul Yardley at lunch that day . . . he seemed different from the other kids; I couldn't put my finger on it. What was different about Paul? He reminded me more of the kids back in Chicago, maybe because he put mayonnaise on a bologna sandwich.

"I'm named after Saint Paul; I'm the token Goy, but I might as well be a Yid, this whole place is all Yids."

"Do you like Minnie Minoso?" I asked.

"Yeah . . . Minoso is terrific . . . he sure put the Go Go into the White Sox." Paul knew a lot about baseball. I enjoyed talking with him at lunch. He said he even knew how to throw a curve ball.

Paul was the bat boy for the Miami Beach Flamingos, the minor league baseball team that played a few blocks from our school. I was impressed! He said he would take me with him one day after school to watch the team practice. He told me that Minoso used to play for the Havana Sugar Kings, the Cuban team in the Florida International League; that's where he first heard of him.

"Really? I didn't know that they played baseball in Cuba . . . except for Minoso."

"Baseball is big in Cuba," said Paul, "lots of great players there. The Sugar Kings always destroyed the other teams in the Florida league."

Paul was from Brooklyn, a Dodgers fan, but he didn't have a New York accent and he didn't scratch his balls when he talked. However, even though he wasn't Jewish he also referred to colored people as "Shvartzahs." Noone ever used the terrible word, "nigger"—that was a redneck term, used only in Miami—the other side of the causeway.

I was having a good time at lunch, talking to Paul, discussing baseball, laughing, and showing him that I could name every starting player on the Dodgers. But the laughing stopped when Buddy Macker walked up to our table. Macker was over six feet tall and very popular with the girls. He always bragged that he had the "biggest dick in the eighth grade." He stood there and said nothing; he just looked down at me . . . one of the shortest kids in the eighth grade. Soon, he was joined by several other tough looking kids; they all stared.

"Hey fag," said Macker. "Do you know what LSMFT means?" The big kids stood there, scratching their balls, waiting for my response.

"Yeah sure . . . . Lucky Strike Means Fine Tobacco."

Macker laughed; they all did . . . and they walked away.

"Forget it," said Macker . . . "he's too young to understand."

Howard Lefkowitz walked out from behind the big kids—his usual hiding place. He looked at me and shook his head to show disappointment, but said nothing.

"Hey Shmuck! Loose Sweaters Means Floppy Tits!" Howard stood there scratching his balls; the big kids were still in the cafeteria watching . . . he had to look cool.

"Oh . . . I get it." I laughed. Then I started to scratch my balls . . . . whatever it took to be accepted.

"No . . . not with the right hand." Howard laughed. "You scratch your balls with your left hand. You use the right hand to pick your nose."

After lunch I had a few additional classes, and my experience was the same in every class; I was way ahead of the other kids—especially in Math, English, Geography, and History. In History I disagreed with the text book and disputed the teacher's comments about the morality of the Pilgrims.

"If the Pilgrims were such virtuous people how could they burn women at the stake?" I asked.

"Because, they were strong, God fearing people, and they believed that they were acting in God's best interest," said the teacher.

"So were the Nazis," I responded, "Hitler was a Catholic." I learned that from Michael Bernstein . . . he knew everything about the Nazis.

"Young man . . . how can you compare the Pilgrims with the Nazis? The Pilgrims were very righteous people; the Nazis were evil fanatics . . . and Hitler was not a Catholic; that mad man was an atheist."

She was wrong about the Pilgrims and also about Hitler, but I knew it was time to shut up. I didn't want to get in trouble, not on my first day of school. My father taught me that the Pilgrims were intolerant zealots who thought that their religion, and only their religion, was the path to salvation. They were very dogmatic people and my history teacher was probably descended from them; she thought she knew everything about everything.

Manny Lefkowitz gave me a secret "thumbs up" . . . anyone who disagreed with a teacher had Manny's respect. I think anyone who scratched his balls in public had Manny's respect. My circle of friends was growing: Manny, Howard, and Paul. It wasn't looking so bad, after all.

My first day of school ended and I immediately left for home. I couldn't wait to tell my father about the Pilgrims and my argument with that dumb history teacher. I loved discussing history with my father. He read a lot about the Civil War and the Russian Revolution and the history of the Jews; he would frequently challenge traditional convictions about history. He told me, many times: "History is written by the winners and it isn't always written right." He told me about the Romans and the Huns, and the life and times of Jewish people in ancient Rome and the Scopes trial, and the Inquisition, and the Pilgrims.

"Myron . . . history looks at the Pilgrims through rose colored glasses . . . the popular belief is that they came to this country for religious freedom. Truth is, they came here for religious domination. With the exception of Roger Williams, they were not very tolerant people." I read a short biography of Roger Williams . . . he was a Pilgrim, but he was a great man. He wanted to compensate the Indians for stealing their land. I wonder what he would say about the 6 P.M. curfew for Negroes in Miami Beach?

I once questioned the importance of studying history, why dwell on the past? Shouldn't we focus on the present and the future? My father certainly wasn't the type person to "cry over spilled milk."

"It's only normal to make mistakes," said my father, "but it's 'dumb' to make the same mistakes twice. An English philosopher in the 18th Century once said: 'those who don't know history are doomed to repeat it.' Look at Hitler; he invaded Russia and suffered huge casualties, same exact fate as Napoleon. Its hard to believe that Hitler didn't avoid the same mistake."

As I walked home I counted the number of sidewalk squares between Ida M. Fisher and the James Manor, never stepping on the cracks between the squares. "Step on a crack . . . and you'll break your mother's back." I took exactly two steps per square and I lived one mile from school (5,280 feet); squares were each five feet . . . that meant there would be approximately 1,050 squares . . . or 2,100 steps. When I reached square #400 I realized . . . I forgot all about my meeting with Miss Baker. I bet she never expected me to know V = 4/3 Pi R Cube. She probably wants me to become a student assistant, like Harold Lorber.

CHAPTER 4

THE HOLY GHOST

What were the responsibilities of a student assistant? I wasn't sure. I'd ask Harold Lorber, maybe today at lunch. Surely, that's why Miss Baker wanted to talk to me. She seemed very impressed when I knew the formula for the volume of a sphere. I wanted to be a patrol boy back in Chicago, directing traffic on a street corner, but those jobs were reserved for eighth graders. I was an assistant patrol boy in the seventh grade, but never got my own belt and badge. If I stayed in Chicago another year and I would have had my own corner with a younger kid working as my assistant.

I walked to school on my own that day, and as I passed the Miljean Hotel, two buildings south of the James Manor, I bumped into Dick Solomon, a boy from my homeroom. He remembered me and introduced himself.

"You're the guy who put Miss Baker in her place yesterday."

"What do you mean?" I asked. "I was only answering her question, about the volume of a sphere."

"She doesn't ask those questions to see how smart 'you' are . . . she asks difficult questions to show how smart 'she' is . . . . and you messed up her act."

"Do you live here at the Miljean?" I asked Dick.

"Yeah, my step-father is the manager. I'm from Boston . . . you're from Chicago, aren't you?"

Talking to Dick was a unique experience; I had never heard a Boston accent before. New Yorkers kind of muffled their "R's" but Dick completely eliminated them. I was convinced that the Boston alphabet only had twenty five letters. Some of his pronunciations were very strange.

"Pahk the Cah in Hahvahd Yahd," that's the old Boston joke. "We can't say that sentence," said Dick.

And "car key," "khaki" and "cocky" . . . . All three of those words sounded the same when said by a Bostonian. Dick said each of them, one at a time, they were identical. We laughed and had fun walking to school together. He thought my Chicago accent was also funny, kind of like I was gargling while talking. What was he talking about? There was no such thing as a Chicago accent; we spoke perfect English, the way it was supposed to be spoken.

"Do you know Howdy Doody's real name?" asked Dick. "You know, the dumb puppet on TV."

"Uh, no," I responded.

"Its Hello Shit!" Dick cracked up laughing. He laughed so much that his nose began to run. He had a great laugh. I began laughing too.

"Are you Jewish?" I asked Dick. He had very light blonde hair, he was shorter than me, and looked like a "shagitz." A shagitz is a Yiddish word for a Gentile boy.

"We're Orthodox. My parents go to shul every Saturday. My Bar Mitzvah is coming up in November; you've gotta' come."

Oops . . . that was a sensitive topic! I didn't like to talk about Bar Mitzvahs; I was embarrassed. It was six months before my thirteenth birthday and I was not going to be Bar Mitzvahed. I didn't want to tell my new Orthodox friend. In Chicago, as my father reminded me, we were very assimilated. None of my Jewish friends or cousins were being Bar Mitzvahed. I would soon find out that in Miami Beach it was much different; the New York Jews were more religious than we were in Chicago. It was unheard of for a Jewish boy in Miami Beach not to have a Bar Mitzvah. Finally . . . the dreaded question: Dick asked about my Bar Mitzvah.

"Uh . . . er . . . um, we just moved here this week, and its kind of late for me to start Bar Mitzvah training, so I guess I'm not going to have a Bar Mitzvah."

"That's horrible. Unless you read from the Torah you won't ever be a man, at least not in the eyes of God." Dick said that he was going to tell his parents and maybe his Rabbi could help put together an "instant" Bar Mitzvah for me.

I reached into my lunch bag and grabbed an early snack . . . a few potato chips.

"Here Dick . . . d'ya want one?"

"Lemme' see the bag. Only if they're kosher . . . gotta' have a U with a circle around it."

"No U," I observed, "but its got a little K in a circle. Is that OK?"

"No . . . only the U is kosher for the Orthodox. I guess the K is OK for other Jews, but we're super strict kosher."

Dick showed me a shortcut to school, cutting across Espanola Way, a neat Spanish looking street; I felt like I was in Havana. As we walked into school together—talking about which food was kosher and which was traif—he put his arm around my shoulder. I didn't find it very unusual, my father did that all the time, but a few kids started laughing and called us "homos." Even Howard Lefkowitz laughed; he didn't like Dick Solomon. Howard liked me; I was his new friend, but he didn't like sharing me with "Solly"—that was the nickname for Dick in homeroom 8B-3.

"Myron . . . did you forget about our meeting yesterday?" Miss Baker showed a new face today . . . a stern face, and she was wearing an orange sweater, not a sheer see-through blouse like the previous day. And her boobs grew overnight; today they were humongous.

"I'm very sorry, Miss Baker, but I had so many things on my mind." I was hypnotized by the sharp orange points on her sweater; I had trouble concentrating.

"Yesterday was my first day of school. I forgot all about our meeting."

"Myron . . . I want to talk to you about the morning devotionals and your behavior in class yesterday." I could hear her teeth clench and grind . . . what did I do to upset her?

The morning devotionals? That was the dumbest thing I ever saw . . . thirty or more Jewish kids (and Paul Yardley) were forced to recite a prayer in class before school. I guess I wasn't too respectful; I chuckled when we all had to say: "In the name of the Father, the Son, and the Holy Ghost." I also drew a picture of a ghost in a bed sheet filled with holes (he was "holy") and I passed the picture to Howard Lefkowitz. It actually was a good drawing;" I was a decent artist.

Miss Baker touched my chin and instinctively, I raised my head. My eyes, which were transfixed on her immense pointed breasts, were now redirected to her steel grey eyes.

"But, I'm not Christian, Miss Baker . . . why do I have to say those words?"

"Because those are the words of God . . . they were not written just for Christians; they are for everyone . . . and 'your people' need them even more, especially if you want to go to heaven when you die."

"I don't understand . . . why do Jews need to pray to the Holy Ghost?"

"Myron . . . I don't feel like getting into an argument with you. Please take this note and go see Dean Kessler; I think the two of your better talk."

Reinhard Kessler was the Dean of Boys. I had relatives in Denver named Kessler, so I was hoping that the dean was Jewish, but Reinhard was also a German name. Well, ether way, Jewish or German, I was positive that he would understand my feelings. Why was it necessary for Jewish kids to say a Christian prayer? Why was it necessary for any type of prayer? We never had "devotionals" in Chicago. I remember singing Christmas carols with my friends in Chicago; I sang all the words except "Christ the Lord" . . . I only mumbled "lah-dah da dah" when it came to that part of the song.

"There is nothing to discuss," said Dean Kessler, a bald elderly man with shiny black shoes and a bright green sport jacket. He waved a crumpled piece of paper in my face. It was my drawing of the holy ghost. How did he get it? I gave it to Howard Lefkowitz.

"Byron, I see that you were disrespectful during morning devotionals . . . and you made some very un-American comments in your history class; you better watch your tongue young man, or you might be accused of being a Commie or an atheist. Bend over boy, and hold your testicles."

"What!!" Did I hear him right?

"You heard me Byron. Bend over."

"Sir, its Myron."

He took down a large wooden paddle that was hanging on his office wall and gave his stern command

"Don't you go 'sassing' me young man. Now . . . assume the position!"

I bent over, held my testicles, and he gave me one hard whack on the "tush." I couldn't believe this was America; what ever happened to freedom of speech? As I left the room and closed the door I listened closely to hear if Dean Kessler was clicking his heels or saying "Heil Hitler." (Mental note: Send a secret coded message to President Truman; find out if Kessler is a Nazi)

I left the Dean's office and returned to class. Miss Baker was explaining the formula for determining the volume of an irregular shaped object. She called several students to the blackboard, one at a time, and made them each look stupid. She liked to chastise students for not doing their homework; her pointed boobs were sharp reminders of her authority. I kept raising my hand; I knew the answer. I knew all about Euclid; you calculate the volume of an irregular object by measuring the volume of displaced water in a cylinder. "Euclid, Euclid" I said it loud enough for Miss Baker to hear me, but she didn't call on me. For the rest of the year, she never called on me again. I got all A's in math . . . she had no choice; I did well on the exams, but she never called me up to the front of the class. She never asked me to show my work on the blackboard and I was never appointed to be a student assistant. Harold Lorber was called to the blackboard frequently; he rarely had the right answer.

During morning devotionals, for the rest of the year . . . I was respectful; I remained silent and I avoided any type of confrontation with Miss Baker, especially on those days when her boobs were big and pointed. I would never again be paddled. Over the ensuing years many boys at Ida M. Fisher Jr. High were subjected to corporeal punishment; they were paddled by the Dean or whipped on the butt by the lanyard of the gym teacher, or slapped on the knuckles with a wooden ruler. Only the Dean had authority to use the paddle, but any teacher could slap your knuckles, and many of them did. But not Miss Baker, she never used the ruler, she never got her hands dirty, she preferred sending "problem" students to the Dean. I don't think girls were ever hit; but if they wore too much makeup or perfume, or "falsies," they were sent to Alba Layne, the Dean of Girls, a middle age woman who always had a smirk on her face. The girls were required to serve detention. I wonder how the teachers knew which girls were wearing falsies? I stared, plenty of times . . . but I could never distinguish real boobs from fake ones. But, Dean Layne was definitely an expert on the subject. I heard that she would always squeeze to tell for sure.

"Nah, you don't have to squeeze em," said Howard Lefkowitz. "If they don't jiggle when the girl's walking then you know that she's wearing falsies."

Miss Baker often supplemented the prayers or psalms with her own sermons and her own venerating prophecies. She talked extensively about the return of the Messiah.

"Every aspect of our earthly existence has been preordained by God; our life, here on earth is merely preparation for the after life." That was not a very comforting thought. How could anyone accept an ideology that viewed an entire lifetime as a dress rehearsal?

"Then why do we have to look both ways when we cross the street?" asked Manny Lefkowitz, "especially if everything's preordained by God."

"Manny," snapped Miss Baker, "do you want to go ask that question to Dean Kessler?"

"No Miss Baker." Under the desk, Manny nervously scratched his balls.

Most of the Jewish kids were like me; we didn't like "forced" morning devotionals, but we didn't put up a fight; I guess we were kind of like the old people at Dubrows, the old people with white hair. However, Barry Kotzen didn't have "white hair" and he wanted to let it be known, loud and clear, how he felt about the mandatory daily prayers, especially the constant reference to the holy ghost. One morning he volunteered to be in charge of devotionals. Miss Baker gave each "God fearing" student an opportunity to select his or her favorite prayer or Psalm and serve as spiritual leader for the class. This was her benevolent way of "opening the gates to Heaven" for Jewish boys and girls.

Barry read a well known Psalm from Ecclesiastics and made a few revisions to one of the passages: ". . . a time to kill and a time to heal, a time to tear down and a time to build . . . and a time to lie down and be pricked." He read this passionate line slowly, eloquently, like a Shakespearean actor, and he elongated the word, "pricked." The class erupted in laughter; all except Miss Baker, who called us "godless heathens." She also said we were "insolent" and "recalcitrant." I wrote down the word "recalcitrant" . . . I would look it up in my dictionary when I

33

got home. I did that a lot, whenever I heard a word that I didn't understand.

The entire class had to serve two hours of detention. Our punishment was to write, 100 times: "I will not be disrespectful of the Lord . . . so help me God." Since we wrote, "so help me God" . . . and signed our name and address this was a solemn oath between us and God. Miss Baker locked our signed letters in her desk drawer and reminded us that we would roast in Hell for eternity if we ever violated that oath. Barry Kotzen was sent to Dean Kessler. As he left the room he called Miss Baker a "cunt." (Mental note: Which takes precedence, a solemn oath with God or a secret mission commissioned by the President of the United States?)

I never saw Barry Kotzen again; he was expelled from school and was forced to transfer to Whitefield or Lear, one of the private schools for incorrigible students and dummies. In 1951, going to a private school meant that you were expelled from the public school or that you were a "draikup," a Yiddish word meaning "scatterbrain."

After school I walked home with Dick Solomon; I told him about my visit to Dean Kessler's office and how I resented having to pray to the holy ghost.

"Did you get paddled, or just the ruler slap?" he asked.

"Paddled? . . . Shit! . . . usually you only get the ruler the first time."

"Hey Myron . . . here's a funny joke about the holy ghost . . .

"An old Jewish man was hit by a car; he was lying at the side of the road, dying.

A Priest happened to see him, sprinkled water on his head and asked:

'Do you believe in the Father, the Son, and the Holy Ghost'?

'Oye! . . . I can't believe this,' said the old man.

'I'm dying and this guy asks me riddles!'"

"I've got to remember that one," I laughed. "My parents will love it."

"Did you see Baker's tits today?" asked Dick. "I'd like to bite those jugs."

I ignored his question. Didn't he know that those orange boobs were phony, just like the phony Florida oranges? And, how come it was OK for teachers to wear falsies . . . but not the girls?

I wondered if Dean Layne needed a student assistant, to help with the squeezing; that would really be a fun job.

"Have you ever been paddled by Kessler?" I asked.

"Sure, many times. I keep a fat wallet in my back pocket; grab my "baitsim" (*Yiddish slang word for testicles*) and let the son of a bitch paddle away. Nothing to it! Only fags complain."

Dick was lying; I didn't know it then, but eight months later he was paddled badly, for telling Miss Baker that Jesus Christ was nothing more than a fable invented by Peter and Paul. I was only hit once, and it wasn't really that hard. But Dick felt the full fury of Dean Kessler. He went home crying to his mother. The next day his parents came to school, to file a protest. I don't know the details of the encounter but Dick never returned to school. His parents moved across the causeway, to Miami. His stepfather got a new job and Dick transferred to Shenandoah Jr. High School.

That night a visitor came to our apartment at the James Manor; it was Rabbi Meyer Lipschitz, from Dick Solomon's Orthodox shul. Dick told his parents that I was not going to have a Bar Mitzvah. Rabbi Lipschitz volunteered to give me six months of private tutoring if we would join his Congregation.

My father was not religious and had no use for temple membership. "Belonging to a temple is like owning a boat; you never stop getting hit for money." Rabbi Lipschitz became very emotional, almost as if I were converting to Christianity. He made an impassioned appeal in Yiddish: "Vi men iz gevoint oif der yugend, azoi tut men oif der elter." (*that which is practiced in youth will be pursued in old age*). Then he started shaking his fist toward the ceiling and yelling in Yiddish until my mother interrupted, to prevent an argument. She was always concerned about my father's heart condition. She asked the Rabbi to leave. I never had a Bar Mitzvah and in future years my father said that he was wrong. He made me promise that I would force my children to be Bar Mitzvahed . . . . or Bas Mitzvahed if I had daughters.

CHAPTER 5

THE GIANTS WIN THE PENNANT

Most classes during my first year at Ida M. Fisher were essentially a repeat of what I had in Chicago. But Phys. Ed. was a unique experience, very different from the co-ed gym classes of Chicago, where boys and girls played indoor sports and games. In Miami Beach, my Phys. Ed. class was one hour every afternoon, immediately after History, and before General Science. Boys and girls went to separate locker rooms and changed into gym clothes. The rigid classroom control and Puritanical morality, which was prevalent in 1951, was completely abandoned in Phys. Ed. Different rules applied; teachers and students used a different vocabulary and a different code of conduct was in effect . . . . at least for the boys.

Girls went to a separate locker area on the far side of the gymnasium. The boys always fanaticized about sneaking over there, to watch the girls in the showers . . . . but it never went beyond fantasy. The girls wore baggy one piece gym suits. One day, the beautiful Linda Spiegel came to the doorway of the boys locker room with a note for the coach. She wasn't very beautiful that day, not in her loose fitting gym suit; you couldn't even tell that she had the biggest boobs in the eighth grade. Girls played unusual sports like "kick ball" or "ring toss." Ring Toss was a stupid game, similar to volleyball, but it was played with a big thick rubber ring instead of a ball. Girls would just catch the ring and flip it back across the net; it was the forerunner of the

Frisbee, but the ring didn't float in the air. The girls also had instructions in archery, which was supposed to be good for breast development. I'm sure that Linda could compete with Robin Hood, the best archer in Sherwood forest.

The boys wore tan shorts, white T-shirts, and sneakers. "Sneakers" was a New York word, which I added to my rapidly expanding vocabulary. In Chicago we called them Gym Shoes. My list of unique New York words was increasing on a daily basis, mainly from Phys. Ed. class: "boobs, knockers, or jugs" instead of "tits," "franks" instead of hot dogs, "soda" instead of "pop," "pecker, putz, shmuck, or shlong" instead of dick, not to mention "knocked up, feeling up, and shacking up." The Phys. Ed. coaches didn't mind the banal overuse of profanity; it was regarded as "manly" to augment your conversation with cuss words. Visual obscenities were also popular; giving the finger was a normal way to make your point. Even the "F" word would not get you in trouble . . . . as long as you wore proper Phys. Ed. attire and showered before returning to your next class. Phys. Ed. class was the perfect environment for Manny Lefkowitz. He loved walking around stark naked, farting, scratching his balls, saying "pussy" and the "F" word; he was king of the locker room.

Boys had to buy athletic supporters for Phys. Ed., even the youngest boys. I went to Reisler Brothers sporting goods store to buy my first jock strap. "What size do you wear?" asked the teenage sales girl. This was embarrassing; I didn't feel like telling her the size of my private parts.

"Oh . . . I guess about average," I spread my thumb and index finger . . . Of course I exaggerated . . . . quite a bit.

"Not your pecker . . . your waist size." She laughed.

We had three Phys. Ed. teachers, and Coach Mookie Malloy was in charge, or as he liked to say: "Head Cheese." He was a jolly, rotund man, with a deep southern accent and one long connected eyebrow. He constantly laughed and referred to Jesus as the Lord. He was the first person I ever heard to use the expression, "mother-fucker." "MF" was never used by boys at Ida M. Fisher, and in future years, when "MF" became more widely accepted, I wondered if that popular profanity was actually created by Coach Malloy.

"Mookie spookie," as he was affectionately known by some of the boys (but not by me), walked around the locker room wearing only his jock strap, and he farted a lot, even more than Manny Lefkowitz. We all applauded when they were super loud. He was a good person to have on your side; boys went out of their way to be friends with Coach Malloy. If you were one of "Mookie's boys" he would support you, tell you dirty jokes, and when he was bored he'd call you to his office to sit and play checkers. Paul Yardley said that on Jewish holidays, when he was one of the only kids at school, he would sit with Coach Malloy all day long and play Gin Rummy. But if you ever forgot your gym clothes and failed to "dress" for Phys. Ed. Malloy would make your life miserable.

Boys who failed to dress for Phys. Ed. would be humiliated in front of all other students. Coach Malloy would call the boy a "mother-fucker" or a "pussy" and have him strip, totally nude. The boy would then be marched into the large shower room, where fifty other boys would crowd around and watch the public "execution." He would have to bend over and "assume the position"—the same position that Dean Kessler used for paddling—holding his testicles. With Kessler, you were fully dressed; with Malloy you were butt naked. Malloy would tell everyone to take one last look at the little (or fat) white ass . . . . and he gave a quick snap of his lanyard, leaving a U-shaped welt on the boy's butt. A lanyard is a thick braided necklace, worn around the neck of a Phys. Ed. coach. A whistle dangles from a lanyard to reinforce the authority of the coach. Coach Malloy had a gold whistle; the two subordinate coaches had chrome whistles. Only the "Head Cheese" got to wear gold. Unlike Kessler, who made his paddling a private matter, Coach Malloy preferred a public exhibition . . . he felt it made more of an impact on the other boys. Rarely would any boy come to Phys. Ed. and forget his shorts, sneakers, and jock strap.

If you forgot to take a shower before returning to class Malloy only gave you a warning . . . he referred to the "shower problem" as a "minor crime"—the first "offense" didn't warrant the lanyard. But, you were put on "warning status"—he made a note in his grade book. Coach Malloy always carried his grade book with him, even when he only wore his jock strap . . . it was a constant reminder to the students . . . . you didn't want to get on Malloy's bad side a second time.

Taking public showers with fifty boys was not my favorite thing to do, especially when I was twelve years old. Ida M. Fisher shared gym facilities with Miami Beach High School; I was twelve, and not yet developed . . . the high school boys were seventeen and eighteen, fully developed. I did not want to be seen nude by boys who had hair all over their body, especially pubic hair. But, Malloy stood watch on the shower . . . making sure that every boy, from seventh through twelfth grade took a shower before returning to the next class. Coach Malloy also watched to make sure that nothing "funny" happened in the shower . . . lots of jokes about never dropping your bar of soap and bending over. As I walked across the locker room, I always covered my lower half with a towel. Then, when I entered the communal shower, I quickly hung the towel on a hook and immediately turned and faced the nozzle . . . with only my back side exposed to the other boys. The older boys, who were more secure, showered with their backs to the wall and their well developed front sides proudly on display.

◆

The New York Giants were thirteen games behind the Brooklyn Dodgers on September 1, 1951, but the Giants made the biggest comeback in the history of baseball, and by the end of September the season wound up with the Giants and Dodgers tied for first place. There would be a one game playoff, to determine which team would go to the World Series and face the Yankees. However, no matter who won or lost . . . it would be an all New York world series. Almost everyone at Ida M. Fisher was emotionally involved. Howard and Manny Lefkowitz were pulling for the Giants; Paul Yardley was a Dodgers fan . . . even Dick Solomon, who was from Boston, liked the Dodgers . . . and of course, my father was a lifetime Giants fan, from the days of Christy Mathewson.

On the day of the Giants-Dodgers playoff game we had an important touch football game in Phys. Ed. My team was playing for the championship. Most boys in my class were faced with a dilemma, whether to go to school or stay home with a fake illness, so they could watch the playoff game on TV. For me, it was an easy decision . . . I couldn't care less who won the baseball game. But, five or six boys cut class that day, and my team was beaten badly.

Sookie Bauman, a very athletic seventh grader came running on the field shouting: "The Giants won the pennant . . . the Giants won the pennant . . . Bobby Thompson hit a two-out home run in the bottom of the ninth . . . the Giants won the pennant." Our touch football team was losing 21-0, so we didn't mind quitting and forfeiting the game. Almost every boy was too ecstatic or too depressed to continue playing football. I immediately called my father from a pay phone outside the locker room . . . to offer my congratulations. I could barely understand what he was saying . . . he was shouting just as loud as the kids at school. "The Giants won the pennant . . . the Giants won the pennant." That was so unlike him; he never got silly

That was a major event in American sports history . . . Bobby Thompson's legendary home run has often been referred to as "The Shot Heard Round the World." It was like one of those famous or infamous days in history, that people never forget . . . one of those moments in time when everybody remembers exactly where they were and what they were doing . . . like Pearl Harbor Day or the day when President Roosevelt died. Some of the boys were shouting with joy; some were pissed off, they ran around kicking the walls of the locker room. Coach Malloy relaxed his standards that afternoon and let the "minor crimes" slip by without even a "warning." Almost every boy left Phys. Ed. and went to his next class without showering. I remember what I was doing the day the Giants won the pennant . . . I was in the shower room, alone, taking a wonderful long hot shower, with my back to the nozzle and my front side fully exposed."

That night, back at the James Manor, it was "Uncle Miltie Night" . . . the tenants all gathered in the lobby of the apartment building to watch the Milton Berle show on a twelve inch television set. The reception was terrible because we didn't have an outdoor antenna. My job, for which I was paid two dollars, was to stand next to the TV and hold the "rabbit ears" for the entire hour; I was a human antenna. Everybody loved that show, and when the four Texaco service men began to sing the opening jingle the old people at the James Manor joined in chorus. Some sang with Yiddish accents, some sang with New York accents:

"Oh we're the men of Texaco,
we work from Maine to Mexico,
There's nothing like this Texaco of ours.
Our show tonight is powerful,
we'll wow you with an hour-full
of howls from a shower-full of stars."

CHAPTER 6

PREPARING FOR WORLD WAR III

During the next week the Yankees beat the Giants four straight games to win their third consecutive World Series but I didn't watch any of the games on TV. I was still depressed that the White Sox came so close, but were eliminated during the final week of the season. I hated the Yankees, and I hated the Giants, and I hated the Dodgers . . . they were all from New York. But the kids at Ida M. Fisher were happy, even those who were Giants fans . . . because it was still a New York team that won it all; even my father was happy. I could sense that he was beginning to disavow the forty seven years he lived in Chicago; he had a rekindled affinity for his New York roots. And over the next few years he also developed a strong awareness of his Jewish heritage; he even glued a Mezuzah on the front door of our apartment. That stuck me as odd since he ate milk and meat together and never attended synagogue.

The movers finally arrived from Chicago with my bicycle, tape recorder, and accordion. I hated playing the accordion, and I guess I was terrible; even my mother left the house when I practiced. But my father said that a musical talent would serve me well during my teenage years . . . . I would be popular at parties. And an accordion was better than a piano; you could carry it with you. Back in Chicago I had to practice one hour a day; I was also part of a traveling accordion band. We played at free community events, hospitals, and nursing homes. Our best songs were Auch Di Leiber Augustin, The Skaters Waltz, and Lady of Spain. During rehearsals, when we practiced Lady of Spain, we all sang: "Lady of Spain I adore you, lift up your dress I'll explore you." I rember one girl in the band, Edna (I never knew her last name). She eventually convinced her mother that the accordion was inhibiting her breast development; she quit two weeks before our big recital. During rehearsals Edna loved "Lady of Spain" . . . she stood and lifted her dress when we sang our spirited rendition.

I had hoped that I could discontinue the accordion in Florida, and I complained that it was bad for my posture; I began slouching, intentionally . . . but, despite my pleas I was forced to take weekly lessons from Ziggy Bloom, a music teacher who lived in our neighborhood. Mr. Bloom was a World War II veteran, a short plump man with a bushy moustache. He was a great accordion player. He told me that if I was really good with the accordion I could serve in the USO during the next war—entertaining soldiers. That was certainly a better option than fighting in the infantry or in some type of combat position. In 1951 everyone assumed that World War III was part of our destiny; the Korean War was a step in that direction. Eventually we would have to go to war with the "Commie Bastards" . . . . Stalin was just as bad as Hitler and America would soon be locked in WWIII with the Russians or the Chinese, or both. Yeah, I would rather play an accordion in WWIII . . . it sounded a lot safer than hand-to-hand combat. Back in Chicago, Michael Bernstein told me that Russian teenagers were getting daily training with knives and bayonets. They were using captured Nazi soldiers as instructors.

Mr. Bloom said that he entertained troops during the war and never saw a German or a Jap, but he saw lots of Italians. That's because they were great accordion players. Mr. Bloom was Jewish, but he had all kinds of Italian memorabilia in his house—a shelf full of Caruso records and a three-dimensional model of La Scala, the opera house in Milan; you could remove the roof and look down into the building. He drank lots of Italian wine and hung empty straw covered Chianti bottles from his kitchen ceiling . . . and he always said, "Ciao" or "arrivederci" instead of goodbye. He was a widower; he lived alone and loved telling me stories without endings . . . he made me develop creative endings for his stories. He taught me the value of "shared discovery."

The first song Mr. Bloom gave me to practice was "Oh Solo Mio." It was fun to sing that song while I played—the louder the better. The accordion music drowned out my terrible voice and my singing drowned out the terrible accordion music, but together it wasn't as bad as you might expect; I liked it. But, I don't think my neighbors did. When I sang "Oh Solo Mio," the inmates at the James Manor banged tin cups on the walls of their cells: "Hey . . . Dick Contino . . . shut the hell up!." Dick Contino was the world's best accordion player . . . he was amazing with the "Sabre Dance." I also played "Funiculi Funicula" and "Arrivederci Roma." The last two months of 1951 was my "Italian Period" . . . I drank grape juice from Chianti bottles and hung a few of those straw covered bottles from the ceiling at the James Manor. I was really improving with the accordion; even my posture improved, and my mother bought me a black beret. I considered changing my name to Mario. It was an "M" name, so I wouldn't be dishonoring the memory of Morris, my grandfather.

On December 31, 1951, at the James Manor New Years Eve party, I wore my beret and played a few of my Italian songs; everybody sang along when I played "Funicui Funicula." Herman did card tricks and ventriloquism . . . his Charlie McCarthy routine. I never liked Edgar Bergen, the ventriloquist. How could you tell if his lips were moving, he was on radio? I prefered Paul Winchell; he was on TV. The cameras always zoomed in on his lips, and he could make Jerry Mahoney talk even while drinking a glass of water. After Herman finished his act an old lady with a thick Yiddish accent did great impersonations of pigs and turkeys, and a fat man lifted his shirt and made his belly roll in tune to "Roll Out the Barrel."

When we finished our show all the tenants at the James Manor posed for a group photo; I was in the first row, with my accordion strapped on my shoulders.

Ziggy Bloom said I had a promising future as an accordionist; he loved the way I played "Oh Solo Mio" . . . he would put on his beret, his was green, hold a glass of Chianti in the air and sing along with me . . . and he knew the whole song in Italian. He entered me in a radio talent show where I would be playing the new Israeli folk song, "Tzena Tzena." I practiced it for weeks, at least an hour a day, until I was getting pretty good. I distributed stamped, pre-addressed postcards to my classmates, telling everyone to listen to the radio show; I needed their votes to win the contest.

"Have you ever performed in public?" asked Mr. Bloom. "I mean other than your accordion band in Chicago or the James Manor Show?" He was worried that I might get stage fright.

"Well, when I was seven, I sang on stage at Moores, a resort in Wisconsin. Most of the little kids were called up to the stage after dinner; we each sang a song of our choice, along with the band. I sang 'Mairsey Doats" a popular song back in 1946. Of course, I couldn't quite get the lyrics right; it was a tongue twister."

"Were you any good?"

"I thought I was, but the guests all groaned when I sang. I was the fifth consecutive kid to sing the same song." Mr. Bloom laughed and almost choked on his cigar.

At the radio talent show I followed a brilliant sixteen year old piano virtuoso who played a concerto by Mozart; he was amazing . . . . a child prodigy. His fingers flew across the keyboard. I was sick to my stomach; I wanted to vomit . . . I wanted to go home. How could I follow that act? I was so nervous when I played Tzena Tzena on the radio, my hands broke out in a cold sweat. My fingers slipped down the accordion keyboard. I had to start over; I was in pain . . . shaking . . . suffering. When we left the radio studio my father said nothing. I broke out in hives, a nervous reaction. My eyes puffed up; I could hardly see. Aunt Pearlie hugged me; Herman laughed and blew smoke at me. He never stopped smoking, even at the radio studio where they had large "No Smoking" signs.

The next day, back at school, Manny Lefkowitz laughed even louder than Herman. He had listened to the radio show.

"I could play Tzena Tzena better than that on my balls," he roared with laughter; so did everyone else. Everyone had listened to the talent show, even though none of them mailed their postcards.

Two days later my father took down the Chianti bottles and donated the accordion to the Jewish Home for the Aged. I never saw Ziggy Bloom again, except two years later when I saw him entertaining at a very bizarre party; I abandoned my plans to be a USO performer in WWIII, but I was still worried. I was almost thirteen and I knew that in five more years I could be drafted into the army, and by then the dreaded WWIII will probably begin, once Russia started making hundreds of A-bombs.

"I know you're concerned about WWIII," said my father. "But if it happens it will be on two fronts, against the Russians and the Chinese, and there will be many non-combat positions for Americans who are familiar with the Chinese culture."

My father made a good point; Americans knew a lot about Russia since it was a European country and many Jews (myself included) were of Russian descent, but virtually no one knew anything about the culture of China except for Chinese laundries and Chinese food, and most likely, in China they didn't even eat the same Chinese food that we did.

"You forgot about yo yo's and Chinese Checkers," said my father, and he chuckled. "Why don't you go to the library and check out a book about Confucius, his philosophy is the soul of Chinese culture."

"Shouldn't I read about Mao? He's the leader of Communist China."

"I think Confuscious is more important than Mao," said my father "Its like comparing Franklin Roosevelt and Jesus Christ in western culture."

The library was on 21st street, just 2 blocks from our apartment; it was a beautiful building, mostly pink marble with a big glass dome in the middle, and the inside had polished wooden floors that were shiny like mirrors. The librarian helped me find a biography of Confucius and a smaller book with many of his quotations.

"If you really want to learn about the culture of China," said the librarian, "you should read about Mao Tse-tung; he is transforming that tired old country into a vibrant communist state. The ancient man you are reading about was more than two thousand years ago, long forgotten; Mao is the face of the future."

My father and the librarian certainly had opposing views, so I looked forward to reading about the life of Confucius. He lived from 551 BC-479 BC; I took out a pencil and tried to figure out how old he was when he died; he was 72. It was complicated to compute ages during the BC era, you had to do it with backward arithmetic. I wonder how they really dated events in that era. Obviously, before Christ nobody knew that it was BC, the years weren't counted in reverse.

I carried the small book of quotations to school and during lunch I enjoyed reading the philosophy of Confucius. He reminded me somewhat of Benjamin Franklin; they both had hundreds of short clever quips.

"Why are you reading about that strange looking Chinaman," said Miss Baker, my homeroom teacher. "If you want to read about great philosophers of that era you should read about Peter or Paul; they shaped the conscience of mankind."

"How did they write dates in the BC era?" I asked. "In 551 BC no one knew that Christ would be here in 551 years."

"Of course they did," exclaimed Miss Baker, "everyone knew that the messiah was coming, even in China. In fact, one of the three wise men was a Chinaman."

Confucius was a social philosopher, and he believed in loyalty to family and respect of elders. Essentially, he believed in the family as a basis for an ideal government.

"That's where Mao differs," said my father. "Mao is attempting to break up the family and create communes, where children can become indoctrinated in a collective mentality; I don't think Mao will succeed in changing several thousand years of culture."

I also read that Confucius was the creator of the Golden Rule, even though Christians think that it came from Jesus Christ.

The well known Christian version says, "do unto others that which you would have them do unto you," but Confucius said: "Do not do to others what you do not want done to yourself." The Chinese version made more sense. It was simply telling people not to do mean things to other people. The Christian version was not very realistic. What if I ran up to a beautiful girl on the street and started kissing her, just because I wanted her to kiss me? If I did that I would probably get arrested.

My father laughed at my analogy. "I don't think you could use the Golden Rule as a defense in court."

"Maybe not in the court of man," said Miss Baker, "but in the court of God our soul will be judged by the Golden Rule of Jesus, not by the chop suey rules of an ancient Chinaman."

I subsequently found out that there was also a Jewish version of the Golden Rule in the Talmud, and it was almost identical to Confucius. "What is hateful to you, do not do to your fellowman. That is the entire Law; all the rest is commentary."

"Too bad Judaism didn't stop there," said my father, "it's the remaining 10,000 pages of commentary and rules that drove me away from religion."

We sat together at the kitchen table eating bagels, drinking Chinese tea, and reading many thought provoking quotations from Confucius. My father always stressed that I should not be a quitter. Even if I tried and failed, I should just keep on trying. His eyes lit up when he found the following quote from the great teacher:

"Our greatest glory is not in never falling, but in rising every time we fall."

CHAPTER 7

IN SEARCH OF DOUBLE NYMPHS

After school I usually rode my bike to the Miami Beach Library; they had interesting programs for kids. I especially liked one slide show about the ruins of Pompeii. The people in that little town died from vocanic fumes; even dogs were unable to escape the poison death. I sure was glad there weren't any volcanoes near Miami Beach. I also went to the beach a lot, either with Dick Solomon or Howard Lefkowitz, but never with both of them together. They didn't like each other. Howard laughed at Dick's Boston accent . . . he thought Dick talked like a "pompous faggot." Dick laughed at Howard's Jersey accent . . . he thought Howard talked like a "low class degenerate." But, I liked them both and neither of them were Yankee fans.

One day during lunch Howard was telling me lurid stories about a beautiful divorced "shikseh" named Virginia, who lived in his apartment building and loved to give blowjobs to young boys. "A shikseh," said Howard, "is a female goy." And the popular belief was that all shiksehs were hot stuff, especially divorced ones.

"You see," said Howard, "once a woman is married and gets laid she can't live without it no more."

Howard knew a lot, almost as much as Michael Bernstein, but certainly not about Nazis or navigation, and he didn't know as much about baseball as Paul Yardley. But, he was a good teacher; he taught me all about girls and sex and blowjobs, and when he didn't have his body guard, Manny Lefkowitz, hovering over him he could carry on a conversation without scratching his balls or spitting. Even his "Joisey" accent disappeared.

"All divorced women are nymphomaniacs, and divorced shiksehs are double "nymphs"—they can't control themselves," said Howard.

"They go nuts if they don't have it every day. All you have to do is whip it out and they're on their knees. But, it ain't that way at school; most all those girls are Jewish"

According to Howard, Jewish girls were never nymphs; they were too worried about their reputation. But, even Jewish girls will "put out," if you drive a Cadillac. Howard qualified the Cadillac observation; it was only hearsay, something he heard from his mother.

"But why do they call it a blowjob?" I asked . . . "the girl is sucking—not blowing."

"I don't know; go ask Miss Baker." Howard and I laughed.

Howard convinced me to come with him to visit Virginia after school. He said that she had given him blowjobs many times and that she would do me also, as a favor to him. One side of me said this was exciting; another side said it was "sick"—another side said it was scared, very scared.

Howard lived in the lower end of South Beach. We sometimes called that part of town Bagel Beach because lots of old Jewish people lived there. It was the low income section of Miami Beach. He lived in a purple and white tenement on 10th and Euclid, a funny looking apartment building with arched doorways and circular windows. The buildings in Bagel Beach were not new and modern, not like James Avenue. They were built in the 1930s; very old fashioned architecture, twisted columns and glass block windows, relics from another time, another era.

Virginia wasn't home; thank God! I didn't really want to go there; I only went so that Howard wouldn't think I was a fag or a homo.

"My father died a few years ago," said Howard, "and my mom is too sick to work so we're on welfare; that's why we live in a rat trap shit hole like this." Howard told me how he missed Newark, but his mother had lung problems; she couldn't take the cold anymore. As we talked, he put on an apron and started vacuuming the apartment—to get ready for Shabbos—the

Jewish Sabbath. I never saw a boy vacuum before, and certainly never saw a boy wear an apron. I can't believe "he" called me a homo—just because Dick Solomon had his arm around my shoulder.

"Almost everybody is here for the same reason," said Howard. "One of their parents got sick or died and they had to move to Florida. You ever hear of Horace Greely?"

"Yeah . . . he was the newspaper writer in New York that said 'Go west young man.'"

"Yup!" said Howard, "but my mom says that the old people musta' been hard of hearing . . . they all went south, 'specially the old Jews."

Howard read a lot, like I did, but his mother couldn't afford to buy books; he only read books from the public library. We talked about the way colored people were treated in Miami Beach; Howard thought it was disgusting . . . but what could we do about it. In Newark, some of his best friends were colored kids. But, according to Howard, southern Negroes were different, they weren't smart enough to go to the same schools as white kids; that's why they had separate, segregated schools. We talked about how they had to ride on the back of the bus; that was the law, and they had to drink at separate drinking fountains. And, if they tried on clothes in a store, especially bathing suits or underwear, they would have to buy it, even if it didn't fit.

"Myron . . . that's one law I agree with. How can you let a shvartza return a bathing suit after he touched it with his gonads . . . would you let them return food after putting it in their mouth?"

"What are gonads," I asked?

"Your private parts," said Howard, "and shvartzahs shlongs' are so fuckin' huge, they can't wear the same size bathing suit or underwear as white men."

Howard's mother was a little old lady; she coughed a lot and never stopped smoking and she saved grocery store coupons under a huge magnetic Jewish star on her refrigerator. Everytime she placed a new coupon under the star she mumbled a quick prayer. Mrs. Lefkowitz told me that she was working "off the books" as a maid . . . if the government knew she was working she would lose her welfare payments. But, she needed extra money to pay back loans for Howard's Bar Mitzvah. Mrs.

Lefkowitz showed me a an expensive leather bound photo album from the Bar Mitzvah. She beamed with pride, especially when she showed the picture of Howard wearing a yarmulkeh and "talis"—a Hebrew prayer shawl.

"Howard gave me goose bumps when he chanted from the Torah.," said Mrs. Lefkowitz. Smoke came out of her mouth as she relived the details of the happiest day of her life. "His father would have been so proud of him; the Bar Mitzvah is the most important moment in the life of a young Jewish boy. It's his covenant with God."

"Yeah, that's true," I said. "I had my Bar Mitzvah early, at twelve . . . before I left Chicago." I couldn't tell her the truth, that I was not going to have a Bar Mitzvah. She asked me if I would like to read the prayer before dinner.

"No, I can't read Hebrew; at our temple we only read in English." I was getting myself deep into a lie; I didn't like this . . . I wish I had just told her the truth.

"But the Torah is only in Hebrew," said Mrs. Lefkowitz.

"I know, but ours had English translations. They do things different in Chicago; it isn't as Jewish there." That almost sounded believable.

"I hate it here, the way they make you do morning devotionals and pray to the Holy Ghost." . . . I tried to change topics . . . I didn't want to talk about Bar Mitzvahs anymore.

"Those are only words Myron . . . as long as you have been Bar Mitzvahed they can't hurt you . . . they can't get you to convert to Jesus; God will insulate you."

I called my parents and asked if it was OK to stay late at Howard's apartment; I was invited for dinner. Mrs. Lefkowitz said they were having a Friday night dinner with one of their neighbors. What a strange expression, a "Friday night dinner" . . . what else would you have on Friday night? I wondered if she referred to other nights like that . . . Thursday night dinners, Wednesday night dinners?

"C'mon Myron, we have to wash our hands and get ready for Shabbos," said Howard.

Howard and I went to the bathroom and washed our hands, but he wouldn't let me leave the room until he peed and said a brief Hebrew prayer—a special prayer for washing your hands.

"Baruch Atah Adonoi—Elohenu Melech Hah A Lom . . . . Hands and Giants . . . Amen"

It was the traditional Jewish prayer, but with Howard's special ending . . . . a blessing for our clean hands and the New York Giants. Even though they lost the World Series to the Yankees it was a prayer for next year. Howard removed his T-shirt and changed to a clean white dress shirt, his special Shabbos shirt. He loaned me one also; it was disrespectful to God to wear a T-shirt at a Friday night dinner. Howard had hair on his chest and elsewhere. Not me; I was still waiting for hair to grow on my body—anywhere.

"Myron, this is Virginia, our upstairs neighbor," said Mrs. Lefkowitz, "she will be joining us for Shabbos." Virginia smiled, a half smile, kind of like the Mona Lisa; she had full red lips and her hair was cut in bangs hanging down to her eyes. She looked at me but said nothing. I was in a trance, seduced by the far away look in her eyes.

Oh No! A warm surge came over my body and an embarrassing bulge was growing between my legs. I was sitting at Mrs. Lefkowitz's Friday night dinner next to the double nymph and I was sexually aroused. This was a religious ritual; God would be observing every move I make, even my thoughts. I would not stand up to say hello to Virginia. I'm sure Mrs. Lefkowitz thought I was rude. Virginia was sitting on my left, Howard was on my right. He looked down and whispered . . . . "boner, boner, boner."

Virginia was probably twenty five; she was thin and very pretty. She had brown hair and rosy cheeks. I guess if you give too many blowjobs your cheeks turn red. And she had small pointed boobs; in those years, boobs were always pointed. It wasn't until many years later that breasts became round. Virginia wore a brown velvet dress and a dark green necklace; I had a sudden desire to slide my hands all over her dress, not just her boobs . . . the entire dress.

Mrs. Lefkowitz rested her burning cigarette on the far side of the table, covered her head with a lace doily, and lit the ceremonial candles. Then she blew smoke out of her mouth and recited the same prayer that Howard said in the bathroom, but her ending did not make reference to clean hands or the New York Giants. Her prayer concluded with a cough and a blessing for Shabbos.

"Amen," said Howard and Virginia. "Amen." I repeated

"Virginia, look here . . . Myron's got a boner," Howard chuckled and mumbled, urging her to peek under the table cloth. Virginia waited until Mrs. Lefkowitz was in the kitchen slicing the brisket. Then, she lifted the table cloth and looked . . . she really looked. I threw my napkin on my lap, quickly, to cover the humiliating bulge, but it was too late. Virginia saw it . . . and she smiled!. Oh my God! My face turned beet red, like the horse radish that was starting to make me choke.

One bite of the spicy gefilte fish, which Mrs. Lefkowitz smothered with horse radish, and my nose began to run like a faucet. Virginia had the same problem; her nose was dribbling all over her beautiful face. Every time I looked at her she had a napkin in hand, wiping her nose. Of course, I didn't look at her too much; I had a problem, under the table and if I continued looking at Virginia it would never go down. Howard laughed and called us both "goys." I guess shiksahs and non-Bar Mitzvahed Jewish boys were the same . . . neither of us could tolerate horse radish.

"Thank you for inviting me to dinner Mrs. Lefkowitz," said Virginia. "Everything was delicious and eventually I'll get used to the horse radish.

"Hey Howard," said a smiling Virginia, "why don't you and Myron come upstairs for a while?" Mrs. Lefkowitz gave Virginia a strange look; I think she was very suspicious . . . and knew that the double nymph wanted to conclude her Friday night dinner with a special dessert.

"Myron, I think its time that you headed home," said Mrs. Lefkowitz, "your parents will be worried." I thanked Mrs. Lefkowitz and as I left the apartment Howard was flapping his wings and making chicken sounds under his breath . . . "puk puk puk puk."

That could have been my first sexual experience, but I wasn't ready—not even close! I was much too shy to let a girl see my "gonads." I didn't even have pubic hair and Howard did.

I lived on James Avenue until the end of eighth grade and I saw Howard many times, but I always found one excuse or another not to visit Virginia, and not to show Mrs. Lefkowitz the pictures from my "English only" Bar Mitzvah. I told her that the photo album was lost by the movers, the company that transported all our personal belongings from Chicago. It was difficult to live a constant lie, but I didn't want Howard to know that I was scared and I didn't want his mother to know that I was never Bar Mitzvahed. In future years, when I was ready I would search for the double nymph many times, but I could never find her again.

CHAPTER 8

PARTING OF THE RED SEA

Several weeks after my first Shabbos dinner I attended Dick Solomon's Orthodox Bar Mitzvah. I had more exposure to Judaism during these past two weeks than in the first twelve years of my life. I joined the Solomon family as they walked from 19th and James to a very small Orthodox shul on 15th Street. Religious Jews must live close to their shul since they cannot ride on Shabbos. Thus, most Orthodox congregations in Miami Beach were small neighborhood synagogues and the members all knew each other very well. Dick walked with his step-father and practiced chanting in Hebrew, bobbing his head up and down as he walked south on James Avenue. His eyes were closed as he chanted. I followed half a block behind with his grandmother, mother, and Rebecca, his older sister. I was told not to talk to Dick, not to get him nervous; so mainly, I talked to Rebecca.

She was eighteen years old and had a pretty face, but she was a little bit plump, not exactly fat . . . just very curvy and very short and that made her look fatter than she really was. Rebecca had red curly hair, like Little Orphan Annie, the cartoon character. Her eyes were also red; she had been crying for several days. She was being forced to marry a wealthy older man from Boston, a man she had never met. Her mother arranged the marriage and said it was "bashert," a Yiddish word meaning that it was meant to be. Dick's grandmother had difficulty hearing, but when she heard the word "bashert" her eyes lit up; "God 'villing, may I live long enough to see my grandchildren married. Ptu Ptu." She did an imaginary good luck spit on the sidewalk.

"Bubby; I haven't even met the man . . . and he's really old. He has a son older than me!" Rebecca wiped her eyes and swallowed hard; she held back tears. She didn't want to be the center of attention, not on this special day; this day was a joyous occasion, a "simcheh." All eyes were supposed to be focused on her brother.

"Is he Orthodox?" I asked.

"Yes," she replied, and more tears streamed down her face.

Dick had told me that Orthodox men and women never touched each other when they had intercourse. Women draped their bodies in a bed sheet, with a hole strategically placed at the right location. That's probably why Rebecca was crying.

"God didn't mean for men and women to screw like wild animals," said Dick. "Only when the woman is in heat."

"So, I guess Jewish girls don't give blow jobs?" I questioned.

"No fuckin' way," said Dick. "But, some do, and the 'Angel of Death' makes them lose all their teeth. That's a Jewish angel; ain't too many of them. Most angels are goyem."

I pondered for a moment on Dick's observations about blow jobs and especially about the bed sheet with the hole.

"Well, I don't think you're right about wild animals," I replied. "They screw one way all the time. Its only humans who come up with a zillion different positions."

"Yeah! Like how do you know? Been spying on mommy and daddy?"

"Well, I'm not stupid," I responded, "I've seen French post cards. Humans do it lots of different ways."

Dick laughed. "Then there's a great business. You can be the first to make bedsheets for Orthodox Jews with lots of holes."

I laughed, but it wasn't such a bad idea.

Rebecca's grandmother (who had no teeth) offered comforting words in Yiddish: "Beckalah, my precious little flower . . . it is bashert; it is bashert; not to 'vorry . . . . fun krimeh shiduchim humen arois gleicheh kinder." (*From bad matches good children are also born*).

"It is bashert!"

I had only been living on this New York Jewish Island for two months, but wherever I turned I kept hearing that word, over and over . . . "bashert, bashert, bashert" . . . "It was meant to be."

Even my homeroom teacher, Miss Baker, who wasn't Jewish, felt that everything was preordained. I was only twelve, but I just couldn't accept this philosophy; I found it very discomforting. If everything is bashert, then why bother with school or reading or eating well balanced meals?

"How about selecting your own husband or wife?" I asked. "Isn't that a decision that God left for us?"

"Shhh," said Mrs. Solomon, as we entered the small Orthodox Synagogue, and Rebecca squeezed my hand, a thank you squeeze, but she didn't smile.

◆

Men sat on the main level of the shul and women and children were restricted to the second floor. Since I was not yet of Bar Mitzvah age I could chose either location. I preferred being with the women; Dick warned me that the men would look with disdain if I couldn't follow along with the Hebrew reading. Another reason why I wanted to avoid sitting with the men was because I didn't own a tie and jacket. My mother bought me a royal blue Cubavera to wear to the Bar Mitzvah. A Cubavera was a Cuban style jacket which was very popular with the tourists. Essentially, it was a long sleeve multi-pleated shirt, worn on the outside of your pants. I really disliked the Cubavera; I looked like a bongo player in a Spanish band, without the moustache, but my mother said it was half the price of a regular jacket, and a twelve year old boy didn't need an expensive sport jacket . . . "Money doesn't grow on trees."

One good thing about sitting in the balcony, I got to sit with the girls, or at least near the girls. Boys sat with boys and girls sat with girls, but I broke with tradition and I sat at the far left seat in the boys section, next to the girls. There were lots of pretty girls there and they almost seemed normal, they weren't wearing long black coats or yarmelkus or a tallis. They were just wearing black dresses with long sleeves, and they whispered to each other during the service and giggled. They weren't much different from the girls at Ida M. Fisher, but the boys were strange—they were not interested in the girls; they were communicating with God.

The service was almost entirely in Hebrew; some of it was also Yiddish, but without the dots it was impossible for me to know which language they were speaking. It was difficult for me to understand what was happening; it was mainly old men rocking and chanting, "davenen" and singing various prayers. The women hummed in tune with the prayers, but they rarely stood and almost never chanted. Most of the women wore hats or had their heads covered with lace doilies, like Mrs. Lefkowitz used when she said prayers at her Friday night dinner. The Torah was lifted from the Ark and held on the shoulder of a bearded old man. Several of the elderly men walked around the room, carrying the Torah, and all the men on the main level kissed their tallis and touched it to the Torah; they were bonding with God. Since the women and children were in the balcony they were excluded from this holy ritual . . . . they weren't allowed to bond. I thought about that for a while, and I wondered whether or not women ever went to heaven. It sure would be a boring place if it was all old men with beards.

The Solomon family sat on the Beema *(the Altar)* and Dick's step father and Mrs. Solomon walked forward to the Torah to lead the congregation in the first Aliah, a traditional Hebrew prayer. Then aunts, uncles, and friends of the family all took turns walking up to the Beema to chant from the Torah. Finally, it was time for Dick to begin reading from the Haftorah, the weekly section of the Torah which covered one of the Five Books of Moses. I had a booklet, in English, which provided a little insight; the reading for this week would come from "Exodus," the Second Book of Moses. The passage described the plight of the Israelites in Egypt, the escape from bondage and the parting of the Red Sea. Dick sounded great to me; he chanted with passion and seemed to davenen in rhythm with the Rabbi and the Chazen *(Cantor)* and he said all his Hebrew lines with his eyes closed, just like when he walked to shul. When he finished chanting the Torah was returned to the Ark and Dick made his thank you speech. He thanked the Rabbi and the Chazen; he thanked his parents, grandmother, and sister, and then he spoke briefly about the significance of his portion of the Haftorah. His eyes were open when he read his speech. I was wondering, maybe Dick couldn't read Hebrew; maybe he had his Haftorah portion memorized.

"God parted the Red Sea for the Israelites to escape from bondage and find their way to the Promised Land. For Jews of today, the sea has once again parted. We have returned to

Eretz Yisroel (the Land of Israel). May God bless my family, this congregation, the United States of America, and the new state of Israel. Today I am a man. Ahh Main."

"Mazel Tov, Mazel Tov." Every member of the small congregation shouted congratulations to the Bar Mitzvah boy. Children on the second floor began throwing pieces of hard candy at Dick, a ritual designed to signify the sweetness of the occasion. Of course, most of the boys attempted to sanctify the occasion by hitting Dick in the face.

As I watched Dick cover his head, to avoid the bombardment of candy, my mind drifted and I started thinking about the unusual lifestyle of the Orthodox Jews, where men were allowed to bond with God and women weren't. But mostly, I tried to visualize having sex while draped in a special holy bed sheet.

Rabbi Lipschitz then walked forth to the lectern and the flying candy stopped. As he looked to the balcony, his eyes locked on mine; it was obvious, he remembered his visit to the James Manor and the heated encounter with my father. He talked about the significance of the Bar Mitzvah and how a Jewish boy could "never" be accepted in the eyes of God until he passed through the "metaphorical waters" of the Red Sea . . . until he read from the Torah. He said that Moses led the Israelites through the Red Sea but Moses was brought up as an Egyptian and never had a Bar Mitzvah (I didn't know that). Thus, he did not live to see his dream become a reality, to see his followers reach the Promised Land. Rabbi Lipschitz reminded us that the rules of Judaism were very strict; even someone as important as Moses was punished because he never had a Bar Mitzvah.

I stopped listening to the fiery Rabbi and started thinking about Moses, the Jewish savior who never had a Bar Mitzvah. And, since Moses was Egyptian, I bet he wasn't even circumcised. At least I was, and that was Abraham's only Covenant with God. There was no requirement for Bar Mitzvahs; that came a lot later, probably even after Moses. Boy, did I want to stand up and argue with that Rabbi, just like I argued with the history teacher who thought that the Pilgrims were such wonderful people.

"Today we reaffirm the dream of the Promised Land," shouted Rabbi Lipschitz, and he paused and made eye contact with every member of the small congregation, especially me. "Today, the Red Sea has parted for Richard Solomon, who stands before us as a proud Bar Mitzvah, prepared to continue the faith of our people."

He talked about the inevitability of "destiny," "Vos Got tut basheren (*what God decrees*) man cannot prevent." He also preached about the day when the Messiah would "finally" come. "Az meshiah vet kumen (*when the Messiah comes*) all the sick will be healed, but a fool will stay a fool." Once again, he glared at me and repeated his warning, "a fool will stay a fool." The Rabbi reminded me of Miss Baker, my evangelical homeroom teacher; his message was almost identical . . . except that Miss Baker had already found her Messiah. She was just sitting around waiting for a second visit. The Rabbi was anxiously awaiting the first visit.

After the services I congratulated Dick and his family, but I didn't stay for the "Kiddish," the special Hebrew blessings that follow the religious ceremony. As I left the shul I heard Rabbi Lipschitz in the background; he was saying a Hebrew prayer, a Barucha to cut the bread: "Hamotzi lechem min ha'orets." followed by another Barucha to drink the wine. I felt very uncomfortable, very different. I didn't belong here, but I didn't belong in my morning devotionals either. Life was less confusing in Chicago, where you were either a Cubs fan or a White Sox fan and you could eat liverwurst sandwiches on Kaiser rolls.

Hamotzi lechem min ha'orets . . . Go White Sox

CHAPTER 9

THE WONDER MACHINE

Nocturnal Enuresis is the medical term for night-time bedwetting. It is characterized by the involuntary discharge of urine, done unconsciously during sleep.

"Mrs. Lindell, there is nothing wrong with Myron," said Dr. Ricewasser, our family physician in Chicago. I was eight years old and my mother, who regarded cleanliness as godliness, was getting frustrated with my chronic bedwetting.

He gave my mother a list of the common factors which could lead to bed wetting, and one by one they discussed each of the listed items.

- *A Delay In The Development Of The Central Nervous System:*
- *Smaller Than Average Functional Bladder Capacity*
- *Hormone Deficiency—of an anti-diuretic secreted to decrease urine production at night*
- *Genetics-related to the chromosomes*
- *Psychological Factors*
- *Hereditary*
- *Abnormal posterior urethra valves*
- *Neurological disorders*
- *Urine infection*
- *Diabetes*
- *Allergies to certain food*

"I've checked Myron for all of these factors and I don't see anything wrong with him, but I want you to go see Adolph Berlinsky at the University of Chicago Medical School; he is one of the top pediatric psychiatrists in the country." Dr. Ricewasser had already concluded that I had some type of psychological problem and the visit to the renowned specialist was merely to get a second opinion.

For four consecutive weeks my mother took me to Dr. Berlinsky, where I was tested for my ability to insert multi-colored wooden circles, triangles, stars, and squares into appropriate holes. I also had to draw lines connecting dots and discuss my interpretation of ink blots that looked like little aliens holding giant dogs. During the four weeks at the University of Chicago I never saw the doctor's face; he was always looking down at charts. He rarely asked me any questions, and even when he did, I only saw the top of his head. What do you ask an eight year old?

"Myron has no psychological disorder, he is just lazy," said the renowned specialist. His conclusion was based upon my aptitude with ink blots, three-dimensional objects, and multi-shaped holes. "However, I have a few suggestions that might help." He then gave my mother a pre-printed list of bed wetting rules:

- *No liquids of any kind after 6 PM; that includes Jell-O, which is really liquid that has been converted into a semi-solid state;*
- *Mandatory urination at 6 PM and immediately before going to bed;*
- *Wake the child two hours after going to bed for an additional urination;*
- *Send the child to a sleep-away summer camp*

The backside of the memo contained a list or recommended camps.

"Why summer camp?" asked my mother.

"Peer pressure!"

Based upon the advice of Dr. Berlinsky, I was sent to Camp Briar Lodge in Oconmowoc, Wisconsin, two hundred miles north of Chicago. After two humiliating bed wetting episodes I ran away from camp in the middle of the night. I found the main highway and started walking south in search of Chicago. Three hours later I was picked up by a truck and reprimanded by several "Chiefs" and "Warriors." It was an Indian camp . . . all members of the staff had Indian titles. I was then transferred from the main lodge, where all the other "Little Braves" slept, to a small cabin with three other bed wetters. We were supervised by Squish Squash, a mean older woman who cleaned bathrooms at the main lodge. I never knew her real name; the counselors and staff all used Indian names.

I was warned by Chief Grey Cloud, the owner of the camp, not to tell my parents about the attempted escape. If I did, they would tie me to the main totem pole during our evening pow wow and burn off my little toe. That was the normal Indian method for dealing with cry babies. On "Visitors Day." when my sister came to Briar Lodge, I told her everything, how I attempted to run away, how I had been forced to sleep in a smelly cabin with Squish Squash, and how they threatened to burn off my toe. My sister thought those were very funny stories; she loved my imagination.

Not all aspects of camp life were miserable. I liked the evening pow wow . . . as long as I didn't think about my little toe. Two hundred campers gathered around a huge bonfire and listened to stories by Chief Grey Cloud, whose real name was Max Moskowitz.

"Tonight little braves I 'vill tell you how Oconomovalk 'Visconsin got its name." The Chief spoke in an unusual accent, part Yiddish, part Indian.

"Many Moons ago da' Indians in 'Visconsin 'vas looking for a new home, so 'dey followed 'dere chief, and 'dey 'valked and 'valked and 'valked until 'da chief dropped 'mit exhaustion. 'Da chief pointed to 'da ground and said, 'dis is 'da place . . . O-con-no-mo-woc.'"

We all laughed and showed approval of the story by beating our little tom-toms. But, for the benefit of those campers who weren't laughing, Chief Grey Cloud clarified the punch line. "Oconomowoc . . . I can no more walk . . . Get it?"

The only thing else worth mentioning about camp was the delicious Summer Squash. I was often required to eat double portions of a secret Indian recipe that was supposed to stop bed wetting. Unfortunately, it didn't work.

At the end of summer, when I returned to Chicago, Dr. Ricewasser recommended that I see Dr. Isaac Gutterman, a prominent pediatric urologist. After extensive tests, measuring the intensity of my urinary stream, my mother was told that my bed wetting was caused by an improperly developed bladder. In order to strengthen the bladder I was required to engage in an unusual exercise, known as the "Gutterman Squeeze." Every time I had to pee, I was supposed to urinate in a stop and go pattern. It would be my mother's job to ensure that I followed a set of written instructions. However, I was too old for her to go into the bathroom and watch me pee, so she stood outside the door and listened, and directed the process:

"Pee—stop—squeeze—pee—stop—squeeze. Myron, I said stop, you are not stopping; I can hear you peeing."

It sounds easy to apply the "Gutterman Squeeze," but once you start peeing its very difficult to stop. I cheated a lot: I did normal continuous peeing when my mother wasn't around to listen, and I drank after 6 PM, by secretly cupping my hands under the bathroom faucet; I also kept my mouth open when I showered. One time, when I was ten, my mother was so exasperated that she took the wet bed sheet, with the ubiquitous yellow circle, and hung it from my second story bedroom window for all the neighborhood kids to see. When my father returned home from work he was furious. He pulled the sheet back into the apartment and threw it on the floor.

"Dammit Rose! Let the boy alone; 'di tseit iz der bester doktor.'" (*time is the best doctor.*) My parents frequently used Yiddish when they didn't want me to know what they were talking about.

"That's easy for you to say," screamed my mother, "you don't have to clean his 'farshtunken' sheets. How is he ever going to get married? No woman will ever sleep with a bed wetter."

I usually slept on a water repellent flannel sheet, which was placed under the regular bed sheet. A small accident would be absorbed completely by the flannel sheet. But, if I drank water after 6 PM there was a good chance that the bed would be flooded, and the overflow would penetrate to the mattress.

When we moved to Florida I had no accidents during the first six months; that was the longest I had ever gone without wetting the bed. I was hopeful that I had outgrown my problem. Then, on March 19, 1952, the day before my thirteenth birthday, the dry streak ended; I flooded the bed, even the mattress. My mother went crazy! At 7 AM she screamed loud enough for all the neighbors at the James Manor to know my secret.

"Sol, I can't stand this pishing' anymore. I don't know what to do. Lets send him to military school."

That evening two salesman came to our door; they were given our name by an unidentified neighbor. The younger man was a Negro; he immediately showed his police I.D. card, which authorized him to stay in Miami Beach after 6 P.M. He was carrying a special "wonder machine" designed to end the bed wetting problem. The older salesman, a white man, did all the talking. He smoked a pipe, wore a wrinkled tan suit and needed a shave; my parents called him a "huckster."

"Hello Mr. and Mrs. Lindell," the unshaven salesman checked his index card to make sure he was pronouncing our name properly. "And hello Ryan. I am about to change your life forever. In thirty days, or less, this fantastic 'wonder machine' will stop your bed wetting problems." He shook my hand and smiled; he had bad breath.

"Its Myron." I didn't smile.

"How much?" asked my father.

"Let me give you a brief demonstration of this unbelievable product, which was developed by leading scientists in the orient and has been used by many famous celebrities, including Clark Gable, for his son . . . I can give you a list."

"How much?"

The salesman spread a special wired sheet on top of my bed. He connected it to the "wonder-machine" and plugged it into the nearest electrical outlet. "Bed wetting is not an emotional problem, it is not a psychological problem, it is not a bad habit, and it is not the result of laziness." Those were the problems that physicians, psychiatrists, urologists, and Indian chiefs had been treating, and this unshaven salesmen with bad breath said they were all wrong. He knew something that they didn't, and he promised to stop my bed wetting with his "wonder-machine" in less than one month.

"Bed wetting is caused by deep sleep and arousal disorder, and this wonderful device is designed to cure that problem." He poured some water on the electric sheet and nothing happened. He explained that water alone will not activate the equipment, but urine was different than water; it had a high concentration of salt. He then put a teaspoon of salt into the glass and poured a few drops on the bed sheet. A shrill, piercing noise sounded, like the air-raid siren at my old Chicago school that warned if the Russians were attacking.

"Mr. Lindell, this amazing machine normally rents for $300 per month; but this month we are offering a half price special, only $150."

I went to bed that night hopeful that the "wonder-machine" would succeed, where years of medical treatment and Indian remedies had failed. I plugged the machine into the wall and followed the salesman's instructions: I drank two full glasses of water, to ensure that I would have an intentional "accident."

Shortly after falling asleep two involuntary drops of urine dribbled upon the electric sheet. Instantly, the "wonder-machine" responded with an ear-splitting explosion, loud enough to wake all the white hair tenants at the James Manor. Normally, when my mother woke me for a nocturnal trip to the bathroom I would be in a semi-conscious trance, but after the "wonder-machine" blasted its alarm I was wide awake. I went to the bathroom, peed, reset the machine, and returned to bed. We kept the device for the full rental period, but that was the only time I ever heard the bell. It took one night and two drops of urine, and the amazing "wonder-machine" cured a problem that had baffled pediatric psychiatrists and the best medical minds of Chicago and defied the old Indian remedies of Oconomowoc. On the morning of my thirteenth birthday I stopped wetting the bed. Even though I did not have a Bar Mitzvah the Red Sea had parted. I proudly proclaimed to the world: "Today, I am a man!"

CHAPTER 10

THE BADGE OF COURAGE

Corned beef was eaten only on rye, never on white bread, not even on challah . . . even though challah was Jewish bread. We never used mayonnaise on anything . . . only mustard, either Guildens, the spicy New York mustard, or Frenchies, the mild yellow mustard that I ate in Chicago, either was OK, but never mayonnaise; to eat mayonnaise, you would be branded as a "goy" or worse yet, a "goyisher kup." Certain combinations of food were sacrosanct on my Jewish island.

"Its pronounced 'holly,'" said my mother and aunt Pearlie, who were from Chicago, but my father and all the kids at my school called it "challah"—because they were from New York. So, I used the appropriate pronunciation, depending on who I was talking to.

Oscar Meyer hot dogs, which I loved in Chicago, were regarded here as goyisher dogs; the kids at Ida M. Fisher only ate kosher Hebrew National franks, and never with catsup, only with mustard, onions, and relish. Some of the kids also smothered their franks with "kraut." That was a New York combination; I hated sour kraut, but Herman, the man I refused to call my uncle, ate kraut a lot.

"The New York "makkies" put kraut on everything," said Herman, "and this shit ain't half bad." "Makkie" was a derogatory term that Chicago Jews sometimes used when referring to New York Jews. Most Chicago Jews were "assimilated" and had adopted the American culture. Many of them looked down on the New Yorkers, who were more religious and retained customs, mannerisms, and eating habits of Eastern Europe. Calling someone a "makkie" was an insult but it wasn't really a vulgar word. However, calling someone a "kike" was a terrible insult, just as crude as calling a colored person a "nigger." A "kike" was a low class, ignorant "makkie."

Herman used profanity a lot; he frequently referred to people as "kikes," especially people with thick New York accents. I always viewed Herman as an adult, chain smoking version of Manny Lefkowitz, except Herman didn't scratch his balls when he talked. Age sure doesn't always bring maturity; sometimes age just brings wrinkles. I never once heard my parents use any profanity, except for an occasional "hell" or "damn" . . . but never the "F" word. My mother threatened to wash my mouth out with soap if I ever used bad words. I think most mothers used the same stupid threat, but I never once heard of a mother really washing their child's mouth with soap, they would probably be arrested for cruelty.

In Chicago my father used to eat ham on rye at Korbs Delicatessen; I always thought that was a Jewish sandwich because he insisted on good Kosher rye bread, but it wasn't just him, all the Jewish people at Korbs ate ham on rye. But here in Miami Beach no one ate ham, not even my father. I never told Dick or Howard that he ate ham sandwiches back in Chicago; they would think he was a goy. In Miami Beach we ate bagels a lot; I don't remember ever eating bagels in Chicago. My parents also ate a lot of lox; that's where I drew the line. I loved bagels, especially the ones with poppy seeds, toasted and covered with cream cheese and strawberry jelly, but I hated lox. I also liked grape jelly, but not orange marmalade.

We ate at Dubrows with Aunt Pearlie and Herman at least three nights a week; I was no longer bothered by the aroma of pickle juice. One night we went to dinner with my aunt's Canasta friend, Blanche Liebowitz, a fat woman with huge breasts and blue hair . . . it really was white, but she had it tinted silver-blue. My mother scolded me if I ever called Mrs. Liebowitz fat; she was "just a little bit 'zaftic.'" Mrs. Liebowitz was very dark, like the colored women who served behind the counters at Dubrows; she said she was a "sun worshiper." I never saw a white person so dark in my life, certainly not in Chicago. And when she talked, only the right side of her face moved. She had a stroke following the death of her second husband, Norton the "nishtikeit" who left her penniless. As a result of the stroke she lost control of the left side of her face. She dribbled when she ate, and always had a napkin in her left hand.

"You never know, Pearl . . . I might meet that 'special man' here at Dubrows." Blanche paused and took a bite of her hot tongue sandwich. "Stranger things have happened! Did I ever tell you how I met my first husband?" She told that story many times; how she met Moe the "mentsch" back in "the city" skating in Central Park. It was a boring story, and by the end of my first year in Miami Beach I knew it by heart. Moe was dead but Blanche always spoke of him in the present tense.

"From your mouth to God's ear," said Aunt Pearlie. She flicked the salt shaker over her left shoulder, wishing her friend good luck in her search for husband number three.

"What a shame! To have two husbands die on you," said my mother. "So lucky in cards . . . but so unlucky in love."

A few people sitting at the next table were speaking with heavy European accents, Romanian, Hungarian, Polish—they had numbers tattooed on their forearms—horrific reminders of the Nazi concentration camps. They wore their tattoos proudly; it was their badge of courage. I never saw people with numbers on their arms in Chicago—but I saw lots of them in Miami Beach, especially in Dubrows. The numbers all began with the letter "A" or "B." I shouldn't have stared, but no one saw me.

"Why did the Germans hate Jews so much?" I asked my father, not expecting a long lecture. He had a mouth full of corned beef; so did I.

"Germany, between the wars, was in a serious economic upheaval, and the arrogant German mentality needed a scapegoat, someone to blame for their problems, and for losing World War I." My father took a bite of his corned beef sandwich, and just sat and thought for a long time. "Hitler was the leader of a group of hooligans known as the National Socialist Party . . . you probably know them as the Nazis. The Nazis rose to power by telling the German people that their problems were all caused by the Jews. Hitler painted the Jews as the 'common enemy' and got the German people to believe that their country would return to glory if they got rid of the Jews."

"But that's a big lie," I blurted, "Jews were always educated people, everywhere in the world, and throughout history . . .

even in Roman times . . . and they were always peace loving people. How could all the problems of Germany be caused by Jews . . . and what's 'upheaval?'"

"Upheaval is when the bottom falls out, when social order disintegrates, when a country collapses from within, like with the Roman Empire. But, people don't like to blame themselves when things go wrong, its always easier to put the blame on someone else . . . and Jews stood out in Germany; they were different. Its easy to point the finger at someone who looks different and acts different."

Jews stood out! I became obsessed with that observation, as I continued to eat corned beef on rye and latkas with apple sauce. Aunt Pearlie was right; latkas were delicious, especially when they were hot and crispy.

We really stood out in Miami Beach . . . we talked different, we ate different, we thought different. Could it happen here . . . in Miami Beach? Could we have an "upheaval" with hooligans taking over and killing all the Jews. It wasn't that way in Chicago; there I ate liverwurst sandwiches on Kaiser rolls at the German delicatessen. One of my friends was Deitmar Shultz, a German boy who taught me to like liverwurst and bratwurst. Deitmar never called me a Jew and I never called him a Nazi. We both liked baseball.

"Yes Myron . . . it could happen here, just like in Germany. If this country ever had a major crash again, like we did in 1929 . . . it could happen here too."

"But we don't have Nazis here," I said. Then I remembered my secret mission to hunt and eradicate escaped Nazis. I wondered if any of the white hair people in Dubrows were really Nazis?

"Well . . . maybe we don't have Nazis now; not like they did in Germany," said my father, "but they will spring up from the streets if we ever have an internal collapse. We have the KKK and they're no different than the Nazis, they hate colored people and Jews . . . but thank God, they don't have a lot of power in America. But, if we ever fell apart, like they did in Germany, the KKK could easily become like the Nazis."

"Well, I don't think they're that scary," I commented. "They're kind of funny looking, wearing bed sheets and pillow cases with holes."

I wondered if the KKK only wore white, or maybe they had different colors for different occasions; the Nazis had many different uniforms and colors. Michael Bernstein taught me which ones were worn in battle and which were worn at parades or parties.

Henry Streuling, the landlord of the James Manor apartments, walked over to our table; he bowed and smiled and politely asked if he could "dine" with us. He was alone, carrying a tray. Mr. Streuling was from Germany; his real name was Heinrich, but he changed it in America. He was unmarried and he spoke with a squeaky voice, kind of like a woman. His German accent was very refined; he sounded like a movie actor. Unlike most of the other older people, he spoke no Yiddish and didn't eat the same food as everyone else. He ate corned beef on a platter, with boiled potatoes and sour kraut . . . not on rye bread; he put mayonnaise on his corned beef (*yuck*); he drank beer instead of coffee, and when he held his beer glass his pinky wiggled in the air. His black shoes were very shiny, and he always wore short sleeve shirts to display the numbers that were branded on his forearm. He called it his "souvenir from Auschwitz." He seemed to be a nice man, and he was especially nice to me.

"Myron, have your parents taken you to the beach?" Asked Mr. Streuling. "Its only one block from the James Manor; if they are too busy I will be glad to take you."

He looked around fifty years old; I never was good at figuring the age of older people, they all looked the same to me. But, Mr. Streuling had all his hair; he wasn't bald like most of the other old men at Dubrows. Aunt Pearlie always tried be a matchmaker, and that night she introduced Mr. Streuling to her zaftic Canasta friend, Blanche Liebowitz.

"So nice to meet you Henry," said Mrs. Liebowitz. She smiled and bent forward across the table to shake hands with him; her loose fitting blouse revealed uncovered breasts. I tried not to stare. Well . . . maybe I did look, but I wasn't obvious; I peeked through the corner of my eyes. Mrs. Liebowitz's breasts were dark brown on top, the part that she displayed for everyone, but the part that was bared only for Mr. Streuling was as white as her smiling teeth. I never saw two-tone boobs before; I wondered if Mr. Streuling thought they were sexy; I sure didn't.

"So how come you never married?" asked Mrs. Liebowitz. "How come a handsome gentleman like you is still a bachelor?"

"I never got married because 'vimmen' is nothing but trouble," said Mr. Streuling, in a very refined German accent. "I like to go fishin' a lot, and 'vimmen' just complain if you come into dere' house smelling from da' fish."

"Not me," said Mrs. Liebowitz . . . "I love the smell of fish in my house."

"And I am very neat and orderly . . . I vant' an orderly house."

Mrs. Liebowitz fidgeted in her chair, providing Mr. Streuling with a different view of her two-tone breasts. "I always say . . . a place for everything and everything in its place." My mother nodded approval; that was also one of her favorite expressions.

My mother's parents came from Germany, and she knew how to speak German; so did Aunt Pearlie. They were both trying to convince Mr. Streuling, in German, that Mrs. Liebowitz was a good catch, a nice woman . . . . he responded in German. I understood "nine" . . . he said that a lot . . . "nine, nine, nine" . . . . it meant "no." Mr. Streuling was a "confirmed bachelor," that's what Aunt Pearlie called him. She thought that he was very handsome and tried, several times, to introduce him to "nice ladies" but Mr. Streuling always said "nine."

Why were they speaking German here . . . of all places . . . in Dubrows? That's the language of the Nazis. I stepped on my mother's toe under the table; I tried to get her to stop . . . especially with concentration camp survivors sitting at the next table. I stared at the white hair of elderly men and women, survivors with numbers on their forearms. How could those people be here eating, and laughing, and having a good time?

♦

Several days later I went fishing with Herman and Mr. Streuling. We fished from the dock of a waterfront mansion on Star Island, an exclusive island in the middle of Biscayne Bay, half way between Miami and Miami Beach. The view was spectacular, surrounded by water on all sides.

"Henry, are you sure its OK to fish here?" asked Herman. "These homes are patrolled by private security guards."

"Don't worry,'" said Mr. Streuling. "I know the owner of this house; he said its OK for me to fish from his dock."

Mr. Streuling was nice to me, very nice. He taught me how to put live shrimp on my hook without killing the shrimp.

"Don't put the hook through da' black dot," said Mr. Streuling. "That's da' heart; you'll kill da'shrimp. Da' fishies don't bite unless da' shrimp is alive and viggling.'"

He also taught me how to feel the nibble of the fish, not to yank too soon or it will slip away.

"You vait' until you got da' trust of da' little fishie, until he's hooked; den' 'gotcha' . . . reel him in."

Then Mr. Steuling stood at the edge of the pier and began to pee into the bay, and he turned toward me with his penis hanging out of his pants. I closed my eyes; I was embarrassed.

"When you gotta pish, you gotta pish," said Mr. Streuling. "I hope I didn't offend you."

Then, I walked to the far side of the pier and turned my back; I also had to pee.

Mr. Streuling was a great teacher—very patient with me. We caught several fish, mainly Grunts and Yellow Tail Snapper, and when we got home he cleaned them in his kitchen, scraped off the scales and filleted them for cooking. My mother broiled the fish in olive oil and melted butter; they were delicious. Mr. Streuling joined us for dinner; he brought a bottle of German wine.

I couldn't wait to go fishing with him again; what a nice man, even if he did expose his penis, but I guess he really had to pee badly. Then, two days later, I was home alone, playing in front of my apartment, dribbling a basketball between my legs, like Marcus Haynes, the Negro star of the Harlem Globetrotters. Mr. Streuling came by our apartment with a tool box in his hand. He said that my father wanted him to fix our leaky shower.

"Sure, I said . . . come in, I'll show you the leak."

"Myron, I can see that you really liked fishing; ve'll' go again. Next time I take you deep sea fishing; ve'll' go trolling for Blue Marlin and Sailfish."

"Wow! That would be so neat."

"And, it's a shame that your parents haven't taken you to the beach," said this nice man. "I'll take you one day; you'll love the beach."

Then Mr. Streuling turned and twisted the nozzle with a giant monkey wrench and he asked me to hop in the shower, to see if the leak was fixed. I opened the shower curtain and reached over to turn on the water.

"No, take off your clothes, get in the shower . . . lets see if 've got 'da problem fixed."

I didn't like showering in front of the boys in Phys. Ed., and I sure didn't want to shower in front of Mr. Streuling, but he was always nice to me, so even though I was uncomfortable, I wasn't scared. Slowly, I took off my T-shirt, shorts, shoes, and sox. Finally, I took off my underwear. I turned toward the nozzle—the same position that I used in Phys. Ed., with only my back side exposed to Mr. Streuling.

"Looks fine to me, thanks." I hoped he would leave quickly . . . I was not too thrilled standing there nude.

"Turn around Myron, lets see your schmeckle," said Mr. Streuling, as he started to remove his shirt.

Now I was scared; I didn't know what to do. His shirt was removed; so were his shoes and sox. He was only wearing a pair of orange boxer shorts. Where were my parents? I started to cry.

"It looks like your schmeckle is starting to develop. Do you ever play with it?"

"I'm gonna' tell my parents . . . you get out of here," I shouted. I tried to wiggle past him and get out of the shower, but he blocked my path and pushed his arm against my face. I bit his forearm hard, until he began to bleed.

"You dirty little 'svinehount,'" he shouted. "You come here and pish in my bed and stink up my mattress. You ungrateful little bastard! I vas' da' vun' dat got you da' 'vonder machine.'" He sucked the numbers on his forearm, to stop the bleeding . . . and as he wiped the blood from his arm I noticed that his tattoo was different than the ones I saw at Dubrows; his numbers were not preceded by an "A" or a "B." He left the apartment, swearing in German.

I didn't know what to tell my parents; they would never believe me. I had a tendency to exaggerate and they frequently reminded me of the story about the little boy who cried wolf. They liked Mr. Streuling; they thought he was the first German they ever met who was "genteel" and "charming." Most important—he was very clean, and to my mother, all other sins were forgiven if you were clean. I could never tell my parents about Mr. Streuling.

I sat down that night and made a tape recording, which I mailed to Michael Bernstein . . . back in Chicago where they didn't have German weirdoes like Mr. Streuling.

"Hey Michael . . . You know a lot about Nazis. Do me a favor; see if you can find out anything about the numbering system in the concentration camps. You know . . . the tattoos that they branded on forearms. How come some have letters in front of the numbers, like "A" or "B" and some are just numbers without letters? I've got a spooky landlord here in our apartment; he has numbers on his arm but no letters. I want to investigate something about him. Thanks"

CHAPTER 11

NEWS FROM THE OUTSIDE WORLD:
1951-1952

In the Eighth grade my only means of transportation was a maroon Schwin bicycle, so my world was limited to a 2-mile radius of the James Manor Apartments. Anything that happened outside of this little circle was of no importance to me. However, there were a few exceptions! Here is a quick list of some of the significant world events that did have an impact on my life. Well, they all weren't that important. Some of them were just things that I talked about with my parents.

- Topps Company started its first baseball card series—these cards would compete with the Bowman cards that I had been buying in Chicago.
- Minnie Minoso, Willie Mays, and Mickey Mantle were rookies . . . Joe DiMaggio retired from baseball. I saved many Minoso rookie cards, and dumped the Mantle and Mays cards when we moved to Florida. I guess, sometimes in life we don't make the right decisions.
- General Douglas McArthur was fired by President Truman. I listened to the "Old Soldiers Never Die" speech and got all choked up. The general also led a motorcade across the 5th Street Causeway in Miami Beach; the bridge was officially dedicated and renamed—the "McArthur Causeway." This was an

emotional conflict for me: I admired General McArthur, but I was a sworn secret agent, working for President Truman.

- UNIVAC1—the first commercial computer was invented—it would soon be used to predict the winner of the 1952 presidential election. Did they really need a billion dollar computer to predict that election? Ike won almost every state; Stevenson barely carried Illinois.
- Swanson introduced beef, chicken, and turkey pot pies. Now we would eat dinner at home at least one night a week. My mother complained that the kitchen of the James Manor was too small for normal cooking. She kept nudging my father to buy a house. "Don't 'hak mir kain tsheinik,'" said my father. (*don't bother me. literally: don't rattle my tea-kettle*).
- Invention of Tupperware. We could now eat home two nights a week . . . leftover Turkey Pot Pie was not that bad. (see "Swanson" above).
- J.D. Salinger published "Catcher in the Rye". Wow! One of the great books of all time—but my mother thought it had too much profanity.
- Temple Beth Israel of Meridian, Mississippi became the first Jewish congregation to allow women to perform the functions of a rabbi. Dick Solomon and his family marched in front of their shul, carrying posters and protesting this sacrilege. This was the first organized protest march I had ever seen. "What's so terrible about having a female Rabbi?" I asked. "Myron, you ask the dumbest questions," responded Dick. "What if she got her period on Shabbos? How could she lead a congregation if she was on the rag?"
- Julius and Ethel Rosenberg were convicted of selling atomic secrets to the Soviets. "Gotteniu!" said my mother. "For Jews to do something like this—'Gevaldikeh zach!' (*A terrible thing*)"

NINTH GRADE

CHAPTER 12

THE MOVE TO SURFSIDE

We only lived at the James Manor a few months after my frightening experience with Mr. Streuling and I tried my best to always avoid him, not even eye contact. I was positive this weirdo was really a Nazi, pretending to be Jewish.

Why did he go berserk about his shower? Maybe he worked in the "showers" at Auschwitz, as a guard or one of those disgusting jobs where you had to remove dead bodies from the crematories and dump them in mass graves. Too many things about him weren't right, like drinking beer and always bowing when he said hello to women . . . his shiny shoes, dangling his pinkie in the air when he drank, the unusual way that he combed his hair . . . . and eating sour kraut with corned beef. Well I'm not sure about the sour kraut, the New York kids ate kraut with franks all the time. I was still into Nazi hunting; my mission had not yet ended, but I knew enough to distinguish fantasy from reality. Mr. Streuling really was a Nazi; I was sure of it, and I had Michael Bernstein doing research for me.

I kept thinking about beer, and adults drinking beer at restaurants . . . and I remembered a trip to Milwaukee when I was maybe nine or ten. It was a business trip for my father and he brought my mother and me along. No one ever goes to Milwaukee on vacation. We were eating at a big restaurant and I was surprised to see that all the adults were drinking beer from mugs. That seemed so strange; in Chicago adults normally drank coffee or tea at restaurants, or maybe just water. My mother explained that Milwaukee was the beer capital of America and that many of these people were German or of German descent.

"Yeah mom, but why don't you drink beer? You're of German descent."

"Because Jews aren't 'shikkers'," she explained, "not even German Jews." Shikker is a Yiddish word used to describe someone who drinks a lot of liquor. It isn't as bad as being an alcoholic, but to my parents, and to most Jewish people, anyone who averaged one drink a day, either beer, wine, or whiskey, was a shikker.

"Jews are only social drinkers," said my mother, "even my parents—may they rest in peace—never drank beer, and they were Germans." Of course, once in a while my father did like a little shnops." Whenever my mother made reference to either of her parents she always threw in that expression, "may he/she/they rest in peace" . . . so did Aunt Pearlie.

My mother knew how to speak German and Yiddish. My father was of Russian ancestry so he didn't know German, but he occasionally spoke a little Yiddish. Our family name was Skidelsky in Russia but when my grandparents passed through Ellis Island in 1890 the attendant at immigration said, "too many Ski's," so the name was change to Lindelsky. In 1904 my father moved to Chicago along with his mother and a few of his brothers and sisters. Chicago had a large Polish population and my grandmother, Ida Lindelsky, was continuously explaining to friends and neighbors that she wasn't Polish: "No, we are Russian, not Polish, the Russian "sky" ends with a "Y" the Polish "ski" ends with an "I." It was out of frustration that the second "sky" was eventually dropped, and the family name became Lindell.

In 1952 most older Jewish people knew how to speak Yiddish; it was the language of the "Old Country," the language of Dubrows; it was also the language that parents used when they wanted to talk "privately" right in front of their children. But I did pick up many words, especially when they made reference to "da kinder." *(the children)*. To me, Yiddish and German sounded the same, lots of similar words, and both languages sounded like you were clearing phlegm from your throat.

"They are very similar." My mother laughed about my phlegm observation. "Actually, Yiddish is derived from an older form of

German; it sounds the same and has many of the same words, but Yiddish uses Hebrew letters."

"Mom, is Mr. Streuling Jewish?" It was a difficult question to ask.

"As far as I know, he is," responded my mother. "He's got those numbers on his arm, but for a Jew, he sure is a shikker."

I was convinced; Mr. Streuling was a Nazi, but if he actually was, what should I do about it? The line between fantasy and reality had become blurred. How could I notify President Truman? That would definitely lead to additional questions, and I wanted to avoid any type of discussion about the embarrassing and scary shower incident.

Once in a while, in order to avoid seeing Mr. Streuling after school, I would take long rides on my bike . . . always alone. I'd go to the 5th street marina and watch the fishing boats returning to the docks; it was fun to see the excitement of the captains as they unloaded their catch. You could tell which boats caught the giant Marlins or Sailfish, even before they docked; they hung special flags high on their masts, bragging about their success. I'd sit on the pier, alone and I'd go into the bait and tackle shop; in the food section of this little store they sold liverwurst sandwiches on Kaiser rolls, just like I used to eat in Chicago. That was my escape from Mr. Streuling . . . eating liverwurst and reminiscing about Chicago; they didn't have Nazi landlords in Chicago.

◆

Good news, great news, fantastic news . . . my father announced that he had purchased a house in Surfside. Unfortunately, it was way up on 95th street, far from my school, far from my new friends, but it was a house, a big house, three bedrooms, I would have my own bedroom, and another bedroom would be set up as a reading room, and it had a special cedar lined closet for books. And it had three bathrooms! What would we ever do with three bathrooms? What were the odds of my father, mother, and me all needing to go to the bathroom at the same time? And the house was walking distance to the beach, and it was far away from Mr. Streuling. I only had one worry . . . would Mr. Streuling know our new address. I had nightmares about the Nazi shicker. Maybe I should tell Howard or Dick

Solomon about the shower incident. No, they would think I was a fag.

"Here Myron," said my father, "I bought a special present for you, two very important books, Webster's Dictionary, and the Columbia University one-volume encyclopedia. I know you already have a little paperback dictionary, but this one is bigger and better. Keep these books in your end table; use them a lot. Look up new words that you hear in school or in conversation. Also, when you learn about people, places, or events, go to the encyclopedia and get all the facts. And, when you see historical or biographical movies, it's a good idea to refer to the encyclopedia; movies tend to take liberties with facts."

"Thanks dad," I responded. "This encyclopedia weighs at least ten pounds. "Ill use it every day, to exercise my brains and my arms."

"How will I get to school?" I asked my father.

"I'm sure they have a school bus," he replied, "and during the ride to school and back you can bring a book; don't waste time. Myron, the more you read in life, the more successful you will be . . . reading is the key to success . . . and make the dictionary and encyclopedia your special friends."

My father and I frequently sat at the kitchen table and drank tea or cocoa, and we talked a lot about books; he belonged to the "Book of the Month Club" . . . we really got into lengthy discussions about history and religion. He told me about Max Weber and the "Protestant Ethic" . . . if you worked hard everything would be OK . . . in contrast, Catholics believed in a prayer ethic . . . if you prayed hard, everything would be OK, at least in the next life. That was a difficult concept for me to accept, I didn't really believe in a next life, at least not without proof, and what kind of proof could there be . . . photographs?

"But Jews really believe in the Study Ethic," my father noted. "Its my own term, you won't find it anywhere in any books. Jews believe that the best way to succeed in life is through study and reading . . . . lots of reading."

"Dad, do you believe that there really is life after death?"

"Well, I hope that there is," he raised his eyebrows and deep furrows appeared on his forehead; he had a large forehead. I think people with large foreheads are very smart . . . they think a lot. "But, Sunshine . . . we just have to do the best that we can here on Earth and not worry about the next life. Maybe there is an afterlife, maybe there isn't . . . who knows for sure? But, don't get preoccupied about it; the more time that you devote to studying and reading, the more you will enjoy your life."

I told my father how I had become so confused about religion, that my home room teacher, Miss Baker, was spooky . . . she scared me; she was so fervent about God and the Bible . . . and especially the "hereafter."

"Anytime we do anything wrong or bad . . . even if we just snicker and have 'evil thoughts,' she reminds us of the ultimate punishment in the next life. We're gonna' roast in hell for eternity, and she talks a lot about the devil. She calls him Satan."

Then I remembered the barefoot boy with the fishing pole, the boy who gave my father directions, how to find the causeway to Miami Beach. That was the first day at our new home and he warned us that Satan lived in Miami Beach. Most likely, he was talking about Mr. Streuling.

My father put a reassuring hand on my shoulder. "Sunshine . . . its only an illusion. Its what many people want to believe; it gives them comfort. And the fear of roasting in hell for eternity gives them some kind of guidance."

Roasting in hell for eternity . . . . what a horrific image! Even though my father warned me not to become obsessed with thoughts of the afterlife, I was haunted by the vision of a pig roasting for eternity over an open fire . . . with an apple stuffed in its mouth. And as I focused on that frightening image the revolving pig slowly turned into a man with a tiny moustache . . . . it was Adolph Hitler, roasting for eternity on a barbeque skewer. And, in a perverted sort of way, it was a very comforting image.

"How's that for a powerful vision?" I exclaimed. "Miss Baker always rants and raves about the prophets and sages and their 'religious visions.'"

My father laughed. "OK; I can't argue with that vision. You sure have a vivid imagination."

"Sunshine, there's a thought provoking book on religion and the afterlife, 'The Future of an Illusion;' its by Sigmund Freud, but its a little too advanced for you to read right now . . . . maybe next year. Freud is the father of modern psychology, and from his study of human neuroses and childhood fears he concludes that religion is nothing more than an obsession of society. He calls religion a dysfunctional 'illusion' and just like a child must eliminate illusions in order to grow into adulthood . . . society must stop clinging to illusions in order for civilization to progress."

"What do you mean by illusion," I asked, "Is that kind of like magic?"

"That's not a bad comparison," responded my father. "Magic, religion, and illusion . . . very similar. But, don't get me wrong . . . I'm not saying that illusions are always bad. It is from illusions that we set our dreams and our ambitions. Illusions give us hope, and in some sense they keep us going. Illusions hold a special place in human relations . . . as long as they step to the side when reality is needed to move us forward."

"Dick Solomon talks about heaven and hell a lot, and the afterlife, and the price we will have to pay for our sins; he is really worried about the next life, and he is Jewish. How come?" I was confused by Dick's fixation with the afterlife; none of the other Jewish kids ever talked about life after death . . . only Miss Baker was obsessed about roasting in hell.

"That's because he's Orthodox, and they follow the Torah, exactly as it is written, they follow the letter of the law . . . even though our religion is several thousand years old. They cling to tradition as if it is fact!"

"Dick's mother said that the Torah was written by God, and who are we to argue with the word of God; we are only 'mere' mortals."

"The Torah wasn't written by God," responded my father. "The Five Books of Moses were originally handed down from generation to generation, by word of mouth. It was finally put in writing by Jewish religious leaders during a period known as the Babylonian Exile. The Torah is the soul of the Jewish religion, but it was written by scholars and rabbis, not by God."

"Don't tell that to your friend Dick," warned my father. "It will cause problems with his parents and could break up your friendship." I understood what he was talking about; Dick's parents were a little bit strange . . . they never entered a house without kissing the Mezuzah on the door; kind of like Catholics who always crossed themselves. Worse yet, even if a house didn't have a Mezuzah, they kissed their hand and touched it to an imaginary Mezuzah. And in their own apartment, they had Mezuzahs on every room, even the bathroom. My mother said they were "meshugenahs" . . . that's a Yiddish word meaning, a little bit nuts. The Solomons were kosher; they couldn't eat at Dubrows, not even the lox or pickled herring, or any of the Jewish food. That seemed really meshugenah to me. What could be more religious than blintzes or latkas?

"Dick's mother says that every move we make has been pre-ordained by God," I replied. "Actually, Miss Baker, who is a fanatic Christian, says the same thing. So, why should we even bother to study or work hard, our destiny has already been written for us?"

"That reminds me of a good quote from Karl Marx," said my father. 'the more man puts in God, the less he retains in himself.' We study hard and we work hard because nothing is written in advance for us by a divine spirit; we make our own future."

"Why did we move here to Miami Beach?" I asked my father. "Everyone is from New York . . . and they're so religious." I understood why we left Chicago, because of his heart condition. But, why did they pick Miami Beach, why not California? Its warm there also.

"We came here several times as tourists and I got sand in my shoes," said my father. "I really liked it here. And, don't go complaining about New Yorkers; I'm from New York."

Finally, the day of the move arrived; we said goodbye to Aunt Pearlie and Herman, but since they would soon be moving to an apartment in several blocks from our new home it wasn't a sad goodbye with a lot of hugs and kisses and crying. Mr. Streuling came out to say goodbye to us; I was already sitting in the back seat of the car, waiting to get out of that place. I stared at the blue Auschwitz tattoo on his forearm and repeated the numbers to myself

425304

I memorized the numbers and wondered why they didn't have a letter in front of them like the other tattoos that I saw in Dubrows. It was fake . . . I was sure of that. He put the tattoo there himself . . . but he forgot to put a letter in front of the numbers. He was an escaped Nazi "shikker" and he was hiding on our Jewish Island.

"What year were you in Auschwitz?" I felt a little scared even talking to that nut, but my parents were already in the car with me.

"1942 . . . but only for a month; then I bribed a guard, and got out." Henry Streuling smiled and waved as we drove away from James Avenue. I was expecting him to say "Heil" and click the heels of his shiny black shoes. I wonder if "Herr Streuling" and Dean Kessler, the Dean of Boys from my school, knew each other in the Third Reich? Were they both Nazi agents, part of a plot to form the Fourth Reich . . . here in Miami Beach?

The house in Surfside was beautiful, only four blocks from the ocean. My bike was tied on top of the car; it was the first thing I unpacked, and within minutes of arriving at my new home on Carlyle Avenue, I was off to explore the neighborhood. I wasn't looking for Nazis; I was just looking at the stores on Harding Avenue, the quaint downtown shopping district of Surfside, and the beautiful hotels on Collins Avenue. I was going to like it here, but I didn't know anyone; I didn't have any friends yet. Miami Beach went from 1st street to 87th street, and Surfside was the next town to the North; it only went to 96th street, then came Bal Harbour, an exclusive "restricted" village where Jews were not allowed to live. I was told by my parents to avoid Bal Harbour, never to go north of 96th street . . . and of course, never go across the causeway to Miami. Surfside was mostly Jewish, just like Miami Beach, and kids from Surfside went to Miami Beach High School. There weren't many restaurants in Surfside, so we became a normal family and ate most of our meals at home, in our kitchen. We would never eat at Dubrows again; I had grown to like that Jewish cafeteria and years later, when it went out of business, I felt like a part of my childhood had died.

It was June 1952, three months after my thirteenth birthday, and I never had a Bar Mitzvah. I was too embarrassed to tell this to anyone, only Dick Solomon knew, and he had just moved to Miami. We talked once or twice on the phone, but I wasn't allowed to cross over the causeway to Miami by myself, so I never saw Dick again, at least not during my school years . . . . except one time when I bumped into him and his parents at a restaurant. And I didn't see Howard Lefkowitz too often anymore, except in school. He lived on 10th street; I lived on 95th street; it was a long bus ride, over an hour. Howard came up to visit me a few times that summer, to go to the beach or to play ping pong in my garage; he was a great ping pong player . . . but

I never went to visit him; Virginia still lived in his building and I still didn't have pubic hair.

I promised my father that I would water the lawn every day once we moved into the house. I hated that apartment on James Avenue, and the thought of watering my own lawn was a vision of supreme happiness. I set up garden hoses in the front and back of the house with little revolving sprinklers. Every hour I moved the sprinklers ten feet; it was a very time consuming job. But, I promised that I would do this, and I kept my promise, even though it soon became boring. Thankfully, after three days, my father made me an offer; he would have an underground automatic sprinkler system installed if I promised to read five books that summer.

"It's a deal!" He reached on the book shelf of our cedar closet and took down five books, three of them were from his "classics" collection, Huckleberry Finn, the Decline of the Roman Empire, and the poems of Edgar Allen Poe. The other two were recent: "A Diary of Anne Frank" and "A Catcher in the Rye." My mother didn't like me reading "Catcher in the Rye;" she thought it had too much profanity, but my father disagreed. He never used profanity himself but he didn't see harm in reading a book that had dirty words; he felt that it was OK to read profanity, but it was "low class" to actually talk that way; you are judged by the way you speak. He thought it was a good book, a very perceptive book, that I should read it twice, and then again when I was an adult. He really liked that book; so did I.

The Anne Frank diary was very depressing; she was only two years older than me, but she was such an excellent writer. I was a little bit envious of Anne, her beautiful writing ability. But, how can you be envious of a girl who met such a tragic fate at such a young age? I was inspired to start my own diary, but mine wasn't very exciting, just day to day facts, about the weather, and what I ate; there were no Nazis in my life, except maybe Mr. Streuling.

The rest of that summer was devoted to reading, discussing the five books with my father, and punting a football by myself on the street. I had to be the one to retrieve the ball; I didn't have any friends. But, I really became a great punter. I rarely watched TV; the White Sox were a distant second to the Yankees again. Instead of TV, I learned to climb palm trees that summer and open coconuts with my bare hands, it gave me a certain

89

sense of satisfaction . . . . maybe because noone else could do that.

During the uneventful summer of 1952, aside from early morning conversations with my father, mostly about the Roman empire, Jewish history, and the rise and fall of Nazi Germany, my life consisted of reading, memorizing the poems of Poe, punting a football, opening coconuts, and scribbling unimportant trivia in a diary. I also became obsessed with Anne Frank; if there really was such a thing as an afterlife, she was one person I wanted to meet (also Thomas Jefferson and my grandfather Morris; I was named after Morris).

Many times, as I try to understand who I am and how I think, I reflect on that introspective period of my life. It was a boring summer, but it was a time of personal discovery.

CHAPTER 13

¿QUÉ ES EL BURRO?

I had no trouble with any of my classes in eighth grade; I got all A's and a B in Phys. Ed. I never could understand why I got that B, I dressed for class every day and even showed up for the championship game, the day the Giants won the pennant, when many other kids were cutting class, and I showered every day. Maybe I showered backwards, but I did shower. I think you had to be one of Coach Malloy's "boys" or a jock, to get an A; it wasn't fair.

Eighth grade was easy, but ninth grade presented a new obstacle for me . . . Spanish. I discovered that I didn't have natural ability in Spanish; I think that the portion of my brain that was supposed to handle foreign languages was dead, or certainly, it was retarded. I did OK with the first few pages of the text book; I understood "¿Qué es el burro?" (*What is the donkey?*) and I thought the upside down question marks and exclamation marks were neat, they really made a lot of sense, but after that it got much harder; conjugating verbs in many tenses, especially irregular verbs, and those illogical confusing idioms. And double negatives! Lots of double negatives in Spanish. Why couldn't Spanish people understand that a double negative is really a positive?

During the first two weeks of the ninth grade I was spending more time studying Spanish than all other courses combined; I was struggling to get "C's" on tests, and I had absolutely no time for outside reading; I used the long school bus ride to memorize

Spanish vocabulary lists. I was so busy studying Spanish and conjugating verbs that I hardly noticed the Steinberg twins, the new kids on my school bus, who would soon become my best friends, even better than Michael Bernstein. My father said that the future of South Florida would be very Latin, and that I should study hard in Spanish, to get a good job after college. We were so close to Cuba, and now that the war was over, many Cubans were moving to Miami, and not just the Cuban Jews. A few Cuban Jews lived near us in Surfside. My mother used to hang laundry in the back yard and talk to the Cuban neighbor behind our house. I never could figure out how they communicated; my mother didn't speak Spanish and the Cuban lady didn't speak English.

Spanish was taking up all my time. I never got started with my study of cryptography or my investigation of the Nazi tattoo numbering systems, and I hadn't read a book, other than a school book, in two weeks. It really upset my father to see me struggling in a class. Back in Chicago, if I ever had problems he worked with me, helped me with my homework; he taught me to read when I was four, and I knew multiplication tables, up to twelve times twelve, when I was six years old. He even taught me how to multiply a three digit number by a three digit number in my head . . . that took extreme concentration. But, with Spanish he was helpless. So, he decided to take private tutoring in Spanish, to learn it for himself, so that he could help me.

That turned out to be a very fortuitous surprise for me. His Spanish teacher used the same workbook that we used in my class, "El Camino Real," with the same assignments and the same tests. My father quickly pulled ahead of me, since he had a private tutor and moved at a faster pace. After he completed each of his chapter exams, he got to keep the answers. I was able to see them and memorize them, to prepare for my own exams. My exam grades improved from 70's on the first two tests, to 100 on exam 3 and 4; I was cheating . . . but I didn't tell my father. He wouldn't let me keep using his workbook if he knew what I was really doing.

One Saturday morning, a few days after my fourth Spanish exam, around 7:30 AM, a tough bully from my school, Buddy Macker, called me at home; he didn't even start his conversation by saying hello or good morning.

"Lindell . . . you got the 'El Camino Real' workbook, don't you?

"No, I don't know what you're talking about." I denied it.

Macker laughed; he knew I had the workbook. I don't know how. Well, maybe I did have a big mouth and couldn't keep a secret, but I never found out who told him. "Meet me at Liggets Drug store at noon today, or I tell Mr. Schecter." Aaron T Schecter was the principal of Ida M. Fisher and Beach High; he didn't paddle kids; he expelled them from school.

I was afraid to discuss this threat with my father since he didn't know I was using the workbook to prepare for my own tests; he didn't know that I was cheating. So, I agreed to meet Macker. I brought the answers from chapter five.

"Don't bullshit me you little twerp, either you bring the whole fuckin' workbook or you're gonna' get expelled to Lear, with all the morons." Macker raised his fist as he made this threat.

"I have answers for the next test; that's all I got now. I'll get you the rest of the book in two weeks." I started to feel like a fag; I was letting this bully push me around; I wasn't happy with myself. I immediately began plotting for the future; next time I will give this jerk wrong answers on purpose; he wouldn't know the difference anyway. Of course, if I did that he would beat the shit out of me. But it would be worth it.

"How'd you get that book?"

"I got sources." I didn't feel like telling him that my father was taking Spanish lessons.

The next week Macker and I were the only kids in Spanish to get grades of 100 on the exam. Our teacher, Martina Potts, called us "los muchachos brilliantes" . . . the brilliant boys. The other students were asked to repeat "los muchachos brillantes" three times, in unison. After we completed chapter #5 I gave Macker answers for #6, but I made sure that his grade would only be 20%, and of course, I also made sure to surround myself with teachers that day, at least until I could seek asylum in the protection of my school bus. On Friday of week six, Macker got an F on his Spanish exam, the worst grade in the class . . . I got another 100 but I was prepared to pay the price; only a miracle could get me out of this mess.

Over the weekend I never left my house, and never answered the phone. And on Monday morning the miracle happened; an alien landed at Ida M. Fisher. His name was Alberoni Zorzi Dorvilus. He was Greek or Italian, I never was sure, but he obviously wasn't Jewish; Jewish boys never used middle names. He was a huge fat kid, an "army brat" who lived with his father all around the world; he said he was from "nowhere and everywhere." He had a round red face, a blonde crew cut, and pointed ears. That's why he soon became known as the alien; he really liked that name.

The gods were good to me . . . somebody up there really liked me . . . the Alien and Buddy Macker were about to lock horns on that fateful Monday morning. Macker was a bully; he picked on everyone, but he made a dumb mistake in Phys. Ed. He saw the fat, nude alien walking to the showers and he called him "Fat Ass."

"Hey Fat Ass," said Macker, "you look like one of those fukin' Martians in New Mexico."

Alberoni was fat, but he knew judo; he learned that from his father, a drill sergeant in the army. The Alien immediately flipped his body and twisted Macker to the ground; he then wrapped his massive legs around Macker's torso in a scissors hold and squeezed and squeezed and squeezed. Macker's face turned red, then it turned blue, then he blacked out . . . he stopped breathing. Coach Malloy, who was dressed only in his jock strap, ran from his office and stopped the fight; he put his mouth right up to Macker, to blow air into his lungs. He pounded his chest, poured water on his face. Finally, Macker started breathing again.

Coach Malloy looked at the Alien and smiled: "Jesus . . . boy, you gotta go out for the football team, you're a goddamn natural tackle if I ever seen one." The coach's face then got mean and ugly, as he turned to Macker. "And you . . . you little mother-fucker, you get your ass down to Mr. Schecter's office; I'm tired of you being such a friggin' bully." That was one of the few times I ever saw anyone sent to the principal's office . . . that usually meant the death penalty. Macker was expelled from school that day; he transferred to Lear. I never thanked the alien, but he sure solved my problem.

After that day in Phys. Ed., I stopped using the workbook for Spanish; it wasn't worth it. Of course I also stopped getting A's. For the rest of that year I worked hard, really hard, just to get C's. What can I tell you . . . I was a dummy in Spanish, a "retardo" . . . and my father stopped taking Spanish lessons; he said he was an old dog, too old to learn new tricks. Here's something kind of interesting, about my Russian grandmother, Ida Lindelsky, who died long before I was born . . . her maiden name was Seville. Can you believe that . . . a piece of my ancestry is from Spain! We were expelled during the Inquisition, but we sure forgot how to speak Spanish over the next five hundred years.

CHAPTER 14

THE STEINBERG TWINS

"Wouldn't you have more fun if you had someone to catch the football?" shouted Mona Rothstein from across the street. Mona was a very "busty" eleventh grade girl who lived three doors from my house in Surfside. Her mother and mine were friends; they played Canasta together. I kind of liked that word, "busty," that's what my mother said when she described Mona; it was "earthy" and better than saying that she had big tits or big boobs. My mother also said that Mona was a little "yenteh"—a gossip.

My punting had improved over the summer, and now with the start of ninth grade, I could punt the ball high in the air, spin around, and catch the ball behind my back; that was definitely a neat trick. "Friends of my parents just moved to Surfside from Brooklyn," said Mona. "They have twin grandsons, David and Shelly Steinberg."

"I know who they are; they're on my school bus," I said, as I punted the ball and ran twenty yards forward, to catch it. "They have gross New York accents; I don't like them."

"Well . . . I've got news for you . . . you little snob . . . my mother invited them over today, to come meet you." Mona talked down to me like that; she kind of acted like she was my big sister, and whenever I stared at her huge boobs she snapped at me and told me I looked like a "degen," that's short for "degenerate." It was OK to look, but I had to be more discreet about it. Of course, when my parents hired Mona to give me dancing lessons and we danced real close and I pressed my chest against her, that was OK. It was OK to feel her breasts crushing against me, but it was not OK to stare at them; I never quite understood that logic.

"Shit . . . why'd she do that, Mona . . . I don't like people from Brooklyn." I devoted the next fifteen minutes to practicing my punting; I wanted to impress the Steinberg twins.

David and Shelly were identical twins; I couldn't tell them apart, at least not on that first day. They were both short, like me, around 5'2", and they had reddish brown hair and wore matching glasses. Shelly had a thick Brooklyn accent (that's even worse than a New York accent); David's wasn't quite as bad. Until I could tell them apart I needed to listen carefully to know who was who. They were both wearing olive green baggy boy scout shorts, with huge pockets, and pockets on top of pockets, and zippers and loops. Shelly said the loops were called "epaulets." Both of the twins were wearing polo shirts with little alligators on the chest; one was wearing aqua, the other was sort of rose colored. Shelly informed me that these shirts were imported from France and could only be purchased at Saks Fifth Avenue, Burdines, and a few other exclusive stores; they were properly called Chamise Lacostes, named after a famous French tennis player, but it was OK just to call them Lacostes. The Steinbergs never dressed alike; that doubled the size of their wardrobe. One could wear the white Lacoste, the other could wear the red one; the next week they could rotate.

"Punt the ball to me," said David. I let loose with a high booming kick; best one ever. He ran downfield, looked over his shoulder and made a great leaping catch. He passed it back to me and complimented me on my punting ability. "You oughta' go out for the football team; you sure know how to kick the ball."

"Thanks; you should too, you really throw a great pass."

Shelly kicked the ball also, but he was a terrible athlete. He couldn't punt, he couldn't catch, he couldn't even throw a spiral pass; he threw a flutter ball. "Lets see your house," he said, as he tucked his Lacoste into has baggy boy scout shorts. "I heard you have marvelous furniture." Shelly was interested in furniture and fashions, and coordinating colors, and things like that. My mother liked him the first time she met him; my father preferred David.

The Steinbergs lived in Surfside, five blocks from me, the same distance that I lived from Michael Bernstein in Chicago. They lived with their mother, Arnell Steinberg, a short red-haired woman, and their grandparents, Harold and Paula Feinstein, who used to own a clothing store on Flatbush Avenue in Brooklyn. The Steinbergs were both Dodger fans and talked a lot about Duke Snider and Jackie Robinson. Their father died the previous year, just before their Bar Mitzvah. He had a heart attack while sitting in a car, waiting at a red light; he died before the light changed. Its too bad; he never got to see the Bar Mitzvah. He was now just a faded memory.

"His name was Mel," said David. "He was a butcher, but he never made a good living, so we always lived with my grandparents." David was not ashamed to admit that his father wasn't successful in business; he talked about playing catch with him, and going together to the zoo. On the day his father died at the traffic light, he was driving home from the kosher caterer; he had just signed a contract for the Bar Mitzvah, the paper was found crumpled in his hand. Shelly never talked about his father. Shelly was the one who picked out all the clothes for himself and David.

"I don't want David to be walking around like a slob," said Shelly. "Lots of kids can't tell us apart and they might think they're looking at me."

Shelly had a "flair for fashion" . . . and he told me that he had fourteen different Lacostes, every color they made. He talked a lot about the rich kids in the ninth grade, especially the ones who were driven to school by chauffeurs, in Cadillacs, they also wore Lacostes. He loved the huge red "sofa" in our house, but he thought our kitchen set was "dreadful" . . . . it didn't blend with the "decor." He sat down in the kitchen with my mother and together, they discussed ideas for rearranging the living room furniture and they looked at pictures of various kitchen sets in the Miami Herald.

The Steinbergs used a lot of New York words: "sofa" instead of "couch" . . . "cellar" instead of "basement" . . . . "auto" instead of "car" . . . and of course, like all other New Yorkers, "franks" instead of "hot dogs" . . . We argued about the correct way to pronounce Chocolate and Chicago; I pronounced them both like "paw" . . . the Monkey's Paw . . . they pronounced both those words "ahhh", like when a doctor puts that flat stick in your mouth and makes you say "ahhhh." Chicaaaahhhhgo . . . that sounded dumb. We played together with my tape recorder; we sang and recorded songs. Shelly sang "America the Beautiful," it was a riot . . . hearing him sing that song with his thick Brooklyn accent.

We joked around; I told them about sending tapes back and forth to Michael Bernstein, and the research I wanted to do at the Miami Beach Library, on the Nazi tattoo numbering system. David thought that was fascinating; he had seen many concentration camp survivors in Brooklyn, with numbers. Some of his grandparents friends had numbers. Shelly thought it was "stupid and idiotic." Of course, I didn't tell either of them about Mr. Streuling, and my scary experience, and my suspicion that he was a Nazi.

David and I agreed to take the bus to the library the next Saturday, to study all about the tattoos of the Nazis. That really intrigued him, but not his brother Shelly.

"That's the dumbest thing I ever heard," Shelly laughed and said he would join us for the ride, but would go browsing in the "exquisite" stores of Lincoln Road, maybe Lacoste had added some new colors to their alligator "mélange." Shelly was a snob; I was starting to get annoyed by his disdain, or maybe it was just his Brooklyn accent, but I liked David. I planned on calling David at home that evening, to suggest that we dump Shelly and go to the library without him. However, before I had a chance to call, Mrs. Steinberg, their mother, called my house and introduced herself. She told my mother that if I wanted to be friends with one of the boys I had to be friends with both of them; it was a package deal. She was a lot like Shelly; she knew a lot about fashions and colors and after the phone call my mother picked up the dictionary to look up the word, "mélange."

CHAPTER 15

PROTECTIVE CUSTODY PRISONERS

I told David that I wanted to get this real smart kid, Spencer Teichman, to join us at the library, to help with our research. I knew Spencer from "Algebra"—he was the smartest kid in that class; he was the smartest kid in every class. He kind of stuck to himself, but he was a genius; he learned German just so he could read the published works of Einstein in the original language. Spencer and I talked about cryptography once in a while; he said he had read a few good articles in "Popular Science" and would teach me how to decipher secret codes. Spencer also knew how to use the microfilm section of a library. He spoke several languages, not only German. He also spoke Polish and Romanian; his parents were from Romania. They escaped in 1938, the year before the war, when he was only a few months old.

He had an ear for languages and was even teaching himself Esperanto, the international language that President Theodore Roosevelt tried to popularize throughout the world. Of course Spencer had nowhere to practice since no one else spoke Esperanto in Miami Beach, but he didn't care, it gave him a sense of accomplishment to be able to speak a language that no one else could understand. I had the same type of feeling when I made high spiral punts and caught the football behind my back; no one else could do that either. He wore glasses; he was a little round shouldered, and if you got to know him, which very few people did, he had a dry sense of humor. He was Jewish and lived in New York until 1948, when his family moved to Miami Beach, but he didn't have a New York accent and he never referred to New York as the "City" and he never wore Lacoste shirts. Many of the kids at school thought that Spencer was a "geek" and called him terrible names, but that was so stupid. I think they were intimidated because he was so brilliant in every subject.

The next day a tape arrived from Michael Bernstein; his previous tapes said nothing about Nazi tattoos, however, this one began with recorded music playing in the background . . . the theme song from Dragnet, the popular TV police show. Michael was dramatic and liked to embellish his stories with sound effects. The Dragnet theme music was loud; then the music faded, and was replaced by Michael's staccato voice, his best impersonation of the actor, Jack Webb.

> I'm Sergeant Friday;
> homicide;
> Chicago;
> it's a big city;
> lots of crime;
> our job
> to stop it."

(Repeat of the Dragnet theme music)

> Here's the facts ma'am
> just the facts
>
> Auschwitz was the only camp to use tattoos—
> Numbers were started in 1941
> political prisoners had a number . . .
> But no letter
> Gypsies had the letter Z
> Followed by a number
> In May 1944 the Nazis began using a new series of numbers
> All Jews then started receiving a letter in front of the numbers,
> "A" or "B"
> those are the facts
> just the facts"

(Repeat of the Dragnet theme music)

101

The rest of the tape talked about things that were happening in Chicago, about Michael's favorite TV shows, his favorite music, the new school where he was going. He was recently expelled from a third school; he didn't say why. He also talked about his father's business. His father was the Kotex and Kleenex king of Chicago . . . the sole distributor for all drug stores. He was also reading a book how to build a submarine; he wanted to cross Lake Michigan. The tape concluded with a word of commiseration to me . . . the White Sox came in second place again; Michael knew that was upsetting to me. The 1952 World Series would be between the Brooklyn Dodgers and the New York Yankees, another all New York "Subway Series," just like 1951. I put the tape recorder on rewind, to listen to his tattoo facts again; I played the part about the 1944 "A" and "B" letters several times.

I couldn't stop thinking about Michael's tape . . . and about Mr. Streuling and the old white hair people at Dubrows and the numbers on their arms. Mr. Streuling said that he was there in Auschwitz, in 1942; that's probably why his number was 425304; the first two numbers must refer to the year, and his number was not preceded by the letter "A" or "B," unlike the old people at Dubrows. I was beginning to understand the significance of the Nazi numbering system; the old people at Dubrows had "A" or "B" in front of their number because they were at Auschwitz after May 1944. That made sense, only the most recent prisoners would have survived; the war ended in May 1945. But why was Mr. Streuling only there for a month? That didn't seem possible . . . to be able to just bribe a guard and get out. I needed to do more research at the library. I would have to tell David and Spencer Teichman about my suspicions, and a little about Mr. Streuling . . . but not about the shower episode . . . never!

David, Spencer, and I went to the microfilm section of the Miami Beach Library. The library was on 21st street, only two blocks from the James Manor, two blocks from Mr. Streuling. We asked to see newspaper articles relating to Auschwitz. The assistant librarian, Katarina Wolinski, was very helpful . . . She was a concentration camp survivor, a short woman, probably in her late thirties, with red hair. Katarina had warm eyes, and the more I talked to her and listened to her stories, the more I liked her. She had a number on her forearm, a number that began with the letter "B." She was Jewish and had married a gentile man in Poland; he made the mistake of converting to Judaism. He was sent with her to Auschwitz in January 1945, just a few months before the war ended. Katarina was extremely fortunate, she was young and strong and had some previous nursing training, so she was assigned to work in one of the infirmaries at Auschwitz; she was there the day the camp was liberated by the Soviet Red Army in May 1945.

Our microfilm research disclosed a few interesting facts: that Auschwitz was the only concentration camp that used numbered tattoos, and the "A" and "B' letters began in 1944. Before that year the numbers were not preceded by letters. But, I already knew that from Michael's tape. We also found an article in the New York Times that gave sketchy information about a massive purge of homosexuals in Germany during the early part of 1942, the year when Streuling said he was at Auschwitz. The article didn't tell if the homosexuals were sent to Auschwitz, or what type of number they received, but it was logical to assume that if they did have a number it would be without the "A" or "B.". We also found out that the infamous crematorium at Auschwitz-Birkenau was not constructed until late 1942, after the purge of the homosexuals.

Shelly returned from Lincoln Road and joined us at the library; he was carrying a shopping bag from Saks Fifth Avenue and was excited to tell us that he bought two Lacostes, two new colors for his collection; he told Katarina that he loved her blouse, then he listened intently, as she began telling her story.

"I got my number the day I arrived at Auschwitz. Getting a number meant that you were scheduled for some type of job, not for the ovens, thank God . . . 'ptu ptu'" Katarina paused and did an imaginary spit into the air . . . an Eastern European Jewish superstition . . . to ward off the evil spirits. "My mother and father were old and feeble; they never got numbers. My husband was normally a healthy man, but he had a bad cold that week; it was January and the weather in Poland was freezing. On the train to Auschwitz we had no blankets; he was coughing and sneezing the entire trip. The Nazi's didn't have much patience for sick Jews; he never got a number either. I cried and told them he was a gentile, but no one listened. We were called 'Untermenschen'—subhuman!"

Spencer said something to Katarina in Polish, how sorry we were to hear about her husband and her parents. She smiled at Spencer and invited us to come to her office and chat for awhile. She asked to see Shelly's two new shirts.

"Beautiful, beautiful," said Katarina, "Klaider machen dem mentshen" (*Clothes make the man*). We all drank an apple flavored Polish tea and listened to Katarina share painful recollections of her first day at Auschwitz, when males and females were taken to different showers and stripped of their identity. She told us terrifying stories, too brutal to imagine, repulsive stories about her work in the infirmary, and her futile search to uncover details about her husband and parents.

I asked her if she ever saw homosexuals in Auschwitz and I told her a few facts about Mr. Streuling, about his tattoo and about my suspicions; at first I thought he was a Nazi, but now I was beginning to think that he was a homosexual . . . especially since he was at Auschwitz in 1942, the year of the homosexual purge. But, I didn't tell Katarina anything about the shower incident at the James Manor. She said that when she was there, in early 1945, there were very few homosexuals.

"The camp was then a full-time death camp for exterminating Jews; the "Protective Custody Prisoners were all gone before I got there."

"What are Protective Custody Prisoners?" asked Spencer, "we never saw that term in our research."

"Those were political prisoners, communists, and homosexuals; the Nazis took care of those problems before 1944."

"What did the Nazis do to them?" I asked . . . I assumed she meant that they were put to death. I soon learned that I was wrong; it was a lot more complicated.

"Well, if they were Jewish they were usually combined with all other Jewish prisoners and exterminated, but if they were German they had a trial; Germans had the right to a trial."

Spencer was very precise how he worded his next question: "What would happen to German, gentile homosexuals, if they had a trial and were found guilty?"

"They would be sent to prison, usually for a month, then after they served their prison sentence they were remanded to hard labor at Auschwitz, probably for another month." Katarina seemed to think that we "hit on something" with that 1942

New York Times article, it shed some light on why most of the homosexuals were gone when she got to Auschwitz in 1945.

"Are you sure you want to hear the rest of the details; you might have nightmares?" Shelly was the first to say yes; he was very tense, chewing the corners of his Saks Fifth Avenue shopping bag. "Once the homosexuals got to Auschwitz they were sterilized, but those who were pedophiles, those who molested small children . . . were castrated." In the years prior to 1944, Auschwitz was primarily a prison for communists, gypsies, political prisoners, homosexuals, and pedophiles. Many of them died from starvation or disease, but they were rarely put to death. It wasn't until late 1942 that the crematorium was constructed at Auschwitz.

"What's the difference between sterilization and castration?" Normally, I would have been much too shy to ask that type of question to a woman, but Katarina was a nurse . . . at least she used to be one.

"Sterilization of a man usually involved just snipping the tubes to the testicles," said Katarina. "I often worked in the infirmary at Auschwitz, they were still doing a few sterilizations after I got there. I held the hands of male prisoners and tried to comfort them as they screamed in pain; the Nazis never used an anesthetic. Sterilization only prevented the man from reproducing, it didn't terminate his sexual ability. Now, castration," Katarina grimaced, "that involved cutting off the testicles; after that a man's voice would usually get an octave higher and he could never ejaculate."

I felt like vomiting; Mr. Streuling had a squeaky voice. I had cold chills in my legs. Did that mean he was castrated? I tried to blot the image that Katrarina was describing. I was deep in thought . . . which fate was worse . . . the crematorium or castration?

"There's something you aren't telling us." Katarina looked directly into my eyes. She saw more pain and suffering in her life than she was supposed to, and she could see that I was hiding details about Mr. Streuling. "Myron, tell us what you're holding back; tell us everything about this man."

I was starting to like the apple flavored Polish tea, I poured a fourth cup and began to tell Spencer, David, Shelly, and Katarina all about Mr. Streuling, all about the day in the shower. Katarina held my hand; she had heard that kind of story before and she had seen much worse. Shelly stared in space; he dropped his partially eaten shopping bag on the floor . . . and later that afternoon, when we rode the bus back to Surfside, he forgot to bring home his fifteenth and sixteenth Lacoste. David just said: "Holy shit!" He said that a lot.

After I finished my story Katarina hugged me, then she summarized what we already suspected: "I would have to say, based upon what you told me, and based upon this man's number, that he was probably some type of Protective Custody Prisoner, sentenced only for one month at Auschwitz; maybe he was a homosexual, or God forbid, maybe a pedophile." Katarina doubted that Mr. Streuling was Jewish; she felt that it was unlikely that he could bribe a guard and get out so easy. "Bribery was common in before the war, but not in 1942."

"OK" said Spencer . . . "here's the way I see it; Streuling's not a Jew; he's either a homosexual or a pedophile . . . and there's one very definite way that we can find out which one he is." Spencer paused; he said nothing; he kind of smirked . . . we all knew where he was going, but we didn't want to interrupt; we waited to hear Spencer say it himself.

"If his testicles have been removed . . . we know for sure."

"I thought he exposed himself when you went fishing," said David. "You said you saw his penis."

"I closed my eyes," I replied. "but he only unzipped, he didn't take down his pants."

David, Shelly, and I laughed, but we knew that Spencer was right; Katarina also laughed. We were all thinking the same thing, but none of us came right out and said it . . . . how could we ever find out for sure? Who was going to do the investigation of Mr. Streuling's testicles?

"Hey, I have an idea," I broke the silence. "Katarina, how would you like to meet Henry Streuling; he lives only two blocks from here and he's very handsome?"

CHAPTER 16

AND GOD MAKETH THE RULES OF SYNTAX

"The Lord is my shepherd, I shall not want; He maketh me to lie down in green pastures. He restoreth my soul . . . . and I shall not think about Mr. Streuling."

I loved "maketh" and "restoreth" they were such neat words, almost as cool as the upside down question marks and exclamation marks in Spanish. I always wanted to find an opportune time and place to use "maketh" or "restoreth" in conversation or in an essay, but they never seemed appropriate, except for the morning devotionals in my ninth grade homeroom—section 9-3.

"It's a Jewish prayer," said Miss Carter, my homeroom teacher. "You should all really appreciate the Twenty Third Psalm, it was written by David, who was one of 'your' people, the King of Israel." Miss Carter was aware of the fact that thirty four of the thirty five kids in our homeroom were Jewish, all except Paul Yardley, the self-proclaimed "token Goy." "And David was the direct ancestor of our Lord and Savior." She had to sneak in that little commentary, her historical footnote.

"There's something I don't understand," said Howard Lefkowitz. "If Mary was descended from King David, that means she was royalty."

"That's right, Howard." Miss Carter had a big smile on her face. Finally, one of the Jewish kids recognized that Jesus was of royal blood.

"So, then . . . why did she have her baby in a barn?" replied Howard. "Couldn't she just tell the mayor of Bethlehem that she was the great great great granddaughter of King David? I'm sure they could have found her a hotel room."

"Well, to begin with," said Miss Carter. "It wasn't a barn, it was a stable. And, as you know, Bethlehem was very crowded that week; the Jews were taking a census for Caeser Augustus. Maybe Mary didn't want tourists and autograph seekers bothering her. When you're having a baby you want a little privacy."

"Yeah but didn't they have hospitals? I mean, like . . . ." Howard attempted to respond to Miss Carter, but she cut him off before he could finish his comment.

"Howard, stop asking silly questions. Anything you want to know about the Immaculate Conception; its all there in the Holy Scriptures."

We were reminded, at least once a week, that the Lord and Savior was Jewish; it was a compassionate way to comfort us, to reassure us that it wasn't such a terrible sin to be Jewish.

"And, boys and girls . . . the Son of God was Jewish, just like all of you." Miss Carter never came right out and said "Jesus Christ" She tried to respect our feelings . . . in her own way.

"Miss Carter, what's the past tense of 'maketh,' asked Penny Sherman, "is it "madeth"? It just don't sound right."

Penny was in several of my classes. She talked a lot, asked a lot of dumb questions and was always staring into a little mirror to make sure that her hair and lipstick were perfect. She wasn't really that pretty except for her beautiful blonde pony tail, but she had a good personality and was very popular. However, I never felt comfortable talking to her, probably because she was always surrounded by a flock of boys.

"Good question, Penny . . . I guess I'd have to say that holy words transcend time . . . 'maketh' is a word of the Lord; its all tenses . . . past, present, and future. What the Lord 'maketh' was there before the beginning of time and it will be there after the end of time. The word of God is eternal . . . . God is omnipotent."

Manny Lefkowitz, who was sitting at the desk behind Penny, pulled on her pony tail and began laughing at Miss Carter's comments. "Hey, God can't get a boner."

"No, you dumb putz," whispered Penny. "That's 'impotent.'"

I raised my hand to ask a question: "Miss Carter, how can there be an end of time? What comes after the end?"

"Only God, Myron . . . only God! May the Lord bless you and keep you and give you peace." Miss Carter liked me. She rarely asked the Lord to give special blessings for any students, just Paul Yardley and me.

Paul raised his hand and wiggled it in the air . . . he had an important question.

"Miss Carter, did they have Chinese food in Bethlehem? I mean back then, when Jesus was a baby?"

"I don't think so Paul. Why do you ask?'"

"Well, I seen pictures of the three wise men, one of them looked Chinese. And what kind of gift were they giving the baby Jesus? What's Frankensteen?"

Miss Carter laughed: "No Paul, it isn't frankensteen, its frankincense, a type of tree sap. It was used to make incense."

"Well, they also gave him gold," said Penny. "That's cause his mom was Jewish. Jewish moms don't want tree sap."

◆

Throughout my final year at Ida M. Fisher Jr. High School, and during the next three years at Beach High, I would always remain in home room section #3 . . . but the Steinbergs, who just moved to South Florida in the ninth grade, were in section #12, a much better homeroom than mine, with many of the most popular kids, including Freya Rothman, a beautiful girl with a great smile and perfect teeth, who would eventually be crowned "Coronation Queen" an award given to the Beach High girl who was most popular. Popularity actually came ahead of beauty in the election of our Queen; I don't want to imply that Freya wasn't beautiful, she certainly was, but one or two of the other contestants were prettier, like Clara Babbit, but she had a bad reputation, so only greasers, like the "Rebels," the teenage Jewish gang, voted for her. And Linda Spiegel, the buxom girl from my homeroom was also a candidate. Linda was the first girl I ever knew who had big breasts, but by the time she ran for Coronation Queen, she lost her competitive advantage; by that time most of the girls had breasts . . . . and she was a distant tenth in the voting. I voted for Linda because she was in my homeroom and I knew her since eighth grade. But, if I wasn't so biased, I would definitely have voted for Freya.

Sections 1-6 were the South Beach kids, the kids who lived south of 23rd street. Sections 7-12 were the kids who lived north of the dividing line; that part of Miami Beach was often called North Beach. Those kids went to Nautilus Jr. High School in the eighth grade, and were now transferring to Ida M. Fisher. Nautilus only went through eighth grade, so it wasn't a voluntary transfer; all Miami Beach kids merged in the ninth grade and your home room number became a label, similar to the little alligator on your shirt.

In 1952 I moved to Surfside, into the Nautilus school district. I wish I had lived there in the eighth grade; If I had I would now be in one of the prestige sections. Unfortunately, I lived on 19th street, at the James Manor, in the eighth grade (Mr. Streuling's building), so I was branded with my number for life; I would always be in section #3, no matter where I moved. My destiny was forever linked to the South Beach kids, to the kids who weren't as smart as the Nautilus kids (with the exception of Spencer Teichman) . . . to the kids who wore white undershirts to school instead of imported Lacostes. But, my new best friends, the Steinberg twins, were in Section 9-12; so was Freya Rothman. I asked the Registrar if I could transfer to section #12. This was the same woman who skipped me to eighth grade the previous year; surely, she would honor my simple request.

My request was denied. . . . I could not escape from section #3 . . . and the edicts of the Registrar could not be appealed; I remembered what happened when Dick Solomon's parents went to school to protest his paddling . . . you only get two options: private school with the morons or deportation to Miami with the rednecks. Maybe this was just a reminder that the concept of "bashert" wasn't quite so stupid.

Some of the South Beach kids, like Howard Lefkowitz, were on welfare, and some, like Harold Lorber, were Orthodox, and some, like Manny Lefkowitz and Norty Berkowitz, scratched their balls when they talked, but the South Beach kids had one advantage over the wealthier Nautilus kids; they lived closer to school and could walk home every day; the kids who lived north of the library rode on yellow school buses or Cadillacs, driven by family chauffeurs.

Once in a while I reminisce about the fall of 1952, the year of the ninth grade merger; I am convinced that the numeric segregation was a gentile plot to divide and conquer the ubiquitous scapegoats of history. I recall the contrived differences between South Beach kids and Nautilus kids, between kids who were arbitrarily assigned to low number home rooms and those who were placed in the high number sections. I have long forgotten those trivial differences; I can only remember the similarities, the bonding . . . the camaraderie . . . the connection . . . we were Jewish; we were the common enemy and some of our teachers never let us forget that we were different, even when they reminded us that we were the "chosen people."

Miss Carter was tall, with thin lips, which she covered with flesh colored lipstick, in an attempt to make them look thicker. I always thought that flesh colored lipstick was stupid; why bother? And she wore black horn rimmed glasses which encircled green eyes that never looked at you; they looked through you. Miss Carter reminded me of the gaunt, raw-boned woman in "The American Gothic," the famous painting of a rural couple, and she spoke with a southern accent; she told us that she was from Georgia. She wore sheer see-though blouses, just like Miss Baker, but Miss Carter never varied her attire; she never flaunted authority by sprouting phony breasts. She proudly wore her see-though blouse and invited pubescent males to stare at her perfectly flat chest. I think see-through blouses were the required mode of dress and flat chests were mandatory for female teachers at Ida M. Fisher. The only male teacher I had was Coach Malloy in Phys. Ed. and as I already mentioned; he always wore white shorts, a lanyard, and a gold whistle, or just a jock strap when he was inside the locker room. I'm not sure if Coach Malloy even had full length pants; at school assemblies, when he sat on the stage in the auditorium, next to the principal and the deans, he wore his white shorts, with a matching white Lacoste. The shirt was a present from some unidentified "brown nose" kid who wanted to kiss up to him. Calling a kid a "brown nose" was a polite way of saying that he was an "ass kisser."

Morning devotionals in the ninth grade weren't so bad, certainly not like the fervent prayer sessions of Miss Baker, the proselytizing zealot in the eighth grade. Miss Carter wasn't on a mission; she never made us pray to the father, son, and holy ghost; we just concluded our prayers or psalms with "Amen," and she would turn her back to the class and sneak in a quick and private finger crossing on her chest. I always respected her for being considerate. Of course, the time when Harold Lorber, the boy with the yarmelkeh, ended the prayer with Ahh—Main . . . the religious Jewish version of Amen, that was pushing Miss Carter a little too far; she put a stop to that immediately.

Paul Yardley told stories about Jewish holidays, when he was the only kid in class. Miss Carter did morning devotionals, with just him as an audience, and breathed a sigh of relief when she concluded her prayer with an impassioned father, son, and holy ghost . . . when she traced a bold, uninhibited, four cornered crossing on her flat chest while facing the front of an almost empty classroom, kind of like me when I showered in Phys. Ed., boldly flaunting my developing body to an empty shower room . . . the day Bobby Thompson hit his famous homerun.

Miss Carter was also my ninth grade English teacher; she loved reading poems by Poe in class, especially "The Bells." Even though she was very vocal in her views on Jesus and Christianity, she was sensitive to the fact that most of the kids were Jewish. For example, when she read segments of Macbeth in class she made a slight alteration to the boiling cauldron poem . . . that's the part where the witches say, "double, double, toil, and trouble." Instead of saying, "liver of a blasphheming Jew" Miss Carter changed "Jew" to "Ewe" . . . a female sheep. Some kids were offended; they felt that she was comparing Jews to sheep, inferring that Jews were sacrilegious cowards. I think she was just trying to be nice . . . and Ewe rhymed with Jew.

Ida M. Fisher Jr. High and Miami Beach High School were adjoining buildings. Both were Moorish architecture, reminiscent of the Alhambra or a medieval Spanish palace; both had bumpy stucco walls, large circular patios, pink archways with twisted Ionic columns, and open air balconies connecting the classrooms. The two schools shared a common principal, Aaron T Schecter, whose signature I eventually learned to forge, and the same two deans, Reinhard Kessler (the Nazi) for the boys and Alba Layne (the inspector of "falsies") for the girls, and a common cafeteria, auditorium, gymnasium, and locker rooms. And in the north courtyard of Beach High there was a statue of a World War

II soldier, standing with his rifle at his side. The statue was a gift from the Class of 1945, in memory of Beach High alumni who died in World War II.

"Boys and Girls, one week from today is the ninth of January . . . we will be commemorating Robert E. Lee's birthday," said Miss Carter. She stood tall, and brushed imaginary wrinkles off her dress, in honor of the memory of her favorite all time American. "Out of respect for this great American patriot we will be having an essay contest. Take two sharpened pencils and a memo pad; we're going to take a little walk." Thirty-four Jewish students and Paul Yardley, crossed over an open pathway to the north courtyard of the Sr. High building.

"Now, look into the eyes of the soldier, the statue . . . think of the Beach High boys who perished in the war and compose an 'inspired' one page essay." This was the charge from Miss Carter. Most of the kids immediately began to write; they had a lot to say about Nazis and Japs and kamakazie pilots. Miss Carter then interrupted our courtyard classroom and modified the rules. "Pretend that the soldier is dead and he is talking to you from the grave; write your essay as if he is giving you advice." I didn't have any definite thoughts; I just sat on the grass and observed that there were several orange trees growing in the courtyard; I had never noticed that before. They were pretty trees, with little white flowers. Mostly, I just watched the other kids write. Death is scary and orange trees are pretty . . . that's about as profound as I could get.

We had the weekend to work on our essay; it was to be turned in the following Monday, and we would have to sign a sacred oath that we had not received help, not even from our parents, "so help me God." Of course, Miss Carter highly recommended that we buy a Thesaurus and use it extensively. One week later, on the birthday of Robert E. Lee, Miss Carter called Danny Berger and me to the front of the class; ours were the top two essays. We were asked to read our papers to the other students. I was the runner up, so I was the first to read.

I stood behind the lectern at Miss Carter's table and in a slow, somber voice I began to read my essay:

"Once, not too long ago, I was a student at Beach High; I enjoyed eating kosher franks at Penways Pharmacy, with onions and lots of hot spicy mustard, but no catsup. I also loved going to football games and dances. I was a good dancer . . . we did the Jitterbug when I was in school. I had a girlfriend . . . . and we made plans for college and a life together; then came the war. We had dreams that would never be! *(long pause . . . I looked around the room, a cute girl with a pony tail was looking directly into my eyes)* Come—sit by the foot of my statue; I have a story that I'd like to share with you . . . a war story." *(more eye contact with the cute girl . . . I must find out who she is.)*

"During a hard fought battle a general decided to attack the enemy even though his troops were greatly outnumbered. The general felt that if he could instill confidence in his soldiers they would win. Unfortunately, his men knew that they were outnumbered; they were scared. While marching to the scene of the battle the general and his troops stopped at a religious shrine and took time to pray. Then, at the alter of this shrine, the general took out a coin and said, 'I shall now toss this coin in the air. If it lands on heads, we shall win. If its tails, we shall lose. We shall now discover our true destiny.' He threw the coin into the air and all watched intently as it landed. It was heads. The soldiers were so overjoyed and filled with confidence that they vigorously attacked the enemy and were victorious. After the battle, a lieutenant remarked to the general, 'Sir! It is impossible to change your destiny.'

'You might be right,' the general replied, and he complimented the lieutenant for his bravery in battle. However, he did not show the lieutenant the coin, which had heads on both sides."

"So, what are you trying to say?" said Harold Lorber, the religious Jewish boy. "What's the moral of the story? The general tricked his soldiers into having a false sense of confidence. I wonder if Hitler flipped a two-headed coin?"

"No, Harold . . . that's not the message," replied the cute girl with the pony tail. "The soldier is telling us that our worst enemy is fear, but if we believe in ourselves we can reach for the stars."

Her name was Leah Sonnino . . . she was the only one who understood what I was trying to say. Her brown eyes sparkled when she spoke and she had a warm smile. I had seen her before . . . maybe it was in a dream.

"Very nice Myron," said Miss Carter. "Now boys and girls, you are in for a 'real' treat, sit back and listen to the stimulating words of Danny Berger." Miss Carter brushed away imaginary wrinkles on her dress, just like she did when she talked about Robert E. Lee. I was expecting Danny to begin with "Four Score and Seven Years ago."

Danny was a "phony" . . . he always knew what to say, and how to get his way with girls and with teachers. He was one of the few kids to get an "A" in Phys. Ed. Danny was positive that his essay would win, so positive that he wore a white shirt and a tie to class that day; he knew he would be called in front of the class to read his "stimulating" words, maybe even to pose for a photo. He walked to the lectern, cleared his throat and raised his fist into the air.

"Friends, teachers, and classmates . . . lend me your ears. I speak to you from my grave, on the beach of Normandy; I am now at peace, comforted in the bosom of our Lord, with my Bible clutched to my heart. *(Danny Berger was Jewish . . . what a brown nose!)* The graves of Normandy contain many bodies, and all of them are dead. They are all God fearing brave American soldiers who died like me on this battlefield in France to preserve freedom of religion. *(this better improve or I am going to puke)* We killed lots of Nazis so that you can enjoy democracy freely and be a free country and worship God freely. Now, you must carry the torch of the Lord; you must be strong of body, mind, and soul and be prepared to fight the godless Russian atheists in the next world war. You must cleanse your mind of evil thoughts and give thanks to God every day in your morning devotionals because you are nothing without God; you owe everything you are to Him. *(how many God's can this brown nose jerk get into one essay?)* In conclusion, honor your mother and father, like it says in the Bible; listen to your teachers, because they are the guiding light and the word of God, and love the Lord because he loves you. God Bless America." *(puke, puke, puke)*

Miss Carter stood and cried. "Danny, that was like music to my ears; it was wonderful." Even though she was crying she glared at any student who was not applauding; every kid was soon cheering . . . even Leah Sonnino . . . even me. "I'm going to have that hung on the wall in Mr. Schecter's office . . . . And your picture too . . . Oh it is so beautiful."

Miss Carter told me, privately, that she liked my writing . . . that I should review her editorial comments. The bottom of my paper had a few hand written notes . . .

"Good imagery; vivid imagination! I enjoyed your story—faith is everything. If you truly believe that God is on your side, you can accomplish anything."

What was she talking about? That was not my message! I got an "A-minus" on that essay—she took off a few points for run-on sentences. I wrote several short stories and essays for Miss Carter during the year, and I carefully reviewed her little red notes. She liked my stories and always gave me an "A" or an "A minus" but I don't think she always understood what I was saying. She read several of my stories out loud in class and laughed out of context; sometimes she laughed in parts that were supposed to be sad; sometimes she got all teary eyed in the funny parts. And one day, when she stepped out of the classroom, I peeked into her grade book. I was really surprised to see that Danny only had a "C" on his "stimulating . . . music to my ears" essay. Miss Carter was our spiritual leader, but when she graded papers, she was an English teacher.

And I was admonished never to begin a sentence with "and" or "but." But I always violated that rule. "But" is such a natural word to use when you interrupt your thought process and start a new sentence or a new paragraph. And I reminded Miss Carter that many sentences in the Bible begin . . . "And the Lord said." But, she told me that Biblical writing doesn't have to follow the same rules of grammar and sentence structure. How can you criticize God for bad grammar? He wrote the Bible and He is the Father of everything. And God "maketh" the rules of syntax.

CHAPTER 17

THE IMPORTANCE OF BEING NORMAL

Eating five or six dinners a week, at home, was a new experience for me; we were becoming a normal family. During my early years, prior to age thirteen, we always lived in apartments and ate most of our dinners in restaurants; I was used to the freedom of ordering what I wanted. I didn't have to eat the same as my mother or father or anyone else. I just had to make sure that I ordered a "balanced meal" and that I ate my vegetables. But now, living in a house, being normal meant that I had to eat the same food as everyone else, and I had to comply with standardized rules for the proper sequence of eating the meal.

My mother's typical dinner consisted of three food groups: (1) meat, fish, or chicken; (2) a different style of potato every night; (3) some type of canned vegetable or applesauce. I hated cooked vegetables, especially canned vegetables. During my restaurant years I developed the habit of eating the main item first. Then I ate the potato. Then I struggled with the vegetable, rotating the asparagus or cauliflower with my beverage, to wash away the foul taste. My mother usually forced me to finish my vegetables, and not waste food, because children were starving in Europe.

"Hey mom, why don't we send my asparagus to Europe, to save those poor anorexic children. And if its so healthy, and so good for you, how come your pee smells disgusting after you eat asparagus?"

In restaurants I always managed to find some type of vegetable that was moderately tolerable, like summer squash, which I learned to like during my summer at Camp Briar Lodge. But, at home, as we became a "normal" family, I was forced to eat canned mixed vegetables, canned peas, or canned carrots. "Myron, eat a little meat, then a little potato, then a little vegetable . . . then take a little drink . . . . then back to the meat," said my mother. I was thirteen; hair was growing on new parts of my body, but she was giving me fundamental instructions on proper eating.

"Rotate . . . that's the way 'normal' people eat. 'Yeder mentsh hot zein aigeneh meshugass.'" (*Every person has his own idiosyncrasies.*).

When my mother made a big juicy steak, probably once or twice a week, she would dump a ladle full of apple sauce or mashed potatoes right in the middle of the plate, right on top of the steak. My complaints always received the same response:

"It all goes together in your stomach anyway. So what's the big deal about putting it together in your mouth? Myron, you have to learn to eat like 'normal' people."

My mother always chastised me for my strange eating habits . . . and no matter what I did wrong, she found an appropriate Yiddish proverb: "Kreplach essen vert oich nimis." (*One gets tired of eating only kreplach.*)

We all try to find excuses to explain the origin of our personal quirks and idiosyncrasies. I am convinced that the reason I still eat each item of food separately (more than sixty years after the move to Surfside) is because of my early restaurant years; we waited too long to become a normal family.

On the evening of Robert E. Lee's birthday, following the reading of my second place essay in Miss Carter's English class, we were at home, eating dinner. I was at the critical juncture of the meal. The Chicken and potatoes were finished; I would now have to begin the painful process of rotating extra sweet lemonade with canned carrots. Thankfully, the phone rang, the call was for me; I had a temporary reprieve.

It was Leah Sonnino, the cute girl from my English class; she was calling to tell me how much she "adored" my short story about the two-headed coin, that it touched her soul. My obvious response should have been a simple "thank you" but I just sat at the phone, tongue-tied . . . I couldn't even say hello.

"Um . . . uh . . . um . . . uh . . . .

"Myron . . . are you there?" "Hello! Hello!" . . . Leah Sonnino hung up and dialed again; she thought she had a bad connection.

"Thank you," I finally got it out. "Didn't you like Danny's essay; he won the contest?"

"You gotta' be kidding; that was pure garbage, Danny is a bullshitter; everyone knows that he just threw in a lot of Gods and Lords to make Miss Carter happy." Leah went on and on, how she couldn't stand Danny, that he was a "phony four-flusher." "He's only popular because his daddy is a big shot attorney and he lives in a mansion on some island . . . and he rides to school in a huge black limo."

Leah was very pretty; she was shorter than me and had a sexy pony tail. She was also Jewish, but Sonnino sure wasn't a Jewish name.

"We're Jewish, I guess, but aside from eating Jewish food we aren't religious," said Leah.

"Yeah, same with me," I laughed. "I love toasted bagels for breakfast."

Leah liked me; I could tell. We made arrangements to go to a movie on Lincoln Road.

"Myron, would you like to go with me to a movie Saturday?"

"Myron, are you there? . . . Hello!"

"Yes"

"Good . . . lets meet at noon, in front of Liggets Drug store; do you know where that is?" That was the same place where Buddy Macker made his threats of extortion about the Spanish workbook. Why did she pick Liggets? I started to worry; maybe Leah Sonnino was a setup; Macker was now at one of the private schools for dummies, but maybe he wanted revenge.

"Uh . . . why Liggets?" I asked.

"Don't you want to meet me?" Leah purred.

"OK . . . Liggets at noon!" At that moment, on the night of Robert E. Lee's birthday, I observed another one of my idiosyncrasies, even worse than my odd eating habits. When a girl purred I lost my ability to think, argue, debate, or disagree. That inability continued to plague me through the upcoming years of adolescence and adulthood. The conversation was very quick, but thankfully, it was long enough for my mother to dump the canned carrots in the garbage. Although Tupperware was recently invented; word of that horrible household product had not yet reached my mother.

Early the next morning, as I prepared for my first date, I called Shelly and asked if I could borrow a red Lacoste. I planned to wear the preppy red polo shirt with a new pair of Levis.

"No, red is too bold," said Shelly. "It's all wrong; it's too aggressive for your first date. I suggest a soft baby blue Lacoste; it sets a peaceful mood, and it matches your eyes." Damn; he was perceptive . . . it was evident that Shelly would eventually wind up in the fashion world. "And definitely wear new Levis; girls don't want to go out with boys who wear old jeans. They want jeans without a history." Shelly rode over to my house on his bike; he carried a baby blue Lacoste and white shoe polish so that I could cover the scuff marks on my white buckskin loafers.

After Shelly left I called Mona, my "busty" sixteen year old advisor, to discuss my upcoming date. She talked to me like a big sister does to a virginal little brother, and proceeded to bombard me with rules and questions. "Now, you be a gentleman, Myron, don't stare at her breasts, it isn't normal, and don't use profanity; nice girls like boys to be polite and refined. Is she Jewish?"

"What if my balls itch; can I scratch them?" I laughed at her advice. "And . . . yes, she's Jewish."

"Do you think you're funny Myron? I'm going to tell your mother that you're becoming a little punk with a foul mouth. You can never use profanity with a Jewish girl; I guess with shiksas its OK, but nice Jewish boys don't go out with shiksas."

"Kenny Shapiro, the quarterback of the football team is Jewish," I noted, "and his girlfriend is Carrie Collins. She isn't Jewish." I knew I had Mona backed against the wall; Kenny was one of the most popular kids at Beach High; how could she respond to that observation?

"Kenny is just going with Carrie for sex; when you get older you'll see there's a difference between going with a girl just for sex, and going with a girl for the right reasons."

"Don't Jewish girls like sex also?"

"Well of course, but only after marriage."

"How can you wait that long; don't you get horny?" I could talk that way with Mona. We had many intimate discussions; she was my surrogate sister.

"That's what cold showers are for, and I think you should do the same thing; you're becoming a little pervert."

After my briefing by Mona, I made last minute preparations for my first date; I paraded in front of a mirror and examined every detail of my well conceived attire. Shelly was right, the baby blue Lacoste was perfect. I also considered wearing sun glasses; they looked cool. But, that would defeat the purpose of the Lacoste; Leah Sonnino would not be able to see that I had blue eyes.

Saturday morning: Just before I left for the bus the phone rang, it was Shelly, with last minute advice.

"No matter what kind of blouse she's wearing, tell her its beautiful. Wait till you're alone in the movies. Girls love compliments about their clothes. And don't call it a shirt; its a blouse."

The bus ride to Lincoln Road, which could sometimes take as long as an hour, seemed a lot longer that Saturday. I kept myself busy, writing notes on a small memo pad, cryptic reminders of possible topics for conversation, just in case we had nothing to talk about. My father suggested that I discuss recent books; girls liked boys who were intelligent . . . and to make sure to stand up straight; good posture was important. Mona said to talk about music and current events at school, but not to gossip about other people . . . and to smile a lot. "Walk with her on your right side," said Mona. "You've got a crooked tooth on the left." And, of course, my mother offered Yiddish advice. "Far ziseh raidelech tsegai'en di maidelech." (*Sweet talk makes the girls melt.*)

It was now a year since my Shabbos dinner with Virginia, the double nymph, and I was finally ready to explore my emerging manhood; puberty was transforming me into an adult; I was showering, facing the front in Phys. Ed., feeling sorry for the timid younger boys who showered in the backward position. And, unlike some of my gawky friends, who experienced pubescent complications, my changes were evolving gracefully. My voice was getting deeper without the awkward embarrassment of crackling and squeaking; hair was growing in all the right places and I wasn't cursed with bad complexion. I never needed Clearasil, the flesh colored medication that many kids used to camouflage pimples, blackheads, or zits. I wondered how Negro kids dealt with puberty; how could they cover zits with Clearisil?.

Maybe Negroes didn't get zits . . . or did they make Clearisil in different colors?

There she was! Leah Sonnino . . . waiting at Liggets; she was punctual, another good quality. She was wearing a white blouse and a bright red skirt with a poodle sewn near the bottom. It was red! What would Shelly say? She had a very sweet smile, dark brown eyes that sparkled with excitement, and a perky way of flipping her head, whipping her pony tail from left to right. And I remembered Mona's advice; "don't stare at her breasts; it isn't normal." Well . . . that wouldn't be too difficult; Leah didn't have big ones . . . .

"Hi, What's up?" That was my eloquent greeting.

"I love your Lacoste, it brings out the blue in your eyes." Leah Sonnino purred and flipped her pony tail, and the next half hour was a blur; she was in control. She made the important decisions, what movie we would see; it was irrelevant whether I had already seen that movie . . . what type of popcorn I would buy, buttered or plain; where we would sit.

It was dark in the Carib theatre, even darker in the back row. Leah was on my right . . . .

I didn't want her to see the crooked tooth on the left side of my mouth. My arm moved slowly along the treacherous path, inching its way across her shoulder until my hand was hanging in space with no place to rest. The obvious resting place was on her right breast, but Mona was shouting instructions, all the way from Surfside . . . . no touching! Leah is Jewish.

The time was ripe . . . to use Shelly's advice. "I think your blouse is beautiful."

Leah turned and whispered in my ear. "You say the sweetest things." And we kissed. It was a tight lipped, closed mouth dry kiss; it was my first kiss. Then she gently placed my dangling right hand on her blouse . . . on her breast. Shelly was amazing, those were magic words, like "Open Sesame." Leah turned toward the movie and continued eating her popcorn. She ate slowly, one piece at a time.

I began to squeeze her right breast, like an exercise ball that you use to strengthen your grip; she continued eating and watching the movie. As I squeezed her wired bra the cup compressed into a concave shape; it didn't pop back. Her breast was not large enough to fill the bra. In the privacy of our back row she twisted and wiggled her bra until it resumed its normal shape, then she returned my hand to the soft and wonderful resting place . . . no words were spoken, but she smiled. So did I.

We sat that way for the next hour, watching the movie and eating popcorn; I was careful not to indent her bra again. I really wanted to squeeze the left breast also, but the only way I could do that was if we changed seats but that was way too awkward and I assumed that it probably felt the same as the right one.

After the movie we stood in the lobby for a few minutes admiring a beautiful parrot that was perched high on a pole. Some kids were trying to teach the multi-colored bird to say dirty words. We watched for a while and laughed, then we walked together on Lincoln Road, holding hands, Leah always on my right, and we discussed various topics, including books, music, current events, and poetry. Leah loved Poe; so did I, and I was careful with my posture.

"Did you ever live on James Avenue?" she asked.

"Yeah! We lived in an apartment when I first moved here, in the eighth grade."

"We met before, but we never talked to each other" said Leah. "You had a cute little black and white dog and I was walking my grandma's French Poodle."

Leah was the girl with Pepe. She was the girl who stood and watched her white Poodle sniff Mitzi, my Aunt Pearlies dog. That was a long time ago, my first day in Miami Beach, And I remembered the prophetic words of my eighth grade teacher: "Every aspect of our earthly existence has been preordained by God." Maybe she was right; Leah and I were definitely drawn together by an unexplained force.

And when we said goodbye at the corner of Lincoln Road and Washington Avenue (the same spot where we began this memorable day) I kissed her again, my second kiss. I was in love with Leah Sonnino for the right reasons, not for sex.

The next morning I called Leah, to ask her to the upcoming Saturday movie. I planned to wear another Lacoste, maybe royal blue . . . but not red. Unfortunately, she said that relatives were coming to visit; she would not be able to go out with me that week. So, the next Saturday I went to the movies on Lincoln Road with David and Shelly, and in the back row of the Carib theatre I saw Leah Sonnino sitting with Danny Berger; his arm was around her shoulder, but his hand was still in the dangling position. I wanted to turn around and shout instructions: "Hey

Berger, tell her she has a beautiful blouse." But, I just sat there quietly, watching the movie, suffering in silence. On that Saturday afternoon, many years ago, I learned the poetic value of a broken heat; I wanted to write a sonnet to Leah Sonnino . . . but nothing rhymes with Sonnino.

CHAPTER 18

STONE CRABS AND KISHKEHS

The area south of Lincoln Road was commonly referred to as South Beach. Eventually it would become a trendy neighborhood, known for fine restaurants, hot music, "beautiful" people, and art deco architecture. But, in the early 1950's it was home to thousands of older Jewish residents, many of whom were retired and of modest means. Washington Avenue, the commercial hub of this region, was a vestige from another era; Yiddish competed with English as the language of the street. It was a vibrant concourse, exploding with humanity, alive with personality—kosher butchers, bakeries, delicatessens, restaurants, cafeterias—and a "shul" on every corner.

For me, the jewel of South Beach was located at the far southern end of Washington Avenue—"Joe's Stone Crabs"—my all-time favorite restaurant. Every year for my birthday my parents took me to Joe's. A waiter dressed in a tuxedo would tie a paper bib around my neck and give me a metal nutcracker and a tiny cocktail fork; then I dug into a half dozen luscious stone crab claws. Meticulously, I removed the shells and dipped each claw into melted butter or a tangy mustard sauce. After devouring my stone crabs and a platter of hash brown potatoes the glorious conclusion to this birthday treat was the most delicious key lime pie in the world. Eating at Joe's was more than a meal; it was a "happening"—it was better than going to the circus. One time I saw Arthur Godfrey at "Joe's." I had only seen him on black and white TV; he looked strange with red hair.

Another time I saw Jackie Gleason; man was he fat! And one time I did a double take, astonished at who I saw. It was my old friend Dick Solomon and his Orthodox parents. I hadn't seen him in almost a year, not since he moved to Miami.

"Dick, how can you eat here, I thought you're kosher?"

"We are, but the only exception is Joe's."

"But, you told me that when you lived in Boston, you would never eat lobsters."

"Yeah, that's cause' lobsters aren't kosher."

"Well, neither are stone crabs."

"Ain't so," said Dick. "Stone crabs are OK, as long as you use the mustard sauce, not the butter. Don't you know, you can't mix crabs and milk . . . and butter comes from milk."

And Dick's mother raised a claw in the air; she smiled and waved to me.

A few blocks north of Joe's, also on Washington Avenue, was the "Famous," a popular European Jewish restaurant. On top of every table was a bottle of seltzer—so you could make a good "greps" (*belch*) when you finished eating. "Ess Gezunterhait!" (*Eat in good health*) That was the special "blessing" before the meal. Then came a seven course eating orgy. My father was in heaven. He loved that restaurant, but as he always said: "it didn't love him." The long drive home to Surfside was sometimes very unpleasant.

"Rose, stop complaining—just open the windows." Said my father.

It was a huge menu; probably 50 different entrées, but I only liked the kreplach soup and the kishkehs. Kreplach is like Won Ton soup, with chopped meat inside the dumplings. Kishkehs are spicy sliced sausages, made from stuffed derma and several other mysterious ingredients.

"What do you think they do with the leftover food when they clean the dishes at night?" said my mother. She smiled as she took a bite of her delicious kishkehs.

I also drank a lot of seltzer with chocolate syrup; it was much better that way. It was fun to "greps" in public; only at the "Famous" was that allowed. I remember the time I saw Milton Berle—he was sitting at the table next to ours, smoking a cigar. I lifted my seltzer bottle and aimed it at his cigar and said, "Hi Uncle Miltie." He made a funny face and pretended to squirt back at me with his bottle. In future years, when I developed a taste for heavy Jewish cooking, the "Famous" was gone.

Aside from "Joe's" and the "Famous" I rarely went south of my school; Ida M. Fisher was located on fourteenth street. However, on a few occasions, I joined the Steinbergs to visit their great uncle Louie Marcus, the Romanian born brother of their grandmother. He lived in the Nemo on first street and Collins Avenue, a retirement hotel for elderly Jewish people. Although he wasn't my relative, I called him "Uncle Louie," out of respect. Also living in the same hotel was another cousin of the Steinbergs, Tanta Baila, a very solemn elderly woman with sad eyes. She had a faraway look, lost in her memories. Tanta Baila didn't speak any English, but she understood a word, every now and then.

The Nemo attracted many Romanian Jews, but I was surprised to see that none of them spoke Romanian.

"That's because, for hundreds of years we were forced to live in ghettos; Yiddish was our language," said Uncle Louie, "but if we needed to speak Romanian, like to a '*shammus*' (policeman) we could manage."

Sometimes we walked with Uncle Louie and Tanta Baila to "Essens," a nearby Jewish deli, and joined them for dinner. Uncle Louie loved chopped liver with a slice of onion and lots of "shmaltz" (*chicken fat*) which he acknowledged was "a killer.".

"When I die, my grave will say, 'here lies Louie; he ate too much shmaltz.'"

And when we weren't walking we just sat on rocking chairs on the front porch of the Nemo; we rocked and talked and watched a completely different world, where Yiddish was spoken almost as much as English.

"In Romania when I was a boy, I was a peddler," said Uncle Louie, "but what a peddler! When I moved to New York in 1890 I had saved a little money, a few shekels; I opened a grocery store in Brooklyn, the 'Marcus Market.'" Tanta Baila nodded and forced a smile.

"Uncle Louie is worth a fortune," said David. "He retired twenty years ago and started buying buildings here in South Beach. He lives at the Nemo because he likes to be with his friends, and he knows that Tanta Baila also likes it here. They were close as children, in the 'old country,' but after he moved to America they didn't see each other for fifty-five years. She came here after the war."

"In the 'old country' . . . she was . . ." Uncle Louie paused and gathered his thoughts. "She was a happy girl. . . . and such a 'Shaineh maideleh!' (*pretty girl*)"

Some of the residents of the Nemo had lived in Miami Beach since the early 30's, and they enjoyed telling stories about the city—before the island became predominantly Jewish. For them, everything was held together by stories. Of course, if three of them told the same story, you got four different versions; the extra version was what they heard from a friend, "who knew what he was talking about."

"In the 30's almost everything south of Lincoln Road 'vas Jewish, but the north side of the island 'vas all goyem, rich goyem." said Sam Mermlestein, in a thick European accent. Sam was Louie's best friend, and the two of them loved to argue. He was ninety years old and shorter than me, and I was one of the shortest boys in the ninth grade. "At the Roney Plaza hotel they had a sign in the lobby—'no dogs, niggers, or Jews allowed.'" Sam lived in Miami Beach since 1930 and was the "mavin" on local history . . . kind of a self-proclaimed authority.

I knew that Miami Beach had several "restricted" hotels and country clubs, where Jews weren't allowed, but I never knew that the island was once divided, like Korea, with Lincoln Road separating a Jewish South Beach from a gentile North Beach. By the time I moved to Florida, in 1951, Miami Beach was almost entirely Jewish. Of course, even in 1951, there were some obvious distinctions between South Beach and North Beach. The people in South Beach were older and generally less affluent. There were also differences in the architecture. North Beach, with the exception of Collins Avenue, was mainly expensive homes, all the way up to 63rd street. South Beach was much more commercial, with very few private homes. Ocean Drive had many Art Deco style hotels, but the interior of South Beach consisted of hundreds of two story white stucco apartment buildings. They all looked alike.

"Before 1910 most of Miami Beach was owned by John Collins, an old Quaker from New Jersey," said Uncle Louie.

"Isn't there a drink named after him?" asked David.

"That's 'Tom' Collins." Uncle Louie laughed. "I don't think John drank anything stronger than orange juice. Collins Avenue was named after John Collins; he was a farmer, not a 'shikker' but I guess he wasn't a very good farmer. He tried to grow oranges or avocados, I forget which one. Either way, his groves failed. I told you, he was a Quaker, but a farmer he wasn't! Eventually he sold most of his island to a big "macher" from Indiana, Carl Fisher."

Tanta Baila never joined in the conversations since she didn't speak English, but when Uncle Louie made reference to Carl Fisher she had something to say.

"Er zol vaksen vi a tsibeleh, mit dem kop en dred!" (*He should grow like an onion, with his head in the ground!*) And she spit on the ground. It wasn't a "ptu" "ptu" imaginary spit; it was a real spit.

"Damn! She doesn't like Carl Fisher," I responded. "Our school is named after his mother, Ida M. Fisher. Wasn't he Jewish?"

"Jewish? He was a Jew hater!" Exclaimed Uncle Louie.

"Don't be so dramatic," said Sam. "You 'vasn't 'dere. Fisher 'vas still alive 'ven I moved here and he 'vasn't such an anti-Semite. OK, he 'vouldn't sell land to Jews, but the guy 'vas a businessman; he 'vas building a fancy-shmancy' island for goyem."

"Nisht getrofen!" (*So, I guessed wrong!*), Louie shrugged his shoulders and continued with his story.

The old men at the Nemo never missed an opportunity to tell tall tales about Carl Fisher; their eyes lit up when they told about his rags-to-riches exploits; how he used an elephant to promote the island or how he tricked President Harding into staying at his Miami Beach hotel, to get free publicity.

"Carl Fisher was a colorful man," said Uncle Louie, "just like P.T. Barnum, the most famous promoter in American history." Uncle Louie's eyes lit up as he continued telling his story, making comparisons between Fisher, P.T. Barnum, and Superman.

I did a little research on my own—at the Miami Beach library; I wanted to learn more about Carl Fisher. I discovered that Miami Beach was just one of many amazing accomplishments of his exciting life, a fascinating adventure that flirted with disaster. He was a master salesman who orchestrated elaborate spectacles to sell bicycles and cars. He was a pioneer in the automobile industry and was even a race driver.

The library version of the Carl Fisher story was very informative, but Uncle Louie's tale was much more animated. In the library version Fisher didn't have super powers or x-ray vision.

"OK, maybe he didn't have x-ray vision," said Uncle Louie, "but talk about vision! That man could see the future."

In 1904 Carl Fisher, the race driver, held the world's land speed record and in 1911 he developed the Indianapolis speedway and the famous "Indy 500," the Memorial Day race. Because of his love of the automobile he became the spearhead in the creation of the Lincoln Highway, America's first transcontinental highway; also the north-south Dixie Highway. He made his fortune with the acquisition of the patent for an acetylene-burning headlamp in an era before automobiles had batteries. He sold the patent to Union Carbide for $9 million just before it became obsolete.

"Oye! Did he have gelt," said Uncle Louie, "by the time he was thirty-five this mashooganuh' daredevil had conquered the world and he was bored, and $9 million was burning a hole in his pocket, so he married Jane Watts, a fifteen year old shiksah' beauty queen, and set forth on his quest to build the American Riviera.

"Not so fast! Don't start the q'vest yet," said Sam. "Louie forgot to tell you about Gertrude Hassler. Before Fisher could get started in Miami Beach he had to take care of one little problem . . . Gertrude. She 'vas his fiancé and she 'vas Jewish." Fisher dumped her for the pretty little shiksah and he got his tuchus' sued big time. The guy 'vas a son-of-a-bitch but don't go saying he 'vas a Jew hater! Now . . . go on . . . tell about his q'vest."

Uncle Louie tended to exaggerate a lot, but that made his story come alive. He ranked Carl Fisher, Franklin Roosevelt, and Albert Einstein as the three greatest men of the 21st century.

"Don't forget Branch Rickey," said Uncle Louie. "Look what he did for that nice colored baseball player. But, Fisher, what a pioneer! He turned a jungle into a paradise."

That part of his story was very accurate. I read a magazine article that described how Fisher converted the groves of John Collins into a tropical paradise of sand and palm trees. Then he masterminded a dazzling sales campaign. He created the image of the Miami Beach "bathing beauty"—and that image became the centerpiece of his promotional efforts. In the middle of winter he distributed hundreds of photographs of beautiful women in tight skimpy bathing suits, with no stockings or swim shoes. The press ate this up; the "cheesecake" pictures appeared in every newspaper in America. He also sent a press release of a circus elephant plowing through the swamp to build Lincoln Road, the thoroughfare that would soon become the most exclusive retail street in the Southeast.

"But the picture didn't show 'vat 'vas behind the elephant's "tuchus," said Sam. "He used a hundred "shvartzvahs" swinging machetes. That, he didn't show!"

"See, I told you so . . . just like P.T. Barnum," said Uncle Louie. "Barnum also had an elephant."

Fisher owned most of the land north of Lincoln Road, which he subdivided into lots big enough for the wintertime mansions of Midwestern millionaires. Many of the new homes were Spanish in design, with thick stucco walls, red barrel tile roofs, archways, patios, and swimming pools. The Midwest nouveau riche, millionaires from the newly emergent automotive industry, were now looking at the island that Carl Fisher was creating. Palm Beach was for the New York-Philadelphia-Boston rich; the old rich. But this was a different group. Like most resorts catering to wealthy clientele Miami Beach was restricted to whites and gentiles. Jews were not welcome . . . . but, the rules were sometimes relaxed for Jewish millionaires.

"OK, so he wasn't always a Jew hater," said Uncle Louie, "but he only liked Jews with gelt.'"

"Vell' . . . I vouldn't say he liked them," said Sam, "but you know vat' they say . . . money talks."

As a result of his genius the dream became a reality; by the mid 1920's Carl Fisher was one of the wealthiest men in America. His young wife was enjoying their new life of opulence; they had 20 servants. But, Fisher was restless and bored with his new lifestyle. He didn't play golf, and he wasn't the type of man who enjoyed wearing white pants and drinking cocktails with wealthy winter residents.

"Maybe he didn't like the white pants, but he sure became a 'shikker," said Uncle Louie, "and he was 'shtupping' his secretary."

His marriage was falling apart. In 1926 Carl Fisher was divorced.

"That's vat' you get from shtupping' your secretary," said Sam. "Vunce or tvice' OK . . . but you can't think vit' your pecker."

He then bought 10,000 acres at Montauk Point, the far end of Long Island, and made plans for a new adventure. His idea was to build another Miami Beach, a summer retreat for his wealthy friends. However, in 1926, shortly after his divorce and the huge investment in Montauk, Miami Beach was hit by a devastating hurricane. Fisher's world was falling apart. He had cash flow problems resulting from the hurricane; emotionally he was very unstable because of the recent divorce, and Chicago gangster Al Capone had moved to Miami Beach with casinos and speakeasies. Fisher was losing control of his island and his own life.

"It wasn't just Capone," said Uncle Louie. "The mob was moving in. Miami Beach had become infested with gambling, prostitution, corruption, and rum-running."

When the Stock Market crashed in 1929, millions in loans were coming due at Montauk, and Fisher's investors abandoned the project. He was a physical and emotional wreck. He mortgaged or sold everything he owned, but it was hopeless. By 1933 he was wiped out, living alone on a side street in Miami Beach, suffering from cirrhosis of the liver and sixty years of fast living. In 1939 Fisher died, broke, alcoholic, and nearly forgotten, in the city he built.

In 1951, when I moved to Miami Beach the only reminder of Carl Fisher was an obscure monument on Alton Road. A small plaque says: ``He carved a great city out of a jungle." He didn't even have a street or a park named after him and our school, Ida M. Fisher Jr. High School, wasn't named after him either. It was named after his mother, a woman who never set foot in Miami Beach.

"Fisher 'vas ongeshtopt mit gelt' (*Literally: stuffed with money*)," said Sam. "But 'vat a promoter! His dream 'vas to get even richer. Like he needed more money?"

South of Lincoln Road, a different world emerged. The southern end of the island was owned by two brothers, J.N. and J.E. Lummus. They sold their land in small storefront parcels, and in the 1930's, buildings sprouted on these lots as fast as wild weeds. The apartments and hotels of South Beach were made of concrete block plastered with stucco; they went up fast and cheap. The building boom of the 30's continued unabated until the entry of the United States into World War II

"That was mob money!" said Uncle Louie. "the gangsters were laundering syndicate money by throwing up hotels made like 'drek.'"

"Louie, that's just a rumor," said Sam. "But the construction? You got a point! 'A lek un a shmek,' and you got a hotel." (*Inferior work. Literally: A taste and a smell*)

The architecture of South Beach, which would eventually be known as Art Deco, represented more than just a style; it was a reflection of larger social trends. For years, in the sections controlled by Fisher, north of Lincoln Road, real estate covenants prohibited blacks and Jews from owning property. In South Beach, however, there were few restrictions. Most of the small hotels and apartment buildings of South Beach catered to retired or working-class Jewish people. In the years following WWII many wintertime visitors became permanent residents and the anti-Jewish covenants which dated back to the 1920's were impossible to enforce. In September 1951, when I arrived at the James Manor Apartments, Miami Beach had one of the most concentrated Jewish populations in the country.

"You have nothing to do?" asked Uncle Louie. "Why don't you join as at shul next Friday night. After services we have wonderful music and dancing, and lots of young people. Come, you'll have a good time."

"Young people? At your shul!" I exclaimed. That seemed hard to believe.

"Yes . . . lots of young people," he replied. "Several months ago a 'gantser-macher' (*a big shot*) donated money for our youth fund. With money you can even get teenagers to go to shul."

However, even with the lure of a "jumping swinging" Jewish youth group, Uncle Louie couldn't convince us to go to Friday night services at his shul. But, we agreed, reluctantly, to join him and Tanta Baila at a Saturday night Yiddish concert.

The old people in South Beach attended free concerts every Saturday night at Lummus Park—an ocean front outdoor band-shell. David, Shelly, and I sat with several elderly immigrants; we got there early, to get a good seat.

A three-piece Jewish band, directed by a singing clarinet player and a lady who danced and played the fiddle, led several hundred people as they sang "Romania, Romania"—an impassioned Yiddish song about their beloved homeland. The elderly Jewish people stood, except for those in wheel chairs, and they clapped their hands to the music. Some of them danced in the aisles; many of them wept. A few of them even waved little Romanian flags.

"I can't believe these people want to go back to Romania" exclaimed a young woman sitting next to us. "They should be kissing the ground here in America."

"No! They don't want to go back," said David. "They're crying for the relatives they left behind . . . who can never come to America."

Tanta Baila was also crying. And when she wiped her eyes it was the first time I noticed the numbers branded on her forearm—her permanent reminder of the "old country." She looked at David and said: "Oib zein vort volt gedint als brik, volt men saichel hoben aribergain." (*If the world will ever be redeemed, it will be only through the wisdom of children*).

"She's right," said Uncle Louie; he was also crying. "That's why we love the youth group at our shul; children are the future of our people."

CHAPTER 19

THE UNIDENTIFIED PUBE

Schools days always began with a fifteen minute homeroom period, where the passion of mandatory prayers varied, depending on the zeal of the teacher. After completion of morning devotionals we would sit back and listen to a variety of announcements on the Public Address System (PA). Most of the messages were from Mr. Schecter, the principal, consoling the football team for its weekly loss or congratulating the tennis or debate teams for their weekly triumphs. The most memorable announcement of my five years at Ida M. Fisher/Beach High came from Massie Quinn, the old-maid director of student activities, who looked like the Wicked Witch of the West and had a shrill voice like Eleanor Roosevelt. Somebody had secretly slipped an extra memo into her stack of mundane announcements. "Boys and girls, if anyone knows where Mike Hunt is please come to my office."

After "homeroom" we all grabbed our books and scurried in separate directions, depending on what classes we were taking. Unlike northern schools that had interior hallways, the architecture of our buildings did not provide for lockers. We had to carry all books to every class. Danny Berger, the brown nose jerk who won the essay contest and who was now going steady with Leah Sonnino was in a few of my classes, including English and Algebra.

During the first four months of ninth grade our Algebra teacher was Carolyn Kelly, an attractive young woman. However, during Christmas vacation, Mrs. Kelly got pregnant. In 1953, if a teacher was pregnant she was put on "maternity leave" until the baby was born. Impressionable young boys and girls were never exposed to seeing a woman in "that condition." Our only formal education regarding the human reproductive system came by inductive logic, by extrapolating from concepts that we were taught in ninth grade General Science and tenth grade Biology. In General Science we learned about plants; we were given subtle hints that the stamen and pistil had analogous parts on human beings. Biology expanded upon the abstractions of General Science, and we learned about oviparous and viviparous animals; it wasn't too difficult to figure out that humans didn't lay eggs. But worms really screwed up the whole picture, they didn't lay eggs and they didn't need a sexual partner; they were hermaphroditic and reproduced by having their front end engage in intercourse with their own back end. I had always hoped to find a horny worm in Biology; I really wanted to see how that was done.

Mrs. Kelly never even had a chance to say goodbye to the students; one day she was there teaching the quadratic formula, the next day she was pregnant, replaced by Hilliard Klein, a retired army Colonel, who had worked as a substitute teacher in Miami Beach ever since 1947. With the untimely pregnancy of Mrs. Kelly, Colonel Klein finally had his chance to be a full-time teacher (although I subsequently discovered that algebra was not his real love) . . . he was a wonderful story teller, probably in his mid forties, very thin and prematurely bald with a deep furrowed brow and a bushy moustache. He had bulging eyes and he always wore army dress trousers with a military belt . . . the same uniform every day, but he provided variety with unique and amusing ties. He had a sense of humor and liked to entertain, and his ties were part of the act. I remember many striped bow ties, as well as ties with palm trees, Santa Claus, and flowers. And for important holidays he wore a very special tie, a hand painted portrait of Mark Twain, the Colonel's idol.

Colonel Klein told interesting stories about World War II and was a frequent speaker at the Miami Beach Library. He also wrote beautiful short stories; some of them were published in the literary section of the Miami Herald. He was unmarried; his busy life never allowed him to settle down with a woman. He had done many unusual things and had seen most of the world. He reminded me of Mark Twain, a man who had a hundred different jobs before becoming a famous writer. The Colonel frequently made reference to a famous Mark Twain quotation, which in later years, I repeated many times to my own children:

"When I was a boy of fourteen, my father was so ignorant I could hardly stand to have the old man around. But when I got to be twenty-one, I was astonished by how much he'd learned in seven years."

One day in Algebra we took a break from math, Colonel Klein loved to talk about current events. We were discussing King Farouk of Egypt, who had recently abdicated his crown because of a military junta led by Gamal Abdel Nasser, and we began debating the merits of American involvement in foreign affairs, Korea, Egypt, Formosa, Southeast Asia, South America . . . all in an effort to thwart the spread of Communism. We thought it was foolish for the United States to continue giving aid to countries that would turn on us if the opportunity ever arose.

"Why are we trying to be the good guy for all those ungrateful countries?" asked Penny Sherman. "We have plenty of poor people right here in the United States, right here in South Beach. See what happened in Egypt? We gave them all kinds of aid; now they're burning American flags on the street. We should have learned our lesson in Korea. Its time for us to stop trying to save the whole world." Penny had an annoying habit of looking in her little pocket mirror, even when she asked questions in class . . . she was always checking her hair and lipstick.

Instead of responding to Penny's observation the Colonel told a story about two monks and a scorpion. He frequently used allegories to make his point.

"Two monks were washing their rice bowls in the river when they noticed a scorpion that was drowning. One monk immediately scooped it up and set it upon the bank. In the process he was stung. He went back to washing his bowl and again the scorpion fell in the river. The monk saved the scorpion and was again stung. The other monk asked him, 'Friend, why do you continue to save the scorpion when you know it's nature is to sting'?

'Because,' the monk replied, 'to save it is my nature.'"

Colonel Klein was a patient, understanding man, but he had little tolerance for students who disrupted the decorum of his classroom. A few of the ninth grade boys with newly grown pubic hair had invented a little game, designed to amuse or irritate the girls. The boys secretly pulled out a few of their crinkly or curly pubic hairs, which were easy to differentiate from the normal hair that grew on top of the head. The "pubes" were scotch taped to an unsigned index card and placed in an envelope. The envelope was sealed and surreptitiously passed to a girl during class. Usually the envelopes were given to the biggest prudes, girls who were most likely to be embarrassed. Girls would typically giggle, act naïve, or blush when they opened the special "love letter," but in all cases the envelopes were dumped in the waste paper basket after class. I never participated in this game; I didn't want to remove any of my new pubic hairs. I waited too long for their arrival and didn't want to take chances with nature.

"I wouldn't mess around," warned David Steinberg. "My dad was half bald at age 30. That happens to lots of men. Women are lucky; they don't go bald . . . . they can pull out pubes whenever they want."

Unfortunately, none of the girls ever sent any of their pubes in envelopes, except for Ruby Goldfarb, a popular twelfth grade girl. Her name wasn't really Ruby, but that's what the kids called her because her pubes were red. At least that's what I heard, but I never got to see one. Those boys who were lucky enough to get one of the infamous "ruby pubes" saved them . . . they were collector's items.

The envelopes were being passed all around class every day, and the Colonel said nothing, but it was obvious that he knew what was happening. Late in the school year, a month before the end of ninth grade, he reached his breaking point. He waited until all students had left the room, then he thoroughly searched the waste paper basket. The next morning, when we returned to Algebra, we were greeted by six index cards, prominently posted on the side bulletin board. And taped to five of these cards were wrinkled or crinkled pubes. The pubic hairs on the sixth card were different; they were very curly.

"OK, said Colonel Klein, "I see we have a cute new game going on, and I don't think its very funny. I'm a reasonable man, and I understand the 'hormonal imbalance' that is causing many of you to act so boorish. Here is my offer: walk up to the bulletin board right now, sign your name on the appropriate index card, and you will only have to serve two hours of detention. But, if you don't admit your guilt, I will turn over the pubic hair to the police; they have means where they can identify who it belongs to. Everyone has unique pubic hair, just like everyone has unique fingerprints. And, if this has to go to the police you will be expelled from school . . . permanently. You better hope this doesn't get to the FBI; this is a violation of Federal law." The Colonel was very angry; that was the only time I ever saw him get irritated at school. He clenched his teeth; he was especially intense when he talked about "hormonal imbalance."

Five boys immediately walked to the side bulletin board and signed their index card; Howard Lefkowitz and Manny Lefkowitz were part of the group. However, one card remained unsigned . . . the card with the curly pubic hairs.

Across the patios and balconies of Ida M. Fisher and Beach High the kids were all whispering and asking: "Who is the unidentified owner of the curly pubes?" Some kids referred to the mystery man as "Pube Man" and elevated him to the status of Superman or Batman.

"Well, not quite," said Howard Lefkowitz. "Superman and Batman wear their underwear on the outside; Pube Man wears his on the inside. He never comes out of his secret disguise."

By the end of the day everyone at school was buzzing about the unidentified pubes; everyone had a theory. The obvious conclusion was that it must have belonged to a boy with curly hair, since the other pubes were all wrinkled and crinkled, like the letter "M" or "Z." The mystery pubes looked more like "@."

That Sunday morning I was home, hanging around with David and Shelly, using the process of elimination, trying to figure out who the curly pubes belonged to. There were sixteen boys in the Algebra class; we knew who the other five pubic hairs belonged to. That left eleven boys. Eliminating David and me (Shelly wasn't in that class)—there were only nine remaining suspects, but none of them had curly hair.

"Maybe the pubes came from a girl," said Shelly. "Girl's pubes are sometimes very curly."

Just then, as we started to consider the possibility that the curly pubes came from a girl, Mona came running over to my house, banging on the door. She was a gossip and knew all the dirt that was happening at school.

"Guess who the 'Pube Man' is?" Mona had a sheepish grin that ran from ear to ear.

"WHO?" David, Shelly and I all responded in unison.

"Its Danny Berger;" Mona's grin was replaced by the look of evil. "I can't wait to see him get expelled, he thinks he's really hot shit just because he lives in a mansion off the McArthur Causeway and his father is J. Martin Berger, the famous attorney."

"How do you know its Danny?" I asked. "His hair is much lighter than the mystery pubes . . . and it isn't curly."

"Danny has a big mouth; he told someone who told a Maj Joghn friend of my mother . . . . and I found out, and I am positive . . . trust me. And pubes are always darker than the hair on your head . . . unless you have black hair anyway." Mona had black hair . . . she knew what she was talking about.

"Yeah, you're right about pubes being darker," I said. "I'm not blonde down there. But, how can someone with straight hair have curly pubes?"

Mona blushed. "Mine are very curly, and I have straight hair."

"Yeah, let me see one," I said. "Just for scientific observation."

"In your dreams, you little perv," said Mona.

◆

The Steinbergs and I concocted a few plans how to get Berger in trouble, how to tell the Colonel.

"Sometimes when you're hot and sweaty a few pubes fall off and stick to the inside of your underwear," said Shelly. "I'm in Danny's gym class . . . when he goes to the shower I'll run to his locker, find his underwear, and steal some pubes."

"Great idea," said David. "Then we'll mail the pubes to Colonel Klein, along with a note."

"But we can't use our own handwriting on the note," I observed, "or we'll be identified, and we have to wear gloves so that they can't check for fingerprints."

"No good," said David. "The FBI can figure out what type of gloves were used . . . then we get caught and probably get expelled from school."

Shelly then came up with another plan, simply to take a nude photo of the boys in his gym class, when they go to the showers. That would prove that the curly pubes belong to Danny.

"How are you going to take that picture without getting caught?" I asked

"And where can we get it developed?" said David.

After much deliberation we decided to do nothing; we weren't stool pigeons. However, on Monday, when we arrived at school, everyone was talking, everyone already knew that Berger was the culprit. When you had a "big mouth" at Beach High, word got around fast. But, the strangest thing had happened over that weekend; Danny Berger had emerged as a "cult hero." Some of the girls even gave him a nickname . . . "Curly." Later that day he proudly signed his index card with a bold signature, like "John Hancock" and fearlessly made the long trek to Dean Kessler's office to be paddled. The curly pubes stayed posted on the side bulletin board for two weeks and every day girls walked up to Danny between class and at lunch, and secretly told him that he had "cute pubes," much cuter than the crinkled ones, and they giggled and blushed and got all bleary eyed. I really hated the phony jerk.

The day after the pubes were removed from the bulletin board, while Danny was at the peak of his popularity, Leah Sonnino came up to me. I was surprised to see her; we hadn't talked in months, not since that day when I saw her at the movie theatre with Danny. Now she was, standing in front of me, wearing his ring around her neck, and asking me for a favor.

"Myron—you write so well; I wonder if you can do me a favor and write a five-minute speech. Well, it isn't exactly for me. Its for Danny. He wants to run for tenth grade president . . . and he can't use a 'God' speech to get elected." Leah purred and flipped her pony tail . . . she had such a beautiful smile.

"OK Leah, I'll have it for you tomorrow morning. Do you want it typed?"

Several weeks later, near the end of the ninth grade, Aaron T Schecter made his morning announcement on the PA system: "Boys and girls, I would like to congratulate the new president of the tenth grade, Danny Berger."

CHAPTER 20

KIBITZING AT THE CROSSROADS

On the second Saturday of June, 1953, we graduated from Ida M. Fisher Jr. High School. We wore traditional caps and gowns and marched, single file, into the school auditorium. A small orchestra played the inspiring music of Pomp and Circumstance . . . . two hours later we marched out to the powerful Grand March from Aida. But it didn't feel like a real graduation, we weren't going our separate ways; we were just crossing over to Beach High, the adjoining building on the north side of the patio, with the same principal, Aaron T Schecter, and the same deans, Reinhard Kessler for the boys and Alba Layne for the girls. We heard a speech from Mr. Schecter and a "stimulating" address from Danny Berger, our newly elected class president. I didn't write this speech; it was his own creation. He made fourteen references to God in five minutes. And when he concluded, the teachers, deans, and students gave him a standing ovation. Then we left the auditorium and threw our caps in the air. We were now high school students, but most important, it was summer vacation.

"School's out, school's out teacher let the monkeys out"

The summer of '53 was a major improvement over the previous year, when I had no friends and did nothing except read, punt a football, and climb coconut trees. Now, I hung out with David and Shelly every day. I rarely watched TV, and once again, I lost interest in baseball; the Dodgers and Yankees were both running away with their leagues. The White Sox were in their usual position, a distant second to the Yankees. We frequently rode our bikes to the nearby Surfside beach, which was boring (no girls), or to North Shore Park, where we played touch football or basketball. But mainly, we rode buses that summer . . . to the 46th street beach (where there were lots of girls), or to the Nemo Hotel to visit Uncle Louie and Tanta Baila and of course every Saturday morning we rode the K Bus to our holy retreat, the corner of Lincoln Road and Washington Avenue.

Miami Beach is a long narrow island, probably ten miles from north to south and not more than two miles wide; it was easy to get around on the city buses. By the end of the summer I knew from memory the complete routes, schedules, and stops of the K, C, S, and R-Bayside buses. I lived on 95th street, the end of the line. That made it easy when I took the long ride home; I could sleep and not worry about missing my stop; the driver would always empty the bus before turning around to make the return trip. Also, I could take any of the four bus lines since they all stopped on 95th street down the block from Surfside Drugs, where I enjoyed burgers, fries, and gawking at the pictures of topless women in "girlie" magazines. (Note: In 1953 magazines never showed "full" frontal nudity . . . except for some 'black market" French magazines.)

I didn't read a lot in the summer of '53; I was too busy getting involved with the social life of my Jewish island. Of course, I read "A Stone for Danny Fisher," the erotic Harold Robbins novel that added new words to my vocabulary: quivering, throbbing, and pulsating. That was the first trashy sex book I ever read and I couldn't understand why it wasn't banned or censored, why no parents were complaining. Don't misunderstand me; I never advocated any type of censorship, but it just seemed strange that the Dade County School Board was hearing protests from irate parents who wanted to ban "Huckleberry Finn" but nobody was complaining about "A Stone For Danny Fisher." Maybe a book has to be a masterpiece before people want it banned. If it's just garbage no one ever complains.

◆

In ancient times Jerusalem was the crossroads of history, where various cultures meshed, merged, warred, and blended, where civilization matured and suffered through the growing pains of adolescence. In the summer of '53 the corner of Lincoln Road and Washington Avenue was the cultural crossroads of Miami Beach, where a world comprised almost entirely of Jewish people met, shopped, ate, went to the movies, strolled, browsed, and "kibitzed." It was the corner where I experienced some of my own growing pains.

Every Saturday morning I stood with the Beach High kids at our special corner and we watched a vibrant collage of Jewish cultures. Although my demographic distinctions would probably make a historian or a sociologist shudder, here is a personal description of some of the people who populated the crossroads of my Jewish island:

- American born Jews: Lincoln Road was comparable to Fifth Avenue in Manhattan, Rodeo Drive in Beverly Hills, or Worth Avenue in Palm Beach, with elegant stores and fancy restaurants. It was paradise for our parents, especially those who could afford to shop in Burdines or Saks Fifth Avenue. Our parents were generally American Jews, born in this country; and most of them were from New York. Many of the South Beach parents had strong New York accents; North Beach parents rarely did, and if they did they hired "accent reduction" tutors. Through the process of acculturation our parents were assimilated into the larger American culture.
- Elderly Jewish Immigrants:—those from the "old country"—who worked and shopped on Washington Avenue (but not on Lincoln Road). These were the elderly white hair people who fled from the Czar, the Cossacks, and the Russian Pogroms. They came to this country in the early part of the twentieth century. Most of them had foreign accents and spoke Yiddish on the streets; many of them were religious and shopped at kosher butchers. And some of them were referred to as "Litvaks" or "Galitsianers"—those who came from Latvia, Lithuania, Galitzia, or Estonia. However, the word "Litvak" was usually preceded by a modifying adjective, such as "dumb" Litvak, "stupid" Litvak, or "ignorant" Litvak.
- Recent Jewish Refugees:—survivors of the Nazi concentration camps. These people were often referred

to as "displaced persons" or "DP's" and many of them had numbers branded on their arms and could be found at all hours at Dubrows Cafeteria, which served breakfast, lunch, dinner, and late night snacks. I felt very sorry for these people. Herman always made fun of them and called them "green horns." He said that they "just got off the boat." But, Herman attacked everyone who was different.

- Cuban Jews:—As European Jewry attempted to escape from Hitler and were denied entry into the United States many of them settled in Cuba. After the war the United States relaxed its immigration laws and some of the Cuban Jews came to this country. However, the major influx of Cuban Jews occurred in the early 60's, when Castro came to power. Eventually a Cuban-Hebrew synagogue was formed, a few blocks north of Lincoln Road.

- Tourists:—Hordes of Jewish tourists strolled past the crossroads. Only the tourists "strolled." The full-time residents of my island never "strolled;" they walked. When you walk you have a destination in mind, a purpose. But, when you stroll you move at a leisurely pace; you don't really care where you are going . . . as long as you don't miss one of your five daily meals.

You could easily identify the tourists; the men wore pink or lime green gabardine slacks, or orange floral cabana suits with sandals; the women wore pastel sun dresses, cork shoes, and wide brim straw hats. And they all wore sunglasses, even on days that were overcast. The tourists didn't stop and kibbutz, they were just passing by the crossroads, buying painted turtles or coconuts that were carved like the faces of monkeys. They shopped at "Mal Marshall," a store that displayed forty eight different colors of gabardine slacks, one for each state, and the world's largest selection of Cubaveras. In the next few decades many of these tourists would buy condominiums in south Florida; they would retire to Hallandale and Pompano Beach and continue to wear lime green and pink slacks on golf courses. Eventually, they would move further north, to Boca Raton, an elegant city named in honor of a rat's mouth. The glitzy "fun in the sun" image of Miami Beach was embellished by their obnoxious pastel slacks, but they had little to do with the cultural evolution of my island. They were just strolling.

I can only speak with authority about the southwest corner of the crossroads, the meeting place where Beach High kids went to see and be seen, sometimes wearing cardboard Polaroid glasses that we stole from Bwana Devil, the first 3-D movie (which gave me a terrible headache), and the boys were almost always wearing cool Lacoste polo shirts, jeans, and very clean white buckskin shoes (white bucs).

The North side of Lincoln Road was not my world, neither was the east side of Washington Avenue. Sometimes I stood on my corner and watched the adults on Lincoln Road, but I rarely talked to them. I could also see the kosher butchers on Washington Avenue, but I couldn't read Hebrew or Yiddish. In the summer of '53, as I stood on my corner and "hung out," my world was the world of transplanted New York Jewish teenagers who were soon to begin tenth grade at Beach High. My world was the "Sixth Borough" of New York City.

In the early 50's we didn't have shopping centers, so this fascinating Jewish crossroads served as our meeting place. Every Saturday morning Danny Berger was one of the first to arrive, to secure a choice location, a site with a view. I always looked to see if Leah Sonnino was with him, but she was never there. The newly elected president of the tenth grade did not want a girl hanging on his arm, especially one who was more intelligent than him. By 10:30 AM the corner was congested with Beach High kids; it was decision time; which of the four Lincoln Road movie theaters would we attend. The movies usually started at 1:30 PM. We had no fast food restaurants in Miami Beach, no McDonalds, no Burger Kings, not even Royal Castle, the "burger joint" that was popular on the other side of the bay. Lunch usually consisted of a cheeseburger, French fries, and a cherry Coke or a chocolate malt at the counter of Liggets Drug Store. I also liked root beer floats. Some of the more sophisticated kids drank iced coffee; it was a fashionable New York drink.

When we had more money to spend, we could walk down the block to Wolfies for a Corned Beef sandwich on rye; there was no Pizza on Lincoln Road. Pizza was not a part of my youth. I once suggested Dubrows for lunch, the Jewish cafeteria where I ate with my parents when we lived at the James Manor, but the other kids laughed; Dubrows was for AK's ("Alter Kakkers")—a derisive Yiddish term for old people, which literally translates as "Old Shits." The pastel colored tourists liked to go "window shopping" on Lincoln Road; it was their promenade. But, the Beach High kids just liked to stand at the southwest corner of the crossroads and watch the world go by. And, of course, all heads turned if a pretty girl walked past our corner, especially if she had huge pointed boobs. In the early 50's pubescent boys were fixated on boobs; we never looked at the other attractions of the female anatomy, not ever the tush. Of course, in future years that would change.

Rarely would you ever see any of the Beach High teachers on Lincoln Road, since none of them lived in Miami Beach, except maybe Mr. Schecter, who was Jewish, but I never saw him either. I always wondered why he sat back and said nothing about the apostolic morning devotionals of Miss Baker. Some of the kids said that he was "walking a tightrope" since he was the only Jewish principal in the county and Miss Baker had a sister who was a high ranking administrator at the county office; Mr. Schecter didn't want to make waves. One Saturday morning, a few weeks after 9th grade graduation, as I was standing at the corner of Lincoln and Washington, talking to other Beach High kids, I saw Colonel Klein walking in my direction with two little boys, one was Oriental, the other was a Negro. The Colonel was wearing khaki army shorts with a dark green Lacoste and black stockings up to his knees; only a few inches of his bony knees were visible. I had never seen a teacher on Lincoln Road before; he looked out of place. I stared, to make sure it really was my Algebra teacher.

"Ciao Myron, you look like you've seen a ghost." That was the first time I ever heard anyone say "Ciao" since Ziggy Bloom, my former accordion teacher. I wonder if they knew each other during the war? They were both very interesting people, great story tellers.

I walked with Colonel Klein and his two boys to Alfies, a popular store where tourists bought out-of-town newspapers. It was on the west end of Lincoln road and it was generally believed that this store was an undercover bookie joint. The Colonel asked me to watch the boys while he walked into the back of the store; I suspected that he was placing a bet on a baseball game. When he returned he invited me to join him for lunch at a nearby Chinese restaurant.

147

"We eat here frequently," said the Colonel. "They don't give us a hassle. I lose my temper when restaurants refuse to serve Jessie. For God's sake, the boy is only five years old."

Many of the Lincoln Road restaurants refused to serve Negroes. It wasn't the law; it was just their choice. But, the Colonel's other boy, Jackie, had no problems. For some reason, which I could never understand, there was no discrimination against Orientals.

"They're my foster children; I'd love to adopt them, but I'm not married, so the law won't allow it. Good boys, both of them. They were abandoned by their mother and nobody knows who's their daddy."

Jackie was six years old and was extremely adept with chop sticks; he knew how to pick up one piece of rice at a time. I tried also, but I struggled. Both of the boys laughed as a chunk of sweet and sour pork kept falling off my chop sticks. The Colonel told me that he lived in Surfside, near the Steinbergs and that he was Jewish. That really surprised me; I never heard of a Jewish Colonel before. He also talked a lot about Jessie and Jackie who were named in honor or Jessie Owens and Jackie Robinson, and he offered to hire me as a baby sitter if I ever needed the extra money.

"Do you know the history of the crossroads?" asked the Colonel. "Especially the southwest corner of Lincoln and Washington? Do you know about Carl Fisher?"

"Well, I know that Miami Beach was developed by Fisher, but what does that have to do with the corner of Lincoln and Washington?"

"Well, at the southwest corner, where you kids now congregate, is the Mercantile Bank Building and Liggets Drug Store. Originally, that was the site of the Lincoln Hotel, Carl Fishers restricted hotel.

"Wow . . . . Carl Fisher would be turning over in his grave now," I laughed. "His 'gentile only' corner is now a Jewish hangout."

"It doesn't take a genius to realize that this isn't what he wanted," replied the Colonel. "His widow, Jane Fisher, is popular on the banquet circuit telling tall tales about her ex-husband. She has said, on numerous occasions, that Miami Beach, as we know it . . . is not at all what her husband had in mind.

Personally, I think that Fisher was anti-Semitic, but I take my hat off to the man. He built a paradise."

"Myron . . . I heard from your English teacher that you like to write. I'd like to read you a few short stories from my memoirs . . . not sure if I'll ever have them published; they're kind of personal. Mainly, they're about life in the barracks during World War II. Some of the language is very guttural; I don't think the school board would appreciate it if I published a book loaded with four letter words."

"Thanks Colonel Klein; I'd love to read your stories. Yeah, I enjoy writing, kind of an escape for me."

"You wrote that campaign speech for Danny Berger; didn't you?" Asked Colonel Klein.

"Well, its for sure I didn't write his graduation speech." I responded, and the Colonel laughed.

"I counted ten 'Gods' in that speech." Observed the Colonel.

"Well, if you include 'Lords' there were fourteen." I corrected his count. I wanted to ask the Colonel why he applauded if he knew that the speech was such garbage, but I knew the reason. It was his job.

"When someone is running for office," said the Colonel "they need an intelligent and sincere speech; people take the time to listen to what the candidate has to say. You wrote a winner for Danny."

"Yeah, it was a winner," I laughed, "but he sure didn't need my help at graduation; everyone seemed to love his speech . . . even with fourteen 'Gods' or 'Lords.'"

"That's because, once you're elected no one really cares what you say as long as you say it with a big smile and don't offend anyone. We got a perfect example in the White House right now."

The Colonel told me that Miss Carter let him read a few of my stories about Nazis and Auschwitz tattoos, and the dead soldier essay. She wanted the opinion of someone with military experience. Miss Carter was from Claxton, Georgia and found it hard to believe that her hometown was a hiding place for escaped Nazis. He thought I was very observant and he liked my imagination.

"Myron, you should keep a journal; write one page every day."

"Well, I've got a diary; I got the idea when I read Anne Frank last summer. But mine is boring; no Nazis in mine."

"Then, put in some Nazis," said the Colonel.

"Yeah, but my diary is factual; Nazis are fantasy."

"So; what's wrong with fantasy?" The Colonel encouraged me to combine fact and fantasy in my writing, to convert my diary into a journal. He even offered to review the journal whenever I wanted a second opinion.

"Here's a good word for you to look up when you get home . . . '**phantasmagoria.**' And don't worry about the grammar and the punctuation or even the spelling. Just write what you feel . . . every day; even if its foolish or very opinionated. And its OK, to begin a sentence with 'and' or 'but'—once in a while."

◆

In ancient Jerusalem there were many types of Jews: Pharisees, Sadducees, Esenes, and all kinds of religious fanatics, zealots, and weirdoes. Most notably, from this ancient crossroads, the course of history was significantly changed by the dispersion of the Jews and the emergence of John the Baptist, Peter, Paul, and Jesus Christ. I'm not saying these legendary prophets were "weirdoes," they weren't, except for John, he was a little strange! But, they were definitely zealots and they sure left their mark on history. Correspondingly, at the crossroads of Lincoln Road and Washington Avenue, the hangout for Jewish teenagers, we also had a few zealots . . . . but our zealots were extremely weird. The two famous prophets of gloom and doom were Holy Joe and Silver Dollar Jake.

Holy Joe was a short frail man. He wore a long sleeve white shirt with suspenders, a bow tie, and a grey fedora. His uniform never changed, even on the sweltering humid days of summer. And he rode an adult size tricycle with Bibles in the basket and his four year old son in a small rear seat. He was an evangelist, and every Saturday morning he stood on the southwest corner of Lincoln and Washington . . . our corner . . . wearing a sandwich board . . . hoping to convince the young Beach High "sinners" to see the way of the Lord. His sandwich boards always displayed different messages and stimulated thought provoking discussions:

"Jesus is the Answer"

. . . and we always asked: "What is the question?"

"The Lord is Coming"

Lots of clever teenage humor resulted from that message!

"Hey, Holy Joe: If the Lord is coming," shouted one teenage sinner. "Does that mean he beats off?"

"No, shumuck," said Manny Lefkowitz. "That's CUM, with a 'U'."

"So, big fuckin' deal," replied the teenage sinner, "and don't go calling me a shmuck you dumb moron . . . U or O, whats the damn difference? I bet God beats off. Ain't we made in his image?"

Manny gave the kid a quick and powerful punch in the stomach. The boy doubled over in pain and immediately ran away. Nobody could talk like that to Manny and get away with it, especially at the crossroads of our Jewish island.

On one particular Saturday, instead of the usual visionary message, the board contained a question:

"How do you get to the Pearlie Gates?"

Holy Joe expanded upon the question and asked whether you could go to heaven if you observed the Ten Commandments. Obviously, it was a trick question, since the Ten Commandments were of Jewish origin, and we all knew that Jews couldn't go to Heaven. But I seized the opportunity to engage in an evangelical debate. "Yes," I replied, even though I had serious doubts about the after-life, except maybe for holy cows that walked the streets in India.

"Wrong, young man," He bellowed loud enough for everyone at the corner to hear. For a tiny man he had a strong voice. "You only go to Heaven if you believe in Jesus Christ; that is the Eleventh Commandment, the ONLY commandment." He explained that even if you observed all ten of the Commandments faithfully, if you didn't believe in Jesus you were doomed to "rot in Hell for eternity." I wondered if he knew Miss Baker, my eighth grade homeroom teacher; they both prophesized the same destiny for Jews . . . . but she had us roasting, not rotting.

"So, which is it?," said Shelly Steinberg, "do Jews 'rot' in Hell or do they 'roast' in Hell?"

"Good question!" I replied. "I think Miss. Baker was referring to all sinners, regardless of religion, when she talked about roasting. Holy Joe says that 'rotting' is just for Jews."

"Well, if I had the choice," responded Shelly, "I'd take rotting; its probably like never taking a shower. But what happens to Jewish sinners, do they rot or do they roast?"

"Wow . . . that's heavy!" I laughed. "Maybe Jewish sinners get the double whammy . . . they rot and roast at the same

151

time. But . . . what's the difference . . . if you're dead, who cares?"

"I'm not sure I understand what you're saying," I continued my debate with Holy Joe. "Are you saying that if I rape, rob, murder, and covet my neighbors wife I can go to heaven simply by believing in Jesus?" My question was dumb . . . but his prior conclusion was even dumber.

"Yes, that is the beauty of His message; believe in Jesus and all your sins will be forgiven . . . that is what is meant by redemption."

"I like it," I responded. "And I don't have to give up coveting. Where do I sign up?" Several of the kids were laughing . . . those who enjoyed "coveting."

Holy Joe didn't laugh; he gave me a pocket size Bible and wrote a personal message: "Myron, may the Lord always be in your pocket and in your heart, Joe."

Manny Lefkowitz also engaged in debate with Holy Joe, but Manny didn't beat around the bush; he got right to the point.

"If Jesus is the fuckin' Messiah how come the world is so screwed up?" He scratched his balls as he asked that poignant question. We all clustered around Holy Joe to hear his response.

"Because we are waiting for the second coming; when He returns the world will be blessed." Holy Joe crossed himself and looked to the sky, probably praying for Jesus to make his promised return at the corner of Lincoln Road and Washington Avenue, the crossroads of Sodom and Gomorrah.

Manny thought for a moment . . . which was unusual. Manny always had an immediate answer for everything. "Well shit; if He was the Son of God why couldn't He get it right the first time? And, if Jesus came back and saw all the bullshit that is going on in his name, he would fuckin' puke."

"Young man," said Holy Joe. "On that . . . we agree." He then gave an autographed pocket Bible to Manny.

We liked to joke around with Holy Joe, but we were not really mean. In fact, on hot summer days when he had to stand on the corner with his sandwich board we always brought him and his little boy orange juice. But, if he earned "salvation points" or a bonus for converting Jews he would have starved to death; no one took him seriously. I'm jumping ahead a little, but I want to finish with Holy Joe. A year later his son fell off the back of the tricycle and was run over by a car; it was front page news in the

Miami Beach Sun. After that Holy Joe continued coming to our corner, alone . . . . the back seat of his tricycle was empty. We no longer joked with him or at him; we just walked around his sandwich board and said nothing. We felt sorry for the frail little man; he had a job to do.

If Holy Joe was the harbinger of the Lord, the self-anointed incarnation of "good," then Silver Dollar Jake was the embodiment of "evil"—the Antichrist. He was a middle age man, always dressed in a ship captains hat, white pants, and a blue blazer with brass buttons. He was always laughing at the world as he drove a red Cadillac convertible—cruising the cultural crossroads of Lincoln Road and Washington Avenue, seated next to his companion, a full size inflatable female doll—the mistress of temptation.

During World War II (before I moved to Miami Beach) the army used the island as a training location, and during off duty hours the soldiers often crossed the causeway to Miami, to Bayfront Park, where dozens of prostitutes were selling their services. This eccentric man passed out silver dollars to soldiers in uniform, to purchase rubbers . . . that's how he got his nickname. However, by the early 1950's the soldiers were gone; Miami Beach had become a Jewish island and Silver Dollar Jake redirected his efforts. His new mission was to offer guidance to the young Jewish boys, to shelter them from Holy Joe.

"Religion is bullshit," Silver Dollar Jake shouted, as he attempted to attract a Saturday morning audience at the southwest corner of Lincoln Road and Washington Avenue. He was competing with Holy Joe for the attention of the Beach High kids. "Think for yourself . . . the world is your oyster, protect your little 'petzle'." Then he laughed and threw a handful of tiny "rubbers" toward the outstretched arms of several dozen boys. Once he had gathered a large enough assemblage he began his "sermon at the crossroads."

"Once upon a time . . . a holy man . . . probably the spiritual predecessor of Holy Joe . . . met with his faithful disciples to begin evening prayers . . . but a cat who lived in their sanctuary made so much noise that it distracted the congregation. So the holy man ordered that the goddamn cat be tied up during the prayers. Years later, when the holy man croaked, the cat continued to be tied up during evening prayers. And when the cat eventually died, another cat was brought to the sanctuary and tied up . . . to continue the 'sacred ritual.' Centuries later, ecclesiastic scholars wrote monographs about the significance of tying up a cat for religious purposes . . . they wrote sermons about the feline connection with God. Wake up, my young friends! Its all bullshit!"

We laughed at his story and held out our hands . . . begging for more mini rubbers.

"Sorry boys . . . that's all for today. Look for me next Saturday . . . same time, same place. . . . and next time you beat your meat . . . say a special prayer for Holy Joe. Carpe Diem!"

Silver Dollar Jake laughed as he drove north on Washington Avenue with one arm draped around his inflatable girlfriend. And we all laughed with him . . . or maybe we were laughing at him. I knew that those tiny rubbers were just a joke; no one could possibly have a penis that little. I assumed that this strange man had them specially made, just as a gag. But many years later, when I had my first "thorough" medical exam . . . when I was bending over in a doctors office . . . . I discovered the real purpose of a mini-rubber . . . and I heard the distant laughter of Silver Dollar Jake. "Hey shmuck, religion is bullshit but hemorrhoids are real."

♦

The summer of 1953 ended with exciting news from Chicago, my sister Bobbie had a second son, and he was named Michael, after my grandfather, Morris. I was also named after Morris but Michael was a lot luckier than me; he got a great name, a much better name than Myron. I spoke to Bobbie on the phone that night; it was very rare to speak long distance in 1953. It was expensive and the telephone connections were bad; you had to shout.

"Bobbie, congratulations," I yelled, "How come when I was born you let mom and dad name me Myron? And, don't tell me you were only eleven and had no influence. Now, you name your baby Michael. Well, guess what . . . I'm going to call him Myron."

CHAPTER 21

NEWS FROM THE OUTSIDE WORLD: 1952-1953

My world had expanded considerably in the ninth grade; I was now taking buses to every possible corner of Miami Beach. Most events in the outside world had little impact on my life. But, on a personal level, here are a few significant highlights of that year:

- Mad magazine makes its debut and Alfred E. Neuman soon emerges as a cult hero—a precursor to Woody Allen.
- Bridey Murphy story—still no proof of an after life, but maybe we did have a prior life. I started having nightmares . . . In my dreams I had long blonde hair and I was surrounded by thousands of Indians at the Battle of the Little Big Horn.
- University of Tennessee admits its first black student. A story buried somewhere in Section "B" of the newspaper. This should have been a topic for discussion, but it wasn't.
- King Farouk of Egypt abdicated in the wake of a coup led by Gamal Abdel Nasser. "Poor Israel, this is going to mean trouble," said my father. Kids around school all joked and said that this would mean the closing of "Farouk U," the major college in Egypt.

- Ernest Hemmingway published "Old Man and the Sea."—right up there with "Catcher in the Rye."
- Birdseye starts marketing the first frozen peas—a major improvement over canned peas.
- U.S. Supreme Court upholds the decision barring segregation in interstate railways. However, this did not apply to the Dade County buses, which never crossed state lines.
- George Jorgensen becomes Christine Jorgensen—which reminded my mother of another Yiddish proverb: "Ven di bobbeh volt gehat a bord, volt zi geven a zaideh." *(If your grandmother had a beard, she'd be your grandfather.)*
- King George VI of Britain found dead in bed by a servant delivering the morning tea; Elizabeth II assumes the crown. "So, what was the maid doing in the king's bedroom?" asked my mother. "And where was the queen . . . eating honey in the parlor?"
- Mrs. Paul's introduces frozen fish sticks—another easy dinner for my mother to prepare.
- Mr. Potato Head is invented—How could you eat a potato after you created him, nurtured him, slept with him, and told him all your personal problems?
- Richard Nixon's "Checkers" speech. My father liked Ike, even though he voted for Stevenson. But Nixon! That was a different story. "Doesn't this clown ever shave? Hopefully, he'll disappear after Ike serves out his two terms."
- "Anne Frank, Diary of a Young Girl" published in the U.S.—major impact on my life; encouraged me to start my own Diary. It was such a sad story, she came so close to surviving the Nazi concentration camps. But, if she did, the "Diary" never would have been so popular and her message would have been lost forever. So, in a very sad sort of way, I guess it was a good thing that she was killed by the Nazis. If there really is a next life, Anne Frank is one of the first people I want to meet, along with Lincoln and Jefferson. I also want to meet Roger Williams, the founder of Rhode Island. He was the only Pilgrim I liked.

- TV acknowledges pregnancy on I love Lucy—even though Ricky and Lucy sleep in different beds—a modern day "immaculate conception." Is "Little Ricky" the long awaited "second coming?"
- Sony, a brand new Japanese company, introduces the first pocket-size transistor radio. "It will never sell," says my mother. "Who needs to carry a radio in your pocket?"
- Telephone area codes begin. Now, my mother can call my sister in Chicago once a week. Miami Beach is in the new (305) area code; Chicago is (312).
- Sugar Frosted Flakes are introduced by Kellogg's, they are 29 percent sugar. What is the other 71 percent? "Mostly sawdust," says Manny Lefkowitz.
- Pream, a powdered non-dairy coffee lightener is introduced. It keeps longer than real cream and costs less. "Sol, what a pleasure! Now you can stop complaining about lumps floating in your coffee," said my mother.
- Albert Schwietzer wins Nobel Peace Prize. "What do you mean, he isn't Jewish?" exclaims my mother. "Such a good man! Helping all those poor colored people in Africa."

TENTH GRADE

CHAPTER 22

THINK PINK

One week prior to the start of tenth grade, David, Shelly and I went to Burdines, the fashionable department store in downtown Miami; we were shopping for "back to school" clothes. My parents now allowed me to cross the bay, but only if I went with friends and stayed in "safe" locations. I was also restricted to daytime travel. Shelly said the hot new color for Fall was pink; the message of the day was **"think pink."** Burdines was larger than any store in Miami Beach; it was comparable to major New York department stores such as Macy's, Gimbles, and Bloomingdales. We explored every section of this magnificent department store and admired the new fashions. Male and female mannequins were draped in pink . . . . pink shirts, ties, sweaters, jackets, hats, bating suits, and underwear. Even the fancy sporting goods department on the fourth floor featured pink golf balls and golf bags. Shelly and I purchased pink Lacostes with the familiar little alligator while David practiced putting on a pink carpet.

As we were about to take the elevator back to the main floor three Negro boys walked up to us. "Scuze' me, sir" said the shortest of the three boys; his eyes never looked up. "You'se bout' the same size as me. Could you try on this here shirt; wanna' see if I like it?" He handed me a pink Lacoste, same as the one I purchased. All three boys were holding pink shirts.

Burdines, Richards, Jordan Marsh, and Sears, the largest department stores in Miami, would not allow Negroes to try on clothes. White customers were not subject to the same restriction. We chatted with the boys for a while. They were big baseball fans. The youngest boy was proud to tell us that his name was Willie, just like Willie Mays. He was in the eighth grade. The two older boys were his brothers. It was difficult to understand them; they had strong southern accents and their English was very garbled. As we left the store and took the elevator down to the ground level Willie and his brothers said goodbye. I shook hands with Willie and smiled, but I felt badly for him; Negroes were not allowed to use the elevator at Burdines.

We then left Burdines; Shelly and I were dressed in matching pink Lacostes. We walked around Flagler Street, the main commercial section of downtown Miami. Many Negroes were shopping in the same stores. That was very different than Miami Beach. On Lincoln Road you rarely saw Negroes other than those who were working at stores or restaurants. We noticed that whenever Negroes walked in the direction of white people they stood aside, to allow the white person to pass. As a slight protest of this demeaning practice, David, Shelly, and I began to reverse the custom. We stood aside and let Negroes pass us on the sidewalk. However, our little protest didn't last too long. A Miami policeman soon pulled the three of us to the edge of the sidewalk.

"Hey! What're you 'JD's' trying to do?" ("JD" was an abbreviation for "Juvenile Delinquent.") The policeman was irate. He shook us and demanded that we show him identification. We showed our Miami Beach library cards.

"Listen, we do things our way over here and if you don't like it you can always go back to Jew town. But, from what I see, you kikes don't treat the niggahs' much better over there. I don't see no spades' living on the Beach."

I was worried, thinking that we were going to be arrested, but the policemen let us go with only a warning. We then went to a large office supply store to get organized for the upcoming school year. Buying school supplies was fun; It was comforting to get a fresh start in life every September. We purchased three-ring notebooks with five sectional dividers, one for each subject. We also had a sixth course, Phys. Ed. But you didn't need a divider for Phys. Ed., you only needed a new jock strap, and by now I knew the proper way to buy a jock; I was fourteen. Perhaps, the highlight of the excursion was lunch at Royal Castle, eating four grilled mini-burgers followed by a frosty mug of birch beer, and no vegetables. That was my first exposure to a fast food restaurant and I loved it. We made sure to leave Miami before 4 PM. My parents warned me that Miami was a southern city, and it could be dangerous after sundown.

As we rode back to the safety of our island three elderly Negro women entered the bus. They immediately walked to the rear looking for seats. However, the back of the bus was full. David, Shelly, and I rose and let the three women have our seats near the front section of the bus. What could the driver do? Certainly, he wouldn't throw them off and strand them in the middle of the McArthur causeway. The bus came to a sudden stop half way across Biscayne Bay. The driver grabbed the old Negro women and dragged them off the bus.

"Damn, Niggahs' . . . won't stand for no God damn law breakers in here." The driver made this announcement on his microphone; he wanted to make sure it was heard by the law abiding Negroes who were seated at the rear of the bus. "Next thing you know, they're gonna' send their little pickaninneys' to the same schools as white kids . . . and anyone who gives a seat to a niggah' will be thrown off my bus. D'ya hear?"

When I arrived home I received very exciting news, Michael Bernstein would be coming to live with us for the year. He was recently mugged by an anti-Semitic teenage gang in Chicago; they bashed his head with a lead pipe, cut off his ear, and left him lying in a pool of blood. The ear was surgically replaced, but he lost 50% of his hearing in that ear. Mr. Bernstein called my father and asked if Michael could stay with us; they were worried that he would be attacked again by the gang. Two days later I met Michael and his father at the Miami airport. Michael was huge; I hadn't seen him in two years. He was always a few inches taller than me, but now when we walked together we looked like "Mutt and Jeff" the comic book characters; he was a full head taller than me.

I was 5'4", I had only grown two inches since I left Chicago, but Michael was almost 6'. He looked a lot different; even his hair was combed different; it was now in a "D.A." (Ducks Ass)—a hair style worn by greasers—but it was not popular with Jewish kids, certainly not at Beach High. Both sides of the head were combed back and plastered down with lots of grease. The unique feature of the D.A. was the back side; the hair was parted vertically, in the middle of the head, to resemble the posterior of a duck. Most of the Beach High boys combed their hair with a big wave in the front, called a pompadour. My wave was really huge, to help make me look a little taller.

Michael wore a long sleeve black shirt with the collar turned up and a thick black belt with the buckle off center, slightly to the left. "Its worn on the left side, just in case you need to make a quick draw," said Michael. "Lots of street fights and gang wars in Chicago, and your belt is your best weapon, unless you carry a knife." He showed me his white pearl handled switchblade, which had a black and red swastika on the base of the handle. Michael said that it formerly belonged to a Gestapo agent but his uncle, Hymie Rosenberg, took it after he captured the Nazi.

"Let's see where your ear got cut off," I asked, as I rearranged my belt, moving the buckle to the left. I wondered what Shelly would think about the combination of a thick black belt, a huge buckle in the attack position, and a pink Lacoste?

The next day my father drove us to school; he had to register Michael at Beach High and show his birth certificate and other documents to the Registrar. It was the the same lady who skipped me to the eighth grade and turned down my request for a homeroom transfer in the ninth grade. She was very pretty; I noticed that the first day I met her, back in the eighth grade. But it seemed strange, such a pretty woman and she never smiled; she always looked so sad. I reminded my father, "make sure you insist that Michael gets placed in 10-3, otherwise he'll be in one of the North Beach homerooms."

The Registrar seemed stunned. She wasn't sure she heard the request properly; that was the first time anyone living in the North Beach district ever asked to be placed in a low number section. But, she didn't argue and immediately stamped Michael's papers with the number: "10-3." We walked to class together and I introduced him to Linda Spiegel, the girl with the big boobs; of course, by this time, many of the other girls also had big boobs. Michael said nothing, not even to Linda. He just stood there, with his collar turned up. He shifted his mouth into a twisted position and dropped his jaw, ever so slightly; his eyes shot daggers, and he put his right hand to rest on top of his belt buckle, just in case he needed to make a quick draw. He looked cool. Then he walked to his desk. Slowly and intentionally he dropped his five books on the floor; they made a loud thud, announcing his arrival. He squeezed into the little school desk and began combing his shiny D.A.; he continued combing during morning devotionals. The rest of the class recited prayers about our father in heaven who had a hallowed name.

As we reached the familiar passage, "Thy Will be done," all eyes focused on Michael. We all knew what fate awaited him. Immediately after the prayer concluded he was sent to see Dean Kessler. But, he was luckier than me. On my first day I felt the full fury of the paddle; he only got a ruler slap on the knuckles and a warning. He was reminded that incorrigible young men were shipped off to private schools like Whitefield or Lear, along with the morons, and he was told to change hair styles.

"That shmuck's a prick," said Michael. "He went 'ape shit' just because I got a DA."

Michael never did homework, and that annoyed my father. He left the house on weeknights and rode the bus to meet different girls, or he went to parties and came home after midnight. He even carried a rubber; I could see the circle, permanently embossed in his black leather wallet.

"Yeah, Myron . . . you gotta' carry one too," said Michael. "Girls get turned on when they see a wallet with the circle of love."

I was never allowed out on week nights unless it was an important school event; I was always busy with homework, reading, memorizing Spanish vocabulary words, or writing in my secret journal. There were numerous phone calls, back and forth to Chicago, between my father and Mr. Bernstein. But, Mr. Bernstein wasn't terribly worried; his main concern was for Michael's safety, not his grades at school. Michael even had a small TV in his bedroom; I was never allowed to have my own TV.

Weekends were devoted to exploring locations where I had previously been prohibited from going; it was a time of discovery. The Steinbergs always joined us on these exciting adventures . . . like Bal Harbour, where Jews were not allowed. We explored the Kenilworth, the restricted hotel where Arthur Godfrey always stayed. It was impossible to enter the hotel through the front door, which was guarded by a team of Nazi doormen who were trained to prevent entry by Jewish intruders. However, the rear of the hotel was unprotected. We swam one hundred yards offshore and entered the Kenilworth from the ocean side.

Since every hotel guest had an assigned lounge chair it would not take long before one of the life guards discovered that we were trespassers. So, we quickly hopped in the pool and blended with the other guests. Many of the men were walking around the pool area dressed in white linen slacks and silk shirts; they drank rum and Coke or a Tom Collins from a tall skinny glass. Women were lying on lounge chairs smoking from long cigarette holders; they were all thin and glamorous, even the older women were attractive, and none of them were knitting. This was very different than the Jewish hotels, where the men wore floral cabana suits, smoked cigars and played poker, and the women played Canasta or sat in lounge chairs knitting sweaters and afghans.

Michael began flirting with Valerie Church, a very pretty girl from Philadelphia who complained about all the "crude" New York Jews who were "swarming like maggots" on Lincoln Road. Michael agreed with her and said that he was so happy to be staying at the Kenilworth, "a safe distance from 'those' people."

"I mean, like really . . . fat old ladies with bad breath walking around in disgusting pink pants." Valerie squeezed her nose. "And, don't they ever bathe?"

Michael and Valerie went off together, to the beach. I could see them in the distance, standing waist deep in the ocean, passionately kissing. An hour later, when they returned, they were holding hands and she was calling him "Mikie" and "snook-ums" and he was calling her "Val." Valerie invited the three of us to join her for lunch at the poolside café; she offered to charge the bill to her parent's room. We sat at a glass table and drank carbonated French water with a dash of lemon, and ate tuna salad with chilled asparagus; they didn't have corned beef, hamburgers, or kosher pickles at the Kenilworth. We also ate chopped liver on little crackers, but it wasn't the same type of chopped liver that I ate with Uncle Louie and Tanta Baila at their South Beach deli.

"This is pâté of goose liver," said Valerie, and she told us it was "really gauche" to write pâté without using the two different types of accent marks.

"Myron, don't you like the asparagus?" asked Valerie.

"Yeah, I do . . . but I usually eat my vegetables last, after everything else . . . it's a bad habit of mine."

"You wouldn't get away with that at my school . . . they emphasize proper table manners . . . and rotational eating."

"Rotational eating!" I wondered if teachers had advanced training in that area. What were the qualifications to be a teacher of "Rotational Eating?"

Valerie attended an all-girl's finishing school in Philadelphia and planned to go to Wellesley college near Boston when she graduated . . . to major in French Literature. She was very articulate and spoke like a TV news announcer, with perfect diction and a slight hint of an English accent, especially the way that she pronounced her "R's." Under the glass table, she was running her hand up and down Michael's leg, rubbing the bulge in his bathing suit.

"Hi Mikie-poo." She smiled and whispered.

"We have a traditional curriculum in the morning," said Valerie, "you know, English, science, algebra, all the college prep courses, but in the afternoon we have equestrian instruction and lessons in elocution and walking." She chuckled as she described her walking exercises. "Miss Hindenberg, our walking teacher, is a contemptuous German bitch. We call her 'old blimp.'

On Tuesdays and Thursdays we walk gracefully for one hour while the old blimp screams at us . . . 'knockers up girls; keep them pointing above horizontal.' She walks around with a yard stick tapping under our boobs if they aren't pointing just right. And she never changes the music . . . its always 'A Pretty Girl is Like a Melody' . . . that song makes me want to barf." Valerie raised her chest. Her knockers were pointing directly toward Michael's eyes.

After lunch we said goodbye to Valerie and left the Kenilworth the same way we entered, by way of the ocean. However, as we were leaving we told her that we were Jewish and that our mothers wore pink pants and rarely bathed. "Oh dear me! I'm just so sorry for the awful things I said about your people. Really, I am." Michael went to kiss Valerie goodbye, but she turned her cheek and her knockers dropped below horizontal.

♦

One weekend we went to the railroad freight yard near downtown Miami and climbed into an empty box car, the same type of train that the Nazis used to transport Jews to Auschwitz.

David, Shelly, and I huddled in the corner; we were prisoners, on our way to the crematory. And Michael was the SS guard; he stood and shouted "Achtung" and "Schvinehount," he even had an arm band with a Swastika; it was part of his extensive Nazi collection. And he wore a red Lacoste. Except for jeans, Michael only wore red, white, and black, the colors of the German flag.

"The Nazi's made homosexuals wear pink armbands," said Michael. He looked at Shelly, who was wearing a pink Lacoste, and gave a look of disgust. "You . . . in the pink . . . move away from the Jews. When we get to Auschwitz, homos get baked in a different oven."

The train started moving; our fantasy immediately ended. Without hesitation, Michael jumped for safety. David and I quickly followed, but by the time it was Shelly's turn to jump the train was almost at full speed.

"Jump and roll," yelled Michael," as he ran alongside the train, shouting instructions to Shelly. "Hurry."

Shelly jumped and attempted to maneuver into a rolling position, but his head hit the gravel stones at the embankment of the railroad track. He was gushing blood. Michael immediately removed Shelly's pink Lacoste and wrapped it around his head. It was scary; we were worried that Shelly might die from a loss of blood. Frantically, we signaled a police car and were rushed to the nearest hospital. Shelly received fourteen stitches; he would be OK. But, on the bus ride home, his only concern was his pink Lacoste, which had been thrown in the trash. What would he tell his mother?

◆

Many very wealthy people made Miami Beach their winter home; they were called "snow-birds." In the Fall their waterfront mansions were boarded; they were living in New York brownstones or in apartments on Park Avenue, or maybe cruising the Mediterranean. It was fun to climb over the iron gates and search the grounds of these palatial estates. Michael suggested that we "borrow" a small, flat-bottom row boat that was chained to the dock behind one of these mansions. This type of boat was called a "John-Boy;" he knew a lot about boats. We picked up a large rock and smashed open the lock; the boat was ours. We were off, on the first of several boating adventures in Biscayne Bay.

David, Shelly, and I did the rowing; Michael, who preferred to be called, "Captain Mike," sat at the bow of our little boat, with his Nazi compass, leading the merry band of sailors in song:

"Come all ye young fellows who follow the seas.
Singing Way! Hey! Blow the man Down!
And Please pay attention and listen to me.
Give us some time to blow the man down!"

One Sunday morning Herman and Aunt Pearlie came to visit, bringing bagels, lox, cream cheese, pickled herring, smoked fish, and other Jewish delicacies. We sat at our new pink kitchen table, which was recommended by Shelly. We were all enjoying breakfast, except Michael, he never ate anything except hamburgers, but he drank four glasses of milk every day. Sometimes he would drink an entire quart of milk straight from the bottle. I was starting to enjoy new foods, even lox, but not the different types of smoked fish like Chubb's or Sturgeon and I didn't like nova, the watered down version of lox. Nova was lox without the salt; it tasted like rubber.

Sunday morning breakfasts were a Jewish "experience" in my home; we didn't go to shul; we didn't say prayers or wear yarmelkehs, but we ate Jewish food, and the adults used many Yiddish words and phrases. They never had complete conversations in Yiddish, not like their parents generation, and not like the street talk on Washington Avenue, but they sprinkled the breakfast table with colorful idioms and expressions. When Herman drove to the Jewish bakery to pick up a sliced rye bread my mother thanked him: "A gerzent dir· in pupik!" *(Thanks for the favor! Literally: Good health to your belly button!)* Aunt Pearlie complained about her brother, Charlie, who was "farblondzhet" *(confused)*. Uncle Charlie was going to abandon a good business in Miami and move back to Chicago because his wife was homesick for sleet and snow. "Er drait zich vi a fortz in rossel!" *(Is he bewildered! Is he in a fog! Literally: he squirms like a fart in foggy soup.)* This was Uncle Charlie's second wife: "A tsvaiteh veib iz vi a hilserner fus." *(A second wife is like a wooden leg).*

On this particular Sunday morning, somewhere in between an "Oye Vey" and an "Oye Gevald" Michael accidentally said something about Mr. Streuling in front of Herman. I had told

Michael everything about the shower incident and about my library research with Katarina Wolinski, but it was a secret; I didn't want Herman or my parents to know. Herman was a dead beat, but he wasn't stupid; my father always said he was "street-smart." He asked Michael and me to join him for a walk, and before we reached the end of the block he pressured me into telling him the entire story about Mr. Streuling. Herman was a cab driver and he knew a lot of shady people, and he also knew several cops. That always seemed strange to me . . . if you're friends with crooks, how can you also be friends with cops?

"I've got friends at city hall; let me see what I can find out, and don't worry; I won't tell your old man. You know you can trust your ole' Uncle Herman." Herman then made a call to a "Records Clerk" at the Miami Beach Police Department. Fifteen minutes later our phone rang and we found out a lot more about Mr. Streuling.

"He's a fuckin' fruitcake," said Herman. "Streuling's gotta' record a mile long: indecent exposure at the 46th street beach; arrested twice for loitering at Nautilus Jr. High playground." Herman's voice then changed from disbelief to laughter. "I gotta' tell Pearl; see if she still wants to make a 'shidech' with her Canasta ladies."

Within twenty four hours my parents knew all about Mr. Streuling; the "trustworthy" Herman told them everything. Surprisingly, I wasn't punished and I didn't have to listen to a long lecture. My parents called the Miami Beach police and reported the incident, even though almost two years had passed. Two squad cars drove to our house and the neighbors stood on the street and gossiped. I had to give a lengthy deposition to the police; a restraining order was issued, preventing Mr. Streuling from coming near me. "'Vay is mir,' I need this like a 'loch in kop' *(hole in the head)*, said my mother. "And to think . . . he was such a clean man."

The next morning I glanced at the Sports Section in the Miami Herald: The Yankees won the 1953 World Series over the Dodgers; it was their fifth consecutive championship. And on that same morning I sent a secret coded message to former President Truman. I resigned as a Nazi hunter, my work was done, my mission was accomplished. Now, I could focus my energy on finding Communist spies. The commie' pinkos were the new menace to the Free World. Senator Joseph McCarthy from

Wisconsin played on this fear. He gained national prominence by leading a crusade to expose subversive communists in the State Department and the army. However, his brand of militant mudslinging was exposed in the first televised Congressional hearings in U.S. history. "McCarthyism" was ridiculed. I watched the hearings and learned a whole bunch of new words like "repressive, reactionary, obscurantist, anti-intellectual, and totalitarian." Senator McCarthy reminded me a lot of Hitler, but he didn't have a funny little moustache. Unfortunately, many people referred to his witch hunt as fearless "Americanism."

My father told me that during the depression thousands of people in this country, including some of my Chicago relatives, were out of work; they were on "bread lines." It was very common for unemployed workers to join the Communist Party.

"Desperate people during desperate times do desperate things," said my father. "However, when World War II started and the economy improved, they all dumped communism."

In the early 1950s we were engaged in a cold war with the Soviet Union and "I Led Three Lives" soon became my favorite TV show. I was enthralled by the clever exploits of double agent Herbert Philbrick, who walked the tightrope, thwarting the diabolical plans of Communist spies who were lurking in the United States, usually as board members of the Episcopalian Church or at meetings of Alcoholics Anonymous, or at PTA meetings.

Even though I thought that Senator McCarthy was a wacko, I was convinced—we had to stop the Commie' bastards. It was painfully obvious, the Pinko's were trying to overthrow democracy and our American way of life. THINK PINK was a serriptitious Communist plot to brainwash the youth of America. As my first gesture of national pride I dumped my pink Lacoste and pink golf balls into the garbage.

My father didn't seem too worried about the Communist menace; he preferred watching the Lawrence Welk show. We had two TVs; one in the living room and one in my parents bedroom.

"Look Myron, they have an accordion player named Myron Floren. Aren't you sorry you quit?"

CHAPTER 23

FORWARD TYPHOONS

Now that we had our own boat, with Captain Mike at the helm, we were about to engage in many maritime adventures, but before I forget, I better say something about our football team. Who ever heard of high school memoirs that didn't include nostalgic recollections of the "glory of the gridiron?" Unfortunately, our team was really terrible that year; one of the only games we won was against St. Patricks, the Catholic school, and they didn't even have helmets for all their players. They had to borrow a few of ours.

With the start of high school I had to balance many emerging talents; I was an aspiring writer, a mathematician, a philosopher, a historian, a former accordion player, and a successful, but retired Nazi hunter . . . and I was also a good punter, so I asked coach Malloy if I could go out for the team. Because I was only 5'4 and 120 lbs. he misunderstood my request; he thought I wanted to be an equipment manager. Those were the guys who handed towels to the players in the locker room; they also sorted and distributed jock straps before the game.

"No, Coach; I'm a good punter, I wanna' go out for the team."

Coach Malloy looked at me; his bulging eyes examined the full length of my body. He said nothing, but I knew what he was thinking. But he never saw me punt! He didn't know that I could kick a perfect spiral high in the air, spin around, and catch the ball behind my back.

"OK . . . . show up for practice next Monday after school, wear shorts and sneakers, and don't forget your jock."

Then he handed me a private note, sealed in an envelope, which I was to give to the football coach. I immediately began deciding what number I would ask for. After much deliberation I concluded that I would be number "**9**" and over the weekend I practiced writing that number many times. If written properly, "nine" is aesthetic, chivalrous, and defiant; it means "NO" in German. One entire section of my new three-ring notebook soon had the number "**9**" written in a variety of colors and styles. I imagined a whole row of cheerleaders kicking up their legs and screaming when I entered the field; they would all wear the letter "L" to show their love of Lindell, the great punter, and they would flip up their little skirts, and the number nine would be written on nine matching tushes . . . "9 is divine" "9 is fine" "any time with number 9" and Leah Sonnino would come crawling back to me and say "9 is mine." It had to be a single digit number; I didn't want some obscure number like 75 or 68. And absolutely not 69! Kids would never stop laughing at anyone with 69.

Everyone knew that one of the easiest ways to be popular with the girls was to be a football player. Even the "Alien," Alberoni Zorzi Dorvilus, had his pick of the most gorgeous girls, and that guy had the biggest, fattest body I had ever seen. His butt was bigger than a watermelon.

The next Monday, after school I reported to football practice with my secret note from Coach Malloy. I gave the envelope to the football coach and asked for jersey number "**9**" but he had different ideas.

"Shorts and a t-shirt will do for now. You like the number nine? Ok boy . . . give me nine laps around the field."

I couldn't understand why I had to do all that running: i wasn't going to be a full-time player, only a punter, and punters didn't have to be fast runners, nor did they have to be in great physical condition; they only had to know how to punt. As I trotted around the football field I saw the "Alien," our all-city Defensive Tackle. He was fast for a big guy. I ran up to him; I felt important running stride for stride with number "77." He glanced down at me, a little kid who didn't even have a number, and he shifted to second-gear and sprinted away. After the nine laps I joined fifty other football players doing push-ups, sit-ups, leg squats, and jumping jacks. Finally, the coach blew his whistle; calisthenics were ended, or so I hoped. We then ran backward through a gauntlet, where we held the ball and a double file of coaches tried to slap it away. I learned how to straight-arm an opponents face; I also learned how to dodge an oncoming straight-arm. We banged our shoulders against tackling dummies and pushed heavy blocking sleds. Then we ran twenty-yard wind sprints, followed by more push ups and sit-ups. Finally, the ordeal was concluded and everyone shouted and cheered as they ran to the showers. I could barely move: I was in severe agony; my muscles trembled, my bones ached, even my hair was in pain. And as I dragged my body toward the locker room, I heard the coach call my name.

"Lindell: this here note says you're a punter. OK boy, lets see what you can do?" He threw the football in my direction. It seemed to weigh 100 lbs.

"Coach: I'm wiped out; let me show you tomorrow. I can barely move."

By the time I showered and took the city bus home to Surfside it was almost 7 PM. I hardly had the strength to walk from the bus stop to my house; my knees were quivering, my stomach muscles were throbbing, and my arms hung limp at my side. I was hoping that a long hot shower would provide some relief, but the muscles in my hand were too weak to turn the handle. My father suggested using Wintergreen Oil; it was good for soothing sore muscles. He laughed and said I was using new muscles, that I would eventually adjust to the exercise. I followed his advice and turned the shower to maximum heat in order to steam the bathroom. I sat there for twenty minutes, letting my pores expand. Then he handed me a small bottle of a potent green ointment that smelled like peppermint.

I stood alone in the shower rubbing the Wintergreen Oil over my neck, my arms, my shoulders, my chest. The hot liquid started dribbling down my stomach, across my abdomen, settling in the open pores of my private parts. I experienced the most biting agony of my life; the pain was excruciating; my testicles were on fire! I turned the water to cold and tried to soothe the burning pain, but the cold water against the hot Wintergreen Oil was like ice; it only intensified the pain. Then I tried hot water, and that created a scalding sensation. For the next thirty minutes I laid on the floor of the shower stall, face down, biting a towel, muffling a scream that wanted to explode. Thus ended my very brief football career and my desire to be the team punter.

Over the ensuing years I blocked all conscious memory of my one day on the football team. However, whenever I pass through the checkout counter of a supermarket and I reach for a pack of "Life Savers" I routinely select Peppermint or Spearmint, even Buttered Rum or multi-fruit . . . never the Wint O Green.

Our team was the Miami Beach Typhoons, but many of the "red necks" on the other side of the bay just called us "Kikes" or "Jew Boys." Our colors were Black and Gold, and the fight song was "Forward Typhoons" sung to the tune of "On Wisconsin," an inspiring and well known college victory march. I always wondered why we were called Typhoons. Typhoons are violent storms in the Pacific Ocean, near Japan; they never occur in the tropics of South Florida. "Hurricanes" would have been the perfect name, but that name was already taken by the University of Miami. Why couldn't we be barracudas or sharks or something native to South Florida . . . even coconuts! Why were we named after Japanese storms?

As our team lined up to play the Miami Edison Red Raiders, the third ranked team in the state the Typhoon Marching Band played and the students sang:

> "Forward Typhoons, Forward Typhoons
> Crash right through that line
> Make a touchdown every time
> For we have got the team
> Rah Rah Rah!"

If Las Vegas were to give odds on high school football Edison would have been favored by fifty points. The game was on their turf, on their side of the bay, but the Alien was a one man wrecking crew on defense; he forced five fumbles and kept the Typhoons in the game. With one minute remaining the Alien smacked their quarterback in the head with some type of Judo chop. We recovered a fumble at the Edison 1-yard line. We were down 14-10; it was first and goal with four shots to win the game. The Edison kids were stunned; the "Jew Boys" were about to upset the mighty Red Raiders. I remember that moment vividly; it was not crazy and wild, not what you'd expect. Instead, there was a ghostly silence of disbelief. Both sides were tense;

175

anxiously awaiting the next play. Kenny Shapiro, our quarterback, walked proudly to the field of honor. The cheerleaders were jumping and yelling: "Kenny, Kenny, he's our man, if he can't do it no one can" . . . and ten matching drummers stood and pounded a rhythmic beat. Then we all rose in unison and sang "Forward Typhoons" our stirring fight song. There was complete silence on the other side of the field. On first down Kenny Shapiro called his own number, "15," a quarterback sneak . . . and he fumbled. Edison recovered.

On the ride home I sat in our air conditioned bus next to Isabela Cardozo, a Cuban Jewish girl. Isabela had recently moved from Havana and spoke very little English. A few Cuban Jews lived in Miami Beach, but Isabela was the only one I ever met. She had a happy smile and a cheerful personality. We had just lost the game; we were depressed, but Isabela was bubbly and full of life. The Edison kids were standing by our bus, taunting us, calling us "dirty Jews," and extending middle fingers, their expressive way of wishing us a safe trip home.

This was Isabela's first football game; she reveled in the excitement. Then, she opened the window and in very broken English . . . sang a passionate rejoinder to the wiggling middle fingers:

> "We're froma' Beach
> Couldn'ta' be prouder
> Can'ta' hear us now
> We yell a little louder"
> We're froma' Beach
> Couldn'ta' be prouder . . ."

Isabela turned to the other kids on the bus, she waved her arms, and with body gestures she urged us to join her in singing. At first, we just yelled back at her: "Shut up! Shut the window. You're letting out the air." But, her enthusiasm was contagious, and on the long ride back to our island, we were led in song by a girl who could barely speak English. I don't think Isabela even realized that we lost the game.

The next morning our principal came on the P.A system and congratulated the team; he said we had a "moral victory" (whatever that was) . . . What was so "moral" about losing? And during the remainder of the football season we had many moral victories.

CHAPTER 24

THE FINAL VOYAGE OF THE NIÑA

Fourteen year old boys don't normally get wrapped up in fantasy, and they don't spend their weekends paddling around Biscayne Bay in a row boat. However, in the the Fall of 1953 Michael Bernstein was staying at my house, hiding from a teenage gang in Chicago, and he didn't share my interest in football. We were growing apart; our boyhood friendship was fading. Michael didn't like hanging out on the corner of Lincoln Road and Washington Avenue and he didn't know one word of Yiddish except for "putz." He used that word a lot.

Michael refused to join the Steinbergs and me when we visited Uncle Louie, Tanta Baila, and Sam Mermlestein and he never ate corned beef sandwiches, chopped liver, and blintzes. In order to find common interests with my old best friend I went through a brief nautical period in my life.

When we were on the boat Captain Mike was in charge. And he wore his white captain's hat with pride. He barked orders to the Steinbergs and to me, we were his faithful crew. "Swab the deck, hoist the anchor, pull in the lines." We never called them ropes . . . . we were sailors. They were "lines." We learned to tie square knots and we talked about the bow and stern of our proud vessel, and Captain Mike looked through his Nazi binoculars, first to the port then to the starboard side.

"Excuse me Captain Mike," said Shelly. "Which is left? Which is right?"

"Shut up, you little putz, and keep rowing."

Our boat was christened in a naval ceremony with a smashed Coca Cola bottle; it was launched and named "the "Niña"—that's Spanish for "little girl." It was named in memory of the third ship in Columbus' first expedition to America, the missing ship that never returned to Spain.

Our "galley"—where we stored the food and rations—was a plastic ice chest. We carried Cokes and peanut butter sandwiches. The "head" was the side of the boat, where we could pee whenever we wanted.

"But, if you wanna take a dump," said Michael. "Hop overboard; do what you gotta' do."

One memorable adventure was the exploration of Indian Creek Village. This private and exclusive village was an island connected to Surfside by a bridge, but access was denied to everyone except residents and invited guests. An armed guard with black shiny boots stood watch at the entrance; his job was to protect this restricted enclave from intruders, especially intruders of the Jewish persuasion. But to the crew of the Niña his presence did not serve as a deterrent; it was only an invitation. The route by land was blocked, but we could enter Indian Creek Village with our boat. Just as Columbus sought a nautical route to India, our challenge was to explore an island where even our parents were barred.

A complete circumnavigation of the island took less than an hour; we counted forty castles and chateau's clustered around a golf course. We made note of our discovery in the Captain's log. In one palatial back yard we observed a party, people were dancing. Captain Mike set our course; we were on a mission of surveillance.

"Lets see what those putzes are doing?"

It was early in the morning; we made a quiet landing at the beach-head and camouflaged the Niña with leaves and tree branches. We renamed the island "Atlantis"—the legendary lost continent, and claimed the island in the name of the United Nations. Then we spread black mud on our cheeks and foreheads and crawled on hands and knees across a vacant lot until we reached the yard where we had seen the party. We didn't speak; we only used hand signals, with Captain Mike leading the way. The final barrier was a seven foot tall Hibiscus hedge, with hundreds of pink flowers, and a few bees. It was impossible to see over the hedge, but we were lying on our stomachs and were able to see between the narrow trunks of the pink bushes.

land ho—I see signs of human life

Then I heard a familiar sound that I had tried to blot from my memory. The band was playing "Tzena Tzena," the last song I ever played on the accordion. Tzena Tzena was the song that ended my musical career. I stretched my head through a clearing in the hedges to get a closer look. But, even before I saw his green beret and smiling face I knew it was Ziggy Bloom, my old accordion teacher. My head was exposed between the hedges; Captain Mike was pulling back on my legs, but I continued to lie there quietly humming along with Mr. Bloom. Damn . . . he really played that song well.

At least one hundred people were sitting at round tables in the backyard of this imposing mansion; they were eating, laughing and drinking. On on a portable wooden dance floor a dozen or more children and adults were holding hands in a circle, singing, and dancing to the lively Israeli folk song.

This was a restricted island, where Jews and Negroes were not allowed to live. However, on the morning of our secret exploration we saw white people, colored people, Jews and gentiles together . . . laughing and kicking their legs in the air. We were looking at the future; this was a glimpse of America as it was meant to be, how Thomas Jefferson envisioned the pursuit of happiness. This it how it would be . . . someday. But, for the moment, we were sure that these people were in violation of several local ordinances. We peed on the empty lot, marked our spot, and scurried back to the Niña. Captain Mike told us his plans for our next journey, and as we paddled home we sang together . . . very much out of tune:

> ". . . Tzena, Tzena, join the celebration.
> There'll be people there from every nation.
> Dawn will find us dancing in the sunlight,
> Dancing in the village square."

THE CROSSING

Our most memorable adventure was the final voyage of the Niña. On this fateful Sunday morning in the Fall of 1953 (461 years after Columbus' first voyage) Captain Mike charted a course for a bold and daring expedition, we would be the first Caucasian teenagers to cross Biscayne Bay in a John-Boy, from Surfside to Miami, a four mile voyage. Our names would be enshrined in the maritime Hall of Fame, along with Columbus, Vasco da Gamma, Henry Hudson, and Sir Francis Drake. We packed extra Cokes and ten peanut butter sandwiches—four smooth and six crunchy.

The first hour was uneventful, it was a hot sunny day and we quickly exhausted our supply of Cokes. Then came the rain. In South Florida a cloudless day can often explode into a tropical squall. We used the ice chest to scoop water from the boat; we feared that the Niña would go down in the middle of Biscayne Bay.

Captain Mike bellowed orders: "Aye laddies, keep scooping or we're heading for Davey Jones locker."

We were all decent swimmers, but not good enough to swim two miles in a monsoon. We were approximately two miles from Miami and two miles from Surfside, past the "point of no return," but we were only one quarter mile south of the Broad Causeway and the town of Bay Harbor. So we aborted our plans and changed heading. We dumped the peanut butter sandwiches overboard and frantically rowed on a northerly course. I thought of Santiago, Hemingway's hero in the "Old Man and the Sea," and I realized that "nature is more luck than a set of rules, for it can shift back and forth with the greatest of ease." We hoped that eventually we would reach the causeway, but the rain was coming down in gusts, our visibility was limited, and we felt the fury of the sea.

Not long after we headed north, we heard a loud horn from an approaching boat; it was the Bay Harbor nautical patrol. They had seen us and were coming to tow us to safety. A deep voice trumpeted through the storm: "You in the row boat; throw us a line."

We were towed to shore and immediately escorted to the police station. They took our fingerprints and we were interrogated. I wasn't sure if this was a rescue or if we were being arrested for stealing the row boat. We let our captain do the talking.

"We were playing in a vacant lot alongside the bay", said Michael, "and we saw this boat adrift. It looked like fun, and thanks for rescuing us. Can we call our parents?"

It was almost an hour until my parents and the Steinberg's grandparents arrived at the Bay Harbor Police station; Herman was at my house when the police called, so he joined them. While we were waiting, sitting at the station in our wet bathing suits, a reporter from the Miami Beach Sun arrived and interviewed us; our story would be in the morning edition of the newspaper. In order to be consistent with the story that we told the police, we let Michael do all the talking. Its funny, how parents react in different ways to the same event. Herman was puffing on a cigarette, coughing and laughing, my father compared our escapade with his boyhood adventures playing on the Brooklyn Bridge, and my mother couldn't stop screaming and crying; she called us "hoodlums."

"Myron," she cried, "someday, when you have children . . . may they all grow up just like you." I heard that curse many times during my adolescent years.

The Steinberg's grandparents were shaking, too nervous to say anything. They weren't upset that we almost drowned at sea; they were upset because David and Shelly might now have a criminal record. Herman knew the Police Captain; they talked privately and no charges were filed. The event was officially recorded as a rescue.

Monday morning the headline of the Miami Beach Sun read . . . "Teenage Boys Rescued at Sea." The newspaper article began: "Myron Tindell, age fourteen . . . ." Damn, they didn't even spell my name right and why was I listed first, the reporter only interviewed Michael? In 1953 not much was happening in the world, and even less was happening in Miami Beach. The final voyage of the Niña was big news.

Several days later Michael and I had big fight over a candy bar. I wish I could embellish these memoirs with a more profound reason why our friendship came to an abrupt end. It would sound so much more mature to say that we had some type of philosophical conflict or maybe a clash over a girl, but it was just a fight over a Hershey bar. He pulled the candy away from me and called me a putz. Then I smacked him on the head with a pillow; the pillow broke open and hundreds of little feathers went flying all over his face, in his nose, and in his mouth. He was coughing and gagging, and when he regained his composure he punched me in the face and my nose started bleeding. My mother ran to the rescue; she put a cold wash cloth on my nose and told me to lie down with my head back. While I was being treated Michael was making a collect call to Chicago.

The next morning Mrs. Bernstein arrived in Miami Beach, and for the remaining six months of the tenth grade Michael lived with his mother at a hotel and we never spoke again. We passed each other every day in home room and in several classes but we avoided eye contact. At the end of the school year he returned to Chicago.

CHAPTER 25

BIOLOGY: THE STUDY OF LIFE

"**B**i' means two and 'ology' means the study of something, like archeology or geology" said Margaret Hunt, our Biology teacher. "So, the first half of this course will be devoted to the study of plant life and the second half will be all about animals."

I was bored with the study of plants, probably because of my lifelong aversion to vegetables. I memorized different plant parts, like the stamen and pistil, and I learned all about the process of photosynthesis, but I could never say that word without lisping. I got A's on the plant tests because I was good at memorizing lists, but I didn't really learn anything. The only thing that fascinated me was **chlorophyll**, the green stuff that was the foundation of plant life. During the year when I was studying Biology, a chlorophyll fad was taking place in America.

People were buying green toothpaste; consumers were convinced that chlorophyll was the new wonder drug, that it would cure diseases and prevent cavities. As would be expected, Lacoste immediately came out with a new chlorophyll colored polo shirt and Shelly was first in line to expand his growing mélange.

Even soap had turned green, as well as salves and ointments to eliminate acne and hemorrhoids. Little children were fed chlorophyll tablets before they went to school and older men who suffered from impotence took chlorophyll injections. Ouch! However, the green fad came to a crashing end when an article in "The Journal of the American Medical Association" pointed out that grazing goats virtually lived on chlorophyll and they smelled worse than pigs.

Then came the animal half of the course. I was fascinated with the dissection of worms. Miss Hunt, our matronly Biology teacher, was also my tenth grade home room teacher, and she was another religious fanatic, almost as bad as Miss Baker, but at least Miss Hunt didn't make us pray to the Holy Ghost. During morning devotionals she preached the Biblical theory of Creation and during Biology she taught Darwin's theory of Evolution. I once asked her how she could reconcile the different theories. She didn't have a problem, she merely said that Darwin explained the evolution of animals, "how" life was created, all the intricate details of "ooze and mitosis," but the Bible explained "why" life was created, the spiritual purpose of man. That sounded very reasonable and I respected her attempt to deal with irreconcilable differences. However, the two sides of Miss Hunt sometimes clashed . . . and her internal conflict enriched the classroom lectures.

"Darwin examines the creation of life, but only 'this' life . . . he does not address the 'next' life. The Bible is the sole authority on life after death."

"Is there any proof of life after death," asked Howard Lefkowitz. "I mean, like fossils?"

"Proof is something that Darwin looks for," said Miss Hunt, "and I support the need for proof, as it relates to his theory. But, our belief in the next life is based on faith. Sorry, Howard, no fossils from Heaven and, for a very good reason; nothing is dead in Heaven . . . Heaven is eternal."

"My father said that Darwin's theory is just a theory," said Linda Segal, "but like all theories its just theoretical."

"No Linda, that's a misinterpretation of the word 'theory,'" said Miss Hunt. "Go check it out in a dictionary; there are two definitions. In common usage your father is correct, 'theory' means theoretical, an unproven idea. However, when used in the context of science a 'theory' is based on a hypothesis which is subjected to verification by empirical evidence. A scientific theory isn't theoretical."

After a preliminary discussion of Darwin, Miss Hunt began her clinical explanation of the process of reproduction; this was the part of the course that we eagerly waited to hear, the part that appealed to most kids . . . except those who loved plants.

"Slower please," said Manny Lefkowitz, as he fumbled through his note book "I want to write this all down."

"Conjugation is a temporary cytoplasmic union," Miss Hunt read from her lecture notes . . . careful to avoid eye contact with the students, "with exchange of nuclear material that is the usual sexual process in ciliated protozoans."

We all chuckled when she said "sexual"—that was the only word we understood. I was surprised to learn that "conjugation" was a sexual term; I only knew about conjugation as it related to Spanish verbs . . . and I sure didn't know that semen was nuclear. Maybe that's the cause of two-headed babies.

"So, did man really evolve from the worm?" Asked Maxine Schwartz, my dissection partner. Dissection was a process that required two people; one to hold the worm and the other to do the slicing. I was the slicer.

"Yes Maxine . . . man did evolve from the worm, but 'only' because God ordained the process." That was how Miss Hunt answered any conceivable question related to a biological phenomenon. First, she would support the scientific explanation, "how" it occurred; then she would go off on a tangent and discuss the Biblical interpretation of "why" it happened. Her dual explanations served to sanctify and deify any biological process, even the merger of the sperm and the egg, which only occurred because it was ordained by God. A few of the kids were of the opinion that men and women had some control over the merger, a process that was covered in throbbing-quivering-pulsating detail by the various pocket-book novels that we read . . . . but we didn't dare to disagree with Miss Hunt.

"God created heaven and earth, and all the seas," said our Biology teacher, "and it only took Him six days; he rested on the seventh day . . . but days were longer during biblical times, and in those six glorious days he created the one celled animals, then the fish and the bugs, and eventually, the humans. The Bible and Darwin are 100% consistent, but this is where Darwin leaves us hanging. We need the Bible to give us additional insight. Darwin says that the human being is the highest order of the evolutionary process, and then he stops . . . but those were just cave men he was talking about. However, the Bible traces the evolution of humans, from Adam and Eve, through the Garden of

Eden, through paganism to Judaism, and eventually Christianity, the highest form of spirituality."

"How did Christians evolve from Jews?" asked one skeptical Jewish kid. We were all fascinated by the ability of Miss Hunt to blend the Theory of Evolution with the Theory of Creation. If she were on the jury at the Scopes trial, she would have supported both sides.

"Obviously, Christians are not a biological change from Jews, even though Hitler thought so, but Christianity is a 'divine' evolution. Jesus adopted the revelations of Moses, and went one step further." Miss Hunt liked the Jewish kids in our Biology class; we were of the same species and phylum as Christians, even though we were of a lower spiritual order.

We learned how to use the microscope in Biology and were taught how to set up slides and view a human hair. After receiving instructions from Miss Hunt we were sent to the lab and told to remove one hair from our head, to examine the hair under a microscope. The lab was an unstructured area where students were free to experiment and dabble without the supervision of a teacher. Naturally, half the boys in the lab chose to extract a different type of hair, those from below the belt. Manny Lefkowitz was even more imaginative; he went to the bathroom and returned with a few drops of semen. One by one, everyone in the lab viewed Manny's slide and marveled at his sperm cells, even the girls stared in the microscope and blushed. There were hundreds of little "spermies"—they had tiny tails and were squiggling in a frenzy without any direction. They were lost, frantically searching for an egg to fertilize. Manny was a nutty guy; it was easy to understand why his sperm were a little bit crazy.

Miss Hunt was a popular teacher at Beach High and her reputation extended beyond Biology. With a name like Hunt, she inspired the poetic talents of many young boys. Her name rhymed with one of the most well known "dirty words." In Phys. Ed., where any type of language or profanity was allowed, boys often marched to the football field in military columns and sang spirited songs in tribute to Miss Hunt.

> "I've got a teacher named Miss Hunt
> She's got a pimple on her cunt
> Sound off—
> Left, right . . ."

One time in Biology, Miss Hunt used the word "penis" in a discussion about the reproductive process of donkeys. We never discussed the reproductive process of humans, but were told that it was similar to donkeys, except donkeys had four legs and humans had two, and the penis of the donkey was considerably larger. In the rear of the room, Manny Lefkowitz scratched his balls and mumbled: "hee haw . . . hee haw."

We all tried to keep a straight face and not chuckle; most of us had never heard the word "penis" used in classroom conversation before, although we had read it many times, especially in "A Stone for Danny Fisher," where we underlined that word, and many other dirty words with red ball point pens. Yellow highlighters had not yet been invented; they would eventually replace the red ball point pen as the favorite instrument for emphasizing words like penis, vagina, orgasm, and ejaculate.

One of the girls was outraged; she walked out of the class and filed a complaint. Miss Hunt was called down to the principal's office. In future lectures she was more careful; she would never again say "penis." When absolutely necessary she would refer to the male reproductive organ as his "thingie". The word "penis" was an awkward word. In the language of the tenth grade it was difficult to decide when and where it was appropriate. It was much too vulgar for Biology, or any other class, but it was too clinical for conversations with other kids. It was not a spoken word, except with a doctor or your parents. It was a word reserved for books, similar to words like: "erudite," "ides" or "phantasmagoria".

Maxine Schwartz also said "thingie" as she raised the magnifying glass and scrutinized the dorsal side of our worm. "Where is the thingie?"

I told her that I had this secret fantasy, to watch a worm have "intracourse." She never heard that word before and I told her I made it up; it's the process of having sex with yourself.

"That's called masturbation," said Maxine.

"I know what masturbation is," I replied, "but worms are hermaphrodites. They reproduce by having intercourse with themselves, so I call it intracourse."

From across the table Manny Lefkowitz whispered. "Hey! That's probably why they say 'go fuck yourself.'" Maxine and I laughed and continued to examine our worm, but even with the help of a magnifying glass we were unable to locate the "thingie."

"And which is the female side," said Maxine. "Where is the thingette?"

Maxine was in the school band and was very pretty, at least I thought so, even though some of the boys called her "spider woman" because she had hairy arms. She had red hair, beautiful ruddy cheeks and a warm smile, but what really attracted me to Maxine was her laugh; she laughed a lot and whenever she talked to me she put a hand on my shoulder. She played the glockenspiel in the school band; that's a small metal set of chimes, like a miniature xylophone. And she marched near the front of the band, not far behind the drum major and the majorettes. That year, the popular marching song at football games was the "Gillette Razor Blade March."

To look sharp, every time you shave (*bong*)
And feel sharp, and be on the ball (*bong*)
Just be sharp, use Gillette blue blades
for the quickest, slickest shave of all (*bong*) (*bong*)

So, on four distinct occasions, when the one hundred piece marching band stopped and paused, Maxine had the spotlight to herself and kids in the stadium sat on the edge of their seat in total silence. If she hit the wrong note at the bong she would screw up the whole song. But, Maxine never missed. At ten football games that year, as the band played the same Gillette Razor Blade March, she hit her four bongs with precision. That's all Maxine ever did in the band; she marched and she hit four notes on her Glockenspiel, and for doing that she got free rides to all games, and went on trips to Nassau and the Cherry Blossom Festival in Washington.

"Myron, would you like to come over to my house Saturday night and study for the Biology exam? My parents will be out late . . . real late."

Maxine lived on North Bay Road, one of the most exclusive parts of Miami Beach, in a huge waterfront mansion constructed from coral rock and pink marble. The long illuminated driveway in front of her house crossed over a canal. The bridge was bordered by Corinthian columns topped with headless statues of nude Roman gods and goddesses.

"How come the gods don't have 'thingies?" I asked, "they're all chopped off."

Maxine laughed—she laughed a lot. "The prior owners thought it was gross to see a bunch of hanging dicks in their driveway."

"Yeah, but they didn't chop off the vaginas," I responded.

"Well, that's different. The female statues all have their legs together, you can't see the holes." Once again, Maxine laughed.

The house was so big it had a name, "San Francisco del Mar," in honor of Saint Francis of Assisi, whose spiritual life inspired the Franciscan order of monks and the associated vows of poverty. But, it sure didn't look like Maxine's family ascribed to the same vows.

"That's because we're Jewish," said Maxine. "Only monks have to follow those vows."

On the upper right corner of front door, immediately below a pair of gothic gargoyles, was a large silver mezuzah with six turquoise stones forming a Jewish star. And inside this stately castle, at the far end of an immense living room, was a white concert grand piano, the largest piano I had ever seen. I told Maxine that I knew how to play the right hand of a piano; it was the same keyboard as an accordion. I wanted to play Oh Solo Mio, but she continued the tour. She laughed a lot and touched my shoulder as she told me the history of her enormous home.

"My grandfather bought 'San Fran' in 1930," said Maxine. "There were lots of bargains during the depression. But, most of the waterfront homes had covenants preventing sale to Jews so he changed his name to Swarz and said he was German. After he purchased the house he changed back to Schwartz; they couldn't stop gramps. My 'bubby' wanted to change the name of the house, she didn't like using the name of a Catholic saint, but gramps insisted on keeping the old name as a reminder of the anti-Semitism in Miami Beach."

The "Florida Room," a glass enclosed den located in the rear of the mansion, had a beautiful panoramic view of Biscayne Bay and the Miami skyline. And . . . hanging on the wood paneled wall, framed in gold, was the original deed to San Francisco del Mar. Maxine proudly showed me the infamous covenant

> *"Said property shall not be sold, leased or rented in any form or manner, by any title, either legal or equitable, to any person or persons other than of the Caucasian Race, or to any firm or corporations of which any persons other than of the Caucasian Race shall be a part or stockholder."*

"But this covenant only talks about non-Caucasians," I noted. "It doesn't say anything about Jews."

"I know," said Maxine. "Gramps said that in those days Jews were considered to be non-Caucasians."

The tour concluded in Maxine's bedroom, which was bigger than the living room in my house. We hopped on her large circular bed and began reading our biology book together. That was the first time I had ever seen a circular bed.

We studied all about one celled protozoan, protoplasm, and cellular fission, and I don't know who grabbed who first but we started kissing. Of course, Maxine was completely in charge, and she kept referring to the most private part of my anatomy as "George" . . . and my very brief adventure, which was a lot less than a sexual experience, concluded with four potent bongs from a glockenspiel reverberating in my head.

Then, after more discussion about biology and protoplasm we left the circular bed and went downstairs to the living room I played Oh Solo Mio on the concert grand piano, using the right hand only, and Maxine accompanied me with her glockenspiel. We both sang and laughed and she touched my shoulder.

"Its more than just hitting the right notes," said Maxine. "Its all in the touch . . . you need a special flick of the wrist and lots of practice to get a really passionate bong."

"Oh yes," I smiled. "You've got the touch."

We continued seeing each other the next several weeks, always in the dark, but we never went "all the way." She was a "nice Jewish girl" and wanted to remain a virgin until marriage, or at least a "technical" virgin, which was almost as good.

Maxine had a long list of rules, what was normal and what wasn't, and as she got to know me better, the list got longer, and as the list got longer she didn't laugh as much, and she didn't touch my shoulder anymore. When we ate lunch together in the

Beach High cafeteria she made fun of the way I ate, especially when I struggled with vegetables; she said that the way I ate "wasn't normal" . . . and she even started to criticize my clothes, especially my color combinations. After awhile I realized that I was not in love with Maxine, certainly not like I once loved Leah Sonnino; Maxine said that she didn't love me either.

A month later, after a band trip to Nassau, Maxine started going steady with a tuba player, but we still remained dissection partners for the rest of the year. Frogs were much more challenging than worms; Maxine named our first frog "George."

"Thanks, Maxine," I said, "but if you still like George how come we broke up?"

"Myron, it annoyed the hell out of me to watch how you ate vegetables . . . . I told you that a thousand times . . . it isn't normal."

CHAPTER 26

SHOP: PREPARATION FOR ADULT RESPONSIBILITIES

In the tenth grade girls were required to take Home Economics (Home Ec.) and boys had to take "Industrial Arts" (commonly referred to as "Shop" . . . . whatever that meant!) we were nearing the completion of puberty, being groomed for a productive maturity where we might perpetuate well defined gender distinctions; we were being prepared to assume adult responsibilities. Girls learned how to coordinate a well balanced meal from the three basic food groups. In addition, they baked cookies, cakes, and brownies and made aprons, pot holders, and men's ties; they also learned how to iron, knit, crochet, embroider, mend, and darn holes in men's socks. And boys learned important manly skills, how to work with power tools like the lathe, band saw, jig saw, and drill press.

Our Shop teacher was Homer Calhoun from Tuscaloosa, Alabama. He had a southern accent and it was sometimes impossible to understand what he was saying because he always had a wad of gum in his mouth, even though there was a school rule against chewing gum in classrooms. His favorite word was "Bullshit," which he converted into an elongated three-syllable word . . . "Buuullll-sheee-it." He frequently reminded us that he was "compassionate to Jews" because we were the "Chosen People."

Mr. Calhoun was probably in his mid fifties and he didn't know the first thing about using any of the power tools. He made it clear on the first day of class: "The only little fuckers' to touch the God-damn power tools will be 'y'all' with prior experience. How ya' ever gonna beat your meat if you get one of 'your pinkies chopped off? The rest of you do whatever the hell you wanna' do the rest of year, but keep your fuckin' hands outta' trouble." The language and decorum of Shop was "mature"—similar to Phys. Ed. Any type of profanity was allowed, but Mr. Calhoun had several Commandments posted on the bulletin board:

- **Thou Shalt Not** utilize power tools unless authorized by the teacher
- **Thou Shalt Not** chew gum while working on the power tools.
- **Thou Shalt Not** use power tools unless wearing protective goggles
- **Thou Shalt Not** leave the room without a pass signed by the teacher or the principal
- **Thou Shalt Not** ridicule the creative efforts of fellow students
- **Thou Shalt Not** sleep during class
- **Thou Shalt Not** disobey orders from your teacher

I was decent with a hammer or a screwdriver, but I didn't know the first thing about lathes and band saws so I was assigned to the group of boys who were prohibited from standing within ten feet of any power tool. Mr. Calhoun called us the "stay out of trouble" boys and we quickly become known as the "SOOTs." David Steinberg was also a SOOT, as were approximately 50% of the boys. Shelly was in the same class; I don't know how he convinced Mr. Calhoun, but he made it into the power tool group; we called them the "PT's" and we always laughed at that nickname, which was also used to describe girls who were "prick teasers."

During the first two weeks of the school year I sat around in shop and tried to read a book or do homework from other classes, but the noise of the power tools was deafening. It was impossible to make use of that time for anything that required concentration. The next two weeks, I just sat around and stared at the wall. Then, during the final two weeks of the "grading period" I put my head on my work table and slept, even though I knew I was in violation of the "No Sleeping" Commandment. However, my grade on the first report card was "A;" I did what I was supposed to; I stayed out of trouble. In the "Teachers Comments" section of the report card, Mr. Calhoun noted: "Hard working student."

The school year was divided into six 6-week grading periods, and I knew I couldn't continue like this for the rest of the year; the boredom of doing nothing was killing me. So, I conceived a clever idea how to sneak out of Shop without a pass. I would go to the Home. Ec. Lab and visit Zondra DiMara Feinberg. I was introduced to this very buxom girl by Maxine Schwartz; they were close friends. When Maxine dumped me for the tuba player she eased her conscience by introducing me to her best friend.

"Myron, you'll like her . . . and she's got plenty upstairs."

"She's smart?" I replied

"Yeah, that too. But, you know that's not what I'm talking about." Maxine giggled.

Zondra DiMara was called "ZD" by most of her girlfriends; she had a great personality and we joked around a lot, but the main reason why I wanted to visit her, aside from a break in the boredom, was because she knew how to bake fantastic chocolate chip cookies, and they were delicious if you ate them hot, right out of the oven.

My plan was simple, but ingenious. Every day at least one or two boys were given bathroom passes signed by Mr. Calhoun. When the boys returned they dumped their used passes in the waste paper basket. Thus, when my Shop class met, at 10:00 AM, there would probably be several discarded passes already in the basket . . . from the prior classes. I needed David Steinberg as an accomplice; David would talk to Mr. Calhoun and get him to face away from the waste paper basket. Once I found a pass I would sneak out of the classroom and go immediately to the Registrar's office, where a bottle of ink eradicator was always on top of the service counter. I could make the necessary modifications to the pass, run over to the Home Ec. Lab, meet with ZD and enjoy her hot cookies. Altough I didn't know ZD that well it wasn't difficult to convince her to be part of my adventure; she thought it sounded like fun.

The plan worked to perfection, I used the liquid ink eradicator, wiped out the other boy's name and replaced it with my own. I also replaced "Boy's Room" with "Home Ec. Lab" as the "authorized" destination. The Registrar's office was completely empty except for the sad, but attractive woman who sat behind a typewriter. She was busy at work and didn't even notice that I was in the office. Then I scurried to Home Ec. and used my "admission pass" to get in the lab; normally boys were not allowed in this "all girls" room.

ZD was waiting for me and the cookies were hot and fantastic; we chatted for a while and laughed. Maxine Schwartz was also in the room; she was making a tie for her tuba boyfriend. Even Leah Sonnino was there. I hadn't seen her in a long time, but whenever I did, I felt really depressed. She was talking to a few other girls, eating chocolate chip cookies. She still had a pony tail, but looked a little different, maybe because she wasn't smiling and was heavier than when I last saw her, probably from too many cookies. I thanked ZD and moved into the final phase of my brilliant plan. I returned to Shop, and walked into the classroom, confident that I had committed the perfect crime. I made sure to wipe any chocolate from my mouth; I was very meticulous.

Mr. Calhoun was standing in the center of the room with a big grin on his face, waiting for my return. So were all of the other boys in the class.

"Welcome back Mr. Ink Eradicator, you sure have fuckin' chutzpah,'" said Mr. Calhoun. He shook my hand and laughed; all the boys laughed.

Boy, have you got "chutzpah!"

It seemed strange to hear a redneck use a Yiddish word to tell me that I "had balls;" 'chutzpah' sounds funny with a southern accent. Putz' and 'shmuck' were also part of the everyday vocabulary of Mr. Calhoun, but he turned them into two syllable words.

I was relieved to see that Mr. Calhoun wasn't upset. In fact, he laughed so hard he could hardly speak. Apparently, the Registrar, who was working at her typewriter, saw me using the ink eradicator and got suspicious. She secretly followed me to the Home. Ec. Lab and with her walkie-talkie she contacted Mr. Calhoun, informing him of every move I made.

"Great plan, Mr. Ink Eradicator," said Mr. Calhoun, "the best gol-dang' plan I ever seen." And he continued to laugh. On my second report card I received another "A" in Shop, with a note in the "Teachers Comments" section: "Very creative young man." For the rest of the school year and for my remaining years at Beach Hi, whenever Mr. Calhoun saw me he called me "Ink Eradicator."

PENNY FOOTBALL

In Shop we didn't sit at traditional classroom desks with useless ink-wells. Instead, four boys were assigned to a work table which was six feet square. The table was extremely thick and sturdy, designed to withstand the strongest blow from a hammer or other hand tool. But the "SOOTs" weren't doing anything worthwhile with our tables, so David Steinberg and I invented a game to alleviate the boredom. We expanded upon a popular form of penny football that boys often played on rainy days in Phys. Ed. But, our game was much more elaborate; it took several days to develop the rules and a two-page typewritten set of instructions. The game required full use of the six foot table as a playing field; one team consisted of eleven copper pennies, and the opposing team consisted of eleven lead pennies. Lead pennies were used during WWII, and in 1953 many of them were still in circulation. A special six-foot long ruler, which we called the "pushkie" was used to slide the pennies across the table. Each side would arrange their pennies in clever and imaginative offensive or defensive formations, with one penny designated as the "runner." The object of penny football was to push your "runner" across the table in four downs without being tackled by an opposing penny.

The "runner" was painted red, blue, green, or whatever color the team captain wanted. But, once a color was selected, no other team could use that restricted color. Mine was light blue; that was my favorite color ever since my date with Leah Sonnino.

The game quickly became very popular among the "SOOTs" and a league was formed, with twenty teams. Each team had a different color and a different name. My team was the

"Bell-Boys"—it was a name that had relevance to Miami Beach, the tourist capital of America. The brown team was called the "Brown Bombers," a tribute to Joe Louis, and the pink team was "Think Pink." David's team was the "Stein-Burgers." That was a great name, even better than mine. Surprisingly, Mr. Calhoun liked penny football and he entered the league. His team was the "Coon-dogs." Soon the "SOOTs" were having much more fun that the "PTs" and one by one the kids who were using the power tools broke rank; they abandoned the lathes and drill presses and joined the penny football league (the PFL). However, if the "converts" wanted to join our league we made them pay a price for admission. We needed little goal posts, designed just like real ones, with little cross bars. So, we utilized their skills with the power tools. The former PTs also made new improved "pushkies" and fancy wooden scoreboards. In time, the only two boys who continued working with the power tools were Shelly and Maynard Krumplestein.

Shelly remained oblivious to the excitement of penny football; he didn't let the noise and cheering disturb his concentration. He preferred working alone, making many "one-week projects." One week projects could be started on a Monday and finished by Friday. Since he now had the lathe entirely to himself he became extremely productive, and made six laminated salad bowls, constructed from walnut and pine. They were two-tone and beautiful. He even gave one to my mother, to blend with the new dishes that he helped select. He also made two dozen hand painted wooden hangers, color coordinated for his growing collection of Lacoste polo shirts. I was a little jealous; the hangers were neat. I was also becoming a collector of the multi colored alligator shirts.

Maynard Krumplestein followed a different approach in Shop. Instead of making many little projects, Maynard worked the entire school year on one huge task . . . building a bar for his parent's den. It was fifteen feet long and it had a counter covered with hundreds of little pink and turquoise mosaic tiles that spelled out "Krumplestein." On the back side of the bar Maynard constructed drawers, compartments, nooks, and crannies. There were special places for glasses, bottles, and all kinds of paraphernalia. He needed the entire six weeks of the first grading period just to draft plans; it was a magnificent project. Normally, supplies such as wood, paint, varnish, and mosaic tiles had to be divided among all students, but in our class Maynard had 90% of the supplies; Shelly had the other 10%. Most of the year Maynard sat in a corner, sanding or staining boards. He didn't talk much, not to any of the students, not even to the teacher. But, Mr. Calhoun always patted him on the shoulder and said, "y'all keep up the good work Maynard." Eventually, all the "SOOTs" patted him on the shoulder or on the head and told him to keep up the good work.

As the school year was coming to an end, Mr. Calhoun urged Maynard to hurry up and finish. The PFL playoffs were coming soon and his bar was taking up too much space. Finally, Maynard finished the magnificent bar, and we held a party to celebrate the occasion. Mr. Calhoun even invited the Home Ec. girls. They brought chocolate chip cookies and a few cakes with orange frosting that said, "Congratulations Maynard." The boys bought cokes and ice cream. It was a great party. ZD was there, and her cookies were better than ever. Maxine also came to the party and she told me all about the tuba guy—how normal he was—that he loved vegetables, and she giggled and asked me if I had been taking good care of George.

"Yeah, and he said that he missed you." Maxine laughed and touched my shoulder. She hadn't touched me in a long time.

I looked around for Leah Sonnino, but she wasn't there. I asked a few of the girls if they knew where she was. There was a hush; no one wanted to say anything. Then one girl said that Leah was "knocked up" and was thrown out of school.

"Who's the father?" I asked. I assumed it was Danny Berger. But, the girl said that Leah had a "gang bang" with ten boys.

That seemed impossible to believe. I was stunned—but I forced myself to stop thinking about Leah—this was Maynard's day. Everyone was patting him on the shoulder and marveling at his magnificent bar. Finally, Maxine asked an interesting question:

"Maynard; how are you going to get it home?'

"Damn, I never thought about that." Maynard stared in space; he looked bewildered.

During the final week of the school year Maynard worked feverishly to disassemble his bar and make room for the penny football playoffs, which were eventually won by the Stein-Burgers. My Bell-Boys came in second; Calhoun's Coon-dogs came in last place.

I remember Shop fondly; it was an unusual experience. But, it did little to prepare me for adult responsibilities. In later years I attempted to teach my children how to play penny football, but they preferred video games where neurons and micro-bytes zipped and zapped each other on a TV screen. And, from what I've seen, not too many of the girls ever mastered the art of sewing or darning.

CHAPTER 27

B-56: THE BUMPY ROAD OF YOUTH

We huddled on the corner of 95th and Dickens in pre-dawn Surfside, boys in one group, girls in another. We stood there, half asleep, too tired to talk to each other, awaiting the morning sun and the arrival of B-56. The big yellow school bus was driven by Rosie Callahan, an elderly Irish lady with gray fizzy hair, who earned extra money by serving vegetables in the cafeteria. The school bus followed a circular route, and circles have no beginning or end, except in the mind of the bus driver. Rosie chose to make 95th street, my corner, the last stop for her circle—the last stop for morning pickups. Thus, by the time I entered B-56 there was no guarantee of a seat during the one-hour trip to school

The first morning of the school year was the slowest since all kids had to show Rosie an official authorization slip. By the time B-56 arrived at 95th street and I proved that I was a legitimate passenger all seats were occupied; I wasn't too happy having to stand during the entire trip to school. It was a long, miserable, bumpy ride and it wasn't even an air conditioned bus. I had to do something, I didn't want to stand every morning for the entire year. So, that night when I got home, I told my parents about my problem. However, I carefully structured my complaint in the form of an ultimatum.

"I'm so exhausted from being forced to stand all the way to school on that horrible, sweltering, bumpy bus; I'm sorry but I just can't set the dinner table tonight, or help with the dishes, or take out the garbage."

This was a "win:win" argument . . . if my parents couldn't do anything to help with the bus problem, at least I could be relieved of a few evening chores. My father immediately called Ben Seligman, our family attorney, and Mr. Seligman called a friend of his on the School Board, who called Aaron T Schecter, our principal, who called Rosie.

The next morning, as B-56 arrived at 95th street, Rosie walked off the bus and greeted me. She then took my hand and escorted me to an empty seat in the front row. The seat had a small sign, "Reserved for Myron S. Lindell" When the door was closed and I was seated, Rosie used an exaggerated Irish brogue to make the following announcement on the microphone:

"Myron's mommy and daddy called and complained to Mr. Schecter. Poor Myron! So, we have reserved this very special seat for him."

I wasn't quite sure how to respond to this sarcasm, so I just stood up, turned and faced a bus full of half awake kids . . . and I smiled. Then I raised both arms in the air, my best impersonation of President Eisenhower. I waved "V" signs with both hands and I kissed Rosie on top of her grey fizzy hair. I was rewarded for this special kiss; the front seat in the bus was designated as my special morning seat for the entire year.

"Nice going," said David Steinberg. "You sure got chutzpah!"

However, the only kids who supported me were David, Shelly, and a few of my friends. Most of the other kids called me a pussy or a fag.

"Only fags complain," said one of the older boys. "A real man got the balls to keep his mouth shut and put up with shit."

I learned an important lesson that morning, a confusing paradox. If you stand up and assert yourself; if you try to initiate change, most kids will call you a fag. But if you sit on your ass and do nothing you will be regarded as "strong" or "brave." Of course, I was only observing teenage behavior. Certainly, adults didn't think the same way.

The morning ride on B-56 was not very eventful. At that hour we weren't fully awake or alive; many of the kids were sleeping. The loudest noise on the bus was the occasional snoring or farting from some of the boys. Girls never snored or farted. I was always mystified by that difference between the sexes. How come girls never farted, not even when they were asleep?

"Cause' they've got wider pores," said Shelly, "specially' the pores under their armpits. Why do you think girls need to wear perfume?"

Some of the older girls slept with their collars turned up, to hide embarrassing hickeys. But, if a boy had a hickey he would sleep with his shirt unbuttoned, to proudly display his sexual memento.

Since I had the special front seat for the rest of the year I was always the first to leave the bus at school, and I never forgot to kiss Rosie on top of the head—she became my friend; she looked out for me.

"Myron, you make sure to come to the cafeteria today; we're serving Summer Squash, your favorite. Unfortunately, its asparagus tomorrow, but I'll give you an extra helping of roast beef."

The afternoon trip was a much livelier experience; it was the time to find out everything about everybody; it was gossip time, and it didn't matter if the rumors were true or not. On the return trip the kids were awake and excited. I heard lots of stories about Clara Babbit, the tenth grade "slut" who gave blow jobs to the older boys. Apparently, her braces created problems and several boys were complaining.

"You can get penis cancer from too much metal scratching," said one of the older boys; he seemed to know what he was talking about. "But a little scratching, if done right . . . can send you to heaven and back." The younger boys looked at him with envy. We tried to imagine what it would feel like to have our dicks scratched by Clara's braces. She was experienced; she knew how to do it right.

Clara's nickname was "Hurricane Clara" and she was immortalized with a poem.

> "The winds blow East
> The winds blow west
> But Hurricane Clara Blows the Best"

Clara wasn't the only one who had a "special" school bus song; so did Billy Rawls. He was a weird, cross-eyed boy, who drooled a lot and frequently exposed himself in public. One time

202

Billy was caught masturbating in the library; he was suspended from school for two weeks.

> "Billy Rawls, Billy Rawls
> Running through the halls
> Billy Rawls, Billy Rawls
> Playing with his balls"

There was lots of snickering about Dee Dee Cooperman, a very unattractive girl, whose family owned the "Star of David" funeral home. Several of the boys were saying that Dee Dee loved to screw in a coffin. And, I also heard a little more gossip about Leah Sonnino, that Danny Berger really was the guy who knocked her up. Kids were saying that Danny's father, a big time attorney, gave money to a bunch of football players; he bribed them to say that they had a 'gang bang' with Leah.

"Yeah, I know four guys who wrote letters saying that they banged Leah," said one of the girls on the bus. "Too bad I'm not a guy, they were each getting two hundred bucks just to write a bullshit letter."

There were also rumors about Brock Tyler, the handsome new English teacher, that he was "screwing" two beach-hi girls. One was Leah's best friend, Mavis Koninberg, but no one was sure about the second girl. I had suspicions that it might have been Leah.

And when there wasn't good gossip or rumors . . . we sang on the bus. I'm sure kids, everywhere, sang cute little ditties to break up the monotony of a school bus ride, but not like ours; ours were special.

> "If your name is Davey, join the Yiddish navy
> Fight, fight, fight for Kosher Ham.
> No more dirty dishes, just gefilte fishes
> Fight, fight fight for Kosher Ham"

The older kids, who were making plans to go to college, sang a few fraternity songs:

> "Oye, oye, oye . . . Zeta Beta Toi
> What have they done vit' my little boy?
> Take him to college and teach him to write
> Now he goes vit' shiksahs on Yom Kippur night."

ZD, the buxom girl who made the great chocolate chip cookies in Home Ec., was also on my bus, and I often sat next to her on the ride home. We talked a lot; she had a great sense of humor and a terrific laugh. It was a contagious laugh, and she always made jokes about her huge boobs, which she referred to as "gazongas." When Rosie hit big bumps her "gazongas" jiggled like jello. A two-mile stretch along the bus route was being repaired; the road was full of pot holes. When we bounced over that section of the trip all eyes focused on ZD. I felt uncomfortable sitting next to her; the older boys gawked and made stupid jokes.

◆

One Friday afternoon near the end of the school year I was sitting next to Flo Loerber on the school bus. Normally, I avoided Flo; everyone avoided her. She was a sarcastic eleventh grade girl with a foul mouth . . . and she was the only girl I knew who had two holes pierced in each ear. She liked to be different.

"You're really a dumb ass," said Flo. She spoke loud enough for half the bus to hear. "Aren't you the 'shmuck' who got caught using ink eradicator in the Registrars office?"

I didn't know how to cope with this offensive girl. I responded in a very quiet voice, barely loud enough to be heard by Flo. "Well, if it wasn't for the Registrar, it would have worked."

"That's what you think." Flo continued shouting. "Boy, you're stupid!" She was actually an attractive girl, if you took the time to look. But, because she was such an offensive person no one ever bothered to look.

"Your shop teacher is shtupping' the sweet little Registrar; that's why you got your balls busted." Flo was a "know-it-all" who lived a few blocks from me; she was the only girl I ever knew who I wanted to punch in the nose. And, I never was a violent person, certainly not with girls. Maybe it was the way she talked—her annoying nasal inflection. Maybe it was the demeaning way she glared and shook her head when you were speaking, to let the world know that she didn't agree with one word you were saying. She talked down to everybody.

"The Registrar!" I exclaimed. "She's so hung up on rules. I can't believe it!"

"Believe it, its true!"

"Impossible!" I repeated my disbelief.

"Well, smart ass, my phone is on a party-line with Eloise Cordess. The cutesy Registrar lives here in Surfside . . . and I can tell you stories all about her 'itchy pussy.'"

"I thought party-lines don't exist anymore."

"Well, it looks like you thought wrong. If you had half a brain you'd be dangerous." Flo lifted her glasses and scrunched her nose; the ultimate put-down. It was her way of telling me that my intelligence ranked somewhere near the level of pigs. "I can't believe you're such a 'shmendrik' to use a bottle of ink eradicator on a hallway pass, right in the Registrars office, right on her desk. And, if you think I'm bullshitting about Mr. Calhoun come to my house tonight at eleven; that's when the lovers always talk."

"O.K, I'll be there; I gotta' hear this myself." The truth is, I wasn't really interested in finding out lurid details about Mr. Calhoun and the Registrar. If they were having an affair that was their business. I wanted to know more about Flo. I was intrigued by her caustic personality. Why was she such a bitter person? And . . . . for some dumb reason, I was attracted to her.

"Now listen . . . dickhead! Pay attention to these details, unless they're too complicated for your little pea-brain. The front door of my house will be locked; everyone will be sleeping at eleven. Don't ring the doorbell. You gotta' climb the wall on the north side of the house to a second story balcony. My bedroom has a door to the balcony; I'll be waiting."

It was a Friday night; I was allowed to stay out late on weekends, but I had to come up with some excuse for my parents, especially if I wanted to be out after midnight. I told them I was going with a few friends to a Frankenstein movie on Lincoln Road; I wouldn't be home until well after midnight.

Flo lived in an older home, built from large coral rocks. That was a popular style of construction in Miami Beach and Surfside in the 1930's. It was easy to climb to the balcony. She was seventeen, two years older than me and half a head taller, and she had the body of woman! She stood there in the open doorway wearing a sheer nightgown with no bra, like a model from a lingerie catalog. She saw me staring and quickly opened the upper half of the nightgown, exposing full white breasts.

"Here! Get a good look, pervert, but no touching." Flo snapped at me. She shook her body and taunted me by wiggling her breasts. An instant later she covered up. "That's enough! You've had your thrill, and don't even think about telling anyone on the bus."

Flo whispered instructions; she showed me how to quietly listen to the party-line telephone conversation between Mr. Calhoun and Eloise, the Registrar. The lovers both had strong southern accents and mumbled a lot; it wasn't easy to understand what they were saying. It sounded like they were making plans for a trip to Key West, on a weekend when Mr. Calhoun's wife would be out of town.

"I'm counting the days till I see you again," said Eloise. Her voice was very sad. "Homer, my darling. Its so lonely without you . . . . and I have such an 'itchy pussy.'"

"Sugar, you're the only thing that keeps me going," said Mr. Calhoun. "I can't go on living with this witch anymore."

". . . and take good care of Jeremiah." Eloise had a nervous laugh.

I put my hand over the telephone and whispered to Flo. "Who's Jeremiah—his Dog?"

"No, you asshole! That's his 'shlong.'"

"That's nice!" I smiled. "a biblical name."

I soon learned that Jeremiah wasn't circumcised.

"Only Jews and stinkin' Arabs get snipped," said Mr. Calhoun. "I've seen Schecter pissing in the mens room. No way I'd have my cock chopped off like that."

Eloise laughed, the first time I ever heard her laugh. "So you stare at Mr. Schecter's dick in the mens room?"

After awhile the conversation got boring; lots of grunting, groaning, sighing and heavy breathing . . . . all with a southern accent. We then stopped listening to the lovers and went out on the balcony. Flo put on a robe and we sat on rocking chairs and talked. She told me that she lived with her mother and grandmother. Her father was killed in World War II; he died at the Normandy invasion, June 6, 1944. His landing barge was hit by a German mortar shell.

"He never made it to the beach. Daddy was blown to shreds; the pieces were buried in the American cemetery at Normandy. I was seven when he died. I should remember more about him, but I don't. My only memories come from pictures." Flo stared in space, searching for lost memories. "Hey! Today is June 4th. Sunday is the tenth anniversary of D-Day. I call it death day."

"If you were seven, you should remember something about him" I said. "I remember many things when I was seven."

"Well, I was only five when he left home; when he went off to war. The only thing I remember about him is really stupid. He used to pull down coconuts for me, from a tree right here in our backyard. He opened them with his bare hands, but I don't remember how he did it. When he brought me the coconuts he scratched under his arms and made funny monkey noises."

"Really!" I exclaimed. "I used to open coconuts by hand the first summer I moved to Surfside. You get a certain sense of satisfaction; its just you versus nature."

"Jesus Christ! He said that too! I asked him why he didn't use a hatchet, and he said he got a 'sense of satisfaction' doing it with his bare hands. Damn! He used the same exact words you did. This is spooky; I totally forgot about that . . . a 'sense of satisfaction.'"

"Flo, get dressed and come downstairs," I said. "I want to show you something."

"I can't go out at midnight."

"Do you know how to climb down from the balcony?"

"Yeah, of course!"

We descended the coral rock wall and went to the back yard. I asked to see the palm tree where her dad used to pull down coconuts. It was a strange looking tree. In the decade since he died it had grown without direction, in a somewhat twisted diagonal shape. I climbed to the top and picked two big coconuts. I shook them first, to make sure they were ripe. If you hear lots of milk sloshing on the inside you know they're good. I handed Flo the coconuts. Then I scratched under my arms and did a subdued monkey call. I didn't want to wake her mother or grandmother.

"You're nuts! It's after midnight." Flo smiled. She was very pretty in the moonlight; I never saw her smile before.

We took our coconuts and walked to a quiet street corner, two blocks from her house. When you don't use tools you need a hard pavement to crack open the coconut. I prefer sidewalks instead of streets; concrete is harder than asphalt. You stand and grab the coconut in two hands, the same way that the center on a football team holds the ball just before he snaps it to the quarterback. Then you throw the coconut straight down, making sure only the point smashes against the ground. Accuracy is more important than strength. It might take a few throws before the husk splits open.

After three shots at the pavement the outer shell of my coconut split and I displayed my accomplishment. "There you go! Lets see you do the same thing."

Flo grimaced and let out a menacing grunt as she smashed her coconut down to the ground. She surprised me; it only took one throw. We then sat next to each other on the sidewalk, under the light of a street lamp. We didn't say a word; we were busy ripping away at our coconuts, separating the messy husk from the nut.

"Is this the way your dad did it?"

Flo put her arms around me; she began to cry. She stayed there holding me for a long time. Finally, she dried her tears on my shirt.

"That's the first time I ever cried for him. When daddy died I was angry; its hard to cry for someone if you hate them. He left me and mom."

We then shattered one of the nuts on the sidewalk, letting the milk go to waste. Neither of us liked coconut milk. I had a Boy Scout knife attached to my keys so we cut off white chunks of coconut and "dined" together at our sidewalk café. Flo talked about her father; she had never talked about him before. His middle name was Samuel; same as mine, and she talked about her fears and dreams, and why she had such a hostile defensive attitude.

"I get lost in wishing," said Flo, "I wish that my dad didn't go away to war, that I could be with him again, or that my mom would get married again and be home with me, and I wish that boys would like me."

"Let me tell you a story," I said, "I heard it from my father, when I was little, its about this boy named Billy, who met a magic geni on the beach. Billy was granted one wish, and he thought and thought and finally said, 'I wish to have three wishes.'"

Flo laughed, "that was very clever."

"Was it?" I asked. "Once Billy got the three wishes he used each of those wishes to wish for three more. Now he had nine wishes, and then he used each of those wishes to wish for three more."

"That's twenty-seven," said Flo, "Whats the moral of the story?"

"Wait," I replied, "it gets more interesting. Billy spent his whole life accumulating wishes; he never went out, he never took chances; he just horded wishes and saved them in a box. When he died his relatives opened the rusty old box, which was hidden high on a closet shelf; they found one million unused wishes."

"I get it," said Flo, "you're saying that I should take chances, that its better to have a few setbacks in life, rather than hiding in a shell and waiting for happiness to find me."

It was now 2:00 AM; I had to get home. Flo kissed me on the forehead and thanked me for teaching her how to open coconuts. She climbed the coral wall back to her balcony and waved goodbye.

"Myron, I'm sorry for pulling down my nightgown; I was a bitch."

◆

Monday afternoon, on the ride home from school, I sat next to Flo. We didn't talk about coconuts or the Normandy landing, we just screamed and shouted to be heard above the noise. Two more days and the school year would be over. It was louder than usual that afternoon. However, it was always loud on the afternoon ride of our school bus; laughing, screaming, and singing were allowed on B-56, even limited profanity was O.K, with the exception of the "F" word. Rosie gave us our space, she let us have fun, but she had a few of her own rules, which she rigorously enforced: no food, no drinks, no gum, no spitting, no smoking, no "intentional" farting (indadvertent farting was allowed), no throwing things, no kissing, no making out. And once you picked a seat, that was it. No moving around. Nevertheless, despite these rules, boys sometimes persuaded girls to sit on their laps, particularly during the bumpy part of the afternoon trip. "Faster Rosie; faster, faster. Hit those bumps!" And Rosie always obliged. We loved the bumpy road of youth.

CHAPTER 28

KINGDOM BY THE SEA

On the final day of tenth grade we received report cards. I had one unbelievable surprise and one major disappointment. The huge surprise was Spanish II, where I had an "A". I was shocked: The only sentence I knew after two full years of Spanish was "¿Qué es el burro?" However, a major portion of the grade was based on an exhaustive research project. We were required to compile a report on the history, art, religion, music, literature, topography, climate, and culture of a Spanish speaking country. I chose Mexico and went to the Mexican consulate in downtown Miami. I picked up over 100 different tourist information booklets, and spent several weekends working on a huge cut and paste project, which I mounted on multi-colored paper with sectional dividers. When it was completed, my report was over two hundred pages; most other kids turned in ten page reports. In addition, my report was bound in a wooden album that Shelly constructed for me in Shop. I would have made it myself but I wasn't permitted to touch any of the power tools. The album was made of laminated walnut and pine, with an inlaid model of the Mexican national emblem, an eagle perched on a cactus plant, holding a serpent in its talons. It was battery operated; if you pushed a button the eagle raised the serpent in the air. Mr. Jacobson, the Spanish teacher was speechless; he had never seen a report like that before, and despite my mediocre grades on exams, he gave me an "A" for the year. He even entered my Mexican report in an academic fair

210

in Miami. I received a ribbon, second place behind a jar of pig fetuses in formaldehyde.

I was extremely happy with my grade in Spanish II, but I was in a major depression about my grade in English. I only received a "B." That upset me very much; English was my favorite class, even more than History. I tried to be creative, using material from my journal to write imaginative short stories. Mr. Tyler, the young teacher, read some of my stories in front of class and used them to discuss the concept of allegories and metaphors. However, even though he praised these stories he always scribbled critical red comments on the bottom of the paper; he took off points for dangling modifiers, misuse of the semi-colon and apostrophe, and run-on sentences. But, unlike my ninth grade English teacher, he didn't criticize me for beginning sentences with "and" or "but."

One day he began class by reading my story about Isabela Cardozo, the vivacious Cuban Jewish girl who encouraged us to sing after we lost the football game to Miami Edison.

"What's more important, our own perception of the world, or reality as seen by others?" Mr. Tyler walked around the room, attempting to stimulate class discussion.

"Reality is truth," said Linda Spiegel. "You can't go around life making decisions based on personal feelings." Mr. Tyler stood behind Linda, rubbing her neck and shoulders while she was talking.

"I, I think . . . um, uh." Linda stammered. She appeared to be uncomfortable, receiving a massage from Mr. Tyler in front of 35 students. "I think Isabela was just a confused girl, like Don Quixote with those stupid windmills. That was the first time she ever experienced the excitement of a football game, she didn't know what was happening."

"So what?" said Penny Sherman, the popular girl with the long blonde pony tail. "Isabela had fun; everyone else was miserable. I like her perception of reality; it's better than the truth. Isn't that kind of like religion? Religion doesn't have much to do with reality either."

"That's a terrible analogy," said Mr. Tyler. He stopped massaging Linda's neck and walked behind Penny. He began braiding her long blonde hair as he made a few comments about religion. "Penny, religion is based on faith; don't confuse faith with fantasy."

"Why not?" I thought, but I kept my mouth shut. A classroom debate about religion would mean an automatic trip to Dean Kessler and his paddle, or maybe even expulsion. It was my short story so I let the other kids do the talking.

Mr. Tyler liked to stand behind the person he was addressing; he directed his discussion to the back of their head. That was kind of weird. Of course, when talking to a pretty girl he augmented his comments with lots of touching and rubbing.

"I agree with Penny," said Howard Lefkowitz, "Isabela reminds me of my grandmother. She's senile and lives in an old folks home—doesn't even remember her own name. But she's always smiling. She's happier than anyone I know."

I received grades of "A minus" on almost every essay in my English class, even the one about Isabela. Then came the final module: "Julius Caeser," the Shakespeare play. We were all assigned the role of different characters and had to read our lines in class. I was the Soothsayer; I got to say, "Beware the Ides of March" . . . and I said it well, with a creepy crackling voice. But, aside from that one fantastic line it was a crummy part. Howard was lucky, he got to be Marc Antony, and every day at lunch he practiced reading the famous "Friends, Romans, Countrymen" speech.

"I thrice presented him a kingly crown, which he did thrice refuse." Howard garbled the words, trying to sound like Marlon Brando.

"What if Marc Antony offered the crown four times?" asked Shelly. "What comes after thrice?"

"How the fuck should I know?" replied Howard. "I never even heard of thrice before this dumb-ass play."

Shelly should have had that part . . . he was really fascinated with the Roman culture, especially their fashions. "I wonder if they wore underwear under their togas?" asked Shelly.

"Well, certainly not Fruit-of-the-Loom, with elastic waistbands," I laughed. "They probably wrapped an extra sheet down there."

"I don't think so," replied Shelly, "every time they'd pee they'd need to unwrap the sheet . . . unless the sheet had a special hole in the front."

"Hey Shelly," I laughed. "Do you think the 'cool' Romans had little alligators on their togas?"

"Maybe lions; the Romans really had this thing for lions."

I only needed a grade of 85 on the final exam to get an "A" for the year. Unfortunately, my grade was 80; Latin was too much like Spanish; it was impossible for me to distinguish one name from another. I couldn't remember who was the second senator to stab Caeser. I knew Brutus was first, but I got confused with Cicero, Cassius, Casca, Cinna, Cato, Claudius, Calpurnia, and Clitus—they all sounded alike.

"I'd hate to go through life named Clitus," said Penny. "Can you imagine the nicknames you'd get?"

"Yeah! They'd probably call you 'Clit,'" I replied, "But, what about guys named Dick or Peter? And don't you think its kind of weird how Mr. Tyler braids your hair and talks to the back of your head?"

"Weird! You've got to be kidding. That man is so dreamy; he really knows how to charm a girl."

"Well, you don't see any of the female teachers touching the boys."

"Jeez! That would be gross," replied Penny. "Who'd wanna be touched by a flat chested old maid, but Mr. Tyler is such a hunk."

◆

I attempted to arrange a private meeting with Mr. Tyler to discuss my grade, but he left for summer vacation the day after school ended, to a Greek Island where they had nude beaches but no telephones. And he didn't even leave a forwarding address. My mother tried to offer some solace, and reminded me that the "A" in Spanish was really a two-letter increase (I was expecting a "C") while the "B" in English was only a one-letter drop. However, I put so much of myself into my journal and the short stories. The English grade was a serious blow to my creative enthusiasm. Colonel Klein read most of the stories and helped with the imagery, but never with the grammar. He never criticized the run-on sentences or the dangling modifiers. He reminded me that Mark Twain wrote extremely long run-on sentences, and that being creative meant that you had to be different. He encouraged me to keep writing, and not to let the "B" upset my summer vacation.

During the summer of 1954 I didn't watch much TV because the White Sox were not in contention for the pennant. The

Cleveland Indians were fantastic, with the best record in the history of baseball, and the Yankees were in second place. It was nice to see Yankee domination finally come to an end. However, most Beach High kids were from New York, so they were all were cheering for the other New York team, the Giants, who were leading the National League.

I frequently went to the 46th street beach that summer, especially during the first month of the vacation. Since I had a fair complexion I didn't tan; I just turned various shades of pink or red, and got blisters and peeled a lot. I always used gobs of white zinc ointment on my nose, but it didn't help. My neighbor, Mona, who had just graduated from Beach High, also went to the same beach, and she had a car. She drove the Steinberg's and me to a drop off point, one block from the beach; it wouldn't look cool for her to be seen driving with fifteen year old boys in the car. If we couldn't get a ride home with Mona we took the bus, but that was a miserable ride. It was messy and itchy to ride the bus with your body and clothes sticky with sand.

"Myron, carry a book." That was Mona's advice. "It looks cool; impresses the girls."

While at the beach, I never set my blanket anywhere near Mona; her circle of friends was much older than mine. She hung out with a group of college guys who wore sunglasses so they wouldn't be obvious when they stared at her boobs. She liked to get there early and select a central location where she could lay on her back and display her well endowed bosom. I had known Mona for two years; she was a tease. The fine print on top of her bathing suit said "look but don't touch."

Most of the girls wore the same unwritten message . . . but not Zondra DiMara. The message on top of ZD's two-piece bathing suit said, "available for the summer." Her "gazongas" were inviting and tantalizing—and so were her chocolate chip cookies.

"Hi Myron, what are you reading?" ZD bent over my blanket and her "gazongas" blocked the sun.

"'Self-Reliance' by Emerson," I responded. It was a small paperback, easy to curl into the pocket of a bathing suit, and whenever possible, I said: "to be great is to be misunderstood" or "a foolish consistency is the hobgoblin of little minds." Those were great opening lines. Other boys were carrying "The Old Man and the Sea," which was also the right size for a bathing suit pocket. "Old Man" was the first book I ever read in one sitting;

I loved it and read it twice. But that was a special book, I didn't want to carry it to the beach and get the pages wet or sandy. I also memorized a few poems by Poe and the Preamble to the Constitution, but I never had occasion to use the Preamble. "We the people," just wasn't a good opening line to break-the-ice with a new girl . . . but Poe was magic.

I asked ZD to sit on my blanket, to listen to my passionate rendition of "Annabel Lee." That was one of my favorite poems. She leaned forward, in an effort to intercept every word. Tears swelled in her eyes and her "gazongas" expanded when I paused and whispered: "She was a child and I was a child, in this kingdom by the sea."

After listening to "Annabel Lee" ZD invited me to her house; she wanted to hear more poetry. She also wanted to learn all about transcendentalism. The invitation was even more enticing when she told me that her parents were out of town for the weekend and she had the keys to their car. I thought about the temptation of her "gazongas." Once again, I would be seeing a girl for the wrong reason.

Later that night, when I got to her house, I suggested that we just stay home; I would help her bake chocolate chip cookies. But, she thought it would be fun to go cruising around town in her parent's car . . . . even though she didn't have a drivers license. She drove up and down Collins Avenue and Lincoln Road, and then to an isolated farm in North Miami where she parked behind a barn.

"You sit in the drivers seat," said ZD. "I can't make out from the left side. Do you know any other poems by Poe?"

"I know 'The Bells.'" I responded. "I learned it last year in Miss Carter' class." ZD was enchanted by the Runic rhyme. "Tintinnabulation" can be a very erotic word, if used properly . . . and at the right time. After the melodic moaning and groaning of the bells we kissed and swirled tongues and probed the deepest part of each other's throat. I was captivated by her huge breasts, but the lower half of her body was off limits; it was defended by an impenetrable latex undergarment that extended from the waist to the thighs. Different girls had different rules. With Maxine you couldn't touch the upper half; with ZD, you couldn't touch below the waist. When she was aroused her nipples protruded. I was fascinated; I never knew that girls had nipple erections. I pressed down on them and they retreated—like little turtles returning to the safety of their shells. I was reminded of Leah Sonnino and her concave bra. And as I continued with my examination of the inverted nipples my mind drifted to the other side of Biscayne Bay; I wondered if Leah had her baby. She was only 15, much too young to be a mother, I wanted to be with her . . . to help her.

Then, I was startled and snapped out of my trance as ZD started making loud animal noises. She abandoned me for her "real lover"—George. ZD was Maxine's best friend, so she knew all about George even before they met. She leaned over and began whispering to him in a soft sensual voice, asking what pleasures he would enjoy. George gave her a long list.

My eyes were closed and I was in ecstasy as she began to wiggle her tongue in my right ear and gently caress George. Then, all of a sudden . . . . I had the weirdest feeling, like both of my ears were being licked simultaneously. It was a three dimensional sensation. This is what Poe must have meant when he wrote about the jingling and the tinkling—and in the "balmy air of night" I was captured by the "gush of euphony" voluminously welling, swelling, and dwelling—and the throbbing of the bells, bells, bells. Then I heard a dull, droning sound . . . . "Moooooooooooo." My head was spinning. Total bliss! ZD screamed! I opened my eyes and on my left side a cow had strayed from the barn; through the open window it was twisting its huge tongue in my left ear.

♦

The next evening ZD and I were lying on her living room floor; her parents were still out of town. It was a depressing evening; a swirling wind was rattling the glass louvers on the jalousie windows. I was reading "The Raven" in a ghostlike voice, while struggling to open hooks on the back side of her oversized bra; I had not yet mastered the art of one-hand bra removal. Then, on this "midnight dreary" she grabbed my hand and said: "Take thy hand from off my bra, and take thy form from off my floor! Quoth the Raven, Nevermore."

ZD ended our brief relationship; she said she liked me, but only as a "friend." That was the polite way for a girl to dump a boy.

"A friend?" I responded. "You sure seemed like more than a 'friend' behind the barn."

"Yeah, and until I started playing with George you sure seemed like you were a million miles away."

I met a few more girls that summer in my "kingdom by the sea" and I continued with my performances of Poe, but never again with the same success.

CHAPTER 29

MYRONS, MYRONS, AND MYRONS

"What's in a name?" It was Shakespeare who penned that immortal question. "That which we call a rose by any other name would smell as sweet." That's easy to say if your name is William or Will, or Willie, Bill or Billy, or if you have an impressive nickname like "the Bard." But, unless you've gone through life with a name like Myron you can't really understand what I'm talking about. I've always believed that we set our own course in life; we are masters of our destiny. But, with a name like Myron your opportunities are limited. Did you ever see a leading man in a movie named Myron? Or a baseball player? Or a wrestler? When I was a little child playing outside with my friends my mother would stick her head out the window and scream for me to come home. Her shrill voice stretched my name into a three syllable word.

"My-ur-in . . . My-ur-in . . . hurry home; we're going out to dinner."

How can you be a master of your own destiny when your friends call you "My Urine?"

The Summer of 1954 had taken a few turns for the worse. The Steinbergs left town for a month and my brief relationship with ZD had come to an abrupt end on her living room floor. My father compounded the problem by deciding that it was time to discontinue giving me an allowance.

"Myron, I was working to help support the family when I was nine. You're fifteen now; you're old enough to get a summer job.

Bring me the newspaper; I'm going to teach you how to read the 'Help Wanted' section."

My first job was at the Tropicana motel, a few miles north of Surfside. I worked from 1:00-5:00 PM as a cabana boy around the pool, serving orange juice to the guests and cleaning up at the end of the day. The orange juice part of the job was fun; several of the guests gave generous tips. But, the cleanup work was backbreaking. I had to collect one hundred lounge mats and stack them in an aluminum storage shed. My boss was Dirk, the life guard. He was a very tan man with a blonde crewcut and no hair on his chest or back. His muscular body was covered with tattoos and his only job was to walk around the pool area flexing his muscles and "shmoozing" with the female guests, mainly the older women, and he wore a red bathing suit that was smaller than my jock strap.

"Fanny, it's a good thing I didn't bring my daughter to Florida," said Rachel Rubinowitz, as she reclined on her poolside lounge chair, embroidering "RR" monograms on a set of matching pink towels. "She would go nuts for that gorgeous 'shaigetz.' Will you look at that bathing suit. Oye. It leaves nothing to the imagination, not even his religion."

"Rachel. Can you keep a secret? Of course you can." said Fanny. "Tomorrow morning at nine, when Harvey is still sleeping, I have an appointment with Dirk. He gives massages." Fanny smiled, as she shared her secret with Rachel, but her eyes never looked up from the purple and blue blanket that she was knitting for her granddaughter.

"Fanny . . . find out if he gives a discount for two," said Rachel, as she countinued embroidering the "RR" towels.

At 3:00 PM Dirk piled five lounge mats on my shoulder and aimed me in the direction of the storage shed. After twenty painful trips to the shed I learned the answer to my favorite Spanish query: "¿Qué es el burro?" That night when I rode the bus home from work I was unable to sit in an erect position, my shoulders and back were throbbing, I was in agony.

"Rose, go look in the medicine cabinet," said my father. "See if we still have any Wintergreen Oil."

"No dad, not that! Just a hot shower, but no Wintergreen."

My father extolled the virtues of pain and suffering; he felt that the Tropicana job was an excellent opportunity for me to mature, to learn to appreciate life.

"Wisdom comes from reading," he repeated his prophetic advice, which I heard hundreds of times in my youth. "But, from stacking lounge mats you also get a little wisdom."

The wonderful thing about having two parents is that you can always seek a second opinion. After my father completed his long discourse on the philosophical value of sweat, toil, and hard work my mother sat down with me on the couch. She put a hot towel around my neck and brought me a root beer float with two scoops of vanilla ice cream.

"You poor dear; I didn't raise you to schlep lounge mats. My father, may he rest in peace, would turn over in his grave if he knew that his namesake was schlepping lounge mats for fat 'alter kakkers.'" She had a sympathetic cry in her voice. "Sol, bring us the 'Help Wanted' section."

My next job was at Pix, an inexpensive ladies shoe store on Lincoln Road. The new style for women was a cork platform shoe held in place by clear plastic straps. The shoe was designed to make a woman look taller and to display her bare feet. In 1954 women didn't reveal their legs, and pointed bras often conveyed a bellicose image of the breast. Naked feet and painted toe nails were the seductive form of female sexual exposure.

"Myron, look at this shoe," said Hershel Glickman, the manager of the store. "'Vat do you see? 'Gornisht!' Like a 'shmuck I bought five hundred pairs of this 'chazzerei.' Five hundred pairs!" Mr. Glickman always wore long sleeve shirts and walked around the store with a clip board in his hand. As he spoke to me he analyzed several pages of inventory turnover reports. Unfortunately, his inventory of cork shoes was not turning over.

"But, not to worry. I had a dream! Good ideas; they sometimes come in dreams. I saw Carmen Miranda, the Brazilian Bombshell. Why Carmen Miranda? Good question! Listen closely; I'll tell you."

Without letting go of his clip board, Mr. Glickman put both hands on my shoulders and looked straight in my eyes. Then, he provided the visionary answer for his Carmen Miranda question. "Myron, that beautiful lady 'vas standing there, stark naked, singing 'South American Way.' She 'vas in her birthday suit . . . except for the fruit basket on top of her head. It 'vas a message from above. Fruit! Vimen' love fruit."

My job was to staple tiny plastic bananas, cherries, apples, or strawberries on top of each shoe, to turn "chazzerei" into gold. I sat alone in the back of the store, in a hot, dusty room. I spent six days sweating and stapling. Five hundred pairs of boring platform shoes were being resurrected from the dead.

On the seventh day I began sneezing; my nose started to dribble, my eyes turned red, and I could barely breathe. I left work early. The next morning I called in sick and went to our family doctor.

"The boy is seriously allergic to dust," said Dr. Heimowitz. "He can't continue working in that type of environment."

"See, I told you so," said my mother. "Now, you won't laugh when I keep telling you that cleanliness is godliness."

Two days later I applied to be a bag boy at Food Fair, a large supermarket three blocks from my house. I hated leaving the job at Pix. I really liked Mr. Glickman; he was funny, but under his witty façade I saw a hint of sadness in his eyes.

"I know the manager of Food Fair," said my mother. "Let me talk to him, and that store is so clean, you can eat off the floor."

"Mrs. Lindell, I appreciate the fact that you are an excellent customer," said the Food Fair manager, "but you've got to understand my position. Fifty boys are applying for the job and we only have three openings."

The manager's name was Myron DeLuca. My mother was very persuasive; it didn't take long for her to convince him that Myrons of the world have a special bonding; they are soul brothers. He had a moral obligation to hire me.

I wore a bow tie at work, a little paper hat, and a plastic Food Fair badge with my name and greeting, "Hi, I'm Myron L; its my pleasure to serve you." And I had to call every customer sir or ma'am.

My first assignment was to walk up and down the aisles, returning misplaced items to the proper shelves. It was much more challenging than I anticipated. Where does horseradish go? With mustard, catsup, and other spices? With cheese, sour cream, and chilled dairy items? In the Jewish section with matzos and gefilte fish?

As I pondered this decision I heard my name being called on the public address system: "Myron, please come to cash register four, we need help." I put the bottle of horseradish on a shelf in the produce section, next to the fresh radishes; that seemed like a logical place. I scurried to cash register four; so did two other bag boys. All three of the new bag boys were named Myron.

Myron K was seventy years old, maybe older, a retired man who was working as a bag boy in order to supplement his pension and Social Security. A bag boy's income is mainly from tips, and its all cash.

"You're writing this down in a journal?" exclaimed Myron K. "Well, you better not use my real name, and don't go telling people that I cheat on my taxes. OK! So I don't report everything. What are they going to do, put an old fart like me in jail?"

The third new bagboy was Myron Peterson III. He was nineteen and the third generation Myron in his family. He was tall and muscular, with dark eyes, and his black hair was cut in an exaggerated style of crew cut known as a "flat top." Myron III lived on the other side of the 79th Street Causeway, in a section of Miami known as Little River. After three attempts at the eleventh grade he dropped out of Miami Jackson high school. He had plans to be a career bag boy.

"That's not true," said Myron III. "I'm also gonna' work part-time in the meat department. I'm not always gonna' be a bag boy. Some day I'll be a meat manager."

Later that day I was asked to join Myron III in the meat department, an eerie refrigerated room in the back of the store. I wore a warm Food Fair jacket and maneuvered between rows of hanging cows, all tattooed with blue numbers. I imagined that I was in the laboratory of Dr. Mengele, the Nazi "Angel of Death." He was conducting grotesque experiments on the frozen carcasses.

I was searching for Myron III, but I couldn't find him. From the far corner of this chamber of horrors I heard a faint groaning sound. Then I saw him, sitting behind a frigid cadaver. Myron III was squatting on a little stool; he was masturbating. I was stunned; I didn't know how to react. I just stood there, frozen . . . like the slabs of chilled beef that were hanging from the ceiling.

"Big deal, so you know I beat my meat." Said Myron III. "I'm sure you do too."

I refused to respond to his comment. Whether I did or not, it was none of his business. "So, what kind of work are we supposed to be doing?"

"Well, if 'you' wack off . . . you're gonna go to fuckin' hell, but not me." Said Myron III. He smirked and chuckled.

"Why not; do you have a special deal with God?"

"You're 'fuckin A' I do; Jesus died for my sins, not for yours." Myron III rose from his stool and zipped his fly.

"Are you telling me that Christians can beat off and Jews cant?" I asked.

"Well, we ain't supposed to either, but I go to this church in South Beach and confess to Father Timothy. I say a few Hail Mary's and put seven dollars in the poor box and all is forgiven."

"You must be kidding! Are you really going to tell your priest that you beat off in the meat department at Food Fair?"

"Beating off is a sin," said Myron III, "but doing it at Food Fair don't make it worse. Father Timothy don't need all the fuckin' details."

"But seven dollars each time you beat off, thats really expensive," I said. "Couldn't you get a better deal?"

"It ain't seven dollars each time," replied Myron III, "if I beat off every day, that's only one buck each time. You really suck in math."

"Actually, I'm very good in math." I replied, "Why don't you go to church every other week, that would cut the cost down to fifty cents each time."

"Every other week! Are you crazy?" replied Myron III, "do you think I want to roast in Hell?"

I was serious about the job at Food Fair; I worked hard and saved my money. I was hoping to buy a car for my sixteenth birthday, which would be in another nine months. Flo Loerber lived a block from Food Fair, so on work days I hung out at her house for lunch. We became friends; I no longer had to enter by climbing the side wall. One morning, on the way to the Surfside beach she stopped by Food Fair just to say hi. It was 7:45 AM—Bag boys came to work fifteen minutes before the store opened. My morning job was to return misplaced items to the shelves. Myron III was responsible for the meat department, to adjust the thermostat on the refrigerator and spread saw dust over the floor. He loved that job, alone in his favorite room until 8:00 AM.

"Hi Myron," said Flo. "Why don't you introduce me to your friend." Her smile was directed to Myron III, who was standing next to me. Flo looked very sexy; she was wearing tiny shorts, teasing us with a hint of her cute white tush.

"Oh . . . he's Myron also." I tried to introduce the two of them, but Myron III had already run off to the meat department. Flo suggested that I bring him to lunch; she thought he was handsome.

Later that day we sat around the kitchen table at Flo's house. She made salami and cheese sandwiches and root beer floats; she knew how much I loved root beer. Myron III said that we were the first Jewish people he ever met and he liked us . . . but he felt sorry that we would be going to hell when we died. It was the fate of all Jewish people, even nice ones like us.

"How do you know that Jews all go to hell?" said Flo. "Last time I checked, there were no reports from the dead."

"Shit! That's the damn reason why they got separate cemeteries for Jews and Christians" responded Myron III. "That's how Saint Peter knows which souls go up and which go down, but it ain't the body that goes anywhere; only the soul."

"What if someone lies?" said Flo. "What if a Jew bribes a cemetery guard and gets buried in a Christian cemetery?"

"Yeah, I guess that would be confusing," said Myron III, "but Saint Peter got assistants; they check for things like that."

"So, I don't get it," said Flo. "Is Jesus the son of God or is he God?"

"He's both," said Myron III, "that's why he's called the father and the son."

"So, who was Joseph?" I asked.

"He was Mary's husband but not Jesus' father. Mary and Joseph didn't screw. They didn't even sleep in the same fuckin' bed; kind of like Lucy and Ricky."

After a brief discussion of cemeteries, religion, and the next life, Myron III shifted the conversation to his favorite topic . . . . "meat." He then gave a lengthy discourse on the grading system for beef, including the granularity of fat.

"Fat is what gives the meat flavor," said Myron III. "Its also what makes some dicks thicker than others."

"I heard that's heriditary," said Flo. "If your dad has a little one so will you, and there's not a damn thing you can do about it."

"No, that ain't true," said Myron III. "In Africa the tribes do a special dick stretching exercise on baby boys."

"Why in Africa?" Flo asked. "I thought colored guys are huge."

"Well yeah, of course they are," responded Myron III, "but that's because the jungle bunnies do dick stretching; they do it when they're babies. What they do is tie a heavy rock or stone to a piece of string—then hang it from the little dick—then the tribe bangs on drums and does lots of dancing round' a fire."

"Ouch! That must hurt," I replied.

"Shit yeah," said Myron III. "But don't ask me, I never needed no stretching. Hey! I ain't bullshitting. The African tribes' been doing dick stretching for billions of years."

"But size doesn't matter," said Flo. "Why do they go through that pain?"

"Size don't matter? Like hell it don't." responded Myron III. "I mean, like why do broads get their tits enlarged? Cause it matters baby, it matters."

"Well, maybe you're right," said Flo. "But only indirectly. I think if a woman has large boobs she feels sexier and I guess it's the same for guys with big peckers. And, if you feel sexy you act sexy . . . and you become sexy. Its all psychological, but yeah, in that way I guess that size does matter."

Hey Myron," I interrupted. "Sorry to break up this fascinating discussion, but we gotta' get back to work."

Later that evening I called Flo on the phone to see what she thought of "Three" . . . that was his nickname.

"Yeah, he's really a hunk . . . but the guy's a space cadet. The only thing he knows is Jesus and meat."

That was the only time the three of us ever had lunch together. Obviously, Flo and Myron III had nothing in common. I continued having lunch at her house every day for the next several weeks—just the two of us; Myron III ate lunch after I returned to work. Flo and I had interesting conversations, talking about many intellectual topics, like history, music, philosophy, and religion. I told her about Freud's theory, that religion was just an illusion. As might be expected, our discussion of Freud eventually shifted to penis envy and sex. Unfortunately, when we talked about sex I didn't have much to contribute to the conversation since my experience was very limited. However, I did tell Flo about Maxine and ZD, how they both talked to my penis and gave it an affectionate name.

"That's a cute name," said Flo. "You should change your name to George. Myron is a better name for a penis."

225

"You're just jealous," I replied. "Because you don't have a pet name for your vagina."

"Is that so?" Flo responded. "I think Myron III might disagree with you." She paused and chuckled. A wicked grin lit up her face. "And Myron IV is so cute . . . I have better conversations with him than with III."

♦

I hated my name! I complained many times to my parents: "Why Myron?"

"Yes dad, I know . . . you told me a hundred times, I was named after my maternal grandfather, Morris."

"Sunshine, it could have been worse," replied my father. "Mother wanted to name you Morris."

"But, what about Mark, Mitchell, Mathew, Michael? They're great 'M' names. Mickey Mantle and Minnie Minoso even got a double M's. Why Myron?"

"When we got around to picking 'M' names," responded my father, "in the summer of 1938, a man named Myron Taylor was in the news. He was in charge of a U.S. delegation that was trying to save German Jews from Hitler."

"Really? I didn't know that. Well, he sure did a lousy job."

CHAPTER 30

DREAMS, CANASTA, AND OVERTOWN

Bag boys can make good tips if they give customers a few extra paper bags. But you can't be nonchalant when you "sneak" the bags into their car . . . you have to let the customer know that you are risking your job . . . your career. The extra bags are a special favor. I learned that trick on my first day of work. And, if you commiserate with the elderly Jewish customers the tips are even better. You had to listen to the customer, listening was very important . . . and you had to learn to groan and say "Oye, what 'tsores!' I wouldn't wish that on a dog!" Myron K, the elderly bag boy, also taught me a few good jokes with Yiddish punch lines.

"Myron, timing is everything. Listen to an old man . . . and from bagging groceries you can make a few bucks. When you start to put the bags into the customer's car, when you are alone in the parking lot, that's the time to set them up with the joke. Then, pause just before the punch line . . . the pause is everything. Go watch Jack Benny . . . he is the master of the pause. Open the palm of your left hand as you deliver the Yiddish punch line . . . and practice your pronunciation. I'll help you with the Yiddish words."

After one month of saying "ongepatshket" and "mishpocheh" I was able to save $500; my father contributed matching funds and by the middle of August I had $1,000 put aside in a special "auto account" and a few hundred dollars to carry me for the rest of the summer. I quit the job after the Steinbergs returned from their vacation and spent the last two weeks of the summer playing Canasta at Colonel Klein's house. Canasta was a woman's game. Worse yet, it was for old women. So that part of my social life remained somewhat of a secret, just like the bed wetting of my youth. My Canasta experience began one morning as the indirect result of waking up with a severe cramp in my leg. I jumped out of bed and leaned against the wall, stretching my calf to alleviate the excruciating pain. Then I got on my bicycle and started racing around the neighborhood. Fast peddling helped. I decided to ride to the Steinberg's house for breakfast; that was the only place I could go at 6:30 AM. As I passed Colonel Klein's house, just a block away from the Steinberg's, I saw the Colonel standing on the front porch kissing goodbye to a short woman with red hair. I didn't mean to spy on him, but I was there, right in front of his house; we couldn't avoid each other.

"Myron, what are you doing out so early?" said the Colonel. He was obviously nervous and embarrassed. "I'd like to introduce you to my friend, Katarina Wolinski."

Katarina was the assistant librarian from the Miami Beach Library, the Auschwitz survivor. She was the lady who helped me with the Nazi tattoo research when I tried to find out about the background of Mr. Streuling. Almost two years had passed since that day at the library. I hadn't thought much about Mr. Streuling anymore, not since the police issued the restraining order.

"Uh, Hi, Katarina. Its great to see you again," I responded. I was even more embarrassed than the Colonel; it was obvious that Katarina had slept the night at his house. She walked to my bicycle, greeted me with a hug, and told me that she had been promoted to head librarian.

"Oh! You already know each other?" exclaimed the Colonel. "She was . . . uh . . . uh . . . teaching me how to play Canasta. Yeah! Canasta! Great game." He stood there on his front porch, smiling like a little boy who just got caught with his hand in the cookie jar. I sat there in his driveway, on the seat of my bicycle.

"Canasta? That's a woman's game!" I exclaimed. Certainly, Mark Twain could come up with a more creative alibi.

The Colonel laughed. "I know it's a woman's game, so don't go telling all your friends. But, it's a good game. I like it better than Poker or Pinochle, or the so called men's card games. If you can find a partner, come join us this evening; we'll teach you how to play. It takes four to play Canasta." He told me that he had known Katarina for several years. He met her at the Miami Beach Library where he sometimes read his short stories to senior citizen groups.

"You should come by one Saturday," said the Colonel, "they would love to hear you read your story about the Wonder Machine."

"Uh . . . no! Not that one," I responded. "Maybe when I'm fifty."

I said goodbye to the Colonel and Katarina and rode to the Steinberg's for breakfast. I didn't normally go riding around town at 6:30 in the morning, so I called my parents. I didn't want them to worry. I told the Steinberg's about the Colonel and Katarina, but we swore not to tell anyone else. Shelly asked what she was wearing; he really liked Katarina. Later that day I rode my bike to Flo's house, but not until after lunch. Flo liked to be alone with Myron III, her new lunch companion. Her refrigerator was now stocked with beer, ham, white bread, and mayonnaise.

"So what's the secret name for your vagina?" I asked. Flo blushed, but refused to tell me. But I saw doodlings on a crumpled piece of paper lying on her kitchen table. It had the name "Millicent Muff" and "Millie" scribbled many times.

"I heard you saw Myron IV on your first day at work," she laughed. "That must have been embarrassing; I would die if I walked in and saw a guy jerking off."

"Well, it certainly didn't bother him; he has religious immunity. I can't believe you're messing around with that moron; I thought you said you wanted a guy who you could talk to?"

"Well . . . . I talk to Myron IV," replied Flo and she laughed. "Eventually, I'll find a guy 'for the right reasons.'" I was surprised to hear her use that expression. Those were the guiding words that Mona, my advisor, had hammered into my head.

"Guys use girls all the time, just for sex . . . and its OK for them," said Flo. "I don't believe in a double standard."

Flo talked a lot about Myron III and his aspiration to be a meat manager. And she even talked about Myron IV.

"He's . . . how shall I say it?" Flo blushed. "He's . . . . a little different! He isn't circumcised."

"I guess his mamma wanted to make sure that Saint Peter didn't think he was Jewish," I responded.

I was fascinated and started asking all kinds of questions. I had never seen an uncircumcised boy in the Phys. Ed. shower, certainly not one with an erection. "What's it like?" I asked. "Is it much different than a Jewish one? Doesn't the extra skin get in the way?"

"Well, Myron IV is the first dick I ever saw. I mean, not counting pictures in 'National Geographic,' but I do agree . . . when its just hanging its funny looking, looks kind of like a **pink anteater.**"

We both laughed at her description. I told Flo that I was invited by Colonel Klein to join him and Katarina to play Canasta, but I needed a partner. Flo knew the game; her mother and grandmother played frequently. She agreed to join me that evening.

"Myron, if I ever told the kids on the school bus that you play Canasta, you're life would be ruined. By the way, if you like Canasta you gotta' try Mah Jongg."

"You won't tell . . . or I'll tell all about the anteater."

We walked to the Colonel's house at 7 PM; he lived two blocks from Flo. His two boys were away at camp; that's why he was able to have Katarina sleep over. It was a small white stucco house, built in the 1940's, with a red barrel tile roof and glass block windows in the bathroom. All the walls in the living room and dining room were covered with memorabilia from around the world; the Colonel loved to travel. I was fascinated by a replica of the Rosetta Stone, which was standing in the corner of his living room. The Colonel had recently been to London and brought back this souvenir from the British Museum; it was his prized possession.

"Hi Myron," said Katarina "and she greeted me with a hug. Who's your lovely girlfriend?"

"Flo Loerber," I responded. "But we're just friends. Her boyfriend's name is also Myron . . . actually, he's the third generation Myron in his family; his name is Myron III."

"Don't go telling people he's my boyfriend," said Flo. "He just hangs out at my house for lunch."

"And I bet you love the way he hangs." I mumbled under my breath.

"The Rosetta Stone is the key that unlocked the mystery of translating Hieroglyphics," said Colonel Klein. "Here, look closely, the text on this replica appears in the form of Hieroglyphics, the religious language of ancient Egypt. It also appears in Demotic, the everyday Egyptian script of the late 1700's, and Greek." As I examined the stone Flo and Katarina went out the back door of the house, into the backyard.

"What does it say?" I asked.

"The stone dates back to approximately 200 BC; it contains a decree praising King Ptolemy V. The identical inscription is written three times, in the three languages. It isn't so important what the stone says, but its from the writing on this stone that we can now understand every detail of ancient Egypt, how they behaved and how they thought. From this translation Egyptologists eventually managed to read most everything that remains of the ancient writings."

"That's fascinating! I've always had an interest in cryptography . . . I'm good in math, but I stink in foreign languages, so I never pursued my interest." The Colonel then showed me an instruction booklet that came with his Rosetta Stone. It showed step by step procedures for using Greek to decipher Hieroglyphics.

"Hey guys, enough with the Hieroglyphics," said Katarina, as she and Flo came into the living room carrying platters of mangoes and avocados just picked from the Colonel's fruit trees. "Lets play Canasta."

Katarina was the dealer and began explaining the game as she distributed the cards. "This is a team game; the object is to communicate with your partner."

"My mother said that some people cheat," said Flo. "Partners touch feet and communicate under the table . . . they use tapping codes."

"That's true," replied Katarina, "and some use special eye blinking codes. But, is winning everything in life? If you abandon your morality its hard to feel good about yourself."

As we played a practice hand, with all cards face up, Katarina gave detailed instructions. I was confused with the threes, which ones were bonus cards and which ones were used to freeze the deck.

"No, you simpleton . . . you got them backward," said Flo. "The red ones are the bonus cards and the black ones are useless, not much good for anything."

"Do you ever feed him ants?" I whispered.

"Ants! Who?" asked Flo.

"The pink anteater!" Flo kicked me under the table.

At first the game was very confusing, but after we played a few hands, with Flo constantly berating me, the rules began to make sense. Maybe it was beginner's luck, but I was the big winner. I picked the pack and dominated the game; I had a handful of Jacks. Even though Flo was my partner and should have been happy with our team success, she lost interest when I became the center of attention and she was removed from the action.

"Why do they call the prince card a Jack?" Flo asked. "I never heard the word 'Jack' used anywhere except in cards."

"A Jack isn't a prince," said Colonel Klein. "It's a medieval English word used to describe a common man, like a lumber jack or a jack or all trades. Originally, the picture cards were Kings, Queens, and Knaves, but when they started putting abbreviations on the corners of the cards, it was confusing to use 'K' for King and 'Kn' for Knave . . . it was easier to use 'J' for Jack."

"So Flo, tell me about your boyfriend, Myron III," said Katarina, as she began to spread her cards on the table.

"He's not really a boyfriend; I just see him once in a while. I'm not going to get involved with a career bag boy."

"Flo, you better be careful," said Katarina. "You're much too young to get pregnant. I hope Myron III uses protection."

Flo sat there, with her mouth half open, much too embarrassed to respond to Katarina's comment. She gagged on a slice of avocado. "No, not really. But, we're very careful. He . . . uh . . . . pulls out . . . before he . . . uh . . . you know."

"Listen, we're not moralizing to either of you," said Katarina. "We just don't want to see you get in trouble or get V.D. Boys all hate to use prophylactics, but until you get married you should always carry them. That goes for both of you."

"Myron III said that white guys don't need rubbers," said Flo. "He said that only jungle bunnies can give you the clap." I froze in my seat! Obviously, Flo didn't know about Jessie, the Colonel's Negro foster child.

"Flo!" The Colonel raised his voice. "That's a terrible hate word. I'm very disappointed with you . . . talking that way."

"What's so bad about 'jungle bunny?' I didn't say nigger."

"Would you like it if people called you kike or dirty Jew?" asked the Colonel.

"Of course not, but I didn't say nigger. For God sake . . . I only said jungle bunny; lots of kids say spear chucker or coon or spade. I don't see what's so terrible, and my bubby and all her friends always say shvartzah."

The Canasta game came to an abrupt end. The Colonel clenched his teeth and said nothing . . . but his eyes said everything. He was irate! The ensuing silence was extremely uncomfortable. Finally, after he regained his composure he suggested that we might want to take a trip with him to visit a Negro relative of his foster child. He said that it would be a very enlightening experience, that neither of us had any real insight as to the living conditions of the Negroes in Miami.

◆

Early that Sunday morning the Colonel, Katarina, Flo and I crossed over the causeway to Miami and drove through an overcrowded Negro neighborhood known as Overtown—but the more popular name was "Colored Town." Some of the bigots often called it "Nigger Town," but you rarely heard anyone from Beach High use that horrible term. Men were drinking beer, sitting on stairways in front of decrepit wooden shacks; most of the homes had tar paper roofs and broken or boarded windows. Children were running on the street without shoes, babies were playing on the sidewalk completely naked. Barking dogs were unleashed in packs. There were flies, lots of flies. I couldn't believe this was America and it was only across the bay from my beautiful island. I was five miles from Miami Beach but I felt like I was in India or Africa or on another planet.

We entered a dank, dimly lit wooden house that reeked from the foul odor of urine. We were greeted by a gregarious overweight Negro woman with a warm smile and a gold front tooth. Her name was Annabelle Stevens; she worked as a maid for a Jewish family in Miami Beach and she was the aunt of Colonel Klein's children, even the oriental boy.

"I hear the Colonel been teaching you'se chilin' how to play Canasta," said Annabelle. "Mighty fine game. Me and my lady friends, we play it all the time here in 'colored town,' just like the white folks do." She squeezed two glasses of orange juice, one for me and one for Flo, and I noticed that she used California oranges, not Florida oranges. That was the first time I had California oranges in the three years since I moved from Chicago.

233

"I just learned the game," I responded, "but my mother and my aunt have been playing for years. They play several times a week." I asked for another glass of orange juice; it was delicious.

"I learned it from the white folks where I work. The Jewish lady, she be playing it a lot. She play every day. I hear too, that you is the one who baby sits my nephews." I was confused; how could Annabelle also be the aunt of the Colonel's oriental foster child?

"They're both your nephews?" I asked.

"Well, my little sister, Flora Mae, she got herself too many boyfriends . . . some of them be colored, some be white, some be Chinamen. Don't know where Flora Mae be today . . . who she be shacking up with . . . . she done picked up and left several years ago. Don't even get no post cards no more. She was a bad seed, even when she be a little girl. My mamma always said she got the devil in her."

"So, how did you get to meet the Colonel?" I asked. I was curious about the connection between Colonel Klein and Annabelle. How did he come to be the foster parent of the two boys? Annabelle looked at the Colonel to see if it was OK to give me the details. He nodded his head, giving approval.

"Flora Mae, she be a pretty woman and she liked messing round' with older men . . . and the Colonel . . . . Well . . . he be one of her boyfriends. So, when she done left home, Jessie and Jackie come live here with me . . . ain't no telling who their daddy be, happened long before the Colonel. But, you see what kind of house I got, and I work all day for the Jewish lady on the Beach. Ain't got no time to take good care of them. Plus, I got four of my own little ones to feed; don't know where their daddy be. The Colonel, he be a saint. He give a fine home for little Jessie and Jackie, a fine home."

Annabelle opened her wallet and showed us her Police Identification card, her authorization to be in Miami Beach after 6 PM. I was disgusted by that law; it was repugnant for a Jewish island to retain such an antiquated racial policy. I understood the origin of the law; it came about in the early days of Miami Beach, the Carl Fisher era, when it was an exclusive resort for white gentiles. But, why wasn't the law eliminated now that Miami Beach was predominantly Jewish?

"No . . . you got it wrong," said Flo. "The Miami Beach law isn't just for Negroes. Everybody has to have a permit in order to work in the city, regardless of race. I saw an article in the 'Miami Beach Sun.' It's just a police work permit; it is not a racial law."

"Listen chillin' . . . there be one truth . . . and there be the other truth," said Annabelle. "Do you understand what I say? The law, it apply to white people too. But, the police, they only be stoppin' the colored folks on the Beach to look at the I.D.; they never be stoppin' whites . . . not unless they'se trouble makers."

"That's called 'selective enforcement,'" said the Colonel. "And if you read the precise wording of the law you'll see the that the Miami Beach police identification requirement is carefully geared to those types of jobs where Negroes commonly work. I'm talking about baggage handlers, chauffeurs, maids, boot blacks, etc."

Annabelle nodded her head in approval and poured another glass of orange juice for me; she saw how much I loved her freshly squeezed juice, but her warm smile was replaced by a haunting far away look.

"I had this dream," she said. Then she looked down at her feet; I couldn't see her eyes. "It was a crazy dream . . . . made no sense at all. I was a rich white lady, sitting in my backyard by my fancy swimming pool in Miami Beach, my finger nails polished real pretty and I be smelling like a bunch of fresh petunias . . . I was fixin' me some ice cold lemonade and playing Canasta with my lady friends. In my dream I didn't know that I was a colored lady just dreaming. I was only a white lady playing cards. Then suddenly I woke up and found myself lying here in bed, a colored person once again, but I wasn't sure if I was awake or still dreaming. Then I thought to myself . . . 'am I really a poor colored lady who dreamt about being white, or am I a rich white lady dreaming about being colored?'"

"I don't get it," said Flo. "You are who you are . . . I don't understand your dream."

The Colonel interrupted Flo: "Don't you see, Annabelle's dream is like the Miami Beach Police ID card . . . like she said, 'there be one truth and there be the other truth.' Annabelle sees the reality of life in Overtown every day of her life and she also sees life in Miami Beach . . . she sees two realities. You and Myron only see one reality . . . I brought you here today to show you the other reality, how different life is on the other side of the bay."

The Colonel then reached in his wallet and gave Annabelle a few $20 bills. We all said goodbye; it was time to return to our island. Annabelle gave me a bag of California oranges and a few large peanut butter cookies to Flo. She told us to come visit her again. I never realized that the Negro section of Miami was so run-down. My father was right, it was definitely the obligation of my generation to stop bigotry in America.

During the last two weeks of summer vacation it rained almost every day; it wasn't beach weather, so I played a lot of Canasta at the Colonel's house, or just fooled around trying to decipher the Hieroglyphics on his Rosetta Stone. Katarina was usually there in the evenings; Flo was always smiling, enjoying her summer with Myron IV although she really didn't care much for Myron III. I never went back to Annabelle's house again and I felt guilty. But I often thought about her and her dream. I then started having similar dreams . . . kind of makes you think. Just what is real? Maybe my whole life is a dream. I wonder where she was able to get California oranges; maybe they were just an illusion; my illusion.

CHAPTER 31

NEWS FROM THE OUTSIDE WORLD:
1953-1954

I was now allowed to take buses to Miami, Coral Gables, and other nearby cities. My world had expanded, but it was still limited by the bus routes of the Dade County Transit Authority. Here are a few significant world events that either impacted on me directly, or were topics that we talked about at dinner.

- Chevrolet begins production of the Corvette—for the first time in my life I fall in love with a car. I have a new goal in life—someday I will own a 'Vette.
- Edmund Hilary and Tenzing Norgay become the first humans to reach the summit of Mount Everest. My mother was reminded of the time when she went to the top of Pikes Peak. "Such a dangerous trip! We risked our lives to drive to the top of the mountain and what for? We went to this little restaurant and the coffee tasted like mud!"
- Sugar Smacks completes with Frosted Flakes; increases sugar content to 56 percent. "Myron, if you eat that 'chazzerei' your teeth will rot," said my mother.
- Tito becomes president of Yugoslavia—"Look at that," said my father, "this guy's got 'chutzpeh' he's backtalking to the Kremlin."

- Joseph Stalin dies at the age of 73. Classes are interrupted at Beach High; his death is announced on the P.A. system—big time applause in every classroom.
- The first 3-D movie is shown: "Bwana Devil" Every kid steals a pair of cardboard Polaroid glasses; we look cool standing in front of Liggets Drug Store on Saturday mornings with our matching 3-D glasses.
- Con-Tact paper is invented—every drawer in my house is immediately lined.
- Jacqueline Bouvier married John F. Kennedy, the son of Joseph Kennedy. "The old man was a 'ganef,'" said my father.
- U.S. district Judge Grim rules that NFL can black out TV home games.—this ruling would have severe future impact on my life . . . but not in 1953.
- Supreme Court rules Major League baseball exempt from anti-trust laws (7-2 decision) as it is a sport not a business. I was hoping for a different decision—hoping that they would break up the Yankees.
- Dow Chemical creates Saran Wrap. This was a horrible invention . . . especially when combined with Tupperware (which was already in wide use) My mother stops throwing leftover vegetables into the garbage.
- To counteract the threat of television, Hollywood thinks big and develops wide-screen processes such as CinemaScope, first seen in the Robe, starring Richard Burton. "Such a handsome man! Is he Jewish?" asks my aunt Pearlie.
- Cheez Whiz is introduced by Kraft. This stuff is great to squirt on Ritz Crackers . . . for quick after-school snacks.
- Ethel and Julius Rosenberg, who were convicted in 1951 of selling American atomic secrets to the Soviet Union, are executed. "Just because their name is Rosenberg doesn't mean they're Jewish," said my mother.

ELEVENTH GRADE

CHAPTER 32

THE GRAND MARCH

"Good morning boys and girls, my name is Ina Madison, like the president who drafted the U.S. Constitution. I will be your home room teacher throughout the eleventh grade." She was a petite, soft spoken woman, probably in her early forties. At last, a teacher who was shorter than me! I was now 5'6" but still one of the shortest boys in my home room.

Miss Madison had a warm smile and short wavy blonde hair, highlighted with a few grey streaks. I always thought she looked like "Miss Liberty," the face on the old style dimes that were in circulation before President Roosevelt died. Her blue eyes were circled by tiny wrinkles. Crows feet radiated from the corners; they were truthful eyes. She was dressed in the standard attire for female teachers, a loose fitting black pleated skirt and a transparent white blouse that offered a view of her full length lace slip and a perfectly flat chest. Her skirt hung long and straight, not like the Beach High girls who inflated their skirts with heavily starched crinolines. Some of the more fashionable girls wore two crinolines at the same time. It was with great difficulty that they shoved their multi-layered petticoats under the tiny school desks.

"I'm also an English teacher," said Miss Madison, "so I will be working with you in English literature. My passion is Shakespeare, Keats, Shelly, Dickens . . . and creative writing. My goal this year is to share my enthusiasm with you." I knew I was going to like her . . . and I really loved her attitude about morning

241

devotionals. She replaced mandatory Bible reading with silent meditation.

"God and religion are personal," said Miss Madison. "I think students should each have the right to pray or not to pray according to their own conscience. So, during this one minute break please be silent, respect those around you, and let your heart and soul guide you as you deem appropriate; you might want to give thanks for something . . . anything."

During my moment of silence I gave special thanks to the 1954 Cleveland Indians for beating the dreaded Yankees for the American League pennant. And I thought about Annabelle, the Negro aunt of the Colonel's foster children, especially about her dream, and I gave thanks for living in Miami Beach. Life sure was horrible on the other side of the bay, even though they could buy California oranges. Then, on that first day of the eleventh grade, the one minute of meditation was interrupted by four bongs of a glockenspiel on the public address system. It was an announcement by our principal, Aaron T Schecter.

I hadn't heard the sound of a glockenspiel in almost a year, not since my sexual initiation with Maxine Schwartz, but I immediately experienced the Pavlovian effect of the four vibrant bongs. I got an erection under the desk. Quickly, I put my books on my lap. The four bongs were to haunt me at many unexpected times during my remaining two years of high school. Whenever Mr. Schecter wanted to interrupt class with an important announcement he used a recording of Maxine playing the glockenspiel . . . a C-Chord followed by the passionate resonance of high C.

"Good morning, this is Mr. Schecter . . . I would like to welcome everyone back to school. Your homeroom teachers will be distributing a mimeograph copy of the Pledge of Allegiance. President Eisenhower has made an important change in the Pledge, so make sure to read it carefully. The phrase, 'one nation, indivisible' has been changed to 'one nation, under God, indivisible.'"

We then stood at attention to recite the revised Pledge. Thankfully, the music of the glockenspiel was not repeated at the conclusion of Mr. Schecter's announcement. We stood with our right hand covering our heart and mumbled the familiar lines . . . "I pledge allegiance to the flag of the United States of America . . ." with special emphasis on the new words . . .

"under God." And the crows feet around the corner of Miss. Madison's eyes seemed to deepen. It was obvious, at least to me, that she wasn't thrilled with the revision. Several months later God also began to appear on newly minted American coins—which were redesigned to include the phrase "In God We Trust"—and many people were suggesting that "God Bless America" should become the new national anthem. Actually, I liked "God Bless America," it was much easier to sing. I never could reach the high notes in the "Star Spangled Banner." I wondered if the religious fundamentalists who were urging Congress to sanctify "God Bless America" knew that the composer, Irving Berlin, was Jewish? However, I don't think that would bother them. They didn't seem upset that Peter and Paul were both Jewish. Even Jesus was Jewish! So was Mary, his virgin mother, and Joseph, his non-biological father. I wonder if God is also Jewish?

I never understood how the foundation of a religion could be built upon a biological absurdity—an immaculate conception. Of course, my religion wasn't much better—Judaism evolved from a geophysical absurdity—the parting of the Red Sea. I had a hard time accepting religious dogma on blind faith. Why did Christianity have such a fear of degrading the image of Jesus by representing him as a man? Moses was never portrayed as a deity, even though he did have several conversations with God. Why do we need religion anyway? Why can't we just be good people . . . and believe that certain truths are "self-evident?"

Jefferson didn't need any reference to God in the "Declaration of Independence." He felt that the unalienable rights of man were "self evident." The defining document of our American democracy, the nation's most cherished symbol of liberty, is not based upon God or religion, it is based upon the "Laws of Nature and of Nature's God." I kind of wondered what Jefferson meant when he talked about "Nature's God"—that seemed like an oxymoron to me. The Declaration intentionally avoids the word, "God." The only inference to a divine authority is indirect and nebulous . . . the "Creator" who endowed us with the unalienable rights. But, our founding fathers clearly left it to our own judgment to define this elusive concept. I didn't need to think too hard; my creators were Sol and Rose Lindell, my parents. I felt badly for Colonel Klein's foster children, they would never know the identity of their father, and they probably would never see their mother again. But, they had the Colonel and they were being raised in Miami Beach, not in Overtown. They were living Annabelle's dream . . . they were being raised as white children. And, some day they would learn how to play Canasta and if they wanted real orange juice they could cross the causeway and visit their aunt.

After the "Pledge of Allegiance" we sang "My Country Tis of Thee"—another dumb ritual that bothered me. It always baffled me why we sang the National Anthem at sporting events, but in school our musical tribute to liberty and freedom was set to the tune of "God Save the Queen," the British National Anthem? As I recall, the "Declaration of Independence" listed at least a dozen reasons why King George III was a tyrant. We split from England; why couldn't we come up with our own original song? Why not "Yankee Doodle Dandy" or "America the Beautiful." I loved singing about "fruited plains" and "purple mountain majesties." Do we really have any purple mountains in America?

The home room period lasted fifteen minutes, then we scattered to our various classes. I crossed Pennsylvania Avenue, the street in back of the school; my first period was Phys. Ed., which for the next six weeks would be in the gymnasium. The class was co-ed; boys and girls were having a great time taking very structured group dance lessons.

Approximately fifty boys lined up, single file, on the north side of the gymnasium, and an equal number of girls stood anxiously in line on the south side. From across the large room I could hear the girls cackle and giggle—and the rustle of crinolines. Selena Garcia, the female gym teacher, addressed the group and bellowed instructions, rules, and restrictions. Most important, boys and girls were required to maintain a respectable distance from each other. Miss Garcia raised her hand and fully extended her thumb and index finger, approximately six inches.

"Look closely . . . . This is how far apart you should be . . . and I will be checking."

"That's about half the size of my dick," whispered Manny Lefkowitz to a few boys that were standing next to him in line. `

"Yeah, you wish," chuckled a new boy in our class. Manny instantly responded with a powerful punch to the stomach. The new boy doubled over in pain . . . and grunted. Manny held him firmly by the shoulders to prevent him from falling to the floor.

"What's going on over there?" Coach Wes Gallagher shouted and blew his gold whistle. Coach Gallagher was responsible for supervising the boys. He was the new head coach, brought in to replace Mookie Malloy, who had been transferred to another school.

"I'm teaching the new boy how to bow properly before a young lady," responded Manny.

The girls were asked to remove their crinolines, to stack them in the bleachers. Boys were told to turn their backs and count to one hundred; we weren't allowed to watch the girls wiggle out of their huge undergarments. Several of the girls who were wearing two layers of petticoats became very irate and refused to cooperate; they walked out of the field house mumbling under their breath . . . "fuckin' dyke!"

"Today we will begin with the Fox Trot," said Miss Garcia, and after three weeks we will move on to the Rhumba, Tango, Jitterbug, and Square Dancing." The short squat woman was dressed in extremely tight red shorts that rode up the middle of her huge buttocks. And she wore a white Lacoste, the same type polo shirt that the male Phys. Ed. teachers wore . . . with a little alligator resting on top of one of her monster boobs. Miss Garcia and Coach Gallagher did a brief performance for the class, demonstrating the "box step"—forward, forward, side, together—with perfect posture, always six inches apart, but because of Miss Garcia's huge boobs the only way Coach Gallagher could stay six inches away was by fully extending his arms. The two Phys. Ed. teachers looked like robots as they danced to a recording of the "Tennessee Waltz"—sung by Patti Page.

"OK Boys and girls, that's how its done," said Miss Garcia. We applauded politely.

The buxom gym teacher then continued with her instructions: "As we play the next song I want you all to march lively to the front of the room, turn to the middle and greet your partner . . . boys bow, girls curtsey, and begin with the box step . . . forward, forward, side, together . . . . and keep the proper distance." Once again, she spread her thumb and index finger . . . to remind us of the "required upper-body separation." The two coaches then demonstrated the proper way to bow and curtsey.

"Hey!" said Manny Lefkowitz, "Miss Garcia didn't say nothin' bout' lower-body separation."

This introductory process was called the "Grand March," and every boy and girl looked across the room and did an instant count to try to determine who his or her partner would be. I did a quick count; I was thirteenth in line. The thirteenth girl was huge and her boobs were even bigger than Miss Garcia's. I secretly slipped out of line and maneuvered to the fifteenth spot. The fifteenth girl was short and very pretty. Many of the boys were doing the same maneuvering, changing their position in line; so were the girls.

Coach Gallagher carefully placed the phonograph needle on the next Patti Page song. The Grand March began and once the marching commenced it was too late to shift positions. Unfortunately, despite switching to the fifteenth spot, I still wound up with the huge girl. Her name was Martha Anne Wurkmeister; she had really big arms, short blonde hair, and she wiggled her huge rear end when she danced. Several boys stared at Martha Anne's musical derriere and sang in harmony with the Patti Page record. "How much is that doggie in the window . . . the one with the waggly tail? Arf! Arf!"

Martha Anne was taller than me, stronger than me, and she insisted on leading when we danced. "I get nauseous dancing backwards," she said, "same as riding backwards on a bus." I struggled, trying to keep up with her. Even though she was immense she was a graceful dancer. However, I gave new meaning to the trite expression, "two left feet." It was really confusing, attempting to dance backwards—the girl's part. Martha Anne also tried to teach me a few swirls and twirls and various types of dips. Although we were supposed to maintain a six inch separation her huge boobs made it impossible for me to watch my feet . . . I was having difficulty with the box step. I kept stepping on her toes. When it came to the end of the song and we did a dip, I did the boy's part . . . I refused to let a girl dip me to the floor. She was heavy, very heavy, but I used both arms . . . making sure not to drop her.

"Carpe Diem," said Manny Lefkowitz. He laughed as he danced alongside of us. That's what Silver Dollar Jake always shouted to the Beach High boys when he cruised around in his convertible . . . "seize the day." I recognized Manny's voice, but couldn't really see him. My face was buried in Martha Anne's gigantic bosom.

We then switched partners; it was Manny's idea. He couldn't stop gawking at Martha Anne's huge breasts. My new partner was Harriet Mintz, the fifteenth girl in the Grand March, the one I originally hoped to get as my dance partner. Harriet was thin, with big eyes and high cheekbones, like a model, and she let me lead even though I stepped on her toes several times. After three Patti Page songs we began dancing to "Too Young" by Nat King Cole, a slow romantic song. Harriet started to grind the lower half of her beautiful body against mine . . . but we carefully maintained the six inch separation above the waist.

The next song was by Rosemary Clooney . . . "Come On-a My House" and Harriet looked in eyes and smiled. She ran her tongue slowly across her upper lip. "Myron, would you like to come to my house after school to practice dancing ?"

Before I had a chance to respond to that unexpected invitation the public address system interrupted . . . . four potent bongs on the glockenspiel. Yikes! Immediately . . . . I ran to the nearest men's room to hide. The power of Pavlov was a self-evident truth that Jefferson forgot to mention. I returned, a few minutes later, but it was too late. Harriet found another dance partner; it was the new boy, the boy that Manny Lefkowitz had punched in the stomach. For the next fifteen minutes I watched the two of them glide across the floor; he was an excellent dancer. They were like Fred Astaire and Ginger Rogers—other kids just watched and marveled. Damn, they were good! When the class ended I saw the boy jotting Harriet's address on a piece of paper; he would be going to her house after school, to "practice."

"Hey! That's your girl," said Manny. "I gave her to you. Just say the word and I'll give that 'homo' a knee to the nuts."

◆

That night I told my mother that I was a klutz, that I embarrassed myself in Phys. Ed. and I needed dance lessons. The next evening I began a series of private lessons at the Arthur Murray studio on Lincoln Road. My dance teacher was Esmeralda Cifuentes, an exotic Cuban woman who wore gold spandex pants that clung tightly to a well rounded backside. She had stark white complexion, almost ghostly looking, and long black hair. Her eyes were outlined by gobs of mascara and her full lips were coated with bright red lipstick. She looked like a vampire. I had never seen a woman that white before.

"You're very pretty," I told her, while staring at my feet, concentrating on the proper footwork for the box-step. "How come you wear so much makeup?"

"Because I vant' to suck your blood," she smiled and pretended to lunge for my neck. I think Esmeralda was able to read my mind. "And don't look at your feet . . . look at the señorita's eyes when you're dancing. Dancing is foreplay; it is a prelude to amour."

"Yo quiero chupar tu sangre." I repeated Esmeralda's Dracula line in Spanish . . . and we both laughed. She was an excellent dancer; she wiggled her hips as we danced . . . sort of a Latin twist to the Fox Trot, and she didn't maintain a six inch separation. I felt the hard points of her bra as she pressed her body against mine.

"Myron, you move like a robot; you're too stiff. Relax; move your hips, loosen up." She put her hands on my hips and forced them to swivel as we danced, "forward, forward, side together . . . wiggle . . . back, back, side, together, wiggle, wiggle, wiggle." We also spent a little time doing the Rhumba; it was the same box step as the Fox Trot but with smaller steps and a lot more wiggling. Esmeralda reached around my hips and grabbed my butt . . . she squeezed and forced me to shake and wiggle.

"Shake your culo, shake it, shake it, shake it." Esmeralda sang in tune to the Latin beat.

"Culo?" I never heard that word.

"Its Spanish . . . for butt, ass, rump . . . shake it 'mi amour,' shake it."

I kept trying to relax, but I couldn't get it all together; it was impossible to wiggle my "culo" and dance at the same time. However, after four lessons I began to improve; my feet and "culo" were finally working together. I couldn't wait to do the Rhumba in Phys. Ed.

I also practiced dancing after school with Flo . . . I loved giving her Rhumba instructions; she had a very firm "culo" . . . great to squeeze. Even though Flo was in the 12th grade she didn't have any experience with boys, other than her summertime fling with Myron III—and I'm sure they didn't do too much dancing. Flo couldn't stop laughing when I told her about my reaction to the glockenspiel bongs on the P.A. system . . . especially in Phys. Ed.

"Same thing with Myron III," said Flo. "All I gotta' do is start talking about porterhouse steaks and he gets a hardon. Do you guys think with your dick?"

"Well . . . I can't help it. The glockenspiel does that to me. But, I didn't get a hardon when Esmeralda squeezed my 'culo' . . . and let me tell you, she is damn sexy."

During the remaining weeks of the dance module Phys. Ed. became my favorite class, especially when we started doing the Rhumba. I was good, and I discovered that wearing a jock strap to dance class neutralized the power of the glockenspiel. I wasn't going to let Mr. Schecter cut in again. One time Miss Garcia stood next to me and watched closely as I did the rhumba; she was marveling at my ability to wiggle my "culo," a rare talent for a white Jewish boy.

"Young man, are you Spanish?" she asked. But, before I could respond she pushed my dance partner aside and cut in. Other students watched and applauded as we did an inspired rhumba. The short, buxom woman also knew how to wiggle her "culo."

After we finished dancing I told Miss Garcia that my grandmother's maiden name was Seville. "Part of my ancestry comes from Spain; way back at the Inquisition."

"That's why you know how to rhumba so well," She responded. "Why don't you join me at the cafeteria for lunch; I'd love to hear more about your heritage."

"That was 500 years ago," I chuckled. "But, it sure didn't help me in Spanish class."

"That may be so," said Miss Garcia, and she smiled as if she knew me very well. "But certain wonderful attributes of Spanish behavior are hereditary, not just the ability to rhumba."

I didn't have the slightest idea what she was talking about; there was nothing Spanish about me. I didn't even like Arroz Con Pollo or other Spanish food, but she sure seemed intrigued when I told her about Ida Seville, my Spanish grandmother. However, I didn't join Miss Garcia for lunch; she was a strange woman and I didn't want to be seen having lunch with her at the school cafeteria.

When I got home I told my father about the discussion with Miss Garcia and we talked about Ida Seville, his mother. We also talked about my emerging talent as a rhumba dancer, and he asked if I would like to resume accordion lessons. I instantly rejected that idea but told him that I would consider taking piano lessons; I enjoyed my one experience with the white grand piano at Maxine's house, but in retrospect, I think it was the total experience that I enjoyed . . . the piano was just the culmination of an exciting milestone in my life. I thought about it for awhile but decided that I wasn't prepared to make the commitment. It would require at least one hour a day practice time. As I look back at the mistakes I made in my life—not taking piano lessons is one of my major regrets.

CHAPTER 33

A TALE OF TWO CITIES

"It was the best of times, it was the worst of times, it was the age of wisdom, it was the age of foolishness." Miss Madison sat on top of her desk and read to the class. She read softly, but with feeling; she loved Dickens. Her legs dangled from the desk, short legs that weren't long enough to reach the floor. Peeking out from the bottom of her long black skirt were cork platform shoes topped with little plastic bananas. How about that! Those were Pix shoes, the shoes that I had stapled the previous summer. My nose tingled as I thought about the seven days when I sneezed and stapled in the dusty stockroom on Lincoln Road, when I created shoes that would liberate women from the bondage of their puritan shackles. Mr. Glickman, the store manager, sure knew what he was talking about . . . women loved fruit on their feet, especially demure, prudish women who covered every remaining part of their body with drab garments.

"Dickens talks about the social evils in London and Paris," said Miss Madison. "That's why the book is entitled 'Tale of Two Cities.' Dickens was greatly influenced by Carlyle's 'French Revolution.' In fact, he is reputed to have said that he read Carlyle's history five hundred times."

It seemed strange to hear Miss Madison talk about Dickens and Carlyle in the same sentence. I lived on Carlyle Avenue in Surfside, only one block away from Dickens Avenue. Shawna Goldstein, the prettiest girl at Beach High, lived on Dickens. Shawna is a Hebrew name; it means "beautiful"—it was a perfect name for the most beautiful girl I ever knew. Her full name was Shawna Rose Goldstein—but Jewish girls rarely used middle names, not like Christian girls who were called Emmy Lou or Mary Beth—so most people just called her Shawna. Too bad . . . Shawna Rose was such a beautiful name. She looked like Elizabeth Taylor, the movie star, same smile, same black hair, same gorgeous green eyes. During the first few weeks of the school year Shawna rode my school bus, but there was no way to talk to her; it was impossible to get past the throng of boys that hovered around her. She was only fourteen, in the ninth grade, and she loved to flirt with the twelfth grade boys. I looked at her from across the bus and she looked at me . . . I stared at her astonishing green eyes and I sensed that behind her coquettish facade she was a sensitive and perceptive girl.

The residential streets of Surfside were named after famous American and English authors and poets. Heading west from the ocean, the streets were in alphabetical order: Abbot, Byron, Carlyle, Dickens, Emerson, Froude, Garland, Hawthorne, and Irving. Then came Biscayne Bay, the western border of my Jewish island. David and Shelly Steinberg lived on Byron.

"Dickens wrote this book in 1859," said Miss Madison, "approximately seventy years after the French Revolution." She paused to adjust her tiny reading glasses. "But he saw many parallels between London and Paris. He depicts both cities as rife with poverty, injustice, and violence due to the irresponsibility of the ruling elite. He felt that the smoldering discontent of the working class in London might eventually explode in an upheaval on the scale of the French Revolution."

I knew very little about Dickens, other than Scrooge and Tiny Tim, and I liked to say "Bah Humbug" at Christmas; so did many other kids. I raised my hand and asked to comment on Miss Madison's observation.

"I haven't read a 'Tale of Two Cities,' but they never had the revolution in England. They still have a limited monarchy." Miss Madison looked at her seating chart to figure out my name.

"Myron . . . read the book first, then we can talk. You're right in one respect . . . during the years following Dickens they never cut off the head of the king or queen in England, but the Western world endured industrial revolutions, not only in England but in the United States, Europe, and Russia . . . . especially Russia. And, the Russians used bullets instead of the guillotine on the Czar and his family. Yes Myron, you're partially correct. During the years following 'Tale of Two Cities,' the western democracies did not execute any monarch. But, the exploitation of the working class led to the emergence of several new 'isms'—fascism, socialism, and communism in Europe . . . . and unionism in America."

I enjoyed listening to Miss Madison when she read from Dickens, and I especially enjoyed her explanations and commentaries. I thought of two additional "isms" to add to her list—racism and anti-Semitism—both of which were very prevalent in Miami and Miami Beach, my two cities. Miss Madison was an intelligent woman, a very progressive thinker . . . but why was such an intelligent woman wearing those dumb plastic fruit shoes? I never bought presents for teachers, certainly not in high school, but I wanted to buy her a more "intelligent" pair of shoes. I was positive . . . at that very moment, Mr. Glickman was in the dusty stockroom at Pix, telling his latest assistant about his Carmen Miranda dream. "Women all love fruit."

That Saturday, the first weekend of the eleventh grade, Shelly suggested that we go swimming at the Venetian Pool in Coral Gables.

"It's the world's largest coral rock swimming pool," said Shelly, "we've got to go see it."

David, Shelly, Flo, and I took the K Bus to Lincoln road; then we transferred to another bus which let us off in downtown Miami, then a third bus took us to Coral Gables. From the time we left Surfside it took two hours until we finally reached the Venetian Pool. It really was immense, big enough for several hundred people to swim at the same time. Kids were running all over the place, swimming, jumping, laughing, and spitting. Lots of spitting! Even girls were spitting. And everyone spoke with a southern accent. I felt like I was in Alabama or Georgia.

"Hey, y'all know where the shit house is?" asked a tall thin boy. "I gotta' take me a wicked dump."

"Oh, you poor little sugah-pie," said Flo. "Go make your sweet little ol' poo-poo right behind the big pink building?" Flo smiled at the tall boy . . . and he smiled back to her.

"Where'd you learn that phony southern accent?" I laughed

"My mom works at the downtown Sears, I just kinda' picked it up from the people who work with her."

We then took turns climbing the huge coral rocks; some of them were over twenty feet high. We stood on top of our mountains, pounding our chests and shouting like Tarzan. Then we plunged into the ice cold water of the pool. Flo screamed as she jumped; her loud shriek could be heard from all corners of the enormous pool. She had a great body and looked fantastic in her two-piece bathing suit. We also explored several dark, creepy caves. I wore swimming goggles and had a clear view under the water. In one isolated cave under a waterfall I saw a tall muscular boy. He was standing and kissing a girl.

From my hidden vantage point, in a remote corner of the cave, I continued to watch the underwater show. Finally, I couldn't hold my breath any longer; I rose to the surface for a quick gasp of air. The boy saw me and yelled:

"Hey punk, get the hell out of here or I'll bust your fuckin' nose."

Several seconds later the girl also rose to the surface; her face looked familiar, but the cave was dark and it was difficult to see clearly. I wanted to go closer and look, but I didn't feel like getting into a fight with the boy, so I swam away very quickly.

Adjacent to the swimming area was a small snack bar where they sold Cokes, non-kosher hot dogs, and cellophane wrapped slices of fruit cake from Claxton, Georgia. I laughed when I saw the fruit cake and told Flo about my Nazi hunt . . . and Claxton.

"My mother works with lots of red-necks," said Flo, "at their Chtistmas party they eat fruit cake doused with brandy and whipped cream. You might be right; I think most of them are Nazis."

Next to the snack bar were two drinking fountains, one for white people, the other for colored. There were also signs posted near the main entrance, informing Negroes that they were not allowed to go swimming in the pool. How could thirsty Negroes ever drink from the "colored only" drinking fountain at the Venetian pool if they weren't even allowed past the iron gate at the entrance? I assumed that the colored fountain was for Negro employees, but I didn't see any Negroes working around the pool. Before we left for home I searched all around the recreational area; I wanted to find the girl from the cave. Eventually I found her lying on a blanket with the tall boy. It was Shawna Goldstein! Why would such a popular girl be giving a blowjob in the Venetian Pool? Maybe that's why she was so popular.

The bus ride home was long and uncomfortable. I couldn't stop thinking about Shawna; I really was disillusioned. I thought she was such an intelligent girl, such a "perfect" girl; I was so positive. Eyes never lie! How could I be so wrong?

"Don't be so critical," said Flo. "She is very young, and didn't you say that your 'precious' Leah Sonnino let you squeeze her little titties in the Carib theatre? Besides, that guy is Jimbo Lang, probably the biggest athlete in the state of Florida."

"I only squeezed one of them," I replied. "And talk about big! That guy's got the biggest dick I ever saw."

Flo chuckled. "So I've heard! The girls all talk about him. The guy has nothing between the ears . . . but they say he's got a lot between his legs."

We didn't get home until after dark and my mother wasn't too happy about my day at the Venetian Pool. She had warned me never to go swimming in public pools because of the threat of Polio.

"But mom, you don't complain when I go to the beach . . . why are you so nervous about the Venetian Pool?" Maybe I had stumbled upon a cure for the dreaded disease. Maybe an injection of salt water from the Atlantic Ocean was the antidote for Polio.

On Friday nights I went to the University of Miami football games at the Orange Bowl. What a dumb name for this world famous football stadium; oranges didn't even grow in South Florida. They grew several hundred miles north of Miami, in the Orlando area. The only fruit or vegetables that grew in abundance in South Florida were avocados, mangoes, tomatoes, and coconuts. The "Coconut Bowl" would have been a much better name for the stadium.

I went by bus with the Steinbergs and a few other friends from Surfside: Arnie Dombrowski, Josh Broden, and Dingo McGuffie. Dingo was not Jewish and he annoyed me. He always used the expression "your people" when he talked to us and he called Jewish girls "Jewesses." Dingo had trouble dealing with the fact that gentiles were a minority in Miami Beach. He was anti-Semitic, but in a subtle way. When I first met him he always camouflaged his prejudice by making saccharine generalizations about Jewish people: "Jews are all very smart; Jews are the best lawyers; Jews are the best doctors; Jews are all very rich; Jews are never criminals."

"Hey Dingo," I interrupted . . . "What about Julius and Ethel Rosenberg . . . and Meyer Lansky?" For once, I was proud of a few famous Jewish criminals. "And my friend Howard Lefkowitz lives in a dingy old apartment; he and his mom are on welfare."

The University of Miami was an all white college with an all white football team. In fact, their star player was named "Whitey" Rouvierre. Occasionally, a northern team had one or two Negro players, but the other southern colleges were all white. The stands at the Orange Bowl were segregated. The stadium, refreshment stands, and restrooms were reserved exclusively for white fans, except for one half of the end zone, where special bleachers were designated for colored people . . . with blue plastic out-houses.

"This place should be called the 'white' bowl," I observed. "They don't even grow oranges in Miami. And, its disgusting how the Negroes have to use outhouses."

"I heard you can't even flush the outhouses," said David.

"Of course not," said Dingo, "nigger crap has to be thrown in the dump; it don't flush like white shit."

"What's white shit?" I snapped at Dingo. "Is your shit white?"

"Since when are you such a nigger lover?" responded Dingo. "Just walk into one of those outhouses and take a whiff . . . see if you live to talk about it."

It really turned my stomach when I looked across the field at the Negro section. As I watched the Miami versus Georgia football game I began to reflect on our reading assignment in Miss Madison's class . . . the "Tale of Two Cities." Miami was reminiscent of Paris, rife with poverty; living conditions in Overtown were horrible. It was a racist southern city—not much different than Claxton, Georgia. Miami and Miami Beach were very dissimilar cities, but identical in several respects . . . somewhat like London during Dickens time and Paris during the French Revolution.

What would Dickens think about the blue outhouses at the Orange Bowl and the "colored only" drinking fountains at the Venetian Pool? What would he think about Overtown, where Annabelle lived? I sat with my friends watching the football game at the Orange Bowl, but my mind was in Paris—the storming of the Bastille by the poor people. Can it happen here? In Miami?

"Let them eat watermelon," shouted the mayor of Miami, as an angry mob of Negroes dragged him to a guillotine on top of a blue plastic out-house.

◆

Monday morning, back at school, I couldn't shake off the horrible memory of the Venetian Pool and the Orange Bowl as we continued our discussion of "A Tale of Two Cities."

"Dickens talks about smoldering discontent in London," said Miss Madison, as she addressed the students. "But lets focus our attention on our own little island. Do you see any current laws in Miami Beach that remind you of London during the Dickens era?"

"Yeah! The 6 PM work permit," said David Steinberg. "Its disgusting! It should be repealed."

"I'm sure it eventually will be," said Miss Madison, "but must we obey such a law in the meantime? It is a racist law . . . even though, on the surface it appears to be benign. Do we really have a moral obligation to obey laws that are blatantly wrong?"

"Well, if we don't . . . we go to jail," responded David. "Do we have a choice?"

Miss Madison then began to read from a copy of Henry David Thoreau's essay on Civil Disobedience. She didn't' read the entire essay, just one page which she had marked with a paper clip.

"Unjust laws exist: shall we be content to obey them, or shall we endeavor to amend them, and obey them until we have succeeded, or shall we transgress them at once?"

◆

"So, what are you saying?" asked Dingo McGuffie ". . . that we should pick and chose, which are good laws and which are bad ones? Personally, I don't see anything so terrible about a work permit law . . . it helps cut down on crime in Miami Beach."

"I'm not suggesting that you take the law in your own hands," responded Miss Madison. "I'm just tossing out the same thought provoking question that Thoreau asked one hundred years ago . . . around the same time that Dickens wrote a 'Tale of Two Cites.' It's a very good question, and to be honest, Thoreau himself didn't really answer it. He just raised the question; something for us to ponder . . . but, in the long run . . . if

America is ever going to eliminate racism its going to take a grass roots protest movement, you won't see radical change initiated by the 'ruling elite'—they're too concerned about opinion polls and approval ratings. Change will begin with the people—just like the poor people of Paris when they stormed the Bastille—then Congress will react."

I raised my hand and interjected my thoughts. I told Miss Madison and the class about my reaction to seeing segregation in the Orange Bowl and the Venetian Pool.

"Its terrible the way we treat the colored people," I observed. "Its wrong and we all know its wrong . . . but we say nothing. We're all from the north, most of us . . . we know better. One day soon the Negroes are going to revolt, and it might get violent."

"We ain't got no problems," said Dingo McGuffie. "Its only in Miami that they have those racial laws that you think are so terrible . . . not here on the Beach."

"Yeah, sure" said Howard Lefkowitz, in a very cynical voice . . . "are you telling us that we don't segregate Negroes at the public beaches or in Memorial Field?" Howard was referring to the stadium where Beach High played its football games.

"Whatcha' talkin' 'bout' Lefkowitz?" said Dingo. "Ain't no signs at Memorial Field saying 'white only'—Negroes can go to the games all they want."

"Of course not," responded Howard. "The signs are 'unwritten' in Miami Beach. Football games are all at night, after the curfew, after Negroes are forced to leave our little white island."

"Nothing racist about the police permit law in Miami Beach," said Eddie Sawyer, a new gentile boy at Beach High. "It makes everybody have a permit if they wanna' work here at night, not only the niggers, and they got their own special beach on Key Biscayne."

I didn't like Eddie calling the colored people "niggers."

"Whats your problem?" said Eddie. "Nigger is just a nickname for Negro, ain't nothing wrong with that word. Is Shwartza any better?."

"Its pronounced 'Shvartzah,'" I responded, and I chuckled (on the outside), but on the inside I knew that Eddie was right.

Eddie lived in Surfside and rode my school bus. He had a blonde flat top, lots of pimples on his face, and he wore polo shirts without little alligators. Eddie and Dingo soon became close friends. Now that Dingo had a Christian ally he discontinued his superficial flattery of Jewish people. He became extremely hostile and made many offensive generalizations: Jews are terrible athletes; Jews have little dicks . . . and the Jewesses look like douche bags and don't give no blowjobs."

Shawna Goldstein, the prettiest girl at Beah Hi, was Jewish and she gave underwater blowjobs at the Venetian pool. She was now going steady with Jimbo Lang, who was all-city in football, basketball, and track, but was even more well known for his humongous penis. He was also Jewish. Shawna and Jimbo contradicted every one of Dingo's anti-Semitic stereotypes.

Four weeks later, as we concluded our unit on Dickens, each student was required to write a brief critique. I knew that Miss Madison empathized with the poor people of Paris—so did Dickens—at least in the early part of the book. The easiest way to get an "A" in English would be to write a stirring essay about the "smoldering discontent" of the oppressed working class. But, after I read the book I came away with a different perspective on the French Revolution. I began to feel sorry for the "ruling elite." I liked Miss Madison very much, and she liked me . . . but I wasn't sure if she would like me after my essay; I was about to take a controversial position.

"Boys and girls; I'd like to read Myron's paper to the class," said Miss Madison. "Even though he doesn't share my view of the French Revolution he has a lot to say . . . and leaves us with a lot to think about."

"Dickens was obviously influenced by Carlyle, but his outlook on revolutionary violence differs significantly. Unlike Carlyle, he can no longer see justice in street violence. He abhors mob rule and institutionalized terror. With the storming of the Bastille and the murdering or imprisonment of the members of the 'ruling elite,' Dickens' earlier portrayal of the poor does an about-face. The people had been, up to then, exploited, gaunt, and submissive. Now they were a howling, breast-beating band of bloodthirsty demons. A celebrated cause became mob rule. Once an abused people, they now use their power to destroy all that is not a part of them. They discard the crosses around their necks for miniature guillotines. And the once oppressors now go to their deaths as martyrs."

After class Eddie Sawyer and Dingo McGuffie came up to me privately and told me that they liked my paper.

"We got the same fuckin' situation in Miami," said Eddie, "also here on the Beach. If we give the coons too much freedom they're gonna' take over and start raping white girls; they're animals, no different than the poor people of Paris."

It really bothered me, that those two bigots liked my critique; they didn't even read the book. They only read the illustrated "Classic Comics" version.

I always sympathized with people who were oppressed, but after I read Dickens' gruesome description of the French Revolution I began to have second thoughts about my emerging liberalism. Dickens painted a gruesome picture; I was opposed to violence, mob rule, and guillotines . . . even in the name of a good cause. But, under certain conditions I could see that Thoreau offered the best response to oppression—that it would be OK to intentionally disregard unjust laws. Gandhi, in India, was obviously a proponent of Thoreau's theory. Gandhi used hunger strikes and non-violent civil disobedience to achieve independence for his country. He believed that the way people behave is more important than what they achieve; that's just the opposite of Hitler's theory, that the ends justify the means. Gandhi achieved his objectives without chopping off any heads, without any assassinations . . . . except his own.

Miss Madison gave me an "A" on the paper . . . and throughout my remaining two years at Beach High we became very close and we frequently disagreed. I was very liberal, mainly because of the influence of my father, but Miss Madison was even more liberal. She taught me how to argue and stick to the issue without turning the argument into a personal attack on the other person. Unfortunately, most people don't know how to do that; they go ballistic and take it very personal if you disagree with them, especially Eddie Sawyer.

"No, Eddie," I commented. "Giving Negroes equal rights doesn't mean they're going to start raping white girls."

"Myron, you're a fuckin' nigger-lover, just like all the commie shmucks at this Jew school. Talk, talk, talk . . . but I don't see you bringing no black-ass niggers home for dinner."

Eddie was right . . . I was "talk, talk, talk." I had no Negro friends and I never brought one home for dinner. I wanted to tell him about the time I modeled a pink Lacoste for a colored boy at Burdines or the time I gave up my seat for an old lady on the bus, but I didn't bother. It was easier just to walk away.

◆

As I rode home on the school bus that afternoon I saw Shawna Goldstein sitting alone. Now that she was going steady with Jimbo Lang, wearing his ring around her neck, the boys stopped swarming around her. I sat next to Shawna and we talked. We talked about Dickens and Carlyle and Emerson . . . the authors, not the streets.

"A foolish consistency is the hobgoblin of little minds," said Shawna, and she tucked Jimbo's ring under her blouse. "That's Emerson!"

"Yeah, I know," I chuckled, "the mass of men lead lives of quiet desperation; also from Ralph."

I couldn't believe that I was actually talking to Shawna Goldstein . . . looking directly into the most gorgeous green eyes I had ever seen. I was very confused . . . . my mouth was working independent of my brain. I was babbling . . . trying to be cool and impressive, but my thoughts were introspective and insecure. What chance did I have with this beautiful girl? None! Then, somewhere in the depths of my subconscious, Silver Dollar Jake threw mini rubbers and began shouting advice . . . . "Carpe Diem" . . . "Seize the day" . . . and I began to recite another passage from Emerson.

"These roses under my window make no reference to former roses or to better ones; they are for what they are; they exist with God today. There is no time to them. There is simply the rose; it is perfect in every moment of its existence."

"That's beautiful," responded Shawna, and she made sure that Jimbo's ring remained hidden beneath her blouse. "Self-Reliance, by Emerson. I've read it several times. I've read at least one book or poem or essay by Abbot, Byron, Carlyle, Dickens, Emerson, Froude, Garland, Hawthorne, and Irving . . . everyone of the Surfside streets."

I was impressed; it was hard to believe that such a gorgeous girl could also be so intelligent . . . . so "perfect."

Then we played a game for the rest of the bus ride; we tried to name authors or poets for the remaining letters of the alphabet . . . just in case they ever wanted to expand Surfside beyond Irving.

Joyce, Keats, Longfellow, Melville, Nietzsche, Orwell, Poe . . . . Q caused problems; Shawna refused to accept Ellery Queen, the mystery writer.

"No good, that's just a pen name, not the author's real name."

"So what. Mark Twain is also a pen name."

"OK," said Shawna, "but I sure wouldn't name a street after him. Queen is another way of saying fag."

The next few letters were easy, Rosseau, Shakespeare, Tennyson. "U" was impossible, the game would have ended so we had to modify the rules. Many ancient manuscripts were listed as "author unknown" so we agreed to allow "Unknown" to be an allowable author, but that sure would be a dumb name for a street.

"Not really," said Shawna, "isn't there a tomb for the unknown soldier."

Voltaire and Whitman were easy . . . then we reached Dickens Avenue, Shawna's bus stop. The game ended before we could attempt "X." Good thing. That would be even harder than "U."

"Goodbye Myron. It was fun." Shawna smiled when she left the bus. I watched her walk home. She removed Jimbo's ring from its hiding spot and placed it proudly on top of her blouse, and I stared in space, lost in my thoughts. It was impossible to come up with an "X" author.

That night, at 10:00 PM, the phone rang in my house . . . it was Shawna.

"Xenocrates begins with 'X' . . . he was a famous Greek philosopher, a disciple of Plato. Good night."

I smiled and made a mental note to myself . . . tomorrow I must go to the library and look up Xenocrates; I'll find a few good quotes to impress Shawna. And I have to find authors or poets with "Y' and "Z."

CHAPTER 34

XENOCRATES

I didn't find anything about Xenocrates at the school library, so I called my friend Katarina at the Miami Beach Library. She couldn't find any quotes either but told me that Xenocrates was born in 396 BC in Chalcedon, near modern day Istanbul, and was the head of the Academy, the school of philosophy that was founded by Plato. He wasn't really an original thinker; his duty as the head of the Academy was to promote a codification of the views of Plato. He believed that human beings had a threefold existence: mind, body and soul—that people die twice, once on Earth, then for a second time on the Moon when the mind separates from the soul and travels to the Sun.

"Hi Shawna Rose, this is Myron," I called her on the phone to talk about Xenocrates.

"I did a little research about your X-man, the Greek philosopher."

"Really! What did your find?"

"You and I are destined for each other," I responded. "Not in this life, but after we die our mind and soul will separate from our body and move on to the moon. You will be my girlfriend on the moon."

"So, what happens to our body?" asked Shawna.

"That gets buried and left behind, back here on earth. A body without a mind or soul isn't much good for anything." I was alluding to Jimbo Lang, her muscular boyfriend.

"So . . . in this lifetime I will enjoy the earthly pleasures of Jimbo's amazing body, but in the next life I'll enjoy your mind and soul?" Shawna laughed.

"How long do you think you'll be satisfied with a body without a mind and soul?"

"Well . . . . until the end of the school year," responded Shawna, in a somewhat flippant voice. "Then he goes off to some college. Jimbo has scholarship offers from over thirty colleges."

"I've tried that before," I said. "Sex without love only kept me coming back for a few weeks; then it got boring."

"Listen Myron . . . I'm fascinated with Xenocrates, but, no lectures, please. I get too much of that already from my parents."

"OK . . . I'm sorry." I didn't know what else to say. She was right; I had no business preaching morality to her. I hardly knew her. I was really at a loss for words . . . and I was afraid that my new friendship was about to come to an abrupt end.

Finally, I broke the awkward silence with a line of poetry . . . another passage about roses; I did my homework before I called Shawna.

"Red Rose, 'Shawna' Rose, proud Rose of all my days! Come near me, while I sing the ancient ways." I stuck the word Shawna in the poem . . . it wasn't in the original version.

"W.B. Yeats," she laughed. "He was a famous Irish poet . . . or maybe he was English, and you definitely improved the poem by adding Shawna. O.K., you got the 'Y' . . . give me a second. Damn, 'Z' is a tough one. How about Zorro or Zeus?"

"J'accuse," I replied. "That's French for 'I Accuse.'"

"Oh, of course." responded Shawna. "Emile Zola, the French author. He was challenging the French judiciary in defense of Alfred Dreyfus."

Shawna was the smartest girl I ever met, and also the prettiest. She invited me to her house that evening and told me to bring a few friends. She was having a party—her parents would be out of town—and she wanted to introduce me to one of her girlfriends. Jimbo never went out on week nights, so he wouldn't be there. David, Shelly, and I went to Shawna's house by bike. But, we hid our bikes in an empty lot and walked the final block. It was OK to be seen walking to a girl's house but it wasn't cool to go there by bike, not in the eleventh grade. Most guys in the eleventh grade were sixteen and could drive a car. But, the Steinbergs and I were only fifteen and didn't have a drivers license.

Shawna had two personalities. When she was alone with me I liked her; she was fascinating and extremely intelligent. But, when she had an audience of dimwit girlfriends she was a self centered twit who talked down to everybody. Her boyfriend, the great athlete with the fantastic body, was revered as the king of Beach High, so Shawna regarded herself as a queen; she became Queen Shawna.

"Jimbo says that the football team will be excellent this year . . . and he probably will make all-city again, maybe even all-state. Jimbo has scholarship offers from all the finest colleges in the country. Jimbo is getting a Jaguar convertible soon; I won't be riding the school bus much longer." Queen Shawna stood in the middle of the living room twirling the large gold ring that hung around her neck, she was the center of attention, and she continued to brag about Jimbo, how great he was in football, basketball, and track, especially about his state record in the broad jump.

"Why don't you tell us about Jimbo's 'main' attraction," said Shirley Segal, as she slowly peeled a banana . . . and the girls all began to chuckle.

"Well." Shawna smiled and paused; it was a long pause. "I guess I'd have to say its somewhere between stupendous and incredible."

Several of the girls stared in space as they repeated Shawna's proud description: 'somewhere between stupendous and incredible.'"

It was a boring party; kids sat around puffing on cigarettes, trying to see who could make the most creative smoke rings. Morton Mandel, a thin boy with a bad case of acne, was the champion. He shaped his mouth into an exaggerated circle and gently tapped his cheek with his index finger. A large smoke ring floated into space; it hovered near his face waiting for the next part of the act. Then he blew a rapid stream of little smoke rings through the opening of the big circle. Everyone applauded. Great trick! For his finale he exhaled smoke slowly out of his mouth, in an upward direction. The smoke crawled over and around pimples and zits, and disappeared into his nostrils. Several seconds later the same smoke came out of his mouth, for a second trip back up to the nose.

"Its called 'French Inhaling,'" said Morton. "I learned it from the colored bus boys at Currys restaurant. I work there on weekends."

"Gross!" Said several of the girls . . . . and they giggled. "Teach us how to do it." Four or five girls clustered around Morton and lit cigarettes; he was now the main attraction; he even stole center stage from Queen Shawna.

No one talked about anything of interest, except for Brenda Singer, the girl that Shawna wanted to introduce to me. Brenda was very cute, with a teasing smile and a brown pony tail somewhat like Leah. She was wearing a pink poodle skirt, a matching poodle on her blouse, and was discussing the Classic Comics version of a "Tale of Two Cities," especially the gory pictures of heads rolling under the blade of the guillotine.

"I think 'decapitation' is such an exciting word . . . I love it," said Brenda, and her eyes lit up. "I bet it was thrilling to watch heads being chopped off, rolling down the street. They should invent a smaller version of the guillotine. It could be used for rapists and sex perverts." She crashed her hand on the dining room table—an exaggerated Karate chop—pretending to hack off the extended index finger of her left hand. "Whomp!"

"Ouch," said David Steinberg. He laughed and grabbed his crotch with both hands. "That sure would make you think twice before you unzipped your fly. You know . . . they do make a small guillotine. My grandfather has one to clip the tip of his cigars."

"I love big fat cigars." Brenda looked at David and smiled. "they're so masculine."

Several minutes later David and Brenda were holding hands as they left the party. They walked into the darkness of the back yard to pick fruit from the avocado trees . . . and maybe to discuss guillotines and cigars.

Damn! David moved quickly . . . I was hoping to talk to Brenda, but he got to her first. And it didn't take Shelly long to get friendly with Shawna's other friend, Shirley Segal; they also disappeared into the night. All the good looking girls were being grabbed up while I sat in the living room watching Morton do stupid smoke tricks. Actually, I shouldn't say they were stupid. Morton was not handsome, but he still managed to capture the attention of several pretty girls. I wonder if I could have been an attraction at parties if I stuck to the accordion? Probably not! No one liked accordion music, but maybe if I had learned to play the piano . . . . that's what the advertisements for piano lessons all said . . . "be popular at parties." But, Morton did it with smoke tricks.

In addition to cigarette puffing, many of the girls gossiped about who was dating who and whether or not they were "going all the way." They also talked about the clothes, shoes, and purses of other girls, and what kind of car every boy was driving. They ridiculed Miss Madison's shoes, especially the plastic fruit. I kept my mouth shut . . . I didn't want the girls to know that I was the one who stapled the fruit on those shoes. It was all gibberish, and I really didn't like Queen Shawna.

And several of the girls who weren't grabbed up and taken to the backyard were babbling about the new TV show, "Queen for a Day." What a dumb show! Some poor disheveled woman would tell Jack Bailey, the host, about her tale of woe and if hers was the most pathetic story she got prizes. One woman lost her home in a fire; she needed a refrigerator to feed her children who were suffering from malnutrition and Rickets. Another woman told a story how her car was stolen; she needed a new car to get to the hospital every day for therapy. She was recovering from a stroke and her left eye twitched when she talked. The Rickets lady beat the stroke lady . . . louder applause from the audience . . . she got her refrigerator. The stroke lady got a big hug from Jack Bailey, a kiss on her non-twitching eye, and well wishes for a speedy recovery, but no car.

Morton finished his smoke tricks; he was now in the back yard, making out with a very pretty blonde girl who had perfect complexion. I sat alone in the dining room, eating avocadoes filled with peanut butter . . . the only remaining girls were those who were obsessed with "Queen For a Day" . . . and Queen Shawna.

"I've got to go," I told the queen. "I'm not supposed to stay out late on week nights."

"No, don't go Myron. Lets sit on the front porch for awhile."

We sat and talked; this was the Shawna I liked . . . Shawna Rose, not Queen Shawna. She told me that she didn't want the other girls to know that she was intelligent; it didn't look cool, but her secret passion was reading. She made me promise not to tell anyone that she enjoyed reading, especially her girlfriends.

"None of them read, except for those trashy romance novels. They underline words like 'quiver' or 'orgasm' . . . and they giggle."

"Well, books are also good for posture," I chuckled. "I met a gentile girl at the Kenilworth; she told stories about walking exercises at her finishing school. The girls walked to music with books on their head and knockers pointed horizontal."

"Oh, I know about 'knockers up,'" said Shawna. "I go to modeling class once a week. My mother doesn't stop reminding me that I look like Elizabeth Taylor. She even had me make a professional composite; I've been in a few magazine advertisements, mainly underwear pictures in the Sears catalog when I was ten."

I looked into her green eyes, which were beautiful in the moonlight. I didn't say anything; neither of us did . . . we both just sat there looking at the moon and we held hands.

"Shawna, you are the most beautiful girl I have ever known . . . and the most intelligent. Why are you so afraid to let people know you're smart?

"Maybe some day I will," she replied. "But right now I'm having fun, and what's so terrible about being popular?"

"Too bad about Brenda," said Shawna. "I told her all about you; you've got to move quicker at parties. Brenda and Shirley are my two best friends, and you let them both get away. Myron, you've got to move quicker."

"Yeah, you're right . . . . I know. But, I guess I'm a little shy at parties."

"Girls like guys who are self-confident." That was Shawna's advice. "Look at that guy with the smoke tricks . . . you could play 'connect the dots' on his face but he did great with the girls."

It was 10:00 PM, so I said goodnight. David and Shelly remained at the party . . . in the back yard. Then Shawna tucked Jimbo's ring under her blouse; she put her arms around me and we kissed. It wasn't a French kiss, just a tight lipped one, like with Leah Sonnino. But it was a long kiss.

"Good night Xenocrates," she said, and she looked up at the full moon. "Next life, up there . . . the mind and the soul . . . . I'll be your girl."

Two weeks later Jimbo Lang got his Jaguar convertible and Shawna never rode the school bus again. Queens don't ride school buses.

CHAPTER 35

THE CATCH

The New York Giants were underdogs in the 1954 World Series even though Willie Mays was the best all around player in the major leagues. The Cleveland Indians had a fantastic pitching staff: Jim Lemon, Early Wynn, Mike Garcia and the great Bob Feller . . . and they compiled the best single season record since the legendary 1927 Yankees, the Babe Ruth-Lou Gehrig team. Some sports writers were predicting that the Indians would sweep the series; they were calling them the greatest team in the history of baseball. I really wanted to see the Indians demolish the Giants, even though my father was a Giants fan; I couldn't wait to see all the arrogant New York kids at school finally shut up. They acted like they owned baseball; the Yankees had won the last five World Series and now the New York tradition was being upheld by the Giants.

David and Shelly came to my house; we watched several world series games together. The Steinbergs were from Brooklyn and were Dodger fans, but in this series they were loud supporters of the Giants. I also invited Morton Mandel to join us; I wanted to learn how to do his smoke tricks. I liked Morton; he told fascinating stories about working with the Negro bus boys at Currys restaurant. He was the only guy I knew who had Negro friends, other than Colonel Klein and his Negro foster child.

"No Myron, you can't just blow the smoke out your mouth," said Morton. "First you gotta' inhale, deep down into your lungs."

I tried inhaling, but I gagged and coughed. I didn't really want to learn how to smoke, only how to do that neat trick. It sure was good for parties. Unfortunately, since I didn't smoke and didn't know how to inhale, I couldn't get the trick to work.

The World Series didn't last long; the underdog Giants won in four straight games. They swept the "best team in history" and kept the title in New York for the sixth consecutive year. The media went nuts over one catch by Willie Mays. It was a good over the shoulder catch of a long fly ball by Vic Wertz, but I wouldn't say that it was the greatest catch ever made. However, sports writers from New York were calling it "THE CATCH" . . . all upper case letters . . . the greatest catch in the history of baseball. New York sports writers had a way of claiming that everything done by a New York baseball player was the best in history. Joe DiMaggio's 56 game hitting streak was "the streak," Bobby Thompson's home run was "the shot heard round the world," Gehrig was the "Iron Man," Ruth was the "Sultan of Swat," and now, "the CATCH."

One Friday after school Morton called and invited the Steinbergs and me to be his guests at Currys Restaurant. However, David and Shelly said that they were going to shul with their Uncle Louie and Tanta Baila.

"My mother's making us go," said David, and he didn't sound too happy. "Uncle Louie says that his shul got great parties for teenagers after the services. Yeah, sure!"

"Teenage parties at a shul?" I questioned David's statement.

"Yeah," he responded. "They even got a 'colored' band. At least that's what Uncle Louie says. Some rich guy is paying for it . . . a 'bennyfactor.'"

"No David," I chuckled. "Its called benefactor."

Since the Steinbergs couldn't join me I asked Flo; she wasn't seeing Myron III anymore. She had a scare; her period was late. Luckily, it was a false alarm, but she decided not to tempt fate anymore.

"No more messing around for me," said Flo. "From now on I'll stick to masturbation."

"What?" I exclaimed. I wasn't sure I heard her right. That was the first time I ever heard a girl admit to masturbating.

"Yeah Myron, you heard me right. And that's all I'm gonna' do 'til I get married. You guys think you got a monopoly on everything that's fun. Well, girls also like to get off, and we

270

drink and cuss and spit. The only thing we can't do is piss against a tree."

"I can do that," I laughed. "I can even write Myron in cursive."

Currys was on Collins Avenue and 74th Street, only a ten minute bus ride from my house. It was a very popular restaurant and extremely inexpensive. They served seven course meals for a little over a dollar. The most expensive entrée on the menu was the steak, only $2.95. I really wanted to order the steak, but I was Morton's guest; I didn't want to be rude, so I ordered the Spanish Mackerel, the cheapest dinner.

On the patio in front of Currys a large crowd of people were waiting to be seated. Two fat Negro women dressed like Aunt Jemimah walked around passing out hot biscuits, rolls, corn sticks, and banana fritters. I devoured four or five of the banana fritters. Once inside the restaurant, the main attraction was watching the Negro bus boys clean the tables. The boys were extremely fast and made table changing into a unique form of entertainment. Every time one of them went to reset a table the customers all stopped eating. They took out their watches and urged the boy to set a new speed record. One very tall boy, who looked like Harry Belafonte, was the champion. His hands were a blur as they flew across the table . . . he flipped forks, knives, and plates like a Blackjack dealer at a casino. He cleared and changed a table for four people in twelve seconds. Then, for the grand finale of his amazing act . . . he banged a spoon with his fist . . . the spoon flipped and flew eight feet into the air; he spun around and caught the spoon in his mouth. Everyone stood and applauded; the boy smiled and bowed to his audience and many of the people walked over and gave him tips. What a great show! What a truly amazing catch . . . much more impressive than the Willie Mays catch.

"Wow . . . I've got to learn to do that!" I exclaimed. "That's even better than smoke rings."

"That guy is a hunk!" said Flo, and she smiled at the bus boy. "He's the most gorgeous guy I've ever seen."

"Hey!" I interrupted, "I thought you were going to stick to masturbation?"

Flo kicked me under the table.

After Curry's closed we hung around to chat with Morton. Several other boys from Beach High were also at the restaurant and we started playing poker. Flo loved poker and was very good; she was good at all card games. The handsome bus boy also joined the game; his name was Francis Montgomery, but everyone called him Monty, like the British general from World War II. Monty was from Jamaica and spoke with a very polite English accent. We played poker for a few hours then we went back into the kitchen to see if we could scrounge up some food. Unfortunately, the chefs had all gone home and the refrigerators were locked.

"Monty . . . are you religious?" asked Flo. She stared at the huge gold cross that hung from his neck. His shirt was half unbuttoned, revealing an extremely muscular chest.

"Not really; this cross was a present from my great grandmother. I wear it out of respect for her . . . she was once a slave. To be perfectly honest, I'm quite cynical about religion and God . . . especially about God."

"Don't you believe in God?" asked Flo.

Monty laughed. "Man is supposed to be made in God's image . . . that's what it says in the 'Good Book.' But, I don't buy that drivel. I think that man conjured God in his own image. Yes, I believe in God, the same way that Emerson believed in God. 'The god of the cannibals will be a cannibal, of the crusaders a crusader, and of the merchants a merchant.'"

"But, there is only one God," said Flo, "and everyone is made in his image."

"Hogwash!" said Monty. "In case you havent't noticed, 'I'se' a nigger . . . and the omnipotent 'one God' he be a white man."

Flo laughed. "Good point! . . . and 'I'se' a woman . . . . God is a man."

"Flo, why don't you read Plato's 'Republic,'" said Monty. "you can skip most of it, just read his 'Allegory of the Cave,' its very profound."

"I read it," I responded. "Plato says that what we see and hear is not reality. He feels that we can only learn truth through logic and reasoning."

"Yes sir! That's exactly how I feel about God," replied Monty. "Where's the reality of God? All I see is a simple dream that defies logic or reasoning."

We all liked Monty, especially Flo. He was handsome, articulate and extremely well educated . . . a colored bus boy who read Emerson and Plato, but the way life was in south Florida, I felt sorry for him. He was destined for a life of racial discrimination. But the blockheads at Shawna's party, who did homework assignments by reading "Classic Comics" and watched "Queen for a Day," were destined to have a home in the suburbs and a life of Canasta, Cadillacs, and crinolines.

We decided to grab a late night snack at Moe's Deli, a few miles south of Currys, and everyone crammed into Morton's car. Flo sat in the back seat on Monty's lap. It didn't take long until the two of them were kissing. It was hard to believe, only a month ago, during our Canasta game at Colonel Klein's house, she referred to Negroes as "spades"—now she was making out with this handsome boy from Jamaica.

"Watch out for his hands," warned Morton . . . and he laughed. "Monty's got the world's fastest hands . . . he can remove your bra in five seconds."

"Faster than that!" Flo chuckled, as she broke away from a long passionate kiss.

As we drove to the restaurant I realized that we were looking for trouble. Moe's Deli, like most restaurants in Miami Beach, wouldn't serve Negroes. I was feeling very nervous; my stomach started to rumble, like when I played the accordion on the radio. Morton was an easy going guy, but I if they refused to serve Monty he would probably explode; I think I would too. I anticipated that we were about to get into a fight; we might even get arrested.

We pulled into a parking space in front of Moe's but before Morton stopped the car Flo said, "It's getting late, why don't I run in and get sandwiches to go." Everyone agreed and my stomach settled down. We picked up a few chopped liver sandwiches and took Monty home to Liberty City—a dilapidated Negro section in Miami. Monty lived in a wooden house with boarded windows and a tin roof. He said goodby as he left the car. He kissed Flo's hand and thanked us for the ride to Liberty City. It was obvious; he was too embarrassed to invite us into his home.

"Damn bastards," said Morton, as we drove back to Miami Beach. "We serve Negroes at Currys; we even had the Harlem Globetrotters one night, the whole fuckin' team. But most of the restaurants on the Beach refuse to serve Negroes. Bastards!"

The ride home was very quiet; we didn't even listen to music on the radio. Flo put her head on my lap and fell asleep, and I put my hand on top of her head and stroked her hair. I felt good about my relationship with Flo. Even though I was two years younger, I was her surrogate father, her confidant, much like Mona was my advisor before she went away to college. And as we crossed the causeway back to our beautiful island, I stared at the dark abyss of Biscayne Bay. Thomas Jefferson was wrong! All men are not created equal; Monty had the misfortune of being created as a Negro. I wondered if Jamaicans 'conjured' God in the image of Harry Belafonte. It was a long drive home, and I thought about Monty's spoon trick; maybe with a lot of practice I could learn how to make that amazing catch.

I never saw Monty again. Morton told me he moved with this parents to Chicago; they were very unhappy living in Miami. Too bad I wasn't speaking to Michael Bernstein any longer; I bet he and Monty would have liked each other. Michael also had fast hands.

CHAPTER 36

THE PUNCH

The first Beach High football game of the year was against Miami High, our traditional rival. It was played in the Orange Bowl, which was really a stupid place for that game. Two thousand fans sat in a stadium that seated eighty thousand. And I couldn't understand why the game was regarded as a "rivalry." You can't call a game a rivalry unless there is some degree of equality between the two teams, some degree of competition, like the New York Giants and the Brooklyn Dodgers or the Americans versus the Russians in the Olympics. But the series against Miami High was extremely lopsided, hardly a rivalry. The two schools started playing each other in the mid 1920's and during the ensuing three decades Miami High won every game, except for one tie, and they always won by routs. In 1950, the year before I moved to Miami Beach, the game ended in a 7-7 tie. That was big news in Dade County; that was the first time Miami High ever played a local team and did not win.

The Miami High "Stingrays" were an awesome powerhouse; even their nickname was scary. They were named after a menacing triangular fish that lurked close to the beaches of South Florida. What a great name! And they dominated Florida football. But, part of the reason why they were so good was because of their illegal recruiting. If a great athlete lived outside the Miami High school district, their coaches would approach the parents of the boy and try to get him to transfer. They had a very convincing selling point; Miami High football players received the best college scholarships.

Unfortunately, they even convinced Alberoni Zorzi Dorvilus to cross the bay and become a Stingray. Alberoni, the "Alien," was the all city, all state, all world defensive tackle from Beach High—the monster who unknowingly saved me from Buddy Macker back in the ninth grade.

I went to the Miami High game with the Steinbergs, Dingo McGuffie, and a few other kids from Surfside. Prior to the game we went to a pep rally in the school patio; we were all given black and gold pom poms and cardboard signs that said, "Beat Miami High." Mr. Schecter, our principal, made a stirring speech . . . the same speech he made every year before the start of the season, before the Miami High massacre.

"Its how you play the game that counts, not whether you win or lose."

Then, special school buses transported us to the game and we sang fight songs as we crossed the McArthur Causeway. "We're from Beach . . . couldn't be prouder." I thought about the bus ride home from the Edison game the previous year, when the vivacious Cuban girl, Isabela Cardozo, led us in cheers. I hadn't seen Isabela since that game. I asked around and no one knew what happened to her; she came and went very quickly. That was common at Beach High. Several of the kids who I met during my first three years were no longer there. Miami Beach was a very transient city. Many people moved there because of the wonderful climate; their parents hoped to find some way to make a living. But, if they couldn't find a good job or if their business venture failed they returned to New York, or wherever they came from, or they crossed over to Miami; it was a bigger city with more opportunities.

However, with the Alien it was different; his parents did not move to Miami. He still lived in the Beach High school district but he was provided daily transportation to school in a small private bus. Everyone knew that Miami High was breaking all kinds of rules with the Alien, but no one enforced the law. Most members of the Dade County School Board and the city council were graduates of Miami High. Even the mayor of Miami was an alumnus and a fanatic Stingray fan.

Although the Beach High vs. Miami High game wasn't a "rivalry" in the pure sense of the word, it was a tradition in

South Florida. Every year the local football season began with this annual massacre. It was a Fall ritual, similar to the bull fights in Spain; you knew who was going to win but you went anyway, to enjoy the artistry and courage of the matador when he slaughtered the bull.

The Alien looked intimidating as he led the Stingrays out of the tunnel in the west end zone of the Orange Bowl. He was dressed in his imposing midnight blue uniform . . . matching blue pants, jersey, and helmet; he was "77" the same number that the immortal Red Grange wore at the University of Illinois.

"I attended only one football game in my life," said my father, "and it was probably the most famous game ever played. I went with my nephew, Harry and a few of his friends at the University of Illinois. We drove downstate to Champaign to watch the Illini play the University of Michigan. Michigan was a big favorite, but a sophomore at Illinois named Red Grange was the star of the day. He ran for six touchdowns and Illinois won the game. After that game Grange became known as the 'Galloping Ghost' and 77 became the most well known number in football history."

The band played "Forward Typhoons" and we all rose for the kickoff. It was a great kick, down to the Miami High goal line, but a fast little scat back, even smaller than me, followed a wall of blockers around end and ran 100 yards for a touchdown. The huge scoreboard at the Orange Bowl showed that only several seconds had elapsed, and the score was Miami High 7—Miami Beach 0. We all assumed that it was going to be another terrible football season.

Then Miami High kicked off to us, and we were smothered at our own two yard line. On first down we threw a long pass to Jimbo Lang, our all city end, and it looked like he was going to run all the way for a touchdown. Unfortunately, he was caught from behind by the Alien at the Miami High ten yard line. It was hard to believe that a monster who probably weighed 300 pounds could be that fast.

I saw Shawna sitting at the fifty yard line, in a section reserved for the girlfriends of the football players; they were all wearing matching gold jackets. They liked to call themselves the "golden girls" but most kids called them the "Gold Diggers."

"The Jeweses got that name cause' they spread for bread," said Dingo McGuffie.

"Spread for bread?' What's that mean?."

"Dumbass! They put out for guys with dough." Dingo replied. "Duh! They make bread from dough."

"So, your're telling me that gentile girls don't go down too?"

"Only whores," responded Dingo, "but they give goddamn great blowjobs, something you ain't never gonna' get from no Jewess. And they swallow!"

"Why's that so important?" I asked. "Swallowing is only after you're done."

"Bullshit! Unless a girl swallows it's a waste of time."

And Shawna (who probably swallowed) was standing and cheering when Jimbo made his long run. The other golden girls jumped and shouted and hugged her. The Queen was in her glory. She looked extremely sexy wearing her shiny gold jacket and very tight black pants. The pants came down only to her knees; they were called "pedal pushers."

We had a good halfback, Steve Gordon, who was also on the track team, one of the fastest 100 yard sprinters in the state . . . his nickname was "Flash." On first down Flash Gordon ran to the left, but was tackled at the two yard line by the Alien. On second down he ran to the right, hoping to avoid the Alien, but the monster followed him across the field and stopped him at the goal line . . . . only inches to go.

We called time out and the quarterback went to the sidelines to confer with the coach. The band played "Forward Typhoons"—all of the Beach High kids stood and sang. I had a feeling of déjà vu; this was the Edison game repeating itself . . . the game where we fumbled away the opportunity to upset the number three team in the state.

"I smell fumble," I said. "I sure hope we don't try a quarterback sneak again."

Unfortunately, my premonition was right. We did try a quarterback sneak and we fumbled. And Dingo McGuffie laughed; he laughed so hard that tears came streaming from his eyes. Even though he went to Beach High Dingo could not get himself to root for a team comprised of fifty Jewish players. I had the urge to dump my Coke on his head, but I contained my anger.

For the remainder of the first half we did a decent job stopping the highly touted Stingrays. Surprisingly, we had a very good defense. And we even managed to have a few good drives of our own, but we couldn't score. Jimbo caught several passes, and every time he did, the goddess jumped and cheered. At halftime we were only losing 7-0; it was a very good game. I went to the refreshment stand with Dingo and tried to talk to Shawna, but she was surrounded by the other golden girls; they were all laughing and smoking . . . she ignored me.

"Ha! The little 'kike' bitch doesn't even know you're alive," said Dingo.

Without hesitation I punched Dingo in the nose, right in front of all the golden girls . . . that got Shawna's attention, but she still wouldn't break away from her friends and talk to me.

"You call that a punch, you faggot Jew?" Dingo laughed. "My little sister can punch harder than that." Dingo had a bloody nose but he didn't punch back. I followed him to the bathroom and stood there as he washed his face in the sink. I felt like an idiot; I lost my cool . . . I exploded. I'm not sure if it was because he ripped into Shawna and called her a bitch or because he called her a kike. I hated that word, especially if it was used by someone who wasn't Jewish. I guess colored people felt the same way about the word, "nigger" if it was used by a white person. I went to apologize to Dingo and shake hands. But he wouldn't accept my apology.

"Kike! Kike! Kike! You'll all roast in Hell. Dirty Jew bastards! And your little cunt friend goes down for Jimbo, everyone knows it. Every damn one of them gold diggers . . . they all 'put out' for the jocks and for that new English teacher. Fuckin' Jewesses!" Dingo spit at my feet.

I wanted to yell back at Dingo . . . "We don't roast in Hell . . . only Christians roast. We rot." But, I didn't think Dingo was in any mood for humor; I let him have the last word. We both walked out of the bathroom and returned to watch the second half of the game.

The second half began as badly as the first half. Miami High kicked off; we fumbled. They scored. In a matter of seconds it was 14-0. The rest of the game was fairly close ; we couldn't score even though Jimbo caught a few long passes, but we played great defense. Miami High had two long drives; we stopped them both times, but they got a couple of field goals. The final score was 20-0, a lot more respectable than the routs from the previous three years.

279

As I left the stadium to return to our bus, a girl in a golden jacket came up to me. She puffed on her cigarette and didn't say a word. Then she handed me a folded note; it was unsigned.

"Great Punch Xenocrates
If you get to the moon before me, find a nice crater.
Ill join you."

CHAPTER 37

BLACK AND GOLD FOREVER

The next football game, after Miami High, was against St. Patricks, the Catholic high school in Miami Beach. Their nickname was "the Shamrocks" but we called them the "pattycakes." That was the team we always beat, even when we were terrible. We all laughed as the offensive and defensive players of St. Pats stripped to the waist and exchanged jerseys on the middle of the football field. They couldn't afford enough uniforms for the entire team. We won 56-0; it was great being on the winning end of a rout. In prior years we lost quite a few routs to the "big four" teams in Miami: Miami High, Edison, Coral Gables, and Jackson. Now, we had the chance to beat up on some pathetic team; it was fun. And every time we scored the beautiful Shawna Rose stood and hugged the other golden girls. The next seven games were in the Gold Coast Conference, against various teams from south Florida, not nearly as good as the "big four." We won them all; we were a powerhouse in our conference.

A few of the teams in the Gold Coast Conference had great names. I always had respect for teams with good names, maybe because I hated the name "Typhoons," maybe because I hated the name Myron. The Hialeah Thoroughbreds were named in recognition of the famous local race track. Hialeah boasted that they had the only high school band in the country without a military type of uniform. They wore long red jackets, shiny black boots and black hats, just like the houndsmen at a fox hunt. The

Ft. Lauderdale team was called the "Flying L's." No one knew what a flying "L" was, but they had a neat emblem on their uniform, a big blue and white "L" with wings. And the Key West "Conchs" were named for a mollusk that was indigenous to the southernmost point in the United States. People born in Key West are called conchs, but we called them the "conch suckers."

The final game of the year was scheduled to be against the Tech High Blue Devils, a home game at Memorial Field. If we won that game we would play for the conference championship. Tech was an unusual type of school; it offered special industrial or clerical programs for kids who were not going to college—for boys who wanted to be plumbers or electricians, or girls who wanted to be secretaries or stewardesses. Tech also was the school where girls were required to go if they had babies or if they were married. I always wondered why married girls were forced to go to Tech, but married boys were still allowed to attend any of the other local high schools. The star pitcher on the Beach High baseball team was married, but his wife was forced to go to Tech. Lots of tough kids went to Tech. It was a small school but they had a good football team.

The City of Miami Beach was so excited about the unexpected success of our football team that it organized a special parade on the Saturday prior to the Tech game. I volunteered to work on the Junior Class float committee, so did David and Shelly. We also had three girls on the committee; Candy Blatz and Josie Levinson were short and a little on the plump side, and the third girl was Harriet Mintz, the pretty girl from my Phys. Ed. dance class; she was now going steady with "Fred Astaire." That's what we all called the new boy who was such a great dancer. Our job was to build a float for the parade. We covered a large flatbed trailer with chicken wire which we stuffed with hundreds of crinkled wads of gold crepe paper. Then, with black crepe paper, we created banners on both sides of the float, proudly displaying our theme:

LETS MOW EM DOWN

Candy and Josie were dressed in black Typhoon football jerseys and tiny gold shorts that clung tightly to their oversized butts. They stood on the float and pushed a huge golden lawn mower, symbolically attempting to mow down Harriet Mintz, who represented the evil enemy, the Tech High Blue Devil. Harriet wore blue leotards. She had horns, a blue painted face, a pitch fork, and a long tail hanging from her very cute tush. I wore a black t-shirt and sat in the rear seat of an open convertible during the parade; it was fun to wave to the cheering crowd. Our car towed the float and I looked back a lot, to enjoy the close up view of our devil's bouncing tail. David and Shelly sat next to me and we threw candy to hundreds of people who lined Collins Avenue. The parade was exciting . . . and we kept shouting our theme. "Lets mow em' down. We're from Beach . . . couldn't be prouder!"

The Typhoon band was the first marching group in the parade; they played their stirring rendition of the Gillette Razor Blade song. But, I was prepared. Just before Maxine hit the four bongs on her glockenspiel I covered my lap with a football helmet. The band was followed by fifty proud football players dressed in gold Typhoon jerseys. Then came a purple and pink city of Miami Beach float, with several models in bathing suits sitting on top of a huge plastic flamingo. Immediately behind the city float were troupes of Girl Scouts and Boy Scouts, followed by the Golden Girls, who were led by the beautiful Shawna Rose. The girls wore matching black and gold outfits and they shouted . . . **"Wreck Tech."** The girls did nothing in the parade except walk and wiggle . . . . and look gorgeous.

Then the parade stopped abruptly. Police cars flew past our float. Flashing blue and red lights! Ear piercing sirens! Several of the Golden Girls were screaming and crying. Something had happened! What? We weren't sure, but we knew it was bad. Miss Quinn, the activities director from Beach High, ran past our float shouting that the parade had been canceled. She had a terrible look of horror on her face, but she refused to tell us what had happened.

"Turn around. Turn around. Go back to the assembly area. The parade is over."

Back at the assembly area I saw Shawna talking to a reporter from the Miami Beach Sun, the local newspaper. I crowded around a large group of kids to hear the details.

"It was horrible," said Shawna, and she paused to take a deep breath. "I saw the accident close up. My marching group was right in back of the Boy Scouts. His name is Arnold Pritikin, he is . . . . uh . . . . was in my home room . . . I'm in the ninth grade. My name is Shawna Rose Goldstein . . . that's spelled S-h-a-w-n-a." Shawna paused again, while the newspaper reporter jotted down the correct spelling of her name. "That's with a 'W' not a 'U.' Arnold was supposed to be marching with the other Boy Scouts, but he ran away from his group and tried to hop on the pink float . . . a moving float. And he fell off . . . and smashed his head on the street." Shawna began to cry; tears ran down her beautiful face. As she was talking the newspaper photographer took her picture from several angles.

"Don't move! I wanna' get that shot a few more times," said the photographer.

"I heard the thud." Shawna made sure not to move her head as she continued with the story. "Blood splattered everywhere. I was right near him when it happened . . . it's the worst thing I ever saw in my life. If only I was quicker, I could have saved him." She cried some more and the photographer changed lenses and took more pictures . . . mainly close ups.

The next day the *Miami Beach Sun* featured two pictures on the front page . . . one picture was a Boy Scout lying face down in a pool of blood; a larger picture featured the face of a grief stricken golden goddess who looked like a young Elizabeth Taylor.

There was talk of canceling the Tech game, but if it was called off we would not get to play for the Gold Coast championship. Thus, a decision was made to continue with the game, but to dedicate it to the memory of Arnold Pritikin. Prior to kickoff, instead of playing the Gillette song or Forward Typhoons, we all stood in silence and listened to "Taps" . . . a very sad trumpet solo. Everybody cried.

We scored quickly; a pass to Jimbo Lang made it 7-0 and Queen Shawna hugged the other golden girls. I had binoculars and looked across the field; I was trying to find Leah Sonnino. I had heard that she had a baby girl and was now attending Tech High. Then I saw her. She was standing, wearing a blue sweatshirt, talking to a few other girls. She was smiling and looked happy and still had that playful way of flipping her pony tail when she talked.

For the remainder of the first half I stared at Leah with my binoculars, trying to summon enough courage to go over and say hello. Finally, at halftime I did it . . . I walked around the small stadium, to the refreshment stand on the other side of the field, the enemy side. It was a mistake. I never reached Leah. I was intercepted by a few Tech High kids who took turns punching me in the stomach; that was Blue Devil turf. I fell to the ground; I was lying face down . . . they began kicking me. Fortunately, a policeman broke it up.

"Hey kid. What are you . . . . a dingbat?" said the cop. "Get back to your own side . . . with the other Jews."

The final score of the game was 7-0; I sat there in pain until it was over, and didn't tell anyone about my halftime adventure. I went to that game with the Steinbergs and Dingo McGuffie. Dingo wasn't talking to me, not since I punched him at the Miami High game, but David was friendly with him . . . so he joined us at the game. Dingo looked at me and grinned; he knew what happened at halftime. He had friends at Tech High.

"Damn right; I got good friends at Tech." Dingo finally talked to me. "And those Blue Devil girls love to suck cock . . . even that little Jew bitch that you went to visit loves to suck cock." I wanted to punch Dingo again, but I clenched my teeth and said nothing.

The final game of this glorious season was for the championship of the Gold Coast Conference against Key West. We beat the "Conch Suckers" during the regular season and were confident that we could beat them again, and we did, 14-7. Jimbo was the most valuable player of the game; he scored both of our touchdowns. After the game we tore the goal posts down and carried them six blocks, from Memorial Field to the corner of Lincoln Road and Washington Avenue; we were the champions, and leading the parade was Jimbo, with Queen Shawna riding high on his shoulders.

The next sport after football was basketball; Jimbo swapped shoulder pads for black and gold shorts and a matching tank top that revealed his broad shoulders and muscular arms. And the cheerleaders bounced and shouted: "Jimbo, Jimbo, he's our man . . . if he can't do it no one can." And, the word around school was that most of the cheerleaders had first hand experience with Jimbo as "their man." The girls cheered and swooned and waved golden pom poms and Jimbo signed autographs for his growing legion of groupies.

But, where was Shawna? As the basketball season began she was gone.

"She moved back to New York," said Shirley Segal. Smoke blew out of her mouth as she talked; a cigarette hung from her lips. "She got a contract with a modeling agency . . . they saw her picture in the paper after the parade."

"That's not what I heard," said Brenda Singer, as she borrowed Shirley's cigarette to light her own. "I heard that she got knocked up and moved to New York to have her baby."

I never found out which story was true and I never saw Shawna Rose again. Shirley Segal became the new leader of the Golden Girls and the new girlfriend of Jimbo Lang. And later that year Shirley went with her parents to Cuba, a popular vacation spot where abortions were legal. Then, with the start of track season, Jimbo changed uniforms again, it was time to defend his title as the state record holder in the broad jump, and he also changed golden girlfriends. Brenda Singer took her turn, and others waited in the golden line and they smiled as they repeated the immortal words of Shawna Goldstein: "somewhere between stupendous and incredible."

CHAPTER 38

ADVANCED CONJUGATION

Due to an administrative error I was accidentally registered in Spanish III in the eleventh grade, an elective course that I never would have selected on my own. I hated Spanish; it was my worst course in high school. Students were only required to take two years of a foreign language, and I struggled through Spanish I and II; the nightmare was supposed to be over. Why was I in this third course? Spanish III was designed for the serious Spanish students. Unfortunately, once again I had to battle with the school Registrar, the same woman who wouldn't allow me to switch from section 9-3 to 9-12 in the ninth grade. But this time I would be dealing from a position of power; I knew more about Eloise than she wanted anyone to know. I knew all about her "itchy pussy," I even knew that her pet name for Mr. Calhoun's penis was Jeremiah. If she gave me a rough time I could also play rough . . . whatever it took to get out of Spanish III.

"Excuse me, Miss Cordess, I think there's some kind of mistake. I never elected to be in Spanish III." I began my attack slowly . . . but I was prepared to pull all punches; I would not lose this battle.

"Yes Myron, you're right," responded the Registrar, as she turned the pages of her record book. "It was a mistake, probably because you had an 'A' in Spanish II; not many students had an 'A' in that course."

I was happy that she was quick to admit her mistake; It looked like the battle would be won without a fight, especially when she took out a list of open courses where I could transfer.

"Hmm. Lets see . . . most sections at 11:00 AM are closed; we have a very limited selection available at that time slot. You can take Latin I or French I. Or, if you play a musical instrument you can take Band."

"Do they have accordions in the band?" Anything was better than Spanish III, even the accordion. Unfortunately, my choice came down to Latin I, French I, or Spanish III. I decided to stick with Spanish III.

"Buenos dias," said Señora Johnson, our Spanish teacher. "The primary emphasis of this class will be advanced conjugation of 500 verbs, regular verbs and irregular verbs . . . in many different tenses. And, as a side project we will translate an abridged version of 'Don Quixote' from Spanish into English. Translation will be a year long project; one page a day for the entire school year."

Oh no! Not another year of this . . . I dediced to go back to the Registrar and transfer out of Spanish III. I called Flo on the phone to discuss my strategy . . . it looked like I would have to play rough with Eloise Cordess. I was going to walk into her office and say one word: "Jeremiah" and threaten to tell Mr. Schecter. That would get me out of Spanish III.

"Not so fast," said Flo. "Guess what I just found out? Mr. Schecter is also banging Eloise—on Tuesdays after school—in his conference room. They call their weekly fun day 'Terrific T-Day' and she calls his dick 'T' . . . probably because his middle initial is 'T.' So, don't go using your 'Jeremiah' strategy. One more thing—Schecter and Calhoun know about each other—they arranged to bang Eloise on different days. You sure can learn a lot of great shit from these party lines."

The next day I returned to the office of the Registrar and asked to switch to Latin I, I already knew Veni, Vici, Visi and E Purblus Unum, and Latin students got to wear neat togas to class once in awhile. But, it was too late . . . Eloise wouldn't let me make the change.

"What is there about NO that you don't understand? Myron, please close the door on the way out."

"Yes, Miss Cordess," I replied. "Thank you anyway." I thought about "Terrific T-Day." Where did they do it, on the floor or the conference table? It was hard to envision Mr. Schecter having sex on the floor or on a table. Actually, it was hard to envision Mr. Schecter with his tie removed. He probably did it with his tie on.

"In French and Latin the students all call me Madam Johnson," said our middle age Spanish teacher, "but in here I prefer to be addressed as Señora Johnson." This stern, matronly woman had never been married and everyone assumed that she was still a virgin.

"But, I thought you only used Señora for a married woman," said Spencer Teichman, the boy genius who helped me with Nazi tattoo research in the ninth grade. Spencer was brilliant and I had great respect for him, but he was a little strange . . . a loner. "Don't you always use Señorita for unmarried women?"

"No Spencer, that's not necessarily true, responded Señora Johnson. "Mature women should be referred to as Señora regardless of their marital status . . . it's a term of respect.".

Peter Broden, one of my neighbors from Surfside, leaned across the aisle and whispered to a few classmates. "How about if she's a virgin? Is she still a señora?" They all laughed, a subdued laugh . . . under their breath.

"I heard that Peter; I might be an old geezer but I still have good ears. And a woman's virtue has no bearing on her title." Peter's face turned red and the entire class laughed, but not Señora Johnson. Peter was an outstanding student in Spanish; he even knew how to roll his tongue and trill the R's, something very few Americans could do, especially Jewish kids.

"Rojo, blanco, y azul . . . those are the colors of the flag," said Señora Johnson; then she pointed at the blackboard. "Black is Negro . . . just like the English words, Negro and Nigger."

"That's not a nice word," exclaimed Candy Blatz. "My mother said we should never use the "N" word . . . of course, Negro is OK, but not the 'igger' word." I knew Candy from the homecoming "Float Committee"—the parade where Arnold Pritikin was killed. She was a nice girl and we had long conversations while we were decorating the float. I was definitely thinking about asking her to the movies but she was dating Peter Broden. The reason Candy was in Spanish III was to be with him; they tried to take all classes together.

"No Candy, it isn't really a bad word. Nigger is just an idiomatic colloquialism derived from the root word for black. Spanish people often refer to Negro children as Negritos or

Negritas. The English equivalent would be Nigger. Of course, we all know that the Negro differs from the Caucasian in several respects, not only skin pigmentation, but their hair, nostrils, and lips are significantly different, and the mental capacity of the Negro . . . well that's another story, but fortunately, we are still living in a different school district . . . so we don't have to deal with that issue."

"But, what about Brown versus the Board of Education?" asked Peter Broden. "Why aren't the schools in Miami Beach integrated? The Supreme Court recently ended the separate but equal doctrine in Kansas." Peter was planning to be an attorney, he was an outstanding student in Spanish and in all other courses.

Señora Johnson appeared uneasy with this question. It was obvious that she wanted to get back to conjugating verbs. "Peter, I'm sure we would have no problem allowing a few well behaved Negroes to attend this school, provided that they showed that they were ready for acculturation into white society, and if they bathed regularly, but only if they lived in Miami Beach. However, they all live on the other side of the bay, so its really a moot issue. But, I question whether the Supreme Court decision follows the will of God. If God wanted all men to be the same they would all be the same color; I see nothing immoral or discriminatory about separate but equal."

I couldn't believe what I was hearing; how could a teacher say that conditions such as those in Overtown and Liberty City were equal . . . or that segregation was the will of God. I wanted to shout out and tell her that she was a bigot, but I kept quiet. However, I knew I was wrong; my silence was an endorsement of her bigotry. I was no different than the "good" Christians in Germany who sat back and let the Nazis kills the Jews. I was no different than the old white-haired Jewish people in South Beach who q'vetched in Yiddish, but only to each other.

Danny Berger was also enrolled in Spanish III. He laughed when Señora Johnson said "negrito." He raised his hand to make a cultural contribution to the discussion.

"My dad calls them 'pickaninneys,' but I like 'negrito . . . great word . . . I guess it means 'little nigger.' But how do you tell the negritos from the negritas? They all look alike." Several of the students laughed.

"Turn em' upside down," shouted Manny Lefkowitz . . . and the laughter turned into howling.

I had avoided all contact with Danny during the past year and a half, ever since I wrote the speech that helped him become tenth grade president. I hated him for getting Leah Sonnino pregnant and dumping her. Even when he nodded to me in Spanish class my typical response was just a grunt . . . which was even less than a nod.

Señora Johnson frequently lost her patience when students came to class unprepared . . . which was almost every day.

"Darn you kids, don't you ever study your verbs? Darn-it Manuel *(Manny's Spanish name)*, if you keep doing so darn poorly with conjugation I'm going to send a note home to your mother and father."

"But, Señora Johnson, I'm working my damn ass off. I just can't understand this shit."

"Manuel!" exclaimed an irate Señora Johnson. "If you ever say the 'D' word in here again I will refer you to the principal." Wow . . . she was really angry.

"Its OK to let off anger and frustration once in a while and its only natural to use cuss words. I'm not chastising you for saying 'ass' or 'shit,' but never—ever say D-A-M-N . . . it is blasphemy to take the Lord's name in vain. That's why I always say darn or darn-it."

"What's D-A-M-N?" Manny whispered to Danny Berger. "I never heard of Dam-n."

"No, dumb-ass," said Danny. "The 'N' is silent."

"Who you calling dumb?" said Manny. "Its stupid to spell 'damn' with an 'n' and then not to even say the goddamn 'n' when you talk to people."

"Well, lots of words are like that," replied Danny. "Hey, the 'b' in 'dumb' is also silent, but I don't think they got too many silent letters in Spanish."

Advanced conjugation was extremely difficult and demanding. Every day we were assigned five new verbs to memorize. The next day we were quizzed on the conjugation of one of the verbs in present, preterit, imperfect, subjunctive, future, present perfect, and past perfect tenses and we had five minutes to complete the quiz. Then Señora Johnson carefully read the solutions to the class and we were asked to grade our own test with a special red pencil.

"OK muchachos, take out your red pencils," said Señora Johnson, "and grade yourself as I read the correct answers. And I don't want to see anyone making changes to the quiz or erasing anything."

"Why only muchachos?" asked Candy Blatz. "How about the muchachas?"

"No Candy," responded Señora Johnson. "Even though we use muchachas as the plural of muchacha, in a mixed group the male noun dominates—like real life, where males have been chosen by God to serve as leaders for the descendants of Eve."

None of the special red pencils had erasers, so it was impossible to change an answer during the grading process. But Danny Berger used a special red pencil which had black lead secretly inserted in one end. Thus, as Señora Johnson read the solutions to the quiz he flipped his red pencil to the black side and made modifications to create a perfect paper. He got away with his cheating the first several times, always getting a perfect 100. However, Danny wasn't content with his success; he liked to brag to other kids, to prove how clever he was . . . like when he bragged about his curly pubic hairs in Colonel Klein's class. But, this time his big mouth got him in trouble. Señora Johnson heard about his cheating and caught him making changes during the self-grading process. She was vicious in her attack.

"Danny, you're just like all the other deceitful Jews. You and your darn racketeer father, always finding a way to scheme and cheat. That's why the Germans hated the 'chosen people.'"

On the inside, I was chuckling, happy to see the phony Danny Berger finally get in trouble. But, I was furious with the anti-Semitic comments of Señora Johnson. Without raising my hand, I blurted my displeasure.

"Señora Johnson—how can you say such terrible things about Jewish people just because one student cheated on a test?"

Señora Johnson stared at me; her face got taut. She had a look of hate in her eyes. Thirty-five students looked at her, and at me. There was a long uncomfortable silence as everyone waited for her response to my question. Then, without saying a word in English or in Spanish she walked over to my desk and grabbed me by the collar . . . and she also grabbed Danny. We were both escorted to the principal's office.

Danny and I sat in the principal's conference room for two hours, waiting for our meeting with Mr. Schecter. Several large signs were posted on the walls, reminding students that talking was not allowed. However, I didn't need a reminder; I hadn't talked to Danny since the ninth grade and I didn't plan on talking to him now.

Finally, Danny wrote a brief note on a piece of paper. He folded the paper and passed it to me.

"Thanks for defending me . . . that took guts!"

I didn't want his thanks. My comments had nothing to do with him. I considered sending a brief note back to Danny, to inform him that I was not defending him . . . but I didn't think he would understand, so I tore his paper into tiny pieces and dumped it in the waste paper basket.

I explained the entire situation to Mr. Schecter and he agreed with me, in principle, but told me that I was wrong to criticize a teacher in front of other students.

"Young man, your teacher was very upset about the cheating incident and she obviously said things that were inappropriate, but that doesn't give you a license to be rude. You could have spoken to her in private, after class."

I was required to serve two hours of after-school detention.

"Make it any afternoon except Tuesday," said Mr. Schecter. "I reserve that day for special meetings in the conference room."

It wasn't a bad punishment, but Danny really got in serious trouble. He was permanently expelled from Beach High and forced to transfer to Lear private school . . . along with the dummies and incorrigible kids. He continued to hang out at the corner of Lincoln Road and Washington Avenue on Saturdays, where he had previously been king of the "Crossroads." Now he was regarded as an outsider, a kid who wished that he was a Beach High student. We called those kids "wannabes." Lots of Jewish kids from the private schools and from Miami were "wannabes" and hung out at our corner. Everyone continued to say hello to Danny, but it was only a perfunctory greeting, much like the forced smile that we gave to Holy Joe after his son was killed in the auto accident.

I worked hard in Spanish III, very hard, and struggled with the daily memorization of verbs and the painstaking translation of Don Quixote. Every night my father quizzed me on the conjugation of the assigned verbs, and the following morning at 6:30 AM, just before I left for school, he gave me another quiz. At the end of the first six-week grading period my average on all tests and assignments was 90, just barely an "A." However, I only received a grade of "C" on my report card. I met during lunch time with Señora Johnson to complain about my grade. She was very abrupt, and told me that I received a two-letter grade reduction because of my impertinence in class, the day that I criticized her anti-Semitic comments.

"But, that isn't fair," I complained. "I served two hours of detention as my punishment. Why must I also have my grade reduced? I had an average of 90; you said that you only needed 90 to get an A."

"Myron, if you don't think I was fair," replied Señora Johnson, "go talk to Mr. Schecter . . . you darn 'chosen people' all stick together." She chuckled and chewed on a celery stalk coated with mayonnaise, "He's available every day except 'Terrific T-Day'—in Spanish its called marvelous 'Martes.'"

I didn't go to see Mr. Schecter; I thought it would be a waste of time to complain, but I wanted to warn him to be careful. His secret was out. I thought about sending him an anonymous letter. I would cut words out of a newspaper and paste them on a piece of paper . . . that way no one could ever trace the handwriting back to me.

Mr. Schecter BE CAREFUL
Señora *JOHNSON* KNOWS ABOUT
Terrific T Day
A friend

As I walked to the cafeteria I stopped and watched several boys who were standing next to the World War II statue in the school patio; they were singing to a couple of girls—a contrived variation of a popular song.

"If I gave my heart to you . . . I'd have none and you'd have two . . ."

The girls laughed . . . so did I; it felt good to laugh. I joined the boys in their serenade, trying to get my mind off of Señora Johnson. I knew that I was headed for another miserable year in Spanish. When I got home I looked in my encyclopedia, I wanted to learn why Jews were called the "Chosen People."

CHAPTER 39

REBELS RULE DOLLY'S

David and Shelly Steinberg and Josh Broden came over to my house, looking to organize a game of touch football. Josh was a good student but his main interests were girls and sports, and he could throw a football a mile. He would stand in my back yard and throw the ball over the roof of my house, and it landed across the street.

"I called Arnie Dombrowski," said Josh. "He's going to meet up with us in Bal Harbour at the field next to the Church By the Sea. He said he'll bring a bunch of kids to join us, including 'your buddy,' Dingo McGuffie. We're going to play against some goys from Bal Harbour."

Twenty kids showed up for the game, nine Jews from Surfside and Dingo, and the ten kids from Bal Harbour. Bal Harbour was a snooty restricted town; Jews weren't allowed to live there, but we didn't think there would be any problem playing touch football on an empty field. If the police came to question us Dingo would be our spokesman; he was the token gentile on our team. I always got confused with Bal Harbour and Bay Harbor, the two towns that were adjacent to Surfside. Bal Harbour spelled harbor with a "U"—a very pretentious spelling. My mother called the residents of Bal Harbour "hoitey toitey blue bloods." Bay Harbor was a Jewish town, situated on two little islands in the middle of Biscayne Bay, just west of Surfside. Bay Harbor spelled harbor without the U. I guess that was the Jewish way of spelling, without the blue blood.

"That's crazy," said Shelly. "with food the 'U' means kosher, but with harbors the 'U' means goyim."

Jimbo Lang also joined us, but only as a coach. We were not allowed to touch him; he was like a "sacred cow," the protected athlete of Beach High. If anyone injured him they would have major problems back at school. Jimbo was obviously the strongest, fastest, and most athletic guy on the field, but he was just a bystander, watching the game and having fun acting as our coach. This was the first time I ever met him close up; I only knew him from the stands at football or basketball games, or from stories I heard from Shawna Goldstein. Of course, I did see a very private close up view of Jimbo, underwater, when he was with Shawna at the Venetian pool. I sure hope he didn't remember that incident.

We scrunched together in a huddle on the sidelines. Jimbo gave instructions. "OK kid, you in the blue shirt, here's the play." He was talking to me, but he didn't refer to me or any of us by name. Gods don't talk to ordinary mortals on a first-name basis. "Run fifteen yards downfield and make a sharp cut to the left and stop dead in your tracks. Then shout, wave your arms, and scream for the ball . . . then run deep. And you, with the red shirt, I heard you got a strong arm . . . once the guy in the blue shirt starts to scream, look directly at him. Pump twice and then heave the fuckin' ball. This play is called P-42 Left-Long. I caught five TD passes off that play."

No one spoke when Jimbo was talking; everyone was in awe of the best football player in the history of Beach High. But, there in the huddle . . . I had one burning question. "So, why did Shawna move to New York?" I asked. "Was she pregnant?"

Jimbo laughed. "Can't rightly say why she moved . . . but I got tired of the same pussy every night . . . it was time to change. So much pussy and so little time. Now make that cut and curl real sharp and scream for the fuckin' ball . . . Hup! Hup! Lets go team."

The play worked . . . I cut, screamed, and ran deep. Josh Broden did two pump fakes and let it go long. It was a perfect spiral and landed right in my hands; I took it in for a TD. Then I fell in the end zone and rolled around with my teammates celebrating our quick score. Jews 7 . . . Goyem 0. But, a large hand reached into the pile and yanked the ball away from me.

"OK you little Hebes' . . . time to move your kosher asses out of here," said a Bal Harbour policeman. He turned south, facing Surfside, which was just across the street, and punted the football back to our little Jewish town. It wasn't a very good kick . . . I could do much better. "Now get the hell out of here Jew boys, and go back to Surfside where your belong."

Dingo chuckled and spoke privately with the policeman. I don't know what they said but they both laughed. We then crossed the street and the two policemen stood and watched, to make sure we left the hallowed grounds of their restricted town; the Bal Harbour kids laughed and shot "birds" at us . . . extended middle fingers. As we stood on the sidewalk, safely back in Surfside, we turned our rear ends to the policemen and the snickering goyem. We dropped our pants and flashed nine matching white Jewish asses . . . a row of moons . . . . our response to the eviction. Dingo was the only one who did not participate in the special message.

Then we quickly pulled our pants back up; everyone except Jimbo. He took advantage of this opportunity to display his extremely long penis, which Shawna Goldstein once referred to as "somewhere between stupendous and incredible.'" He knew boys all talked a lot . . . what better way to advertise his special attribute to the girls.

"Jesus H. Christ!" said one of the guys, in disbelief, "that's a fuckin' salami you got hangin' there."

I picked up the football and turned toward the laughing kids and the two cops in Bal Harbour. I let out my anger by kicking the ball back into enemy territory. It sailed high over their heads, deep into the restricted grounds of the forbidden city. The other kids were still staring at Jimbo's dick; they missed the punt, but Jimbo saw it.

"Damn, kid, that was the longest punt I ever saw. How come you ain't on the football team? By the way, haven't we ever met before? Have you ever been to the Venetian pool in Coral Gables?"

"Venetial pool? Me? No . . . I've never been there." I gave a menacing look to David and Shelly Steinberg, for them to keep quiet. They were with me the day I saw Jimbo getting a blowjob in the cave.

Just then I felt a sharp thud on my head; I saw stars, and I fell to the ground. One of the Bal Harbour kids threw a large rock from his side of the street and it hit me in the back of the head. Blood was gushing all over my clothes, onto the sidewalk. The police ran over quickly, wrapped a shirt around my head and pulled me into their patrol car.

"Shut up Jew boy . . . we're getting you to St. Francis hospital . . . you've been hurt bad. You damn Jews; always causing trouble. That's what happens from too many centuries of inbreeding."

At the hospital a nurse shaved my head around the wound and washed the area. I sat for a long time with an ice pack on my head and counted the nuns and the nurses walking by the emergency room. The nuns outnumbered the nurses three-to-one; I was convinced . . . Catholics were more concerned about the next life than the present one. Finally, a doctor arrived. His name was Sheldon Eisenman. It felt comforting to have a Jewish doctor, especially at a hospital that had more nuns than nurses. Dr. Eisenman gave me an injection, a tetanus shot, and wrapped a bandage around my head. I looked like the drummer boy in that famous Revolutionary War picture, the one with three wounded patriots playing fifes and a drum.

My parents then arrived at the hospital; my father looked very white and scared and my mother was crying.

"Myron, what happened?" shouted my mother. "Oh, don't talk, the doctor said you should relax; don't get stressed out."

I was OK on the ride home; I had a real bad headache, but other than that I was in good condition. But, when I got home I had trouble breathing; I felt faint, my knees were weak, and my heart rate slowed down. I could barely speak.

"Get me back to the hospital, something is wrong with me; my heart feels like its about to stop."

"He's allergic to the Tetanus antitoxin, said Dr. Eisenman, as he gave me a shot of adrenaline to restore a normal heartbeat. "Make sure he never again has a Tetanus injection, it could kill him."

I was only fifteen; it was scary to hear any mention of death, very scary. But, I marked those words of caution indelibly in my memory; never again would I allow doctors to give me a Tetanus shot. When I got home from the hospital, the second time, I told my mother how we were evicted from Bal Harbour. She went nuts and called the police "bastards, sons-of-bitches, and Nazis."

"Sol, isn't there anything we can do about this?" asked my mother. "Can't you talk to Ben Seligman; he's your attorney. Can't he do something?"

"Rose . . . Seligman is a real estate attorney, not much he can do. Besides, Bal Harbour is a restricted town, the police have the legal right to keep Jews out."

"Dad, I agree with mother. We should do something about this, how can they get away with that? I can understand the Kenilworth hotel not allowing Jews, but how can a whole city be restricted? This is America."

That night I had an unexpected visitor. Jimbo Lang came to my house in his red Jaguar convertible; he even called me by first name.

"Myron, I just wanted to see how you're doing. You were really gushing blood today . . . . I got scared."

"I'm OK Jimbo, its nice of you to come by. Thanks." I was surprised to see him; I didn't picture him as a sensitive, caring person.

"Myron, how would you like to join 'Rebels?' You know, the gang that hangs out at Dolly's. We could use a good punter on our team. I'm not allowed to play, so I'm the head coach."

Dolly's was a very popular open air restaurant near Beach High, where many of the tough kids ate lunch. It was a haven for Jewish boys who tried to put on a façade, who tried to look like they were greasers. The boys at Dolly's wore white tee shirts with packs of cigarettes wrapped under rolled up sleeves, and an extra cigarette stuck behind their ear. Most of the boys at Dollys smoked Lucky Strike or Chesterfield, but the Rebels smoked Camels. If you weren't a Rebel you weren't allowed to smoke Camels . . . that was their brand.

"Thanks Jimbo, but I can't see myself as a Rebel, I don't even smoke."

"Well, I don't either, but that's because athletes ain't allowed to smoke. And if you're going to be the team punter they'll let you in without smoking."

The following day I joined Jimbo at lunch; he introduced me to Chuck and Toby Weinstock, the owners of Dolly's, and he told everyone that I was the "best fuckin' punter" he had ever seen. There were lots of greasy looking "hoods" at Dolly's, but only two girls, a smiling red head in a straw cowboy hat and a blonde who was wearing a tiger striped hat; she was sticking the tip of her tongue into a large Coke bottle. Both of the girls were very sexy.

"Give Myron a burger and fries, and a large grape cooler," said Jimbo, "its on me." I loved the grape cooler, it was an extra sweet version of grape soda served in a huge glass that looked like a flower vase, but if you drank the whole thing you would pee all day long. And the other Rebels welcomed me to the group, but told me that I couldn't become a member until I went through a formal initiation process, even if I was being sponsored by "the great" Jimbo Lang.

"Well, OK . . . but I don't smoke cigarettes."

I thought back to the eighth grade, when Manny Lefkowitz, Norty Berkowitz, and several other kids stood around scratching their balls. Three years had gone by; most of the former ball scratchers were now in Rebels, the Jewish teenage gang, and had taken up new vices, like smoking, beer, and sex. Of course, I also liked girls, but aside from my brief flings with Maxine Schwartz and ZD, I didn't have any other sexual experiences to talk about. There was also my lingering memory of Leah Sonnino and that one kiss on the front porch with Shawna Goldstein. But, I refused to smoke and the taste of beer made me sick. Life was much simpler when all you had to do to look cool was scratch your balls and spit.

"Hey Chuck, toss me a hard boiled egg," shouted Corny Krepach, a fat, pimple faced kid, as he sipped on a gigantic lime cooler; coolers came in many flavors. Most of the Rebels called him Kreplach . . . like the Jewish soup.

"OK, Kreplach, anything for one of my boys," replied Chuck, "here comes your egg."

Kreplach reached in the air and made a one hand grab of the flying egg. But, Chuck had a sense of humor . . . it wasn't hard boiled. Splat! The raw egg ran over Kreplach's outstretched hand; everyone in Dolly's had a big laugh, especially Chuck.

"Toby, give Kreplach a wet towel and an extra burger," said Chuck, "its on the house . . . . he's a good sport."

Just then, amid the laughter, the multi-colored Wurlitzer in the corner of Dolly's began to blast the popular new song, "Rock Around the Clock." Dolly's didn't have a dance floor, it was a small, open air luncheonette, but the new sound by Bill Haley and the Comets got the kids on their feet, out to the sidewalk . . . One Two Three O'Clock Four O'Clock Rock.

There weren't any girls at Dollys, except for the two slutty "babes" sitting in the corner . . . it was a rough crowd, not the place where "nice Jewish girls" wanted to be seen. But on that fateful day any girl who happened to be on the sidewalk, walking by Dollys, was grabbed by one of the boys . . . and Rock and Roll began, between the twisted columns and pink archways of Espanola Way, one block west of the hotel where Desi Arnez first introduced Babalu to America. But that was during the decade before I moved to Miami Beach.

"Damn! This new sound is hypnotic," said Toby, "it's captured the kids . . . . kind of reminds me of the Charleston, when I was young." Toby took hold of Kreplach's hand, the one covered with raw egg, and pulled him to the sidewalk.

"Lets Rock Daddy-O." Goodbye Pattie Paige, goodbye Perry Como. Worse yet . . . goodbye Rhumba . . . . No more forward, forward, side together. I feared that my dance lessons at Arthur Murray's were about to become useless, almost as useless as my ability to open coconuts. But, I could still punt a football . . . and I was about to become a member of Rebels.

◆

"Hey Lindy, you ever got a blow job?" asked Irv Fishkin, the leader of the Rebels; he was a thin, weird looking guy with hollow cheeks. He rolled up the sleeves of his shirt and wore a black vest that matched his pants. Because his name was Fishkin and because he had a face that looked like a fish, Irv was called "Fish-Face" or if you knew him well enough you could just call him "Fish" . . . even the teachers at school called him by one of those names, and he always reminded people that Fish-Face was one word, a hyphenated word. At the mention of "blow job" the two girls immediately jumped up from their table in the corner of Dolly's and grabbed the the back of Fish-Face's black vest.

This was like the famous story from "Arabian Nights," where Ali Babba said "Open Sesame" and a giant door immediately opened and a room full of treasures were on display. Fish-Face said the magic words "Blow Job" and Wow! . . . I was ready for my room full of treasures.

It looked strange to see a guy wearing a vest in Miami Beach, since the weather was typically in the 80's or 90's, and very few of the classrooms at school were air conditioned. Even if you only wore a t-shirt you would be sweating by the end of the day. But, the leader of Rebels was expected to dress that way. He called the two girls his "babes" and said that once I became a Rebel they would be glad to give me a blow job whenever I wanted one or I could watch them "do each other." Fish-Face was my new hero; he had magical powers, just like Ali Babba.

"But, Lindy . . . only BJ's or hand jobs . . . they don't go all the way with you or nobody else, they only put out for me." Everyone in Rebels had a nickname and it looked like I was going to be known as Lindy; I was about to become a crony of Jimbo, Kreplach, and Fish-Face.

The girls looked at me and smiled. Bubbles, the red head, had a mouth full of silver braces. Oh no! That's how you get "penis cancer." She was chewing bubble gum; I could see a big pink wad rolling over her tongue. The girls kissed each other and Bubbles passed the gum to Bam Bam, the blonde. Then Bam Bam walked over and stuck her wet, sticky tongue in my ear. It was her erotic invitation for me to become the new punter for the Rebels football team. Thankfully, Bam Bam did not have braces.

Normally, a new member of Rebels had to eat at Dolly's and "pledge" for at lest three months prior to initiation; you had to save receipts from the little luncheonette. But because I was sponsored by Jimbo I was allowed to skip the pledging process and go directly to initiation. My old friend Howard Lefkowitz was also being initiated as a Rebel, but neither of us fit in with the group.

"I'm here only because Manny wants me to join," said Howard. "He say's 'you ain't nobody at Beach less' you're a Rebel.'"

"But, what do 'you' want Howard? Do you really think you belong with this group? Do you really want to join?"

"I ain't got much choice; I live here in South Beach, with most of the other Rebels. Where you live . . . up with all the rich kids in Surfside, you don't have to face these guys every day. You got a choice . . . Do ya' understand what I'm saying?"

THE INITIATION

We met in a warehouse in South Beach, down near fifth street; it was owned by the father of one of the Rebels. We lined up against a cold concrete wall, completely nude, except for our shoes and socks. There were ten of us, ten pledges. We were all scared and you could see goose bumps on our arms. And thirty Jewish Rebels sat around watching, drinking beer, laughing, and smoking Camels. Bubbles and Bam Bam, the "babes" of Fish-Face also watched. You could hear them giggle and pop their bubble gum. A few of the nude boys turned their backs and began yanking on their penises, trying to look a little more impressive for the two girls.

"OK Myron," said Fish-Face, "here's a riddle for you. "An Italian plane crashes in Idaho; all the passengers were from France. Where do you bury the survivors? What country?"

"You don't bury survivors," I responded.

"OK guys," said Fish-Face, "this here boy ain't as dumb as he looks. Now, here's the first big test of the initiation, to see if you truly qualify to be a Rebel. Its called the 'Olive Race.' You pledges will be divided into two teams, five on each team. Bubbles and Bam Bam will be the official olive starters; they will stick a black olive up the ass of one guy and a brown olive in the other guy . . . and they'll make sure that its in good and tight. These two guys are your lead men . . . Then, the lead man of each team, black and brown, will run to the first Coke bottle and without touching the olive, squat, spread your cheeks, and drop the olive in the plate next to the bottle. If you miss the plate, pick the olive up with your mouth and put it in the plate. No hands allowed! Then, once the olive is in the plate the second member of the team will squat on top of the next bottle. You can see, we've put black or brown olives on top of every bottle. Then squat and work the olive up your ass . . . and no fuckin' hands allowed. Then you run to the third bottle and plate. The first team to finish the relay is the winner."

"What do we get if we win?" asked Howard. He was staring at the girls and was starting to get an erection. Howard couldn't wait for the race to begin; he volunteered to be the lead runner on our team.

"You get BJs from Bubbles and Bam Bam . . . but why don't you ask what happens to the losers?" said Fish-Face, and most of the Rebels began to laugh. "The losing team has to eat all ten olives."

"Hey guys," I interrupted . . . "I don't like black or brown olives, why can't we use the green ones . . . I like the little ones with red tongues sticking out." No one laughed.

"Lindy . . . shut the fuck up," said several of the Rebels, "this ain't no joke. If you don't want to be a Rebel you can walk right now. We only want guys who are committed . . . who belong . . . even if you can kick the shit out of a football."

"Hey, go easy said Jimbo, the only Rebel who wasn't smoking or drinking. We need him if we want to beat the "River Rats." That was the Christian gang from Little River, a run down neighborhood in Miami. They were a tough bunch of hoods who frequently drove over to Lincoln Road on Saturday mornings, looking for fights. The River Rats hated Jews . . . their mission in life was to terrorize Jewish girls; they were the descendants of the Cossacks . . . . the Pogroms . . . the reason why my ancestors moved from Minsk and Bialystock to America.

"Jimbo . . . I know how important it is for you to win that game," replied Fish-Face, "but principles come first, if Lindy ain't happy with the olive race then he don't fit in and he can pick up and leave right now."

Jimbo was the hero of Beach High, the idol of every boy, and the romantic dream of every girl, but he wasn't the leader of the Rebels . . . Fish-Face was. I was having second thoughts about joining the gang; it was obvious, I didn't fit in and would only be a welcome member on fourth down when they needed a punter. If my father ever saw this group of semi-literate airheads he would be furious. None of them knew what a book was . . . . This was all wrong.

"Listen guys," I said, as I stood up and covered my torso with a towel. "I would be glad to punt for the Rebels anytime you need me, but this isn't for me . . . good luck, good bye." I ran into the bathroom, got dressed, and left the room. Howard turned his naked body so that I was the only one who could see his secret hand gesture. He gave me a "thumbs up" approval.

"Bye bye Lindy baby," said Bubbles. She opened her eyes real wide and blew a large pink bubble.

"I guess you don't want no blow job," said Bam Bam. And thirty Rebels started to laugh. Actually, only twenty-nine laughed. Jimbo shook my hand and wished me good luck.

"Good luck kid," said Jimbo, "I hope you know what you're doing."

I rode the bus home; it was late and it was a long trip from South Beach to Surfside. I sat by myself and thought about my decision to quit the Rebels; I wasn't sure that I did the right thing. I had that problem a lot . . . I often made major decisions and then agonized and spent days second guessing myself. But, maybe its better to make a wrong decision than none at all . . . like many kids who just talked and talked and complained and never did anything.

During that long bus ride I fanaticized about getting a blowjob from Bam Bam and Bubbles or maybe from both of them at the same time, if that was possible, and I tried to imagine all the sexual combinations I could invent with the three of us together . . . with one of them hanging by her legs from the chandelier, like the girl who hangs from the flying trapeze . . . and I thought about Jimbo; I felt sorry for him . . . he was trapped by his body. He would have been better off in life if he wasn't such a great athlete. Maybe its impossible to have a great body and also a great mind; look at Albert Einstein! He had the ugliest hair I ever saw. But Shawna Goldstein sure proved that it was possible for a girl to be gorgeous and brilliant. Of course, she did her best to hide the fact that she was probably the smartest girl in school. And Spencer Teichman was clearly the smartest boy I ever met in my life, but everyone regarded him as a geek, and that really upset me. There was noone I respected more than Spencer; I really wanted to be his friend but he kept to himself.

In the tenth grade I went out for the football team; punting could have put me on a fast track to popularity, even better than the accordion, but I quit the team after one day. Now, once again, my ability to punt a football could have been "open sesame" for me . . . but I walked away.

CHAPTER 40

THE MELTING POT

None of my friends were born in Miami Beach, nor were their parents . . . most came from New York. That's why we frequently referred to our little Jewish island as "The Sixth Borough." Of course, my family came from Chicago, but only by way of New York. The lower East side of Manhattan was the first American home for the Lindelsky's of Russia . . . who eventually became known as Lindell.

My father, his mother, two brothers and a sister, moved from New York to Chicago in 1904, but his remaining five brothers and sisters stayed behind in New York. Fifty years later, with all of my father's siblings deceased, he was the only linkage between the young generation of Lindells from New York and Chicago . . . who otherwise would not know each other. The meeting place for the New York and Chicago branches of the Lindell family was Miami Beach. Many of the relatives came to Florida during the winter, and my house became the Sunday "melting pot" for the second and third generation relatives.

"Uncle Sol, lets go eat some Chinks," said cousin Bernie Lindell from New York. Bernie came to Florida twice a year, once around Christmas time, with his wife Della, and their son Justin. Bernie also made another trip south in April, alone. My mother said he was a womanizer, that he didn't know how to keep his zipper closed but my father defended Bernie and said he needed a break to help preserve his sexless marriage.

"He's a good provider and he's good to his son," said my father. "And before you call Bernie names, what about your brotherinlaw Herman? He flirts with anyone who wears a skirt."

My father never let anyone say anything bad about any Lindell relative . . . he was Uncle Sol, the "Godfather" to at least one hundred nephews, nieces, grand nephews and grand nieces. And there were even a few great-grand nephews and nieces.

On Bernie's April trip he would stop by our house to spend a few hours chatting with my father, but we never got to see any of his girlfriends. My mother said they "rented by the hour," that's why we never met any of them. In December, when Bernie came with his wife, we saw a lot of him and his family, always for Sunday Chinese dinners. That's what the New York relatives meant when they said . . . "lets go for Chinks." But first, before dinner—Bernie and my father went into my parents bedroom, behind closed doors—to discuss various real estate investments.

"Uncle Sol . . . I see that you and Aunt Rose got the same sleeping arrangement that we do . . . separate beds." Bernie laughed.

"Well, I'm sixty-four," responded my father. "What's your excuse? You're only forty."

"Why the Hell do you think I come to Florida in April?" Bernie shrugged his shoulders in disgust.

Bernie's son, my cousin Justin, was a year younger than me. He had bright red hair, which was common among my relatives. My father had red hair when he was younger, before I was born; so did his sister, my Aunt Jenny. Justin had a thick New York accent and all he ever talked about was sex. He liked to brag a lot.

"The girls think I got a 'beautyful' cock . . . fat, like a knockwurst," said Justin, "and they go 'ape' for red 'pubes.'"

I didn't like Justin, but I liked my other New York cousin, Ethan; I liked him a lot. He was my age. Ethan looked a little like me, maybe because his grandfather, my Uncle Nathan, was practically a twin brother to my father. When I was six years old and went to New York I was confused seeing Uncle Nathan and my father sitting next to each other; I couldn't tell them apart. My relatives said that I stared at both of them, bewildered, and started crying.

Ethan and Justin were first cousins but rarely spoke to each other. I tried to be friendly with both of them but it was difficult, especially if they were with me at the same time. Their fathers were brothers, Bernie and Milt Lindell; they were very close to each other, but Ethan and Justin had nothing in common.

"The Chinks is much better in the city." Justin whined, in his obnoxious New York accent.

"What city?" I responded. I knew he was talking about New York, but I didn't like his pompous attitude . . . as if New York was the only city in the United States.

"Shmuck! How dumb can you be?" responded Justin. "I'm talking about New York . . . the center of the universe."

"Well, if it's such a great city with such great 'Chinks' why do you come here every winter?"

"Because those winters are colder than a witches tit. But that don't mean I gotta' like this hick town. You ain't even got no baseball team."

From December through March a typical "Lindell Sunday" began around 4:00 PM . . . my relatives liked to eat early. Everyone gathered at my house, then they drove in a caravan to the Lime House, a popular Chinese restaurant in Sunny Isles (just north of Surfside). Twenty to thirty relatives would meet . . . Lindells from Florida, New York, and Chicago, but only my father's side of the family. The owner of the restaurant, a short friendly Chinese man named Lee Chang, wore a short sleeve white shirt, a black vest, and a bow tie. He always greeted us with a polite bow and a big smile.

"Hello, Mister 'Rindell' so nice to see you and your family . . . welcome to the Lime House . . . I have two special round tables all set up for you."

My father loved the combination platter—egg rolls, pork fried rice, won ton soup, and chicken chow mein. I preferred shrimp instead of chicken. It cost a dollar extra, and I even ate the Chinese vegetables combined with the shrimp. Everything was smothered with hot Chinese mustard and sweet and sour sauce. I learned to eat the mustard from my New York relatives.

"It puts hair on your chest," said Cousin Bernie.

"Don't use too much," said my mother. She was afraid that Chinese mustard would turn me into a "womanizer" like Cousin Bernie.

After dinner Mr. Chang and I had our own special competition; he promised to give me a free orange sherbet if I could beat him in a math race . . . . adding the Lindell dinner bill. I was very quick at adding columns by hand, and he used an old fashioned Chinese abacus. He always won, until I learned a special mental technique for grouping numbers into combinations of ten. Then, one day I surprised him . . . and everybody else, I beat the abacus. Mr. Chang was stunned; but no one was more stunned than my father.

"Sunshine, I know you like writing and history . . . . but I think you should consider being an accountant. I never saw anyone add columns so fast. I can't believe you beat the abacus!"

After desert the Lindell motorcade traveled back to my house where we had a huge thirty-cup coffee machine primed and ready to go. My job on Sunday mornings during "relative season" was to go to the Jewish bakery and buy bobka and strudel.

"Myron—buy the plain bobka—no one likes the chocolate type. And make sure that the struedle is fresh. Squeeze it . . . if the crust cracks it's stale. And get two loafs of sliced rye bread with seeds."

My mother worked in the kitchen, making coffee and slicing the pastry, and my father, the family "godfather," sat in his big easy chair . . . and one by one each of the "blood" relatives gave him a hug and a kiss. He was loved by all of his family. I looked forward to the time in life when I would have a large family of my own and become the patriarch. I was jealous of my father. Maybe it wasn't jealousy . . . it was admiration; I wanted to grow up just like him. He was the most important person in the world to me, a kind, loving, understanding man, and no one could ever say a bad word about any member of his family . . . he would jump to the rescue. You couldn't even poormouth the husbands or wives of the Lindells. We called them the "water" relatives.

Everyone loved Uncle Sol, even the "water" relatives . . . and as my father received all this adulation, my mother continued slicing rye bread, bobka, and strudel, and I sat on the floor playing checkers with cousin Ethan. Sometimes, just to be obnoxious, Justin would wait until we were well engrossed in a game, then he'd kick over the board. One time Ethan and I were out on the street, throwing a football, and Justin came running into the house screaming and telling everyone that I had been hit by a car. He got some type of perverted pleasure by scaring the hell out of all the relatives.

"OK everybody, the coffee's hot; come and get it," said my mother. The adults went to the dining room for coffee and cake, but the little children sat on the floor by my father's feet, or on his lap. He told them stories about his brothers and sisters, Jenny, Nathan, Morris, Harris, Rachael, Abraham, Sam, and Ann . . . their grandparents. He told stories about the first generation of the Lindell family, when they "just got off the boat" . . . the "Gay Nineties," life on the lower east side of Manhattan, playing on the Brooklyn bridge . . . or the Bowry, the dangerous Italian section . . . fighting with the "dagos" . . . or crossing Delancey, to the Irish neighborhood . . . fighting with the "micks." And he sang to the children; he sang the songs of his youth . . . "Sweet Rosie O'Grady," "By the Light of the Silvery Moon." The little cousins loved "unca" Sol and his stories; he hugged them and kissed them . . . and my mother "slaved" in the kitchen. Those were her words . . . "slaved." When the relatives left the house my mother yelled a lot; she didn't like being the "slave" for thirty Lindell relatives every Sunday.

"When we moved to Florida I didn't think I was going to be the slave for all your damn New York relatives. Do I need this? If you want your precious family here on Sunday, hire a maid." None of the Lindell relatives ever hugged or kissed my mother, except for a quick hello or goodbye kiss on the cheek . . . . but you could tell, it wasn't from the heart.

Although my parents still continued to see Aunt Pearlie and Herman, they never combined relatives from my mother's side of the family with the New York Lindells. I think my father was embarrassed to include Herman with his family. His New York relatives were educated and very refined; they talked about books and quoted from ancient Greek philosophers. Many of them were lawyers, doctors, or college professors. One of my cousins, Hannah Lindell, was a former member of the radio show, "The Quiz Kids," and she competed against Joel Kupperman, one of the most famous child geniuses in history. Hannah spoke with a phony British accent. So did cousin Gary Lindell, who knew differential calculus at nine years old. The New York relatives talked about sending their children to Harvard and Yale and then to finishing school in Paris. In contrast, Herman was a cab driver; he didn't know anything about Greek philosophers or calculus. He was loud and crude and used mediocre ventriloquism to make the lamps and ash trays talk. He thought it was hilarious to have an ash tray use the "F" word. When we went out with Herman and Pearlie it was frequently to Gallaghers, a Steak restaurant in North Miami, or the Rascal House, a large Jewish restaurant. We also went with my mother's other sister, Esther, who had recently moved from Chicago to Miami Beach, along with her new husband, Willy, who really got pissed off if you misspelled his name.

"God dammit! Spell it with a fuckin' 'Y,'" shouted Willy, "only shvartzahs use 'IE.'"

Aunt Esther was a strange woman, with bulging green eyes and bright red hair, and she wasn't very nice to me. My mother often referred to her as a simpleton. She had worked for twenty years selling ladies hats at Marshall Fields, the major department store in Chicago. Now, at the age of forty, she finally got married. Her husband, "Willy—with a Y", was skinny, tiny, and one of the dumbest people I ever met. He always wore a cowboy shirt with metal tips on the collar, a belt with a huge Indian head buckle, and a bolo tie that looked like two silver tipped shoe laces.

I wish I could think of one nice thing to say about Willy, like maybe he was kind or funny, but my only lasting memory of Willy is that he always got confused between his left and right hand . . . Herman got him a job as a cab driver, but he couldn't learn the street system in Miami Beach and got fired. How hard is it to figure out a street system that starts at first street and increases to eighty-seventh street as it goes north? And, the whole island isn't more than a couple miles wide.

"Its Willy on the phone," said my mother. "He's lost again."

I got on the phone to give him directions: "Willy . . . . If you're calling from the corner of 71st and Collins just keep heading north . . . we're on 95th street, in Surfside . . . 24 more blocks. North . . . . that's the direction you'll be facing if you keep the Ocean on your right. . . . that's the hand you 'write' with. Yes . . . the Atlantic, not the Pacific."

Herman, Pearlie, and Willy smoked a lot, especially Herman. I hated to be in the same room with them; it was hard to breathe. Oh yes . . . I just thought of one nice thing to say about Willy. He was clean; my mother appreciated the fact that he always dumped his ash tray in the toilet before he left our house. To my mother, if you were clean, all other sins were forgiven. But Willy coughed up phlegm a lot, and spit on the street.

"Stop making fun of Willy," said my mother, "at least he doesn't cheat on his wife, not like one of your 'educated' New York relatives."

While the New York Lindells loved Chinese food and socializing at my house, the Chicago Lindells were passionate card players . . . poker, bridge, canasta, kalukee, and gin rummy. Herman and Pearlie also loved cards, so my parents carefully planned their Sundays; it was OK to blend my mother's family with the Chicago Lindells, but not with the New York relatives. And, even though the New York Lindells didn't play cards, it was always acceptable to blend them with the Chicago Lindells . . . after all, they were "blood" relatives linked together by Unca' Sol.

Sundays, during the winter months was "Lindell season," New York and Chicago relatives spent the evenings kissing my father, drinking coffee, and eating chinese food at the Lime House, but throughout the rest of the year, on Sundays, the living room in my house was transformed into a card room, with several tables going at once. My job was to serve coffee, bobka, and strudel at the various tables, and giant Hershey bars to Aunt Pearlie. Card players loved to eat, but they didn't like to interrupt their game, even for food. They were very serious about cards . . . especially Herman.

One time when Herman lost a big hand of poker, when his full house was beaten by four of a kind, he got so upset that he kicked the table to the ground. Poker chips and cards flew all over the room. I was sleeping on the couch and was startled when I heard the noise. He was screaming and cursing, so was aunt Pearlie. She was embarrassed by his terrible temper tantrum. Herman was wearing Bermuda shorts, and his right leg was bleeding profusely.

"Herman, get in the bathroom," shouted my mother. "You're gushing blood all over the carpet."

"Fuck the God damn carpet," Herman responded, and he continued with his rage and threw a glass of gingerale against the wall.

After that episode we didn't see Herman for several months; my father wanted nothing to do with him. But, my mother still continued to see her sister Pearlie in the daytime, to have lunch together, or to go shopping on Lincoln Road. Then one Saturday morning Herman came driving his taxi up Carlyle Avenue, where I was playing touch football with my friends. He was alone.

"Hey Myron . . . you wanna' learn to drive? You're almost sixteen, time to get your license. How else you ever gonna' get some pussy. Hop in, I'll teach you; lets surprise your old man."

Herman was a good teacher; I would never have expected that. He had a lot of patience. I kept stalling the engine as I fumbled with the clutch on his taxi. In 1954 if you passed your driver's test with a standard-shift car you would get an "unrestricted" license, you could then drive any type of car. But, if you took the test with a hydromatic car your license was "restricted "—you were not allowed to drive shift cars. It would have been so much easier if I learned how to drive with automatic transmission, but Herman insisted that I should learn to drive a shift car.

We drove over to the Church by the Sea in Bal Harbour; that's where I had played football and was evicted by the police. The parking lot was empty; it was a good safe place to learn to drive . . . back and forth, shifting, sputtering, and stalling . . . until I drove a complete circle around the church. I did that for about an hour, then I was ready to make my debut on Carlyle Avenue, to display this new talent for my parents and friends.

I honked the horn in Herman's taxi as I drove past my house; I was at the wheel. I was driving. My parents both stood on the front porch and applauded. My friends were still playing football on the street, and they stepped aside to let me pass. The Steinberg's hid behind my father's car, an exaggerated gesture to show their fear. Herman was welcomed back into my house; he hugged my mother and shook hands with my father. It was nice to have Herman back in the family; maybe he was loud and crude but he had a kind heart . . . sometimes.

It was December 1954, the beginning of relative season; I would be taking my driving test on March 20, 1955 . . . my sixteenth birthday. But if I was to pass that test, I needed a lot of practice, and despite the fact that my father had a great deal of patience, he was not good at teaching me how to drive. Every time I cut a right turn too sharp and drove over the curb he almost had a heart attack. And when I made left turns too close, finding myself head to head with oncoming traffic, he covered his eyes.

Cousin Itsie from Chicago was 22; he was in town for the month of December. I think Itsie's real name was Itzak, named after one of our great grandparents from Russia. I could understand why he never used his real name. Damn! It was even worse than Myron. My father gave Itsie a job, working a few hours a week as my driving teacher. My father also recruited cousin Julie, who was on vacation from New York; she was 21 and drove an Austin Healy sports car. Julie was extremely pretty, with dark piercing eyes; she looked somewhat like Esmeralda Cifuentes, my old dancing teacher . . . and it was fun to drive her little convertible. But it didn't take too long until cousins Itsie and Julie decided to spend their days together at the beach. I lost both of my teachers. Everyone called them kissing cousins and warned them not to "go too far."

"You better watch out," said my mother. "When cousins 'go too far' it can lead to children who are insane." Itsie laughed; Julie blushed.

"Rose, they're only second cousins," said my father, "same as Franklin and Eleanor Roosevelt, and their children didn't grow up insane."

"Well, maybe not, but one of them became a Republican."

Later, in private, Itsie told me that Julie was the "best piece of ass" he ever had . . . "She's the wildest Jewish girl I ever laid. Damn! You should hear her scream when we screw."

"What does she say?" I asked.

"Beats me," said Itsie. "I can't understand her fuckin' New York accent. But, tell Uncle Sol, not to worry . . . I'm using rubbers. No chance of getting Julie knocked up."

"Yeah," I laughed. "Otherwise your baby would be your third cousin."

Finally, the big day arrived, March 20, 1955, my sixteenth birthday. I drove to the license bureau with my mother, father, and the Steinbergs. I took a number and waited. It was a long wait, almost two hours. I sat in the white section. Colored applicants waited in another section; they sat on wooden benches. At last, my name was called over a speaker system, and my hands began to sweat.

"OK young man, here are the ground rules" said the driving instructor, as he made several notations on a sheet of paper. He adjusted his clipboard and gave me directions, where I would be driving and how I would be graded.

I looked in the rear view mirror; my father and mother were standing together, holding hands. That struck me as odd; they were not an affectionate couple. I had never seen them holding hands before. The Steinbergs were waving and wishing me good luck. Then I twisted my body into the proper position. I stepped on the clutch, eased the car into reverse, and turned my head completely around; you're not supposed to use the rear view mirror when driving in reverse, and I made a mental note of the distance between my car and a black car that was parked on the right.

I inched backwards, slowly, turning the wheel to the right, careful to avoid hitting the black car, and then . . . crunch! My front left fender smashed into the car on my left. I had focused all my attention on the car on the right side, I completely ignored the car on the left.

"OK Son . . . that's it. The test is over," said the instructor. I never even made it out of the starting block; I bombed the test, and it cost my father $150, that's what he paid to the owner of the car that I hit, to avoid going through insurance. When we got home Herman laughed; he always laughed when I screwed up.

"Why are you laughing?" I said. "You're the one who taught me to drive."

Herman started chiding me, singing like a ten year old kid. 'Myron flunked his driving test . . . Myron flunked his driving test."

Two weeks later I returned, to take the test again. This time I didn't have a large entourage, only my father, and I passed. Perfect score! And I was sitting with $1,000 in a bank account; I was ready to buy my first set of "wheels."

CHAPTER 41

WHEELS TO FREEDOM

Now that I was sixteen and had a drivers license I was about to buy my first car; I was ready to spread my wings and fly.

"No, say it right," said Herman. "You're ready to unzip your fly . . . and let your little wing-ding see the world." Herman then put his cigarette on the edge of our dining room table; that always bugged my mother . . . and he used ventriloquism. He made my crotch say: "Help! Let me out of here. Help! Let me out of here."

"Herman, don't be so crude," said my Aunt Pearlie, but my father laughed . . . and advised me to always carry rubbers in the glove compartment.

"You know the old Boy Scout motto," said my father. "Be prepared."

"C'mon Myron," said Herman, "lets look in the Herald Classified . . . see what you can find for 1,000 bucks. But don't expect no T'bird."

We found an ad for a used 1954 Chevy' convertible; they were asking $1,500. Hopefully, we could bargain them down to $1,000. I went with my parents, Herman, and an envelope filled with ten $100 bills.

"Our best offer, our only offer, our final offer is $1,000," said my father. He was much too strong; he didn't allow any room for negotiation.

"We'll take $1,200 . . . not a penny less."

"No, lets go," said my father, and I almost cried. I loved that car, a neat brown convertible with a white top and tan leather seats. And it was automatic. I knew how to drive manual transmission, but if I had a girl in the car that would tie up both of my hands. I definitely wanted automatic.

"Please dad, they're only asking another $200. Please loan it to me; I'll pay you back this summer. I'll go back to work at Food Fair."

"Myron, there are more fish in the sea, more cars, more convertibles. Learn to be a little tougher in business."

"Sol, let me see what I can do," said Herman, and he walked into another room and spoke privately with the owner of the car. He wasn't in the room for more than five minutes. When he came out . . . the car was mine. I was so excited I ran and hugged Herman, probably the only time in my life I ever did that. It was a very quick hug! Herman rode home with me; my father drove with my mother in their car.

"Myron, don't tell your old man, but I slipped the guy an extra $200. Next summer pay me back."

Herman was definitely crude and sometimes he was mean, but occasionally he had a warm spot in his heart. However, I never saw anyone smoke so much, and the coughing was getting ugly. I wanted to tell him not to smoke in my new car, but I didn't want to say anything to upset him. I planned on buying some saddle soap when I got home to really clean up the leather . . . . and some type of spray to get rid of the cigarette odor.

I slept in the car that night, in the garage; it was the most exciting night of my life. I couldn't wait to drive to the Steinbergs in the morning, to show them my beautiful convertible . . . and I would also drive to Flo's house. I wish Shawna Rose still lived in Surfside; I would have shown her also. At 5:00 AM I woke up with an aching back; it was very uncomfortable sleeping in a car, even with the wonderful fragrance of leather seats. I spent the next two hours washing my car, including the canvas top and the beautiful whitewall tires.

Gasoline was twenty cents a gallon and I would need at least ten gallons a week to commute to school, so I quickly organized my own group of riders, David, Shelly, Flo, and my cousin Phyllis Posner. I charged them each one dollar per week, to cover the cost of gasoline, with a little extra for my services. It was a nice arrangement, but my cousin Phyllis didn't like Flo and soon backed out of the group. Phyllis was very proper, never even said damn or hell; her main concern in life was which fork or spoon to use when she ate. In contrast, Flo couldn't say a complete sentence without one or two cuss words. They both lived on the same block, only three houses apart, but they really clashed. Phyllis couldn't see past Flo's profanity; she couldn't see that Flo was a very good person, and Flo couldn't see past Phyllis's affected personality, that she wasn't really a pompous ass. I always tried to see through a facade, to understand the real person. I was quick to recognize that Shawna was an extremely intelligent girl, even when everyone else saw her only as a sex goddess, and I eventually recognized that Jimbo Lang had something between his ears, although not as widely publicized as what he had between his legs. I even saw a little good in Herman.

That Monday night, at 8:00 PM, I called Mickey Cohen, a very cute girl with long blonde hair; she had a great smile and I was always attracted to girls who smiled. She lived on Emerson Avenue, two blocks from my house. I didn't know her that well but I had a car, a convertible, my own set of wheels, and I was ready to start dating.

"Hi Mickey, this is Myron Lindell."

"Who?"

"I ride your school bus. Well . . . I did ride it, until yesterday. Now I have a convertible. I'm the guy with blonde hair; I live on Carlyle Avenue, two blocks from you."

"Oh yeah, I think I know who you are. You wear glasses, don't you?"

"No, that's Arnie Dombrowski. Maybe you know me from American History, I'm in your class, I sit next to Spencer Teichman."

"The geek?"

"He isn't a geek; he's just a loner. I think when you're that smart you don't relate to your peers. Maybe you just don't have peers."

"Why do you need a pier?" asked Mickey. "Not everybody likes fishing. Listen . . . I can't talk anymore . . . I really gotta' go."

"Uh, Mickey, would you like to go out with me this Saturday night?"

"Oh gee. I've got other plans, I'm sorry."

"How about Sunday?"

"I don't go out on Sundays."

"How about next Saturday?"

"I don't make plans that far in advance. Bye Byron."

"It's Myron, not Byron."

"Oh. Sorry."

I called again the following week and this time I was really shot down; not even an attempt to be subtle.

"No Byron! And stop calling me."

♦

Two weeks later I got into one of my many debates with Luther Burkhead the teacher of my American history class. I loved history and read many history books and historical novels; I hated it when teachers tried to simplify the causes of conflicts, especially the Civil War.

"I know what you're saying, Mr. Burkhead, Lincoln was certainly a great president, a statesman, a philosopher, and an inspiring leader, but he was not the great emancipator. He was not a martyr for the Negro people."

"Myron . . . it was Lincoln who freed the slaves. Don't you know that? And in the Lincoln—Douglas debates he opposed slavery."

"Yes sir, that's true, but once the war began Lincoln only had one objective, to save the country, and if the threat of freeing the slaves would bring the war to an end, that was his strategy. I'm sure, if retaining slavery would have appeased the Confederacy, Lincoln would have gone that way; anything to preserve the union."

"Myron, you have a warped view of history. You regard Lincoln as some type of sleazy politician, like a door-to-door salesman."

"Mr Burkhead, Lincoln is my favorite president, but he didn't fight the Civil War to end slavery; he fought the war to keep the country together. Our history book simplifies his motives and glorifies the whole war."

"Young man! That war was a holy crusade." Then, in a muffled voice, Mr. Burkhead began singing the Battle Hymn of the Republic: "Mine eyes have seen the glory of the coming of the Lord." He stopped singing and pounded a fist on his desk. "Lincoln was a great man, and great men are not the product of history; they make history. It sounds to me like you've been

319

reading too much Karl Marx. You better be careful; that atheist garbage can warp your brain."

What a jerk! Hitler and Stalin also made history. Does that mean they were great men? But, Mr. Burkhead was right about one thing; I did read the "Communist Manifesto" by Marx. However, I thought that the concept of communism was idealistic nonsense; it clashed with normal human behavior. "From each according to his ability, to each according to his need" was just as unrealistic as "turning the other cheek" if someone punched you in the nose. I wonder what Mr. Burkhead would say if I told him my opinion, that Communism and Christianity were very similar ideologies? I'd probably be expelled from school before the day was over.

♦

That day, after class, Mickey Cohen talked to me in the hall . . . first time she ever talked to me in person.

"Myron, you really know this history stuff. I'm impressed. If you still want to go out with me, I'd love to go. I heard you got a beautiful convertible. I really love the feel of the wind in my hair . . . driving along the beach."

The logical side of me said to give her a great big NO . . . "sorry Nickey, I'm busy . . . . Oh, excuse me, its Mickey, isn't it?" But, how could I say no to a girl with such a beautiful smile?

"When? What time? I'll be there!"

Mickey greeted me at the door of her house with an inviting smile and a hug; she was wearing a red plaid skirt and a white sleeveless blouse.

We went to a movie on Lincoln Road, and she put her head on my shoulder and squeezed my thigh everytime there was a scary part. After the movie we put the top down in my convertible and went cruising along the southern end of Miami Beach. We parked by the bay and looked out at the commercial fishing boats in the harbor and the distant lights of the Miami skyline; it was a beautiful sight. And we talked about American history and the Civil War. I soon realized that Mickey was a "draikop," that's a Jewish airhead . . . she thought that Jefferson Davis wrote the Declaration of Independence and that Lincoln was a man of many talents . . . that he invented the automobile.

"Isn't that why it's called the Lincoln?" She asked, "and why did we attack the Germans at Pearl Harbor?".

I was going crazy; I couldn't continue with this conversation. "Myron, I have a wonderful offer for you. If you let me copy off you during the next history test I will make you very happy." And she made an erotic slurping sound.

My father had warned me about situations like this. "Myron, be careful . . . a stiff penis has no conscience." I heard his words of advice . . . loud and clear.

"Mickey, that's a fantastic offer, best I ever had, and you are really a beautiful girl . . . but I don't cheat on tests."

"I'm not asking you to cheat," said Mickey, as she slid her tongue over her moist upper lip. "Just keep your test paper on the right side of your desk . . . uncovered. You won't be doing anything wrong. And I promise . . . you won't be disappointed." More slurping!

This was a difficult decision, a lot harder than quitting the Rebels. I had flashbacks to the time when Buddy Macker bullied me into helping him cheat in Spanish, But Mickey was using a different approach. Actually, I think I might have allowed a real girlfriend to copy off me, like Leah Sonnino or Flo, or Shawna Goldstein, but not Mickey. I didn't like what was happening. I turned on the ignition and drove back to Surfside. No words were spoken during the long drive home.

Finally, as I walked Mickey to her front door she broke the long silence. "Boy, are you a shmendrick!" (*Yiddish word for fool*).

The next day I told Flo about the incident and she hung on every word; she started breathing heavy when I described Mickey's position, with legs up on the dashboard . . . . I discovered that I had a talent . . . I was a good erotic story teller. Flo was getting aroused.

"You sure got balls Myron. Most guys would give anything for a blowjob."

"That's easy for you to say," I responded, "but at least you've had some experience; I'm still a virgin. Well . . . except for petting with ZD and Maxine; if you want to count that."

Flo was making plans to go to college, she had been accepted at the University of Miami and would start classes in the fall. Her only decision was whether to live home or in the dorms. We sat together on her bedroom balcony and read brochures from the university and looked at all the pictures.

"I know I might sound weird, most girls want to get away from home and live in the dorms. But, I like it here. I get along great with my mom and bubby. I don't want to live in a smelly dorm with a bunch of horny dykes."

"Flo, you're the most sensitive person I know, even if you do have a foul mouth once in a while. You have something special here at home, a real closeness; I think you're cool."

We hugged and Flo looked into my eyes; it was the first time we ever kissed. Then, abruptly . . . I backed away.

"No, I want to always be your friend. If we do that it will change, forever."

"Damn, Myron . . . why are you always so logical. lets go crack some fuckin' coconuts. Either that or my dildo!."

"What's a dildo?" I asked

"It's a rubber dick."

"You have a rubber dick!" I exclaimed. I knew she masturbated; she told me that once before, but I thought girls just used their fingers or Coke bottles.

"Yeah . . . he sleeps in my end table. His name is Stanley."

"Wow, you should call that thing King Kong . . . that's huge," I exclaimed. "You're going to have a hard time finding a guy to compete with that monster dick."

"Well, I don't put the whole thing in; it feels best just rubbing against my clitoris. That's the sensitive spot."

"Its called CLI'toris," I corrected her. "Not cliTOR'is . . . . it doesn't rhyme with Delores."

"You're nuts," said Flo. "I'm a girl . . . don't you think I know? Its definitely cliTOR'is. You don't see me telling you how to pronounce scrotum. And, by the way, in case you're interested, the plural of scrotum is scrota."

"Wow, that's a great word to know, if you're a movie critic for French films. But, I think that scrotum is already plural, like 'deer' . . . a guy's got two balls in there."

"No, its singular." Flo corrected me. "Two balls, but they're together in one scrotum."

"Hey . . . I got a real hot idea." Said Flo, and her face lit up with an evil grin. "I'll use Stanley and let you watch if you let me watch you jerk off. That ain't really sex; we can still be friends."

As I sat there, with a growing bulge under my jeans, unable to think logically, Flo stood in front of me and began removing her clothes.

"No. That's sex." I jumped from the couch. "If you let me watch you do that its gonna' kill our friendship."

Flo smiled and ignored me; she licked Stanley very slowly, from top to bottom, but I didn't stick around for the show. What was wrong with me? Why did I always walk away from great opportunities, like Mickey Cohen or the Rebels? What was I waiting for?

♦

I never drank liquor, but that night I did. I was extremely depressed. I went to the cabinet where my father stored several bottles of whiskey. He told relatives that Haig and Haig was his "best stuff" so I filled a shot glass and downed it quickly. Damn! That tasted terrible. Then another shot of whiskey . . . then another. I wanted to get drunk, but it didn't happen. I just got sick to my stomach and vomited in the toilet.

The next morning Flo called to see how I was doing. "Yeah Myron, you're right. You're always right. You can't be a lover if you're a friend. Oh, by the way . . . I looked up "clitoris" . . . your pronounciation is correct, but so is mine. OK . . . yours is listed first, but it sure sounds dumb to me."

Once again I remembered my father's words of advice . . . "a stiff penis has no conscience." He was wrong . . . on two separate occasions my stiff penis did have a conscience.

♦

That Saturday night I had no plans, neither did Flo. So we went cruising in my new convertible. It was great driving across the 79th Street Causeway, one of the most beautiful sights in Miami Beach, with the wide open bay all around us. We parked at "Peckers Point," a secluded peninsula that jutted out into Biscayne Bay . . . it was a popular passion pit where teenagers went to watch the "submarine races." That was a popular way of saying that they were going to make out. Some kids used other terms, like "hankey-pankey" or "moofkie-poofkie," or if they wanted to gross you out they'd wiggle their little finger in the air and talk about "stinky—pinky." Yuck!

The top was down in my convertible and the radio was blasting the new blockbuster hit, "The Ballad of Davy Crockett." And every time the song finished it came back on again, and again, and again. DJ's sometimes did that . . . play a song over and over all night long. It was kind of crazy, but the kids loved it. Flo and I sang along; It was a great song. Davy Crockett had captured America; it was one of the most popular songs in history. I really wanted a coon skin cap, but I was too old. Boys who go out with girls and think about sex don't wear coon skin caps.

Those who parked at "Peckers Point" for romance gazed at the beautiful moon over Miami, but Flo and I were in a nutty mood; we just sang Davy Crockett, over and over . . . . very loud.

"Born on a mountain top in Tennessee greenest state in the land of the free lived in the woods till he knew every tree killed him a 'bar when he was only three . . ."

"Shut up," shouted teenagers from the other cars; they were busy making out . . . some were way beyond first base, well into heavy sex. Those with Nash Ramblers had already converted their back seats into beds.

"Davy, Davy Crockett . . . king of the wild frontier," we continued singing. And everyone began honking their horns; Flo and I ignored them and began laughing. Then a tough looking guy got out of his car, zipped his fly, and started walking toward us. In a flash, we "tore ass" out of there, laughing all the while.

"Lets go to Fun Fair," I suggested, "I love their hot dogs." Nothing like a kosher dog with spicy mustard and onions. Fun Fair was a popular hangout on the 79th Street Causeway, not too far from "Peckers Point." It was a big open air arcade, with miniature golf, bumper pool, skee ball, and lots of pin ball machines. I was the skee ball champion of Fun Fair, no one could beat me at that game, and I was also very good at bumper pool But, I liked Fun Fair mainly for the hot dogs, best in town. Unfortunately, this popular Jewish hangout was sometimes terrorized by the "River Rats," the teenage gang from Little River.

We pulled into Fun Fair and I wasn't very observant. If I was I would have noticed twenty or thirty motorcycles in the parking lot; not many kids from Beach High rode motorcycles.

"Hey Jew boy, nice wheels," said one of the River Rats. And a short skinny guy grabbed Flo and began to kiss her. Flo screamed; we were surrounded by at least twenty River Rats, all dressed in matching black leather jackets. Several of them laughed and began singing their special version of a popular song: "If I knew you were coming I'd have baked a 'kike.'"

"I bet this broad will love being banged by a real man," said a big fat River Rat, and he put both of his hands around Flo's neck and started grinding his pelvis against her butt. This was a nightmare . . . and it was all happening in full view of everyone . . . Fun Fair was an open air arcade. The employees were standing behind counters, serving food and drinks, pretending that they didn't see what was happening. I was afraid that Flo was going to be raped . . . maybe, me too.

Several of the River Rats then dumped their leftover hot dogs, pizza, French fries, and Cokes into my open convertible. There wasn't much I could do to protect my car, but I grabbed Flo and pulled her away from the fat guy. I put my arms around her to shelter her from him, and he threw his coke in my face. Then he walked away laughing.

"Get the hell out of here Jew boy," said the leader of the gang, as he combed the greasy sides of his D.A., "or you'se gonna' watch your babe get fucked in the ass. I love to watch Jew bitches squeal when they get corn-holed."

He didn't have to say it twice . . . we were out of there fast. Flo was crying; her hands were trembling. I couldn't believe this was America, that there was so much hatred of Jews. What did we ever do to them? We didn't kill Jesus . . . the Romans did . . . . and even if we did, that was two thousand years ago. . . . Jews don't still hate Spain for the Inquisition . . . . and that was only five hundred years ago. OK, maybe we still hate the Nazis, but that was just yesterday.

When we got to Flo's house we parked along side the garage and began to clean out the car; it was late at night, but she insisted on helping.

"Myron . . . don't let food sit overnight, otherwise your car will smell like shit in the morning."

Just then her mother came outside crying.

"Bubby's had a massive heart attack . . . she's at Mt. Sinai hospital. Its looking bad."

Flo screamed and hugged her mother.

CHAPTER 42

SITTING SHIVA

Two days later the phone rang at 7:00 AM; it was Flo. Her grandmother died and they already had the funeral. It was a private funeral, only for the immediate family.

"Myron, we need an extra man to form a 'minyan. We only got nine men here for the 'Shiva' . . . we need a tenth. Can you come to my house right away?"

"OK, I'll be right over, but you better check with your Rabbi to see if I'll do, I was never Bar Mitzvahed."

"You're OK," responded Flo, in a very sarcastic voice. "I already asked him; all males over thirteen are OK for a minyan, you don't even have to be Jewish, you just need a dick."

That seemed hard to believe. Flo, a Jewish female who was Bas Mitzvahed and knew how to read Hebrew, was not allowed to be part of a prayer service for her own grandmother. Damn, she didn't even eat ham or bacon. But, it was OK for me . . . and I wasn't even Bar Mitzvahed. That didn't seem right.

"Stop by the Jewish bakery and pick up a bobka," said my mother. "You don't go to a 'shiva' without food."

I drove to the bakery, picked up a bobka and a dozen bagels and then went to Flo's house. It was nice having a car to get around, a lot more convenient than riding a bike. Flo looked bad, her eyes were red, she had been crying all night . . . and she hugged me when I arrived.

"You taught me to cry Myron; before our night with the coconuts I never cried. I just put up my cold front and ignored the fuckin' world. But, I guess its better this way."

"Thanks for the bobka," said Flo's mom, "now go join the men; they need you for the minyan."

Several of the older men, the more religious ones, used 't'filin' when they prayed. Those are leather straps that are wrapped tightly around their arms. And they each draped a large white and blue talis over their head, the traditional Hebrew prayer shawl. I wore a yarmelkeh and joined the men as they recited the "Kaddish"—the mourner's prayer. But, I was silent, I couldn't read Hebrew. I didn't belong at the minyan'—I was standing in a place that belonged to Flo.

"It isn't Hebrew," said the Rabbi. "The Kaddish is in Aramaic; that was the language of Israel when the prayer was written. But, it sounds a lot like Hebrew."

Later in the day the Steinbergs came over; also Colonel Klein and Katarina. Katarina was wearing an engagement ring; she and the Colonel were going to be married in June, the week after school ended. I hadn't seen the Colonel that much in the eleventh grade; Miss Madison had been reviewing and editing my journal and other writings. The Colonel was usually with Katarina in the evenings and on weekends; I didn't think it was right to bother him.

"Myron, you remember Annabelle, the boys' aunt," said the Colonel. "Well, she was at the wrong place at the wrong time; she got caught in crossfire at a robbery in her neighborhood. Poor, sweet lady, she died two weeks ago; she wasn't even forty years old."

"Oh, that's horrible," I responded. "Didn't she have four children? What's going to happen to them?"

"They're with me now," replied the Colonel, "and I guess its up to the courts, but Katarina and I want them to live with us. After we get married we'll adopt Jackie and Jessie and also all four of Annabelle's children."

A steady stream of people came and went throughout the day, each bringing food, but none brought flowers. Jewish people don't bring flowers to a shiva, nor do they put flowers on a grave, and I sure don't understand that. What's so bad about flowers? When Jewish people sit shiva, one week of mourning following the death of a loved one, friends and relatives come by the home of the deceased, to pay their respect. I guess the bereaved are not supposed to cook or work. That must be why the visitors all bring food. And the older relatives told stories, their memories of Flo's grandmother when she was a little girl in Europe and in New York.

From what I understand, when Catholics have a wake its really depressing . . . except for all the flowers; the grieving room looks like a florist shop. And the Catholics delay the funeral until a week after the death. Jews get it over quickly; the funeral is usually the next day, unless that's a Saturday, then it's put off until Sunday. But the shiva isn't really a miserable week. Many of the friends and relatives try to bring cheer into the lives of the family . . . and they tell Jewish jokes.

"So, did I ever tell you the von' about old Jake?" said an eldery Jewish man. "For his 75th birthday his friends got him a 'kurvah.'"

"What's a 'kurvah?'" I murmured to Flo.

"A whore."

"Anyvay' . . . the 'voman comes knocking on Jake's door and asks: 'Vould you like super sex?'"

"At my age . . . . I'll take the soup," responds Jake.

Everybody laughed . . . even Flo and her mother.

It seemed hard to believe . . . Flo's grandmother had just died and people were telling jokes and laughing. At first I thought it was terribly disrespectful, but I guess laughing helps to ease the pain. A shiva is a celebration of life; friends and relatives gather together to relive wonderful memories; it is not at all similar to a wake.

I'm sure I must have been at a shiva before this one, but I have very faint recollections. If I was, I was only a child. But, this one struck close to home, and I was part of it. I helped slice cake and pour coffee. And I even told a couple of jokes, Yiddish ones that I had learned from Myron K at Food Fair.

"Yes, its true," said the Colonel. "Jewish shivas are less morbid than Catholic wakes, but, Catholics have a more optimistic view of the next life."

"What do you mean?" I replied, "Catholics and Jews both believe in an afterlife."

"Yes and no," replied the Colonel. "Jews certainly invented the concept of Heaven in Genesis, but it's not a major aspect of the religion. The Catholic religion seems to be preoccupied with life after death, where all sins will be forgiven. I say it facetiously, but Catholics regard their earthly life as a dress rehearsal for the hereafter."

"I've said the same thing," I observed, "but if Catholics have such a strong belief in the next life why are they so depressed at the wake? The departed one is off to a better place."

"Good point." The Colonel laughed. "However . . . . the afterlife has two final destinations, and the one 'down below' isn't exactly a 'better' place. Actually, I think that people at a wake aren't really crying for the deceased; they're crying for their own loss . . . for an emptiness in their own life."

"Well, maybe a Catholic funeral is kind of like a graduation," I observed. "The dead person is being promoted to the next level. They really should play graduation music at a Catholic funeral."

"Do you think that Jews and gentiles get along better in the next life," I asked, "assuming that there is a Heaven?"

"I hope so," said the Colonel, "but according to Christians, there aren't any Jews in Heaven. All you have to do is look at the horns on the statue of Moses. It was the Pope who insisted that Michaelangelo put the horns there."

"Yeah, you might be right." I responded. "Like what Holy Joe says . . . 'the only way to go to Heaven is to believe in Jesus.' So, maybe there are two Heavens, one for Christians and one for Jews . . . but then, what about the Moslems and the Hindus, and all the other religions? I cant believe that there are hundreds of Heavens; that would be worse segregation than we have in this life. And what about the Negroes? I mean, gentile Negroes. Do they go to a different section of heaven with different drinking fountains? They believe in Jesus, same as the white Christians, so shouldn't they get into the main section? Next time I see Holy Joe I've got to ask him about that."

"Death is frightening," said the Colonel. "Maybe there are no drinking fountains in heaven. We're much better off to focus on life—it's not as confusing."

"I never read Dante," I replied, "but I heard that his Inferno had many sections; he sure felt that there was segregation in hell, but I don't think he talked much about segregation in heaven."

Shelly then entered the room, wearing a black Lacoste. He always knew how to dress right, for every type of occasion. He was carrying a large pitcher of piña coladas, the popular tropical drink. He was a huge hit and kept going back to the kitchen for one pitcher after another. The guests were getting tired of coffee. Jews don't drink beer at social functions or at Shivas. I know that's a generalization; I'm sure many Jews like beer, but certainly not my family, nor my friends at Beach High. Piña coladas seemed to go well at a Shiva. Even Flo and her mother drank several tall glasses. I think Flo drank too many tall glasses.

"Now I know for sure. I'll be living home during college," said Flo, and she slurred when she spoke. She definitely had too many piña coladas. "I can't go away and leave my mom living home alone."

"Myron, I got a dumb favor to ask you. I just gotta' get out of here for a while. Will you climb that tree in my backyard and get me a coconut. This one's for bubby."

Flo and I walked to the far corner of a parking lot, on the back side of Food Fair. She was wearing a fancy black dress, high heel shoes, and nylon stockings, but that didn't stop her from smashing her coconut on the pavement. She then sat on the ground in a clumsy position, not caring that I could see up her dress . . . she wasn't sitting like a lady.

She grabbed the coconut and screamed in anger as she opened the husk and ripped away at the inside. She was driven by rage. Finally, the nut was removed and Flo heaved it against the side of the building. It cracked into a hundred pieces.

"Thanks Myron, for being with me. Now, I have to go back home and hear a few more Yiddish jokes . . . and maybe I'll have another piña colada. Thank God, I've got Stanley waiting in my end table."

331

CHAPTER 43

THE AGE OF REASON

On April 12, 1955, near the end of my Junior year, four early morning bongs blasted on the PA system and as a matter of habit, I immediately put my books on my lap . . . Mr. Schecter made his morning announcement. It was a wonderful announcement! "Dr. Jonas Salk has developed a vaccine to prevent Polio and the federal government is going to implement a plan to inoculate every child in America. The dreaded disease has been defeated."

"He's Jewish? Isn't he?" Asked my mother.

"He sure is. Mecheieh!" *(Yiddish: Super Joy)* My father beamed with pride.

"Now, can I go swimming at the Venetian Pool?"

Several days later the PA system interrupted class again, but this time it wasn't good news. On April 18, 1955 Albert Einstein died. My father was extremely sad and put an American flag in our front yard.

The next morning I used a small brush and painted $E=MC^2$ on my T-shirt; so did many other boys. The most brilliant scientific mind of the Twentieth Century was gone.

"He was a great man," said my father, "and it's too bad, but people will remember him as the father of the nuclear age. What history will fail to mention is that Einstein was a pacifist."

The Miami Herald ran a huge tribute to Einstein, along with a full page of his famous quotations, mainly about time, space, matter, energy, and relativity. But, I was particularly impressed with Einstein's views on religion. They kind of summed up my own personal belief.

"A man's ethical behavior should be based effectually on sympathy, education, and social ties; no religious basis is necessary.

Man would indeed be in a poor way if he had to be restrained by fear of punishment and hope of reward after death."

"Einstein had his own conception of God," said my father. "He didn't believe in the Biblical interpretation, that God made man to serve the lord. He believed in a cosmic God that created the universe . . . but, beyond that, he believed that we were in control of our day-to-day decisions."

"That makes sense to me," I responded. "I met this Jamaican bus boy at Curry's who kind of thought the same way."

"I didn't know you had any colored friends," my father responded. "You never told me about him."

"Oh, he's not really a friend. I only met him once. He used to work with Morton Mandel."

"Myron, don't get me wrong, I see a lot of good in religion, and naturally, I'm partial to Judaism, but I also see a lot of superstition and fanaticism. Its funny, but when we look at great literature we have no problem reading between the lines, searching for metaphors and hidden meaning . . . like the <u>fish</u> in the Old Man and the Sea, or the <u>whale</u> in Moby Dick, or the <u>raft</u> in Huckleberry Finn. But when we read the Bible, which is also great literature, we tend to take everything so literally, such as Moses parting the Red Sea or Noah and the ark. I think you will get much more out of the Bible if you read it figuratively; look for the underlying message."

I wondered if there were hidden metaphors or symbolism in "A Stone For Danny Fisher," the popular trash novel that all of my friends were reading. Even Manny Lefkowitz read that book. Maybe phrases such as "throbbing penis" or "pulsating vagina" have hidden meaning; those were the words that we all underlined in red. Maybe they were metaphors representing some type of idol worship or cosmic power. What exactly is a cosmic power?

"Dad . . . Who wrote the Bible? I just can't agree with my teachers . . . that the Bible was written by God." I didn't ask him about the metaphors in "Danny Fisher."

I joined my father in the kitchen; we both sat in pajamas, drank tea with lemon and went though a whole box of Ritz crackers. He knew a lot about Israel and the ancient wars with the Assyrians and Babylonians, he knew a lot about Jewish history.

"Most religious scholars think that the Bible was written during the Babylonian exile, I've told you that before . . . that was shortly after the reign of King Solomon, somewhere around 500 BC. Israel was split into two kingdoms. The southern kingdom was conquered by the Babylonians, the Temple was destroyed, and many of the political and religious leaders were sent in exile. Prior to the exile the religion was passed down from generation to generation by the high priests . . . everything was by word of mouth. But, during the exile, Jewish leaders were afraid that the religion would die; it was then that the Five Books of Moses were formally written. Christians refer to these books as the Old Testament; Jews refer to them as the Torah or the Bible."

"Some of my teachers say that Moses wrote the first five books of the Bible," I noted. "But hows that possible, Exodus talks about his death and burial?"

"I think you answered your own question," replied my father, and he chuckled.

"One of my teachers says that America is going the same way as Rome; gambling, liquor, and prostituion will destroy our country. He says that low moral standards led to the fall of Rome and the same thing will happen here."

"Tell your teacher than the Roman Empire lasted for 1,000 years . . . we should only be so lucky. On second thought, you better not say that; you know what happened in the Eighth grade, when you ripped into the Pilgrims." My father laughed as he poured me another cup of tea, this time with honey instead of lemon.

During the final few weeks of the school year Flo dropped out of sight. I called frequently, asking her to go riding in my car, but she always had one excuse or another . . . and I heard that she frequently went to a synagogue in South Beach by herself, sometimes for many hours. I was worried that she might retreat, back into her shell, like when I first met her. The school year was almost over and I spent most of my time studying for final exams. Grades in the junior year were more important than the twelfth grade; these were the grades that the colleges looked at when they evaluated your application. So, I studied hard and my only break from studying was when I washed my car. I washed the car four or five times a week, but I put off dating until the summer; I was hoping to get all A's, except in Spanish III, where I didn't expect to get more than a C. I wound up with 4 A's, a C in Spanish, and a B in Phys. Ed. I just couldn't figure out how they graded you in Phys. Ed. If you weren't on one of the athletic teams it was almost impossible to get an A.

I stopped by Food Fair the day after my last final exam and spoke to Myron DeLuca, the store manager, to see if I could work as a bag boy that summer. I had promised to repay Herman the $200 he loaned me to help pay for my car.

"Myron, the job is always yours . . . whenever you want. Its hard to find good bag boys, especially ones named Myron. The customers love you, especially the old Jewish ladies, but you've got to learn what goes where when you return food to the shelves."

Myron K, the elderly bagboy, still worked at Food Fair. Myron III had been transferred to the regional office in Georgia, he was training to be a meat manager. I was glad to see that he was doing well, and really glad that he was no longer working in Surfside. I worried that Flo would go back to him, as an escape from her depression.

My new advisor and confidant was Myron K; he was a sensitive, very funny old man. And my repertoire of Yiddish humor improved . . . so did my ability to empathize with the "tsoris" (*problems*) and "mazel" (*good fortune*) of elderly Jewish customers. The tips were outstanding; all I had to do was listen well . . . listening was the key to success . . . and respond appropriately with "oye gevald" or "mazel tov." I repaid the $200 to Herman in two weeks.

The customers at Food Fair were primarily Jewish, but many French Canadians also lived in Surfside, in the luxury oceanfront apartments. One day I helped a very pretty French lady wheel her grocery cart to her hi-rise. She had wild and bushy reddish brown hair and wore a green dress, high stockings, and lots of lipstick and perfume. I could smell her from twenty feet away; she smelled like lilacs.

When we got to her building a doorman in a red blazer opened the door and she asked me to come upstairs and help unpack the bags.

"I can't," I replied, "I have to get back to work. I work on tips."

"Here, young man, here's ten dollars; help me up with the groceries. I live on the 15th floor."

I was astounded. That was an amazing tip. For ten dollars I would do anything she wanted . . . even cook her lunch. Once I put the grocery bags on her kitchen table she gave me a knife and asked me to chop onions for a tuna salad. There were several pictures of Jesus and the Virgin Mary hanging in the living room, and a gold magnetic crucifix was used as a memo holder on her refrigerator door.

I tried to play it cool, not to say anything stupid; this was the biggest tip I ever received in my life and if I was smart, this lady could probably be my weekly customer . . . . so I began chopping onions. She told me that her name was Simone Pasquier; she was forty-six, originally from Paris, but she moved to Montreal after the War, then to Surfside. Her husband was part of the French resistance and was killed two weeks after the Normandy invasion. I said nothing . . . oye gevald would not be appropriate (she wasn't Jewish).

I continued chopping onions and listening to her story; I was a good listener (thanks to my training from Myron K). She told gruesome stories about the Nazi occupation of Paris and how the German soldiers abused French women, including her. And as she told her story she stared directly into my eyes; she was crying . . . . either from her tragic story or from the onions.

She sat with one foot raised up on a chair; I could see all the way to her black panties. Even though she was a middle age woman she was really very pretty. Then she put one hand on my knee while her other hand began stroking my neck. She told me I had beautiful eyes and invited me to join her for lunch. She put another $10 bill on the kitchen table, slightly out of my reach.

"Um! Uh! . . . thanks, but I really have to get back to work."

"OK mon cherie, I am so sorry. Maybe next week we talk again, you are a handsome young man. I shop on Mondays, I will look for you. Au revoir." Simone leaned across the kitchen table and offered me a perfect view of her breasts; she was not wearing a bra. Then she removed the $10 bill from the table, folded it in half, and slowly put it down the top of her dress.

As I was leaving her beautiful ocean front apartment I stopped for one final look. Simone had her back to me but her head was half turned; she was smiling, an extremely seductive smile . . . and she was unzipping the back of her dress. I was mesmerized; staring at the beautiful French lady. Then, quickly, before she turned around . . . I ran out of her apartment and wheeled the shopping cart toward the golden doors of the elevator.

♦

Since I had already earned enough money to repay Herman I cut back to a three day schedule, and I stopped working on Mondays. But, Simone spoke to Mr. DeLuca to find out which days I would be working; she changed her shopping day to Tuesday.

"Mon cherie . . . comment allez-vous? How have you been?" Simone smiled as I began to bag her groceries; she was wearing a lot of lilac perfume and very tight pants. Once again, she asked me to wheel the bags to her apartment, and as we walked along Collins avenue she stroked my head and shoulder, but this time I refused to go upstairs. I gave the bags to the doorman. The tip dropped to a quarter, and that was the end of Simone; she soon found another, more accommodating bag boy.

I felt strongly that having sex with a middle age woman was just as bad as letting a girl copy off my exam in exchange for a blowjob. I certainly was anxious to end my virginity, but I had well defined expectations. Simone was not what I wanted; I wanted my first sexual experience to be an unforgettable milestone in my life. I wanted to see fireworks and shooting stars.

As I walked back to Food Fair I remembered my first Shabbos dinner, in the eighth grade, when Howard Lefkowitz's mother shared passionate memories of his Bar Mitzvah. She called it his "Covenant with God." I never had a Bar Mitzvah; I wanted the loss of my virginity to be my own special covenant. And I didn't want my covenant to be with a 46 year old French woman!

I told Myron K what happened with Simone and he said that he suspected what was going on. He had been working for over a year at Food Fair and was well aware of the adventures of the "hot French lady." Every bag boy in the store knew about her and many tried to position themselves to wheel out her groceries . . . but she did the picking. Simone selected the bag boy of her choice.

"Too bad I'm an alter kakker,'" laughed Myron K, "she's never picked me. That woman is a little meshugeneh; she loves young boys. But, you sure cut off a weekly annuity."

◆

After work I frequently went to Fun Fair with some of the bag boys. But ever since the scary incident when Flo almost got raped, I always checked twice for parked motorcycles. And even after I settled in at the game room or the food counter I listened carefully for the roar of approaching motorcycles . . . no telling when the next "pogrom" would occur. The River Rats were a very mobile gang, like the Cossacks . . . they hated Jews; they called us "Christ Killers" and they painted swastikas at Fun Fair and on Lincoln Road. Whenever the Rebels tried to retaliate it was impossible to find them. They had no hangout, not like the Rebels with Dolly's.

I made extra money at Fun Fair that summer in the game room. Some kids were really stupid when it came to gambling . . . they bet on anything and everything, even if they had no chance of winning. I was excellent in Skee Ball and not too bad in bumper pool, so I did quite well hustling bag boys and other kids in those two games. However, I was smart enough to avoid betting on pinball machines, or other games where I wasn't so good.

"Myron, you're a chicken," said Arnie Dombrowski, a friend of mine from school who worked year round as a bag boy. "You only bet on the games where you're good . . . you never play pinball for money."

"Arnie, I bet to win. Why should I bet on pinball. I'm not any good with those games?" Arnie didn't grasp my logic, he regarded gambling as some type of gentleman's sport, like the fox hunt or croquet . . . with rules of etiquette.

Actually, its wrong to say that I engaged in gambling. For me, Skee Ball and bumper pool were a reliable second source of income. When you know that you're going to win that's not really gambling. And, when I saw someone who was better than me in bumper pool I left the room . . . I wasn't out to prove anything. If I couldn't beat the guy I cashed in on my winnings and had another hot dog. But, with skee ball it was different . . . no one ever beat me in that game.

Arnie always liked to call me "Kemosabi." That's what Tonto called the Lone Ranger. It was probably an Indian word meaning, "friend."

"Myron, did you hear the joke about the Lone Ranger and Tonto when they were surrounded by one zillion Indians?" asked Arnie.

Damn . . . I heard that joke one zillion times, from every kid at school. But, Myron K told me never to interrupt someone when they were telling a joke, that was their moment to shine. And, absolutely never shout out the punch line.

"No Arnie . . . how does it go?"

He then rattled off the names of many Indian tribes, Apache, Comanche, Cherokee, Arapaho, Navajo, Sioux. And, he reminded me that Sioux was spelled with an "X."—"the're French Indians." I wanted to tell Arnie to leave the Navajos out of his joke . . . they were farmers, not fighters.

"Anyway . . . The Lone Ranger knew that there was no possible escape from the zillion Indians, so he turned to his faithful Indian companion and said: 'Tonto, Tonto . . . what should we do?' And Tonto responded: 'What you mean WE—white man?'"

I laughed—really loud. Arnie was my friend.

One night several guys from Rebels were in the game room at Fun Fair watching me play bumper pool. They stood around, saying nothing. They all had turned up collars and puffed on Camel cigarettes. The Rebels tried to look like greasers, but they never really scared anyone. Actually, everyone welcomed them to Fun Fair. If they were there, you knew that the River Rats would not attack.

"Hey Lindy, I hear you're good in bumper pool" said Heshie Hornbein. Even though I never became a member of the gang they still continued to call me Lindy. Everyone in Rebels had a nickname . . . even those who almost became a Rebel had a nickname.

"Yeah, I'm not bad," I responded, and I purposely missed a shot, and another shot. I didn't want to look too good; I knew he was getting ready to challenge me to a game.

"Make it five bucks, Lindy," said Heshie, "best two out of three games." Fifteen Rebels and six bag boys crowded around the table to watch the match. So did a lot of girls.

Heshie played a very aggressive game . . . always looking to make extremely difficult low percentage shots, but never bothering to block my shots. He was very good; he could make shots that I would never attempt, but he paid no attention to defense. Therefore, I decided that I would completely ignore offense; I would play a 100% defensive game, making every effort to block Heshie's shots . . . not to even attempt a shot of my own unless it was a very easy high percentage shot.

"Damn, Lindy. Don't you ever attempt a shot?" said Heshie. "At this rate the game will go on all night."

He was right. Bumper pool normally takes five minutes for a game, or less. However, I played a deliberate, conservative strategy . . . and I won two games in a row, but it took almost an hour.

"OK Lindy, here's your damn five bucks." said Heshie, and he threw a five dollar bill on the pool table. "Rebels don't never welch on bets. But, I don't like the way you play . . . you play like a pussy."

He sounded just like Arnie Dombrowski, like there was some type of chivalry associated with gambling . . . a right way and a wrong way to win.

"OK Heshie . . . I'll give you a chance to get even; double or nothing. Lets play three games of skee-ball; if you win once I give back your five. But, if I win all three games you owe me another five."

"That sounds fair," replied Heshie, but everyone could hear the nervousness in his voice. Even the Rebels knew about my reputation in skee ball.

I won the first two games by huge margins. Then, before we started the third game, Arnie Dombrowski walked over to me and suggested that we talk in private.

"Kemosabi, if you beat this prick, you're looking for trouble. Listen; I'm giving you good advice; throw the third game. Heshie's got all his buddies watching."

I heeded the advice of my trusted Indian companion; I let Heshie win the third game . . . and when the game was over he shook hands with me. "Nice try, Lindy, but you weren't quite good enough to be a Rebel or to beat a Rebel." Then he put his arm around my shoulder and led me to the food counter . . . he treated me to a hot dog and a chocolate egg cream. Egg creams were a popular New York drink . . . . Chocolate, milk and seltzer, lots of chocolate. I sat with Heshie and the other Rebels and we all joked together. A few of them scratched their balls when they ate.

"Lindy, did you hear the one about the boy in the prehistoric family?" asked Heshie.

Of course I did—from Myron K. It was part of my Food Fair repertoire.

"No Heshie—how does it go?"

"A little boy in a prehistoric family comes home from school with an 'F' in history. His dad yells at him. How can you get an 'F' in history? What's there to learn?"

"Great one Heshie, I love it." I laughed.

Arnie turned to Heshie: "I don't get it. History ain't no easy class."

"Hey Arnie . . . . Hello!" responded Heshie, in a sarcastic voice. "Prehistoric means 'before' history. Like the boy's dad said, they didn't have nothing to learn."

"Yeah, I know that," said Arnie. "But didn't they learn bout' dinosaurs and stuff like that?"

◆

One night I saw Flo at Fun Fair with some older boys who were wearing yarmelkehs and long sleeve white shirts; they had 'tzitzis' (*fringes*) hanging from their belt. She barely talked to me. The next morning I called Flo at home . . . I wanted to have a serious discussion. "Flo, we've got to talk. What's the problem?"

"Myron . . . we don't really have that much in common anymore; I'm in college, you're still in high school. I know, we used to be friends, but I've grown a lot lately. And, I've found God this summer . . . my life has changed."

"Damn! You're only in summer school . . . and you live home. How much growing up could you do in six weeks? And, I'm good friends with a bag boy who's over 70 . . . that's a little bit older than your kosher boys. And a 46 year old French woman tried to seduce me. I think I'm growing up quite a bit this summer."

"Myron . . . you still just think about sex. Wait til' you go to college; wait till' you find God; then you'll know what I'm talking about."

"Why . . . . Do you stop thinking about sex once you're in college? And I thought you agreed with Freud, that God was just an illusion."

"No . . . not really! That was just you who said that . . . I didn't know enough to disagree with you; you're the one who reads every fuckin' book. But, I'm taking Psychology now . . . and Freud isn't quite the genius you think . . . . I bet you didn't know that he developed all his theories from analyzing dreams of neurotic wackos.' Does that make him an expert on God and religion? And, I sure as hell don't agree with him about penis envy."

"Well . . . of course not! You've got Stanley waiting in your end table."

(SLAM)

Flo hung up the phone . . . and that ended our conversation . . . . and our friendship.

I didn't talk to Flo again that summer; she found God and I didn't fit into her spiritual plans. She was obviously depressed by the death of her grandmother and she escaped by finding new friends, religious Jewish boys who wore long sleeve white shirts and yarmelkehs. She even dressed different and wore lipstick and earrings. I hoped she didn't start smoking or drinking; I hoped that she remembered the pleasure of smashing coconuts. I thought about climbing up her balcony for a late night visit, but I knew that she really wanted to make a break from her prior life, and that included me.

◆

My best friends, the Steinbergs, also had good jobs that summer and made a lot of money. David worked at Perry Chester, a very expensive women's shoe store in Surfside, and every time I saw him he was holding hands with a gorgeous girl. They were all tall, very tall, and they all looked like models.

"How do you do it David? You don't even have a car."

"It's a trick I read in a sex manual from India. Its called the Kamasutra. When I'm on my knees, helping a girl try on her shoes, I cradle her foot in my hands and start massaging her toes and heel with my thumbs. If you know what you're doing and hit the erogenous zones . . . they can't say no."

"Jeez . . . you gotta teach me that trick." I responded, and I made a mental note to look up the word "erogenous." "So far I've drawn blanks all summer . . . just Simone, the horny French lady. I told you about her. But, I couldn't do it with anyone that old."

"Forty-six! Yuck!" said David. "No way I could get a hardon with someone that old. Betcha' her pussy is all dried up. Oh, shit! I almost forgot to tell you . . . Guess who I saw in the store the other day? An old man in a white silk shirt and super shiny shoes was with a little girl; she was probably twelve or thirteen. While I was helping her try on shoes the man was touching her leg, her neck, her ears. He was pawing all over her; weird looking guy with a squeaky voice and a thick German accent. And when they left I heard the little girl call him 'Mr. Streuling.' It was your old buddy . . . he found himself a girlfriend."

"Jesus Christ! Last thing I want is for that degenerate to find out where I live. Listen David . . . if you ever see him again, don't talk to him."

Why was Streuling messing around with a little girl? I thought pedophiles only liked boys. This didn't make sense. And . . . if he really was castrated how could he still be a pedophile . . . with a boy or with a girl? Maybe I was wrong; maybe he still had his testicles. Strange man . . . I sure didn't want to see him again.

♦

Shelly worked for the Miami Beach sanitation department, scraping barnacles from the underside of the McArthur Causeway. He made good money but his grandparents forced him to quit after one month; the back of his neck was turning green and he was developing an ugly cough. Once he quit, so did I, and we spent the rest of the summer together, sneaking into the Fontainebleau, the elegant new hotel in Miami Beach.

The Fontainebleau had a fantastic pool area, with platform diving boards, a ping pong room, and lots of girls . . . mainly tourists from New York. But the pool was reserved exclusively for hotel guests. It was protected by several security guards. However, Shelly and I found a way to get past the guards. We used the same method that we used to sneak into the restricted Kenilworth Hotel—we went to the public beach on 46th street and swam fifty yards offshore. Then we entered the Fontainebleau pool by way of the beach, the unprotected back side of the hotel.

After we snuck into the pool area we blended with the hotel guests . . . we played ping pong with the boys or Canasta with the girls. Canasta was an easy way to meet girls; Shelly and I were the only boys who played the game. And my Rhumba lessons finally paid off; barefoot Latin dancing was very popular at the poolside bar. The New York girls were really "wild" . . . they were away from home, on vacation, and didn't care about their reputation, and they loved the way I wiggled my tush.

"Yeah, I'm Jewish," I told one of my Rhumba partners, "but my ancestry is from Spain. Its in the blood."

One day after playing Canasta at the Fountainebleau Shelly and I ate lunch with Sondra and Sonia Sorkin, buxom twins from Great Neck, Long Island. They were wearing two piece bathing suits that barely covered the important parts of their chubby bodies. Shelly and I ordered cheeseburgers and pineapple smoothies.

"No . . . . no cheese," exclaimed Sondra. "that's 'traif.' You can't mix 'fleishik' (*meat*) and 'milchik' (*dairy*) in the same meal."

"Why not?" I responded. "Even without cheese, the meat isn't kosher anyway?"

"No way," said Sonia. "Our parents wouldn't even let us sit at the same table with you if you ordered a cheeseburger."

"OK . . . . Make them plain burgers." We changed our order. The sisters mumbled a quick Barucha' (*Hebrew blessing*) before we ate our hamburgers.

"The hotel is pronounced Fontaine . . . bluh," said Shelly, "I took French and our teacher went nuts if we said blue or blow."

The sisters took turns saying "bluh" and as they chuckled their boobs jiggled.

"I heard you got a twin brother," said Sonia. "The two of you should go out with Sondra and me; that could be wild."

"Yeah," responded Sondra. "If we swapped partners, just think of all the combinations. And what if everyone went 'both ways?'"

Shelly and I stared at two beautiful pairs of well endowed bosoms . . . they were both adorned with matching gold mezuzahs.

"Shelly, I got a question to ask you," said Sondra, and she smiled. "Its kinda' personal, so you don't have to answer if you don't want to."

"Is your . . . uh . . . your . . . uh . . . your 'you know what!' I mean, yours and your brothers! Are they identical?"

Before Shelly had a chance to answer this poignant question Sonia interrupted: "Hey, its really sweltering; why don't we all go in the ocean."

Shelly said he wanted to stay around the pool and watch a fashion show by a French designer; he was coming out with a "vibrant" new line of bathing suits, all in chartreuse, a popular new color.

"That's nice," said Sondra, "The French are very creative people, they invented the brassiere, the Ferris Wheel, the pencil and . . . ."

". . . the ménage à trois!" exclaimed Sonia, as she abruptly ended her sister's history lesson. "C'mon Myron, lets go swimming."

Sonia, Sondra and I swam far from shore. We swam until the water was up to their mezuzahs. Then Sonia stopped, mumbled a quick barucha, and started to kiss me; so did Sondra . . . and it really got confusing . . . everyone was grabbing everyone and I thought of the well known passage from The Three Musketeers . . . "One for all and all for one."

"They were French guys," said Sonia. "Viva la French!"

Then Sondra started screaming, really loud. "Jesus Christ! Oh My God!"

She saw a shark! One glimpse of the shark fin gliding on the surface of the water and the three of us swam full speed, back to the beach. After that terrifying experience I stopped sneaking into the Fontainebleau by way of the ocean . . . and I never saw Sondra and Sonia again. Their parents got scared and returned to Long Island.

It was now mid-August, only one more week and summer vacation would be over. I told my father that I was very confused; why did Flo get so involved in religion, and why were the Sorkin sisters so afraid of eating cheeseburgers? He suggested that I read "The Age of Reason" by Thomas Paine. I struggled with the book; it was difficult to understand. I was confused with Paine's style of writing and all the quotes from the Bible.

I stopped by Colonel Klein's house one afternoon to discuss the book. The Colonel was now married and Katarina lived with him, along with his two boys and Annabelle's four orphaned children. The house was completely redecorated; it no longer looked like a war museum, even the souvenir Rosetta Stone was packed away in the garage. It was now a dormitory, with bunk beds in the living room.

"The 'Age of Reason' is really a sequel to 'Common Sense,'" said the Colonel. "In 'Common Sense' Paine argues for democracy as the logical form of government to replace monarchy. Then, in 'The Age of Reason' he uses the same type of logic to argue for the elimination of religion."

"So, was Paine an atheist . . . like Freud?"

"No, not at all . . . he was a Deist. Atheism teaches that there is no God. Deism rejects the Bible and the revelations of religion but does not reject God. Paine, Jefferson and Franklin, the founding fathers of our country, shared the same vision of God. More recently, Einstein expressed similar sentiments . . . that God lives spiritually in the soul of Man."

I thought about Flo; she found God by wearing lipstick and going to synagogue with Jewish boys who wore yarmulkes and long sleeve shirts . . . and I thought about the kosher Sorkin sisters, who flaunted golden symbols of God between large sun tanned breasts . . . and Simone, the French lady who seduced teenage bagboys. Her God was a magnetic crucifix on the refrigerator door. God was all around me . . . . even the River Rats were inspired by God; they were on a holy crusade to cleanse my Jewish island of "Christ Killers."

As I look back to the summer of '55 I think it was then that I also found God, but my God was the God of Jefferson, Einstein and Paine . . . and my God said it was OK to eat cheeseburgers; it was even OK to fool around with "well endowed" twin sisters in the ocean . . . but it was not OK to let a girl copy off my exam and it was not OK to sell my soul to a middle age French woman.

CHAPTER 44

NEWS FROM THE OUTSIDE WORLD: 1954-1955

My world is still limited to bus routes, until March 20, 1955 . . . but I expand my horizons to Broward County, just north of Dade. Here are a few key events that had some type of impact on my life or on the lives of my family.

- Sports Illustrated is first published—how will they find enough sports news to fill a weekly magazine? What are they going to write about, bowling and roller derby?
- A test program using sterilized males wipes out screw worm flies on the Caribbean island of Curacao in only 4 months. "Maybe someday, this research will lead to a cure for Cancer," "says my father. "Yeah, maybe." I responded, "but only on screw worms."
- Ernest Hemmingway won the Nobel Prize for Literature. The whole family takes a trip to Key West. My father and I drink Cokes at Sloppy Joe's, the bar where Santiago had the arm wrestling match.
- French colonial rule in Vietnam weakens when Viet Minh rebels take Dien Bien Phu. Vietnam is divided into northern and southern regions. "I hope we don't start sending money," said my mother. "We have enough poor people in this country to worry about"

- Ralph Lauren, a Jewish boy in the Bronx (same age as me), trashes his Lacoste collection and proudly proclaims to his friends, "I had a dream . . . . some day polo ponies will replace the little alligators on these shirts." His friends laugh at the dream. "Ralphie . . . Shmuck! When was the last time you saw a Jewish boy playing polo?"
- Ray Kroc goes to California and also has a dream . . . at the end of a rainbow he sees two golden arches . . . "some day thin tasteless processed beef patties will replace thick juicy burgers." His friends laugh at his dream. "Ray . . . Shmuck! Who's gonna' eat tasteless processed patties?"
- Hold the pickle! Hold the lettuce! Here comes another dream . . . . The first Burger King opens . . . in Miami. But, I don't like these burgers; not nearly as good as Royal Castle. Too much lettuce and tomatoes . . . and they use mayonnaise.
- Catholic Church declares that watching Mass on TV does not fulfill obligations. I wonder if Einstein or Paine would have supported that conclusion? What would Freud say?
- Dr. Roger Bannister of England becomes the first person to break the four minute mile; his time is 3 minutes, 59.4 seconds. Six tenths of a second and he becomes a living legend. He is eventually knighted by Queen Elizabeth, "Sir Roger," an honor that never was bestowed on Dickens, Darwin, or Shakespeare.
- M&M Peanut Chocolate candies are introduced—but it was too late for me. I was already addicted to the plain M&Ms.
- The Butterball brand and the self-basting turkey are introduced. Through genetics, Swift develops a broad-breasted bird without the tough tendons and uses a hot-water bath to remove feathers.
- Dr. Sam Sheppard's wife Marilyn is murdered (he is accused of the crime)—was this where they developed the TV show, "The Fugitive?"
- Play Doh is invented—never allowed in my house—much too messy. What is the difference between Play Doh and Silly Putty? I never played with either one.

- Nash-Kelvinator and Hudson Motor Car Co. merge to form the American Motors Co. Nash Rambler was the famous car which had a back seat that folded into a bed . . . very popular at "Pecker's Point.".
- Colonel Gamal Abdel Nasser seizes power in Egypt and signs a treaty with the British under which the British will withdraw from the Suez. "Oye! This means trouble for Israel," says my father.
- General Electric introduces colored kitchen appliances. Bye bye white . . . Shelly runs over to our house, excited with the announcement. He and my mother decide on mustard, as the new color for our kitchen. Of course, that means that we would have to replace our pink dishes.
- A hydrogen (fusion) bomb is detonated on Bikini, a tiny atoll in the Pacific. This is the most horrible weapon of mass destruction in the history of mankind. In honor of this horrific, terrifying event an itsy witsy teenie weenie yellow polka dot bathing suit is designed for girls. Very popular with the tourists at the Fontainebleau. "Why polka dots?" said Shelly, "Little alligators would be much sexier. And why yellow? Yellow represents cowardice. Green would be better; Mother Earth—fertility."

TWELFTH GRADE

CHAPTER 45

THREE BRAINS ARE BETTER THAN ONE

I arrived early for the first day of twelfth grade, very early . . . before 7:00 AM, and parked my convertible close to school, with the top down. I sat high in the front seat, wearing my black and gold "Senior 56" pin prominently above the alligator on my new sienna Lacoste . . . the latest color . . . a shade of brown. And to complete my "super cool" image I chomped on an unlit sienna colored pipe. I didn't smoke but it looked very sophisticated to have a pipe in your mouth when you talked. After all, I was a senior, and I was now six feet tall, no longer a little shrimp. Yep! Six feet tall, but skinny as a rail.

Many of the boys were wearing Yankee or Dodger hats. Another subway series was about to start, the fourth in the last five years. Maybe the New York domination of baseball was good for me . . . during my high school years I was never glued to the TV. My main diversions were reading and writing . . . and now girls were also high on the list. I was surprised to see that Miss Madison was my home room teacher again; normally we had a new teacher every year. She gave me a big hug and welcomed me back to school.

"Myron, I met an old friend of yours this summer, Hershel Glickman, the manager of the Pix shoe store on Lincoln Road. He said that you did wonders for his business, even though you only worked there one week. His fruit shoes are a huge success and he told me to say thanks. He also said that you should stop by his store one day after school . . . he wants to talk to you."

Miss Madison raised her long black skirt a few inches, smiled, and proudly displayed her new cork shoes; she switched from bananas to apples. Linda Spiegel also hugged me (but she wore fancy Italian shoes), everyone was glad to see everyone. This was the beginning of our final year of high school. We were the Class of '56 and we kept repeating the cool new expression . . . . "we got it made in the shade."

Just then, while hugging Linda, the familiar sound of the glockenspiel heralded the first PA announcement of the new school year. Four potent bongs reverberated above the clamor of the classroom. Linda's arms were wrapped around my sienna Lacoste; it was impossible to run and hide . . . impossible to grab my text books for cover.

"Myron! Oh my!" Linda tightened her grip around my waist and blushed. When she returned to her seat she whispered to a few girlfriends. They all giggled.

The first announcement of the new school year came from Aaron T Schecter. "Good morning boys and girls. For those of you who don't know me, I'm Mr. Schecter, your principal . . . welcome back to school, and a special welcome to the new seniors . . . the senior class of 1956."

"Yo, yo, daddy-o." The whole classroom erupted; fists clenched, thumbs pointed up. "Seniors rule . . . we are so cool!" I was especially cool in my sienna Lacoste . . . so were seven other boys who were also wearing sienna.

Massie Quinn, the "old maid" director of student activities made a few announcements on the PA. . . . she urged students to sign up for various projects and committees. I hated her horrible shrill voice, especially early in the morning, but that disgusting shriek was the perfect antidote for the "power of the glockenspiel" . . . . which is probably why Miss Quinn was a middle age spinster. How could any man ever have sex with that woman?

The next announcement came from Andy Nathanson, our newly elected senior class president. He also welcomed the students back to school and discussed some of the upcoming social events, football games, pep rallies, and dances. I liked Andy; he had been in several of my classes. He was really smart; not quite as smart as Spencer Teichman, but Andy combined intelligence with personality. One thing I noticed about Andy . . . he was a very good listener. One time when I was making an oral presentation in World History, describing ancient architecture, the various types of Greek and Roman columns, Andy's eyes were glued to mine; his face was extremely expressive and responsive. He hung on every word of my presentation; his head was constantly nodding approval. He could have been a great bag boy.

The next speaker was Cody Goldstrich, the Vice President of the Senior Class. Cody was also the president of my homeroom, section 12-3. Later that day Cody told me that he was informed by Miss Quinn that the Beach High constitution prohibited him from holding both offices simultaneously. He was forced to resign as homeroom president.

"Myron, why don't you run for homeroom president?" said Cody. "I'll talk to the other kids and help you get elected." I had never held any elected office at Beach High; this was my final chance.

My opponent was Tommy Duke, who's only exciting quality was his biceps. During the next several days, as we campaigned for election, Tommy wore a black sleeveless T-shirt to school . . . . the same one every day.

"Hey, you don't see no chick with big tits dressin' like a fuckin' nun," said Tommy. "Like the old saying goes . . . . If you got it, flaunt it." And he crossed his arms across his chest and displayed his muscular arms.

Tommy was nineteen; he was from the Class of '55 but had to retake the twelfth grade. He wasn't exactly stupid, but he was extremely lazy and never studied for tests.

"I really got the royal shaft," said Tommy. "It don't prove nothing if you study your ass off for a test and 'ace it.' I bet Einstein didn't have to study none for tests."

Tommy won the election, 18-17. He made a short acceptance speech in front of the class and flexed his biceps, kind of like Ike, when he flashed his fingers in the "V" sign. Damn! Tommy had great arms. Every girl voted for him, except Linda Spiegel.

"Myron, when did you grow so tall . . . and so cute?" Linda looked up into my eyes and smiled. "Gosh . . . I remember when you first came here. You thought I was the teacher; you were so little. But . . . you sure aren't little anymore." Linda blushed.

That day after school I drove to Reisler Brothers sporting goods store and bought a new jock strap and a pair of dumbbells; I decided that I had to do something about my scrawny body;

I was a walking bean pole. During the four years since I moved from Chicago, I had been working on my intellect, but ignoring my body, it was now time to begin pumping iron . . . serious pumping. And I also needed some type of diet supplement to build up bulk; I looked like Ghandi during one of his hunger fasts.

"Young man, if you vant' to be a Charles Atlas drink this high protein mix every morning," said the elderly Jewish salesman at Reisler Brothers. "Mix vit' a glass of milk, two raw eggs, and a banana. And give a squirt of Hersheys. Not too much . . . just a 'bissel.'"

So, every morning I made my banana-chocolate power mix for breakfast and after school I did two hours of curls and lifts, working on the biceps, triceps, quads, and shoulders. Then I did sit ups, push ups, and leg squats. Then more curls and lifts until I dropped from exhaustion, with my arms shaking in pain. And, I completely eliminated reading and studying.

Six weeks later . . . . the first report card was a disaster, three B's and three C's. With the exception of Spanish, those were the only C's I ever received on a report card . . . . and my father stared at the three C's. He took out a piece of paper and a pencil and began writing the letter C . . . large C's . . . . and he said nothing. He just kept writing C's. I had a strong feeling that I was about to be grounded, not allowed to drive my car for a week or a month or maybe until the next report card.

"Rose, please make a full pot of tea. Myron and I are going to have a long discussion."

"Dad, I'm just looking for balance in my life. So far, all I've ever done is study and read, and write . . . I'm six feet tall, 140 pounds; I look like an Auschwitz survivor."

"Are you jealous of that muscular boy who beat you for homeroom president?"

"Well, yeah . . . I am! That guy just stands there and flexes his biceps and the girls all swoon . . . they all go ga-ga over him."

"I thought you said that Linda Spiegel likes you. It sounds like she is impressed by your intelligence."

"Well . . . that's a different story, but trust me . . . it wasn't my intelligence that prodded her to vote for me."

"So, if you had huge biceps all your problems would be solved," exclaimed my father. "What do you want in your tea . . .

honey or lemon?" He reached in the pantry and grabbed a box of chocolate chip cookies, and poured an extra large cup of tea.

"Let me tell you a story . . . . I heard it from my father when I was even younger than you . . . Its about a poor Jewish stonecutter in Minsk, back in the old country . . . his name was Lazar Abramowitz.

"Lazar was miserable, dissatisfied with himself and with his position in life . . . even though he had muscular arms and shoulders. *(I thinkt my father just threw in that part of the story)* One day he passed a wealthy merchant's house. Through the open doorway, he saw many expensive possessions and important visitors. 'How powerful that merchant must be!' thought Lazar the stone cutter. He became very jealous and wished that he could be like the merchant. To his great surprise, Lazar suddenly became the merchant, enjoying more luxuries and power than he had ever imagined, but envied and disliked by those less affluent than himself.

Soon a high official passed by, carried in a velvet chair, accompanied by attendants and escorted by soldiers beating drums. Everyone, no matter how wealthy, had to bow down before the procession. 'How powerful that official is!' thought Lazar. 'I wish that I could be a high official!' Then he became the high official, carried everywhere in a velvet chair, feared and hated by the people all around.

It was a hot summer day, so Lazar the official, felt very uncomfortable in the sticky chair. He looked up at the sun. It shone proudly in the sky, unaffected by his presence. 'How powerful the sun is!' he thought. 'I wish that I could be the sun!' Then Lazar became the sun, shining fiercely down on everyone, scorching the fields, cursed by the farmers and laborers.

But a huge black cloud moved between him and the earth, so that his light could no longer shine on everything below. 'How powerful that storm cloud is!' he thought. 'I wish that I could be a cloud!' Then he became the cloud, flooding the fields and villages, shouted at by everyone. But soon he found that he was being pushed away by some great force, and realized that it was the wind. 'How powerful it is!' he thought. 'I wish that I could be the wind!' Then he became the wind, blowing tiles off the roofs of houses, uprooting trees, feared and hated by all below him.

But after a while, he ran up against something that would not move, no matter how forcefully he blew against it—a huge, towering rock. 'How powerful that rock is!' he thought. 'I wish that I could be a rock!' Then he became the rock, more powerful than anything else on earth. But as he stood there, he heard the sound of a hammer pounding a chisel into the hard surface, and felt himself being changed. 'What could be more powerful than I, the rock?' he thought. He looked down and saw far below him the figure of a poor Jewish stone cutter."

I drank two full cups of tea and ate the entire box of cookies. It was a good story; envy is stupid and leads to even more envy.

"Dad, I will never get a 'C' again . . . never." We hugged . . . and I kept that promise; I put the dumbbells on the loft in our garage and eventually threw them out when they got rusty.

Although my father and I usually discussed history, philosophy, religion, and school, he sometimes gave me more "personal" advice, especially since I was now taking more of an interest in girls.

"Myron, now that you're getting interested in girls, here's a little tip, and I speak from experience. Watch a young lady eat an ice cream cone and you'll have a pretty good idea how she'll be in bed."

◆

Several days later, on the way home from school, I stopped by Pix to say hello to Mr. Glickman. He had told Miss Madison that he wanted to talk to me. I should have gone sooner but I was always a procrastinator.

"Myron? Is that you?" said Mr. Glickman. "You've grown so tall . . . I hardly recognize you." We shook hands; Mr. Glickman was not a hugger. "But, oye . . . so skinny!"

"Boitsheck . . . look at me, a fancy-shmancy silk shirt, diamond cufflinks and a gold vatch' . . . I owe this to you, and to Carmen Miranda. Go figure?" Mr Glickman grabbed my head and kissed me on the forehead. I guess I was wrong . . . he was a hugger.

"Myron, come . . . sit vit' me at Dubrows . . . lets 'nash' a little. You vant'—I'll buy you a nice tongue sandvich.'"

"I hate tongue; how about corned beef?"

I hadn't been to Dubrows in years, not since we moved to Surfside. Even though I spent many Saturday mornings hanging out on Lincoln Road, just a few doors away, none of my friends would be caught dead in the "alter kakker" cafeteria. The distinctive aroma of pickle juice reminded me of aunt Pearlie, Herman, and Blanche Liebowitz, my aunt's canasta friend. Its funny how smells can trigger memories.

"Say, before I forget, I have a little bonus for you . . . a year late." Mr. Glickman opened his wallet and flashed a thick wad of $100 bills. "Here . . . take one of these. Now go to Mal Marshalls and buy some nice clothes. Girls like a young man who dresses like a Beau Brummell. And vhy' don't you eat your vegetables. No vonder' you're so skinny"

"Wow! Thank you very much Mr. Glickman. By the way, talking about girls, I have a crazy question to ask you . . . since you're in the shoe business. I have a friend who worked at a shoe store last summer; he said that the easiest way to pick up girls was to massage the erogenous zones on their feet when they're trying on new shoes. Have you ever heard of that?"

"Vats' an erogenous zone?" asked Mr. Glickman. "Look here, its done vit' da' thumbs." Mr. Glickman then lifted a large roll from the basket on our table and gave me a quick demonstration, how to massage the balls of a woman's foot.

"That's how I got da' first Mrs. Glickman in bed, ven' I was a young man, working at a shoe store in Hamburg. Oye, those were vild' times, between the wars. Don't ask . . . . You don't vant' to know."

"The first Mrs. Glickman?" I interrupted his demonstration. "So you're married to your second wife now?"

"No . . . I'm on the third Mrs. Glickman. I met my second vife' the same way as the first one . . . vile' massaging her foot at the shoe store. Oye, vas' she a vild' one; she loved to have vipped' cream and shnopps all over her body ven' we made love. OK, one and two overlapped a little . . . . I vas' 'shtupping' number two vile' still married to number one. But, I vasn't really cheating . . . me and number one, ve' vasn't' sleeping together no more."

"So, how did you meet number three?" I asked. "Another foot massage?"

"Ven' I came to America number two was dead. Its a tragic story . . . Son—of-a-bitch Nazi's! Ptu! Ptu!" Mr. Glickman did an imaginary spit on the floor.

"Do you have any children," I asked

"No! I don't want to talk about that." Mr. Glickman was very abrupt. I obviously touched a sore spot, and was careful to avoid that subject during the remainder of our discussion.

"Myron . . . do you know the difference between men and vimen'?" Mr. Glickman broke the awkward silence. "No . . . don't even try to answer. How are you supposed to know? You don't even know your own petzle yet! Here, let me tell you. Vimen' make decisions from the heart . . . especially about love, they are very romantic; they vant' men that give them flowers and ride vite' horses. Men are much more complicated. I know . . . vimen' don't think so; they think that a man's brain is in his pecker. But . . . like I said, men are very complicated. Ve' have three brains. Yeah! . . . one of them is in the pecker, that's the brain that got me into my first two marriages. But, men also have a brain in the head; we sometimes are very logical. I said, 'sometimes,' not always. Vimen' never use the brain in their head . . . it doesn't function."

"Where is the third brain?" I asked.

"In the heart, like vimen,' but men don't use that brain too much, ve' don't look for vimen who ride vite' horses.'"

"So, which brain got you into your third marriage?"

"The von' in the head . . . she's a good cook, keeps a clean house, a 'balebosteh' (capable homemaker). But . . . but . . . . vell,' lets just say . . . . the pecker ain't vat' it used to be . . .

useless for shtupping and not much good for pishing. Myron, it's the shits getting old. Don't ask."

"Isn't it possible to ever have all three brains going at the same time . . . . the head, the penis, and the heart?"

"Vhy' bother?" Mr. Glickman shrugged his shoulders. "Vimen' never even attempt to use all three."

"I had all three going once." I responded, "back in the ninth grade . . . with a girl that I only went out with one time. I'm sure of it . . . all three brains said 'yes.'"

"Then vhy' did you let her go? Shmuck . . . that girl and you vere' 'bashert.' Listen to a vise' old man . . . . I know vat' I'm talking about."

"Say Myron, you vant' to come vurk' for me? After school? Veekends'? You can vurk' up front vit' da' customers, . . . and I'll teach you how to give a good foot massage."

"Thanks for the offer Mr. Glickman, but I didn't do so well on my last report card . . . I have to get my grades back up."

Mr. Glickman said goodbye and he gave me a pair of fruit shoes for my mother. He was a nice man; I really liked him, and he knew a lot about love and life. I finally understood why I was obsessed with my memory of Leah Sonnino. She touched all three of my brains. Now that I had my own car maybe I should try to find her again.

CHAPTER 46

A NIGHT IN THE SLAMMER

During the next six weeks I put my social life on hold, except for football games; I went to all the Beach High and University of Miami games with the Steinbergs and Josh Broden . . . but no girls. I promised my father and myself that I would improve my grades, so I put in long hours studying and memorizing lists. Other kids were going nuts watching the annual New York World Series, but not me. This year it was the Dodgers and the Yankees . . . and the Dodgers won. Naturally, they were deified by the New York sports writers. In future years the 1955 Dodgers would be known as "The Boys of Summer." I hated that title! Why wasn't every team that won a World Series called "The Boys of Summer?" How come only New York teams and players were awarded special titles of distinction? I think if one of the players from the Yankees, Dodgers, or Giants made a good piss it would be immortalized by the New York sports writers; it would be called "The PISS." I had been going to this school of transplanted New Yorkers for five years (including the two years at Ida M. Fisher) and every damn year a New York team won the World Series. I lost all interest in baseball, even the White Sox.

The big excitement in my life . . . also for the Steinbergs and Josh Broden, was receiving our letters of acceptance from the University of Florida. We were all going to be "Gators" and we bought matching blue and orange UF t-shirts. Next year, Josh and I would be roommates in Gainesville, and the Steinbergs would room with each other. Hopefully, we would all be on the same

362

floor in Tolbert Hall, the freshman dormitory . . . along with many other kids from Beach High who were also going to Florida.

"My father has connections with TEP," said Josh. "I can get us both invitations to Spring Frolics."

"Whats that?" I asked, "I knew nothing about college fraternities.

"It's a big weekend, when all the frats at UF invite prospects. I've heard they have wild entertainment. It will be great in G-ville Myron . . . me and you roommates and frat brothers. And lots of pussy; sorority girls love to put out for guys in frats."

As the growing legion of future Gators walked across the patios and open balconies of Beach High we greeted each other with the popular new expression: "See you later alligator."

The Miami vs. Florida football game was a bittersweet experience in 1955. We had all been diehard fans of the University of Miami but now we were wearing blue Gator T-shirts. It was very uncomfortable rooting against the Hurricanes when they opened their 1955 season against the Gators. We couldn't do it! One last time, I cheered for Miami over Florida, so did the Steinbergs and Josh.

The next report card was fantastic, five A's and a B. No matter how hard I tried, it was impossible to get an A in Phys. Ed. And, of course it helped that I was no longer taking Spanish.

"Congratulations Sunshine," said my father, and he gave me a big hug and $20 for extra spending money. "My CPA, Seymour Rosenblatt, needs someone to work part time. I told him how fast you were at adding columns. Would you like a job? His office is on Lincoln Road, just a few blocks from your school."

"What can I do at an accounting firm? I don't know anything about accounting."

"It will be good experience; better than working as a bag boy."

Actually, I would have preferred working for Mr. Glickman at Pix. Learning to give a good foot massage to a girl would be a very useful skill . . . it could serve me well in college. What could I learn working at an accounting firm? However, the pay was really great. I agreed to work after school and on Saturdays at Rosenblatt, Unger and Polsky, Certified Public Accountants. But, one bad part of the job . . . I hated wearing starched dress shirts; it was much too hot. Mr. Glickman from Pix was the only man I knew who always wore itchy long sleeves, even on the hottest days of summer.

I was greeted by Seymour Rosenblatt, the senior partner of the CPA firm.

"Myron, your father is a good client, and his attorney, Ben Seligman, is an old friend of mine. Its nice to have you on board. But first, I want to tell you a little something about professional ethics and client confidentiality. Working here, you will learn a lot about many clients of the firm . . . some of them are prominent people . . . . some are a little on the 'shady' side. But what you find out must never leave this office. The backbone of the accounting profession is based on trust and ethics."

"Thank you Mr. Rosenblatt. Don't worry; I'll never say anything to anyone about firm business, not even to my parents."

"Call me Seymour," said the well dressed middle age man, "and I really have to see if you're as fast with adding as your dad says. You know, when I was your age I was always the champ. Back in college I was treasurer of my fraternity. Probably a dozen former frat brothers became clients . . . and some are quite successful."

Seymour then poured me a cup of coffee. He was wearing large gold cuff links and a monogrammed white shirt, "SSR" on both sleeves.

"What's your middle name?" I asked, and I crossed my legs and took a sip of coffee. As I sat there, chatting with the senior partner of this prestigious accounting firm, I felt very important.

"Its Solomon, like the wise Jewish king, same as your dad." Seymour looked directly in my eyes. "Myron, you're Sol Lindell's son . . . I am trusting you. Now, finish your coffee. We'll have one of the girls teach you how to use the adding maching."

My primary job was to double check the computations of the three CPAs, to add long columns of numbers. I leared how to "foot" worksheets and financial statements—how to "cross-foot" vertically and horizontally—and it didn't take long until I was extremely fast with the adding machine. Nothing left the office until it had my unique stamp of approval . . . a purple letter "M" bisected by an equal sign. It was an original design . . . I created it.

I was meticulous as I ticked and footed with my special purple pencil; I was the only one in the office with purple . . . even the partners were not allowed to use my exclusive color, not even Seymour. Four secretaries worked for the firm and I was doing much more complex work than any of them . . . except Trixie.

She ran the office. But, the three assistant secretaries resented the fact that I was on a first name basis with the partners.

"Trixie also calls him Seymour," said Bruce Polsky, a short, very overweight partner, "but that's only because she sucks his cock at night. But, aside from Trixie, this here's a man's firm, and its a man's profession . . . the girls all call us mister. I'm gonna' talk to Trixie. Don't look right for them to be calling you Myron . . . they should give you proper respect."

One afternoon I was working in the file room with Joanie Vozella, the youngest of the secretaries. She was the tallest girl I had ever seen in my life. I had heard that Joanie was "AC-DC"—she went both ways—with girls or boys. That seemed so confusing. Without a penis, how can girls have sex with other girls?

Joanie and I were alphabetizing client files in black metal cabinets. I was working on "A-M" in the upper drawers and she was bending over, organizing the "N-Z" files. Joanie was nineteen, a senior at Tech High in Miami—enrolled in a work-study program learning to be a secretary. Polsky told me that she was expelled from school for posing nude in a French "girlie" magazine. She was forced to transfer to Tech and had to repeat the twelfth grade. The secretaries chuckled when they talked about Joanie, especially when one of them said that the magazine needed an extra long centerfold.

Most of the kids at Tech High had some type of problem and were enrolled in industrial arts or clerical work-study programs. That's where Leah Sonnino was going to school, at least she was there a year ago, when I saw her at the football game.

"Joanie, do you know a girl named Leah Sonnino?"

"Yeah sure, she's my best friend, a real cute Jewish girl." Joanie smiled and twirled the large cross that was hanging from her neck. "Leah's doing an internship at a car agency near downtown Miami. How do you know her?"

"Oh, we're old friends from Beach High. I went out with her back in the ninth grade . . . . a long time ago. Well, if you see her tell her that I said hi . . . if she even remembers me." I had a far away look in my eyes when I reminisced about Leah.

"Myron, I might be a dumb shiksah, but I got a feeling that you still have a crush on her."

"A crush? Now? Not really! But, I sure did like her back then . . . she was the first girl I ever dated. Actually, she was the first girl I ever kissed."

"OK, I'll talk to Leah. The two of you would make such a cute couple."

Joanie turned away from me and continued organizing client files. She was wearing a very short skirt. I had never seen a skirt that short before, it was at least two feet above her knees . . . and when she bent over to reach the lower drawers of the file cabinet I saw her black panties . . . they were pulled tightly up the crack of her butt, exposing full white cheeks. It was difficult to concentrate on my work; I couldn't stop gawking at Joanie's beautiful round tush. That was the first time in my life I felt more attraction to the back side of a girl than to her front.

"Myron . . . stop staring at my ass," said Joanie, in a very businesslike voice. I wondered if she had eyes in back of her head; she remained in the bending position, organizing client files and tax returns, unconcerned that her semi-nude butt was on full display. "I don't put out for guys at work. Just ask Polsky; he's been trying to get in my pants ever since I got here."

"Polsky! He's old enough to be your father," I exclaimed, as I returned to the job of alphabetizing client files. "He probably can't even get a hardon any more."

"Don't bet on it; these old farts can still get it up for a young piece of ass." Joanie laughed and talked about Polsky, how the "fat degenerate" kept trying to hump her in the file room. However, I wasn't concentrating on what she was saying. My eyes and mind were transfixed on a file that surfaced to the top of Joanie's pile. The client's name was typed in large white letters on a black background . . . .

STREULING, Heinrich *(Henry)*

My curiosity got the best of me; I opened the file and started browsing through the pages; I knew a lot about tax returns. A big part of my job was to double check the computations on all 1040's prepared at the office. I didn't know anything about tax law but I knew how to check arithmetic and I knew which numbers went where. The first thing I did when I looked at Mr. Streuling's file was to make a mental note of his home address; he now lived at the Nemo Hotel in South Beach. Hey . . . . that's where the Steinberg's Uncle Louie and Tanta Baila lived; what a small world! He was still unmarried (that was to be expected) and the line where you are supposed to list "income from wages" was blank, which meant that he didn't work for the James Manor any longer.

His income was entirely from a partnership, "Sardera and Associates" . . . and it was huge, $200,000. (How did he get rich so fast?) Only four years ago he was working as the landlord of a small apartment building. Of course, one thing was really puzzling. Why would someone making so much money live in a run down hotel in a low income neighborhood? However, Uncle Louie was also very rich and he liked living in South Beach. But, Uncle Louie lived there to be close to Tanta Baila and his Romanian friends. Streuling wasn't Romanian; he wasn't even Jewish. This didn't make sense.

I also noticed that Streuling claimed a $100,000 charitable deduction, but the tax return didn't show any details. That was a mistake! When you make big contributions you're supposed to list the name of the charity. I definitely would have flagged this error with my purple pencil, but Streuling's tax return was prepared before I worked for the firm.

"Joanie . . . do me a favor. Down in one of the lower shelves, is there a file for a partnership named Sardera and Associates?"

"You better watch out," said Joanie, "the partners will go nuts if they see you snooping in the files. But, yeah . . . here it is. Looks like it's a pretty new client. The new clients all have white letters on a black tab."

SARDERA, et. al.

"What does 'et. al' mean?" I asked.

"I think its Latin," responded Joanie. "It means 'and others' . . . we use it a lot with partnership files, instead of listing the names of all the partners. Some of the big partnerships have over a hundred partners."

I did a quick look though the tax return; the partnership was formed in 1954 and it used a P.O. Box in Miami Beach as a mailing address. There were three partners: Vasco Milé Sardera, J. Martin Berger, and Henry Streuling.

Sardera, the primary partner, lived in Lisbon, Portugal. J. Martin Berger lived on Star Island in Miami Beach; only millionaires lived there. Berger was one of the most prominent attorneys in Miami Beach. He was also the father of my old nemesis, Danny Berger. It was impossible to determine the nature of the partnership business, but all of the income came from one source, a corporation known as "GSRFF, Inc." Joanie and I searched further in the cabinets to see if there was a file with those initials. Unfortunately, we couldn't find anything remotely similar.

Streuling hadn't bothered me in four years; I wasn't on a vendetta to find details about him . . . so, that was the end of my superficial investigation. But I sure was curious . . . how could that pervert be making $200,000 a year?

Later that day Trixie spoke to the three assistant secretaries and instructed them to call me Mr. Lindell. Even Joanie was required to call me by my last name. It was very awkward working at Rosenblattt, Unger and Polsky. The partners treated me with respect because I was a male. However, even though I did all the math checks the secretaries regarded me as an office boy, a "gopher" . . . go for coffee, go for Kotex, go for more toilet paper. I was only sixteen, the office errand boy, but the secretaries were required to call me "Mr. Lindell." It was obvious, they weren't too happy with this contrived formality. With the exception of Joanie, they were all twenty or thirty years older than me, but I was instructed to address them by first name and to refer to them as "girls." Every time I accidentally referred to one of the secretaries as a "woman" Polsky corrected me.

"Myron, we've got some hard working 'girls' here at the office . . . especially' that hot Amazon with the incredible ass, and they all know their place. Lets keep it that way. OK?"

♦

One Saturday afternoon I received a call at work from my mother; she was crying hysterically.

"Myron, hurry home . . . daddy had a heart attack. The ambulance is on the way to the house."

A chill ran through my body, down through my legs. I think, maybe that was also a heart attack. I never experienced that feeling before in my life.

"My father's had a heart attack . . . I have to get home," I told Marty Unger, the middle partner, and asked if he could drive me home. I knew that I couldn't drive a car . . . not the way I was shaking.

"I'm sorry Myron, but I have an appointment with an important tax client, one of Seymour's old fraternity brothers. You have a car; you're OK . . . just drive carefully. And don't worry, we won't dock your pay."

My hands were cold and sweating as I drove north on the beautiful tree lined Pine Tree Drive. I was going 70 in a 25 mile-per-hour zone, but I felt like I was crawling. I wanted to floor the accelerator and fly . . . but I had enough common sense to know that I wasn't in full control. I kept saying to myself . . . . "calm down, calm down . . . be careful." Then a delivery vehicle from a shoe repair store cut across the front of my car, making a left turn from my right side. The vehicle was a small motor scooter, encased in a fiberglass shell; it was brown, shaped like a man's shoe. I hit the motorized shoe, full speed; I didn't even have a chance to step on the brakes . . . I never saw the teenage Negro delivery boy . . . not until I hit him. And the boy went flying into the air. He did a mid-air flip and landed on the grass, on my left. Miraculously, he landed on his feet. The fiberglass shoe was demolished but the boy appeared to be unhurt.

"Are you OK? I didn't even see you. Thank God you're OK."

"Yeah, I'm OK . . . but man, you were really burning rubber." The boy was probably sixteen, my age, and didn't have a scratch. He was even laughing. "Sweet Jesus, I made one hell of a flip . . . would get me a perfect ten if I did that in the Olympics."

A crowd of people gathered around us, including the residents of the home where the boy landed. They all saw the accident . . . clearly, I was at fault. Even though the boy made a careless left turn, I should have been in control of my car; I should have been able to avoid the accident. But, most important, everyone saw that he was unharmed. That was all that really mattered. I could never live with myself if I killed anyone. According to Florida law you are supposed to report an auto accident to the police and wait for them to come to the scene of the accident . . . but I was anxious to get home. I was under extreme pressure.

"Listen, I've got a crisis at home; my father just had a heart attack. I can't sit here and wait for the police. Here, write your name and phone number on this paper." I handed a piece of paper and a pencil to the boy. He wrote his name and number.

Then, I tore the paper in half and wrote my name and number on the other half . . . and gave him the portion with my name. I shoved his portion of the paper in my wallet; I never even bothered to read his name or phone number.

"If the police want to talk to me I'll be at Mt. Sinai Hospital, but you have to understand. I can't sit here waiting. I'm needed at home. But, you're OK, and I'm sure my insurance will cover the damages; I just have to go." I also asked the owner of the home if he would call the police; I told her why I had to leave and how to find me. I realized that I was probably violating the law, but what else could I do?

Just as I pulled into my driveway the ambulance was leaving my house. I hopped in back and sat along side of my father. We held hands for the rest of the trip . . . his hand was very cold. I didn't tell him about the accident. My mother was sitting alongside of me, crying. Her hands were trembling. None of us said anything.

Three hours after we arrived at Mt. Sinai hospital two Miami Beach policemen came and arrested me. I was charged with "leaving the scene of an accident" and was taken to the city jail. Before I left the hospital I gave my mother the folded piece of paper with the name and phone number of the boy I hit. I was only allowed to be alone with her for two minutes, so I quickly explained what had happened. I told her to contact Mr. Seligman, our attorney, to give him the paper . . . but not to tell my father. Then, I tried explaining to the police the severity of the situation, how I was needed at the hospital, and that the boy was unharmed.

"Unharmed!" exclaimed the police. "Why that little nigger was almost killed. An ambulance came and took him to the hospital. He's right here at Mt. Sinai . . . and you better pray that he lives. Otherwise you'll be facing manslaughter charges. We got laws here that protect people from crazy punk drivers . . . they even protect niggers."

I sat in the back seat of the police car, with my hands handcuffed behind my back, like I was some type of dangerous criminal and I started to cry. I wasn't crying about my own situation; I knew that the charges against me would be resolved, once Mr. Seligman got into the picture, and I knew that the boy was OK. I was crying about my father. He was in critical condition. I wanted to be there with him, and with my mother.

Once we arrived at the police station I was pulled and dragged from one room to another. All they had to do was tell me where to go; I wasn't resisting them. But, I was on their turf . . . they had to let me know who was boss.

"OK, book the little shit and throw him in the slammer," bellowed a gruff looking cop.

I was then pushed into a cell with three men. One of them was a huge Negro man with a completely shaved head. His name was Bubba. Oh no! I heard what happened to young boys when they were locked in jail with older men. I maneuvered into the far corner of the cell, but one of the other men, a sleazy looking guy with a pencil thin moustache, was rubbing his crotch and looking directly at me. He was smiling. I was petrified. Just then the guard came to our cell and delivered four trays; it was dinner time. Immediately, I conceived a plan for my survival. Slowly, I edged next to Bubba and asked if he would like an extra dinner. I told him that I wasn't hungry.

"Why, thank you dude. That's mighty kind of you." He was the biggest man I ever saw in my life.

Finally, at 7:00 AM Mr. Seligman came to bail me out. Of course, throughout that very long night I never closed my eyes. I sat as close as possible to Bubba; his huge shoulder made a very comfortable pillow.

"Mr. Seligman, I never was so happy in my life to see a friendly face. How is my father, and how is the Negro boy?"

"Your dad is OK, but it was a serious heart attack. He'll probably be in the hospital for a week. But I don't think I can get your charges dropped; we're going to have to tell your story to the judge. I'm doing my best to get an early court date; best to get it over with fast. And, don't worry about the boy; he obviously had an attorney tell him to check into the hospital to build up a Workman's Comp. case . . . he's trying to squeeze out as much money as possible."

Mr. Seligman tried, but couldn't get the charges dropped, but he did get a hearing within two weeks: "The City of Miami Beach vs. Myron S. Lindell." The Negro boy, William Jefferson, appeared as a witness for the city and told the judge that I never even bothered to check and see if he was hurt, that I just drove away, with my top down, screaming that I would be at Mt. Sinai Hospital.

Mr. Seligman began his cross examination. "Mr. Jefferson . . . after you landed on your feet . . . after you made a very dangerous illegal left turn cutting off an automobile . . . did Myron stop and ask you how you were?"

"No sir . . . as I done told the judge, he never stopped . . . he just yell out that he be going to Mt. Sinai hopspital and he just keep right on driving."

"Did Myron ask you what your name was? What your phone number was?"

"No sir; he drive away . . . never stop."

And as the boy made that obvious lie he turned and looked directly into my eyes . . . and he stared at me . . . . then he looked back at the City of Miami Beach attorney . . . and shook his head left/right . . . the universal gesture for No.

"No man . . . that ain't the truth . . . I was told to say that by my boss. But, none of what I said be the truth. Myron stopped and stayed with me for ten minutes, maybe more; he made sure I was OK. Then he told the lady at the house where I been hit to call the police . . . he wrote his name and phone number on a piece of paper and told me that he be going to the hospital.".

The judge then interrupted. "Young man . . . how do we know that you're telling the truth now?"

"Here's proof that I'se telling the truth."

The boy then took a folded sheet of paper out of his wallet . . . it had my name and phone number written in my handwriting. It was the paper I gave him at the accident. And Ben Seligman displayed the other half of the paper, with "William Jefferson" written in the boy's handwriting. The two torn pieces of paper fit together . . . like the pieces of a puzzle.

"Myron, come here to the bench," ordered the Judge. Mr. Seligman and I both walked forward.

"I hope your dad is feeling better now, and I want you to know, I understand what you must have been going through. I'm dropping the criminal charge, 'leaving the scene of an accident,' but the other charge, 'wreckless driving, will be imposed, and that will mean three points on your driving record, but there won't be any fine. Myron, you should never have driven home that day. Since you couldn't get one of the people at your office to drive you, you should have taken a taxi. You acted judiciously after the accident . . . but the accident happened because you weren't in full control of your vehicle. Now, be more careful in the future."

As we left the courtroom I went over to the Negro boy to thank him for changing his testimony but he wouldn't talk to me until both attorneys walked away.

"William, thank you very much; I could have gone to jail."

"No trouble man . . . but the name ain't William, its Willie . . . and it's the least I could do for an old friend."

"An old friend? Me? Do you know me?"

"Yeah, I do," said Willie. "Back at Burdines, bout' two years ago . . . you was the only white boy who'd help me. Don't you remember, you tried on a pink alligator shirt for me? No other white person would even talk to me."

"Oh my God, yes . . . I remember. We talked about Willie Mays . . . he was your idol. And you had two older brothers."

"Back then I did . . . but one of them been killed in a street fight."

I shook hands with Willie and told him how sorry I was about the accident and about his brother. I wrote down his phone number again, and said that I would call him. It was so bizarre how our paths had crossed after two years. I walked away from the courtroom kind of tingling with goosebumps; I remembered a movie I had seen where the people were all pieces on a chess board. They all thought they were making their own decisions, but they weren't. Some guy, up above, was looking down on the world and making all the moves . . . and now, that guy just moved the black pawn in front of the white knight.

I didn't feel comfortable working at the accounting firm anymore, so I gave two weeks notice and quit. The main reason I quit was because I had bitter feelings toward Marty Unger; he should have driven me home the day when I got the phone call from my mother. He could have, at least called a taxi. My head wasn't on straight; I wasn't thinking. Another reason why I quit was because I hated the way they treated the women at Rosenblatt, Unger and Polsky.

My father supported my decision to quit, but he criticized me for joining the crowd. He thought it was terrible to treat older women as if they were inferior to men.

"Yeah dad, I know . . . I called them 'girls, broads, or babes' . . . . but, but, but . . . . that's what I was told to do."

"That was the same excuse that the Nazi's used at the Nurenberg trials," responded my father. "Following orders isn't always a valid defense."

CHAPTER 47

RENDEZVOUS WITH DESTINY

After my father had the heart attack his health began to deteriorate. He napped every afternoon on the living room couch; I always looked closely to see if he was breathing. And after dinner he took long walks, alone, sometimes more than an hour. My mother and I worried when he was gone too long; he was becoming forgetful and losing his sense of direction. Many times I got in my car to go looking for him, just in case he was lost. He aged a lot. His hair, what little he had, turned from grey to white, and I frequently saw him slip a nitroglycerin pill in his mouth . . . a blood thinner, when he had chest pains. I spent a lot more time at home with him; he was only 65 but he looked a lot older. Worst of all, he discontinued his membership in the Book of the Month Club and began watching a lot of TV.

"Sunshine . . . my eyes aren't what they used to be; its getting difficult to read small print. And my concentration is shot to hell. The idiot box is all I've got left . . . my attention span is fifteen minutes, at best."

My mother played Canasta four or five nights a week; I stayed home with my father and we watched TV together. Fortunately, his limited attention span never caused a problem since TV shows all bounced back and forth, from one story line to another. It was obvious, the emerging American TV generation had the same attention span as a sick old man. I felt fortunate—my early childhood was before TV; I was greatly influenced by my father and I became an avid reader. OK, I occasionally read comic books . . . but that was still reading.

Even though my father and I watched a lot of TV we still talked about school and history. He loved the history of the Jews and the Romans. He said that he would miss me when I went to the University of Florida . . . that I should study hard; accounting would be a good major, with history as a minor, and then maybe law school. Whenever he told me how much he would miss me I got a lump in my throat, but he never told me to stay home, to go to college in Miami. He was happy for me; Florida was a very good university, and he said that I should consider joining a fraternity, it had its advantages . . . especially for a Jewish boy in Gainesville, a small college town in the middle of Florida. In fact, he even called Seymour Rosenblatt and arranged to have me invited to a special weekend in Gainesville, where the various fraternities would be recruiting high school seniors to be future "pledges."

It was late in the school year; I had just turned 17—only two months until graduation. Josh Broden and I drove to Gainesville for a preview of the University of Florida campus. Thanks to Seymour Rosenblatt, I was invited by Tau Epsilon Phi to participate in fraternity "rush" weekend; Josh got an invitation through one of his father's friends. This was a wonderful opportunity, a chance to get a bid to TEP, a very popular Jewish fraternity. As fraternity "prospects" we were expected to be on our best behavior. We had to act cool, talk cool, and dress cool. Indoor attire was limited to black, blue, or khaki pants, a long sleeve white shirt with a button down collar, and a "rep" tie . . . . those were the ties with multi-colored diagonal stripes. Outdoor attire was plaid Bermuda shorts, very clean white Keds, and a Lacoste polo shirt. It was absolutely forbidden to wear a "cool" TEP t-shirt. That would be very presumptious, since we had not yet received a coveted "bid" from the fraternity.

The fraternity brothers took us to dinner, twenty-eight "cool" Jewish "prospects. I wore a blue and white rep tie, and smoked a matching blue pipe. I didn't really inhale, but I kept puffing on the pipe, blowing out cherry smelling smoke. I was very cool! I was excited at the prospect of getting a bid to TEP . . . to be a "Greek." Fraternities and sororities all had names using Greek letters . . . so the brothers or sisters were called Greeks.

We went to a BBQ restaurant that served pork sandwiches and spare ribs. The evening began with the TEP chaplain leading us in Hebrew blessings for bread and another blessing for wine—lots of wine. He concluded the solemn prayers with a brief Jewish-Greek observation.

"We are all Jews, but up here in G'ville we are also 'Greeks'—the blessing over wine is a special prayer, an ancient Hebrew prayer to Adonoi, but we also pay homage to fuckin' 'Bacchus' the Greek god of wine."

We drank a glass of very strong wine and said "TEPs are tops, Hail Bacchus, L'Chaim." Yuck! I hated that wine.

"You're gonna' have so much pussy in G'ville, your dick's gonna' fall off," said the next speaker, the half-drunk fraternity rush chairman. "That's what happens when you become a TEP . . . cause TEPs are tops." His exciting prediction was greeted by a loud chorus of cheers from the brothers and the recruits: "TEP's are tops, bring on the pussy!"

"And, don't forget this advice," the rush chairman continued with his welcoming remarks. "You're here to get a college degree; too much pussy can really kill your grades. I mean, Hell! We all love pussy . . . but just remember the 4-F's . . . . find em, feel em, fuck em, and forget em."

FFFF

"Are we gonna' get Jewish pussy too?" asked one of the prospects. "Back home we only get shiksahs."

"That ain't so easy," said the rush chairman, "unless you drive a T-Bird or a Vette, but you don't really want Jewish pussy; trust me on that. When you're in your final semester and you start thinking about careers and marriage, that's when you start going out with the Jewish girls."

Dinner was awkward; BBQ spare ribs are messy, and I was wearing a long sleeve white shirt. It doesn't look cool to have smelly sauce all over your clothes. I ate slowly and carefully. After dinner and several glasses of that disgusting wine, and a continuous chorus of "TEP's are tops," we heard speeches from three middle age Jewish faculty advisors. The professors took turns selling us on the benefits of "going Greek."

"Greeks get better grades, especially TEP's, said Abe Zuckerman, an accounting professor. "They have more fun, meet the sorority girls, and develop lifelong friends. Most important, they cultivate future business contacts. When you leave this place its important that you got a good education; "what" you know is a stepping stone to success, but even more important than that is "who" you know, and that's what TEP is all about."

I learned a new word—"networking." Dr. Zuckerman also lectured about ethics and morality and spent several minutes trying to explain why they were not the same thing. I failed to see the difference. He then told us that it was time for us to grow up, to cast aside silly games and childhood fantasies; he concluded his speech by telling us why "Jews and Shvartzahs" had to stick together . . . . "We are both persecuted minorities," said Dr. Zuckerman, "Jews have a moral obligation to defend Shvartzahs." Everyone applauded when he finished his speech, but instead of clapping our hands we snapped our fingers; that was the "cool" Greek way of applauding. I joined in the finger snapping, but I was unable to get a good snap from my left hand. I made a mental note of "things to do" . . . "learn to snap the fingers on my left hand."

After dinner the faculty advisors walked around the room, talking individually to the twenty-eight "prospects." Dr. Zuckerman spoke to me. "Myron, I heard from Seymour Rosenblatt that you're pretty fast with addition; so am I. We have to go head to head one day, but lets see how good you are after you 'chug-a-lug' a pitcher of beer." Dr. Zuckerman then invited me to enroll in his accounting class during the next school year, when I would become a Gator and a TEP.

"Myron, you make sure when you get to campus you sign up for ACC-101, I take good care of Seymour's boys." He put his arm on my shoulder. "Its like this . . . . my first name is Abe, it begins with an 'A' . . . and Zuck begins with a 'Z.' I know everything about this little hick town, from 'A' to 'Z.' And listen to the TEP brothers, they keep the pledges posted, which professors to take . . . and which ones to avoid. Lots of Jew haters up here. Do you have any questions?"

"Are there any colored students here at UF?" I asked.

"Shvartzahs? Students?" The professor chuckled. "Not that I know . . . but we sure could use a few on the football team."

"But, you said that Jews and colored people should stick together."

"Of course they should," replied Dr. Zuckerman, "but I was referring to life after college, not here at UF. Son, this isn't Miami Beach or New York; they eat grits up here and they put mayonnaise on everything, probably even on pussy. I've got nothing against colored people, in fact I'm an investor in a Shavartzah night club in Miami."

When we returned to the "frat house" the recruits crowded in the living room—everyone was smoking—the brothers all wore white shirts, rep ties, and very cool fraternity pins. The president, a thin boy with black curly hair, made a brief speech telling us about the perils of being a Jew in Gainesville and why we needed TEP to make our collegiate experience tolerable. Then he led us on a tour of the modern, air conditioned building, through several very clean bedrooms and down a white hallway with tan marble floors. We looked at the "Wall of Fame," an impressive display of TEP group photos dating back to the 1920s. Two faces on top of the 1930 photo immediately caught my attention. The president was J. Martin Berger, Danny Berger's father, and the treasurer was Seymour Rosenblatt, senior partner at Rosenblatt, Unger, and Polsky.

After the tour was concluded we returned to the living room. The fraternity president removed his tie and snapped his fingers; he was a sensational snapper. He snapped with both hands, loud enough to get eighty noisy boys to shut up and listen to him. "OK men, is everybody ready for 'showtime?'" All the brothers snapped their fingers and shouted in unison: "Showtime! Showtime!"

Showtime was a bizarre TEP "tradition" dating back to the 1920s. The president introduced two gorgeous women, both around thirty years old. One woman was a beautiful negro with short curly hair; she painted the left half of her face white, divided right down the middle of her nose. The other woman was white, a blonde; the right half of her face was painted black. I think there was supposed to be some spiritual meaning for the black and white coloring.

The ritual began with the bi-colored women drinking beer from large green bottles . . . and the brothers began a droning chant: "Chug-a-lug, chug-a-lug, chug-a-lug."

Then, the women began kissing, dribbling beer on each other, and undressing. I stared; I had never seen brown nipples before, except pictures in "National Geographic." When the women were fully naked they got down on the floor, on a king size mattress. All the frat brothers started snapping their fingers and shouting . . . . "showtime." I had a terrible view; I was in the back of a smoke filled room, standing behind several dozen tall "brothers" and three faculty advisors. I stretched my neck to see what the women were doing, but I couldn't see a thing—of course I heard lots of moaning and groaning.

"The beer part is a tradition," said one of the older frat brothers, "it dates back to some type of slave legend from the Southern plantations before the civil war."

Then, the negro woman stood up, stark naked; her beautiful body was doused with beer, and she said that she wanted one of the "prospects" to join her on the mattress. Immediately, every boy lowered his head to avoid eye contact; there were no volunteers.

"Just as I thought," and the woman laughed. "You nice Jewish boys are afraid of screwing 'shvartzahs'—afraid the color will rub off on your little white dicks."

When showtime was finished the naked women grabbed a few towels and went into separate bedrooms. Many of the boys stood in line, waiting to pay $10 for a few minutes alone with the woman of his choice . . . the color of his choice. Josh was second in line; Dr. Zuckerman was first. But I left the living room and returned to the marble hallway, to examine the "Wall of Fame" in greater detail; I didn't want to lose my virginity at a fraternity gang-bang.

When the weekend was over Josh and I drove back to Surfside. We were excited about the prospect of going to the University of Florida, excited about TEP, excited about networking. During the long drive home I practiced snapping the fingers on my left hand—I was beginning to get the hang of it. Obviously, this was a talent that was necessary if I wanted to become a TEP.

"Man oh man, that shvartzah was chocolate delight," said Josh. "She gave the best blow job I ever had."

"Didn't you fuck her?" I asked.

"Are you nuts," said Josh. "this white dick don't go sloppy seconds in a black pussy. I got her phone number. She goes to Miami a lot and works in a colored strip joint; her name is Flora Mae."

Flora Mae! My heart almost stopped; I was stunned. This was the missing sister of Annabelle Stevens; the mother of the Colonel's adopted children. During the ride back to my Jewish island I continued practicing left-hand finger snapping, but I couldn't stop thinking about the beautiful Flora Mae and her brown nipples. I kept debating whether or not to ask for her phone number, whether I should tell the Colonel, whether Jessie and Jackie should get to meet their real mother. After much deliberation I decided that Katarina was their only mother; I never asked for the phone number.

Two days after I returned from Gainseville my father had another heart attack. Fortunately, it wasn't as severe as the one that put him in the hospital, but the doctor ordered him to stay in bed for two weeks. I realized that even though my best friends were all going to the University of Florida I couldn't leave home, not with my father's health deteriorating so badly. I drove across the bay to the University of Miami and filled out an application form.

"Myron, you cant live your life for your father," said Josh Broden. "You should go to Florida, it's a much better college than Miami and its close enough, you can drive home five times a year. And TEP will be a blast." Josh snapped his fingers to remind me of all the networking I would be missing.

"I can't do it Josh. I could never study; I would be nervous every time the phone rang. I just can't do it."

I gave Josh my blue and orange Gator T-shirts; I replaced them with several green Hurricane hats and shirts.

I was no longer working for Rosenblatt, Unger and Polsky; I really resented the partners at that firm . . . but I did enjoy certain aspects of my work experience. I learned a lot about proof reading tax returns; it was fun finding arithmetic errors. Obviously, I didn't see any future in being a bag boy, or in working at a shoe store, but I saw potential in public accounting, or better yet, some combination of law, accounting, and taxation. One afternoon I called the office to thank Seymour Rosenblatt for arranging my invitation to the TEP weekend. I also wanted to talk about career opportunities in taxation. Seymour was helpful and very nice, but he was only nice because my father paid him an accounting fee. The partners in the firm were all cordial if you meant "billable hours" to the firm . . . otherwise they were abrupt and insensitive. I'm sure he charged that phone call to my father.

"How did you like Showtime?" asked Seymour. "That's a cherished TEP tradition, goes back before I was in college. And, did you meet Doctor Zuckerman? He was my accounting professor. Talk about speed with addition, old Zuckie was lightning."

I thanked Seymour again, but I didn't tell him that I would be attending the University of Miami. We chatted for fifteen minutes, exactly fifteen minutes. Seymour had a small fifteen minute sand-clock on his desk; he computed client bills in quarter-hour multiples.

After our brief discussion I asked to talk to Joanie. With my mind all wrapped up in my father's heart attack, the trial, and my trip to Gainesville, I never followed up with Joanie, to get Leah Sonnino's phone number . . . . I thought it would be nice to see Leah again. I had my chance with Simone, the French lady, also with the "Showtime" strippers and with Mickey Cohen . . . probably even Flo. But, I had this strange feeling that someone else had already written the script, that my sexual future was indelibly inscribed in some type of holy book, like the book that rabbis talk about on Yom Kippur—I could only lose my virginity with Leah.

"Hi Myron," said Joanie, "Glad I don't have to call you Mr. Lindell anymore . . . and I'm really glad to hear you won your trial. Shit! You could have gone to jail; you poor dear."

"Thanks Joanie; you're sweet. Listen, did you ever tell Leah that you know me, that I was working with you?"

"Jeez . . . I forgot to tell you . . . . I'm so sorry. Her eyes lit up when I mentioned your name, but after you stopped working here it slipped my mind. Leah works as the receptionist at Miami DeSoto-Plymouth, just across the Venetian Causeway, near Sears. Myron, she said that back in the ninth grade she realled liked you. Why don't you call her at work."

"Oh, one more thing Trixie is retiring at the end of the month and I will be the new head secretary. Bruce recommended me to Mr. Rosenblatt . . . I'm so excited."

"Bruce? No longer Mister Polsky? Hmm!" I chuckled. "I guess you'll be putting in lots of late night work."

"That's for sure," Joanie laughed, "and Bruce is going to rent me a cute little efficiency apartment near Lincoln Road; its walking distance to the office and only two blocks from a really neat old Catholic church where I can say Confession."

"Boy, I can't get over you Catholics," I said. "I just don't buy the idea of sinning and confessing and doing the same sins again and confessing again."

"Well, I don't see that you Jews are so perfect," she responded. "You sin and never confess; you just keep on sinning."

"Listen Myron, you told me about that guy who beat you for homeroom president because he had big muscles. Well . . . you're lucky, you're good in math and you write well. That guy had big biceps, that's all he had . . . and I got a gorgeous ass. Don't be so fuckin' judgmental."

Joanie was right; I was very judgmental. Maybe I was immature, but I didn't buy the argument that you can only play with the cards you're dealt. That's a cop-out on life. Joanie had a nice, outgoing personality. OK, maybe she wasn't the smartest girl in the world, but her ass (which was truly fantastic) wasn't her only quality.

I now knew that Leah worked at Miami DeSoto-Plymouth, but I decided that instead of calling on the phone I would find out her work schedule and stop by in person. A face to face meeting would be better, not as awkward. I called the auto agency to find out when Leah would be working, but I didn't want to give my correct name.

"Hello, my name is Fred Cole. Do you have a girl named Leah Sonnino working for you? I found her wallet and a little note which seems to indicate that she works at Miami DeSoto-Plymouth."

"Yes, Miss Sonnino works here. Why don't you give me your phone number; we'll have her call you."

"I prefer to stop by your place, to give it to her in person. When will she be working?"

"You can come in anytime you want; we'll make sure that she gets the wallet."

"No . . . I want to give it to her in person. There's money in the wallet."

"She's here all day Saturday and Sunday, most anytime."

Three years had elapsed since my date with Leah; I was almost a full foot taller, and I think I was more intelligent and more mature. But, I was extremely nervous, maybe even more nervous than the day when I went with her to the Carib theatre, the day when I carefully selected a wardrobe that highlighted my blue eyes. I wondered if her breasts had grown; I was excited . . . . I was about to lose my virginity; I could sense it. I made sure to carry several rubbers, a few in my wallet and a few in the glove compartment of my car; they were special ribbed rubbers, the package said that they were designed to give the woman extra pleasure.

But, buying those rubbers was really difficult. I went to Surfside Drugs, a few blocks from my house, and just as I began to whisper to the pharmacist . . . to secretly slip me four packs from behind his high security counter, I was greeted by the shrill voice of Lottie Rothstein. Mrs. Rothstein was the mother of my old friend Mona; she was the town gossip and one of my mother's Canasta friends.

"Myron . . . what are you doing here so early in the morning?" Mrs. Rothstein could be heard from across the store.

"Good & Plenty, Good & Plenty," I responded, as I shook a box of candy coated licorice. "Early morning sweet tooth . . . . I love licorice in the morning."

I bought the candy and immediately left the drug store; I drove three miles, to the nearest source of rubbers.

After I purchased several boxes of multi-colored rubbers I drove to the Stag Shop, a trendy men's boutique in Coral Gables. A tall effeminate man helped me select the appropriate wardrobe for my upcoming rendezvous with destiny. The man had silver horn rimmed glasses, wavy gray hair and an unbecoming delicacy about him . . . he floated around the store with his right forearm bent in an upward position and his hands dangling limp at the wrists.

"If you want to make a favorable impression with the young lady you must wear shades of blue; you have such lovely eyes. I suggest this stunning blue madras shirt with the itty bitty touch of red . . . and couldn't you just die for this button down collar? Long sleeve, of course." He looked at my skinny arms and my underdeveloped biceps and repeated his suggestion . . . "Definitely, long sleeves!"

"Thirty dollars for a shirt!" I never saw such an expensive shirt in my life. "What's it made of? Gold threads!"

"Young man, this is madras, from India. It is guaranteed to bleed."

"Bleed? What does that mean?"

"When you wash the shirt the colors will run together . . . . to make a warm sensual blend."

"That doesn't sound good to me. I like the colors just they way they are now . . . why would I want them to run together?"

"That's the beauty of madras . . . the blending of the colors is so delicious and special . . . . You will be telling your little sweetie that your heart bleeds for her, and if she ever cries, let her wipe her tears on your sleeve. Oh—I'm getting goosebumps."

"OK . . . and what type of pants should I wear? Are jeans OK? I mean, new jeans!"

"Oh, heavens to Betsy . . . absolutely not. Let me show you our new line of hopsack . . . very delicate light blue, the latest in men's fashion. But, don't even think about jeans. And you absolutely must get a pair of Bass Weegan loafers, either cordovan or black . . . 'weegies' are timeless and classic."

I wound up spending $100 at the Stag Shop . . . but I really looked great. Now I was ready to see Leah.

Saturday morning at 9:00 AM I doused my face with Old Spice, put a pack of peppermint Life Savers in the glove compartment (definitely not Wint-O-green) . . . along with the ribbed rubbers. I drove slowly. After my accident with Willie and his mororized shoe, I knew that my driving was horrible under pressure. At 10:15 AM I pulled into the parking lot behind Miami DeSoto-Plymouth; the lot was empty—and I entered the showroom through two impressive glass doors.

There she was, with the same cute pony tail that I remembered. The salesmen were all wearing red cabana suits and straw hats; the agency was having a "fun in the sun" car promotion, and Leah was barefoot, wearing a long black skirt with a tiny matching top . . . very tiny. Her thin stomach was exposed; she had a cute belly button. And she was still short, just like in the ninth grade, with the same gorgeous smile that I had dreamt about many times over the years. Time had stood still. Whoever it was that said you can never go back was wrong; I went back and nothing had changed. What I remember most from that magic moment was staring at Leah's naked belly button; I should have had a burning desire to grab her and hug her, but I didnt; I just had a powerful urge to kiss her belly button.

And as I gathered courage to walk over and talk to Leah I hid behind an artificial palm tree and watched her lick a chocolate ice cream cone; she licked very slowly, and I remembered the advice of my father: "Watch a girl eat an ice cream cone and you'll have a pretty good idea how she'll be in bed."

"Hi Leah . . . its me, Myron. How have you been?" I was so cool! I was carrying an unlit blue pipe; it matched my eyes and my light blue hopsack pants.

"Oh my goodness, Myron! I can't believe its you. You're so tall. Wow! And you still have beautiful blue eyes." Then she purred and did a little pony tail flip . . . still the same magic; she was in control. Déjà vu all over again. This is where I left off three years ago.

"Um, um, um, your friend, Jeanie . . . I mean Joanie, told me you work here." I dropped my pipe—tobacco spilled on the floor.

"Joanie is my best friend; she is a real sweetheart. So tell me about yourself . . . I bet you now have big plans for college," said Leah, as she bent over and helped me clean tobacco from the floor. "And do you still write a lot?"

Leah was really excited to see me. Her eyes sparkled; she couldn't stop talking. "Oh my God, Myron, its so great to see you again; I've thought about you many times over the years . . . I've wanted to call you, but I didn't think you wanted any part of me; I was so mean to you and nice Jewish guys don't date girls who live on the wrong side of the tracks, except for the wrong reasons, and I just love your hopsack pants and your shirt, especially the little hint of red, but be careful, madras bleeds when you wash it . . . those beautiful colors run together, and . . . ."

I interrupted, in order to answer her questions, "I had plans to go to the University of Florida, but my father had a heart attack, so I changed my mind; I'm staying home, I'll be going to UM. And, yeah . . . I still write a lot. I've been keeping a daily journal for years. I even wrote about the day we went to the movies at the Carib."

"I'd love to read your journal. Every night I try to read in bed for an hour; I never watch TV, except for the late night news. I remember the essay you wrote in Miss Carter's class, the story from the dead soldier . . . the two-headed coin. It was beautiful. I guess I flipped the wrong coin. If I had gone out with you the next week my life could have been so different."

"I also like to read in bed," I responded. "What do you read?"

"Lately, I've been reading a lot from Plato," said Leah. "People don't realize that he was very romantic. Here, listen to this quote: "Every heart sings a song, incomplete, until another heart whispers back. Those who wish to sing always find a song. At the touch of a lover, everyone becomes a poet."

"That's beautiful," I responded. "The only thing from Plato that I read was the 'Republic,' and except for the 'Allegory of the Cave,' I thought the rest of the book was too simplistic."

"It was OK," said Leah. "but I sure didn't agree with his philosophy in the 'Cave.' We see and feel with our eyes and our heart; logic and reason are useless in matters of faith and love."

"I hope you're wrong," I responded. "logic and reason are what separate humans from animals, we have the ability to think with our brain and our conscience."

"Not when you love someone," said Leah. "Then it all comes from the heart."

There weren't any customers at the auto agency so Leah asked to take a half-hour break. We walked out to the parking lot and sat in my car. We had to catch up on three years of our lives . . . and we only had thirty minutes.

"You know I have a baby, don't you?"

"Yes. A girl."

"Danny was the father, but he tried to say that I went down for the whole football team. That was a big fuckin' lie. The rotten son-of-a-bitch didn't want to get stuck with child support. That's why I need this shitty' part-time job."

"I heard that but I never believed it."

"It was impossible to fight him in court; his father is a big attorney in Miami Beach . . . and some of his clients are gangsters. They made a lot of threats . . . scary people."

Leah paused and took hold of my hand. We didn't kiss; we just held hands as she talked about her bad experience with Danny Berger's father. Of course, I already knew a lot about J. Martin Berger—I knew that he was partners with Henry Streuling; I also knew that he was a fraternity brother of Seymour Rosenblatt—but I didn't bother to talk about those people. I wanted to focus completely on Leah. I just listened and kept looking at her beautiful face.

"I saw you one day in my Home Ec class," said Leah, and she smiled. "You were eating cookies with ZD. I wanted to go over and say hi, but you were busy. That girl had huge boobs, but look at me, I still can't fill an A-cup."

We reminisced about the day at the Carib theatre; neither of us could remember the name of the movie, but we had vivid recollections of a multi-colored parrot that was perched on a pole in the lobby. All the kids took turns trying to teach the bird profanity . . . especially the "F" word.

"Fuck you mac . . . fuck you mac," I flapped my wings and pretended to squak like a parrot . . . and Leah laughed. Then, she took my hand and put it on her breast . . . just like she did in the ninth grade. I was getting a second chance, to go back and start over . . . and this time everything would turn out perfect.

"Here . . . squeeze. Watch! The bra still won't pop back."

I think this was the moment when I should have told her that she had a beautiful "blouse" . . . when I should have kissed her . . . but I didn't. I wanted to freeze the moment forever. I said nothing . . . . I just squeezed.

Finally, I broke the silence: "Um . . . Uh . . . I saw you last year when Beach played Tech, from across the field. I walked over at halftime, to say hello, but I ran into a bunch of 'hoods' from Tech. They convinced me to go back to the Jewish side of the field."

"I didn't want to go to Tech," she replied, as she ran her finger nails lightly on the back of my neck. "But once I got pregnant I was forced to transfer. I hate it here; lots of street gangs, lots of drinking. My dad was so pissed he called me a whore and ordered me to get an abortion. I refused! Its not that I'm opposed to abortions; other girls can do what they want, but I really wanted to keep my baby. So the bastard picked up and left home."

Leah was shivering, maybe because of the tiny halter top that she was wearing. I held her hand as she continued with her story. It was the happiest moment of my life, just letting her talk . . . and talk . . . and talk.

"I live here with my mom. With my father gone we both have to work, and we go to shul in Miami Beach every Friday night. We were never religious before I got thrown out of school. I was surrounded by hundreds of Jewish kids at Beach High, but I barely knew I was Jewish, except for eating bagels and lox. Now, thank God for religion. Religion has helped me so much. I was such a mess; I really wanted to give up on life."

"I'm not religious," I commented, "but I'm glad it helped you. Are you Orthodox?"

"Hell no! We don't go around kissing doors, but I believe that someone up there hears you and can help you, but only if you ask for help. Mom and I belong to a Reform temple on 41st Street."

Leah stared in space and smiled. "My little girl is named Ruth, one of the few female names in the Bible. Ruthie is all I live for. Nothing else matters anymore. She'll be two on July 30th; we have the same birthday, and she looks a lot like me."

"She must be beautiful; I'd love to see her." I responded. Leah turned toward me and we kissed . . . but this time it wasn't a dry tight lipped kiss like at the Carib theatre; this time it was wet, with probing tongues and heavy breathing.

"You know, you were the first girl I ever kissed," I broke the long passionate embrace to come up for air. "I'll always remember the back row of the Carib Theatre."

"Myron, are you still a virgin?" Leah smiled and put her hand on my leg, but carefully avoided touching the very impressive bulge in my new hopsack pants. Now I knew why hopsack was better than jeans . . . it was a stretchable fabric.

"Well, I came close a few times, but so far I haven't been lucky." We both laughed.

"I guess if I was the first girl you kissed . . . its only right that I should be the first girl you . . . . you know what I'm saying. Some things in life are meant to be; those little dogs knew it a long time ago. Don't you remember how they were sniffing each other back on James Avenue?"

"You and me? Here? Now?" I didn't know how to react or what to say. But, thankfully . . . I had a few ribbed rubbers in the glove compartment.

"No, silly . . . not here! Your first time has to be really special, with romantic music, a warm bubble bath and lots of wine. What type wine do you like?"

"Oh! Red, white, blue . . . I'm patriotic." Actually, I hated wine, except maybe Manishevitz, the sweet Jewish wine that was popular at Passover.

"Mom and Ruthie will be sleeping at my grandma's Monday night. Why don't you come over at seven? And bring your toothbrush; I hate kissing stinky morning breath." Leah smiled and wrote her address and phone number on a piece of paper; she looked into my eyes and we kissed again. I felt so strong holding her in my arms.

"Hey Leah, now that you're religious, is there a special 'barucha' (*blessing*) when you take a bubble bath? I mean, isn't it like a 'mikvah?'" (*a ritual bath for Jewish women*)

She laughed. "You might be right; I'll ask my rabbi." We sat together in the car for a long time, a lot longer than thirty minutes, and she told me all about her life, how it wasn't turning out like she had hoped. Her laughter soon turned to tears. I didn't have Kleenex or a handkerchief, but I let her dry her tears on my sleeve, on my new madras shirt.

"Myron, I never met a boy like you. Most guys just like to bullshit and brag; I think I could fall in love with you."

I didn't want this moment to end. I couldn't believe this was happening. It was so surreal. The guy up there who moves the pieces on the chess board was bringing us together. Finally!

Once Leah stopped crying she struggled to tell me the most unpleasant details of her life, details that I didn't really want to know, but I held her hand and continued listening.

"After that horrible experience with Danny and the threats from his disgusting father I really flipped out; I used sex as an escape; it was an easy way to forget my rotten life, to feel loved . . . kind of like drunks who drown their sorrow in booze. Then I found religion, thanks to Joanie."

"Joanie? But, she isn't Jewish."

"I know, she's Catholic, but Joanie went through some rough shit when she got expelled from school, same as me. She told me that Confession really helped her."

"Confession? Not for me," I responded. "Some day I'll tell you about a bag boy who used to work with me at Food Fair."

"Myron, I was really a mess; I did some awful things, but if you heard that I went down for Mr. Tyler, the English teacher, that's a damn lie."

"Yeah, the kids talked a lot about him, especially on the school bus. I heard that he was banging two girls from school; one was your friend Mavis Koninberg."

"Only two?" Leah interrupted me. "Believe me, there were a lot more than two, like Penny Sherman, the stuck up snob with the blonde pony tail, and half the Golden Girls. How do you think those air heads got A's in English? Also some fat gym teacher with huge tits; I forgot her name."

"Selena Garcia?"

"Yeah, her," Leah chuckled. "They did it in the alley behind the girl's locker-room. Mavis saw them doing it 'doggie style,' grunting like pigs in heat."

"I thought Garcia was a lesbian; she's the one who set all the rules in dance class."

"No, she's AC-DC," responded Leah. "Lots of girls go both ways; also some of the girls' gym teachers."

"Yuck! I sure wouldn't want to screw Garcia. But, how did Mavis happen to be in the alley and see them?"

"Tyler got confused; that was supposed to be Mavis' day."

"What's 'doggie style?'" I asked. It probably made me look stupid to ask a dumb question like that, but I felt comfortable with Leah; it was OK to let her know that I was inexperienced.

"Wait till' Monday night," she whispered in my ear and smiled.

I wanted to ask Leah if she and Joanie had sex with each other . . . but I avoided that question. I remembered how Flo got so pissed when I made fun of her dildo. I wonder if Leah also had a dildo. I couldn't wait to see what she was going to name my penis.

"Myron . . . I'd love to sit here talking with you all day; you are so easy to talk to, but I gotta' get back to work. I'll see you Monday night, and don't forget to bring prosthetics."

"I think you mean prophylactics," I chuckled, "prosthetics are wooden legs."

"Damn! I never get that word right . . . probably why I got knocked up."

Then, Leah kissed me on the forehead and returned to the auto showroom, and as she disappeared behind two large glass doors she flipped her pony tail and blew a kiss.

On the drive home my three brains got into a serious debate. Mr. Glickman was right . . . . I did have three brains.

◆

"Tell her to call me Jacques," said a voice from inside my hopsack pants, "and spell it right, with a Q."

Then, in a contrived French accent, my penis began to sing like Maurice Chevalier: "Every little breeeeeze seems to whisper Leah Leah Leah."

"Yes, yes, yes," said the palpitating brain in my heart, "don't let her get away again."

"You must be kidding," said the brain in my head, "the girl is a slut . . . probably even a dyke."

♦

For the next two days the only thing I could think about was Leah Sonnino and my upcoming rendezvous with destiny—the end of my virginity—and her gorgeous smile. We would have to do it with the lights on; I wanted to see her beautiful face while we did it. I wonder if she wore her hair in a pony tail during sex. I'll bring a whole bunch of rubbers, just in case I accidentally break a few of them. I heard if you weren't careful that could easily happen, especially if you weren't experienced, and I sure wasn't. I practiced at home, putting them on with the lights on and the lights off, with my eyes closed, using only one hand, either hand. I was ready. Which rubber should I use? Which color? Too bad I didn't have a blue one to match my eyes.

We'll do it four times, first in the bubble bath, then with me on top, then her on top, and the final time has to be doggie style. It sounded like she really loved that position. I reached in my end table drawer, grabbed the dictionary and looked up "doggie style." Damn! Nothing there. I'll have to call my old friend Howard Lefkowitz; he knew all about sex.

♦

"Shmuck!" said the brain in my head. "While you're looking in the dictionary check out 'quicksand.' Do you want a two year old daughter? What about college? You're only seventeen. Use your fuckin' head."

"Shut up," said the brain in my penis. "For the last seventeen years that's all he's done . . . always used his fuckin' head . . . and what did it get him? He could have been making big bucks from the horny French broad and getting a little 'Voulez_Vous'_on_the_side._The boy is seventeen . . . and still a virgin! Now its my turn. If you cant find a blue rubber use the purple one."

"Hey Jacques-strap," replied the brain in my head. "Once you're inside her she won't know if you're purple or orange. And, shul every Friday night? You gotta' be kidding!"

391

"Pat-pat! Pat-pat! Pat-pat!" The brain in my heart was pounding. "Jacques, you got my vote, and don't worry about shul. Leah can go with her mom; it will be so much fun to stay home and read to little Ruthie."

♦

And voices were swirling inside my very confused head . . . At the forefront was Miss Baker, my evangelic eighth grade teacher. Her eyes were glaring . . . her phony orange boobs were pointing at my face. "Myron . . ." Every aspect of your earthly existence has been preordained by God." Then Holy Joe hopped off his tricycle and stood next to Miss Baker. He crossed himself, looked to the sky, and told me that the Lord is my shepherd, that I should lie down with the Jewess in a green pasture and let my rod and staff comfort me. The frail man tugged at his bowtie and smiled. "But, don't worry about her cup, it definitely won't runneth over."

Rabbi Lipschitz, the fiery Orthodox Rabbi, wiggled inbetween Holy Joe and Miss Baker; he put his ams around their shoulders and bellowed an impassioned warning: "Vos Got tut basheren (*what God decrees*) man cannot prevent."

Mitzie and Pepe were barking, Silver Dollar Jake was throwing mini rubbers at my feet and laughing, "Carpe Diem, seize the day," and Mrs. Solomon, the orthodox mother of my eighth grade friend, was waving a stone crab claw in the air. "It is 'bashert,'" she shouted, "Leah is your destiny, but don't do it in the bubble bath; God will cut off your petzle if you copulate in a 'mikvah.'"

Then, Colonel Klein walked in front of everyone, along with Katarina and their six adopted children. They were all holding little white boxes, eating Chinese food with chop sticks.

"Myron, you are the sum total of the decisions that you make in your lifetime . . . you write your own destiny . . . . the choice is yours."

That Monday night at 6:00 PM I called Leah and canceled our date; but I kept all the rubbers in the glove compartment of my car. Then I buried my head in my pillow and cried. Maybe I made the wrong choice, but it was my own choice, without any type of divine intervention.

CHAPTER 48

THE T-SHIRT REBELLION

I got so engrossed telling about my auto accident, Joanie, Showtime, and Leah . . . that I forgot to mention the t-shirt rebellion. That was probably the biggest event in the history of Beach High. The rebellion was triggered by student reaction to an incident involving Jemele Davenport, a very unpopular teacher. Miss Davenport taught a course in U.S. Government; a twelfth grade class. I guess the best way to describe this very strange teacher would be to expand on a simplistic description of life in Miami Beach in November 1955, seven months before I graduated from high school.

"The world consists of two types of people, those who think that the world consists of two types of people and those who do not think that the world consists of two types of people." Obviously, this little bit of homespun philosophy sounds stupid, and I forgot where I heard it, but it was actually a pretty good snapshot of my world and many of the teachers that I encountered . . . . especially Jemele Davenport.

Miss Davenport couldn't say a complete sentence without reference to some type of black vs. white conflict. And, like many of the female teachers at Beach High, she was a flat chested spinster with a wardrobe consisting almost entirely of long black pleated skirts, semi-transparent white blouses, and full length lace slips. She envisioned every cultural and political phenomenon as a clash between two mutually exclusive ideologies or adversaries: Federalists vs. Anti-Federalists,

Communism vs. Democracy, Lincoln vs. Douglas, Caucasians vs Colored people, Republicans vs. Democrats, rich vs. poor, management vs. labor, industrial workers vs. farmers, God fearing Americans vs. atheists, patriots vs. anarchists, Catholics vs. Protestants, Jews vs. Christians. It was a long list, separating the forces of good and evil, separating heaven and hell.

"Didn't Marx say the same thing?" asked Howard Lefkowitz. "He talked about class stuggle and the conflict between the Bourgeoise and the Proletariat."

"Howard! How dare you . . ." Miss Davenport raised her voice. "This is a course on American Government, democracy and the Constitutional history of the United States. I don't care what some godless Communist had to say about conflict."

Although Miss Davenport was not interested in the Marx-Engle concept of social conflict, she developed an entire course based on her own simplistic "black-white" theory. Most significantly, she contended that every amendment to the U.S. Constitution was a political reaction to social, economic, or moral conflict.

"Prohibition occurred when the moral leadership of America stood up and took a stand against dissipation," said Miss Davenport. "Unfortunately, FDR and his 'New Deal' socialists had no concern for morality . . . prohibition was eventually repealed. That was a sad day in American history, a victory for the forces of evil."

Miss Davenport argued that the most pressing domestic conflict of the mid-50's was the clash between the emerging generation of "rock and rollers" (led by Elvis Pressley) and the faithful "guardians of decency" who adhered to the Christian values of Robert E. Lee.

She envisioned the Elvis vs. Lee battle as a serious internal threat to democracy and our system of government. Miss Davenport frequently used her platform as a Government teacher to blend religious dogma and moral values with political history. She taught us about the ingenious method of checks and balances that were built into the U.S. Constitution, how the American government was comprised of three branches, each with its own powers and limitations, kind of like the popular game: "Rock-paper-Scissors." She also taught us that religion was the "unwritten" fourth branch of government, the spiritual safeguard of our system of democracy.

"Laws, without faith, are merely the insincere use of pious words," said Miss Davenport. "Without the moral influence of God, laws are nothing more than cant. Even in ancient Greece democracy failed. The Greeks had brilliant philosophers and mathematicians, but the populace bowed to idols and marble statues. That's why their experiment with democracy failed."

"What about separation of church and state?" asked Howard Lefkowitz.

"Certainly, that's one of the most important aspects of our system of government," replied Miss Davenport. "Religion is not a direct part of checks and balances; we separate church and state. But, like I told you, religion is the unofficial fourth branch of government; it is the moral fiber of democracy. Without a firm belief in God, we are like ships at sea, adrift without a compass. It is the fear of God that allows mankind to know the difference between good and evil."

"I understand what you're saying about religion and democracy," said Penny Sherman, "but what's so bad about rock and roll? I mean . . . its only music . . . and Elvis is soooooooo handsome."

"Handsome!" Exclaimed Miss Davenport. "Penny, I don't see anything handsome about watching the vulgar gyrations of a man's pelvis. Its Devil music and it will lead the world toward Armageddon . . . as prophesized in Revelations 16:14-16. The 'rock and rollers' threaten to destroy morality in America. Boys and girls . . . all you have to do is look at the spelling of his name . . . ELVIS . . . its almost the same as EVIL. Open your eyes."

Miss Davenport had a subliminal fear of Evil-Elvis, the antichrist. She dwelled on the fact that the name "Elvis" sounded like the letter "L"—and "L" rhymed with "Hell"—the location where sinners would rot or roast for eternity. The mere mention of Elvis infuriated Miss Davenport below the threshold of consciousness; she vented her hostility and her fear of Armageddon with a passionate onslaught of "L" words. They were great words for my journal; I wrote them all down and tried to use each one of them in an essay: "lewd, lascivious, licentious, lickerish, lustful, lurid, lecherous, libertine, libidinous."

None of those words were new to me; I had heard them all before, except 'lickerish," but never at the same time; never in one sentence. Elvis sure got Miss Davenport "livid."

"That kind of music is OK for colored singers," said Miss Davenport, "but not for a white Christian boy from Tennessee."

"Excuse me, Miss Davenport," I raised my hand. "How do you spell 'lickerish?'"

"Myron, I am not talking about candy! No need for you to learn to spell that horrible word."

Needless to say, I was worried about my grade in Government; Miss Davenport had obvious contempt and disdain for the letter "L"—and Lindell not only rhymed with Hell—but it began with an "L" and ended defiantly, with two more "L's."

The exact opposite of Miss Davenport was J. Linus Jackson, my twelfth grade English teacher, who had a completely different outlook on life, death, and world events. "Social interaction is very complex," said Mr. Jackson. "Its all too easy to fall in a trap, to try to find simple solutions for complex questions. People are always looking for a quick fix that can solve all problems or explain any phenomenon."

"That sounds just like religion," said Linda Spiegel, who tried to sit next to me in every class . . . especially during PA announcements. "I think its so stupid the way we look for God to answer all our problems . . . . God is our 'quick fix.' Some kids even pray to God to win football games. But, the dumb thing is that kids on the other side are also praying for victory. So who does God listen to?"

"Lets not go there Linda," said Mr. Jackson, and he laughed about the football observation. "Its not a good idea to get into a classroom debate about religion, that's a sensitive topic for many people. But, as long as you brought up the subject . . . let me just say this. Many scholars, scientists, and poets feel that the concept of heaven and hell is an oversimplified dichotomy. For example, Milton, in his epic 'Paradise' poems, refers to 'purgatory' as an intermediate level between hell and heaven and Dante had many levels in his Inferno."

Mr. Jackson was a graduate from the University of Virginia, and during the summers he was working to complete his PhD at some Ivy League college. He spoke with a deep southern accent and idolized Thomas Jefferson (so did I). He also reminded us that he was an "emancipated southerner." He liked to use that word a lot . . . "emancipated."

"The Negro was 'emancipated' by the Civil War, but most southern whites weren't. They're still living in the past . . .

thinking it was all a bad dream, that the South will rise again. Pardon my pun, but we cannot and must not view issues as black and white . . . the truth usually lies somewhere in between, some shade of gray. Try seeing both sides of an argument. There is almost always some element of truth on both sides."

"Well, that's not how we're learning Constitutional History," said Linda. "Our Government teacher said that every Amendment to the Constitution was the result of social or economic conflict."

"No, Linda, it isn't quite that simple," said Mr. Jackson. "Here, let me read something from Mao Ts-tung, the leader of Communist China. Although he is a strong proponent of Communism, he breaks from the simplistic schism of Marx. Mao doesn't view history as a simple conflict between the Proletariat and the Bourgeoisie." Mr. Jackson then reached in his jacket pocket and began reading from a little red book.

"A simple process has only one pair of opposites, while a complex process has more than one pair. Various pairs of opposites are in turn opposed to one another. In this way all things in the objective world and human thought are formed and impelled to move."

I wanted to raise my hand and tell Mr. Jackson about my interpretation of "showtime" in Gainesville, how "black and white" was used to emphasize the bonding of all people, regardless of race. That sure wasn't how Miss Davenport envisioned "black and white." I think Mr. Jackson would have enjoyed hearing about "showtime," but not in the classroom, so I kept my thoughts to myself. In retrospect, its too bad I didn't end my virginity at the TEP house . . . a spiritual black and white experience would have been something to remember for a lifetime!

◆

I also took typing during my senior year: I could type 75 words-per-minute on a timed test. Typing class was a relaxing and refreshing mid-day break from "senioritis," the disease we got during our senior year, after we had been accepted to college and grades didn't matter any more.

"The quick brown fox jumped over the lazy white dogs."

I probably typed that sentence two hundred times. Florida Vickers, our typing teacher, loved "quick brown fox" . . . it contained every letter of the alphabet. Believe it or not . . . that really was her name, "Florida," like the state. She was younger than the other teachers and very pretty; she probably was the only female teacher who smiled all the time. However, like all the other female teachers, she often wore see-through blouses that revealed a full slip and a flat chest. Of course, for a typing teacher, you would expect her to be flat. And, for obvious reasons, girls with big boobs never took typing. Miss Vickers didn't say much. However, in order to inspire the class and improve our typing speed she kept reminding us that the complete works of Shakespeare could be created by rearranging the letters of "quick brown fox." We all groaned when she made that ridiculous statement.

I didn't do much thinking in typing class; it was a time to relax my brain, to exercise my fingers, and just space out. I guess the only thing I thought about was Florida's name, whether she had sisters named Georgia or Alabama. There was an Israeli boy at Beach High whose name was Meyer Sonenshein. If Florida married Meyer her name would become Florida Sonenshein. I liked that name and when I had nothing to do I practiced typing it . . . . forward and backwards.

Manny Lefkowitz practiced typing **"Mona Colona"**—that would be the name of Mona Lisa if she married the comedian, Jerry Colona.

"What about Hope Lang, the actress," said Manny. If she married Bob Hope she would be **Hope Hope**, ain't that a pisser?"

"Yeah Manny," I replied. "But, what if Hope Hope hoped for something . . . . Then it would be Hope Hope hopes."

Manny chuckled, scratched his balls, and practiced typing Hope Hope hopes.

I wondered whether Florida earned the same salary as the other teachers. She didn't do that much. She just smiled and watched us, to make sure we kept typing. "Keep typing . . . keep typing; keep those fingers moving. This isn't study hall." That's about all she ever said, aside from her occasional reference to Shakespeare and quick brown fox. I really didn't belong in typing;

I already knew how to type, but there were very few electives in the twelfth grade, and there was no way in Hell that I would take Spanish IV. Actually, the real reason I took typing was because the lab was the only air conditioned classroom in the school. Air conditioning was a relatively new invention and window units were very expensive. Even in my house we only had one unit, in my parents bedroom. On hot humid nights I usually slept on the back porch, wearing ugly boxer shorts . . . . jockeys gave me jock itch. We lived four blocks from the ocean; you could feel the breeze on our back porch, especially at night. At school, all classrooms except the typing lab used large built in ventilation fans above the front and rear doors, but the fans did very little to cool the room . . . they only circulated hot muggy air.

Because of the terrible heat and humidity of South Florida, the typical attire for boys was either a polo shirt, preferably with a little alligator, or a short sleeve sport shirt with a T-shirt underneath to absorb the perspiration. The sport shirt was worn open, to the second button, to display the "cool" plunge of the T-shirt, which was either a crew neck or a v-neck. Boys only wore v-neck if they had a lot of chest hair that they wanted to display. Tough kids opened the shirt down to the third button.

The county dress code prohibited boys from wearing a T-shirt without a sport shirt, but that rule was never enforced . . . not during my first four years at Ida M. Fisher and Beach High. Girls had their own fashions, but they weren't as well defined. In late 1955 many girls were wearing hoop skirts and crinolines and some were wearing ankle length dresses, usually pastel shades of yellow, blue, or pink, and they all wore shoes with Italian names like Papagallo or Capezio. They carried white basket purses made of painted wicker.

What I remember most from those hot sticky classrooms was getting prickly heat and jock itch . . . not very pleasant memories. Both of my arms would be covered with hundreds of itchy little pimples. And the more I scratched, the worse it got, until both arms got wet and gooky and very red. Jock itch was even worse. I blotted that memory forever; I don't want to talk about it, but for some strange reason girls were immune from jock itch, they never perspired down there; not even the fat ones.

"That's cause' girls ain't got no sweaty gonads hanging between their legs," said No Neck Nissenbaum. "They get good ventilation with skirts, 'specially if they ain't wearing no panties."

No Neck was one of the Rebels; he got his nickname for obvious reasons. He was 6'4" and his head was connected directly to his shoulders.

"How can you tell if a girl's not wearing panties?" I asked.

"Well, it ain't always easy," said No Neck, "usually, they walk around with a stupid smile on their face. I guess a little breeze 'down there' makes a girl happy."

"Do you know a girl named Mickey Cohen?" I asked. "She's always smiling."

No Neck began to laugh. "That chick loves to give BJs, and I ain't never seen her wear panties, cept' maybe in the winter. And, look at Vickers, the typing teacher, always has that dumb ass grin on her face, specially' when she talks about the quick brown fox."

"Hey, I think you're right. She's the only teacher that always smiles in class."

"Well, she ain't smiling for no cock," said No Neck. "Vickers' is a fulltime lezzie."

"Really?" I responded. "She doesn't look like a lesbian."

"Duh!," said No Neck. "Why do you think she always eats lunch with the girl's gym teachers, especially Garcia?"

"Well, maybe its because she's younger than the other female teachers, expect for the gym teachers."

"And maybe its because Garcia got monster boobs," said No Neck. "Lezzies love to suck on big tits."

Although I laughed about Garcia's monster boobs I couldn't believe his suspicions about Vickers. I know she wasn't as smart as my other teachers, but she was really nice.

No Neck spelled his name without a hyphen, unlike Fish-Face, the leader of Rebels, who was the only one allowed to use that symbol of distinction, and despite his crude observations, No Neck was a good student.

"I'm so fuckin' bored," said No Neck, "I got accepted at UF. I can't wait to get out of here and start college."

To alleviate his boredom No Neck decided that he would make life miserable for Jamele Davenport, our Government teacher. Miss Davenport was an eccentric woman who lived in her own black and white world . . . and she was allergic to perfume.

"If any of you girls dare to wear perfume in my class, you will be suspended from school," bellowed Miss Davenport. "And the same thing goes for you boys; no after shave lotion, especially Old Spice."

No Neck arrived at school very early one morning, 6:00 AM, even before the janitors. He climbed over the protective chain link fence and went to the third floor, to Miss Davenport's classroom. Then he poured half a bottle of Old Spice on the large ventilation fan in front of the room and the other half on the back fan. The fans would not be turned on until the start of first period, at 8:30 AM.

Fifteen minutes after class began Miss Davenport had a seizure. I was a student in that class; I watched with horror as she almost died. She gasped for air, clutched at her neck and turned blue. Then her eyes rolled back in her head and she fainted. Several boys quickly ran to the front of the room, grabbed her and dragged her to the balcony, where she could breathe fresh air. I helped; I held one of her legs. No one laughed, not even No Neck, when the ambulance came to school and two men in white coats carried Miss Davenport away. She needed an oxygen mask to breathe. Throughout the day and after school, everyone talked about the incident. We tried to be polite and sensitive, and not laugh. But, on the inside, I think some kids were holding back laughter. Miss Davenport was really a strange woman; she would be perfect for Mr. Streuling. One good thing about that "match" . . . they would never reproduce, unless immaculate conception was still possible.

The next morning four bongs of the PA system set the stage for a very stern announcement from Mr. Schecter. Linda Spiegel immediately stared at my lap before I could grab my books; so did a few of her friends, and they all chuckled.

"We know who did this terrible thing to Miss Davenport," said Mr. Schecter. You could hear the anger in his voice. "And that hoodlum has been expelled from school . . . permanently. Its too bad; this young man was only several months away from graduation. This was a very juvenile thing to do, and if Miss Davenport had died he would be facing manslaughter charges. I am happy to report that Miss Davenport is resting comfortably at home, and will be back to school in a few days. But, let me warn you, all of you, if anything like this ever happens again, there will be some serious repercussions around here . . . a lot more than perfume will be hitting the fan. Do you understand what I am saying? Do I have to spell it out for you?"

Later, that day, as a retaliatory measure, the Dean of Boys, Reinhard Kessler, clicked his heels and began enforcing the no t-shirt rule, a regulation that had been "on the books" for many years, but never taken seriously. And the first boy he caught was Corey Kaplan, the captain of the tennis team and vice-president of National Honor Society.

Corey came to school that day wearing a sport shirt over a t-shirt, but it was an extremely hot day. In Miami Beach it sometimes gets very hot, even in late November. During lunch Corey stripped down to his undershirt; so did his two buddies. And Dean Kessler caught the the three boys walking in the Sr. High patio, not far from the beloved statue of the World War II soldier.

"Corey, come to my office immediately . . . also, you two punks." Kessler was wearing his green blazer even though it was a very hot day. Most kids assumed that he slept in that jacket, that he even wore it when he had sex. Of course, we had doubts whether Nazis ever had sex, except when they raped Jewesses. Kessler was virulent in his attack on Corey and his friends, he had a stern look on his face, like Heinrich Himler, the infamous Director of the SS. Dean Kessler was close friends with Jamele Davenport; he was also a strong advocate of the theory that the world was divided into two distinct groups . . . good people and evil people and you didn't have to be a genius to figure out where he placed Jews, even Aaron T Schecter, his Jewish boss.

"I am sending you three trouble-makers home; you are in violation of the county dress code. You know damn well that you are not allowed to wear t-shirts without a sport shirt. Tomorrow, make sure you come to school properly dressed or you will be expelled permanently. I don't understand 'you people' . . . you come here from Russian and Poland and think you can just take the law in your own hands."

Kessler stood at perfect attention as he continued with his tirade: "Haven't you noticed, we have a big statue in New York harbor welcoming foreigners to our country. We open our doors; we even promote some of you to become high school principals, but you don't show any respect for law and order. You saw what happened in Germany; that's because 'you people' are trouble makers wherever you go . . . and good law abiding citizens won't stand for crap."

"Gee, Dean Kessler," said Corey, in a very sarcastic voice. "Now I understand what led to the Holocaust; German Jews were probably wearing t-shirts to school."

"Don't be a damn wise ass," said Dean Kessler, "just because you have a scholarship to Princeton. I have a good mind to talk to their Dean of Admissions. Don't go testing my patience! For Christ sakes, when are you people ever going to learn; you are welcome guests in America, but this is still a Christian country; we are God fearing people and we don't want a communist revolution."

"Huh?" responded Corey. "Are you saying that wearing t-shirts on a hot day is the first step in a communist overthrow of our government?"

"Corey, get the hell out of here, and don't go calling it 'your' government. It will be a cold day in Hell when we elect one of 'your people' to be president of the United States of America."

That night Corey and his friends began a telephone campaign, looking for support from all their friends, and friends of their friends. They had a plan, but it required assistance from hundreds of other boys.

"OK, here's what we're gonna' do," said Corey. "Tomorrow we'll all go to school wearing only a t-shirt . . . . no sport shirt on top. The Nazi jerk doesn't have the right to enforce that dumb rule . . . and if we stand united they can't expel everyone." The t-shirt phone message was circulated from boy to boy . . . but I guess I wasn't in the loop; I didn't know anything about the proposed "T-shirt rebellion."

"I've got a cousin who works at the Miami Herald," said one of Corey's friends, "I'll clue him in; this can be a great story."

"Great idea," said Corey, "and I have a friend who works at WTVJ."

On the morning of the rebellion I wore a short sleeve paisley shirt with a crew neck t-shirt underneath. And as I pulled into a parking spot a few blocks from school I immediately noticed that almost every boy was only wearing a white t-shirt. As soon as I heard the details, what was happening, I ran back to my car and removed my sport shirt . . . I joined the t-shirt rebellion; so did half the boys at Beach High and Ida M. Fisher, the two adjoining schools. Nothing like this had ever happened before.

We were protesting against something; I wasn't quite sure what, but it was an organized protest. I wish I could look back and say that we marched or stood up for the rights of Negroes, or fought to eliminate forced prayers in school, but we drew the battle lines and made our stand at a grass roots level . . . . our right to wear t-shirts to school.

Mr. Schecter came on the PA (*without the glockenspiel*) and told every boy who was wearing a t-shirt to go home, to come back the next day wearing a proper shirt.

"If you don't leave the building in the next fifteen minutes you will be suspended from school."

Fifteen minutes passed and none of the boys in my homeroom left. In fact, almost all of the boys who were wearing sport shirts removed them and joined the protest.

Thirty minutes later Mr. Schecter came back on the PA.

"All teachers . . . please write down the name of any boy who is still in your classroom wearing a t-shirt without a sport shirt. Tell them that they are now officially suspended from school."

Approximately one thousand boys were suspended and left the two buildings. We all congregated on Pennsylvania Avenue, the street immediately behind the school. The girls were not part of the protest, nor were the boys who were "properly dressed." They weren't suspended, but they all ran out of school to watch the protest. The crowd swelled to approximately two thousand, maybe more.

Several of the boys built a large bonfire and constructed a grass filled dummy to look like Dean Kessler. The dummy was dressed in a green sport jacket, just like the blazer that Kessler always wore, and it was hung in effigy. Eventually it was thrown into the fire. Corey Kaplan was the hero; he ran in front of the bonfire and threw rocks at the burning dummy. He stood bare chested and raised his white t-shirt high above his head.

"Freedom . . . freedom . . . freedom," he shouted, as he waved his t-shirt in the air. It was our symbol of liberation; it was our battle flag. Remember the Alamo, remember the Maine, remember Pear Harbor, remember the t-shirt!

Two thousand kids began chanting . . . "freedom, freedom, freedom,—t-shirts forever." Many of the boys removed their t-shirts and waved them back and forth; the shouting intensified. I was hoping to watch some of the girls pull off their blouses and join the protest . . . . so were most of the boys. It didn't happen. Penny Sherman, the well dressed girl who never went anywhere without her makeup mirror, wiggled out of her two starched crinolines and threw them in the fire. Linda Spiegel followed Penny and kicked off her expensive Italian shoes.

On the other side of the bonfire Dean Kessler stood tall and arrogant, surrounded by sixty teachers. None of them said anything; they stayed on their side of the fire. But Mr. Schecter was not there. Where was the principal of our school at this time of crisis? After ten minutes newspaper reporters from the Miami Beach Sun arrived to observe the protest . . . then came reporters from the big Miami newspapers, the Herald and the Daily News . . . . and camera crews from the TV stations. This was the biggest news story ever to come out of Beach High.

"What are you kids protesting?" asked one of the reporters.

"Our right to wear t-shirts to school," shouted several very angry boys.

"I know that . . . but what do the t-shirts represent? What is the bigger underlying issue?"

"Represent? Huh?"

And the chanting continued . . . . "freedom, freedom, freedom."

Several police patrol cars pulled up to the bonfire; intimidating looking men in blue uniforms and plastic face masks soon stood side by side clutching their night sticks. Several of the policemen held large dogs on leashes . . . ferocious Doberman Pinschers with face muzzles. I had a horrible feeling that this was going to get ugly, that someone was going to get hurt, maybe even killed.

Just then Mr. Schecter climbed out of one of the patrol cars and walked to the student side of the bonfire. He was wearing a dark blue suit and a red tie and he was carrying a police "bull-horn"—a battery operated megaphone. He had an angry scowl on his face. A few boys, hiding in the safety of the mob, screamed out and called Mr. Schecter a faggot, a pussy, and a few other obscenities, but our principal said nothing . . . he just stood in front of the police, glaring at the throng of students.

Then, Mr. Schecter removed his suit jacket and threw it to the ground. Slowly, he took off his tie and opened the top two buttons of his long sleeve white shirt. He never lost eye contact with the students; his face was taut, but he said nothing. I was positive that he was about to elaborate on the threat that he made on the PA . . . when he talked about Miss Davenport and the perfume incident . . . "shit was about to hit the fan." But, what happened next was completely unexpected. Several thousand students watched in total silence as Mr. Schecter took off his dress shirt. He stripped down to a white undershirt, it was a v-neck . . . . and he paused, a long pause, just like Myron K always did before he reached the punchline of one of his jokes. Then Mr. Schecter threw his dress shirt into the bonfire and without too much emotion, he spoke quietly into the bull-horn.

"Its really damn hot in this school. We absolutely must install air conditioning in the classrooms. But, until that happens, I'm going to allow boys to wear white t-shirts to class. What the Hell! Girls too." Now, lets all get back inside the building." Mr. Schecter then walked over to Corey Kaplan and shook his hand. Everybody applauded (*except Dean Kessler*) . . . and the bare chested Corey led the parade back into school, walking side by side with our principal, who was only wearing a t-shirt. Colonel Klein was the first teacher to break ranks with his colleagues; he removed his tie and shirt . . . and threw them into the fire. J. Linus Jackson, the emancipated Virginian, ripped off his tie and joined the Colonel, so did Miss Madison, who threw her fruit covered Pix shoes into the fire.

Colonel Klein, Mr. Jackson, and the barefoot Miss Madison walked arm in arm, as they returned to their classrooms, and Brock Tyler, the handsome English teacher, kissed Penny Sherman on the forehead . . . he also hugged several Golden Girls. In the rear of this momentous procession Florida Vickers and the very buxom Selena Garcia were holding hands and smiling. This was the "Storming of the Bastille," the poor people of Paris had taken to the streets. We made our point, whatever it was . . . change was in the air.

CHAPTER 49

THANATOPSIS

The next morning, December 1, 1955, was my father's 65th birthday. He bragged about the fact that he was finally eligible to collect Social Security. I sat at the breakfast table, eating a toasted bagel and drinking a cup of hot cocoa; I was reading the front page of the Miami Herald, the feature article was all about the t-shirt Rebellion . . . with photos of the bonfire and boys in t-shirts. There was even a picture of several gorgeous Golden Girls clustered around Mr. Tyler. My father chewed on his unlit cigar and smiled; he was reading an obscure article in a back section of the newspaper about a Negro woman named Rosa Parks; she lived in Montgomery, Alabama and refused to give up her bus seat to a white man.

"We challenged the system and we won . . . and we did it without any violence. For the next few days the boys strutted around the patios and open balconies of Beach High in t-shirts, defiantly in violation of the county dress code. Even though girls now had permission to wear t-shirts, they realized that Mr. Schecter was just kidding. Girls never wore t-shirts, so they couldn't share our sense of victory. Therefore, they organized a little protest of their own. Many of the girls decided to wear sunglasses inside the classrooms—that would violate another school board rule. But this time the Dean of Girls, Alba Layne, had learned how to deal with harmless demonstrations of adolescent self-expression; she simply wore sun glasses herself

The t-shirt and sunglass fads lasted three days. By the following Monday life was back to normal at Beach High and Ida M. Fisher. I thought about Rosa Parks in Montgomery; I wondered whether her life could ever be back to normal. I wish I knew her address; I wanted to send her a letter. What a courageous woman!

My favorite class in the twelfth grade was English, especially the module on early American poets. And of course, I had a great deal of respect for J. Linus Jackson, the emancipated Southern teacher; he knew a lot about American poetry.

"Many critics regard Thanatopsis as the first important American poem," said Mr. Jackson. "William Cullen Bryant was only seventeen when the original version of the poem was published, the same age as most of you. Amazing, for a young boy to have such a profound sense of spirituality. He was a descendant of John Alden, one of the original Pilgrims, but he rejected Puritan dogma for Deism."

I knew something about Deism . . . about Thomas Paine. In the "Age of Reason" he really ripped into religion; Jefferson was also a proponent of Deism and he intentionally left God out of the "Declaration of Independence" . . . except for a confusing reference to "nature's God." "Excuse me Mr. Jackson," I interrupted. "Deists don't believe in religion, but Thanatopsis begins with a reference to 'communion' . . . that's a very religious word."

"Good point Myron," responded Mr. Jackson, "but 'communion' is a word in the dictionary, go look it up; it means connection or close association. Yes, Catholics use it to mean a connection with Jesus Christ, but that version of the word is always shown with an upper case 'C'. In the context of Thanatopsis, Bryant uses it to illuminate man's connection with nature. He is telling the reader to go out and listen to nature when thoughts of death come. He believes that people are only here for a short time before death takes them away and their bodies become a part of nature."

That was similar to the belief of Xenocrates, the ancient Greek philosopher. He also believed that after death the body became part of nature, but only the body. Xenocrates had the mind and soul moving on to the moon. Maybe Jefferson and Paine conceived the idea of Deism from Xenocrates.

"Listen to Bryant's painful image of death," said Mr. Jackson, "in the early part of the poem"

> When thoughts of the last bitter hour come like a
> blight over thy spirit, and sad images of the stern
> agony, and shroud, and pall, and breathless darkness,
> and the narrow house, make thee to shudder, and
> grow sick at heart—go forth under the open sky, and
> list to Nature's teaching . . . .

'Bitter, blight, sad, stern agony, shroud, pall, breathless darkness, shudder, sick' . . . he gets his message across, doesn't he? Death is scary!"

"Now, listen to the last nine lines of the poem, a new message evolves."

Then, in his rich baritone voice, Mr. Jackson read the final nine lines of Thanatopsis. We all sat back, mesmerized by his dramatic performance.

> So live, that when thy summons comes to join
> The innumerable caravan which moves
> To that mysterious realm, where each shall take
> His chamber in the silent halls of death,
> Thou go not, like the quarry-slave at night,
> Scourged to his dungeon, but, sustained and soothed
> By an unfaltering trust, approach thy grave
> Like one who wraps the drapery of his couch
> About him, and lies down to pleasant dreams.

"That doesn't make sense," said Shelly. "That can't be the same poet. He is now comparing death to a pleasant dream. What happened to bitter, blight, and agony? He can't make up his mind."

"Well, Shelly, no one ever said that death is an easy concept to accept," responded Mr. Jackson. "But, you are very insightful; this 'almost' is another poet. The final nine lines of Thanatopsis were written seven years after the original publication. Bryant is now a little older and a lot wiser, and he's had more life experiences. Thanatopsis is a poem about death; the word itself is Greek . . . I'm not sure of the precise translation, but it is 'related to death.' However, the real message of Thanatopsis is to live life to the fullest."

"Yeah, I dig the final nine lines," said Manny Lefkowitz. Underneath his desk he nervously scratched his balls . . . old habits are impossible to break. "But why bother with the whole poem?" Manny always had a way of getting right to the point. "This Bryant guy babbles all through the poem about nature this and nature that and how disgusting death is . . . then seven years later he writes nine new lines and says, forget everything I wrote before; it really ain't so bad. When you're ready to die just put your blanket over your head and go to sleep . . . . don't make no sense to me. And none of it rhymes . . . how can you call this a poem? I liked the Bells much better; tintinnabulation is a cool word."

Mr. Jackson laughed. "Yup . . . tintinnabulation is a cool word. Does anyone know what it means?"

I knew, but I didn't want to raise my hand; I didn't want to look like I was sucking up to the teacher. No one answered the question, so Mr. Jackson provided his own definition, using a very vivid example.

"Whenever an announcement is made on the Public Address system here at school it is preceded by four melodic chimes . . . that is tintinnabulation."

Well . . . I'll be damned! I didn't know that . . . I sure had an intimate relationship with those chimes.

"That's the sound of a glockenspiel that you hear," said Mr. Jackson, "the same musical instrument that embellishes the marching band at football games. Don't you feel a kind of reverbertion go through your body when you hear the tintinnabulation of those chimes?"

Linda Spiegel immediately commented: "Why don't you ask Myron, he has his own special communion with those chimes." And she giggled; so did a couple of her girlfriends.

"I used to," I whispered to Linda. "But now I take cold showers." Linda laughed; so did Mr. Jackson. I guess I whispered too loud.

"Well . . . that's not exactly what I had in mind," said Mr. Jackson, "but maybe Poe did. He was a very earthy man."

After English my next class was Phys. Ed. We were now playing soccer every day . . . . which I always regarded as an extremely unnatural sport. How can you engage in an athletic

410

activity without using your hands? That's like holding a ping pong paddle in your mouth or using your nose to spread mustard on a hot dog.

"Or like scratching your balls with your teeth," said Manny Lefkowitz.

"Yeah, you wish you could do that," said Linda Spiegel, and she laughed.

"You're damn lucky I can't," responded Manny, "or you'd be out of a job."

"Keep dreaming," said Linda. She refused to let Manny have the last word, but I suspected that behind her defensive façade Linda really liked Manny. He was very insightful, in his own crude and candid manner. And Manny definitely liked Linda, he was always staring at her big boobs.

I was now a senior; I was comfortable walking naked in the locker room or in the communal showers with my front side exposed. But many of the younger boys suffered from locker room shyness . . . they walked around with towels draped around their waist and faced the wall when they showered. I always felt a sense of compassion for those boys; I knew what they were going through. One day in Phys. Ed., as we were all running around naked in the locker room, my heart stopped . . . . I saw a frightening face peering into the window, gawking down at the younger boys. The window was high above the showers . . . . at least 10 feet above a room full of naked teenage boys . . . mostly Jewish boys.

It was Mr. Streuling. His hair had turned white. At first I wasn't sure it was him, but that was a face I could never forget. He was four years older, but it was definitely him. And he saw me, . . . but hopefully, he didn't recognize me. I was almost a foot taller than when he saw me naked in the shower at the James Manor.

I ran to Coach Gallagher and told him about the face in the window, but I didn't tell details about my prior experience with Mr. Streuling.

"Coach Gallagher, there's a man staring in the window. He's very creepy looking."

Immediately, Coach Gallagher and fifteen boys ran outside the locker room to try to find Mr. Streuling. We got a brief glimpse of the back side of a man with white hair climbing over the chain link fence, but we didn't get a view of his face.

Later that day, after school, I went to the principal's office; I told his secretary that it was extremely important for me to talk to Mr. Schecter.

"His next available opening is tomorrow after school . . . I'm sorry, but he's in the conference room, in the middle of an important meeting."

Damn! This was Tuesday—"Terrific T-day." I picked the wrong day to ineruupt the Principal.

"But, its urgent; its about a criminal matter." I wasn't about to let this office guardian keep me from talking to Mr. Schecter, even on Tuesday; this was much too important.

"OK, young man," said Mr. Schecter, as he nervously adjusted his tie and buttoned the top of his shirt. "What is this urgent criminal matter that's so pressing that you had to interrupt my meeting?" The only other time I was in Mr. Schecter' office was when I criticized Señora Johnson for her anti-Jewish generalizations. I hope he didn't remember that incident; I didn't want to be regarded as a trouble maker.

"Mr. Schecter, a man was staring in the window at the boys locker during gym class . . . he was gawking at the naked boys, mainly the younger boys. And, I know who he is; he has a criminal record."

"Did you tell Coach Gallagher?"

"Well, I told him that a man was looking in the window, but I didn't tell him who the man was or that I know him, and I definitely didn't tell any of the criminal details."

"Oh lord! This can mean trouble, let me get my girl in here," said Mr. Schecter, and he flipped the intercom switch and called for his secretary.

"Gert, please clear the conference room and put the beer bottles back in the refrigerator. And go get Coach Gallagher . . . tell him to come to my office right away. We have an uncomfortable situation here."

Coach Gallagher was breathing heavy when he arrived at the office; he ran all the way from the boys locker room. He was dressed in his white shorts and polo shirt, and nervously twirled his lanyard while Mr. Schecter opened the office refrigerator and took out a few bottles of Dr. Pepper. His secretary also joined the conference; she took notes in a spiral memo pad.

"OK Myron . . . slowly, lets hear the whole story. Tell us everything you know about this man; I have to know everything . . . then we're going to call the police."

I sat there quietly, I was the center of attention. I hated Dr. Pepper and I didn't know where to begin my story.

Mr. Schechter was aware of my nervousness. He reached across the conference table and handed my bottle to his secretary. "Gert, give Myron a 7-up or a root beer. Looks like he doesn't like Dr. Pepper."

"Make it root beer," I thanked Mr. Schecter and started telling him and Coach Gallagher all about my scary incident back at the James Manor and about Mr. Streuling's criminal record, but I didn't think it was necessary to talk about my Nazi tattoo research at the library.

"Does he still work at the James Manor? Is he still the landlord?"

"I don't think so . . . I haven't seen him in four years. But, I think he might be living at the Nemo Hotel on first street."

"Did you ever file a police report on this man, about that incident?"

"Yes . . . but not until two years after it happened. I was with the police for at least two hours telling them every detail; its probably all on file with the Miami Beach police department. Oh yeah . . . one more thing, when I filed that report the police issued a restraining order; Mr. Streuling isn't allowed to come near me."

"Myron . . . call your parents and tell them what's happening," said Mr. Schecter. "Go use the phone in the Registrar's office; she left work early. I think we're going to be here for quite some time, telling all of this to the police."

"I'd rather not tell my father, Mr. Schecter, he has a bad heart condition. Let me just call home and say that I'm staying extra late at school to listen to a special speaker or something like that."

Fifteen minutes later the police arrived, two cars with sirens blasting. The leader was a plain clothes detective named Antonio Bellazio; he was followed by two uniformed policemen. The policemen had highly polished black shoes, just like the shoes that Mr. Streuling always wore . . . and they walked with perfect posture. Detective Bellazio was round shouldered; he was wearing a wrinkled tan suit, his striped tie was loose and and his shoes were not shiny. We walked to the boy's locker room to view the scene of the incident; Detective Bellazio walked with a slight limp and he asked me a lot of questions. I showed him the window where I saw Mr. Streuling and the approximate location where he climbed over the fence.

"Jim, go to the radio and call for a team of dusters," said Detective Bellazio and he wrote instructions on a small piece of paper. He gave the note to one of the uniformed policemen. "I want a complete set of prints from the window and the top of the fence. And . . . bring in a couple of dogs to sniff for semen . . . 'peepers' like to 'get off' while watching."

"Excuse me sir," I interrupted, "but I don't think you're going to find any semen?"

"And how do you know that?"

"Because I don't think that Mr. Streuling has testicles."

"Doesn't have testicles!" Detective Bellazio, Mr. Schecter, and Coach Gallagher, repeated my observation in disbelief.

"OK . . . I can see there's a lot more to this story," said Detective Bellazio, "tell us about Mr. Streuling's testicles. Where did they go?"

"I think the Nazi's cut them off; he was a Protective Custody Prisoner at Auschwitz, but he isn't Jewish. He was a pedophile . . . that's what the Nazi's did to pedophiles. His tattoo from Auschwitz is 425304 . . . I memorized that number for life."

"Well, if he had his nuts cut off he wouldn't be peeping at young boys," exclaimed Detective Bellazio. "There goes your theory."

I then told complete details about my Nazi research at the Miami Beach library, the microfilm records, and Katarina . . . . but I didn't say anything about the information I discovered in the client files at Rosenblatt, Unger and Polsky. I remembered the lecture from Seymour Rosenblatt on trust and ethics . . . "nothing should ever leave this office." I was sworn to confidentiality, the "ethical backbone" of the accounting profession.

Detective Bellazio had a very serious look on his face . . . he shook his head and clenched his fist; he was quiet and extremely introspective. Then he snapped out of his trance and chuckled:

"Well . . . I guess we've got to get out an APB for an elderly man with white hair, who might not have testicles." Bellazio laughed, so did Mr. Schecter. "Listen . . . . don't none of you talk about this to no one. No need to get everyone scared shitless . . . we'll investigate Streuling and keep you posted. We'll check out the restraining order. And, of course, you call us if anything new happens at your end. Myron . . . especially you! Anytime . . . middle of the night. I think there's more you're not telling me. And, when you feel up to it, call me."

Detective Bellazio put his hand on my shoulder and handed me his business card. He discontinued the stern "cop talk" and lowered his voice almost to a whisper. "Myron, be careful. This man might be dangerous. But, I never heard of a castrated man who was still a peeper. The Nazi's had 'quick justice'—they knew what they were doing. If Streuling really was a pedofile they would have castrated him and he wouldn't be bothering young boys anymore. I think you're assuming that he was castrated just because he has a high pitched voice. I've dealt with weirdoes like this before . . . this man sounds like a looney-bird!"

The next evening I received a phone call at home from Detective Bellazio.

"Hello Myron, this is Antonio Bellazio, MBPD . . . we've done a little checking on Streuling and you're right, he does live at the Nemo Hotel. But, we didn't come up with any prints at the school, and no semen . . . so we got no case on him. Listen . . . we examined your deposition on Streuling and the restraining order was only for six months. We're going to have to meet with you and your parents so you can get an extension."

"Do I have to get my father involved in this nightmare? He had a recent heart attack; can't I just come to your office with my mother?"

"Yeah, that's OK, but we must have one parent since you're underage. Come to my office tomorrow at 10:00 AM."

"There's a little more we found on Streuling. In 1942 Auschwitz wasn't just used for homosexuals and pedophiles; it was also a processing center for many types of misfits, including lesbians, bi-sexuals, and the mentally insane. The Germans needed more hospital space for wounded soldiers; that was the middle of the war and Hitler didn't have much patience for wackos, even if they were German."

"Were the mentally insane also castrated?" I asked.

"No; they were only sterilized, and I'm sure you can guess when Streuling arrived in the US?"

"Of course! 1942" That was a simple question; the first two numbers of his Auschwitz tattoo were 42.

"Yup . . . I think your buddy might still have his nuts." Bellazio laughed. "Sounds like the nuts got to keep their nuts!"

I also laughed, but it wasn't a "ha" "ha" laugh; it was a nervous laugh. I was definitely scared. "I read the 1942 New York Times article," I said. "It didn't mention anything about lesbians, bi-sexuals, or the mentally insane."

"Well, it sure don't make no sense for a castrated man to be peeping and messing around with little kids," said Detective Bellazio. "There's got to be another explanation. Maybe Streuling never was at Auschwitz; maybe he put the tattoo there himself."

"That's crazy," I responded, "why would anyone do that?"

"Ain't so crazy," said Bellazio, "no way in hell the US would grant a visa to a German in the middle of the war, especially a queer or a pervert. But, a Jew just out of Auschwitz . . . yeah, no problem."

"Then all you've got to do is check out his tattoo," I replied. "Can't you do some type of ink test? Can't you compare his tattoo with ones that you know are genuine?"

"Ink test!" Bellazio laughed. "Myron, you've been reading too many comic books. Sorry, the lab at the bat-cave is closed."

◆

I went to police headquarters the next morning, along with my mother and Herman, but we didn't tell any of this to my father. Herman was street smart; my father always said that about him, and he had friends at the police department. He was a good person to bring along.

"Hi, Princess, you're getting prettier every time I see you," said Herman to the police dispatcher, an unattractive woman who was at least fifty years old. She smiled and blew Herman a kiss.

"Hello there Hermie," she chirped. "How's my lover boy?"

As we went upstairs on the elevator I asked Herman why he was flirting with that woman; Aunt Pearlie was a hundred times prettier.

"Myron," said Herman, and he coughed. He was coughing a lot lately . . . too much smoking. "If you flirt with a 'piece of ass' you're wasting your time; every other man is also flirting

416

with her. But, if you flirt with a 'mieskeit' *(ugly person)* you got a friend for life."

We walked down a long hallway that smelled like disinfectant, almost like a hospital, until we reached the small cluttered office of Detective Bellazio. The office was furnished with a cheap metal desk, matching grey shelves, and several uncomfortable folding chairs for visitors . . . but the view was beautiful, overlooking Biscayne Bay.

"Hi Tony," said Herman, "Myron's my wife's nephew . . . I came along to help."

"No problem Herman. Hope you're keeping out of trouble."

It was reassuring to find out that Herman and Bellazio knew each other. It seemed that wherever I went, whatever I needed . . . Herman had a foot in the door.

"I heard that the old restraining order was only good for a few months," said Herman. "That's the problem using a damn real estate lawyer for a criminal matter. I knew Streuling too . . . . Me and Pearl used to live in the James Manor, back in '51 and '52. He seemed like a nice guy . . . very polite, bowed a lot, and spoke like a fruitcake." Herman then tried to imitate the falsetto voice of Henry Streuling.

"Do you think Myron is in any danger?" asked my mother.

"Its hard to say, Mrs. Lindell," said Bellazio. "Perverts go for little children, not boys that are as tall as Myron; he's a full grown man. I've said it once, and I'll say it a hundred times, sickos' are hard to predict, very hard. But, I don't think Myron is right about Streuling . . . if he really was castrated by the Nazis he wouldn't be bothering little boys and girls anymore. That's what's so baffling about this case; this ain't your normal nut."

My mother cried: "Don't you go telling this to daddy, he has a bad heart."

♦

A few weeks later, on a Saturday morning, I joined the Steinberg's to go to a Bar Mitzvah in South Beach, at Temple Beth Sinai. The Bar Mitzvah boy was their cousin Donald Marcus, who had recently moved to Miami Beach from Brooklyn. Uncle Louie and Tanta Baila were also there, along with many other Steinberg relatives.

This was a Conservative synagogue; families sat together, prayed together, and danced together. I felt much more comfortable here than at the Orthodox shul where Dick Solomon had his Bar Mitzvah, where men sat on the first floor and women were restricted to the balcony, just like colored people who had to sit on the back of the bus. I sat with David and Shelly. Uncle Louie and Tanta Baila were on the 'Beema'—next to the Rabbi. I wondered how they got those special seats of honor.

After Donald made his Bar Mitzvah speech the Rabbi delivered a sermon about life and death and Anne Frank. He also talked a lot about the importance of living life to the fullest, the message of Anne Frank. That was the same conclusion that Mr. Jackson emphasized when he discussed Thanatopsis.

"When in life you are in the midst of death," said the Rabbi. "Anne ultimately ended up in Bergen-Belsen camp in Germany, after being evacuated from Auschwitz in October, 1944. As starvation. cold and disease swept through the camp's population, Anne's sister developed typhus and died. A few days later, in April 1945, Anne also succumbed to the disease. Two weeks after she died the camp was liberated by the British. She was fifteen years old. When in life you are in the midst of death . . . make the most of what time you have here on earth. Love God, find comfort in God . . . but find strength in your own soul. Amen. Good Shabbos!"

After the rabbi said "Amen" everyone moved from the sanctuary to a beautiful room decorated with baloons and flowers and we all held hands in a huge circle and began doing the "Hora," and we drank wine, and ate lots of "rugalah" (*Jewish pastry*). I did the Rhumba with several girls. This was a fun synagogue; teenagers were dancing; little children were running, laughing, and doing the "Hokie Pokie" and the "Bunny Hop."

"Are you sure you're Jewish?" asked one of my Rhumba partners. "You move your tush' like a Cuban."

"Yeah, I'm Jewish," I responded, "but part of my ancestry comes from Spain."

I loved to use that line. Girls really got excited when I told them I had Spanish blood, it inspired them to tell me all about their fears, inhibitions, and secret desires. But this was the first time a girl ever exposed her personal life on the dance floor of a synagogue.

"Nice to meet you." The girl shook my hand. "I'm Mindy Marcus, Donald's cousin from Brooklyn. I hope you don't freak out, but I'm about to have a catharsis."

Mindy slurred as she spoke; her breath smelled from wine and she had an irritating Brooklyn accent.

"Can you believe it, my fuckin' boyfriend broke up with me while he was still inside of me?" Several people on the dance floor turned and stared at us; this annoying girl was really loud.

"Jesus, what horrible timing." I lowered my head and mumbled. "You must have been shattered."

"Nah! He had a tiny pecker, and it was always slam-bam-thank you maam, but you know the old saying, if your puppy dies you gotta' find a new puppy." Mindy stared at my swiveling hips. "Maybe even a Spanish puppy."

"I think that only refers to puppies," I whispered, "not boyfriends."

I did my best to be sympathetic, but I wanted to get away from this nut, so I made an excuse to walk over to the head table, to congratulate the Bar Mitzvah boy and his family

"Hi Donald, I'm best friends with your cousins, David and Shelly. Mazel Tov."

I circled the table and said 'Mazel Tov" to Donald's parents and other relatives from Brooklyn. Then, a bearded man in a white yarmelkeh walked over to the Marcus table and squeezed firmly on my hand. He had a German accent and spoke in a high pitched voice.

"Hello Myron . . . my, how tall you've grown."

It was Henry Streuling. I felt a cold chill in both of my legs.

"Um, Um . . . hello." I tried to say something cool or intelligent, but my lips wouldn't move.

"I heard that you had an accident," said Mr. Streuling. "I'm glad my little buddy is OK."

"I'm not your little buddy," I exclaimed.

"Not you!" Mr. Streuling laughed. "You almost killed the boy who drives the shoe-mobile; that little black sambo takes good care of my shoes."

I pulled my hand from his strong grasp and walked to the far side of the room, next to the table with all the rugalah. I sat there staring in space and eating.

"Hey, whats the matter?" said a very drunk Mindy Marcus. "I saw you sitting here alone; you look white as a ghost."

"Hi Mindy. I think I had too much to eat, and it looks like you've had too much to drink." I held both hands to my stomach and pretended that I had an upset stomach. "It was great meeting you, but I'm gonna' go home now."

"Oh! That's too bad. I wanted to invite you back to my hotel. We're staying at the Nemo and I have my own room. Well, I guess I gotta' go find another puppy."

I looked for the Steinbergs; I was scared and wanted to leave the party, to get far away from Streuling. However, David and Shelly said they were having fun and wanted to stay longer, so I drove home without them.

As I left the temple I noticed a huge bronze plaque mounted on the wall of the lobby. The plaque listed the names of people who made large donations, and the top name was Henry Streuling; he contributed $100,000 to the "Jewish Youth Fund." This was the same amount that he claimed as a deduction on his tax return, but it just didn't make sense. I was positive that Streuling wasn't Jewish.

When I got home my father was sleeping on the living room couch with a multi colored blanket wrapped across his body. He seemed so at peace. Gently, I lifted him and helped him to his bedroom, then I took out my dictionary and looked up the word "catharsis."

CHAPTER 50

BANCO DE PORTUGAL

Early the next morning I drove to a nearby pay phone. I didn't want my parents to hear my conversation with David. I had difficulty keeping my composure as I told him that I saw Streuling at the Bar Mitzvah . . . that he squeezed my hand and scared the hell out of me . . . . and that he was a big shot at Uncle Louie's Synagogue.

"Holy shit, you better call the police," said David. "Damn! When I saw him with the little girl at the shoe store he looked weird. I should have known, Streuling's got 'gelt.' Only rich people shop there."

"Yeah, you're right," I responded. "I'll call the detective who's handling the case. Oh, by the way, your cousin Mindy is really strange."

David laughed. "Myron, you missed the boat last night, that girl is a nympho, and she thinks you're some type of hot Spanish lover; she wanted you to be her 'puppy.'"

"I know; she invited me back to her hotel, but I was so spooked after seeing Streuling, I would have been a lousy puppy."

"Well, Shelly and I were great puppies, but she didn't stop talking about how you moved your tush like a Cuban."

"The three of you!" I exclaimed. "I can't believe you and your brother had a threesome with your own cousin."

"No, that's sick. We just took turns, one at a time . . . and Mindy's only a distant cousin. I'm not even sure how we're related."

"Well, it wasn't only because of Streuling," I said. "I could never 'get it up' for another girl; I just can't get Leah out of my head."

"That's what I thought," said David. "Listen, if you love that girl so much, then go back to her, otherwise you gotta' move on. You know how Mindy keeps saying that she needs a new puppy? Well, so do you; I never saw you so miserable."

"David, you're right . . . of course you're right. But it isn't that simple."

It was 8:00 AM on a Sunday morning, probably too early to call Detective Bellazio, but he told me to call him anytime I had information about Streuling. So, after I finished hearing details about the gang bang at the Nemo I put another dime in the pay phone.

"Hello, Detective Bellazio," this is Myron Lindell. "I saw Mr. Streuling yesterday at a Bar Mitzvah. It was at Temple Beth Sinai on Second and Washington. He came up to me and said hello. But, the way he said it . . . very weird."

"Did he make any threats or touch you?"

"No. No Threats . . . I was shaking hands with all the relatives of the Bar Mitzvah boy and I mistook Streuling for a relative, but he squeezed my hand real hard, and wouldn't let go; he got creepy, the way he looked into my eyes, the way he talked."

"Well, there ain't much I can do about that," responded Bellazio. "The new restraining order doesn't cover this type of situation; you were both attending the same function. Get me something to go on and I'll nail the fuckin' pervert, but just saying hello in a scary voice ain't enough."

"OK, I understand," I responded. "He didn't do anything so bad at the synagogue, but listen to these facts, and here's a few new things I discovered:

(1) Streuling isn't Jewish—I'm positive of that!
(2) His name is listed on top of the bronze plaque at Beth Sinai—he gave a $100,000 donation to the synagogue
(3) He has a record of indecent exposure arrests
(4) The donation was to the Jewish youth fund."

"Myron, all he has to say in court is that he wanted to clear his conscience and make up for his dirty past. That's why he donated all that money to a youth fund. You got nothing."

"But why to a 'Jewish' fund? This man isn't Jewish. He drinks beer, he kisses ladies hands, he bows, he puts mayonnaise on corned beef, he likes fishing. And why would a guy who has $100,000 to donate live in a dump like the Nemo Hotel?"

"I told you before, these child molesters are strange cats; impossible to understand what makes them tick." Detective Bellazio was very abrupt; maybe I shouldn't have called him on his private line on a Sunday morning.

It was obvious; I wasn't getting much help from the police. Bellazio was losing patience with me. I then came up with another idea . . . maybe I should call Joanie, at Rosenblatt, Unger and Polsky, and get another look at Streuling's tax return. Although I had already seen that file, it wasn't really an in-depth search. What else could I find? I had to figure out what the "GSRFF" corporation was all about. That was the source of the partnership income, the missing piece of this mystery. But "GSRFF" was not a client of the CPA firm.

Then it hit me . . . Yes! Yes! Yes! "**NETWORKING**" Of course! There was somebody else I forgot to check. I never looked at the tax return of Streuling's partner, J. Martin Berger. He was Seymour Rosenblatt's fraternity brother at the University of Florida (Class of 1930). I was willing to bet that the illustrious Miami Beach attorney was also a tax client of the CPA firm. I needed to talk to Joanie again, to examine Berger's tax return, but she was close friends with Leah, maybe even an "AC-DC" friend. Most likely, Leah hated my guts. She would never ask Joanie to help me! I was a real jerk; I shouldn't have broken our date at the last minute. Leah probably spent a lot of money buying bubble bath and wine. But, even if she was pissed maybe she would like me to dig up a little dirt on J. Martin Berger . . . the father of Danny Berger, the bastard who screwed up her life

So . . . I decided to call Leah. This was a very private call, even more private than the calls to David and Detective Bellazio. Once again, I had to use the pay phone next to the neighborhood gas station. Ten cents was a small price to pay for unlimited privacy.

"Hi Leah. This is Myron. I'm really sorry I broke our date . . . I, uh, like you a lot . . . more than you know . . . and, uh, if you spent lots of money on bubble bath or wine I'll pay you back . . . and . . . uh."

"Myron, I understand' . . . you don't have to apologize; you're not ready to make a commitment to a baby daughter. Don't worry about the bubble bath, I already used it, and we have a dozen bottles of Manichevitz at home, that's the only wine I like."

"Me too," I laughed, "but just the sweet grape flavor."

"Well, sometimes I like beer." Leah chuckled. "When I sleep at Joanie's its really a blast to get wasted."

I was careful, not to ask Leah if she and Joanie had an AC-DC relationship. I had a definite purpose for this phone call and I didn't want to get side tracked, but I couldn't stop thinking about Leah and Joanie kissing each other, with beer dribbling down their naked bodies.

"Say, Leah, do you remember how you came up to me when you started going steady with Danny Berger and asked me to do you a favor, to write a campaign speech for him?"

"Yeah, sure; I really appreciated it."

"Well, I need a favor from you now; I know you're probably mad at me but I really need your help."

"Hey! That was almost three years ago. I already offered you my body, what more do you want?" She chuckled; I was glad to see that she wasn't angry.

"I'm trying to look up some information in the client files at the CPA firm where I used to work. I need Joanie to let me in after hours, and if you talk to her I think she'll say OK. Its really important. By the way, in case you're interested, one of the people I'm investigating is a guy named J. Martin Berger . . . ever hear of him?"

"Of course! That's Danny's father." Why are you getting involved with a scum-bag like that?"

I didn't want to tell Leah too much, but I had to tell her something if I wanted her to talk to Joanie. "I think Berger is involved in some type of crooked business with a really strange nut. The weird guy is a pervert who was peeping in the boys locker room at Beach High. . . . and I think there might be enough information on Berger's tax return to prove whats happening."

"That would be fantastic," exclaimed Leah, "I'd love to see you stick it to that son-of-a-bitch. But you gotta' be careful, he's got a lot of connections with the Mafia and some colored hoods . . . and I know what I'm talking about. OK; I'll talk to Joanie . . . . we're really close."

"Joanie is really nice," I responded. "she told me that you're her best friend."

"Hey, I've got a question that's been bugging me," said Leah. "I laughed my ass off when I heard that Danny got expelled from school for cheating on a Spanish test, but why did you try to help that shmuck?"

"Oh yeah! I forgot all about that," I responded. "That was almost a year ago. Boy, I sure was stupid to get involved in that mess, but I wasn't defending Danny. I just got so pissed when our Spanish teacher starting making anti-Semitic comments. I couldn't hold back my anger."

"That's funny," said Leah, "Why would anyone make anti-Semitic comments about Danny? He and his parents never went to shul; they didn't believe in God or religion or anything. The only thing they worshiped was money."

Leah and I continued talking and laughing and reminiscing. There was such excitement in her voice; you could "hear" her smile over the phone. Then, all of a sudden, her voice changed. There was an uncomfortable lull in the conversation. Leah spoke in a far away dreamy voice, "Myron, you would have made a wonderful daddy for Ruthie."

That was the first time I ever thought about myself as a father. "Leah, you're the only girl I ever loved and I would love to be a daddy for Ruthie." That was also the first time I ever told a girl that I loved her. "But, I just turned seventeen; I've got to finish college first."

"Yeah, you told me that already. Damn problem is you get too logical about love and I get too romantic, but I'll really be hurt if you don't come to our birthday party; Ruthie and I both have the same birthday, July 30."

"Oh sure; Ill be there, I promise." But I was lying. I had to lie, otherwise Leah would not ask Joanie to let me in the CPA office.

"Myron, do you remember the poem, 'The Bells' by Poe?" Leah continued speaking in a very sad voice. "We learned it in Miss Carter' class—back in the ninth grade."

"Sure! I really loved that poem, one of my all time favorites."

"Mine too," said Leah. "I knew it by heart. I was pregnant with Ruthie, very depressed, very scared, and Danny's father was making terrible threats. I kept reciting 'The Bells' over and over . . . kind of an escape from all the shit that was happening in my life. Then, one night I had a strange dream—in my dream I was chanting that haunting poem, and when I reached the word 'tintinnabulation' you were standing next to me ringing a bell. You didn't say anything . . . but I had this feeling that you were reaching out, trying to help me."

"I was." I murmured, and a lump came to my throat.

"Myron, do you know the meaning of the Jewish word 'bashert?'"

I paused and took a deep breath. "No, I never heard that word."

I wanted to keep talking to Leah about "bashert" and about her dream. I also wanted to tell her about my dreams; she was in many of them, but I was at a pay phone and people were waiting in line.

"Leah . . . I have to get off the phone. Thanks for your help. I'll see you at your birthday party."

I was in love with Leah and I knew it was all wrong . . . but that damn Chess Master wouldn't let her out of my life. I was positive, that sneaky son-of-a-bitch arranged to have Joanie bend over and expose her gorgeous tush in the file room at Rosenblatt, Unger, and Polsky . . . that was the link back to Leah. How could this be? This contradicted my conviction that I was master of my own destiny. I had read Plato, Emerson, and Freud; I should not believe in the childish nonsense of a supernatural power. Then it hit me . . . . of course! The Chess Master did not control my life; he simply moved pieces on the board. He opened doors and created opportunities, but always, I was the one who had to make the next move.

♦

Later that week Joanie let me in the office at midnight. We were the only people in the building; even the cleaning ladies were gone. Joanie looked very pretty that night; she dressed a lot more mature now that she was head secretary. And even though she was only nineteen, she looked very grown up. We talked about her new job as head secretry but mostly we talked about Leah, and I couldn't stop staring at Joanie's long, beautiful legs.

"Myron, I don't know why I'm doing this. If I ever got caught I'd lose my job, probably get arrested, and I already got a fuckin' police record. They'd throw the damn key away. But, anything for Leah. That girl doesn't stop talking about you, and what the hell does 'bashert' mean?"

"Oh, it's Jewish superstition," I responded. "Some people think that little dogs can predict the futue."

"That's what Leah said," Joanie chuckled. "Dumbest shit I ever heard . . . and you guys laugh at Catholics for saying Confession! Hey, if those dogs are right and you and Leah get married, I want to be maid of honor; I've never been to a Jewish wedding."

"Why do you have a police record?" I asked. "What happened?"

"Nothing serious. Three years ago I was giving head to four old farts; they were paying twenty bucks each. Then one of their jealous wives pressed charges and I got booked for prostitution, but thankfully, I was only sixteen and didn't have to serve time, but its on the books. That's why I gotta' be careful and stay out of trouble."

Joanie took hold of my hand and led me to the file room, a depressing chamber crammed with black metal cabinets; her hand was shaking.

"Five minutes, no more, then we gotta' get out of here," and in the darkness of this eerie dungeon she kissed me on the forehead. Although I was focused on my mission, to investigate the tax return of J. Martin Berger, I had a sudden desire to grab Joanie; I wanted to feel her long legs wrapped around me. Too bad she was Leah's best friend; this gorgeous girl would have been a perfect "puppy" . . . right there, on the floor of the file room.

BERGER, J.Martin

I was right; J. Martin Berger was a client of the CPA firm, and his file had black letters on a white tab, which meant that he wasn't a new client. His tax return listed over $1 million income from his law firm, several rental properties, including a building in Miami Beach called the "1849 property." The James Manor was at 1849 James Avenue. That probably explained the connection between Berger and Streuling, the former landlord of the James Manor.

He also had investment income from a lounge in Overtown and $200,000 from "Sardera and Associates," the same amount that was reported on Mr. Streuling's tax return. However, under a schedule of miscellaneous income one very small item caught my eye: "$10 Director's Fee" from "GSRFF, Inc." It looked as if Berger received a nominal fee for serving as the director of the corporation that funneled huge income to Sardera and Associates. But, I was still in the dark on several points. What did "GSRFF" stand for? What did the corporation do? What kind of business?

"I'm scared," said Joanie. "I'm going to get a few beers from Bruce's liquor cabinet; I'll be in the waiting room to keep watch. Hurry up."

As soon as Joanie left the file room I immediately began making thermofax copies of three tax returns: J. Martin Berger, Henry Streuling, and Sardera and Associates. When I finished I folded the copies, put them in an envelope, and hid them under my shirt. I didn't want Joanie to know that I was taking them out of the office, but if I was ever going to provide information to the police I would need to prove my allegations, whatever they might be. However, I still couldn't figure out the whole picture. What were Berger and Streuling doing? How were they making so much money, and why did Streuling donate $100,000 to the youth fund at Temple Beth Sinai. Most important . . . there was one missing piece in this puzzle . . . what was GSRFF?

I carefully put all the tax files back in the cabinet and returned to the waiting room, which was being protected by the very nervous, well dressed watchguard.

"Joanie . . . thanks so much, I really owe you a favor." She smiled and looked down into my eyes.

"Leah told me that you're part Spanish." Joanie's speech was very garbled. She already finished three bottles of beer. "I never met a Jewish guy with Spanish blood. You know what they say about hot blooded Spaniards; great in bed. They know how to make señoritas happy. Ole! Ole!"

Once again, just like that bizarre experience with Mindy Marcus, the mere mention of my Spanish heritage inspired a girl to have a "catharsis"—at least this time I knew what the word meant, and what to expect. I tried to pull the beer bottle away from Joanie; she was drinking too much and telling me more than I really wanted to hear.

We hugged, a long hug; then I dumped the empty beer bottles into the trash. Leah was lucky to have such a good friend, but I felt so alone as I left the waiting room of Rosenblatt, Unger, and Polsky. It was almost 2 AM, but Lincoln Road was still alive with tourists; older people were holding hands and strolling along the promenade of their dreams. I joined the silent parade and tears came to my eyes when I passed the Carib theatre, the site of my first date with Leah. I was walking away from the girl who should have been my destiny, who should have been the mother of my children. It all could have been so different if Leah had gone out with me the next Saturday. I looked at the old people; they were really happy, but Leah and I would never grow old together; we would never hold hands and walk on Lincoln Road. My sadness turned to anger. Where was the fuckin' chess man back in the ninth grade? Why did he let this happen? When I got home my parents were sleeping, and for the second time in my life I drank several shot glasses of my father's best Scotch, and after I vomited I took a shower and went to sleep.

◆

The next morning I told David and Shelly about the tax returns and we discussed strategy. What else could we do in our expanding investigation of Mr. Streuling? How could we find out more about the "GSRFF" corporation? We checked the telephone book, white pages and yellow pages, but couldn't find a listing for any business with that name. We also called the Greater Miami Chamber of Commerce and the Better Business Bureau, but had no success.

"Its an abbreviation," I said. "Impossible to find it in any of the normal directories. 'G' probably stands for something like 'General' or 'Greater' . . . . Like Greater Miami . . . but the second letter would then be an 'M' . . . I'm stumped."

"How about 'Good' or 'Grand?' said Shelly. "Or 'Giant' or 'God or 'German?'"

"German!" I responded. "Hey! Maybe? Streuling is German."

"Did you make copies of the tax returns?" asked Shelly.

"No," I lied. I knew that it was illegal to steal copies of a tax return so I never told that to anyone, not even to David and Shelly.

"What about your uncle Herman?" asked David. "You told me he's got friends everywhere. Maybe he can find out?"

"No! I don't want my father to know anything about this; if we tell Herman it gets right back to my father."

"I have an idea," said David. "Lets have lunch with my Uncle Louie; he keeps his ear to the ground at the Nemo Hotel, and he's on the board of directors at his temple. Maybe he knows something about Streuling; that spook is definitely a big "macher' at Beth Sinai and so is Uncle Louie. Four seats on the Beema are named after him and Tanta Baila."

"I thought you had to be dead to have seats named after you," I replied.

"Hmm . . . yeah! So did I. Well, I think this makes more sense. Uncle Louie doesn't have to wait till the next life to use his seats."

"That's probably why he got to sit next to the rabbi during your cousin's Bar Mitzvah," I responded. "I wonder how many seats Streuling got for $100,000?"

"For that much money they'll probably name a building after him," said David, "maybe the whole temple, like Temple Beth Streuling."

♦

David, Shelly, and I met Uncle Louie and Tanta Baila for lunch at Essens Deli, home of the world's best matzoh ball soup. And we were joined by Louie's friend, Sam Mermlestein, the renowned maven and yenteh' *(gossip)* who knew everything and everyone . . . and if he didn't, he had a friend who did.

I told the whole story again, about Mr. Streuling, the tattoo on his arm, and his police record, and of course, everyone cringed when I got to the part about his testicles. Of course, I didn't bother to talk about Detective Bellazio's latest theory, that Streuling might really be a Nazi, pretending to be a Jew. I didn't want to scare the old people.

"Sam, shut up and listen," said Uncle Louie, "let me do the talking."

"A braireh hob ich?" *(Do I have a choice?)* responded Sam.

"Henry Streuling is wonderful with the kinderlech *(children),*" said Louie, "a regular pied piper. In all my life, never did I see such a kind and good man . . . a Jewish Santa Claus. The little ones, they love him. Everyone at the shul loves him! Such a good man."

"Louie, are you a 'meshugeneh?' *(a little bit crazy)* said Sam. "Are you listening to vat' Myron is saying? Don't be such a 'kunyehlemel' *(naïve)* . . . the man had his baitsim' chopped off by the Nazis; he's a faigeleh.' Don't give us vit' the Santa Claus. You know as vell' as I do . . . 'a chazer bleibt a chazer!'" *(A pig remains a pig!)*

Sam was calling Streuling a fag and a pig; Uncle Louie was calling him a Jewish Santa Claus, and I was starting to re-think my "pedophile" theory. Maybe I was wrong. If Streuling really was castrated by the Nazis why was he so interested in little children? And why Jewish children?

"So . . . just because he had his baitsim cut off, does that make him a bad person?" asked Uncle Louie. "I've been to many Bar Mitzvahs and parties at the shul; Henry Streuling is always up front leading the children in the 'hokie pokie' or the 'hopping bunny.' And, what a mitzvah' he did for Baila and her friends from Romania."

"What did he do for Tanta Baila?" David asked. "And, its not the hopping bunny . . . . It's the 'Bunny Hop.'"

"He helped Baila and her friends get thousands of dollars from the Nazis, from some type of special bank fund."

"Do you remember the name of the fund?" I asked.

"Like I should know?" Uncle Louie shrugged his shoulders. "Ask Tanta Baila . . . . get it straight from the horse's mouth."

Tanta Baila spoke very little English, but she could follow the gist of our conversation. She encouraged me to eat first, to enjoy the pastrami sandwich. She told Louie that she had letters and legal documents back at the hotel, about some type of Nazi recovery program, but first, I had to eat, especially my vegetables. If I was ever to meet a nice Jewish girl I needed a "little meat on my bones."

Tanta Baila gave me her motherly advice. "A lung un leber oyf der noz." *(Stop talking yourself into illness! Literally: Don't imagine a lung and a liver upon the nose).* Then she leaned over and cut the fat off my pastrami sandwich.

The three older people carried on a long conversation in Yiddish; they got into a heated argument. I could only pick up a word, here and there; they kept saying "meshugeneh" and "shmaltz." It seemed like their main concern was the excess fat on the pastrami; they weren't terribly concerned with my research about Mr. Streuling.

"Didn't you all get a little bit suspicious?" I asked. "Your Jewish Santa Claus doesn't speak a word of Yiddish? Isn't that kind of unusual? And he uses mayonnaise on corned beef."

"Not at all," said Uncle Louie. "Very few German Jews speak Yiddish, not like the Jews in eastern Europe. But mayonnaise on corned beef? 'vay is mir.'"

"The German Jews thought they vas' big shots," said Sam. "They only spoke German; they vas' too good to speak Yiddish. But look . . . vat' good did it do them? Ven' the Nazis came they vas' Jews, just like the Jews that only spoke Yiddish."

My mother's relatives were German Jews. I knew what Uncle Louie and Sam were talking about. At my cousin Phyllis' house they had Easter Egg hunts, and at Christmas they had a tree . . . and they sang "Come all Ye' Faithful" and "Silent Night." They didn't even muffle their mouth when they sang "Christ the Lord." My father sometimes told me that my grandfather Morris, my maternal grandfather, liked to boast and call himself a German, even though he lived most of his life in America. He died in 1937—I was named after him. I bet if he lived another few years he would have changed his opinion of the "Fatherland."

"Don't be so critical," said Uncle Louie. "Most German Jews were like that. Germans are very arrogant people . . . why should Jews from Germany be any different? That's what comes from too much assimilation."

When we got back to the Nemo Hotel Tanta Baila took out a metal strongbox where she had saved many important papers. She showed us a copy of a form letter that was sent from the Banco de Portugal in Lisbon to the "German Survivors Restitution Foundation of Florida." The letter was entirely in Portuguese, and even with my three years of Spanish, it was impossible for me to understand anything. But, I was able to read the name of the bank officer who signed the letter. His name was Vasco Milé Sardera. He was the Portuguese partner in Sardera and Associates.

"Myron . . . look! Look! Look!" exclaimed Shelly . . . . "German Survivors Restitition Foundation of Florida."

GSRFF

That's it . . . that's the phantom corporation."

We jumped in the air like nutty children . . . we were putting the pieces of the puzzle together. Then, at the suggestion of Uncle Louie, we brought the letter to the hotel bellhop, a Cuban teenager. Maybe with his knowledge of Spanish we could get it translated. Unfortunately, even though Portuguese is similar to Spanish the bellhop wasn't much help. Finding someone to read Portuguese in Miami Beach would be extremely difficult.

"Esperanto!" shouted David. He was so excited he could hardly speak. "Holy shit! Only one person in Miami Beach speaks Esperanto . . . and I bet he also speaks Portuguese."

"Spencer Teichman!" David, Shelly, and I all said the name in unison.

Several days later we returned to the Nemo with Spencer, the smartest kid at Beach High.

"Of course I read Portuguese," said Spencer. "Its one of the Romance languages, with many of the same root words as Spanish, French, Italian, and Romanian."

"Romanian!" exclaimed Uncle Louie. "What does Romanian have to do with Portuguese?"

"Both languages are derived from Latin," said Spencer. "I believe that the word 'Romance' is a reference to 'Roman' and so is "Romanian." Give me the letter; lets see what its all about."

Spencer wasn't quite as brilliant as I thought; he constantly referred to a pocket size Portuguese-English dictionary. It took him almost an hour to translate the letter. Finally, after we all finished a chopped liver sandwich (without shmaltz) on rye bread and a bowl of Tanta Baila's kreplach soup, Spencer was ready to discuss the letter.

"Vait one minute," said Sam. "I have to 'pish' . . . Oye! Vat a mystery! Don't start vitout' me . . . . sometimes it takes more than a minute."

"It seems as if there is lots of money in this Portuguese bank," said Spencer. "The letter doesn't say how it got there or where it came from, but its being set aside as restitution money for concentration camp survivors, but only if they file proper claims through authorized companies like the German Survivors Restitution Foundation."

Tanta Baila searched further in her metal strongbox and found a few more letters, all written in Portuguese, all signed by Vasco Milé Sardera. None of the letters mentioned Streuling. Damn! I was hoping that the letters would provide some type of trail back to that pervert. Spencer rolled up his sleeves and continued translating—and Tanta Baila served more kreplach soup—and Sam made several trips to the bathroom and he didn't stop saying "Oye! Vat' a mystery!"

"Well . . . this is kind of confusing," said Spencer, I'm not sure if these letters are talking about money or gold. But, it seems as if Germany froze many bank accounts just before the war, probably a lot of it was Jewish money . . . that's just my guess, and they shifted everything to the national bank of Switzerland. Then in 1945, during the final days of the war, hundreds of millions of dollars were transferred from Switzerland to Lisbon, Portugal . . . probably to the Banco de Portugal."

"How much of a claim did you file?" Spencer spoke slowly to Tanta Baila, in Romanian.

Tanta Baila only spoke Yiddish, like all other Romanian Jews, but she lived in Romania her entire life. If necessary she could understand a little Romanian.

"Henry Streuling helped me file a claim for $20,000," said Tanta Baila (in Romanian) "lots of paperwork . . . but all I ever saw, after all the paperwork, was $2,000. And he also helped a few of my friends with their claims. Henry is such a good man, so patient and so clean Every day he shines his shoes . . . they look like mirrors. You don't see men shining their shoes in America, not like the old country. And he is so good with the 'kinderlech,' they all love him."

"Spencer," I interrupted. "Ask her whether her $2,000 check came from "GSRFF" or from Streuling's partnership. Who signed the check?" It really disturbed me that Tanta Baila called him a "good man." The guy stole $18,000 from her but she thought he was some type of saint . . . and Uncle Louie regarded him as a Jewish Santa Claus. I guess if you're good with little children everyone thinks you are a wonderful person. Tanta Baila sounded like my mother . . . impressed with Mr. Streuling just because he was super clean.

Tanta Baila wasn't sure about the source of the $2,000, so she looked in her checkbook, where she made a careful record of every deposit. She found a notation for the $2,000 deposit, but her records were not as good as I had hoped. They didn't show whether the money came from "GSRFF" or from Streuling's partnership—still no evidence that Streuling was involved in any type of scam.

"Only $2,000. Holy shit! They took a huge cut," said David. "That doesn't sound kosher."

"Yeah," exclaimed Shelly. "Sounds like Tanta Baila's been robbed, big time, and the guy in Portugal . . . seems like he's in on it too."

"I think he's more than just 'in on it,'" I noted. "I think he's the brains of the operation; that's where all the money comes from."

I was now ready for the next step in my investigation . . . fantasy had turned to reality. I began to organize all the documentation. I borrowed the Banco de Portugal letters and made thermofax copies at a local office supply store. Tanta Baila then found several letters from GSRFF, Inc. they were all signed by J. Martin Berger, the president of the corporation. I copied them also. But there were no letters or paperwork from Sardera and Associates, Streuling's partnership and nothing with Streuling's signature.

Two-thirds of the triangle was obvious

(1) Vasco Milé Sardera and the Banco De Portugal—that was the source of the money;
(2) The German Survivors Restitution Foundation of Florida "GSRFF"—that was the authorized agency that processed the restitution claims.

But I had nothing to prove what part Streuling played in Tanta Baila's claim, other than her personal statements. However, several days later Uncle Louie helped complete the triangle. He went to the bank and obtained a micro-film copy of the $2,000 check that she deposited in her account.

(3) The check to Tanta Baila was written by "Sardera and Associates" and was signed by Henry Streuling.

The triangle was complete!

One week later I drove back to the Nemo to return the various letters to Uncle Louie and Tanta Baila; of course, I kept copies of everything. I was greeted by Sam Mermlestein.

"Hey, boitshick, have I got some news for you. You think that Sam Mermlestein is just gonna' sit on his old 'tuchas' and let these ganefs' get avay' vit' murder. Here, take a look."

Sam provided me a list of seven names, elderly Jewish residents of the Nemo hotel, all members of Temple Beth Sinai, all Auschwitz survivors . . . . and next to each name was their phone number, their Auchwitz tattoo number, the amount of the restitution claim and the amount of the final settlement. In each case, the settlement check from Sardera and Associates was exactly ten percent of the original claim. Sam also provided thermofax copies of the seven checks, all signed by Henry Streuling.

As I examined the list Sam stood next to me, looking over my shoulder, grinning from ear to ear.

"Not such a 'dumkop' . . . huh? If I said it once, I said it a thousand times . . . 'a chaser bleibt a chaser!'" *(A pig remains a pig!)*

"Jesus Christ! This list is great," I exclaimed. "Where did you get it?"

"Vell' I'll give you a clue. It vasn't from Jesus Christ." And his grin got even bigger.

My file was growing . . . and it also included copies of three tax returns: Henry Streuling, J. Martin Berger, and the Sardera partnership. I was becoming a real detective, like Sergeant Friday, the TV cop from Dragnet.

But, I had guilt feelings when I thought about my vow of confidentiality to Seymour Rosenblatt. "Nothing shall ever leave this office" and I wasn't quite sure about my next step. Should I take all this evidence to Detective Bellazio? That's probably what I should have done, but Bellazio didn't seem too interested in dealing with this matter any longer. He was definitely annoyed with me. I even thought about calling the FBI or maybe President Eisenhower, and the more I anguished over my decision the more frightened I became. I was very scared about having to testify in court against a famous attorney with Mafia connections and a charismatic pervert with shiny shoes who probably didn't have testicles. Finally, I decided that the best way to deal with this nightmare was to hide my well documented "German Restitution" file at home, on the top shelf of my cedar lined closet . . . behind books that no one ever read.

CHAPTER 51

MUSIC OF THE DEVIL

The aroma of cedar is very invigorating, very uplifting . . . but its only a temporary high. You can't hide in a tiny cedar lined closet forever; it burns your eyes. I stood on a chair, reaching the top shelf of my closet; I found a secret place to hide the Berger-Streuling-Restitution file . . . behind a stack of Passover Hagadahs—paper back religious books that we never used. Tears streamed from my bloodshot eyes. I didn't know which way to turn. The right thing to do was to go to the police with all my evidence . . . but I was scared; I was in over my head . . . way over my head. I just wanted to walk away from this mess . . . like I walked away from so many other bad situations . . . . I quit the accordion, I quit the football team, and I even quit "Rebels," three opportunities to be popular. But, none of those situations were dangerous. None were scary like the Berger/Streuling discovery. This was a nightmare. The only solution was to walk away again . . . What else could I do?.

"My-u-rin, come to the phone," shouted my mother, stretching my name to three syllables. "Its for you." I wiped my burning eyes and left the protective shelter of my cedar lined closet.

It was Willie Jefferson, the Negro shoe delivery boy. After the trial I intended to call Willie, but once I discovered that he was Mr. Streuling's "little buddy" I decided to avoid problems.

"Yo, Man! . . . You wanna' hear what real music sounds like?" said Willie, "not that Pat Boone crap . . . You gotta' hear Little

438

Richard; he wails from the soul. I got tickets to the rock and roll concert at Dinner Key."

The Miami Herald had a feature article about the upcoming concert, which would be held at Dinner Key Auditorium, several miles south of downtown Miami. Tickets were being sold to Negroes and whites, it was going to be the first major integrated event in Miami and several white supremacy groups were protesting, even a few local churches were opposed to the concert. But the churches said that they were not protesting for racial reasons; they thought that Negro music was the music of the devil.

"This new music is inspired by the devil," said the pastor of a large Miami church. "It elicits promiscuity and concupiscent desires from young people, who have all they can do to control their emerging sexuality."

The mayor of Miami promised to provide police support, to ensure that the event would be peaceful.

"Say, Willie . . . you still work on Lincoln Road. Why don't you come up to my house on Friday after work; sleep over and I'll drive to the concert on Saturday. Bring your brother too . . . we got plenty of room."

"OK, but it won't be easy," said Willie. "Mack ain't got no work permit."

"I live in Surfside, not Miami Beach," I responded. "We don't have the same disgusting law. By the way, how did you get tickets to this concert? I bet they're expensive.

"Oh, they be a present from a nice old German dude at the Nemo Hotel. I make sure his shoes be looking good. Man, this guy really loves his shoes."

Even though I already knew that Willie took care of Mr. Streuling's shoes I felt uncomfortable using tickets that were a present from the pervert. Maybe Willie was Steuling's latest boyfriend. However, Miami Beach is a small island; I couldn't walk around scared of everyone who knew the Santa Claus of Temple Beth Sinai . . . I decided to ignore this coincidence; I didn't ask Willie any questions about Streuling.

♦

"Myron! What kind of lunatic are you?" exclaimed my mother, "What will the neighbors think? Having two colored boys sleep here! Do I need this?'"

"Rose! How can you talk like that?" My father got up from the living room couch and came to the rescue. "I don't want Myron growing up to be a bigot . . . he can invite any friend he wants to sleep here."

"But Sol . . . the neighbors. Those are my friends. You've got your relatives; all I have are my friends."

My mother made an interesting point; my father had no friends, other than his relatives, but he had a lot of relatives, so he didn't need to go looking up and down the block for approval. He didn't care about the gossip and petty prejudices of neighbors on Carlyle Avenue. I guess when you don't care about the opinion of neighbors you can make decisions just the way you see things. I thought only little kids changed their behavior because of peer pressure . . . . I guess I was wrong.

"OK mister Abraham Lincoln, you want to be the new emancipator, go ahead . . . but don't expect me to feed them." My mother started to cry. "Some day, I hope you have children . . . just like yourself. That is my wish for you." That was my mother's ultimate curse.

"Mom, I'm not trying to free the slaves; I'm just inviting a boy and his brother over. We're going together to a concert to hear the new colored music."

"Colored music! Regular music isn't good enough for you? Whats wrong with Eddie Fisher, a nice Jewish boy . . . or Pat Boone? Or the McGuire Sisters? Such adorable shiksahs."

My mother wiped her eyes, took a deep breath, and continued in a more serious voice. "Myron . . . I am not opposed to you having a colored boy friend. I don't want you to be a bigot . . . we are all minorities, Jews and Negroes, but one thing leads to another. Next thing you know you'll be dating one of them . . . maybe wind up marrying one. Do you think you'll be happy married to a colored girl? Where would you live? In a white neighborhod? In a colored neighborhood? And what about your children . . . what will they be, white or colored? What kind of life are they going to have? Are you being fair to them?"

"Mom . . . I just want to go to a concert; I don't want to marry a colored girl."

440

I called Colonel Klein and told him about the concert; that I was inviting Willie and his brother to stay at my house. I asked for suggestions; what should we have for dinner . . . I really only knew stereotypes about colored people, that they liked fried chicken and watermelon. But stereotypes are just exaggerations; the Colonel had five Negro children living in his house. He would know.

"They eat the same food as everyone else," said the Colonel, and he laughed . . . "whatever you eat is OK with them. But, stay away from fried chicken and watermelon . . . they will probably regard that as an insult."

"Myron, why don't you and your friends come over here for breakfast Saturday morning; I'd love to hear more about this concert. This new music will do more to bring the races together than any court case or legislation. Social change always comes from the people . . . and the people are speaking."

Willie and his brother Mack joined my father and me for dinner. My mother served fried chicken, but she ate standing up.

"Mrs. Lindell, why don't you sit down?" said Willie.

"Uh . . . someone has to serve the food."

My father got in a long discussion with Willie about baseball; they really hit it off well. They were both Giants fans and loved Willie Mays. Willie didn't know much about the history of the Giants and enjoyed hearing my father's stories about the old days, Christy Mathewson, Rube Marquad, and Roger Bresnahan, Giant legends from another era. And my father also talked a lot about the old Negro league, Satchell Paige and Josh Gibson. Willie was fascinated; he knew very little about the history of Negroes in baseball, not even about Jackie Robinson.

"I'se glad you be feeling better Mr. Lindell," said Willie, "and I'se really glad I got to meet you . . . us Giant fans are soul brothers, don't matter none if we be white or colored."

"Willie . . . I always take a walk after dinner," said my father. "Come join me . . . you'll like hearing about Mugsy McGraw, the tough old Giants manager."

Mack, the older brother, didn't talk too much and when he did it was difficult to understand him . . . his speech was very garbled. He went to the living room, where my mother was watching TV, and they both laughed together, watching the Honeymooners. Mack doubled over and howled when Ralph

Kramden feigned a punch to his wife . . . "One of these days, Alice . . . Pow! I'm gonna' send you to the moon."

"Lookie here, missa' Lindell, this be a knuckle sandwich." Mack smiled and made a big fist.

The next morning I went to the Colonel's house for breakfast, along with Willie and Mack. We sat at two long picnic style tables on the back porch . . . eleven of us. Katarina didn't walk around and serve, not like my mother. It was buffet style; everyone helped themselves to a variety of fruit, cheese, eggs, bacon, bagels, and Danish pastries.

"Don't none of you Jewish people ever thank the Lord before you eat?" asked Willie. "In my house my grandma always says grace first . . . she slap my hands if I be eating without saying blessings."

"Different people show their respect for God in different ways," said the Colonel. "Orthodox Jews say prayers before meals . . . a whole series of prayers. But we are not very religious; neither is Myron's family."

"Don't seem right to me," said Willie. "If you don't show no respect to God, you be heading for trouble."

It was a beautiful day so we decided to spend a few hours at the Surfside beach . . . It was only one block from the Colonel's house. We borrowed a few of his bathing suits and walked to the ocean . . . . the Colonel, me, Katarina, one oriental boy, and seven Negroes.

That turned out to be a big mistake . . . five minutes after we spread our blankets and set beach umbrellas in the sand two Surfside police cars drove up to the beach. Riding in one car was the arresting officer; in the other was his backup. We were told that we were in violation of some type of local ordinance . . . "inciting a riot."

"Inciting a riot!" The Colonel exclaimed . . . "All we've done, so far, is spread blankets and stick goddamn umbrellas in the sand . . . we haven't even gone in the water yet."

"I'm sorry sir," said a police officer who wasn't much older than me. "But we want to cut off problems before they happen. We don't want a riot here in Surfside. I don't mean to sound like a racist, but you know as well as I do . . . many people around here are very prejudiced. Why don't you just take your colored boys to Virginia Beach; it's a very nice beach especially for Negroes . . . and it's the same ocean."

"I don't want to go to Virginia Beach, that's miles from here. We live in Surfside, we pay taxes here; this is our beach. We aren't leaving."

"Hilly, it isn't worth it," said Katarina. "Lets go home . . . you can lose your job if you get involved in a mess like this. You have six children to feed now; you can't be such a free spirit anymore."

"So, you're telling me that once you take on 'family responsibility' you have to accept ignorance and intolerance, that I have to be spineless and put up with this bullshit?"

Katarina didn't answer . . . . It was only a rhetorical question; the Colonel knew what he had to do.

"OK . . . OK . . . Willie, do you know how to play Canasta? Lets go home . . . we'll teach you and Mack a fun game." And under his breath he mumbled: "Narrow minded bigots!"

"Don't you go worrying none, Mr. Klein," said Willie. "This all gonna' change soon . . . just you watch."

The Steinbergs joined us that night for the concert; this was exciting. I had heard records by Fats Domino, Little Richard, Frankie Lymon, and Chuck Berry; they were great. But, I had never seen them in person. Our parents hated colored music, and the juke boxes in Miami Beach only played white music, but one of the Negro radio stations played colored music and the kids loved it. Didn't make much difference to us whether the singer was colored or white . . . "Long Tall Sally" was super great; so was "Johnny B. Goode." Talking about juke boxes; I once saw one at a luncheonette in Miami that had a hand written little sign scotch taped on the inside of the glass:

"We only play music by white performers . . . if you love Niggers, take one home to lunch."

I was going to tell Willie about that horrible sign, then I reconsidered. It would be stupid to tell him; I'm sure he knew about racial discrimination a lot more than I did. He knew, first hand . . . that he couldn't ride the elevators at Burdines or Sears, that he had to stand back and let white people pass on Flagler Street. I remember how, at fourteen, he never looked me in the eyes when we talked. Now, two and a half years later, we were becoming friends and he still looked at my feet when we talked. A whole generation of Negroes were growing up with a terrible inferiority complex. They were treated like second class citizens, and until white people gave them respect as equals they never really would be equals . . . . no matter what laws were passed. As Colonel Klein had always said, change would have to come from society . . . government is only a reflection of social values; you cannot legislate kindness.

Normally, when I went anywhere wearing jeans I wore white sneakers, usually Keds. But, I noticed that Willie and Mack always wore black high tops, the type that had a white circle on the ankle. I had a pair also; I usually wore them for Phys. Ed. or when I went to the park. However, for this very special concert I decided that I would dress like Willie and Mack; I wore my Charles Taylor black Converse shoes.

Across the street from Dinner Key Auditorium, the largest arena in Miami, hundreds of white people stood and sang church songs and little children, dressed in white Sunday school outfits, held posters:

"Little Richard is the Anti-Christ"
"Negro music is not God's music."

Fortunately, it was a peaceful protest. But that's probably because there were at least thirty armed policemen separating the teenagers from the church people. And there were newspaper reporters and TV cameramen everywhere. But, I think they were disappointed; a good riot would have made a much better story for the 11 PM news. The funny thing is . . . all the teenagers were on the same side of the street, white kids together with colored kids. I thought of my father and Willie, they bonded because of their mutual love of the New York Giants. And, that night, at Dinner Key auditorium, the white kids felt the same type of closeness to the Negro teenagers because of our mutual love of Little Richard, Frankie Lymon, and Chuck Berry. It was colored music, but it wasn't only "their" music . . . it was "our" music too. It was the music that separated my generation from my parents. It was the music of emancipation and it was the music that united all teenagers, regardless of race . . . except for the geeks who liked Pat Boone and the McGuire Sisters. They would probably grow up to be Republicans.

We had great seats, tenth row center. and all around us were thousands of screaming teenagers . . . . white kids, colored kids, sitting together, not like in the Orange Bowl, which had a separate section for Negroes. Actually, we weren't "sitting" . . . we were standing for the entire concert. How can you sit when Chuck Berry goes nuts on stage? "Johnny B. Goode" makes you jump to your feet and try to copy that impossible dance. I couldn't do it . . . they never covered that step at Arthur Murrays. But Willie could . . . so could Mack, so could all the colored kids.

After Chuck Berry the next performer was Frankie Lymon and the Teenagers . . . he was only 14, three years younger than me, and wow, what a great voice. The group opened with "Why Do Fools Fall in Love," and Frankie hit a high note that made all the girls scream, even the Jewish girls from Miami Beach. Then he took off his shirt and ran to the front of the stage; he grabbed the hand of a white girl in the audience. That was probably the first time in Miami that a colored entertainer ever danced on stage with a white girl. I was positive that Frankie's sexual dancing would lead to a riot, that white kids would rush on stage to "rescue" the girl.

The police also anticipated problems; and when Frankie jumped in the air and landed in a split they reached for their pistols and ran to the front of the auditorium. Fortunately, there was no riot; no one ran on stage. In fact many kids started dancing along with Frankie.

"Ooooh shit, I gotta' teach you how to boogie." Willie laughed when he saw me dancing in the aisle with a colored girl. "Man, this is rock-n-roll; not the Rhumba."

Then came Little Richard and "Long Tall Sally" . . . a wild and crazy song about a tall skinny flooziee who was having fun in the alley with Uncle John . . . who had been cheating on Aunt Mary. That was the song that brought white and colored kids together. "Listen to the people," said the Colonel, "and you'll see the future." And the people were speaking . . . my generation was "finally" speaking . . . not with words, but with actions that were more genuine than words. Hundreds of Negro and white teenagers were dancing with each other in the aisles.

"Again . . . again." Everybody shouted . . . "Long Tall Sally!" Little Richard flashed a huge smile . . . he banged on the piano; he gyrated, and he sang the music of the devil.

We're gonna have some fun tonight,
Gonna have some fun tonight.
We're gonna have some fun tonight,
Everything will be alright.

CHAPTER 52

A TIGRESS TO THE RESCUE

"Hello boitshick, its me . . . Sam Mermlestein. So tell me, vat's happening vit' Streuling and Berger?" Sam called me at home on a Saturday morning; two weeks had passed since he gave me the list of names, the seven people from the Nemo hotel who were swindled by Berger and Streuling. Sam's list was safely filed with the other Berger/Streuling papers, hidden on the top shelf of my closet . . . . they were starting to smell from cedar.

"I did just like you," said Sam. "I made copies of letters and checks from all seven people. Like I told you before, every check was signed by Mister Santa Claus . . . . Herr Streuling. | "

"Listen Sam . . . I have a lot of evidence, but I don't know. I don't think the police are going to believe a kid . . . and Berger is really a big time lawyer. I don't think we can pull this off."

"Myron, I smell cold feet. You remind me of a lot of these alta kakkers vit' white hair, who sit back on their rockers and just 'k'vetch' about everything. All you hear is 'vay is mir' and 'oye gevald' . . . but they never get off their fat tuchas. If you let this die those ganefs vill' keep on svindling' people. You've got the papers to nail the bastards."

"OK . . . . Let me think about it. I'll get back to you." . . . but the only thought I had was to burn the files! One day later Sam called again.

"That's enough time to think. Now you get your tuchas and all your papers together and come here . . . meet me at 10:30

at the lobby of the Nemo. I have an important person I vant' you should meet . . . and Louie's nephews, bring them vit' you; I vant' the three Musketeers together. Myron, you know those shirts you kids vear,' the vuns' vit' da' little alligators? You better vear' a yellow vun'."

Sam was very perceptive . . . he knew I was scared. This was more than I wanted to deal with, certainly not by myself. I called Spencer. I needed his help with translations, just in case there were more Portuguese letters.

"No way Jose!" said Spencer. "I didn't mind investigating Streuling, the psycho, but not Berger. I'm trying to get a scholarship to M.I.T. and I don't need to look for trouble. Berger can really mess up my life. I've seen this guy's picture in the paper. He's the lawyer for Don Carbonelli, the head of the Miami Mafia."

The Steinberg's weren't too enthused about joining me either, but Sam was best friends with their Uncle Louie, so they were obligated to come to this clandestine meeting. I packed all my Berger/Streuling papers in the trunk of my car, all except the three tax returns. Those stayed on the top shelf of my cedar lined closet.

We made the long drive to South Beach; we were all very nervous. Who was the important person that Sam wanted us to meet. Maybe it was J. Edgar Hoover, the Director of the FBI, maybe even Elliot Ness . . . . the real Elliot Ness, not the actor from the "Untouchables."

The Nemo had a very large lobby; it was easy to find a corner where we could sit and have a private conversation, especially at 10:30 on a Saturday morning when just about everyone was at shul. We were greeted at the front door of the hotel by Sam and a well dressed woman in her mid-twenties. They were joined by my old friend, Flo Loerber, who I hadn't seen in over six months.

"Hi Myron. So nice to see you again," said Flo. "I'm working part time with the B'nai B'rith." Flo shook hands with me, very proper, very businesslike. Our friendship sure had deteriorated. "This is Eileen Jacobs; she's an attorney with the ADL, the Anti Defamation League, that's part of B'nai B'rith."

"My father belongs to B'nai B'rith," I responded, "but I never heard of the ADL."

"It's a pleasure to meet you Myron," said the young attorney. "Flo's told me a lot about you and please call me Eileen. Actually,

I don't work for B'nai B'rith or ADL; I work for a law firm that's been engaged by ADL to do some investigative research." Eileen was wearing a dark skirt and a matching jacket, a woman's business suit, and her short blonde hair was parted like a man. She stood and shook my hand; she had a very strong handshake. Her business card read: "Greenberg, Goldberg, Rosenberg & Co, Attorneys at Law" . . . lots of Bergs.

"I'm sure you realize I want to talk to you about J. Martin Berger and Henry Streuling. I also want you to know, up front, Sam is my grandfather, and he has given us all the details and a lot of paperwork; I've also seen copies of your reports on file with the Miami Beach Police. It seems you've been a busy young man—checking out some of the same people and the same Portuguese bank that we've been investigating." Eileen pointed to a large black briefcase that was attached to Flo's wrist by a metal handcuff. I remembered wearing handcuffs the day when I had the auto accident and went to jail; they hurt.

"That's only a small portion of our documentation," said Eileen. "We have a dozen more boxes back at the office. You and Sam uncovered seven or eight restitution claims; we found at least fifty more, all initiated by Henry Streuling . . . all members of Temple Beth Sinai."

I glared at Sam; I was upset that he called an attorney, even if it was his granddaughter. Now, there was no way to avoid going to the police. Sam shrugged his shoulders and made a funny twist of his face. His body language was clear . . . he did what he had to do. He had seen too many older Jewish people who just complained, and did nothing . . . . especially in the "Old Country." He didn't want the Berger/Streuling file to die on a bookshelf in my closet.

"Boitschik . . . My little 'Eilie' is a 'Shana Maideleh,' a blind man can see that . . . vat' a tuchas!' But Oye . . . she is one smart cookie' . . . . Cornell . . . Chicago law school. Don't you vorry' none . . . she vil' nail deze' gonifs'. Just you vatch!"

"Shhh!" Eileen sat down and put her finger over her lip, a gesture for her grandfather to stop talking . . . it was her turn. I listened intently to what she was about to say, but not until I got a quick peek at her "tuchas." Sam was right!

"Myron, before we talk about these two men, I want to tell you a little something about B'nai B'rith." She then turned to her grandfather. "Zaide' . . . you'll appeciate this; its about

Romania." Eileen was intense as she discussed the history of B'nai B'rith.

"In 1870 there was a wave of violence against Jews in Romania. A man named Benjamin Peixotto, a former B'nai B'rith president, met with President Grant, in Washington, and told him of this problem. Grant appointed Peixotto to be an honorary US counsul to Romania, where he served for five years without a salary. That set the stage for decades of advocacy by B'nai B'rith for Jews around the world, and for Jewish causes."

"Peixotto! Vat' kind of Jewish name is that?" asked Sam. "You sure he vasn't Italian?" Eileen nodded to her grandfather, but the stern young woman did not smile; she was all business. I listened intently to her story about the B'nai B'rith . . . I also tried to decide who had a better looking tush, Eileen or Joanie. Of course, Joanie was sexy on both sides; Eileen tried to look like a man on the front side.

"In 1913 a B'nai B'rith member named Leo Frank was framed for murder in Georgia." Eileen grimaced, as she began telling about the origin of the ADL. "Frank was later lynched by an angry mob. After that horrible incident the Anti-Defamation League was formed. The primary mission of the ADL was to battle bigotry in the US, all kinds of bigotry, not only anti-Semitism."

Shelly interrupted, "I wouldn't exactly call the phony operation of Berger and Streuling 'bigotry.' Yeah . . . of course, I understand the purpose of the ADL . . . but isn't this more of a police matter, or maybe the FBI?"

Eileen paused and looked at Shelly; then she looked at me. At first she said nothing; she just shook her head, tightened her lip, and made an obvious look of disgust. "Unfortunately, speaking as an attorney, I can see two sides to this scam; taking a 90% commission is certainly exorbitant and unconscionable, but it isn't illegal. There are no laws setting definitive limits in this area. We're walking on untested waters! What is the proper fee for assisting a concentration camp survivor in the filing and processing of a restitution claim? Who knows? Its never been done before. The ADL is looking at a much bigger issue, much bigger than getting a conviction against two very horrible men. Let me give you a broader perspective to help open your eyes to the real problem."

Flo took the handcuff off her wrist, opened the briefcase and removed two files. I was sitting across the table but because of my experience working in the file room with Joanie, I could instantly read the upside down titles of the two files. One said "J. Martin Berger," the other said "German Gold." I knew all about the German gold from the Portuguese letter that Spencer Teichman translated.

"She's a bright young lady, even though I have to wash her mouth with soap once in a while." Eileen looked at Flo and touched her shoulder. "Flo's going to make a fine lawyer one day." Flo smiled, but she looked embarrassed.

"Myron . . . here's the big picture.," said Eileen. "We're talking about something very new, survivor restitution programs. And this Banco de Portugal that you discovered is one of the participating banks, but there are others, especially in Argentina and Switzerland. There is an obvious need for Federal legislation to guide and assist in the restitution process . . . . to regulate those who provide help, and to place limits on fees. The ADL is testifying before Congress in a few weeks. We will be asking the government to take more of a proactive role in this process, and hopefully, to provide federal funding for audits and enforcement."

Eileen was worried that a police investigation could generate unfavorable publicity in the newspapers and on TV. Berger was a community leader and a prominent Jewish philanthropist. A front-page story might taint the integrity of the restitution process; it could alienate many members of Congress. Certainly, it would not help the ADL in Washington.

"Are you saying that we should just forget about this whole thing?" I asked. But, as I asked this question I thought about my own apprehension . . . isn't that exactly what I wanted to do? I was hiding all the files and tax returns in my closet.

"No Myron . . . . I'm not saying that we should back off," responded Eileen. "What I'm saying is that the ADL has to resolve this matter behind the scenes, without going to the newspapers. We want to stop Berger and Streuling . . . and believe me, we will stop them. But, these two con men are just the tip of the iceberg. Hundreds of millions of dollars from German bank accounts were transferred to Switzerland, Portugal, and Argentina. Those accounts are now being investigated and we're doing our best to make sure that this money is properly distributed to survivors or their families. People like Berger and Streuling are a cancer, they must be stopped . . . but without ugly publicity." I was very impressed with Eileen; she was a brilliant woman.

"That's great!" I said. "I'm really glad the ADL is doing this. I hate to sound like a chicken, but I know this is way over my head. This all started out as an adventure, investigating a weird man. We were just having fun at the library. Then, little by little, the pieces of a puzzle kept falling in my lap; I wasn't on a mission to stop him. Don't get me wrong, I'm glad I found all this information . . . but there isn't a whole lot I can do. The police would never believe a kid."

"You're definitely right," said Eileen. "But don't get down on yourself; there's no crime in being chicken. Its smart to be scared. Look at little dogs; they bark at alligators. Those dogs would be a lot better off if they were 'chicken.'"

"I'm curious," I said. "You've done a lot of your own research. Your file is ten times bigger than mine." I looked at Flo's briefcase and smiled. "How did a sleazy pervert like Streuling get to be friends with a big time attorney like J. Martin Berger?"

"Berger is the owner of your old apartment building, the James Manor . . . and Streuling managed the building. But, you should have figured that out, you looked at their tax returns."

"How did you know that? I never told that to anyone?" Oops . . . I did tell someone. I told the Steinbergs every detail about the tax returns, including the '1849 property,' and they probably told their Uncle Louie . . . who probably told Sam Mermlestein . . . . who definitely told Eileen Jacobs. However, I never told the Steinbergs that I made copies of the tax returns.

"Hey boitshick' do you think my granddaughter is a dumkop?'" said Sam.

"Myron, you're a very good detective," said Eileen, "and I'm willing to bet that after you looked at the tax returns you made copies. And, that's the purpose of our meeting today. Everything else you found we already know; we have hundreds of pages of documentation. We know every detail of Streuling's sordid youth in Hamburg and his criminal record here in Florida, but we don't have copies of tax returns; the ADL really could use those documents to tie this all together . . . to establish a trail connecting Berger, Streuling, and the Sardera company. The sad thing about this whole situation is that Streuling and Berger did not break any laws. The only one who can go to jail is you. I'm sure you know; its against the law to steal copies of tax returns from the office of a CPA."

"But . . . but . . . . I wasn't stealing the copies," I responded. "I wanted evidence to give to Detective Bellazio. You're an attorney; can't you just get copies directly from the IRS?"

Eileen changed her tone of voice; she stopped talking like a historian and became a very stern attorney; I was facing a serious dilemma. From a moral-ethical perspective, I wanted to help the ADL and give them copies of the tax returns . . . but I didn't want to violate my promise of "confidentiality" to Seymour Rosenblatt. However, a much bigger problem was the legal dilemma. If I didn't turn the tax returns over to ADL I could get in serious trouble with the police, but if I gave the tax returns directly to the police I could get in even bigger trouble. I sure got myself into a horrible mess.

"I'll give you the social security numbers," I stated. My voice was shaking. "You'll need those numbers to request the tax returns . . . . or maybe you can go to the CPA firm and just ask Seymour Rosenblatt? He's big in Jewish charities. I'm sure he'll help."

"Forget the IRS," replied Eileen. "Tax returns are 'privileged information,' damn near impossible to get them released unless it involves national security, and don't count on your old boss. He's buddy-buddy with Berger. They're partners in a sleazy strip joint in Overtown called 'Showtime.'"

"Showtime!" I laughed. "Boy, can I tell you stories about 'showtime.' Yeah, I guess you're right. You're not going to get any help from Seymour. He and Berger were fraternity brothers in college, class of 1930. Hey, is one of the partners in 'Showtime' an accounting professor from the University of Florida, a guy named Dr. Zuckerman."

"You're a real Sherlock Holmes," said Eileen. "I can't believe you found out about Zuckerman and the TEP connection. Most of our information is very confidential, so I'm not at liberty to disclose too much to you, at least not until after the Congressional Hearings. But, I can tell you about 'Showtime,' that's public information. Zuckerman is a partner, and so is Don Carbonelli and a few Mafia gangsters. "I guess Rosenblatt, Berger, and Zuckerman have a few Italian friends."

Eileen looked at me and smiled, the first break in her stern façade; she knew how scared I was and she was trying to put me at ease. She really was pretty when she smiled; I wondered why she wore her hair parted like a man, it made her look matronly, like most of the female teachers at Beach High.

"Hey . . . . Smartie pants . . . . Va't about me?" said Sam. "Vat' vas' I . . . chopped liver?"

"Yes Zadie . . . . You were also a big help." Eileen hugged her grandfather.

And while Eileen and Sam were hugging Flo removed a hand written letter from the "J. Martin Berger" file. The letter was on three-hole notebook paper, the same type paper we used in school, and it was signed by Leah Sonnino. How was that possible? I felt knots in my stomach. Why was there a letter from Leah in that file? I didn't know what to say; I certaintly didn't want to get Leah in trouble and I didn't want Joanie to lose her job or go to jail. Despite my immediate impulse to ask questions about Leah I switched topics and started talking about the bank officer from Portugal.

"What can you do about Sardera, the guy in Portugal? It sure looks like he's the leader of this whole operation."

"Not much, we aren't an enforcement agency," said Eileen. "And not much we can do to help the people at Sam's temple recover their money, but the legislation that we're recommending to Congress will mandate closer scrutiny over foreign banks involved in the restitution process. We're hoping to prevent this type of problem in the future."

"Oh, before I forget." I interrupted. "I've got a question that's driving me crazy. Why did Streuling give so much money to a synagogue youth fund?"

"It got him a foot in the door," responded Eileen. "Elderly Jewish people love and trust a man who is good with children; its part of the culture. Children are the hope and future of the Jewish people. Streuling's donation paid for Negro rock and roll bands to perform at synagogue parties every Friday night; that attracted many teenagers to attend religious services."

"Holy shit!" said David. "Shelly and I went to a few of those parties. They were great; loaded with girls."

"Streuling became a leader at the synagogue," said Eileen. "He was a member of the Board of Directors; even the rabbi embraced him. Every move that Streuling made was part of a carefully orchestrated business plan; he even learned how to read a few Hebrew prayers. Don't forget, many of the congregants at

Beth Sinai are Romanian survivors of concentration camps and it was easy for Streuling to spot potential customers; they had numbers branded on their arms. He had a ready made shopping list at the temple."

"But, Streuling isn't Jewish. Don't you have to be Jewish to be a member of a synagogue?"

"Technically, yes!" replied Eileen." But when you join a synagogue, as long as your check doesn't bounce you don't have to answer the four questions, and you sure don't have to show proof of your briss."

"I see! This is starting to make sense," I responded. "I bet the old women also loved him because he's super clean. If they're anything like my mother, they probably walk around all day long saying, 'cleanliness is godliness.' And, talking about 'foot in the door'. Streuling is a nut about shiny shoes."

"So am I." Eileen laughed and pointed to her shiny black leather shoes. "I spend half my salary on shoes; over one hundred pairs. And it doesn't hurt that Streuling is well mannered; he knows how to charm the old ladies."

"One hundred pairs!" I exclaimed. "Do you have any fruit covered platform shoes?" I was only kidding about the cork shoes from Pix; No way that this brilliant young attorney would buy those dumb shoes.

"Certainly! The whole collection," replied Eileen. "Apples, cherries, coconuts, all of them . . . and yes, before you ask, I met with Hershel Glickman, and I talked to him about you. Unfortunately, I'm not allowed to tell you details of that conversation except for his Carmen Miranda dream . . . . which you already know." Eileen chuckled. "That sexy old man spent fifteen minutes giving me an amazing foot massage."

"Coconuts! That's a new one," I commented. "Wow! You sure were thorough in your investigation. But, I've got another question, the biggest question of all. Is Streuling a castrated pedophile or did he just put phony numbers on his arm to pretend he was Jewish, so he could get a visa to the U.S? For the longest time I was positive that he was a pedophile. I'm sure Sam told you about all the research we did at the library, but, now Bellazio thinks that the numbers on Streuling's arm might be phony, that he never really was at Auschwitz."

"No, Streuling definitely was at Auschwitz," said Eileen, "We've got proof of that—eye witness accounts from several people who were there at the same time, including Hershel Glickman—but I never saw Streuling with his pants down, so I don't know the rest of the details." Eileen laughed; so did Flo, Sam, and the Steinbergs. But, I didn't join the laughter, not this time! I had been laughing about Streuling's testicles for almost four years. It wasn't funny anymore. Why does everyone laugh when they hear about a man who had his balls cut off? I bet, if I talked about a woman who had her breasts cut off nobody would think that was funny.

"Myron, I don't know how you got copies of those tax returns. You don't have to tell me . . . that's something I don't need to know. But, I promise you this, if you give them to us we won't have to go to court and serve you with a subpoena and we won't have to reveal how we got access to the returns. I'm sure you know, we can't force Rosenblatt to cooperate; CPAs have the protection of client confidentiality. But, you don't have the same legal protection and if this goes to court you will be required to tell the judge how you got copies. If you're protecting other people they will also be dragged into the case."

Eileen and I continued talking as we left the Nemo and walked to Essens Deli; it was time for lunch. We ordered matzoh ball soup and huge brisket sandwiches. My mother would definitely criticize this brilliant young attorney; she talked with food in her mouth. Whenever I did that, and I did it a lot . . . my mother always yelled at me.

"Myron, swallow before you talk. Educated people don't talk while eating."

Eileen kept talking and eating, and she "shlurped" when she swallowed her soup, another bad habit that my mother tried to correct. I was starting to really like this woman, but I was stunned when she started drinking beer with matzoh ball soup.

"Yeah, I learned to drink beer at college," said Eileen. "We drank it like water in the girls dorms."

Although Eileen tried to talk exclusively about the three tax returns I was much more interested in the relationship between Mr. Glickman and Henry Streuling.

"Are Glickman and Streuling friends?" I asked, in complete disbelief.

"Not really," responded Eileen, "but they're both from Hamburg, Germany. Before the war Streuling was a frequent customer at the shoe store where Glickman worked, and of course, they were both at Auschwitz in 1942. Glickman doesn't like to talk about that horrible experience, in fact he always wears long sleeve shirts to hide the numbers on his arm. Streuling is 425304, Glickman is 425111."

It was obvious; Eileen knew a lot more than she was allowed to tell. I couldn't believe that Mr. Glickman was a homosexual. That means he was probably sterilized by the Nazis. I bet that's why he was so abrupt when I asked if he had children.

"I'm really confused about Mr. Glickman," I stated. "Was he a homosexual in 1942? There's no way he was a pedophile; he doesn't have a high squeaky voice. That happens when you get castrated. And . . . and . . . he's been married three times. And, I'm positive that Mr. Glickman is Jewish."

Eileen smiled and chuckled. "Yes, Glickman is Jewish and just because he came up with the idea of putting fruit on women's shoes doesn't mean he's a fruit. Judging by the way he massaged my feet . . . he definitely likes women. Unfortunately, in 1942 he was married to a bi-sexual woman; they were both sent to Auschwitz. The Nazi's violated her sexually and she commited suicide. Germany, between the wars was out of control, even worse than the "roaring twenties" in America. And, of course, as you know, a madman seized the opportunity to manipulate human fears and frailty."

"I'm sure you know about the purge of 1942," said Eileen. "It was directed primarily towards homosexual men and pedophiles. But, the Nazi policy of 'extreme family values' extended in many directions. Lesbians, prostitutes, women who had abortions were referred to as the 'black-triangle.' There's lots of documentation as to how the Nazis dealt with the lesbians."

"What did they do?" I asked. "Is there such a thing as female castration?"

"Oh yes," replied Eileen, "but female castration was not that widespread. Most lesbians were sent to concentration camps where they were forced to spend six months to a year having sex with the male prisoners. This was expected to make these women 'normal.' And in some camps, such as Buchenwald, they did experiments with hormonal implants designed to 'cure' lesbians of their homosexuality."

I was fascinated as Eileen told about female castration and the Nazi treatment of lesbians. I learned a new word:

"**homophobia:** irrational fear of, aversion to, or discrimination against homosexuality or homosexuals."

Eileen reminded me, several times, how important it was for me to give the tax returns to her and the ADL rather than to the police. But, I kept trying to change the topic. I rambled on about anything that was remotely related to Streuling and Berger. I told her all about "showtime" at the TEP house, all the "black-and-white" details. And I talked about Dr. Zuckerman and his "networking" lecture, and in the course of conversation I learned from Eileen that the island mansion where Herman, Steuling, and I went fishing, when I lived at the James Manor, was the home of J. Martin Berger. Finally, after one hour of persuasion, I broke down and told the whole story, how I made copies of the tax returns, how Joanie let me in the office after hours. I even talked about Joanie's sexual preferences, that she was probably AC-DC. Of course, I never mentioned that Leah was her best friend.

"But, Joanie was in the waiting room," I noted. "she didn't know that I was making copies. I hid them under my shirt when I was alone in the copy room."

Eileen promised that if I gave the tax returns to ADL she would not implicate Joanie or me. "Myron, I'm an attorney, I can't be forced to reveal the source of my information, not even before a judge or a Congressional hearing. And, don't be so critical of Joanie just because she fools around with other girls; its very common with young women. I sure remember the girl's dorms at Cornell, that was quite an experience. Believe me, I could tell you stories every bit as wild as 'showtime.'"

"Really? I thought Cornell was such a nice Ivy League school, so proper."

"Hey, don't misinterpret my comments," said Eileen, and her voice got very defensive. "Girls are very 'experimental' with their emerging sexuality, much more than boys."

"OK," I responded, being careful not to seem immature. "I don't need details."

Eileen kept looking at her watch. There was a lull in the conversation, we were done talking about shoes, foot massages, bi-sexuals and female castrations. I could read the mind of this brilliant young attorney; she wanted me to come to a decision. Would I turn over the tax returns to ADL voluntarily . . . or would she have to get a court order? Either way . . . . she was determined to get those tax returns . . . .

"OK, here's what I'll do," I stated. "You convinced me; I wont give the tax returns to Detective Bellazio. I'm going to give them to my father's attorney, Ben Seligman. Then, you can meet at his office, you and one of the Bergs' from your law firm. I definitely want one of the big partners at the meeting. Mr. Seligman will give everything to you, but I'm sure he's going to want some type of letter promising that you won't tell anyone how you got the tax returns."

Eileen smiled and we hugged and I felt the sharp points of her bra pressing against my chest. Why did women wear steel bras that hid the natural softness of their breasts? It sure wasn't sexy!

"Myron, you asked a lot of questions," said Eileen, as she broke away from our embrace. "Good questions . . . . but, you left out one very important one . . . one that I am allowed to answer."

"I did? What was that?"

"You never asked about GSRFF, the restitution foundation. You never asked about that tax return, where it is, or whether we have a copy?"

"I gave up on that," I responded, "GSRFF is not a client of Rosenblatt. Are you saying that you have a copy of that tax return?"

Eileen smiled, a big smile. "Do you know anything about 501(c)(3) corporations?"

"Not really, I never did math checks on those returns. I think they're some type of chartitable or tax exempt organization."

"Precisely," said Eileen. "and those returns are public information, easy to request copies from the IRS. The GSRFF return is filed out of Gainesville, Florida; that's why the foundation isn't listed in the Miami phone book. Berger is the director; that you already know. But, lets see if you can guess who prepared and signed the tax return?"

"Dr. Zuckerman from the University of Florida?"

"Yup! He's the accountant. But, you should have figured that out without my help. Didn't you tell me about Zuckerman's lecture on networking?"

◆

459

Eileen Jacobs was brilliant and very nice, and the more I got to know her, she became prettier, and not just her beautiful tush. She was a dedicated and determined woman, a real tiger . . . . much tougher than Detective Bellazio.

"That's for damn sure," said Flo, as we drove back to Surfside. "I never saw a woman with such tenacity. But say it right . . . . she's a 'tigress.' Her grandpa is right—she definitely has balls. And, that's more than I can say for Streuling."

"She also has a nice 'tuchas,'" I observed, "like her grandpa said." I had visions of Eileen Jacobs, walking naked into the Surfside beach.

Flo went to this special meeting by bus, but now that we were talking again, she asked if I could drive her home. David and Shelly were in the back seat but that didn't bother Flo; she didn't care if our conversation got personal and sexual.

"I really like her," I said. "I wish she was younger. She's the type of woman I hope to marry. You know what I mean . . . . the type of woman I could fall in love with . . . 'for the right reasons.'"

"Sorry Myron," replied Flo, and she chuckled. "You're not her type."

"Of course not, she's twenty-seven; I'm seventeen."

"No, there's another reason," said Flo, "Eileen is a lesbian, and she has a colored girlfriend who is 'DDG' . . . drop-dead gorgeous."

I quickly changed topics; I liked Eileen and I didn't want to hear unnecessary details about her personal life. Eileen was "almost" the perfect woman.

"Flo, did Eileen ever talk to a Negro boy named Willie Jefferson?"

"Yeah! He's the kid that takes care of her shoes; he also shined Streuling's shoes. Sorry, I can't tell you what he said; its confidential."

"OK! I understand. But, I really got an important question to ask. I didn't want to say anything to Eileen, but why is there a letter from Leah Sonnino in the files?"

"There's more than one," Flo responded. "Several months ago Eileen found evidence that J. Martin Berger was involved in this scam. I recognized the name and told her about Leah and Danny Berger and the 'gang bang' accusations. Don't forget . . . you're the one who told me all those stories."

"I know! But that happened several years ago. What does any of that have to do with the ADL investiation?"

"Well—after I told Eileen all the 'gang bang' stuff she figured that if Leah knew any dirt on J. Martin Berger she would love to tell everything she knew . . . and Eileen sure was right. I'm not allowed to discuss those letters, but I can tell you this much, the gang bang crap was a pack of lies, so that Danny could get out of child support. I can also tell you that Leah knew a lot of shit about Berger and his investments. Danny had a big mouth and didn't know when to shut up. Myron, she's a lovely girl; I see why you liked her. I've got her phone number. Why don't you call her?"

"Thanks Flo, but I'm not interested in Leah anymore." I forced a smile—but there was an obvious crack in my voice. Flo understood my real feelings; she put her hand on my shoulder.

I drove north on Pine Tree Drive, very slowly, very carefully, very depressed. No matter how hard I tried to block Leah from my mind . . . . she kept coming back into my life. I wanted to be a master of my own destiny . . . . I really did. But, maybe if something is "bashert" its out of your control.

"Leave me alone!" I said those words silently, as I looked at the Pine Trees that lined this beautiful street; I was talking to the guy up there who was moving the chess pieces, but he simply laughed. He held the white knight in his hand, planning his next move.

Pine Tree Drive was the street where I had the auto accident with Willie and his motorized shoe. It was a picturesque street, lined with tall Australian Pines. These imposing trees were planted in the early part of the twentieth century; it was the dividing line between John Collins and Carl Fisher, the two famous pioneers of Miami Beach. None of us said anything, but we were all proud of our efforts. Now, it was up to the tigress, Eileen Jacobs, and the ADL. It was up to them to stop Berger and Streuling.

After I dropped the Steinbergs at their home Flo started to talk about her new life . . . how she found religion.

"Myron," Flo broke the silence. "I know your feeling about religion, and I don't agree with you; that's why our friendship ended. In fact I'm now majoring in 'Judaic Studies' at UM."

"I thought you wanted to be a lawyer," I said. "I got that impression from Eileen."

"No, not really. I want to be a rabbi. They're starting to allow female rabbis at Conservative and Reform congregations."

"You! A rabbi?" I just couldn't picture Flo Loerber as a rabbi, not the loud mouth girl from my school bus who rarely said a complete sentence without the "F" word. Rabbis don't use the "F" word, and rabbis don't use dildoes.

"Do you remember a boy at school a few years ago . . . Harold Lorber?" Asked Flo. "He always wore a yarmelkeh?"

"Yeah, sure. He was in my homeroom in the eighth grade; ninth grade too. I think he moved back to New York. What about him?"

"Well, he's my cousin . . . his name is spelled Lorber, without the extra 'e' . . . and he didn't move to New York; he transferred to the Hebrew Academy, the religious high school in South Beach. Anyway, I never really got along with Harold when we were kids . . . I thought he was a spook. But I freaked out after I was almost raped at Fun Fair, and when my bubby died I was so alone. Then, Harold came and visited a few times. He convinced me that I could only find comfort in religion; I should tell my problems to God. He told me that God listens . . . but he can't help you if you don't talk to him. I know . . . . you prefer cracking coconuts, and that works for letting out anger . . . but not grief. Lets try to be friends again, but, no talking about religion . . . you're never going to change my mind."

"I always was your friend Flo. Its nice to have you back."

When we got to Flo's house I walked her to the door.

"Hey . . . can I ask a personal question without you getting pissed at me?"

"Sure. What?"

"Now that you're studying to be a rabbi do you still have Stanley in your end table?"

Flo laughed. "Hey, I'm not dead . . . and in case you didn't notice, Stanley's Jewish."

♦

Several days later the Steinbergs called. They heard from their Uncle Louie that Mr. Streuling moved out of the Nemo Hotel. He fled in the middle of the night and left behind three dozen identical pairs of shiny black shoes.

And one night, while watching the 11:00 o'clock news on TV, I saw J. Martin Berger. He was being interviewed by Ralph Renick, the famous newscaster in Miami.

"I am saddened to inform you that I am stepping down as director of the German Survivor's Restitutaion Foundation," said the great philanthropist. "I leave with a heavy heart. Nothing in my lifetime has given me greater satisfaction than to look at the faces of God fearing concentration camp survivors when I presented them with 'full' restitution for the horrors that they suffered at the hands of the godless Nazis. I would like to announce, at this time, that I will be seeking election to City Council in Miami Beach. God bless America."

I wonder if Mr. Berger had ever talked to his son Danny . . . I could help write a great campaign speech.

CHAPTER 53

EMPHYSEMA AND VENTRILOQUISM

A unt Pearlie called our house crying, "Hoodlums from Chicago found Herman. They beat him badly . . . left him lying in an alley with broken pinkies on both hands." Herman had to come up with $5,000 within one week or they were going to kill him. The reason why Herman and Pearlie moved to Miami Beach was because he owed money to bookies from gambling debts and he finally got caught. I rarely referred to Herman and Pearlie by last name because I wasn't sure what it was; they kept changing their name in order to hide from the bookies. In Chicago it was Davis; before I was born it was Davidson. But, in Miami Beach it was changed so many times I didn't even try to remember . . . they were just Aunt Pearlie and Herman.

"Don't worry Pearl, we'll loan you the money," said my mother. "I'll talk to Sol."

"Loan? Let's be honest about this Rose. Ill get this money back when it snows in hell. How much money have I 'loaned' your brother-in-law over the years?"

My father loaned/gave Herman the money . . . and the "enforcers" backed off. But, two weeks later Pearlie called again . . . still crying.

"Herman is going off the deep end, spending every penny he makes at the dog track; he's become a chronic gambler. We're living on peanut butter and jelly sandwiches . . . my lousy salary isn't enough to pay the rent and also food."

"Gambling is like a disease," my father told my mother . . . making sure I also heard the sermon. "If we give your sister money to buy food her deadbeat husband will just piss it away at the dogs or horses. OK, OK . . . I won't let them starve. I'll have Myron bring $100 to the manager of Food Fair. Herman and Pearl can have a charge account . . . $25 a week. That way, at least the money will go for food."

Herman wasn't a drinker. "Jews are never shikkers," said my mother. So my father knew that the money wouldn't be spent on liquor. But, he was a chain smoker; Pearlie too . . . and she was also addicted to one pound Hershey bars. Unfortunately, the $25 per week went mostly to buy cartons of cigarettes and chocolate . . . with the leftover money going for peanut butter and jelly. Of course, Mitzie never suffered, she ate only premium dog food.

Then came another call from Pearlie . . . crying again. Herman was suffering from an advanced case of emphysema. A lifetime of smoking three packs a day finally caught up with him and he was only fifty five. He was in intensive care at Mr. Sinai Hospital.

My mother and I went with Aunt Pearlie to visit him, but my father stayed home. Although my father was only sixty five his health was bad and he rarely left home anymore, except for Sunday trips to the Chinese restaurant with his relatives . . . but that was only during "Relative season." He stopped driving; his eyes were getting bad. I had become the family chauffeur.

Herman was lying in bed with an oxygen tank next to him and a clear plastic mask over his face. He smiled when we came in the room, but he couldn't talk with the mask covering his mouth. My mother kissed him on the forehead. Then Herman removed the mask and asked Aunt Pearlie and my mother to leave the room for a few minutes; he wanted to talk to me in private. It was difficult understanding what he was saying; his chest was congested with phlegm. He could only whisper.

"Congratulations Myron, I heard from Bellazio how you got Streuling by the balls. Sorry! Bad choice of words . . . Good job . . . I'm really proud of you." He reached over and squeezed my hand. His hand was very cold.

"Detective Bellazio! How did he know? I never told any of this restitution stuff to the police."

"Hey . . . you're a smart boy; don't be such a kunyehlemel.' Do you think that dyke from B'nai B'rith was able to put the squeeze on Berger and Streuling without a little help from the cops?"

"Well . . . if Bellazio knew so much, why did he always brush me away? Why didn't the police go after these crooks?"

"Berger is a gantser-macher' in Miami Beach *(a super big shot)* . . . he greased a lotta' palms at City Hall. Bellazio had his hands tied going after him . . . and even though you dug up all that shit, you were just getting in the way. If Bellazio tried to make a case against Berger he could have lost his job. It was much cleaner to get you out of the picture and let an outsider with clout go after Berger and Streuling. On our Jewish island who got more clout than the B'nai B'rith?"

"Yeah; I guess it all makes sense. But, how do you know about the B'nai B'rith and Eileen? No way that Bellazio would tell you all those details!"

Herman winked. "What did I teach you about flirting with mieskeits?'"

Then he put the mask back over his mouth and smiled . . . . and he closed his eyes.

I twisted the corner of my mouth and made my best effort to use a little ventriloquism that I learned from Herman. I attempted to make the oxygen tank start talking.

"Help! Let me out of here. Help! Let me out of here."

Herman laughed . . . and he gagged to relieve the congestion in his chest . . . and he laughed again. A few minutes later Aunt Pearlie and my mother returned to the room and we sat by his bedside for another fifteen minutes, until he fell asleep.

That was the last time I saw Herman.

CHAPTER 54

THE SENIOR PROM

Almost a year had passed since I sat Shiva for Flo's grandmother; now we were hosting a Shiva in my house . . . for Herman. But ours was without a minyan' or t'filin' . . . my family wasn't religious. Of course we had plenty of bobka, strudel, and lots of Yiddish jokes, which is probably what Herman would have preferred. He was even less religious than us. I was tempted to use my mediocre ventriloquism and make the ash trays start cussing, as a final tribute to Herman, but I didn't think our guests would appreciate the humor.

On the first day of Shiva my mother invited Aunt Pearlie to move in with us, along with her dog Mitzie. I enjoyed having both of them . . . but I knew that this arrangement couldn't last too long. My mother had little patience for dog poop on our new wall-to-wall carpeting.

On the third day of Shiva Aunt Pearlie's old Canasta friend, Blanche Liebowitz, came to pay her respects. Mrs. Liebowitz was the short, zaftic' overly tanned woman with silver-blue hair and two-tone breasts . . . our old neighbor who lived near the James Manor. I hadn't seen her since we moved to Surfside.

Mrs. Liebowitz hugged and kissed Aunt Pearlie and handed my mother a box of sugar-free Jewish cookies that tasted like rubber coated cardboard.

"Pearlie, you poor darling," said Mrs. Liebowitz, who was still searching for a third husband, "you should move in with me, down near Lincoln Road. You'll never find a man living way up here in the boon docks."

"Blanche . . . Herman is dead only three days . . . I'm not looking for a man yet."

On the seventh day of Shiva Pearlie and Mitzie moved in with Mrs. Liebowitz, two blocks north of Lincoln Road. Pearlie didn't move there to meet a man; she moved in with Mrs. Liebowitz because she couldn't get along with my mother. During the seven days that my aunt lived with us my mother didn't stop complaining about Hershey wrappers dumped on the floor, dog poop on the carpeting, and cigarette butts all over the house. Aunt Pearlie smoked almost as much as Herman.

. Mrs. Liebowitz and Aunt Pearlie came to my house occasionally, to play Canasta with my mother; I sometimes joined them when they needed a fourth player but I hated it when they smoked . . . . and none of them knew how to French inhale or make smoke rings.

It was now April 1, 1956; I hadn't had a date since my closure with Leah Sonnino; I lost all interest in girls. However, there was only one month until the senior prom and I didn't want to miss my own prom. I thought about calling Leah, maybe just for that one night, but no sex. However, I knew that would be impossible; there is no escape from quicksand.

David and Shelly had girlfriends. David met a very tall girl at Perry Chesters, the expensive shoe store where he worked; he couldn't stop talking about her gorgeous feet, and Shelly was dating a girl who worked in the Lacoste section at Saks Fifth Avenue. He couldn't stop talking about her employee discounts. Josh Broden was dating a very cute Chinese girl who recently moved from Hong Kong to Miami. Her name was Liling Wong and Josh couldn't stop talking (and singing) about her acrobatic ability.

"Liling Wong from Hong Kong loves my big fat Jewish 'shlong,'" Josh sang his crude little song. "She's a fucking contortionist, every bone in her body is double jointed. When we screw she puts both feet behind her head, and not always the same way"

I was immediately fixated with images of Chinese sexual positions . . . . especially flexible girls putting both feet behind their head. Was it really possible?

"Does she talk to your dick in Chinese? What does she say?"

"Only in Chinese, but she won't tell me what she's saying," said Josh, and he laughed. "I wish my dick understood Chinese."

Several days later I was playing Canasta with Mrs. Liebowitz, aunt Pearlie, and my mother . . . trying to focus on the game. But, I was also trying to visualize Liling with her feet behind her head; maybe she had a sister. Then, Mrs. Liebowitz asked a life saving question.

"Myron, would you like to meet my niece?"

I had just taken the pack and I was spreading cards into a dozen carefully arranged melds and blends; it was an intense moment in the game . . . but the zaftic lady with silver-blue hair captured my attention . . . . my ears perked up. I even stopped fantacizing about Liling.

"Whats her name? What's she look like? Yes."

"Its Buny," said Mrs. Liebowitz, "not like the rabbit . . . . its B-U-N-Y; rhymes with 'puny' . . . she's in the tenth grade at Beach High . . . a 'Shana Maideleh.' . . . just moved here from the 'city.' And what a personality!"

Thank God! Bring on puny Buny.

Buny Liebowitz was pretty; not gorgeous and sexy like Leah Sonnino, but she had a warm smile and a soft, sweet voice. I liked her the first time we met. I'm not saying I was in love with her, but she was intelligent and very interesting, certainly not like the dimwits that I met at Shawna Goldstein's party. Buny would never watch "Queen for a Day." She also had big boobs; that was certainly a "plus."

On our first date I borrowed my fathers car, a new Super 88 Oldsmobile; the prom was only four weeks away . . . time was running out, I had to make a good first impression. Buny entered the car and immediately placed her large white basket purse in the middle of the seat. Then she pushed her body firmly against the right hand door. Josh Broden had advised me to check out the location of a girl's zipper before the car door was shut, while the light was still on. The zippers on girls pants were sometimes on the left side, sometimes on the right; they were even on the back or the front . . . you didn't want to go groping and fumbling in the dark. Buny's was on the left, very close to me, but it was blocked by her purse. So close, but yet . . . so far!

"Be careful," I warned her, "the door's liable to pop open."

We went to a movie at the Carib, and in the protective darkness of the theatre I spent the next two hours watching Buny breathe. I stared through the corner of my eyes at the slow and sensual movement of her bosom. I wondered if she had two-tone breasts like her aunt.

"You have a beautiful blouse," I whispered . . . . hoping for magic to repeat.

"Shhh . . . let me watch the movie." Buny crunched on her popcorn and ignored me.

Then, I slowly moved my right hand around her shoulder, inching slowly toward her breast.

"Stop that!" she said. "I'm not that kind of girl."

After the movie I tried talking to the parrot in the lobby . . . Buny pulled me away. She thought it was stupid to teach profanity to a parrot. Then we held hands and walked on Lincoln Road, and I made sure she was on my right side . . . so she wouldn't see my crooked left tooth.

"Myron, why do you keep pushing me to the right when we walk?" said Buny.

Damn! None of my "tried and tested" techniques were working with this girl.

We went to Wolfies, the popular Jewish restaurant; I ordered a corned beef sandwich and a knish. Buny ordered a spinach salad topped with cold asparagus, string beans, and broccoli; everything was green.

"I'm a vegetarian," she informed me.

"Oh, I love vegetables too . . . I always eat my veggies last. You know the old saying, 'save the best for last.'"

"Actually, I'm one step beyond vegetarian," Buny smiled. "I'm a 'vegan' . . . I don't even eat fish or eggs. I don't believe in killing animals."

"How about your shoes? You had to kill a cow to make those shoes."

"No, they're vinyl, a type of plastic. I won't wear leather shoes."

"Do you have any of those cork shoes with the fruit on top? That was my creation when I worked at Pix, and they're not leather."

"Hmm, not a bad idea," she responded "Do they make any with carrots or broccoli?"

"Oops! Sorry to tell you, but that sweater you're carrying is cashmere . . . that comes from a lamb."

"Nope!" said Buny, "Cashmere comes from the soft underbelly of a goat and they dont have to kill the goat to get the wool."

I liked Buny. Mrs. Liebowitz was right; she did have a nice personality. But, how could a confirmed vegetable hater like me find anything in common with a vegan?

"Whats your sign?" asked Buny.

I realized that she was talking about the zodiac and astrology; that was a trendy question that some of the kids were now asking each other . . . like it really mattered how the moon and planets were aligned when you were born. I didn't know the first thing about astrology, nor did I know my sign. I think Leonardo DaVinci was a big believer in astrology . . . or maybe he argued against astrology . . . I wasn't sure. What was my sign? How could I continue this discussion with this very intelligent girl? I wasn't even sure how to spell "astrology."

"My sign? I kind of like the yield sign," I chuckled. "I'm into triangles; I even have an autographed picture of Pythagorus hanging in my bedroom." Buny laughed; glad to see she had a good sense of humor.

"But the yield sign is so indecisive; it isn't quite a stop and it isn't a go . . . kind of a wishy-washy sign. Whats your birthday?"

"March 20th." Buny seemed to know me very well; hard to believe she just met me.

"You're a Pices, on the cusp. Now I see why you like the yield sign. 'Cuspers' are very indecisive people . . . hanging in space between two signs. Your birthday is the first day of Spring; the world is waking from its sleep. You should be a very uplifting, positive person."

"Funny you should mention that . . . about my birthday being the first day of Spring. I always thought that March 20th was the last day of winter. Then, one day I heard on the radio that it was the first day of Spring. I checked it out; its both. March 20th is the last day of winter and the first day of spring. The seasons change in the middle of the day. Maybe you hit on something . . . I often have trouble making up my mind. And even after I make a decision I'm not sure I did the right thing . . . especially with girls."

"Myron, you're a senior; you should be sure of youself by now. What are you gonna' take in college . . . what major?"

"Well . . . . I can't make up my mind; I'll either be a neurosurgeon or a bag boy. I've had a successful career as a bag boy, but I heard that good neurosurgeons can also do OK."

"You're funny," responded Buny, as she slowly ingested a long green asparagus stalk. It was very erotic to watch the asparagus slide down her throat . . . almost as arousing as listening to Maxine play the glockenspiel. Later, at the driveway of her house, I ran around the car to open the door. And as I escorted Buny to the front porch she grasped my hand and cradled it between twin peaks, now covered by a white cashmere sweater . . . . and she gave a slight squeeze.

"I had a wonderful time Myron, except when you got 'fresh' in the movie theatre. Goodnight." No kiss or anything, but I felt that she liked me; it was a sincere squeeze. Maybe I'll do a little research about astrology when I get home. I wonder if she would be interested in learning about Xenocrates and the moon . . . or how to open coconuts? Yeah! Coconuts are fruit; vegans like fruit.

Sunday morning, I wanted to call back and ask Buny to the prom, but I was afraid that I would look overanxious. It wouldn't be cool. Maybe I should wait a few days, probably even a week. But, by Sunday evening I couldn't hold off anymore.

Eight PM—that was the perfect time to call a girl, about two hours after dinner. Parents sometimes got all up tight when you called during dinner, and that could start the whole conversation off on a defensive note. And if you called much later than eight the girl would probably be sleeping. Then her parents really got upset. So, at eight, precisely at eight, I called.

"Uh . . . Buny . . . You wouldn't want to go with me to the senior prom, would you?"

"Yes," she replied.

I ended the conversation immediately, before I screwed things up, and I called the Steinbergs and Josh Broden to tell them the good news. "My senior year is complete. My senior year is complete. I have a date to the prom with Buny Liebowitz."

The prom wasn't until May. I was very undecided; should I go out with Buny every Saturday over the next four weeks or should I space the dates, like every other week? I weighed the advantages and disadvantages of each option.

On the one hand: If I went out with Buny a lot . . . . then, by the time of the prom, we would be a lot closer, that's for sure.

And there's no telling what might happen. I heard that many girls waited until prom night to lose their virginigy. I can understand that: What a glamorous, glorious way to get starterd . . . with gowns and tuxedos and all the fancy frill.

On the other hand: What if she got to know me better and didn't like me? How could I go another four weeks faking it with vegetables? What if she broke the prom date? I would have to start searching all over, and by then all the girls would be taken. Of course, I could always try to find a date at Miami High, but that wouldn't be the same as taking a Beach girl; everyone would know that I couldn't get a "real" date.

I decided to take my chances; I would see Buny every Saturday and when we were together I would force myself to eat vegetables. I also made it a point to tell her that I left a $5 deposit on a tuxedo rental. She would never break our prom date knowing that I could lose that much money.

Four weeks later . . . . In the mirrored hallway of the Liebowitz house, I pinned a corsage on Buny's abundantly filled strapless gown . . . she looked radiant. She was wearing high heel shoes and a bouffant hair style swirled on top of her head . . . like a Dairy Queen cone. She was elegant, glamorous and very statuesque, like Venus Di Milo, the famous statue. Well, not exactly! Venus didn't have arms and Buny's arms were white and soft and very inviting. Don't get me wrong. I don't mean "inviting" in a nasty sexual way. They just seemed like they would feel good wrapped around me, like she would some day be a very comforting mother. And, talking about mothers, her mother was watching, crying, and k'velling' *(glowing with pride)* . . . making sure that I was careful with the placement of the pin and extra careful with the placement of my fingers. And her father was snapping photographas from every possible angle.

"OK son, don't move . . . hold the flowers right there. I want to bounce a trick shot off the mirror on the ceiling."

"Oh, don't worry Mr. Liebowitz, I wont move a muscle."

No way I'd move, not with my hands wrapped around two white orchids—firmly planted in an unchartered region where no man had ever gone before. Of course, I knew in advance that Buny was going to wear a strapless gown, so I carefully planned for this moment. At least four or five times she told me about the gown, I guess as often as I reminded her of my $5 tuxedo deposit.

"Myron, my mother and I picked out this gorgeous violet gown. Mom wanted me to get some mousey dress with spaghetti straps, but I told her I had enough to hold up a strapless gown. Chuckle, chuckle." Everytime Buny referred to that portion of her anatomy she concluded with a giggle.

The florist suggested that I buy a wrist corsage, especially since my date was wearing a strapless gown. But, I rejected that idea. "No, I want the type you pin right up there; should help get the evening started on the right foot."

♦

The prom was at the Seville, one of the new luxury hotels on the ocean; Buny and I doubled with Josh Broden. His date, Liling, felt out of place because she was the only oriental at the prom. Buny also felt uncomfortable; she had recently moved to Miami Beach and didn't know anyone. But, within five minutes the two girls were chatting with each other; they both loved Chinese vegetables. Liling was telling Buny all about different Chinese recipes; I was hoping that she would also teach Buny all about Chinese acrobatics.

"When I was in the eighth grade I read a biography of Confucius," I said. "I liked his family values; the Jewish culture is very similar. One of the Ten Commandments says to 'honor your mother and father.'"

"But we go one step further," replied Liling, "we continue to honor parents even after they die."

"I guess we do also," I replied. "My mother lights yarhtsite candles every year on the night before her mother and father died."

"Ain't that the guy who said all those dumb 'Confucius says' jokes," said Josh?

"They weren't jokes," Liling replied; she spoke with a very refined British accent. "He was great teacher, and culture of my people derived from his beautiful philosophy."

"I read that Confucius conceived the idea of a Golden Rule'" I noted, "even before the version that is used by the west; actually, his version makes more sense."

"That's because Confucius understood human nature," replied Liling. "The Christian Golden Rule is idealistic." She then bowed her head toward me; I interpreted her gesture as a Chinese sign of respect.

"Who gives a fuck about Confucius?" said Josh, as he interrupted my discussion with Liling; he didn't seem too happy that I was engaged in an intelligent conversation with his pretty Chinese girlfriend.

"Hey, did you hear about the new Eisenhower doll?" said Josh. "You wind it up and it smiles and does nothing." We all laughed. "Or the Hellen Keller doll? You wind it up and it walks into the wall."

"How about the Lenny Bruce doll," said Buny. "Wind it up and it laughs at the Helen Keller doll."

Liling sat quietly, she probably didn't know any "windup doll" jokes; neither did I, but the band started to play a Rhumba, this was my moment to shine, and as I dragged Buny to the dance floor Liling looked at me and smiled. I thought it was really neat that Chinese people worshiped their ancestors, and I was positive that they didn't belive nonsense about bad people rotting in hell when they died.

"Wow, you're good," said Buny, as I wiggled and guided her through a series of perfectly executed twirls, dips, and box steps. "You really know how to shake your tush. Where did you ever learn to do Cuban dancing?"

"Its hereditary . . . my grandmother's side of the family comes from Spain; we were evicted in the Inquisition. Her maiden name was Seville . . . just like this hotel."

I expected this magical revelation to impress Buny, hoping that she would start telling me all about her secret desires, but she didn't seem impressed by my Spanish ancestry, certainly not like Mindy Marcus or Joanie Vazelo.

"I'm in Spanish II," said Buny, "I really like that course."

"So did I," I responded. "Spanish was my favorite subject in the tenth grade; I got an 'A' in that course."

OK . . . I wasn't 100% honest with Buny . . . but my lies about vegetables and Spanish were just little white lies. What good would it do to tell her that I hated vegetables or that Spanish was my worst subject? She was impressed with my ability to Rhumba . . . now I needed one good line in Spanish.

"Me gusta tus ojos rojos," I spoke softly in her ear . . . as we danced to a romantic ballad. Buny laughed.

"You love my **RED** eyes? Look again; they're brown."

"OK . . . Spanish was not my best subject. How do you say brown?"

"Marrón," Buny smiled and squeezed my hand . . . . another sincere squeeze. The message was clear . . . she liked me and this lie was forgiven . . . but she still thought I loved vegetables.

After the prom we went to the Eden Roc Hotel and saw a wonderful Negro singer who sounded like Roy Hamilton. He sang "I Believe," and Buny started to cry. She looked beautiful in the dim light of the night club. Her corsage was still in place. Moist eyes sparkled as black masquera ran freely down her cheek; her soft lovely arms were covered by elbow-length white gloves. I put my arm around her shoulder. Then came "Ebb Tide"—and more crying. My groping hand made the bold and daring turn, down from her shoulder toward the forbidden zone. Finally, the showstopper: "You'll Never Walk Alone"—uncontrolled tears, and I stretched my arm, reaching for the "promised land," but my probing fingers were stopped by Buny's immovable white glove barricade.

At Josh's suggestion, the next stop was Baker's Haulover, one of the popular "makeout" beaches.

"Well, OK." Reluctantly, Buny agreed, "but only for a little while; its getting late."

We parked at the beach, facing the void of a starless black sky, and we listened to the sound of invisible waves pounding against the shore. In the rear view mirror I saw that Liling had her legs twisted behind her head. I slumped in my seat, closed my eyes and clenched the cold plastic steering wheel of my father's Oldsmobile. My hands began to sweat as I started to move, ever slightly to the right. Instinctively, Buny moved out of reach, seeking shelter at her favorite door. And from the back seat I heard the unmistakeable sound of a zipper, slowly opening.

OK, I said to myself, as I unsnapped a rented bowtie and threw it to the floor, its my turn. I opened the collar of a heavily starched, multi-pleated tuxedo shirt and slid toward Buny. And as I edged to the right Buny immediately opened the door. "Lets take a walk. I love walking barefoot in the sand."

We walked along the shore, holding hands, feeling the waves rolling over our toes . . . the water was cold. "You're a Leo, aren't you?" I asked.

"Yes, August 1st is my birthday."

"Leo's are generous and warmhearted, creative and enthusiastic, broad-minded and expansive, faithful and living . . . . Uh! I mean 'loving.'" I did my homework before the prom.

Buny laughed. "But . . . on the dark side, Leo's are pompous and patronizing, bossy and interfering, dogmatic and intolerant. However, we have been known to be very compatible with Pices."

"Did you know that Lincoln and Darwin were both born on the same day?" I noted. "And their lives were very different . . . even though they had the same sign."

"Well, they were both great men," said Buny, "and they both lost their mother when they were very young . . . but the alignment of the planets and stars is different in England than in Illinois."

"Lincoln was born in Kentucky, not Illinois," I corrected her; I knew a lot about Lincoln—he was my alltime favorite President.

"Well, either way . . . the stars are different in Kentucky than in England."

"Do you really believe in astrology?" I asked.

"Why, of course I do," said Buny. She smiled and pulled at my hand. We both ran barefoot along the waters edge. "And I believe in green vegetables and waves on my feet."

Then we walked for awhile and we sat on the sand. We kissed once, a closed mouth kiss, then we just held hands and sat silently, staring at the ocean, watching the morning sun rise above the horizon.

CHAPTER 55

POLAR OPPOSITES

I saw a lot of Buny over the next few weeks and we had fun together. I even told her the truth, that I disliked vegetables. At first that upset her, but then she found a new mission in life . . . to convince me to eat healthy "veggies" and I began eating carrots and broccoli, but not asparagus . . . never!

"Yes, same thing with girls," Buny laughed. "Asparagus makes your pee stink."

"But, it doesn't do the same thing to your poop," I observed.

"Of course not," said Buny, "your own shit never smells . . . one of the mysteries of nature."

"No, I've got that mystery solved," I said. "It doesn't smell because you're there right from the beginning . . . it kind of sneaks up on you. But, if you leave the bathroom without flushing and then come back . . . it stinks like shit."

"Maybe yours does!" said Buny. "but vegans don't have that problem."

We studied together for finals and I helped Buny conjugate Spanish verbs. And I taught her how to laugh in Spanish . . . . Ja! Ja! Ja! Can you believe that? I was helping someone in Spanish!

"Do you know how to say 'balls' in Spanish?" asked Buny.

"Which type—the rubber ones or testicles?" I replied.

"Those," said Buny, and she pointed at my crotch. "They're called 'huevos' which means eggs."

"I thought vegans had no interest in eggs" I responded.

"Well, if I was Christian I would," said Buny. "They love pretty colored eggs at Easter, but I still wouldn't eat them, but while we're talking about colors why do you have all those colored rubbers in your glove compartment?"

"Well, you know the Boy Scout motto," I responded, "Be prepared! But, so far, I haven't used any of them."

"But, do you know how to put one on?"

"Yeah, sure . . . but they won't fit you."

"No, seriously, I'd like to learn how to put one on a boy, just in case he's stubborn and refuses. Could you teach me?"

"Only if you teach me how to remove a bra with one hand."

Buny laughed. "OK, that's a deal."

This definitely sounded like fun, a lot more fun than conjugating Spanish verbs. So, we went to Buny's house. I brought several rubbers and I was all set to go upstairs to her bedroom. My "live" demonstration would begin with me putting on the first rubber, then it would be her turn.

"No, here in the kitchen," she stopped me at the stairway. "On the table."

"On the table?" Wow! This really was going to be kinky!

Unfortunately, Buny's plans were different than mine. For the next half hour we practiced rolling rubbers on bananas. She was a quick learner, and after a few attempts she was able to do it with her eyes closed, using only one hand. And, once she mastered the "traditional" technique she rolled the final rubber on a banana with her mouth . . . and I stared with amazement.

"Great job," I complimented Buny. "You have a natural talent, and your final act was awesome. Now are you ready to switch from bananas to the real thing?"

"Nope! I'm a vegetarian." Buny laughed.

I decided that if I ever did it with Buny I would use a green rubber; she definitely loved anything that was green, like asparagus, broccoli, spinach, and brussel sprouts. But, I knew that my chance of having sex with Buny was remote; the two of us seemed to disagree on everything except how to put on rubbers. It was as if we came from different planets. She wouldn't eat chopped liver, corned beef, or hot dogs and I wouldn't eat vegetables . . . and she told me that in her Biology class she was bored with the animal module, but was really fascinated during the unit on plants. Maybe the old adage was true . . . "opposites attract."

"Yeah, I know that expression," said Buny, "but I've also heard that 'birds of a feather flock together' . . . and you and I sure have different feathers."

"Well, maybe with the birds they're just referring to casual friends," I observed. "With romantic relationships I think opposites do attract . . . my parents are very different."

"I always wonder why there is an attraction between real tall men and tiny women," said Buny. "How can they kiss while they're having sex?"

"Well, I can see certain advantages," I replied. "If the guy is ugly, when they screw the girl won't have to look him in the face, she can just kiss his belly button."

"I think you've got a good point," said Buny, and she laughed. "Usually when I see couples where the girl is short and the guy is very tall, he is really ugly."

Then came the lesson on one hand bra removal.

"Your left hand cradles the girl's head, assuming that you're right handed; you gotta' keep your right hand free, and you kiss her. Make it a long wet kiss; you must stop her from talking. Its impossible for a girl to say 'no' when you got your tongue wiggling in her mouth." I followed Buny's instructions; it was a good kiss, lots of tongue wiggling, but I didn't see shooting stars; I didn't even get a bulge in my pants.

"Now, your right hand reaches behind her back, under her blouse," Buny whispered. "Move slowly, delicately. Then you pinch the middle of the bra strap together, and presto . . . let the fun begin."

Unfortunately, Buny wore the demonstration bra on the outside of her sweater. The lesson was good, but not nearly as exciting as I anticipated.

"So, what are you waiting for?" I asked. "When are you going to let the fun begin?"

"Myron, you told me you're waiting for the right girl, one you can love for the right reason, not just for sex. Well, it's the same with me. That's what I'm waiting for."

"Yeah, in principle, that makes sense" I responded. "But how are you ever going to know if its the right person? Isn't it better to find out before you get married, before you make a lifetime commitment? The man I used to work for at the shoe store had three wives."

"I think you can tell more about a person from their horoscope than by sampling them in bed," said Buny. "I clipped this out of the newspaper . . . tell me if this isn't you . . . : I mean, exactly you: 'Your emotional life is not as sticky as some people. You're self conscious, and prefer to be rational and never lose your temper; You're verbal and like to talk things out.'"

"Yup, that's me, but don't ask how I am in bed; so far I don't have anything to talk about, but the horoscope is pretty much true. I don't usually lose my temper, except one time when I punched Dingo McGuffie in the nose. Yeah, I do like to talk things out."

"There's no shame in being a virgin at seventeen," said Buny, "I'm sixteen, still a virgin. At our age we should both just have fun, go to movies, and eat a lot of vegetables."

"I wouldn't use words like 'fun' and 'vegetables' in the same sentence," I replied, "but I guess I am a little obsessed about my virginity. I think a lot about how I will lose my innocence, and who will be the lucky girl. Have you ever thought about how and when you would lose your virginity?"

"Of course; I think about that a lot," said Buny. "I'm waiting for a guy who is really different, but to tell you the truth, I'm not exactly sure what I mean by 'different.' I guess I'll know it when I see it."

"Like maybe a guy with a ten inch dick?" I laughed.

"Myron, you're a pervert," Buny responded. "Girls don't care about the size of a guy's dick; we want a guy who is smart, has a sense of humor and is kind and loving, and it won't hurt if he is also handsome."

Buny was intelligent and fun, and great to talk to, but I wasn't in love with her. I certainly didn't have the same feelings that I had for Leah. My relationship with Leah and Buny were so different. I was in love with Leah, a beautiful girl who slept around with many guys, even with girls, but I turned down the chance to have sex with her. I was afraid that I would fall hopelessly in love. I guess I was smart enough to recognize how dumb I was; that was always one of my strengths. I think it was Shakespeare who said, "To Thine Own Self Be True" or maybe it came from one of the Bibles, either the old one or the new. I never read either Bible, so I wasn't sure, but that poignant philosophy sure explained why I was suffering and why I was staying away from Leah.

And, to erase Leah from my mind, I was trying my hardest to have sex with Buny, a girl who I didn't love, and who wasn't gorgeous. Naturally, this emotional conflict was very confusing and my brain, penis, and heart got into many debates.

♦

"Myron, didn't you listen to Mr. Glickman?" said my brain. "Why did that nice old man chose his third wife? He wanted a 'balebosteh.' I know, sexual attraction is important, but only at first; after a few months the novelty wears off. Buny will be a perfect wife and mother. Think about it dummy . . . what kind of fun will it be having sex on dirty sheets?"

"Good point," said my penis. "Its definitely better to screw on clean sheets."

"Wake me when its over," said my heart. "Sex without love is boring."

"What the hell is wrong with you?" My brain snapped at my heart. "Here's a chance for Myron to get laid without any emotional commitment; he can screw Buny on weekends and still do well in college. That doesn't sound boring to me; it sounds like a very rational balance in his life."

"I'm all for it," said my penis. "Buny will be OK until I meet the right girl."

♦

I followed the advice of my brain and penis (ignoring my heart), and I took Buny to the Surfside beach early on a Sunday morning; sex on the beach would be fantastic, and I brought a blanket (it was green). We were alone; Gentile families were still at church and Jewish families were home preparing for Sunday brunch, and while Buny was jumping in and out of the early morning waves the top of her bathing suit fell off I was surprised to see, she did have two tone breasts, just like her aunt.

"Well, of course they're two-tone," said Buny, and she laughed. "Why do you think some girls go topless to the beach? But you should see my tush' if you really wanna' see white."

"OK—show me!" I responded, and I grabbed her hand, preventing her from putting on the top of her bathing suit, and I

482

kissed her, a long wet kiss and I wiggled my tongue in her mouth so that she couldn't say no.

Buny chuckled as she pushed me away and said "NO!" Then she turned away from me and tied the bow on top of her bathing suit.

It was time for a new strategy. What else could I do?

"Hey, Mr. Chess man, aren't you going to help?"

"Try Canasta," said the Chess Master.

"Jewish girls all love Canasta."

So, we played Canasta with Colonel Klein and Katarina, then with Aunt Pearlie and Blanche Liebowitz. And both times, after we finished playing, we drove to "Peckers Point" (the popular makeout island) but I never got past tight lip kissing, and I never got to use the one-hand bra removal technique.

"Lets play Canasta with David and Shelly," I suggested. Playing cards with the older people wasn't opening any doors . . . or bras.

"That's funny," said Buny. "I can't believe you guys play Canasta."

We played Canasta with the Steinbergs, and Shelly wore a green Lacoste and while we played cards he discussed recipies for making asparagus soup . . . and Buny had a far away look in her eyes . . . and I knew that my relationship with this vegan was coming to an end.

"Mr. Chess man," I said to myself, "I got your next move figured out."

And I was right: The next morning I got a phone call from Shelly: "Myron, is it OK if I go out with Buny? She wants me to take her to a farm in Homestead to pick string beans, and she said that I'm very different.'"

"Yeah Shelly, string bean picking sounds really exciting; maybe next week you'll get to pick tomatoes."

Oh well! Buny and I definitely were not bashert; I guess it wasn't my destiny to be a vegetarian and have sex on clean sheets.

♦

"No big deal," said my heart, "now get your ass over to the phone and call Leah. Don't you realize, you cannot escape from your destiny?"

"You make your own destiny," said my brain. "Wait until college, you'll meet the right girl."

"I'm not looking for the 'right' girl," said my penis, "any girl will do, but I don't know if any girl wants me."

♦

Losing Buny so soon after I ended the opportunity to get back with Leah was a double blow to my ego; my self confidence was shattered. I couldn't even focus on reading, not even the Sunday comics. I considered calling Josh to see if his cute Chinese girlfriend had a sister or a friend, especially one who knew how to put her feet behind her head; too bad Joanie Vazelo was close friends with Leah, that girl was so hot, or maybe I could ask my parents to send me to New York as a graduation present. I could stay with cousin Ethan and be a puppy for Mindy Marcus. I even considered going to Food Fair to look for Simone Pasquiere, the middle age French woman who tried to seduce me when I was sixteen. My high school days were coming to an end and I was still a virgin.

Only three weeks remained until graduation; not much was happening at school; no more tests, no more homework. Seniors were even allowed to sign out of class and go to the library. We could also watch movies in the auditorium; it was a large dark room and it was easy to fall asleep, but you had to make sure that someone woke you once the movie ended. If the lights came on and you were caught sleeping you would have to serve detention. I went to several movies with David, Shelly, and Josh, and of course, I couldn't stop asking Shelly what was happening with Buny. However, he wasn't a "kiss and tell" kind of guy. He preferred to smirk and keep me guessing. But, I was a good detective, and I noticed that three green rubbers were missing from the glove compartment in my car.

Then, on Friday, May 31, 1956, six days before graduation, I was watching a movie with Josh. It was an old movie about the Crusades and during one of the great battle scenes, when a million ferocious Saracens were chopping off heads with their curved swords, Josh told me that he was no longer dating Liling.

"That's terrible," I responded. "What happened?"

"It was driving me nuts," said Josh. "What was the little chink saying to my dick? So I hid a tape recorder in my car and asked a waiter at a Chinese restaurant to translate for me. The damn slut was saying that I was a dumb fuck, and she called my dick 'Shagua'—that means 'idiot' or 'dumb melon.'"

"Wow! Whatta' bitch," I commiserated with Josh. "Can I have her phone number?"

"Yeah sure," Josh chuckled, "I knew you had a hardon for her. She was a good fuck but two months was enough; she didn't shut up about ying and yang."

"I bet you weren't ready for that move," said the Chess master. "That's my graduation present."

After school I drove home in record time and ran to the telephone to call Liling and tell her that I was sorry to hear that she broke up with Josh, and that I was no longer dating Buny, and it would be nice if we got together, but it wouldn't be a "real" date, neither of us were emotionally ready to start dating, and we both needed a good catharsis (that was my favorite new word), and I was a very good listener thanks to my experience as a bag boy at Food Fair. But, I knew that words like "oye gevald" or "vay is mir" would be useless with this cute girl from Hong Kong.

"The best 'medicine' for both of is to have a sympathetic shoulder to cry on," I said, "We aren't ready to start dating; we need time to heal."

"That's so sweet of you," Liling replied, "I really enjoyed our stimulating intercourse at the prom."

That was the first time I ever heard the word "intercourse" used to mean "conversation;" it sounded so unusual and very refined. I had immediate visions of enjoying the more well known type of "stimulating intercourse" with Liling, especially if she twisted her feet behind her head.

"You're the only American boy I ever met who appreciates the philosophy of Confucius. Can you be at my house at seven tonight? My parents are out of town for the weekend; do you like Chinese food?"

"I love it; I go with my relatives to the Lime House almost every Sunday."

I knew it was polite to bring something when you go to a person's house for dinner; I bought flowers and a box of fortune cookies, and I wore my "special" blue madras shirt (with the hint of red) the same expensive shirt that I wore for my meeting with Leah at the auto agency.

485

Liling was very alluring when she greeted me at the stained glass double doors of her house; her long black hair encircled a sad but intriguing face, and I was mesmerized by her catlike eyes. She took the flowers and we hugged in the doorway and I inhaled the scent of her perfume; she smelled like flowers.

"I like your perfume," I said. "What's it called?"

"Peach blossom, imported from China, only sold at Saks Fifth Avenue on Lincoln Road."

"When's your birthday?" I asked, "I know what to buy you."

"Birthday four times a year," said Liling, and she smiled.

She put the flowers in a vase and we sat at the kitchen table, then she gave me a quick lesson how to use chop sticks, and I did OK with the big pieces of chicken but every time I tried to put the rice in my mouth it fell back on the plate. I also drank Chinese beer.

"I like this beer," I commented, "this is the first time I ever liked beer."

"Here, have some more," replied Liling, and she brought two bottles from the refrigerator. "Its Tsingtao, popular in China."

Liling enjoyed telling me about her heritage; one of her ancestors, Shu-sai-chong, was a prominent engineer during the Ming Dynasty. He helped connect many of the ancient walls to build the famous Great Wall. She also talked about centuries of conflict between China and the "barbaric hordes" of Monguls, and the many wars between China and the "ruthless" Japanese invaders.

"When I was seven the war with Japan ended," said Liling (I did some quick math; she was eighteen) "but then came civil war with the Communists and my family was forced to evacuate; we moved from Shanghai to Hong Kong. Today my country is enslaved, but this "Red" tyranny will not last forever; the soul of China is based on filial respect; Chairman Mao is trying to brainwash my people, to make loyalty to the state more important than loyalty to the family."

"You have a charming British accent," I commented, as I stared at her hypnotic eyes, "and you speak so eloquently."

"Thank you," she bowed her head. "I graduated from Victoria Academy, prestigious girl school in Hong Kong. Most teachers came from England; we learned 'Queen's English,' but I still struggle with rules of grammar."

Liling told me that her family recently moved from Hong Kong to Miami; they owned two laundromats and she would soon be managing a third one on fifth street in Miami Beach. For the next hour I sat at the kitchen table listening to this intelligent girl summarize two thousand years of Chinese history. I always loved the study of history but I knew little about China, so I was fascinated when she talked about Sun Yat-sen and the overthrow of the Qing dynasty. At first she was very serious, but after awhile she started to smile and when she spoke with food in her mouth I knew I was going to like her. Then we opened the box of fortune cookies and read poignant words of wisdom.

"At the end of the fortune always say 'in bed,'" said Liling, "much funnier that way."

- *"You will meet the love of your life"* (in bed).
- *"Generosity will repay itself sooner than you imagine"* (in bed)
- *"A dream you have will come true"* (in bed)
- *"Your unhappiness will come to an end"* (in bed)
- *"Give and you shall receive"* (in bed)

We took turns reading the little white slips and we laughed. Liling was beautiful when she smiled; she had very white teeth, and as we read each optimistic prophecy I was hoping it would come true that night (in bed). Then, as if she read my mind, she took my hand. No words were spoken as she led me to her bedroom.

It was a large room with a high ceiling, shiny black furniture with carvings of butterflies and flowers, and an inviting pink bed. We stood in front of her dresser and Liling lit several candles and bowed to a row of family photos. Then she chanted in Chinese. I assumed that she was saying prayers to her God.

"No, I don't worship an invisible God," said Liling, "I light the candles as a token of respect to my ancestors. Westerners often call this 'ancestor worship,' but it isn't really worship; is just a form of personal communion."

"I heard that Chinese people have a different view about the afterlife," I said. "I have difficulty accepting the Jewish belief, and the Christian concept is way too simple."

"My ancestors are 'not' dead," she exclaimed, "they live in my heart and they will continue to live in the heart of my children and my children's children. Death only comes when no one remembers you."

I really respected that beautiful Chinese belief, it made much more sense than our concept of heaven and hell, where dead people either floated on clouds or roasted on hot coals for eternity.

"So, how do you decide who goes to the cloud and who roasts?" asked Liling.

"Jews use an advanced version of Santa's 'naughty and nice' list," I responded, "you're judged based on a lifteme evaluation test, but Christians have a much easier method. All they have to do is accept Jesus and they get an automatic pass to heaven; all sins are forgiven."

"You're funny," said Liling. She forced a smile but I could see that her beautiful eyes were turning red. I sat quietly and watched as she kissed each photo and turned it toward the wall, all except a picture of a very old Chinese man with an usual pipe and a strange looking beard. I was curious, why did one relative get special treatment, but I felt it would be rude to ask questions during this spiritual ritual; then Liling begain to cry.

"I dated Josh for two months," she said, and tears ran down her face; she looked so fragile. "He was first American boy I ever dated; he was crude, inconsiderate, and selfish . . . a real prick. He never even tried to understand the Asian culture. I disgraced my ancestors."

Liling was having an emotional catharsis, and I knew (from experience) that my role was simply to hold her hand and listen, not to offer any type of advice. She told me that she had been so "loving and sharing" with Josh; she washed his car and shined his shoes; she even learned how to say Hebrew prayers over bread and wine.

"Last month I joined his family for a Passover Sedar and I read from the Hagadah; I worked really hard to read a few lines in Hebrew. I learned from old Jewish man in Miami Beach, owner of building where we will open new laundromat. Unfortunately, my Hebrew was not perfect and in front of all relatives Josh laughed at me; he humiliated me."

I couldn't think of anything comforting to say so I just held Liling in my arms and let her dry her tears on my shoulder. The rich colors of my madras shirt began to bleed, a subtle sign of empathy. My head was spinning, probably because of all the beer I had been drinking. Then we kissed, a soft tender kiss, and she ran her finger nails gently on my neck and I pulled her body close to me, but I felt guilty. I was taking advantage of this vulnerable girl, and I heard my father's warning: "a stiff penis has no conscience," but Silver Dollar Jake was much louder, "Carpe Diem, seize the day." And I did!

The kissing became passionate and we rolled on her large pink bed; I was on top, then she was on top, and my left hand was cradled behind her head, beneath her long black hair and my tongue was swirling in her mouth; the aroma of peach perfume was intoxicating, and I carefully applied the "Buny method" of one-hand bra removal, and "presto, the fun began," and before I knew what was happening Liling was talking to my penis in Chinese; she named him Chao Chao, in honor of her beloved great grandfather; his picture was the one that was facing the bed.

I liked that name, Chao Chao was better than George, definitely better than Shagua, and I gave a thumbs up to my new best friend, the great Chess master. "Ooooooh my!" Liling sighed and moaned, and she wiggled her flexible body and twisted both ankles behind her head. Her exotic eyes were closed; she had a look of ecstasy on her sensual face, and she whispered to Chao Chao; it was time to end my virginity, but not until I received last minute instructions from my brain.

◆

"Make sure you use a rubber, but not yellow, you might offend her."

"I hate wearing rubbers," said my penis, "I cant breathe."

But, the biggest problem was my heart, which showed little interest in the momentous event that was taking place. My heart kept reminding me: "Don't forget to bring a nice book to little Ruthie's birthday party."

"Oh, fuck little Ruthie," said my penis. "I can't do what I'm supposed to do if you keep whining."

◆

Thankfully, my penis and brain joined forces and convinced my heart to "shut the fuck up" and finally, at the age of 18 years, 2 months, and 11 days, it happened! And I saw shooting stars and Chinese fireworks, and I stayed in the bedroom with Liling for the entire weekend, except for frequent trips to the bathroom; that was because of all the beer. But I had good manners and always raised the toilet seat when I peed, and I also closed the door, even though Liling peed while I was brushing my teeth. Of course, when a girl pees its very demure and feminine, and you don't see an ugly stream of urine, but when a boy pees its really gross; he stands there and "pisses" just like a dog when it lifts its leg and squirts against a tree.

Then, we played Chinese Checkers (in bed) and I learned about Confucius and Taoism and I marveled at the acrobatic ability of this Chinese girl, and she kept praising me and telling me that I was so unselfish.

"There are forty-eight positions for copulation, known as 'shijūhatte,'" said Liling. "So far, I have mastered sixteen."

"Well, if you want to practice the remaining thirty-two, I'd love to be your partner," I chuckled. "By the way, in America we have fifty-two positions; I've seen them on a deck of cards."

"Here, drink ceremonial tea," said Liling, "is Chinese custom to drink full cup each time you copulate; honor to ancestors."

"Yuck, this is horrible," I said, "can I put sugar in the tea?"

"Oh no!" she replied, "would offend great grandfather."

Liling was a very refined girl and kept saying "copulate" when she talked about sexual intercourse, but she only used the word "intercourse" to refer to intelligent conversation, like when we discussed the Analects of Confucius or Yin Yang. However, even though she was extremely proper she giggled and became playful like a little girl when she selected rubbers from my multi-colored collection; I loved watching her use a Chinese version of "ennie-meenie-miney-moe."

"Yin Yang is ancient Chinese theory," said Liling, "We believe that polar opposites are interconnected and interdependent." I liked that theory; it certainly applied to the two of us. We were definitely "polar opposites" and we were doing a sensational job of interconnecting.

"Its not just a Chinese theory," I responded. "I saw it demonstrated in a mystical black and white ritual in Gainseville; two polar opposites really got interconnected."

490

"I know about 'Showtime,'" said Liling, and she laughed. "Josh told me all about it. That was simply a vulgar show for a bunch of libidinous guys. Yin Yang is very spiritual; it is a blending of souls."

"Libidinous is a great word," I exclaimed. "My Government teacher used it a lot when she talked about American teenagers, and she also had her own theory about polar opposites. She felt that conflict was the force behind all change."

"That's not our belief," said Liling, "Yin Yang are not opposing forces; they are complementary opposites that interact within a greater whole, as part of a dynamic system."

This was all so new to me, so exciting . . . I tried to be proper and polite but I was like an animal in heat; I was trying to make every one of my sexual fantasies come true in one weekend. But, I felt a little guilty and I apologized to the lovely Liling. "I hope I am not demanding too much sex."

"No such thing as too much sex," replied Liling, and she smiled. "Confucius say that some sex is good, more is better, and too much is just about right."

"He didn't really say that," I chuckled.

"No! My beloved great grandfather did," and she blew a kiss toward his photo. Then she put fresh pink sheets on the bed and turned off the lights; it was time to go to sleep.

I wore the bottom half of her great grandfather's black silk pajamas; Liling wore the top, and I held her in my arms and our bodies meshed and blended like two spoons in a drawer, and I realized that there really was such a thing as heaven; this was it!

◆

"Don't get carried away," said my brain. "You're not exactly two spoons; you're more like a spoon and a fork, but I really love the silk pajamas."

"Well, in case you haven't noticed," said my penis, "this Jewish fork has been going non stop with the heavenly Chinese spoon."

"Its just a novelty," said my heart, "but it wont last long. Look at Josh; he got tired of the acrobat in two months."

"How could anyone get tired of this enchanting girl?" said my penis. "But, I sure would hate to be called Shagua."

♦

Saturday morning I woke to the smell of bacon cooking in the kitchen, and Liling served breakfast in bed, on a silver platter, along with a pot of "ceremonial" tea. After breakfast she consulted with her great grandfather. Then she smiled and I followed her into the shower, an elegant room with marble walls, glass doors, and two golden nozzles.

"Why are there two nozzles?" I asked.

"Upper one for washing back and hair, and one with long flexible hose is for special use," Liling blushed, "many ways to use special nozzle."

Then she washed my hair with shampoo that smelled like peaches and scrubbed my back, and I scrubbed every part of her soft, soapy body (while using the special use nozzle). After we dried each other with large towels we returned to the wonderful pink playground and cuddled (under the sheets) . . . and I closed my eyes and traveled to another dimension, a parallel universe where I met my grandfather Morris (after whom I was named).

"I would love to learn about theory of parallel universe," said Liliing, "many Chinese smoke opium in order to cross over to other world."

"Why do that?" I questioned. "We found a much better way to visit our ancestors."

Liling smiled, "I hope your grandfather liked me. Next time you talk to him tell him that I'm going to name one of my goldfish 'Morris.'"

"You must learn some important Chinese words," said the lovely Liling, and she pointed to the lower region of her body. "The Chinese word for vagina is "táohuāyuán, which translates as 'garden of peach blossoms.'

"Peaches are delicious," I responded. "and I really love your perfume and shampoo; I'm sure glad the Chinese didn't name the vagina after cauliflower or limburger cheese."

Liling laughed; she had a good sense of humor. "And we have many words for penis; depends who you are talking to and intended use of penis. In romantic novels we say 'nà huà er,' poetic metaphor for 'the thing that matters' but when talking to children it is more common to say 'xiǎo niǎo,' which means 'little bird' and if we want to be sexual we sometimes say 'guītóu' which means 'turtle's head.'"

"Jewish people have more words for penis than we have fingers," I responded. "There's putz, pecker, shmuck, and shlong, and we say shmeckle or petzle to little children, but I'm not sure if we have a poetic version." I was sorry that I said "shlong" . . . that was the word Josh used in his crude song about Liling.

"Petzle is cute," said Liling, "it sounds like little pretzel, but I hate the word 'shlong;' my ancestors were offended when Josh degraded me with his disgusting song. Do you have any Jewish words for vagina?"

"Good question," I responded, "the only slang words I know for vagina are common English words, and I'm sure you already know them, but I can't think of a Jewish word."

The ancient Hebrews (who created the Western concept of a supreme deity) felt that God had an unpronounceable name; it seems as if they had the same spiritual regard for the vagina. But, that was thousands of years ago. I found it hard to believe that a language as rich and colorful as Yiddish ignored the vagina; we have so many expressive words for other parts of the body. I squeezed Liling's cute little ass and taught her how to say "tuchas," then I stroked her face, head, and belly button and said "punum, keppie, and pupik," and she tried to teach me how to say "táohuāyuán," but I never was good with foreign languages and Chinese was much more difficult than Spanish, so whenever I referred to that very inviting part of her body I always called it the "peach garden" or the "garden of peaches." Thankfully, despite my incompetence with Chinese pronunciation (and chopsticks) I impressed Liling with my ability to use an abacus.

"I never met an American boy who read Confucius and knew how to use an abacus," she said. "You are so urbane."

I thanked her and bowed, and made a mental note to look up the word "urbane" when I got home. I couldn't stop telling Liling that she was beautiful, intelligent, wonderful . . . I even told her that my mother would teach her how to make matzoh ball soup; I was in "Shangri-La."

♦

"Wrong fantasy," said my brain. "Shangri-La is in Tibet; this girl is from China."

493

"Oh, my mistake," said my penis. "Liling was born in Shanghai; I get the two Shangs' confused, but didn't I tell you last night, this is definitely heaven?"

My brain chuckled, "It sure is, but don't get used to this. You're probably going to marry a Jewish girl; this is an impossible act to follow."

However, my penis immediately offered a suggestion: "Maybe I can convince her to convert?"

Then my heart joined the discussion: "Listen guys, I haven't said too much during this Chinese adventure, but I can't believe what I'm hearing. It sounds like you're falling in love with this girl just because she knows how to screw with her legs behind her head."

"Stop making me feel guilty," said my penis, "I know whats really bothering you; you're pissed because you don't think I'll go to little Ruthie's birthday party."

"Don't give me this bullshit about feeling guilty," said my heart. "it hasn't hurt your performance at all."

"Well, so far it hasn't," said my penis, "but I still have half a box of rubbers and I'm running out of steam."

◆

Liling also knew that it was going to be difficult for me to maintain my sexual stamina so she guided me through a series of ancient exercises known as Chi Gung.

"Breathe deep; good to relieve tension," said Liling, as she pulled my legs, pinched my toes, and squeezed my butt. "Also good for full awareness of your being and for much needed energy."

Then, we rested and she sang Chinese love songs about 'nà huà er,' (the thing that matters) while I polished her toe nails bright red and played "this little piggie went to market." When it was time for dinner we called for delivery of Shrimp Chow Mein, which we ate from little white boxes (in bed). After dinner I was really tired but, thanks to the Chi Gung exercises I had enough energy for one final "interconnection." We fell asleep wearing the black silk pajamas, but this time we reversed the position of the blended spoons; I was the front spoon and Liling wrapped her arms and legs around my body.

Sunday was my final day in paradise, and I surprised Liling; I got up very early and brought Rice Crispies, toast, and orange juice and we ate breakfast in bed and listened to the cheerful sound of "snap, crackle, and pop." Then, she consulted with her great grandfather, brewed a fresh pot of tea, and led me to the much anticipated morning shower. After some very pleasant scrubbing we sat on the cold marble floor and she pounded her fists against the bottom of my feet; then she pricked my left heel (no pun intended) with a needle.

"Ouch, what's that all about?" I exclaimed. "That hurt!"

"That's acupuncture," said Liling, "Chinese therapy based on nervous system of body. On third day, is good to give extra boost to keep turtle's head strong."

"Well, I'm glad you didn't stick the needle in Chao Chao," I laughed.

"That comes on fourth day," said Liling, and she smiled.

. . . And the acupuncture worked . . . . It worked very well.

♦

As I drove home I was exhausted but smiling. However, on Monday morning I woke up with a very stiff back; I could barely get out of bed. Those Chi Gung exercises were really difficult, and I wasn't very flexible. In fact, I could never even touch my toes. I called Liling and told her that my back was killing me.

"Oh, you poor dear," said a very compassionate Liling. "Josh always had the same problem. Why don't you try using Winter Green oil, but be careful. Don't let it drip on Chao Chao, and definitely not on Deshi or Qi-Shi." (My testicles were named in honor of two cousins who were killed in World War II.)

One day later I called again and told Liling that my back was feeling better, and I asked if she would like to go to my graduation party, to meet my parents and all my relatives. I knew she loved being close to family and I looked forward to our first "real" date. Our passionate weekend in paradise was amazing (more than amazing) but it wasn't really a date; we were just having a mutual catharsis. How can you call it a "date" if you never even leave the bedroom?

"That is not true," said Liling. "We also went to kitchen and bathroom."

495

She thanked me for being a wonderful listener and for being respectful; she appreciated the fact that I always closed the bathroom door when I peed and said that I helped her get back on her feet.

"But you must lower the toilet seat after you flush," said the charming Liling, "most uncomfortable for girl to sit on toilet with raised seat."

"Oh, I'm sorry," I responded. "I'm not used to sharing a bathroom with a girl."

"I consulted with great grandfather," she said, "he feels I am ready to start dating again. I'm sure you know, he watched over Chao Chao."

"What a nice custom," I commented. "I guess he was kind of like a fairy godfather."

"Oh no, he was much more than that," she replied. "After the first time we made love he told me to give you 'horny goat weed' tea; that's a Chinese aphrodisiac used to enhance the male libido, and I brewed a fresh pot every morning."

"Wow; it really worked," I said. "Don't forget to thank your great grandfather, that was magical tea."

"Yes, I know," Liling chuckled. "It is said that great grandfather was extremely virile until the day he died. At age ninety his greatest delight was playing Chinese Checkers in the nude while making love to two young women."

"That's awesome," I responded. "So, how does a ninety year old man get an erection, by drinking the magical tea?"

"Lots of tea," said Liling, "but much of the magic comes from pretty young women who know how to keep the turtle strong."

"So, tell me," I asked, "I'm dying to know. What did your honorable great grandfather say about me?"

"He was pleased with the splendid performance of Chao Chao; a credit to his name, but he said he worries; we come from two worlds, difficult for people who are so different to find lifetime of happiness. He warned that the novelty of passion only lasts for brief time."

"But . . . but . . ." I argued, "I don't get it. Buny dumped me because she wanted to find a guy who was 'different' and now it sounds like you're dumping me because I 'am' different . . . I thought you believe in Yin Yang and polar opposites."

"Oh, Myron, our weekend was wonderful," Liling had a cry in her voice, "you helped me escape from my depression, but even if I learned how to make matzoh ball soup and you learned how to use chopsticks there would always be a cultural gap. This is so difficult to explain; I really hate to hurt you. I am not looking for a guy who is a contortionist, but I want a guy who can at least touch his toes."

I tried desperately to hang on to this exciting relationship, and I reminded Liling that the board we used when we played Chinese Checkers was shaped like a Jewish star, an obvious sign that our two worlds were united, and my family loved Chinese food, especially my New York relatives, and Jewish women all played maj jong, and I promised that I would put pictures of my ancestors on my dresser and light candles, and I would do stretching exercises every morning, but after I concluded my very convincing arguments and finished begging, the sweet girl from Hong Kong said: "Goodbye Chao Chao. Confucius say: 'Wheresoever you go, go with all your heart.'"

Unfortunately, Liling and I were not bashert. I wasn't destined to have a life of endless sex with a double-jointed girl who could twist her body like a pretzel and knew how to make tea from horny goat weed . . . if only I was more flexible!

◆

"Myron, its got nothing to do with your flexibility," said my heart. "That spiritual girl was very depressed; she needed you to help her move on with her life. You were her puppy."

"Bow wow," said my penis, "I loved being her puppy, but next time I don't want to wear rubbers."

"Don't even think about it," said my brain. "those little balloons are mandatory until you get married."

"Yeah! Yeah! I know," said my penis. "Maybe I should call Liling and tell her that I'll name her peach garden in honor of my beloved great grandmother."

"That wont work," said my heart. "you don't have photos of any of your great grandmothers; in fact, you don't even know their names."

"Don't waste your time," said my brain, "She wasn't even impressed by my 'brilliant' observation about Chinese Checkers, that the board is a blending of the Chinese and Jewish cultures."

"That was such bullshit!" my penis chuckled, "but I've got to remember that line, in case I ever meet another Chinese girl."

That night, when I went to bed I took out my dictionary and looked up "urbane, filial, aphrodisiac, libido" and many new words; my weekend in paradise was a wonderful learning experience. I also did some research in my encyclopedia; I wanted to read about the power of "horny goat weed," but I couldn't find a recipe how to make that magical tea.

CHAPTER 56

GRADUATION

Only one day until graduation . . . . Seniors were instructed to go to the Registrar's office, to line up in alphabetical order and sign various papers. I stood behind Emanuel Lefkowitz (Manny), Howard Lefkowitz, and Joey Lefkowitz, but, Eloise was no longer the Registrar. There were rumors that she got pregnant and was forced to leave. The new registrar, Maria Elena Alvarez, was only 19, and very pretty. All the boys were flirting with her, asking if they could defer graduation for another year. Then, Mr. Calhoun cut in front of the line to introduce himself.

"Hi, you sweet little darling, I'm Homer Calhoun, the shop teacher. If y'all have any problems here, come call on me; I bend over backwards to take care of you girls in the front office. . . . I'm a true God fearing southern gentleman from the old school."

"You bend over backwards! I'd love to see that," said the new registrar and she smiled. "I'm also very God fearing."

"Well, maybe some weekend we can take a religious retreat to Key West," said Mr. Calhoun, "reading from the 'Book of Jeremiah' can be very inspiring."

Mr. Schecter was also flirting with the "sweet little darling." "Maria, you are 'muy bonita' today; don't forget, every Tuesday after school, bring your memo pad and meet me in the conference room. Did I ever tell you that I have Spanish ancestry?"

"But, Mr. Schecter," she said, "Why do I need a memo pad? You told me that I wouldn't need to take dictation when you hired me."

As the line reached "S" I saw Shelly wearing a new Lacoste, a light purplish blue, and David's new Lacoste was aqua.

"Whats that . . . violet?" I asked. "Its almost the same color as Buny's prom gown."

"No, its called Periwinkle," said Shelly, "and David's is Teal!"

I asked Shelly if he knew where to buy Chinese silk pajamas, other than Saks Fifth Avenue; they were very expensive.

"You can always buy rayon," said Shelly, "it's a lot cheaper."

"No thanks," I responded. "That's kind of like the phony Florida oranges."

♦

It was a daytime graduation, held at the Miami Beach auditorium . . . two blocks west of the James Manor Apartments. My high school days were ending within walking distance of the apartment building where I began my life on this Jewish island and not too far from the sidewalk where two little dogs once sniffed each other.

Students were only given a few tickets to the graduation, so my guest list was limited to my parents, Aunt Pearlie, and my sister Bobbie, who drove down from Chicago with her husband and my two young nephews Barry and Michael.

Then, as we entered the beautiful pink auditorium everyone stopped and took photos on the front steps. Parents and relatives posed, hugging the graduating students. We proudly wore our black caps and gowns. I posed with my parents and my sister, also with Aunt Pearlie. The teachers were also there, so I ran over to take pictures with Miss Madison and Colonel Klein, my two favorite teachers.

As the Colonel and I were smiling and saying "cheese" a parade of motorcycles came roaring down Washington avenue. It was the Little River "River Rats," fully dressed in their summer combat uniforms . . . black t-shirts, gloves and boots, and Nazi helmets. They didn't shout at us or extend middle fingers, or do anything illegal, so the police security guards did nothing to stop them. They just drove slowly past the auditorium and revved their engines . . . a loud reminder that they were out there, and this was still their country. Our little Jewish island, situated in the middle of the deep south, reminded me of the new state of Israel, which was a little Jewish country situated in the middle of a hostile Arab world.

Spencer Teichman, the class valedictorian, and Andy Nathanson, the Senior Class President made graduation speeches. Spencer talked about the reason why he taught himself Esperanto and the sense of satisfaction from being a loner.

"Nothing in life is more rewarding than to say to yourself . . . I can do this and no one else can," said Spencer, "even if it means that people regard you as different, even if they laugh at you. Now, our generation will do things that our parents generation couldn't do . . . different things. Our generation will put a man on the moon; our generation will complete the job of emancipating the Negroes, and we will start by eliminating the racist curfew law in Miami Beach."

Everyone in the auditorium stood and applauded except Jay Bierenbaum, the newly elected mayor of Miami Beach. Mayor Bierenbaum sat quietly on the stage and showed little emotion. J. Martin Berger, the famous lawyer, philanthropist, and God fearing candidate for City Council, was also seated on the stage. Once he saw that everyone was standing, he rose and applauded.

"Racism is the residue of slavery; an ugly reminder of a shameful period in our history." Spencer shook his fist in the air; he had a strong voice. "Our generation shall turn this country into a land where all races and all religions will be treated with equal respect, where all men will truly be equal . . . women too, the kind of country that Thomas Jefferson envisioned in 1776. Our generation shall be the generation of hope . . . but we must not be deterred by the cynics and naysayers; nothing will ever be accomplished if all possible objections must first be overcome. Savor this moment . . . today is the first day of the rest of our life."

I was impressed, Spencer really had a lot to say. He was number one in our class and he had a full scholarship to M.I.T. For the past five years this eccentric, round shouldered genius, who spoke Esperanto to himself and wore thick glasses had been a recluse; he never said too much to anybody . . . but today he really let it all out. Way to go Spencer! He received a standing ovation when he finished.

"Shit . . . Spencer's got balls," said Manny Lefkowitz, as he scratched under his graduation gown . . . one final time.

Andy Nathanson, our class president, was the next speaker and he also made a brilliant speech, echoing the sentiments of Spencer. Andy was going to Harvard, and he told all his friends that he would eventually go to law school and maybe follow that with a career in politics. Both students were virulent in their criticism of racial problems in America. Andy was very articulate; he spoke in a slow deliberte voice, whereas Spencer shouted and shook and got very emotional, but they both had the same message. They both addressed controversial social issues, including segregation, forced prayer in the schools, and anti-Semitic restrictions at local hotels in Miami Beach. Andy finished his speech with a special mandate: "We must rip down the signs that say 'no dogs, niggers, or Jews allowed' . . . that is the mission of the Class of 1956."

Then came a very long and patronizing sermon by Mayor Bierenbaum, who talked about God, coconuts, and democracy, and our beautiful purple and pink Jewish island, and how life was so wonderful in Miami Beach, and how proud he was of the Class of 56, and a little more about God. After the mayor finished speaking Mr. Schecter introduced J. Martin Berger, the honored guest, who was about to donate $15,000 for the Beach-Hi air-conditioning fund; that was money he swindled from Tanta Baila.

Mr. Schecter smiled as he waved the $15,000 check in the air. "I am pleased to announce that next fall the patio at Miami Beach High School will be renamed . . . the 'J. Martin Berger' patio.'"

Bullshit! They should have named it the "Tanta Baila" patio . . . . she paid for it.

It was the sixth of June, the twelfth anniversary of D Day and as I sat and watched the packed auditorium applaud the magnanimous contribution of this "distinguished" philanthropist I thought about the memorial statue of the World War II soldier. It was because of my essay about that statue that I met Leah Sonnino, unless maybe it really was bashert. And, I reminisced about the graduation from Ida M. Fisher Jr. High school. That was a contrived ceremony . . . kids weren't really going their separate ways; they were just crossing from one pink building to another one, from a building with a giant gold fish pond to a building with a statue of a soldier.

Unfortunately, the beautiful memorial courtyard would soon be transformed into a living testimony to a racketeer who had a brown-nose son with curly pubic hairs, a son who screwed up the life of Leah Sonnino. The Jr. High graduation wasn't a real graduation, but this one was . . . . this time we really were going our separate ways. When the ceremony ended kids cried, screamed, laughed and threw their caps in the air. And everyone hugged everyone; I even hugged all three of the Lefkowitzes. As we marched out of the auditorium, to the inspirational Grand March from Aida, the "River Rats" made another pass along Washington Avenue . . . waving little Confederate flags. Those were legal . . . Nazi flags weren't. They also covered their heads with white pillow cases, with big holes for the eyes. Those were also legal since they were not identical to the KKK hoods. The mayor was standing in front of the auditorium; he turned his back and pretended that he didn't see the parade of motorcycles.

◆

After the graduation ceremony we went to the Lime House, my parent's favorite Chinese restaurant; my father reserved a private room. At least forty friends and relatives came to celebrate the occasion.

Flo stopped by but wouldn't stay to eat . . . she was now kosher, and the Lime House wasn't on God's list of approved restaurants.

"Why don't you join us," said my father, "just drink water."

"No . . . I can't even sit in a restaurant that isn't Kosher; it wouldn't look right."

"Look right? Certainly, God won't mind . . . as long as you stick to water."

"It isn't God I'm worried about," said Flo, "it's the members of my Shul; if one of them saw me here I would have hell to pay."

Flo gave me a present, shook my hand, and then left. Her present was a tiny sterling silver Bible, the type you put on a coffee table, but never read . . . . it was too pretty to put on the top shelf of a closet.

My sister came to the party (without her husband), and as a graduation present she gave me a round-trip airplane ticket to Chicago. "Myron, I want you to spend time with your nephews. Before you know it they will be grown up and you'll miss out on their childhood." I hugged her and thanked her for the generous present; I really wish she and my nephews lived in Florida.

My mother made the seating arrangements, putting Blanche Liebowitz next to Myron K, my elderly bag boy friend. It was an instant match.

"Blanche, did you ever hear the joke about the rabbi and the preist on the golf course?" asked Myron K.

"No, Myron, I'd love to hear it," and she leaned forward, exposing her two-tone breasts . . . and when she laughed, they jiggled . . . and Myron stared, and not just from the corner of his eyes. Old people don't waste time being subtle

"Myron, I am so sorry to hear that you are a widower. You should come visit me sometime; I make a delicious breast of turkey." She was so obvious when she hung on the word "breast."

"I would love to, but you live all the way down in the boondocks . . . so far from Surfside. It would take 'a yor mit a mitvoch' to get there." *(A long, long time. Literally: A year and a Wednesday.*

Myron K. gave me a graduation present, a book of Yiddish humor. And he inscribed a little message inside the front cover.

"Mazel Tov—and don't forget to pause before the punch line."

Then, my clever advisor whispered in my ear: "Myron, tell your mother to invite Blance to Sufside; I never saw two-tone titties before, but at my age I don't know if I can still get a hardon."

"Myron," I replied, "go to the library and get a book about acupuncture; there's a magic spot somewhere on the left heel."

♦

Colonel Klein and Katarina were also at the party; they gave me a new book written by Senator John F. Kennedy from Massachusetts, "Profiles in Courage." Katarina also told me that she was pregnant. That was exciting news; I hugged her and patted her stomach; so did everyone else, but I questioned that custom. Why do people always hug and congratulate a pregnant woman, but no one ever pats the crotch of a man and says "good job?"

"It's a very inspiring book," said the Colonel. "Keep an eye on this young senator; I think America is going to hear a lot more from him."

Then I asked Katarina if there was a Chinese section in the Miami Beach library, I wanted to do some research on recipes for herbal tea.

"No, it's a small library," she responded, "very few Chinese people live in Miami Beach, but maybe the library at the University of Miami could be helpful. They have quite a few exchange students from Hong Kong and Nationalist China."

Aunt Pearlie bought ten giant Hershey bars, five plain and five with nuts. I appreciated that gift; she couldn't afford much more, and I really wished that Herman was there. Aunt Esther and Willy were invited but got lost.

Willie Jefferson and his brother Mack sat next to the Steinbergs. They gave me a "Little Richard" record album.

Josh had to leave the party early; he was getting a private lesson from the instructor in his Yoga class, an older woman who could stand on her head and do a perfect split. We talked briefly about Liling but I didn't tell him that I just spent a weekend in bed with her.

"Watch out, if you ever go out with her," warned Josh, "she'll bore you to death with all her Ying Yang crap."

I asked Josh about the Yoga classes. That sounded like a good activity for the summer, especially if I wanted to start dating exchange students from China.

David and Shelly sat next to me and they gave me two Lacostes, one black and one white, but Shelly refused to tell me anything about his relationship with Buny. I kept asking him questions and he just smiled; then he asked me if I would like to trade my green Lacoste for his light blue one.

"Sure." I replied, "I love light blue, and you can definitely use an extra green one."

"How was your weekend with Liling?" asked David. "you sure look like you've snapped out of your depression."

"How did you know?" I couldn't believe that David knew about my secret weekend in Chinese heaven; I didn't even tell my parents. I concocted a "lie" and told them that I was going with a few friends to Daytona Beach, to watch an air show.

"Myron, we live on a small island," said David. "Its impossible to keep secrets! Uncle Louie owns the building on fifth street where Liling's parents are opening their new laundromat."

"Are you telling me that Liling told her parents about her weekend with me?" I was really stunned.

David laughed as he answered my question: "Chinese teenagers tell everything to their parents, and I mean 'everything,' its part of their culture; and how is little Chao Chao today?"

"Chao Chao is doing great," I chuckled, "and he sure wasn't 'little' during our amazing weekend. Liling named him in honor of her great grandfather." David was right; I had finally snapped out of my depression. I was smiling, for the first time in a long time.

"That's really a nice custom," said David, "The girls I meet never name my dick after dead relatives; they usually use names of Italian shoes."

Then, David handed me a flat box wrapped with a pink bow. "Uncle Louie said to give this to you, it's a graduation present from Liling." Inside the box was a brand new pair of black silk pajamas from Saks Fifth Avenue, and a card that said "Mazel Tov Chao Chao: Begin your life anew with strength, grace and wonder (in bed)." There was also a typewritten recipe: "How to make horny goat weed tea."

I smiled and realized that I was about to enter a new chapter in my life. The days of punting a football and opening coconuts were over; I was now a high school graduate and I was no longer "innocent," and I was confident that college girls would stand in line once they heard about my Spanish ancestry, and I also knew the secret recipe for horny goat weed tea. Back in the eighth grade, when I first moved to this Jewish island, I wore a beret and played the accordion; I went through a brief Italian period, but now I would begin my Chinese period.

"David, can you do me a favor?" I asked. "Can you get me a photo of your tanta Baila? I'd like to put it on my bedroom dresser."

"Huh? Why do you want a picture of a 95 year old woman? She's old enough to be your great grandmother."

Then, Mr. Chang, the owner of the Lime House, came into our room with a beautiful gift, a shiny black and red abacus, with a set of advanced instructions.

"You try this . . . and you never use adding machine again. When relative season come we race. Next time we both use abacus."

"What's the plural of abacus?" I asked, "abacuses or abaci."

"Either one," said Colonel Klein, "but abaci sounds like a disease."

"You pretty good with adding," said Mr. Chang, and he smiled, "you smart young man but adding is not everything in life; you must also learn how to touch your toes." Damn! David was right . . . this was a small island.

♦

Eileen Jacobs, the attorney who led the ADL investigation, stopped by the Lime House to congratulate me. She was carrying two large books and looked different; I hardly recognized her. Her hair was in a cute blonde pony tail, and she wasn't wearing a dark business suit. She was joined by a gorgeous fair-skinned Negro woman who looked like Dorothy Dandridge, the movie star.

Both women were dressed in jeans and matching **ADLAI-1956** t-shirts. The Negro woman had large breasts and wasn't wearing a bra; you could clearly see the impression of her nipples under the face of Adlai Stevenson. I did a quick look to see if Eileen was also braless, but she wasn't big on top; impossible to tell.

"I heard from my grandfather about your graduation party," said Eileen, "so I stopped by to give you two special gifts . . . something you've earned. Myron, say hi to Shanika. We were roommates at Cornell, now we're living together in Coconut Grove. Shanika is in charge of the Stevenson campaign in Overtown."

"Nice to meet you Shanika," I reached over and shook her hand. "Do you really think he can win?" I gawked at the picture of Stevenson when I asked that question; I probably looked like a geek, talking to her boobs.

"No chance in hell," she laughed, and when she laughed Adlai bounced up and down. "The only one who can beat Ike is FDR, and he's pushing up daisies. But, we're creating a political infrastructure for 1960; Nixon can be beat."

"Yuck!" I responded. "I sure hope you're right. I'd hate to see Nixon become president." Shanika laughed and Adlai jiggled.

Eileen then gave me a beautiful leather-bound book: *"United States Congressional Record—May 31, 1956."* (a very momentous date in my life) The book contained the entire testimony of the ADL regarding the regulation of German restitution programs. Then she autographed the book and gave me a big hug. What a surprise . . . Eileen wasn't wearing a bra, and despite the fact that she was ten years older than me I wanted to leave the party with her and Shanika.

"Here's another book you might like," said Eileen, "especially if you have trouble falling asleep at night. It's a long boring 1949 PhD dissertation from Cambridge University in England."

An Investigation of the Transfer of Jewish Gold and Monetary Funds between German, Swiss, Portuguese, and Argentine Bank Accounts during the final months of World War II. By Vasco Milé Sardera

"I bet you know the author." Eileen chuckled. "The dissertation was supervised by a committee of Cambridge professors and a visiting accounting professor from the University of Florida, Dr. Abraham Zuckerman. Oh, you might be interested in knowing . . . 'Old Zuckie' just took early retirement from the faculty at UF."

◆

After the two women left the restaurant, carrying a six-pack of Tsingtao beer, my mother asked, "Who is that blonde lady? She talks with food in her mouth . . . and the colored girl . . . what a beauty, but can't she afford a brassiere?"

My father then banged a spoon against a glass of water to get eveybody's attention. He raised his glass in the air and made a special graduation toast: "To my wonderful sonny boy, who brought sunshine into our lives . . . congratulations and good luck in college."

"L'Chaim," shouted all of our friends and relatives. They raised glasses of water or cups of Chinese tea; we didn't have champagne. "L'Chaim, L'Chaim. To Life."

"Glad to see you guys finally say a blessing," said Willie. It annoyed him that we never prayed before we ate.

Then my parents gave me a fantastic graduation present, the keys to a brand new Plymouth convertible. I was ecstatic.

"We couldn't decide what color to get you" said my mother. "Dad wanted red, but an adorable Jewish girl who works at the DeSoto-Plymouth agency said that red was too aggressive; she suggested that we buy you powder blue. Such a nice 'shana maideleh,' and so clean! Myron: If you ever listened to me, even once, this would be the girl I would pick for you. But you, mister know-it-all, you're too smart for a 'shidech.'"

That night, as I sat alone in my new car, reading every page of the owners manual (even the Spanish pages) I found a little envelope in the glove compartment. Inside the envelope was a photograph of a beautiful girl with a pony tail and an irresistible smile . . . and a brief note.

"Mazel Tov Myron
Good luck in college
Don't forget, July 30th.
Ruthie and I hope to see you
at our birthday party . . .
and don't think you fooled me.
I'm sure you know what 'bashert' means.
Love, Leah and Ruthie
xoxoxo

CHAPTER 57

NEWS FROM THE OUTSIDE WORLD:
1955-1956

On March 20, 1955 the world was discovered . . . I got my drivers license, my wheels to freedom. To the south, I could drive to the Keys, and to the north I could explore non-Jewish cities like Hollywood, Ft. Lauderdale, Pompano Beach, Boca Raton, and Palm Beach. I could even drive for a weekend to Gainesville. Here are some of the interesting worldwide events of 1955 and 1956, As noted in prior chapters, some of these events weren't really earth shaking, but they were good topics for classroom discussion or table talk with my parents, especially when I searched for an excuse to avoid eating my vegetables.

- Polio shots are given in schools for the first time . . . . which allows me to occasionally go to the Venetian Pool.
- U.S. starts sending $216 million in aid to Vietnam. "Sol . . . what did I tell you?" said my mother. "Mark my words . . . no good will come of this."
- Ann Landers starts her famous column in the Chicago Sun-Times. My mother clips useful columns and puts them on the refrigerator door under a Mickey Mouse magnet. Simone Pasquier, the French Canadian

customer of Food Fair, puts her Ann Landers clippings under a huge magnetic crucifix.

- Richard J. Daley is elected mayor of Chicago and begins a 21-year reign powered by patronage politics. He also begins procreating more Daleys to continue the reign after his departure. Maybe I was wrong . . . . Maybe there is life after death.
- The first home microwave ovens are manufactured by Tappan. They cost $1,300. My mother cannot convince my father to buy one.
- Instant Oatmeal is invented by the Quaker Oats Company. Not bad—with brown sugar and strawberries.
- West Germany is admitted into NATO. Five days later the Soviets counter NATO with creation of the Warsaw Pact, signed by eight countries. WWIII is our future . . . I consider resuming accordion lessons.
- Bella Lugosi (Dracula) goes into a hospital for treatment of 20 years of drug addiction. What do you expect? The guy spent a lifetime (maybe several lifetimes) sucking human blood.
- Birds-Eye introduces Potato Patties—no more potato scrubbing, peeling, or paring. Simply fry patties on each side until evenly browned or you can broil or bake them. An important addition to the basic food groups.
- Its finger lickin' good! Kentucky Fried Chicken. Yuck—it didn't compare to Pick'n Chicken.
- Crest, the fist toothpaste with fluoride clinically proven to fight cavities, was introduced. "Now, can I eat Sugar Smacks?" I ask my mother.
- The National Review appears, edited and published by William F. Buckley, Jr. "Scary stuff," said my father. "These people remind me of Goerhing, Goebles, and Himler."
- The Village Voice begins, founded by Norman Mailer, the weekly publication introduces free-form, high-spirited and passionate journalism into the public discourse. I had visions of an old fashioned duel, with matching pistols . . . William Buckley vs. Norman Mailer.
- Argentina's President Juan Peron is overthrown by a military coup; then he is forced to flee to Spain; then

511

he is ex-communicated by the Pope. When you fall . . . you really fall!

- Seat belt legislation is enacted in Illinois. How can they enforce that law if cars don't come equipped with seat belts?
- Ray Kroc starts McDonalds . . . . maybe the most culturally significant event of the 50's. But, this extremely important event would not have an immediate impact on my Jewish Island. However, within the ensuing generation the golden arches would become the most well known symbol in the world. More than the cross?
- November 12, 1955 Michael J. Fox (Marty McFly) from "Back to the Future" returns to the "Enchantment Under the Sea" dance and introduces Rock and Roll to Chuck's cousin Marvin. However, this fact will not be known until 1985.
- The corticosteroid prednisone is developed. In future years my sister and I will have unpleasant experiences with this medication.
- Congress authorizes all US currency and coins to say "In God We Trust." Didn't Jesus preach that you should render separately unto Caeser and unto God?
- Marian Anderson becomes the first black singer to perform at the Met (NY) . . . Of course, she would need a special work permit if she wanted to sing at the Miami Beach Auditorium after 6 PM.
- Del Monte introduces Stewed Tomatoes and Pineapple Grapefruit drink.
- Disneyland opens in California, but why was Mickey Mouse the designated star of the park? I always preferred Donald Duck.
- No-iron Dacron introduced. Beach High girls who learned how to iron in "Home Ec." can now disregard that talent; it will never be needed, at least not for their husbands clothes.
- Pillsbury creates Chocolate Angel Food Cake Mix—and the Beach High girls, who learned how to bake cakes in "Home Ec." can disregard another talent.

- James Dean is killed in an automobile accident . . . but he is destined to become a bigger star in death than in life.
- 1955 Thunderbird comes to Ford showrooms, at just under $3,000 . . . without options. The Corvette now has competition, and a classic car is born. I would be happy with either one.
- The AFL and the CIO merge and after months and months of deliberation and debate the united organization reveals its creative new name, it would now be known as the AFL-CIO.
- The Ouija Board comes out with a new design. Through the use of spiritual ventriloquism, Herman speaks to Aunt Pearlie from the next life . . . . "Help, get me out of here."
- Pepsident, to compete with the flouride of Crest, comes out with "You'll wonder where the yellow went" ad campaign. But, my mother is sold on Crest . . . . thus I grow up with yellow teeth, but no cavities.
- The U.S. Department of Agriculture formulates the four basic food groups. On my island they were Franks, Pastrami, Blintzes, and Chopped Liver.
- At a fourth of July family barbecue, Milton Levin dreams up the idea for the first Ant Farm, complete with live ants.
- Yahtzee is born. I bought the game; you can't play Chinese Checkers for a whole weekend.
- Soviet troops and tanks crush rock throwing anti-Communist uprisings in Hungary. This inspires a new finger game . . . . scissors beats paper, rock beats scissors, but tanks beat rocks.
- As the World Turns and Edge of Night premiere . . . . and as I write these memoirs, more than sixty years later, the storyline from these soaps continues.
- Actress Grace Kelly marries Prince Rainier III of Monaco in a highly publicized Monte Carlo wedding. "Now there's a beautiful shiksa," says my mother. "What a 'punum.'" (*pretty face*)
- At a reception in the Kremlin, Soviet premier Nikita Khruschev tells ambassadors from the West, "History is on our side. We will bury you." What a host!

- Choosy mothers can now choose—Jif Peanut Butter. Call me crazy, but I preferred chunky over creamy.
- Britain abolishes the death penalty, and they were once so famous for chopping off heads at the Tower of London.
- The La Leche League is founded in Illinois to encourage mothers to breast-feed their infants. The league is opposed by the dairy industry in Wisconsin.
- The last Ringling Bros, Barnum & Bailey Circus under a canvas tent.
- Clairol introduces the "Does She or Doesn't She advertising campaign . . . only her hairdresser knows for sure. "Not true," says Josh Broden, "There's another way to know for sure."
- Certs, the first candy breath mint, is introduced. I always carried a box in my glove compartment along with the package of ribbed rubbers.
- Peyton Place is published. Sale of red ballpoint pens increase dramatically . . . lots of good throbbing and quivering words to underline.
- "Profiles in Courage," by John F. Kennedy, is published. JFK loses in his bid to be Stevenson's running mate, but I knew that he had a bright future. He had TV hair and a charming Bostonian accent.
- A big year . . . . momentum builds in the quest for Civil Rights. "Finally! 'Mecheieh' (*super-joy*)," said my father.

EPILOGUE

If you've read this far in the book, without skipping chapters, you proably realize that I am fascinated by unusual words like "tintinnabulation" and "phantasmagoria" . . . . or "maketh" and "restoreth." Or how about all those "L" words that Miss Davenport used to describe Elvis . . . "lewd, lascivious, licentious, lickerish, lustful, lurid, lecherous, libertine, libidinous?" And, in retrospect, I definitely agree with Flo Loerber, "clitoris" sounds better with the accent on the second syllable, rhyming with Delores . . . and "scrota" is a great word, which I have never had the opportunity to use in conversation.

"Epilogue" is also a great word . . . not to be confused with "Epitaph." Webster defines "Epilogue" as a concluding section that rounds out the design of a literary work. There are also other definitions: For an actor it's a little speech at the end of a play, and in music its the concluding section of a composition. So, I guess I have to say something intelligent and memorable at the conclusion of my high school memoirs. I wish Dickens hadn't already said, "Those were the best of times . . . the worst of times." I could have used that line here. What a perfect description of life in the early 50's in Miami Beach! Those were the best of times for white teenagers . . . . and the worst of times for black people . . . or as we politely called them back then . . . . "Negroes" or "colored" people. "Those were the times that tried men's souls." Paine said that in "Common Sense." That wasn't bad either; a few people were starting to speak up . . . but only a few souls were being "tried." Back in 1951, when I was marching around the breakfast table in Chicago, getting ready to move to Miami Beach, a man named Jack Kerouac began his famous Bohemian odyssey across America. He soon composed

515

a rambling narration of his adventures on a long continuous scroll of paper. Six years later, shortly after I graduated from high school, "On the Road" was published and became the Bible for the "beat generation."

In 1956 . . . . change was just around the corner; we won our right to wear t-shirts to school, J. Martin Berger provided funding for air conditioning in the classrooms of Beach High, and Long Tall Sally brought white and Negro teenagers together at a concert . . . and several years later Bob Dylan wrote his immortal song: "The Times They Are A-Changin." OK . . . maybe in 1956 the times weren't changing a lot, but as I look back at the world of 1956 it reminds me of a pot of water that was just about ready to come to a boil. Under the surface the water was extremely hot, but only a few bubbles had reached the surface, like Rosa Parks, who wouldn't give up her seat to a white man and Corey Kaplan, who fought for his right to wear a t-shirt to school. However, in a few more years the bubbles would explode all over the place, bubbles would be exploding in Mississippi, Selma Alabama, and Washington, D.C. . . . in a few more years we would meet Medgar Evers, Martin Luther King, John F. Kennedy, and his brother Bobby. I mention these great American heroes in the same sentence because they all met the same tragic fate as Lincoln, my alltime hero.

During the summer of 1956, as I prepared for college I took Yoga classes two mornings a week, but Josh wasn't in the class, he left for Gainesville to get an early start in college, and I gawked and stared when the instructor stood on her head and did a split, and I soon developed the ability to touch my toes, but I couldn't do any of the "human pretzel" positions. I also put photos of the Steinberg's tanta Baila on my dresser along with a few of my sacred ancestors, and I learned how to brew horny goat weed tea, and I did lots of reading and memorized a few great quotes by Confucius. Of course, I avoided watching baseball on television; the Yankees and Dodgers were running away with their leagues . . . . another year of total domination by New York teams. And in September, the Yankee pitcher, Don Larsen, threw the first perfect game in world series history. Naturally, the New York media ranked "the PERFECT GAME" right up there with "the sultan of swat, the iron man, the Yankee clipper, the boys of summer, the streak, the catch, and the shot heard round the world.

I also went back to work as a bag boy and one day I saw Simone Pasquiere, the middle age French lady who once tried to seduce me, and I said "hi Simone, can I help you?" Now that I was no longer a virgin I welcomed the opportunity to rent out my body and earn an extra $10 a week.

"Thank you," said Simone, "but the young Spanish bagboy is taking care of my groceries."

"Don't you remember me?" I asked. "You told me about your husband who was killed in the French resistance during the war?"

"I was never married," she replied, "you probably have me confused with someone else."

I was really a great bag boy and I saved enough money to buy an "Ivy League" wardrobe for college. Every new shirt had a button down collar and every pair of pants had a useless little belt in the back. I also went to Overtown several times to stuff envelopes with Willie at "Stevenson for President" headquarters. Shanika was the supervisor and she never wore a bra; that was how she recruited dozens of young guys to work as volunteers; also a few older men. In fact, one time I saw Homer Calhoun, my old shop teacher. I was surprised to see that a God fearing southern gentleman was attracted to a braless black woman. We reminisced about the ink eradicator incident and he laughed and said that I really had "chutzpah" and I noticed that he was carrying a copy of the "Book of Jeremiah."

"Are you going to Key West this weekend?" I asked.

"How the fuck did you know?" said Mr. Calhoun.

"Oh, just a lucky guess."

The nice thing about writing a book of memoirs, you can always go back and read any part over again if you think you missed something. I really felt good writing the chapter about the Wonder Machine, a time of my life that I never talked about, not even with my own children. I guess writing that chapter was my catharsis. Mindy Marcus had her catharsis on the dance floor of a Bar Mitzvah and Liling had hers with both ankles twisted behind her head. I think we all need to occasionally open up and have an emotional release, but I wish my mother were alive to read about that horrible period of my life; I don't think she ever fully understood how hard she was on me.

Like the Condor and the Bald American Eagle, the Miami Beach "TYPHOON" is an endangeared species. I've worked on a few High School reunion committees, compiling mailing directories; it's extremely difficult to locate the "girls" (now grandmothers), who have all changed their names, often more than once. Even some of the boys have changed their names . . . dropping the sky,' vitz,' berg'or stein.' Sadly, as we organize reunions, the "gone but not forgotten" list is getting larger and it's almost impossible to find old teachers to attend our parties. It is also difficult to find people who remember how to Rhumba. For the 50ᵗʰ reunion we found my old teacher from Spanish I, Martina Potts, which I found very astonishing, since she was an old lady in 1952. I bragged about the fact that I now understood a little Spanish. "Yo entiendo un poco Español." I tried to talk to her in Spanish.

Miss Potts startled me with her response: "I don't speak Spanish."

"What! You were my Spanish teacher! And you gave me a 'C.'"

"Well, you probably didn't know how to conjugate verbs."

GLOSSARY OF USESFUL YIDDISH WORDS

	WORD	TRANSLATION
	WORD	TRANSLATION
1	**Alevei**	It's a miracle! Would that it comes true . . . usual reference to the new Jewish state of Israel
2	**Aliah**	Being honored, to read blessing from Torah
3	**Alter Kakker**	Literally: Old Shit . . . commonly used in reference to the old people at Dubrows Cafeteria
4	**Bagel**	delicious Jewish rolls . . . enjoyed by everyone, even the goyim . . . but they put mayonnaise on bagels.
5	**Baitsim**	Literally: eggs. Slang: Testicles
6	**Balebosteh**	Capable homemaker . . . The "perfect" wife . . . As seen by my mother
7	**Bar (Bas) Mitzvah**	Religious Ceremony when Jewish boy (girl) is 13 . . . but don't ask me about mine.
8	**Barucha**	A Blessing
9	**Bashert**	"Meant to be" . . . . I had very serious spiritual doubts about this concept
10	**Beema**	The Altar in a synagogue.
11	**Bissel**	tiny measurement . . . used in my mother's recipies . . . handed down to her from her mother

12	Blintzes	Cheese filled crepes . . . excellent with blueberry sauce and/or sour cream
13	Bubie	A term of endearment . . . pronounced the same as Boobies
14	Bubby	Grandmother
15	Challah	Jewish egg bread
16	Chazen	Cantor
17	Chazzerei	Pigs feet (Junk) . . . Why is this word so similar to Chazen?
18	Chutzpah	brazenness . . . . Slang: Having "balls"
19	Davenen	Bowing and praying
20	Draikop	Scatterbrain . . . . Not quite the same as Dumkop
21	Drek	Literally: dung
22	Dumkop	Dumbell, dunce
23	Eretz Yisroel	The Land of Israel . . . almost always said in connection with the word Alevei.
24	Ess gezunterhait	Eat in good health . . . popular Jewish expression before eating . . . when I was 12 I thought this was a prayer
25	Faigeleh	Literally: Little Bird Slang: homosexual, fairy, fag, pervert
26	Farblondzhet	Confused (similar to Fardreked)
27	Farshtunken	Stinking . . . used by my mother to describe urine stenched bed sheets
28	Futs	To attempt to fix something (a verb)
29	Ganef	crook; racketeer
30	Gantser-macher	A very important person; a "big shot."
31	Gefilte Fish	Usually white fish or carp, mixed with eggs My father insisted, his mother made the best Gefilte Fish.
32	Gelt	Money
33	Gevaldikeh zach!	A terrible thing
34	Gornisht	Nothing . . .
35	Gonif	Crook, thief . . . often used to describe Joseph Kennedy.
36	Gotteniu	Oh God

37	**Goy or Goyem**	Gentile (singular or plural)
38	**Goyisher Kop**	Derisive insult: Literally: Gentile Head
39	**Greps**	Belch . . . encouraged at "The Famous" restaurant . . . . But no place else.
39	**Haftorah**	The weekly section of the Torah, read at Shul
40	**Kaddish**	The Mourner's prayer
41	**Kibitz**	Chatting (similar to 'shmoozing')
42	**Kiddish**	Blessing over the wine or bread
43	**Kike**	Vulgar: worse than a "Makkie"
44	**Kinder**	Children . . . . Kinderlech is even more affectionate
45	**Klutz**	a person who is uncoordinated . . . . I heard this term a lot.
46	**Kop**	One's Head. For a child: Keppie or Kepalah
47	**K'velen**	Glowing with pride . . . happiness
48	**K'vetch**	Complain
49	**Kurvah**	Whore, prostitute
50	**Kunyehlemel**	Naïve, milquetoast
51	**Latkas**	Jewish Potato pancakes
52	**L'Chaim**	Usually used in a toast: "To Life"
53	**Macher**	Important person (a big shot) See: #30 . . . Gantser Macher
54	**Makkie**	Derogatory: Low class Jew See #43 . . . Kike
55	**Matzoh**	unleavened bread . . . . Delicious with peanut butter, but peanut butter is not allowed not during Pesach (Passover)
56	**Maven**	A self proclaimed expert
57	**Mazel**	To have good luck
58	**Mazel Tov**	Congratulations
59	**Mecheieh**	Super-joy, a great pleasure
60	**Mentsch**	A special man or boy
61	**Meshugeneh**	Slightly crazy

62	**Mezuzah**	religious artifact or jewelry . . . nailed in a doorway, or hanging around ones neck
63	**Mieskeit**	Ugly person . . . . Can be used to describe a male or female
64	**Mikvah**	A ritual bath for women, usually after menstration or child birth
65	**Minyan**	Quorem of ten men necessary for holding public worship
66	**Mishegass**	Idiosyncracy
67	**Mishpocheh**	Family, relatives
68	**Mitzveh**	Literally: Commandment Mostly used to mean a good deed
69	**Nash**	A snack (noun); munching between meals (verb)
70	**Nebbish**	A Nobody . . . simpleton . . . . but not to be confused with Nishtikeit
71	**Nishtikeit**	A nobody . . . almost always correlated to one's wealth.
72	**Oneg**	Small party after services at a Synagogue . . . little paper cups of wine and horrible little cookies
73	**Ongepatshket**	Cluttered, overly-done
74	**Ongeshtopt**	Very Wealthy
75	**Oye Gevald**	Cry of Anguish, frustration . . . not to be confused with Oye Vey
76	**Oye Vey**	Dear me. . . . or "Oye Vai is mir" (woe is me).
77	**Pecker**	Slang for penis . . . used mainly by New York Jews
78	**Pesach**	Passover . . . The kids at Beach High ate sandwiches on Matzohs.
79	**Petzle**	See: #84 Schmeckle
80	**Punum**	A face . . . . Can be a beautiful punum . . . or an ugly punum
81	**Putz**	Derisive term—a jerk: Literally: Penis See: Shmuck
82	**Rugalah**	Jewish cookies—cinnamon was my favorite.

83	Schlemeil	A cross between a Klutz and a Shmendrick
84	Schmeckle	Slang for penis . . . usually referring to a little boy
85	Shabbos	The Jewish Sabbath
86	Shagitz	Gentile Boy
87	Shaineh Maideleh	Pretty girl
88	Shana / Shawna	Beautiful . . . Shana is Yiddish; Shawna is Hebrew
89	Shammus	A Policeman
90	Shana Maideleh	Beautiful girl
91	Shidech	A match or marriage . . . to make a Shidech.
92	Shikker	Drunkard . . . "Jewish Shikker" is an oxymoron
93	Shikseh	Gentile Girl
94	Shiva	Seven day mourning period following death
95	Shlep	Verb: to drag. Adjective: bedraggled person
96	Shlong	An extra long pecker
97	Shmaltz	Chicken Fat . . . don't eat it; it's a killer!
98	Shmattah	Old clothes (literally: old rags)
99	Shmendrick	Fool
100	Shmoozing	Chit chat (small talk)
101	Shmuck	Derisive term. Literally: Penis Slang: a Jerk, see Putz
102	Shnops	Liquor (Whiskey)
103	Shnorer	Literally: A beggar, used more often to described someone who sponges off of another
104	Shpilkes	Nervous reaction . . . restless, edgy . . . on pins and needles.
105	Shtup	The "F" word (used as a verb) . . . .
106	Shul	Synagogue
107	Shvartzas	Blacks (Negroes)

108	Simcha	A blessing : good fortune
109	Tallis	Hebrew Prayer Shawl
110	Tanta	Aunt ("Fetter" is uncle, but is rarely used)
111	T'filin	Leather straps wrapped around arms during prayer
112	Torah	5 Books of Moses, the Old Testament
113	Traif	Food that isn't kosher
114	Tsores	Troubles, misery
115	Tuchas	Buttocks . . . but not as affectionate as Tush
116	Tush	Affectionate . . . buttocks (Tushies for a baby)
117	Tztzis	Fringes on corners of tallis, worn hanging from pants of Orthodox man
118	Vay is mir	Woe is me
119	Yarmelkeh	Hebrew Skull Cap. Also worn by the Pope. Why? Don't ask.
120	Yenteh	A gossip . . . usually a female, but could also apply to male gossip
121	Zadie	Affectionate term for Grandfather
122	Zaftic	Chunky, pleasantly plump (but not exactly fat)
123	Fleishik, Milchik, Pareve	Kosher Jews could not eat dairy products (milchik) and meat (fleishik) in the same meal. Neutral food, such as fruit and vegetables, were (pareve) and could be eaten with any combination.

CPSIA information can be obtained
at www.ICGtesting.com
Printed in the USA
LVOW11s1507160717
541557LV00004B/458/P